TORONTO
PUBLIC LIBRARY
YORKVILLE

D0874612

JUL 2 0 2011

TORONTO
PUBLIC LIBRARY
YORKVILLE

JUL 20 2011

RIVER CITY

ALSO BY THE AUTHOR

NOVELS (AS JOHN FARROW)
Ice Lake
City of Ice

NOVELS (AS TREVOR FERGUSON)
The Timekeeper
The Fire Line
The True Life Adventures of Sparrow Drinkwater
The Kinkajou
Onyx John
High Water Chants

PLAYS
Zarathustra Said Some Things, No?
Barnacle Wood
Beach House, Burnt Sienna
Long, Long, Short, Long

FILM
The Timekeeper

RIVER CITY

A NOVEL
JOHN FARROW

TORONTO
PUBLIC LIBRARY
YORKVILLE

HarperCollins*Publishers*Ltd

River City
Copyright © 2011 by John Farrow Mysteries, Inc.
All rights reserved.

Published by HarperCollins Publishers Ltd

First edition

No part of this book may be used or reproduced in any manner whatsoever
without the prior written permission of the publisher except in the case
of brief quotations embodied in reviews.

HarperCollins books may be purchased for educational, business,
or sales promotional use through our
Special Markets Department.

HarperCollins Publishers Ltd
2 Bloor Street East, 20th Floor
Toronto, Ontario
Canada M4W 1A8

www.harpercollins.ca

Library and Archives Canada Cataloguing in Publication information
Farrow, John, 1947–
River city : a novel / John Farrow.

ISBN 978-0-00-200580-7

I. Title.
PS8561.A785R58 2011   C813'.54   C2011-900482-8

Printed and bound in the United States
RRD 9 8 7 6 5 4 3 2 1

FOR JACQUES CINQ-MARS,
1920–, CAPTAIN OF THE NIGHT PATROL (RETIRED),
WHO FOUGHT;

AND IN MEMORY OF JOSEPH GUIBORD,
1808–1869 (BURIED 1875),
WHO THOUGHT.

The earth in its devotion carries all things,
good and evil, without exception.
—*I CHING*

If this sprawling half-continent has a heart, here it is.
—*TWO SOLITUDES*, HUGH MACLENNAN

BOOK ONE

CHAPTER 1

TIME IMMEMORIAL

THROUGH SPACE, TIME AND DEVASTATION, LAND FORMS.
Foursquare, sheer, the cliffs of a muscled terrain stand stalwart to the sea, their dawn shadow a broad river's awning. Tilting northeast, the strata of rock ascend steeply, legacy of a time when rock ripped from rock in fire and blast and polar shift, continent from continent, plates skid loose and from the rupture a hard surface arose from an ocean's buckled floor.

A northerly forge.

Land heaves. Erupts. Ground rolls, in agony sways, then rests awhile.

Along the shore of what would become a grand estuary to and from the sea, three hundred and fifty million voyages around the sun before the diminutive, pale Frenchman Jacques Cartier anchored on the spot, a meteor's impact shattered the earth's crust. As measured in a future epoch, a crater punched a plateau fifty-four kilometres in diameter. Away from the epicentre, the surface crumpled into mountainous waves.

Over eons, the dazed planet wobbled back from the blow.

In another time, the hills were struck again, albeit mildly, a deep, circular lake the residual souvenir.

Upon the plains south of the great river, hills took shape as glacial deposits, the prodigious ebb of tidal ice scrapping rocks into giant rogue waves before setting them gently down at select locations, marking the passage of sluggish time in ceremonial nubs. North of the fault line delineated by the river, ancient rock eroded under the stress of the elements. The oldest mountain range on the continent slumped nearer to the level of the sea

3

again, debilitated by age, in summer mere green hills and under a winter's blanket windswept creases.

One peak formed from vacant space. An empty volcanic crater, backfilled by glacial debris, compressed by ice miles high. The ice receded, the outer lava mould washed away. The tougher inner plug revealed itself and remained ever the more tenacious, a scrap heap of rock to be anointed in time as a royal mountain.

The warm melt of glaciers, the fall of winter snows, the rains of spring and the thunderclaps of summer storms conspired to create a green land. Rivers etched the landscape. Lakes became plentiful. Fish swam the freshwater currents or lazed in the arbour of shoreline trees. Bear and moose, lynx, wolf and deer prospered and found their balance. Caribou roamed the northern pelt. A crafty, industrious creature, the beaver, dammed streams and ponds and constructed community lodges from sticks that rose above the water, altering the landscape for those who depended upon its engineering acumen.

The land's genius lay in its waterways. Loon alighted each spring, forerunner to waterfowl that would arrive and go in great masses to dapple along the shores or dive to the depths of cold lakes. Upon the rivers appeared the first people, eleven thousand migrations around the sun before the present moment, as glaciers receded. Russet-skinned and curious, they travelled in tune to the seasons as did the birds, and a few tribes learned to cope with the vigour of enduring winters. In the far north, the people lived along the shore of an immense saltwater bay, an ocean of ice, where they fished through short, bright summers and in the forests through sunless months trapped and hunted the four-leggeds. They chose to live where the land was unforgiving, where peaceable lives could prosper.

Generations lapsed in this way, one folded upon another.

Where the forests and rivers were generous, the weathers becoming less extreme, tribes competed for land. Those who spoke the language of the Iroquois roamed the great inland waterway and along the rivers and lakes south. To the west dwelled proud Huron and Algonquin, and to the north ruddy Montagnais. They fought the Iroquois when one tribe encroached upon another, and battled for rivers and lakes, for shorelines, for whole forests, and at times the wars were great furies and at other times mere skirmishes among rowdy young men anxious to test their mettle. Generations lapsed in this way, striving to persist.

Time immemorial, so it seemed, lapsed in this way, striving to persist.

CHAPTER 2

1971 ~ 1955 ~ 1939 ~ 1821 ~ 1535

BY MOONLIGHT, TWO WOMEN MOVED AMONG TREES DOWN A STEEP escarpment. Tricky going by daylight, riskier at night. They lugged shovels. A small dog scampered on ahead. Burdened by a backpack, the younger woman used her spade to leap a narrow stream of snowmelt, then stretched out the handle for the eldest to balance herself, pause, and traverse the ditch with a bound. A slippery ascent came next. Against a broad horizontal limb just off the ground at the hill's crest, they sagged, gasping, and caught their breath.

Both waited there. Glanced around.

Then looked at one another.

"Ready?" the elder asked.

The two wore black.

"Ready," the younger responded. Together they groped for a channel through a thicket, scant light reflecting upon patches of snow and ice that had persevered, concealed from noonday suns. On all fours, they scrabbled over the humps of keening grey boulders, their bare lives suddenly exposed.

And entered a silent stand of protective trees.

The women diverged from the customary trails. None were intended for a night passage. They moved wherever their trespass would be the most concealed. Down from the mountain they tramped and skidded, the pooch going on ahead, away from the upper cemetery towards a mid-sized American automobile, maroon, borrowed, a Dodge or Plymouth, parked and empty amid boulders and a cluster of evergreens off the main road that traversed the mountain.

By a culvert, where the mountain's runoff was strong, they cleaned fresh clay from their long-handled spades. When accidentally the pair banged tips, the echo resounded off a face of rising rock and down across the meadows of the dead.

The breath of their exertion billowed in the cool air. Two women and a dog, departing a cemetery in the dark with shovels. What could they have been doing . . .

. . . in the year 1971?

†††

The first warmish winds of the season whooshed down from wooded hills, crisscrossing the still-snowy fields of March all sodden from a swift melt. Black loam showed through in patches. Chickadees chased their tail feathers through cedars and bare maples as animals, both domestic and wild, twitched their nostrils at the secret scent, eyes blinking, the earth's scuttlebutt decoded: *spring.*

Sniffing fresh mud stink, the boy felt it, too. As if regaining faith in a neglected deity, he sensed the possibility of summer again: free time—*no school!*—and games, swimming behind the creek dam, riding a horse into—this year, perhaps beyond—the woodlands. Although the promise of that paradise riddled his senses, the mood did not linger long. By evening, rowdy winds shook the shutters and whistled around the upper dormers of the home in which he had been born, the home in which his father had also been born in Saint-Jacques-le-Majeur-de-Wolfestown, Quebec. Yet the boy's interest in one season's discourse with another had flagged. The game was on the radio. The game! The playoffs were almost at hand. Now was the time to catch every static-encrusted syllable and root for his home team. Now was the time to be consumed by his winter passion—skate, check, pass, shoot, score, in his head, alongside his hockey heroes.

"A goal?" the boy's father inquired, not fully removing the pipe from his mouth but taking up the weight of the bowl in his left hand to speak properly. From Quebec City, *Le Soleil* lay folded on his lap as he caught up on world news in the comfort of an armchair, the big, floppy one with the faded burgundy print of immense roses. A floor lamp's shade, tinted with roses also, these a pastel mauve and a faded yellow, lurched over his left shoulder. Soft light illuminated the pages. The bookcase, built with his own hands into both corners of the wall behind his chair, reached from his knees to the high ceiling and included a short ladder made from the wood of a crabapple tree to assist browsing the higher shelves. Quaint, magisterial, a grandfather clock would have been heard ticking by the father and son had they not turned the radio's volume up so high.

The voice of Albert Cinq-Mars sounded sympathetically gloomy, and the knit of his brow denoted a worry. His son reacted poorly to enemy goals, and in the background the crowd's roar was apparent. The game was underway in Boston—that Bruins fans cheered did not bode well for *les Canadiens*, Montreal's home team.

"A fight, Papa," the eleven-year-old on the floor stipulated. "It's the Rocket."

"Mmm." His father's eyes and mind returned to the paper.

The boy shifted onto his back while he absorbed details of the brawl. Could he ever battle that way, or would courage fail him? He enjoyed roughhouse play as much as any boy, but being in a real scrap was difficult to imagine. Getting beaten up worried him—what could that be like?—but Émile was also afraid of going berserk, punching a boy and, having hit him and hurt him, doing it again. He'd seen others do it in the schoolyard, but could he make someone bleed and cry and, once his foe was bloody and weeping, keep on punching? He was bigger than most boys his age. Would he instead offer his opponent a hand up, a Kleenex for his tears and a sympathetic comment? One of life's curious mysteries.

Just then, a word broke through the roaring and the static that drew his father's disapproving attention back to the game. "Sticks?"

"Over-the-head swings—two!" Émile announced, spinning onto his derrière. He immediately updated himself with the announcer's next words. "Three times! The Rocket! Three times he's hit him with a stick! He's got a teammate's, Papa! He already broke his stick across that other guy's back. He must be pretty damn mad!"

Dismayed, his father shook his head. Grown men, fighting, on skates. With sticks. Barbaric. Yet he plucked the pipe from his mouth and leaned in more closely to the radio. No ordinary punch-up. The game's greatest player—for all Quebecers were agreed on that—the legendary Maurice "Rocket" Richard, had swung a stick three times across an opponent's back, connecting with each fierce swipe.

"Don't say damn," he gently reproved his son.

"Sorry."

"He'll be thrown out," Albert Cinq-Mars forewarned.

The boy made a chopping motion as though administering the blows himself.

Then the radio commentator announced that, in the melee, the Rocket had punched an official.

"A big fine," the father persisted. "This will cost him. He'll be suspended for a few games, you watch." Attentive, he continued to lean forward, although he could never have reconnoitred that the political shape of a nation turned on these events.

"How can the Rocket miss a game? The scoring championship! He's so close."

"Kiss it goodbye now. Not that it matters. The Cup's the main thing."

"I guess so," the boy relented. He felt dejected to think that the Rocket may have blown his chance at the scoring championship, the one feat that had eluded him throughout his career. Incapable of foretelling the future, he could not have guessed that the Cup was now lost also, or that history-making events would soon transpire. As the loss of an individual scoring title was rendered insignificant by the quest for the team trophy, so would that trophy, the glorious, mythic Stanley Cup, emblematic of hockey supremacy, be overshadowed by time's conniving winds.

Young Émile, intently listening in, had assumed that the game was hockey—only hockey, and just a game. Over time, he would learn that he'd been eavesdropping on history in the making, that the fracas on the ice, of the sort that could erupt anytime, anywhere, among any number of players in the sport, would ignite the passions of a people, his people, never to be forgotten over the course of his lifetime, that the cultural fabric of his society was being knit with each swing of the stick . . .

. . . in the year 1955.

†††

On the first day of September, deeply inebriated and almost naked, the premier of the province of Quebec sat in a plush leather chair in the tower of an immense, elegant, Old World hotel, the Château Frontenac in Quebec City. He discussed with a young woman the matter of her virtue. Fetching, yet admirably hesitant, the young lady from the legislature's secretarial pool presented a half-moon face to him, the hidden portion darkened by brown curls that sprang back to her scalp whenever he gave them a tug. When they'd met, he'd pulled a curl before saying hello, and she had looked at him through her one uncovered eye, revealing a half-smile. She'd not yet consented to the fulfillment of their liaison, and had declined to unfasten all her clothing—determined, it appeared, to remain perpetually in half-shadow.

In advance of her compliance, the young lady needed to ascertain the level of this man's faithful interest. In the oratorical gusto for which he was renowned, the premier had roared back, "Not only do I *not* love you, my beauty, but I never shall, nor will I marry you! What else do you wish to hear, sweet girl, to be convinced of my fidelity in this matter? You are, I suppose, with your flashing green eyes and soft pink skin, a lovely creature. I am Maurice Duplessis—*le Chef*! The soul of the French people! I wish to sink my teeth into you—yet draw no blood, impart no serious impression. What more could you possibly need to know, Mademoiselle?"

"Sir. Yes. For instance, do you know who I am?" pleaded the young woman.

"Of course! You're . . . Charlotte, no?"

"Charlene!"

"The green-eyed Charlene! Close enough, no?"

"Do you want to sleep with me, sir, because you like me, or do you want to sleep with me because you're too drunk to care?"

Ah, so that was it, and a good question, one the intoxicated premier now had to worry his way through. Never before had he encountered an objection laced with such pert eloquence.

Just then came a frantic knocking at the door.

Unsteady on his feet, wearing only briefs and socks held in place by garters, Duplessis swung open the oversized door to confront his aide. "Imbecile! What is it? I forbade you to interrupt—"

"—except in the case of an emergency, sir."

"What emergency? Out with it!"

"The Germans, sir. Hitler. He's invaded Poland."

The premier stood in the doorway, swaying, assessing the news. "Young man," he declared, after an interval of a half-minute, "Poland is not an emergency!" And slammed shut the door.

Turning back to the room and his consort for the evening, the most powerful man in the province remarked, "My dear, I am sleeping with you tonight, not because I love you or even know you, not because you are beautiful, although perhaps you are—who can tell under those delightful curls?— but I am sleeping with you because we've reached a moment in history that cannot pass without . . ." He burped, stalled, and swayed awhile. "What was I saying? . . . commemoration. In time you will recall this fateful day. When Germany invaded Poland, you were in bed with *le Chef*! Is that not reason enough to stay the night?"

She considered his take on the matter a moment. Then the lady accepted that the justification met her standard.

Later, smoking, her limbs indelicately akimbo and her round, alabaster face aglow upon the pillow, her hair finally off her face, she inquired of him, "What will become of us, sir? The world?"

Duplessis stretched an arm to retrieve the Scotch. "That, Mademoiselle, remains to be seen."

"I'm frightened."

"My dear, why trouble yourself? We're in greater danger of your cigarette igniting the mattress than we are from Hitler in Poland. Who is your premier?"

"You are, of course. Maurice Duplessis."

"In whose arms do you lie tonight?"

"In yours, sir. Still, I worry. What will I do when you forget me tomorrow?"

"Don't let that happen! Be unforgettable tonight!"

"Oh, sir. What's a poor girl to do with you?"

"No one does anything *with* me, my child. If anything is to be done, I am the one to do it! But don't despair about this war. A week ago, a speaker was quoted in the papers. He declared that, rather than fight on the battlefields of Europe, French-Canadians will fight on the streets of Montreal!"

"That's why I'm frightened," Charlene said. "The uproar."

He sighed, and tousled her curls. He tugged a few and smiled as they snapped back. "That is why you must depend upon your premier. Now come closer, my pet. Let us drink this bottle down."

"What about the war?" the young woman inquired. She inhaled smoke to the depths of her lungs. His penis was deformed. The sight still unnerved her.

"Poland is not a war! What about our bottle?"

In the morning, he'd more fully discover the news. Nations were declaring war, including his own, thanks to that wretched prime minister, Mackenzie King, who'd promised no war only to bound at the chance to declare. Politicians and their promises. They should all be hanged.

Except, of course, himself.

Lines were being drawn, outside the country and within . . .

. . . in the year 1939.

†††

The English were coming. The English were coming. Again! *Les maudits anglais.*

The bishop rarely uttered the words aloud, yet endlessly they'd drum in his head. His sleep had been fitful. *Damn English.* He woke to a new day muttering the phrase out of a dream in both languages. A report of fresh arrivals at the port in Montreal had reached him the night before. For a moment, as he opened his eyes, he yearned to believe that the news had visited him in a dream, that it was all some wretched nightmare, unreal. His perpetual frown furled into a scowl. No dream. More damn English *were* coming. By his perspective the invasion had achieved epic proportions. Would it never stop?

A more troubling issue agitated him as well: what would be required of him before this human brush fire burned itself to ashes?

At the outset, the matter had been less problematic, the convenience of good choices apparent. Canada had oodles of room. Why did Upper Canada exist if not to accommodate the aggravating, infernal English? As well, New York State had agreed to accept stragglers. Americans, after all, were both infuriatingly friendly and encumbered by their own largesse. They spoke the same language, practised a retrograde quasi-Christianity similar to that of these pitiful migrants. Initially, the bishop's conscience had not been disturbed as boatloads of suffering émigrés arrived. He had traipsed down to the docks with his entourage in tow, grand men in their illustrious capes and hefty rings and bejewelled crosses, accompanied by a pod of pale priests in black who'd help their superiors down from the carriages, open a gate, then sweep nosy riff-raff aside. Bishop Lartigue would sagely whisper in the ear of a ragged English representative, "New York, mmm?" And more often, with a knowing wink, "Upper Canada." He'd smile, then shoo *les maudits* on their way.

Quebec was to remain forever French. Any astute interpretation of the terms of surrender dictated that obligation. Yet with the passage of time, the bishop had had to confess that his conscience was growing muddled. The new travellers were not being welcomed into the established societies to the west and south. Malnourished as they emerged from famine in the Lake District of England, they boarded ships to the Canadas. Assailed by illness and catastrophe throughout the crossing, many travellers lost their lives. The survivors who disembarked at the port of Montreal were wretched, exhausted, recently bereft of husbands or wives, abruptly childless. They slumped on the pier in their misery and in their stinking rags and upon their knees begged for a sliver of hope. As if hope had proved to be a commodity only Bishop Lartigue could properly dispense.

"Your Grace," they pleaded. "Your Grace."

As if they were Catholics themselves. Were they Irish? If they weren't Irish, they weren't Catholics in the Bishop's eyes, and if they weren't Catholics they should not be begging food or land from him, much less be pleading for their lives.

Still, word had come back on the fate of the first arrivals he'd dispatched up the St. Lawrence River. A number had perished, including children, the journey too difficult for indigents in their condition. Of those who had arrived alive, so sorry had been their state that they were maltreated at their destination. At the time, the solution seemed perfectly reasonable: point the way to *English* Canada. Move them along, a few shiploads initially, an appropriate response to a regrettable problem. And yet, more shiploads were coming, still more were expected.

In the past, the English had arrived on these shores as soldiers, flaming in the arrogance of their red coats, claiming victories across the continent— including here, in Lower Canada, where trickery, or so those defeated in battle claimed, had earned the day. Who could doubt it? The English were fiendish, arrogant, dour, dim-witted, pompous, dull, foul-smelling and, with striking exceptions, infuriatingly victorious. Who could not despise them? Until this latest foray. Now they were arriving in tatters, skinny, dismayed, their mouths bleeding, their teeth falling out if they spoke too rapidly, their eyes sunken to the backs of their heads like the most pathetic ghouls of hell. Their children— if alive, and often a few had just been born, bred in the holds of ships where rats fed upon the placenta—so sickly that to gaze into their suffering eyes was tantamount to enduring the Lord's own passion. What was he to do with these *English* children?

The new migration altered the political compact, which had been partially adversarial, so that Bishop Lartigue was unsure how to consider the new arrivals or how to conduct himself among them. In his heart he could no longer think of them as *les maudit anglais* with an abiding conviction.

He pushed himself out of bed and carried the immensity of his girth to the door, where, languidly, he scratched his belly and, stretching, indulged in a flagrant yawn. He wore only his white nightdress and the small gold cross on a chain that hung from his neck. In sleep he would lie modestly attired, secure in his humility should death find him in the night, although five rings sparkled upon his fingers. Over the years his flesh had expanded everywhere and he had long since forsaken the idea of slipping any ring loose again. The door opened from its centre. He thrust its two halves apart and snapped his fingers. Young priests scurried, as they should, one to draw his bath, another to attend to his breakfast. Another brushed past him to prepare for his grooming and the formality of his dress. A fourth priest, this one not young but grey-haired and sallow, a year from seventy but closer to death, approached with his eyes downcast and kissed the archiepiscopal ring on his right hand, which the bishop extended while gazing absently elsewhere.

"Your Grace," the skinny old priest dutifully, somewhat fearfully, informed him. "More English have arrived. A ship—"

"Yes yes yes," Bishop Lartigue, in early-morning temper, snarled back. "May I not take my bath in peace? Must you besiege me before my eyes have fully opened!" He took a step toward the man, as though to flail him with an invisible whip.

"Your Grace."

"You fool!"

Bowing, the secretary-priest retreated, his eyes downcast in supplication . . .

. . . in the year 1821.

†††

Drawn by a light nor'easter, pitched against a fair current on the bow, the *Émérillon* plied the river waters cautiously, gaining little more than a half-knot an hour towards the hilly island ahead. Indians at Stadacona had foretold this place, and the French mariner Jacques Cartier knew that he was soon to be confronted by the limit of his exploration for the summer. Cold weather approached, and the Indians had impressed upon him that the island lay surrounded by treacherous rapids. Only the exceptionally brave or the ardently reckless need persevere beyond this threshold, and none by ship.

Masts creaked, sails flogged as the wind shifted, waves gently lapped at the prow. Overhead, geese by the tens of thousands flew in V-formations from one horizon to the next, wave upon wave across the sky, their bellies lit bright orange by the setting sun, their manic honking incessant.

South with Verrazano, Cartier had already proven his mettle, and this was his second exploration with his own command to the north latitudes, to most minds an act of foolhardiness. Both stubborn and astute, he believed that the challenges that faced him here and beyond this island would be greatly superseded by the riches they sheltered.

The trick would be to survive.

Jacques Cartier readily followed his instincts, but he was no fool. A year earlier, he had sailed the coast of an impressive island on a broad, magnificent sea bound by imposing coastlines and an abundance of birdlife and fish. Combining his wits and experience with stories gleaned from Indians, he'd deduced that the current indicated a great river flowing to the sea. Winter stood guard against him, and with the season the wild, frigid winds of the north Atlantic. Having returned to France without exploring what lay ahead, he had spoken of his belief with sufficient zeal—and produced two Indians to corroborate his opinions—that his second voyage was financed and its scale increased. His calculation proved shrewd, for on this next journey he sailed into the inland waterway, which he declined to name. (An anomaly of which his crew took notice. Cartier named an insignificant bay for St. Lawrence, anchoring there on that saint's day, but the mightiest river known to him, the only river upon which he'd sailed a vessel intended for the sea, went unnamed. Most of his men, but not all those aboard, remained puzzled by this.) After a brief sojourn at the native village of Stadacona, he left two ships there and approached, more than a hundred nautical miles south, the place the Iroquois called Hochelaga. In the shank of the evening, with a distant silhouette of the mountain behind which the sun had set, the *Émérillon* dropped anchor to weigh the adventures of morning.

Ducks descended from the sky like a darkening rain and fell upon the broad bays and out from the river's shore.

Cartier stood upon the deck while his men struck sail. In the distance, elevated on a squat mountain, he observed tiny specks. Fires within the Iroquois fortifications. Evidence of habitation in this vast domain bewildered and excited him, and he listened to the robust silence of a continent awakening to his presence.

"Jacques." Only the king's man presumed to speak to him without proper formality.

"Gastineau," acknowledged the captain. Neither did he return the appropriate recognition, failing to use the king's man's Christian name or to address him as *monsieur*. If the courtier considered him a boor for being a mariner, he would allow the opinion to stand, and behave, whenever he felt the need, boorishly.

The two men stood side by side in the vast twilight while seamen worked aloft and along the deck. They were not the sole inhabitants of their planet, but in this realm it was easy to imagine that they persevered among the scant few.

"Come sunrise, Jacques, what are your expectations? What do you hope to find here? In this . . . Hochelaga. The way you speak the name . . . the reverence in your voice. This place is important to you."

Cartier considered a response. How could he explain the magic in the word? Or dare reveal that Indian stories describing the Land of the Saguenay, its access beyond this river island, had seduced him? He had paused in Stadacona only a few days—compelled by the weather, but more importantly by a sense of destiny, a compulsion to prove the island and speak to the Indians there, hear from their lips tales of the marvels over which their island stood guard.

From the outset, Gastineau had been skeptical of the voyage, reticent to accept the potential of a land beyond the sea. Sailors were impudent liars by nature, clever with a tall tale or an outlandish claim of riches calculated to inspire a king's investment. The most resilient among them if confronted by a disappointment, Cartier was also the most persistent, both as an explorer and as a spokesman for his cause. Not a trustworthy combination in Gastineau's mind, an opinion shaken in recent days as a land of astounding scale had arisen before his eyes. The broad hills, the majestic waterway—in all of Europe no river of similar breadth existed. He had already participated in perplexing adventures and conceded that Cartier had never overstated his impressions gleaned from previous voyages. If anything, he should be judged deficient at invoking the continent's majesty and wonders. Upon reflection, Gastineau had come to believe that he now knew why—for no speech could summon this dominion to life. What words could recreate its wild enchantment, pay homage to its particular glory?

Such wonders. Seals by the hundreds of thousands barked at their passage. Whales cavorted in a river far inland from the sea. Seabirds by the millions, their cries louder than the roar of armies. Fish in such thick abundance, at times they reversed a ship's progress.

The shape of the world was being forever transformed.

And what of those they called *sauvages*? Severe in their smoky tepees, asquat in animal skins, gazing coldly upon him, they stank. Such a foul odour that his eyes watered and he veered towards faint. He had no standing in their midst—he could not announce the king's name to assure his passage—yet he had been obliged to sit among them, mindful of protocol. On this side of the sea, his very life, he had come to understand, had to be entrusted to the care and acumen of Cartier.

"Last summer," spoke the captain of the *Émérillon*, and he possessed a slow manner of speech, each word carefully considered, which indicated to Gastineau that he had either to be plotting something or maintaining a rigorous mental diary of his lies, "at the approach of autumn, I stood on an island out to sea. I felt the flow of water between my fingers, observed its ripple despite the tide. This confirmed stories told by Indians of a great river. Now we have sailed its upper portion. My friend, the river will continue for miles without end, through what riches? Ask yourself, how vast a land must exist to provide for such a river? The tributaries, the lakes? Together, all the lakes and streams of Europe are no more than puddles and creeks compared to this river! No man has seen its end, the Indians say. So, we are not passing through a narrow barrier to the Orient, the one Verrazano envisioned. He was searching for what he saw in his mind, failing to comprehend what his eyes could plainly see. What lies beyond us is what the Iroquois say: a land without measure. A land, as you may advise our king, rich in diamonds, abundant in gold."

The king's man nodded and continued to watch down the river for the occasional infinitesimal flicker of fire. With the fall of darkness, he could feel the continent rising in his mind, as though to mirror the immensity of the starry space above them, equally as mysterious and unknown. He felt that he now understood why the captain had named his ship after Merlin, a sorcerer. Yet he was a practical man, and checked himself before he was fully undermined by the poetry of this boundless space. "My dear Jacques, my mind has been opened to the girth of the land, yes. But God has not entrusted my eyes with evidence of treasure."

"All that the natives have told me has been proven true. Why not this?"

The king's man no longer challenged Cartier's logic with any special vigour. During the voyage, he had lost every argument he had pressed and the exercise now lacked merit. If Cartier was leading him, and their king, to gold and diamonds, he no longer wished to be dissuaded of the possibility. Indeed, with the proper inflections, an adroit word, he could recast himself as the true proponent of the enterprise.

Gastineau had guessed Cartier's motive in not naming the river. The mariner had to be hoping that a clever cartographer, or the king himself, would name the river after him. *Fleuve Jacques-Cartier*. The king's man would have none of that. He had gazed upon the map the captain was creating and noticed a small bay that now bore the name St. Lawrence. As soon as they were back in France, he would speak to the cartographers, and, through whatever means necessary, impress upon them that St. Lawrence was the name intended and best suited for this river without end. He wished the mariner no ill, but what extant mortal deserved a river of such immensity named in his honour? Certainly not a ship's captain. If he personally accomplished nothing else on this voyage, Gastineau would sink that ambition to the bottom of the sea.

The travellers gazed upriver into the darkness there.

Unbeknownst to either man, at the smoky village beyond their vision, an Iroquois hunter had arrived on the shore by canoe. He told of a strange canoe the size of a hill seen afloat on the water days earlier, heading upstream. News of similar sightings had previously reached the ears of these men and women. White-skinned men, bearded men, men without women, sea creatures whose wretched seal-stink and sordid wolf-breath had been much discussed among the coastal tribes, men who lived in canoes as tall as trees and travelled from a world beyond the waters, beyond this land in another land, or so they claimed, had found the path down the great river inland from the sea, into the depths of their forests by giant canoe.

This, then, would be their time to meet.

These were Mohawks, one of the six nations of the Iroquois people. They kept watch that night, and awaited morning and the days ahead, their vigil a lengthy one . . .

. . . in the year 1535.

CHAPTER 3

1955

SURGING EAST ALONG STE. CATHERINE STREET, A MOB SWELLED. Thousands spilled from the Forum, where a game between *les Canadiens* and the Detroit Red Wings had been curtailed, initially by tomatoes thrown at Clarence Campbell, the National Hockey League's president. Then stink bombs erupted on the ice. The stench and smoke ignited panic among a portion of the spectators while seeding rage in others. The most angry swarmed Montreal's focal artery, smashing windows, looting shops and vandalizing buses. Hordes exercised their collective muscle by rocking police cruisers until they managed to roll a few upside down, then the mob burned the cars and cheered the flames.

A former prosecutor at Nuremberg, Campbell had brought down a stunningly stiff verdict. Maurice "Rocket" Richard had been suspended for the remainder of the season for swinging his stick three times across an opponent's back. He'd also punched an official. The judgment effectively denied Richard the scoring title. More shocking, his suspension included the playoffs. Montrealers feared the edict would cost their team the championship they were favoured to win. Fans were livid. Once the stink bombs were tossed their rage knew no remorse. Rioters toppled phone booths, stomped on mailboxes and slashed tires. Hundreds cheered each petty misdemeanour as they followed the mischief-makers on foot.

Although it possessed no organizational apparatus, and slogans had yet to catch on, the burgeoning crowd seemed to know that it would find more interesting, more critical targets ahead.

A pair of cops patrolli—   le beat near the Forum were not the first to intervene—others had   le crowd from the building and bullied a few individuals outside—b   re of what had transpired, they were ill prepared for the impendin   ge. Beer-bellied, with a florid complexion, the senior of the two put u   l to block a group of forty raucous men and youths. He demanded th   get off the street and use the sidewalk. "That's what it's there for!" he c   d them, as one might a rascally pack of kids. The men hooted, then ch   and the officer felt both his knees snap before he was trampled underfo

His partner, youthful   limber and less belligerent, escaped the crush by vaulting over the hood   arked car and dashing across the sidewalk into a doorway, emerging to he   s dazed and bloodied mentor back to his feet after the howling band had   sed on. The older man seemed to be under the impression that he still ha   unction to pursue, raising a hand to block the progress of the next thron   gang of about six hundred men, reaching also for his missing pistol—con   ited by a rioter and now indiscriminately being fired in the air.

The junior officer guide his confused colleague away.

The first calculated intervention by authorities outside the building resulted in similar dismay. Fifteen officers ran down a side street and cut the mob off as it moved along Ste. Catherine, expecting that the presence of the uniform and the sight of fifteen truncheons would sober the drunks and bring order to the lives of the reckless. The gang failed to be impressed. Having ransacked a corner grocer, depositing the owner and his wife outside the premises while emptying his backroom, they demonstrated their commitment to the furor by hurling full and half-full beer bottles at the cops, and the blue line of fifteen men buckled and ran.

Their flight charged the atmosphere with conviction. To the men running rampant on the street, they now owned the city.

Bad news for Captain Armand Touton of the Night Patrol. After the sun went down, the city's security rested upon his shoulders, but he had made a reasoned deduction. His detectives were not equipped for this type of operation and could offer no useful support beyond logistics and expertise. He did not find merit in hand-to-hand combat against the rioters.

"We have a choice," he maintained to the officer in charge of the patrol-men. Many of his constables had reported in when an appeal went out over the radio. Others had trundled off to bed as soon as news of the riot was broad-cast—so great their need for sleep that they disconnected their phones. Still others headed for the nearest neighbourhood tavern in order to miss the call from a station commander to return to work.

"Is that right?" Captain Réal LeClerc, in charge of police operations, asked him. "What choice would that be?"

"We can let the rioters break store windows, or we can let them break the noses of our men. I say we let the mob smash glass."

LeClerc was visibly astonished. "Never expected that from you, Armand."

A former commando and prisoner of war, Touton's reputation as a tough guy had been earned and proven often. Months earlier, while driving home in the morning after a particularly hard night, he'd come across Captain LeClerc and his men surrounding a home in the East End. Officers squatted behind police cars and civilian automobiles, weapons drawn. Touton had dashed from his car, bent over, his head down, and crept alongside the uniforms until he found LeClerc. "What's going on?" he asked.

"One man inside. Young punk with a gun. Already he took a shot at his own mother. He missed. His mom, his dad, they got out, but he's a lunatic, his parents say. Sick in the head and body both."

"If he's inside, what are you doing outside?"

The captain had nothing to say to that, managing only a faint shrug.

"I'm going in," Touton announced loudly. "Who's coming with me?"

He looked around. None of LeClerc's men made eye contact with him. This time, he was the one to shrug.

On his way into the lower level of the shabby two-storey crammed together with others identical to it, Touton reached down and gathered a handful of pebbles from the yard. He threw one of the stones ahead of him as he entered. No response. He walked in. He went up a short flight of sagging stairs that creaked underfoot. The first door was open. He chucked a stone inside, then listened to it rattle around and come to rest. Nothing. He went in.

He tossed a stone into the living room on his left and, when he heard no sound, stepped into the room, then moved towards the rear of the house into the adjoining dining room.

Tossing another stone earned him no reply.

At the doorway to every room, he lobbed a stone. At the last, he spotted the shadow of an arm come up. Then a pistol rose into view. Commando style, fast, fiercely, Touton struck first, his massive fist smashing into the youth's face. A left uppercut to the chin snapped the lad's head back. Blood spurted as the gunman bit through his tongue. Touton reeled at the unexpected horror that confronted him there, and he levelled the crazed gunman with another savage right hand.

Motionless, the young man's body seethed with pustules. Foul secretions leaked across his back, and from his forehead down into his eyes. An effect, Touton would later have confirmed, of syphilis. The disease had already chewed up his mind. Touton called in LeClerc to clean up the mess and haul the diseased man away before he awoke in bad temper.

And yet this time, as the riot gained intensity and the crowd grew more brazen and violent, Touton was the one suggesting that the cops pull back, that the conflagration be permitted to run its course.

"Some guy wants to play with matches, douse him with a firehose. A thug wants to put the boots to a citizen, shoot off his left big toe. Later, you can claim it was an accidental discharge. A drunk wants to fire a pistol in the air, aim a warning shot past his right ear. If you miss and hit him between the eyes, too bad for that guy."

LeClerc said no. Newspapers and radio journalists had heralded Touton for his courage against the syphilitic gunman while reviling LeClerc and the rest of the department as cowards. Now he was being presented with an opportunity to show the other man up. "These bums need to be taught a lesson. They can't take over the streets on my watch."

Pondering his options, Touton nodded. "Your choice. If you think you can teach a mob a lesson, be my guest. I'll monitor the radio. Crooks will be going about their business tonight. My guys need to be ready for that." He'd rather allocate his resources to protect critical targets, starting with the banks in the path of the mob's eastward flow.

Officers in overcoats—collars up, hats low over their eyes to suggest to rioters that they were not cops at all, a shotgun tucked under each arm and multiple pistols visible in gun-belts slung over their shoulders—ought to be enough to keep looters from the banks' doors. He also had people on phones, siphoning bank presidents out of their evening baths, demanding that they hire private security to pick up the slack deeper into the night. Touton dispatched detectives to hot spots as they flared up, for all ears—including those of criminals—were tuned to the radio. By now, the whole city knew about the riot. Furious men in every quarter were racing to join the melee, by car or on foot. Those who came by bus would smash out the windows of the coach and beat up the drivers as they disembarked. Sometimes burn the buses. As he had expected, petty crooks were taking advantage of the massive police deployment to knock over small businesses elsewhere in the city. He might not be able to chase down those guys tonight, but his men would nab a few in the act, and afterwards he'd be in a better position to sort through who had done what to whom and drag a few bad guys in.

Between bursts of information and the doling out of orders from his vehicle, Armand Touton kept tabs on the efforts of his colleague Réal LeClerc. The man was in charge of the uniforms, and had managed, despite the evening hour, to cobble together a small army. This proved fortunate, given that his actions had already helped the riot to escalate into all-out war.

†††

A man of thirty-five, thin, agile, in jeans and a short leather coat, standing farther east along Ste. Catherine Street, anticipated the mob's approach. Although of average height, his features were exceptionally striking, distinguished by a prominent, serrated nose and cheekbones like plump pears. The overall effect was a sculpted, even cunning look that barely masked a cherub's propensity for mischief. Continents appeared to come together in his face, as though his ancestry combined native Indian with Asian, and the French of Normandy with a smattering of English aristocracy. A wealthy man's son, he had studied law and been called to the bar, yet had taken no interest in a conventional career. Pierre Elliott Trudeau preferred the work he did these days editing a small intellectual magazine, *Cité Libre,* and had recently stepped away from a job as a legal advisor to a government agency. Hearing radio reports of the havoc, he left the comforts of his mother's home, where he was visiting, to hail a taxi that dropped him off as close to downtown as the driver dared.

Cabs, the radio reported, were being overturned whenever cop cars weren't handy. "That's all right, what they're doing," the cabbie broadcast. "Me, I don't mind. Burn the city, burn downtown. Go to Westmount, burn the English to the ground—know what I mean? But don't burn my cab."

"That's where you draw the line?" Trudeau asked.

"That's my line. I can't go no closer than this."

"Sure you can. Go a little closer."

"My cab is my life to me!"

"That's probably not as true as you think. Don't worry, nobody's burning cabs for a few more blocks."

"You never know!"

"A little farther."

Trudeau got out eventually and walked the last couple of blocks to a public square that appeared to be peaceful and quiet, although an unusual number of people were milling around, waiting. The anticipation in the air felt akin to the charge before an electrical storm. He was sitting up high on the backrest of a bench when he heard a dulcet male voice address him from behind.

"Pierre? I thought that might be you."

In no mood to welcome company, he turned to see who had identified him. A step behind his left shoulder stood a soft-looking man in casual attire, his hands crossed over his tummy in the pose of a child waiting for an elder's sanction to step forward. He wore large, floppy rubber boots, the tongues hanging out, jeans, a heavy wool sweater and a dusky jacket open down the front. He had on a small, black wool cap. Of similar height to Trudeau, the second man possessed a much bulkier build. Only twenty-eight, he appeared likely to become hefty in later years. Already his belly had to be cinched by his belt, and when he exerted himself he'd soon pant. Trudeau had first met him during the Asbestos miners' strike a few years back—the skinny intellectual got into a fistfight, now a legendary battle, while the robust youth cheered him on—then later through the milieu of intellectuals around *Cité Libre,* where the corpulent fellow demonstrated a tenacious, if not a particularly original, intellect. In some circles, he became a formidable proponent of decisive political change as envisioned by the far left. Trudeau held reservations about the man—the two of them were incompatible politically—but on first impression conceded that he liked him. He'd detected a knack for astutely assessing personalities, and an ability to understand how others were likely to think. When the two of them rehashed a meeting that had gone badly, the man adroitly, and bravely, fingered those who lied. Finding him on the square, Trudeau dropped his automatic air of combativeness.

"Father François," Trudeau greeted him. "A surprise. How's it going?"

"Fine, Pierre. Taking in the riot on a midnight stroll?"

On the bench seat, the marks of footprints in snow told that others had sat in a similar position to himself, on the backrest. "Father, are you blind? I'm sitting here, minding my own business."

The young priest emitted a self-conscious chuckle and sat at the opposite end of the bench, on the icy seat portion. "I see the potential arsonist in you, Pierre. You're in the mood to burn down a building. So don't tell me you're here as a neutral observer."

"Observations are neutral? Since when? We see what we want to see, with the slant we prefer. What about you, Father? Packing snowballs with rocks inside? Burning cop cars?"

"Twenty-five minutes ago—like you, I was minding my own business—I was standing alongside a cop car when it burst into flames."

"Spontaneous combustion?"

"Something like that." The priest leaned forward. The night was not too cold for March, but his breath was visible under the streetlights. "I singed my jacket. My first thought: what happens if the gas tank explodes? I tried moving people away, but on a night like this, people have minds of their own. They insisted on encircling the car, cheering."

"And you, incognito with no collar on. You could have said Mass."

"I didn't expect to be attending to my flock this evening."

"Didn't you?" Trudeau dug his hands into his pockets to warm them, not having bothered with gloves. "You usually listen to hockey games, Father?"

"At this time of year, of course. Not you?"

"Tonight, for the first time. But I expected tonight to be different—more than just a game." Both men were distracted by a momentary roar from the approaching throng. "Sports fans," Trudeau scoffed in the sardonic manner familiar to Father François Legault. "Their team scored a goal."

"Another cop car's been roasted," the priest surmised.

"An English store window spontaneously shattered."

The priest eyed the other man closely. While he had been irritated by Trudeau in some discussions before, a timbre to his manner on this night made Legault suspect that he might enjoy his company. "You're not curious, Pierre? You'll walk no closer?"

"They'll be here soon enough."

Father François looked around. In accompanying the mob down Ste. Catherine Street, he had usually contrived to stay ahead of the action, looking for those areas where the police might initiate a pitched battle. In one instance, he coaxed officers to retreat by pointing out to them the discrepancy in numbers. In another, he confronted the wounded on both sides of a fight while they awaited ambulances. "The French and the Catholic are fighting French Catholics. Does this make sense?" he inquired. Lacking confidence in his physical health, he had carried on to this square. Intermittent breathers kept his pulse regular.

"Why be confident, Pierre, of where they'll go? It's a mob. Without a destination. It could turn off anywhere, slide away in any direction."

Across the street from Phillips Square, where they were sitting, a department store, Morgan's, projected its wares in bright windows. Like Eaton's a block away, the store was an emblem of English Canada. Clothing, furniture and cosmetics for the ladies, but the French were obliged to speak English if they expected to be served, and speak it well if they wished to be served politely. A French lady buying French perfume from France had to learn to say *please*, not *s'il vous plaît*.

"Why trouble myself by finding the riot," Trudeau remarked, a nod indicating Morgan's, "when I can sit here in a front-row seat and the riot will find me?"

"Then you'll agree, Pierre, that this evening has nothing to do with hockey."

"Hockey is the flashpoint. But there's more to it. This mob will start selecting targets. When it does, it'll discover its *raison d'être*." Sirens wailed through the night. Above Ste. Catherine Street police cars, hook-and-ladder trucks and ambulances raced by. "Watch. Our rioters will educate themselves as they go. That's already happened, or they would never have bypassed the National Hockey League offices."

"They don't know where the offices are."

"Just as well."

"I'm serious," the priest reiterated. "Someone asked me if I knew where the league office was located. He had a brick in one hand, a beer in the other. I almost answered him before I thought better of it. I offered him a smoke."

"Good of you."

"I traded. A smoke for the brick."

"Quick thinking."

"It's hard to get rid of a brick on a night like this. I stuffed it in a mailbox."

Trudeau blew warm air into his hands. "Father, while this is not only about hockey, I don't see that it has much to do with religion."

"Now you're insulting me. Even in this light I detect the devious twinkle in your eye. What does any of this have to do with the Privy Council, Pierre? You're still employed by the government, no?" Feeling cold, as if the conversation had subdued his adrenaline, the priest stood and stomped his feet a moment. He finally did up the zipper on his jacket.

"I thought you knew. I'm out of work. I quit. But the Catholic Church, Father. Your boss is no mere boss. The Church is your calling."

"The Catholic Church serves the people of Quebec, Pierre."

"Arguable," Trudeau murmured.

"Put it another way then. My flock is in torment. They're rioting. Where else should I be? At home? In bed? Reading *Cité Libre*?"

A large pane of glass shattered, catching their attention.

"Somebody found your brick," Trudeau said.

"They probably used the whole mailbox." Both men smiled. "I agree with you—though, sadly. They'll be here soon."

"The police, too," Trudeau noted. He glimpsed shadows forming on his right.

The priest also spotted the gathering forces. Trudeau, the crafty young fellow, had chosen a ringside seat for the fiercest battle of the night. As he had done before, in the midst of past debates, Father François made a mental note of the man's acumen.

Getting to his feet, Pierre Trudeau hugged himself against the chill. The two men smiled, for both believed that their conversation on this special night had brought them together as possible, if unlikely, friends—closer than before. They stood side by side as sirens wailed louder, nearer, ever more plaintively, and the mob, too, increased its roar. In the chill of the chaotic March night, the men waited patiently for the riot, and history, to seek them out.

✝✝✝

Captain Armand Touton took the call after the riot had been out of control awhile, the resources of his men stretched beyond their usual limit. Half the police presence was now involved in carting the injured to hospital and keeping roads open for emergency vehicles. In hospital corridors, civilians lined up alongside the same cops who had beaten them, and firemen were streaming in, taken out of action by rocks as often as by smoke inhalation.

The call was being transmitted to his vehicle over the two-way, relayed by a harried dispatcher at police headquarters who was also on the phone to another officer. The dispatcher sounded quite young, probably in her early twenties, a civilian fearful that the social order had come to an abrupt halt. She dreaded conveying messages between the two roaring lions.

"I have no time for a goddamned burglary!" Touton yelled back at her. "Tell him to take care of it himself! That's what he's paid to do!"

A delay ensued as his response was passed along.

The young woman's sweet voice squeaked again. "Sir, Detective Sloan says that you've got time for this one. Over."

"There's a riot in progress! Ask that dumb sonofabitch if he's opened a window lately! If he says yes, ask that dumb sonofabitch if he's deaf in both ears or only blind in one eye!"

Another pause. "Sir, Detective Sloan says I'm to tell you in an angry voice that he's calling from the NHL head office in the Sun Life Building. He says I'm supposed to say to you in an angry voice that he knows about the . . . I'm supposed to say it this way, sir . . . 'the goddamned'—he made me say it that way, sir, he insisted on it—he knows about the . . . you know, goddamned . . . riot. Those aren't my words. Over."

This time, Touton took time to formulate a response. Both the Sun Life Building and the National Hockey League offices were supposed to have been guarded, and he had taken charge of that detail himself. Nobody had been allowed to stay in the building, for trouble had been expected, even before the throwing of the first tomato, as the building was an obvious potential target. A break-in would certainly reflect badly on his squad.

"I had guards posted at that site," he said feebly.

In a moment, the young woman passed along his officer's response. "Not enough. I was told to say that, sir. I mean, it's not me saying 'not enough,' it's Detective Sloan. Stand by, please, sir."

Touton hung on. This was his city. A portion of its centre was now in flames. He could still hear the shouts of rioters, although they had moved on from his station, their exuberance echoing like sirens between the buildings all cheek by jowl, two and three storeys high. Smoke lingered in his nostrils, a reminder of that day on the beach at Dieppe, not so long ago, where he had bled, awaiting capture or death as he breathed in smoke and the terrible stench of the dead.

"Sir? Detective Sloan says to tell you that this is bigger than the riot. He just doesn't want to explain why over the two-way. He has his reasons, he says. Over."

With the front door of his vehicle open, Touton stood with a foot up, leaning one elbow on the roof and the other on the door. He clicked his microphone on. "Tell him it's impossible to drive through the mess from here. I'm heading there on foot. It'll take a while. Tell him it better be bigger than the riot or I'll make him smaller than a cockroach. And you can say that to him in your usual sweet voice. You don't have to sound angry at all. Now, *ma chérie*, don't go off on a crying fit. You did just fine. Over and out."

Touton stepped back from his car and slammed the door shut. A detective stepped close to him, but stayed away when he noticed the intensity in his eyes. "Get me a shotgun," Touton ordered quietly, without emotion. When the officer returned with the weapon and a box of shells, he cracked the gun open and deposited two shells in the chambers. He left the shotgun open across his left arm and stuffed the box in his coat pocket. He doubted that he'd need the damn thing, but a mob was a mob, and that merited a degree of caution.

As he walked down Ste. Catherine Street, images of burned-out cars, smashed windows, spaghetti coils of firehose and the hollering, drunken kids hauling away stolen loot angered and saddened him in ways that hadn't fully hit home when he was safely tucked behind the scene at his car. The litter impressed him. How all that debris could be scattered in such a short time was mystifying, as though every object that a rioter could pick up and hurl had been hoisted, smashed and thrown onto the street in pieces. He'd been through chaotic times before. After Dieppe, he was force-marched through Europe and put on display. Citizens stepped from their homes to throw vegetable peelings and human excrement in his face and upon the other prisoners. They hollered fevered insults. Firsthand he had witnessed a mob's frenzy, and privately he was wondering if he urged caution for reasons that were not entirely professional—he did fear mobs, this one included, not for what they might do to him, but for the memories they invoked.

Armand Touton was unaware of the impact of his presence. He was walking down the very centre of the street, a shotgun crooked over one arm, his grey hat on, his charcoal coat flaring out with each immense stride. He was a man in a hurry. To everyone, he was obviously a cop—not only to those who recognized him as the city's most famous police hero—and he was one cop who was not cowering. Respect was accorded to him. Boys who taunted unwary adults shut up as he went by. Men who had been throwing rocks and snowballs that contained ice and stones at firemen kept their arms at their sides. Before them strode a man on a mission, and it appeared to many that the folkloric hero was intent on single-handedly breaking up the riot. While the idea might be deemed laughable by anyone on the street who thought about it, no one stood in his path to prevent him from doing so, either.

Those who knew him only by reputation understood that this was his town, the night shift his time. Montreal was a night city. Its clubs and bars were infamous across the continent. Deprived Canadians thirsty for relief from dull social lives booked business meetings and stopovers every chance they got. Americans arrived for the shows and the gambling and the open prostitution. Hookers freely worked the trains coming into town. Over the years, the act he'd enjoyed the most had been Édith Piaf, who'd played the Sans Souci. He suspected that he'd never see her like again. In any case, the Sans Souci was now closed, the closure part of a trend. Yet only last week Touton had caught Vic Damone at the El Morocco. He loved Vic's voice. He hadn't had a chance to get back to the El this week to hear Milton Berle, but usually the comedians left him cold because his English just wasn't quick enough. Another comedian, Red Skelton, was booked at the Tic Toc. Some of the guys had been talking about him, but he'd rather catch Dean Martin and Jerry Lewis, coming soon to the Esquire Show Bar, or Sammy Davis Jr. who was booked for the Chez Paree. Last year, he had used his influence—one of only a few times, but the owner, a gambler and a hood named Harry Ship, owed him a big favour—to hear Frank Sinatra, also at the Paree.

He wondered if he'd ever see those big-name acts again: by morning, half his city might lie burned or smashed.

Touton liked to catch the stars, but he wasn't much into the club life, the drinking and conviviality. He was never made welcome anyway. He preferred to go, listen, look around, check things out, see who was talking to whom, and leave. Too many cops went down the tubes spending their wages at the Algiers or the Samovar, or hobnobbing with the likes of Jack Dempsey or Rocky Marciano at Slitkin's and Slotkin's, although he'd done that, too—just once, on a dare. Marciano had been in town, and one of his cops had bet that Touton's fists were bigger than the champ's. The cop begged him to go down to the club the next night and measure his closed fist alongside the reigning heavyweight king's. Both men settled for a tie, but the photographers enjoyed themselves, snapping the massive fists side by side on a table, then capturing the two heroes feinting punches. A front page showed Touton cracking a right hook across the champ's jaw. The champ had been smiling. People wondered, though, and the tabloids asked the question, "Could Touton take out Marciano?"

"He's undefeated," the officer had quipped. "I've lost fights. Adolf had me on the ropes, remember?"

The Top Hat. The Copacabana. The Normandie Roof. The Bellevue Casino, where the cover was fifty cents and so was the beer. The Chez Maurice Danceland, where the young people hung out. The Black Sheep Room at Ruby Foo's. So many acts and so much action, and the tough guys visited them all and hatched their schemes. Montreal was a night city, to the consternation of the Church and those who held to traditional values. Of Montreal, Mark Twain had said in the 1880s, "you can't throw a brick without breaking a church window." Now that same brick would bust the windows of bars.

Times change, but times remain the same, Touton believed. Montreal had always been a drinking city, and a brawling city, a city of vice and pleasure as well as one of piety. Ebb and flow. Amid the social strata stood the police, usually corrupt, on occasion righteous.

As captain of the Night Patrol, and an officer intricately linked to the new reformers, Touton was not usually welcomed into the clubs. He'd never be denied entry, either.

A municipal election had been held a year earlier. On that day, messages about disturbances burst over police radios about every twelve seconds. The day might not have been as bad as the one ten years earlier, when seventeen people were shot, but baseball bats and brass knuckles remained in vogue, and polling booths were dangerous places. Valorously, the reformers persevered this time, and won. Jean Drapeau, the diminutive lawyer who'd led a four-year investigation into city corruption, became mayor, and the man who once had been the head of the police morality squad, Pacifique "Pax" Plante, who had closed down the gambling dens and the bawdy houses only to be fired for his trouble, was brought back to the police department as its new director. This returned Touton to a safer position within the department, but now the club owners were being forced to abide by the 2 A.M. closing hour instead of dawn. They were obliged to evict the prostitutes from their premises, and were crying foul. Even the legendary stripper, Lili St. Cyr, who would vamp in her heart-shaped chastity belt before discovering the key, slipped away, drawn to a burgeoning desert oasis of sin and wickedness. Americans wanted to capture the Montreal business for themselves, and Las Vegas was the answer. The local club trade was bad and getting worse, and Touton suspected that many clients were on the streets tonight, their rage having little to do with hockey and not much to do with the complex politics of the day. They wanted to party, to revel in debauchery once again, and as the new administration was curtailing their fun, they wanted to smash anything that looked vaguely official.

Gambling dens were being shut down, and gambling had been the city's second-largest industry behind the rag trade. After-hours speakeasies were cropping up, and they'd be the next to be rooted out and closed. One by one, the bawdy houses were bolting their doors, the women waving to their admirers at Windsor Station as they caught trains to New York. A few of the men who had enjoyed the pleasure of their company were now throwing rocks at cops and overturning police cruisers, forgetting that the cops had been the mainstays of the old regime and that reformers in the department, like Touton, whom they were leaving alone, belonged to an embattled minority.

The rioters had their frustrations. They were taking them out.

Times changed and times remained the same—yet these days something new stirred. A fresh influence had emerged to truly change the way things worked. People's minds were being altered, and for that Touton credited television. Quebecers had only been kneeling before their sets since 1952, a mere three years, but already the impact was palpable. Fewer people came out to the clubs, and Touton had a hunch that TV would do more to close down the city's nightlife than the 2 A.M. closing hour. But something else: through television, French-speaking Quebecers were seeing, for the first time, how English-speaking people lived on the rest of the continent, and that was an eye-popper. That was stunning. They saw that, in comparison, they were wretchedly poor and hard done by. As well, for the first time, opinions were being expressed over French-language television that ran counter to the dictates of the Church. Touton was all in favour of that. He had been to war. He had lived in a POW camp, then marched in a destitute column back to Germany in the depths of winter without shoes and with little clothing. The Germans did not feed their prisoners on that last march, but allowed them time in the evenings to scrounge for their own food. He knew what it was like to be a captive and a scavenger, knew what it was like to be saved on what was, in all probability, to have been his last day alive if not for the sudden appearance of an American tank. He didn't need a priest to tell him what to think. The war had instilled that independence in him, and he believed that if more Quebecers had gone to war, and if the war hadn't killed them, they'd understand that, too. And yet, now, thanks to television, thanks to entertainment rather than war, they were also advancing on the same principles he had attained. They were thinking for themselves. They were questioning authority. And perhaps, Touton considered as he mulled things over, this was why he had not favoured full combat against the rioters, because the riot was a reaction against their restraints, and the people had every right to be mad. They had every right to be furious.

They were poor.

Their lives were hard.

The damn English were always telling them what to do, and now they had suspended the Rocket! Their hero! What else did they have if not the Stanley Cup, and now the *maudit anglais* had conspired to deprive their team!

So windows were smashed. Debris was scattered. Stores were looted. Vehicles were vandalized and fires struck. Captain Armand Touton walked through the melee wondering how all this would unfold, this intoxicated rage, agitated all the while by a cantankerous officer who had insisted that somehow a burglary was more important than the social firestorm before their eyes.

††††

Cops brought in horses.

The mob paused, retreated slightly, and formed a denser unit. Men shouted profanities at the cops or waved their fists or threw icy snowballs or hatched fresh manoeuvres. Nervously, a cautious contingent stepped to the rear, their enthusiasm tempered, while moving to the forefront were unionists, men who had battled cops previously in bloody confrontations. The combatants included men who'd hire themselves out at election time to wreck polling booths or stuff ballot boxes at knifepoint. Politicians and the papers called them goons. They'd fought cops often, sometimes with guns.

Also among their number were the fearless young, their courage found in the tempest of the moment and in the unlimited supply of stolen beer being quaffed down.

Cops manning the line looked across at a few old adversaries they recognized.

The two groups stared one another down.

Waiting.

Anxious horses whinnied.

The cops had no special training with respect to riots, and the only additional equipment they were issued were truncheons. In the past, they had discerned that cops on horseback were able to turn back any crowd. But they were facing men who had fought against horses before, had been beaten back and fled, yet they always itched for an opportunity to try again, believing they could devise fresh tactics.

They could not.

When the cops charged, they charged. The men were pummelled and trampled. Their lines yielded and cracked, yet they had a good number of recruits this time, and the chaos of the scene pulled bystanders into the fray. Riders found themselves surrounded. The youngest of these were terrified. A few panicked, fear travelling through their saddles into the skins of the animals. The horses kicked with their forelegs and spun in circles and kicked with their hind legs as they'd been trained to do. Rioters fell and held their bloodied heads in their hands. Even so, one policeman on horseback was hauled down from behind. The horse bucked and galloped clear.

Other cops swung their truncheons into the mob, concentrating an attack to rescue the fallen rider, and the mob peeled back and cheered themselves and took up the fight elsewhere. Tear gas was fired, but most of the cops were not prepared for the fumes, and a swirl of wind might send the rioters running one minute, the cops the next. The gas then dipped in gusts perplexed by the compress of buildings, and the eyes of the horses went wild, the animals choked and they were ridden off.

Gas swirled skyward, caught in an updraft that lifted it above the huge, bright, blinking Pepsi-Cola sign.

A tired, bleeding cop, down on one knee awaiting rescue or an ambulance, unsnapped his holster and held a hand on the stock of his revolver. Photographed, the picture would serve as a symbol of the battle in the morning papers.

The mob threw stones and bricks they had loosed from the walls of English stores, and they tossed broken glass at the cops and in the path of horses, and they threw snowballs without any harmful ingredients, or harmful effect, as though this were merely a schoolyard donnybrook. The groups charged and retreated and charged again, and a cop swung his truncheon to get Pierre Elliott Trudeau and his friend, Father François Legault, off their bench.

"What're you doing that for? I'm not bothering you," Trudeau complained.

"Get the hell away from here!" the cop cried out and slammed his weapon down hard against the bench, damaging it. He was a man in his fifties with dirt on his face and a wide cut on his chin.

"You're a Frenchman!" Father François shouted at him, as if that came as some sort of surprise.

"So?" the befuddled cop wanted to know.

"Yeah, so?" Trudeau wanted to know as well.

"Why are you striking another Frenchman?"

"Because he's sitting on a bench here! I don't want no goddamned spectators! Are you a goddamned reporter?"

"I'm a priest! You watch your language."

"You're a priest?" the cop asked him, shocked.

"He's a priest," Trudeau confirmed, as though his opinion should be trusted. "A Dominican, of course, but we can forgive him for that, no?"

"You Jesuit elitist," Father François fired back at Trudeau, and chuckled.

"Just get off this bench here!" the cop tried again, not knowing what to make of these two nutcases. Then he capitulated somewhat. "You should go home, Father. We can take care of business here tonight. Tomorrow you can visit the hospitals."

"*You* should go home, not me. Don't bother with your business. Tomorrow you can go to confession."

"What am I supposed to confess? That I'm doing my job?"

"That you were busting Catholic heads for your English bosses!"

"What English bosses?" the cop asked. "What's he talking about? Is he really a priest?" He seemed on the verge of striking them both again, if only to stop their crazy chatter. "He talks like a communist!"

"He's a communist priest. They exist now," Trudeau explained.

"Wake up, man!" Father François yelled at him. "Wake up!"

"I'm awake," the cop answered, confused. "Are you drunk, Father?"

"Are you?"

"I'm on duty!"

"Are you drunk on duty? Ask yourself this question."

"You can't be a communist priest. There's no such thing. It's *impossible!*"

"Why? Because Duplessis won't allow it?"

"The Pope won't allow it!"

"The Pope has problems with Dominicans, though," Trudeau cut in. "They're such a pain in the butt, you know? At least he's not a Sulpician."

"At least you're not either."

"Or a Franciscan."

"What are you talking about?" the cop asked. He thought they might be making fun of him.

"The divisions and subdivisions. If you're a communist, you might be a Trotskyite, or a Marxist-Leninist, or even a Maoist. If you're a Catholic, well, the permutations are endless."

"What's he talking about?" the cop asked again.

"Anyway, Officer, it's been nice talking to you. Don't swing that thing at me again, all right? We're moving back."

"I'll crack your head open if you don't! If I find out you're a reporter, I'll smash your nose!"

"If you like, I'll point out the reporters to you," Father François offered, which won a chuckle from his new friend.

"You'd better move back, too, Officer," Trudeau cautioned him. "We're in the middle of the next charge. Give up the bench—it's not worth bleeding over."

"You're communists!"

"Not quite. He is. I'm merely an intellectual Jesuit Buddhist, with liberal underpinnings and a humanitarian bent. A little hedonism on the side."

"You're homosexuals!"

"I'm a priest! Watch what you say."

"I'm also a lawyer," Trudeau admitted, "but maybe I shouldn't tempt you. I'm also a ladies' man. But, like I said, maybe I shouldn't tempt you."

"Sorry, Father, but get out of here or I'll forget that you're a priest. I'll bust your head! I'll bust the lawyer's head in half."

"Officer," Trudeau persisted, "look around you—you're isolated. Get the hell out of here yourself."

The officer did look around this time and realized that he was alone. The mob had spotted him, and the next charge met in the middle of the square around the bench he'd coveted, the officer flailing wildly at communists and homosexuals and unionists and intellectuals and reporters and lawyers and probably teachers and parents and superior officers and even hockey players who failed to score on crucial breakaways while other cops raced to his rescue and Trudeau and his new friend stepped back as the two forces clashed.

"This changes everything!" Father François yelled in Trudeau's ear above the din. They were not alone in having a conversation, as behind each joust men on both sides argued and tried to figure out what was happening, or what should happen next, although their discussion was singular.

"We can agree on that," Trudeau said.

"It's the beginning of the revolution."

"Actually, it's the beginning of the riot. The riot is part of an ongoing social upheaval. To call it a revolution is to hijack the agenda for your own purposes. You should be ashamed of yourself, a priest."

"I'm a Dominican. We promote new ideas, unlike Jesuit stick-in-the-muds."

"We promote a more rigorous examination, Father."

"So in the end you can clear your conscience for doing nothing."

"Am I holding you back, Father? Do you want to throw a rotten egg?"

"The poor don't have eggs to waste on policemen!"

"Pardon me?"

They were being jostled from behind and had to duck to the side against a building to avoid being pushed into the path of horses.

"Not even rotten ones. The poor don't have eggs," Father François repeated.

"Spare me the rhetoric, Father. Who do you think you're talking to?"

"A rich young Jesuit from Outremont."

"And you, a cozy priest."

"You pulled your punch there, Pierre. You meant to say fat."

"I meant to say what I said, Father."

"Don't call me cozy. I'm here, aren't I? On the front lines."

"The front lines are fifty feet away."

"Close enough. I don't have the heart for battle."

"You're a pacifist?"

"No, I just have a weak heart."

The two men laughed then, and the fight in front of them dispersed in a torrent of snowballs from the young boys in the rear.

✝✝✝

Amid imposing Doric columns, visitors are guided up broad stairs into the Sun Life Building. Scaled-down columns are repeated seventeen floors higher, the overall effect one of solidity and long-term prosperity, as if success can be measured as eternal. True to form, the Sun Life Assurance Company has enjoyed a long and eventful history in the province, its influence at times approximating that of the Church. The first institution Armand Touton had chosen to defend upon deducing that there might be trouble in the streets was the Sun Life, not because he favoured the place, but because it stood out as a likely flashpoint for French rage.

He accosted the first officer he came across guarding an entrance.

"I said to keep people out of here!"

"I did, sir."

"Crooks got in!"

"Not through my door."

"Young man, I bought a new stove recently. Electric. Turn it on, and like magic, the rings on the burner heat up. They get so hot they go red. You can boil water so fast you can turn your kitchen into a sauna in the wintertime. If I find out somebody got through your door, I'll make you sit on that burner."

"My door was locked, sir, and it's still locked. I don't have a key. You have to go down to the middle to get in."

Touton tested the officer's locked door, and confided, "That's good news for your ass."

"Yes, sir."

Only a few cop cars were parked up and down the block, and across the street a number of officers had gathered around a statue to the Scottish poet, Robbie Burns. Touton didn't have a spare minute to investigate how they got to goof off amid the uproar. Across the night sky he heard the sirens of emergency vehicles, marauders roaring and the flagrant honk of car horns in support of the riot.

Smoke from fires and tear gas fumes drifted across the square.

Touton also berated the cop on duty at the middle door, but again received no admission of guilt. "They didn't come in this way, sir."

"If I ask every cop on duty, will I get the same response?"

"I don't know, sir. Maybe."

"I suppose the crooks landed by helicopter." He intended the remark to be both rhetorical and facetious.

"Something like that," the young patrolman said. "I heard it was something like that, anyway."

Touton shook his head as the officer unlocked the door for him. Sometimes young cops could be just so damned stupid they took his breath away.

Downstairs, another cop was waiting to guide him up. The elevator, smooth with a comforting guttural purr, possessed an elegance the policemen rarely experienced. The walls were mahogany and the fittings a gleaming, polished brass.

"Detective Sloan upstairs?"

"I don't know, sir," the patrolman said.

"What do you mean, you don't know?" He doubted that young cops were becoming more stupid year by year, but on this particular night he seemed to be running into the dullest minds in the department.

"He's gone back and forth so often, it's hard to keep track. Sir, I think he's upstairs, but I could be wrong."

"Back and forth between where and where?"

"Between here and the park, sir."

Touton guessed the cop was probably intimidated by his rank and reputation, as well as by his tone, so offered nothing more than rudimentary responses.

"You mean across the street? What's in the park?"

"The dead man, sir."

"What dead man?"

"The one in the park, sir."

"What's your name, Officer?"

The lad took a deep breath and wondered what he'd done to deserve this. "Miron, sir."

"Miron, why is there a dead man in the park?"

"I don't know, sir. I mean, he was murdered, I know that, but I don't know why, sir."

The elevator had reached their floor and the two men clambered out, Touton first. "You're telling me there's been a murder in the park? Detective Sloan is covering both cases?" Actually, when he thought about it for a moment, given that every cop was being stretched beyond the breaking point on this night, that seemed reasonable.

"I think it's the same case, sir."

"What?"

"Just what I heard."

"The burglary in here—"

"—and the murder in the park, sir. Same case."

They'd reached the door to the league offices. "All right, Miron. I want you to stick around and take care of my shotgun. Can you do that?"

"Yes, sir."

"Don't shoot your foot off."

"I'll take the shells out, sir, if that's all right."

"All right. Here's the rest of the ammo. If the rioters come up in that elevator, you have my permission to reload and blast away."

"Yes, sir," the young man said.

Touton shook his head in dismay. Then he thought he'd better say something. "I'm kidding."

"Oh," Miron said. "Okay. I got you."

Touton stepped over glass and tried not to touch the cracked door to the modest office. A crowbar was on the floor. The foyer was surprisingly small, with insufficient room to swing a cat—or a hockey player his stick. Players had to come here for their disciplinary hearings, and Rocket Richard would have been here only a day ago to plead his case. Touton stepped through to the corridor that led to the warren of adjoining offices, and Detective Sloan spotted him.

"What's up?" Touton asked.

"This is big," Sloan said.

"It better be," the senior officer let him know, but he could see the excitement in Sloan's eyes and caught it in his tone of voice.

"All right, from the top, there's been a break-in."

"How'd they get in? We've got guards on every door."

"Through the windows," Sloan told him. At forty-seven, he was considerably older than Touton, but having neither his war record nor his success as a cop, he had become junior to him in rank. His hair was thinning. His face was pinched, as if by adversity. His complexion was pale, as though he rarely experienced sunlight. No matter the time of night, he always had such a smooth jaw that Touton doubted he could properly grow a beard, although he could use one, as his chin was weak.

Touton pushed the tip of his hat back, its usual angle when he was indoors, especially if he was mulling something over. "Are you telling me they flew in here? Because I'm willing to partner you up with that dumb patrolman I met downstairs. Oh . . . let me guess. You're the one spreading the rumour they swooped in by helicopter."

"Give me a break, Armand. Come on. We don't have everything yet, but it sure looks like they got up on the roof somehow, then lowered themselves down to this level by ropes. We know they broke in through the windows—that's a fact. They committed a burglary, took what they wanted and left by the windows also, but this time a few floors down. Then they dropped themselves to the ground by ropes when our guys weren't looking."

"Our guys weren't looking. Of course not. What else did they have to do tonight to keep themselves occupied . . . twiddle their thumbs?"

"Armand, they were guarding the doors. They weren't looking up. Who would? They were watching the street. Coming down, the crooks concealed themselves behind the columns. It's ingenious. They almost made a clean break."

"Almost?"

"Let me show you this first." He led Touton down a narrow corridor, through an office where cops were murmuring amongst themselves, then into a small antechamber that housed the vault. The heavy steel door sagged open and the wall had been blackened from a blast. Touton took a closer look.

"They blew it open?"

"Dynamite. That crude."

"Who heard this? And don't say 'nobody.'"

He already knew what the man would answer. The building had been emptied for security reasons. The walls were as thick as fortress ramparts. In none of the rooms he had just walked through had there been any windows, and there were none in this one.

"Nobody," Sloan said.

"What did they get?" Touton asked him.

Rather than answer straight away, Sloan took a deep breath.

"What?" Touton tried to imagine what the dilemma could be. "The Rocket's stick? A Howie Morenz puck? The Stanley Cup? What?"

"The Cartier Dagger."

"What's that?"

"You should know," Sloan told him. "Not me."

"Why should I know?"

"Because you're French. Campbell's coming over. He can tell you more about it."

"Clarence Campbell? The mob will kill him if he's spotted."

"I told him that. He wanted to come anyway. So I sent a patrol car."

"That's good." Touton shook his head. "If it was me I'd've put a bag over his head."

"If it was me I'd just shoot him," Sloan said. "But that's another story."

"Good point. I hope you sent a couple of guys we can trust."

Both men smiled. Sloan showed him the smashed glass display case in which an invaluable antique knife resided most days. The case was a couple of feet long, and, like the panelling in the elevator, made of a bright mahogany with polished brass trim. The broken glass was thick and scattered in pieces on the floor.

"Usually, during the day, the case is kept in Campbell's office. On display. Even then, it's locked, and secured to the desk it's on, and the desk weighs a ton."

Touton was thinking about something else as he took to examining the heavy door blown partially off its hinges. "Usually, there'd be people up here, right? If not in this office, on the floor. If not on the floor, then in the building. Night shift workers. Cleaners. Lawyers preparing a case. People working overtime on a big project. That sort of thing."

"That's right."

"So if this is some sort of big-time heist—"

"Which it is."

"—then the bad guys took advantage of the riot to break in . . ."

"I believe that," Sloan agreed.

" . . . then how did they know there'd be a riot?"

"I believe that, too," Sloan contested, one step ahead of him.

"You believe what?" Sloan was making no sense.

"Somebody might have started the riot in order to steal the Cartier Dagger."

This was news. Touton had assumed that, in the coming weeks, numerous commentators would be taking a stab at explaining the riot. The frustration of hockey fans, the fury of the French who felt victimized yet again by the English, the social upheaval of a nation wrestling with its postwar restraints, the wrath of the poor—the rationale would be discussed and debated, yet no one was likely to suggest that the entire matter had been a ploy to blow the doors off a vault.

Recovering, Touton said, "Tell me about the knife."

"An old relic owned by Sun Life. It's worth millions. For once, 'priceless' is a word that fits. Originally, it belonged to Jacques Cartier himself—some Indian gave it to him. It's on loan to Campbell for his work at Nuremberg, but just on loan, because, like I said, it's worth millions—or more. He can keep it here as long as he's NHL president."

"What's in it for him?"

"He gets to look at it whenever he wants, I guess. It's a handsome knife."

"How do you know?"

"I've seen it."

"When? Where?" Touton drilled him.

"Tonight. Across the street in the park. The dagger is stuck in the heart of a murder victim. Up to the hilt, right through the breastplate. It's still there right now."

Touton looked at Sloan. His own excitement was rising, and he wanted to suppress it. "You've got to be kidding me," he said slowly.

"Come across with me. See for yourself."

"Lead the way." Touton pulled his hat lower, indicating that he was headed outside, but also that he meant business.

Before they could manage the foray, Clarence Campbell got off the elevator. He was still in the company of the three women with whom he had attended the game, one of whom had received more than her share of tomato splatter. Apparently, the three were not about to leave his side anytime soon, nor would they consent to being left alone by themselves. They were spinsters, and he was a bachelor in need of their care in this, his darkest hour.

The hockey league president held his fedora at his left side, his right hand in his coat pocket. A relaxed posture. Only wisps of hair covered his pate, and his face sagged into his jowls. He had a stout middle. He did not seem to be the sort of man to be keeping the company of three women, but one was his sister and all three were rather dowdy in the style of their day, despite wearing half-veils that hung from their hats, and earrings and bright lipstick. Their coats bulged beneath their waists from the fabric of their dresses and crinolines.

Campbell paused—stopping so suddenly that one of the three women inadvertently stepped into him while she fiddled with her purse. The sight of a shotgun-toting cop at the entrance to his office had shocked him. He took a breath, apologized to the lady who had bumped into him, and carried on.

"Is that really necessary?" he asked the man in blue.

"I'm holding it for someone, that's all," Miron replied, somewhat bashfully as he tipped his cap to the ladies present. "It's not loaded, sir. I'm not planning to shoot anybody with it."

"That's heartening, Officer." He stepped past the policeman and entered the crime scene just as Detective Sloan and Captain Touton emerged.

"Did you *have* to suspend him for the playoffs?" Sloan asked without thinking. "I mean, he's the Rocket, for crying out loud."

"Sloan," Touton said, and the cop shut up. Then he said, "Mr. Campbell."

"It's good to see they have Montreal's finest detective on the case, Captain Touton. The dagger is infinitely valuable. It goes beyond the probable millions it's worth. An historic relic."

"We've found the knife, sir," Touton revealed.

"You have! Oh. That's good news. What a relief. Where?"

"It's across the street. In the park."

"The crooks went to all this trouble just to toss it away in the park?"

"We're still sorting it out. Do you know why anybody would do that?"

Campbell shifted his hat from one hand to the other as he shook his head. "Beats me. People steal things. That happens. But who steals something of value, then throws it away? I'm stumped."

Touton nodded. "We'll have to confiscate the knife for a time, sir. Material evidence."

Campbell did not offer immediate compliance, and instead squared his shoulders. "I'd feel much more comfortable if I received the dagger back tonight, Captain."

"That's not possible, sir. Anyway, your vault's been blown open. You can't keep it safe."

"I see. May I have a look inside? At the damage?"

Usually, Touton would keep civilians out, but this man was the president of the NHL and had been a war crimes prosecutor. In that latter sense, they had both fought the Germans, and had both worked on the right side of the law. "Go ahead, sir, only, please, don't touch anything. I know it's your office, but wait until the boys are done. They're dusting for prints right now."

"Thank you, Captain. Your fast work on the dagger is appreciated."

"Lady Luck got us the knife back. Our investigation is only getting started. Now, sir, another matter, when you're ready to leave—"

"Certainly, Captain."

"Sir?"

"I'll accept your escort, if that's what you're offering." He smiled. "I have the safety of my ladies to consider. I won't be walking around the streets of Montreal anytime soon. If I do, as we both know, I won't get far."

As though he'd been on slow simmer, Sloan barged in again. "Five games, for instance. That would've been a reasonable suspension—pretty severe. Five games would've taught the Rocket a lesson. I could live with that. But the play-offs—"

"Sloan," Touton said quietly.

"If you went to a tavern to break up a fight, Detective," Campbell argued back, "and you arrested a fellow who'd taken a baseball bat and smashed it three times across another man's back, and you'd had to deal with his violence before, what sentence would you expect him to get? Jail time, or a tap on the left wrist?"

"That's different," Sloan complained. "This is hockey, not a public tavern."

"If the Rocket had missed and hit the guy's head, he'd have killed him. Or maybe he did miss . . . maybe he was hoping to hit the guy's head. What sentence would he get for murdering a man on the ice? Or would you recommend that he be let off for that, too, that we just call it hockey?"

"That's different."

"Sloan," Touton hissed.

"Why is it different?" Campbell pressed on. "If people go to a hockey game, or sit in a tavern, they don't expect to see one man try to hack another man to bits."

"It's the Stanley Cup!"

"Sloan, out the door and shut up!" Touton burst out, rather more loudly than he had intended. The detective looked at his superior, then broke off and angrily strode back to the corridor. Touton was stepping around the women to join him when he turned to face Clarence Campbell. "Sorry about that. Like everybody else—"

"No problem, Captain. I understand it's not a popular decision."

"It's your job, I suppose," Touton sympathized. Then he shook his head, and added, "But I don't know . . . the playoffs," as he went out the door.

In the corridor, Touton shot Sloan a glance, but chose to speak to Miron first. "Come with us. Bring the shotgun."

Sloan said, "What? Is the shotgun for me? Look, Armand, sorry about that in there. It just rots my socks, you know?"

"If you were investigating a murder scene, and you knew who the murder weapon belonged to, who would you suspect for the crime?"

Being older, Sloan was not usually put in the position of being tested, and he felt momentarily flummoxed. He particularly did not enjoy being dressed down in front of a uniform. "The guy whose weapon it was, of course, but—"

"So what's different about this case?"

Sloan was still confused, even as he pushed the call button for the elevator. "No, wait, you don't think—"

"I didn't say that."

"Clarence Campbell . . . he's—"

"What? A Nuremberg prosecutor? A big-shot? League president? Therefore beyond suspicion? Okay. That's fine. But it's still his knife in the heart of the victim."

"My God," Sloan whispered as the elevator doors opened and the three men stepped in. "You don't think—"

"I don't, actually. I think his alibi is airtight. He's been busy. Fourteen thousand people were trying to kick his butt. They were joined by another fifty thousand. I don't see him getting here fast enough, although it would have been possible. I also don't see him breaking through upper-storey windows or climbing down to the street by rope. That's pretty funny, actually, when you think about it. On the other hand, he is under attack. Who knows how nimble that makes him? But my point has nothing to do with Clarence Campbell being a suspect or not."

"What's your point?"

"Your head's not in the game. We have a pretty daring robbery here, don't you think? Well planned, well executed, from what I've seen so far. All this to acquire a weapon that was then used to kill a man. Wake up, for God's sake. You can't be going off half-cocked about some dumb-assed suspension."

Contrite, Sloan put his hands in his pants pockets and hung his head most of the way down. As they reached the main floor, he asked, "So you agree?"

"About what?"

"It was a dumb-assed suspension."

"Totally." Touton smiled as they headed outside. "Officer Miron."

"Yes, sir?"

"If Detective Sloan brings up the Richard suspension again, or even mentions the name Rocket Richard—"

"Yes, sir?"

"Load two shells into the shotgun, peel his overcoat off his back and shoot it full of holes."

"Ah, shoot his back, sir, or his coat?"

"His coat, for crying out loud. I'm not asking you to commit murder."

"Yes, sir," Miron agreed.

They were on their way down the outside stairs when Sloan thought to say, "Miron?"

"Yes, sir?" the young cop asked.

"You know he's kidding, right?"

"It doesn't matter," the officer in uniform deadpanned. "Whether he's kidding or not, I'll do it anyway."

Touton laughed under his breath as Sloan gave the young cop a second glance. He might have to alter his initial opinion on the young man in uniform.

With the street blocked off due to the riot, they didn't have to look for traffic as they stepped off the curb and crossed to the park and a crowd of cops. Dominion Square occupied a short city block, a park with the usual complement of trees, open spaces and benches to provide a measure of rest amid the haste of the city. Grass showed through here and there, but snow had been ploughed into piles to keep the walkways clear, and these drifts, hard packed and dirty, would be the last to melt.

The Sun Life was a building associated particularly with the English, and to a degree the park possessed an English motif as well. The Frenchman Laurier, who had been one of the fledgling country's early prime ministers, had a statue here, but another monument paid homage to the fallen heroes of the South African War, which held no interest at all among the French—and not much among the English, either, as it harked back to British colonial rule. The poet chosen to be honoured was Robbie Burns, a Scot who had never set foot in the country. On the steps below the Burns statue, the poet's back to him, lay the sprawled, inert body of the murdered victim.

Cops had driven onto the walkways, and the area was lit by the headlights of their cars. Touton was quickly able to spot the coroner, Claude Racine. A small, wiry man, around fifty-five, with a salt-and-pepper moustache and greying temples, he was wearing a Montreal Canadiens jacket with Richard's famous number 9 across the biceps, perhaps a deliberate ploy to manage his way through the crowds on this night. His trip to the crime scene had been slower than usual, given the ruckus in the streets.

"Claude," Touton said, both to acknowledge the man's presence and to announce his own.

"Armand."

"What do we have here?"

"Go look for yourself. It's not a pretty sight."

Touton was about to do so when the coroner thought twice, put a hand to his chest and stopped him. "Wait." He addressed Sloan. "Does he know yet?"

"Know what?" Sloan asked him back.

"Do you even know?"

Sloan was befuddled. "What am I supposed to know?"

"What is it, Claude?" Touton asked him gently, for something told him that matters in this place might be serious. All he could see from his current vantage point was the dead man's boots.

"Prepare yourself, Armand. You're not going to like it. He's not your best friend or nothing like that, but you know the victim."

Touton stepped around the coroner and moved cops aside to get a proper view of the corpse. He knelt down beside the dead man, and tipped his fedora back from his brow, his sadness palpable to all who could see his face. The coroner crouched next to him. The dead man was square-shouldered and square-jawed, with a boxer's big chest and a drinker's swollen paunch.

"I'm right, aren't I?"

"Roger Clément," Touton acknowledged. "How do you know him?"

"Coincidence. We've been witnesses at the same trials a couple of times."

"He wasn't the accused?"

"A defence witness. Paid to lie. But I'm right? You've been friends?"

"Acquaintances. More or less. I've busted him a few times. We respected each other—that's probably fair to say. He could punch, this guy. A strong man, but I never knew him to really hurt anybody. Even though he was hired to do so, from time to time." Touton glanced over his shoulder at Sloan, standing behind him. "Do you know him?"

"No, sir. He has a record?"

Touton stood up. "He was still a decent guy. Shit. I'll have to tell his family."

"We could send someone," Sloan suggested. "He's only a hood, right?"

Touton was looking up at the highest level of the columns on the Sun Life.

"He was never *only* a hood. I just told you, he was a decent guy. It wouldn't take much for me to have been him, or for him to have been me. We have the same physique, similar background. He's a family man. To his family he was never a hood. He was a father, a husband. Make sure nobody gets to his house before me."

"Yes, sir."

"He was also an ex-hockey player. He played for Chicago, and somebody else. New York, I think."

They waited for him to lower his gaze, and when he didn't, the other cops around him and the coroner also looked up at the Sun Life.

"He could have done it," Touton stated. "He had the balls. The strength. He could have broken in and slid down by rope. But he never could have planned all that. Not Roger. He's not that kind of thief. He would've been hired to carry it out."

"Then he gets back down here and somebody kills him with what he stole," Sloan pointed out. "Makes no sense, no matter how you cut it."

"Unless somebody else stole the knife and he crossed paths with the thief in the dark. Still doesn't make sense, though. To go to all that trouble to steal a million-dollar dagger, then to lose it in a guy's heart."

The coroner returned to the corpse and, with his gloved hands, tried to extract the knife from the body. The weapon did not slide free easily. He had to remove instruments from his bag and use them to slowly extract the weapon, working it loose with difficulty. Finally, the dagger slid up into his hands.

"I wish I could reward you with the crown of England, for pulling Excalibur from stone, Claude."

"I'll settle for a good night's sleep. And a chance to hold this in my hands."

"Interesting, though. Whoever implanted it might have had the same trouble getting it out. Then he might've had to take off before he succeeded."

"That's possible. Look at this thing."

The handle was made of bear bone, the blade of stone. The cutting edge was serrated, not naturally, but had lost its edge over time and was quite jagged. The very tip of the knife had snapped off, Touton noticed.

"Look, the leading edge, the change of colour. I bet that piece is still in him."

"I'll be looking for it," the coroner assured him. "Do you see the jagged edge? That's what made it difficult to extract. It caught on the breastplate, a rib. The blade isn't steel, after all. It's soft. It's only stone."

The bone handle was partially wrapped with hide—very old, so that it was conceivable to think it was original. A remarkable aspect to the knife were the gold and diamonds embedded in the handle. They were not finely cut, but rough-hewn in a primitive fashion. The weapon was now centuries old.

"You'll take care of this?" Touton asked him. "Don't leave it lying around."

The coroner nodded. "There's a safe I can use, back at the office."

"Probably it's more secure with you than at the police station."

"Definitely, I'd say."

Touton grunted.

"All right, I'm going to bag the body now, Armand. Need anything else?"

He moved his chin slightly. "I could use that good night's sleep you were talking about, but that's not going to happen anytime soon."

In the distance, the wail of sirens and the roar of the mob still sounded. Closer to them, fire smoke drifted by and mingled with the exhaust fumes of their cars.

"This could go on for days," the coroner concurred.

"The Rocket should talk," Miron suggested.

"What?" Sloan asked him.

"The Rocket, he should get on the radio. Tell the people to calm down."

"The Rocket! On the radio!" Sloan challenged him. "To save Campbell's ass?"

"He should get on the radio," Touton butted in, lending authority to the suggestion, "to save the city."

The men nodded, understanding the gravity of the situation, when Miron disrupted their mood. "He mentioned the Rocket, sir. Do I get to shoot his coat?"

"You little shit!" Sloan burst out.

Touton glanced at the young cop. "Now you know you goaded him, Miron. That wasn't part of the deal."

"Yes, sir."

"But keep your ears open. You may get to shoot his coat yet."

Sloan glowered at the young guy, then said, "Speaking of the radio, Captain, he has one on him. In his pocket. One of those fancy new transistors. The Regency TR-1."

"Sophisticated. Imagine that, eh? A radio you don't plug in. Damn thing costs fifty bucks, but I might buy one. Anything else?"

"A flashlight and a penknife, also in his coat pockets. A bit of putty. We picked up a woman's kerchief that was lying beside him so it wouldn't blow away. We can't say if it belonged to him or just blew in."

Touton shook his head, then nodded back at the Sun Life. "Look at that building. I don't know what Fort Knox looks like, but it must be similar. Are you telling me he broke into that building with a transistor radio and a penknife?"

Sloan shrugged a little. "He also must have had several long stretches of rope and a few sticks of dynamite."

"Dynamite, a kerchief and putty." Touton blew out a gust of air.

The coroner bagged the knife and placed it in the glove box of his van, which he locked, then he locked the van. He came back for the body, which his assistants had bagged, and, while Touton questioned other cops on the scene, he loaded the corpse onto a gurney. The captain wanted to hear what the other cops had learned or guessed, if anything, and to know if any witnesses had stepped forward. This was a public park, one that was used at night, although, admittedly, the night had been exceptional. The cops confirmed what he'd expected: that the usual thrum of people had been drawn into the cacophony of the riot, and so far only one witness had turned up. That man had spotted a group of adult males, at least two of whom looked old, huddled over the victim. Suspiciously, aggressively, he said. He'd dashed away to call a cop. When the officer went to investigate, the men ran.

"The cop didn't chase them?" Touton asked.

"He did, he says, but they vanished into the mob scene."

Feeling glum, Touton went over to the coroner's van and shut the driver's-side door on him, giving it a slap as the vehicle departed. The coroner drove across the grass and snow, onto the sidewalk, then slowly dropped the van off the curb onto the street and headed south.

The captain of the Night Patrol turned back to the crime scene.

This one was perplexing. He knew that his men were seeing what they were meant to see. The acrobatic robbery, followed by a bold murder with a valuable, stolen weapon. But an aspect that had made the robbery work was the early preventative evacuation of the building due to the riot. Sloan had already made that connection. And another question—why would a thief lie dead, with the stolen prize lodged in his chest? That one was the real puzzle to anyone looking at this.

"Sir! Sir!" Miron called excitedly. Then, suddenly, he reached into his jacket pocket and pulled out two shells.

"What? Did Sloan mention Richard?"

Miron stooped to retrieve a shell that had fallen in the snow, and nodded in the direction the van travelled. Touton shot a glance that way. The coroner's van had been cut off by a car at the intersection with Dorchester Boulevard. Both its front doors were flung open.

"Get down there! Go! Run!"

Touton ran, too, but the younger, lighter man who was free of war wounds dashed ahead of him. Spotting them on the move, Sloan and other cops came running. Touton could see a confrontation around the cars, a tussle, then heard a gunshot. Men leaped into a large, black Cadillac, and the car burned rubber, its tires squealing as the car vaulted away before its doors were closed. Still running, Touton caught sight of a coroner's assistant bent over a body in front of the van, and he yelled at Miron, "Shoot! Fire that thing!"

The young man still had to load the shells. He stopped running to do so, then aimed and pressed both triggers. The right rear tail light popped and went dark, but the fleeing black Caddy continued off into the night.

The echo of the shotgun blast bounced off the Sun Life Building and, across the street, off Mary Queen of the World Cathedral. Touton raced towards the van. His longtime associate, the coroner, lay dead on the pavement. His head to one side, a bullet hole in his temple. Blood streamed down the back of his neck. An assistant held his hand and panted heavily, in shock. Another sat shivering in the front seat. Touton leapt to the second man. "What happened?"

Dazed, the man whispered, "The knife." The glove box lay open. "I had to give it up. He's dead?"

Sloan came running up.

"After them!" Touton shouted out. "Get cars! They're in a black Caddy! Put it out on the radio!"

"Armand, there's no one available."

Touton looked at him and realized that what he said was true. Every cop on duty was fully engaged on this night. He spoke more calmly. "Get a couple of cars. Get after him. Put it on the air. Do whatever you can do. They killed Claude."

Now the cops who had run up were sprinting back to their vehicles. Miron stayed behind and stood beside the captain over the dead man.

"I've got another family to talk to now," Touton said. "What the hell is going on here?"

Miron was hoping he was not expected to answer. His body trembled. He was breathing deeply, his heart thumping in his chest. He had never fired a weapon in action before and was sorry that he had missed. He knew that a shotgun had to be aimed well in front of a moving target, but in the heat of the moment, with the Caddy accelerating, he failed. He stood beside the famous captain, beating himself up, having blown his first big opportunity to impress a superior.

Touton touched his elbow. "In a war, lots of guys, probably three-quarters, never discharge their weapon in battle. Too chickenshit. You did all right, kid. You hit the car. Took out the tail light. Good. That'll help us trace it."

At that moment, an ambulance under full siren raced down Dorchester, carrying wounded from the riot's front lines. Touton watched it go, and wondered again what the hell was going on. His city was in chaos.

He wondered if, by morning, or in a day or two, it might not lie in ruins.

CHAPTER 4

1535 ~ 1534 ~ 1535–36

A BREEZE CAME UP, RIPPLING THE RIVER. ON THE AIR WITH THE rise of the sun also rose the migrant birds—ducks and snow-white geese and black-backed geese larger than any fowl these strangers had seen. Cantankerous calls as cacophonous as a ship's cannons. The rhythmic swoosh of wings louder than the flogging sails of an entire fleet. To look up, gaze upon the long-necked birds in flight, the astonishing breadth of their V-formations, row upon row southbound beyond the horizon, overtook the sensibilities of these sailors as a dread, an awe, not previously experienced.

They sensed their trespass in an unknown realm.

Felt their lives become infinitesimal.

Jacques Cartier ruminated on the significance of the migration as he watched the birds embark in a noisy rush and ascend. "They fly to a destination." Indians claimed that the great birds departed for the winter and, come spring, returned, which indicated that they travelled far enough south to reach a different climate. How great, he pondered, could this land be?

How vast?

He rarely awoke among the first. Cartier had remained ignorant of a ritual that had developed among his sailors. Strewn along the deck, the men greeted first light. They demonstrated no interest in chores, and instead observed the waterfowl, listened to the racket, felt the warmth of the sun on their necks and hands, and in the naked hour breathed, rapt. About to shout a command, the captain let the impulse pass. Standing above his men on the high aft deck, he felt oddly joined with them in the astonishment of this land's mystery. He shared in their privilege.

A cascade of colours across the hills vibrated in the breeze. Wind snatched leaves from their branches, crimson and oranges, a myriad of yellows sashayed down to the riverbank to float among the dabbling waterfowl. Upon this threshold he would cast his fate. Meeting a newer, more powerful band of Indians, he could not foresee how events would unfold. Still, he would endeavour to execute his plan, to perform a feat of magic, to extract a gift from the chief for his king so beguiling that future journeys would be well financed. To do so would require his cunning while meeting a people who no doubt possessed great cunning of their own.

Like a gopher's, Donnacona's head poked up through the fo'c'sle. The Iroquois chief from the village downstream, known as Stadacona, inhaled great breaths of fresh air, a relief from the calamity of rancid pale-skins' stink and other wretched emanations from the crew's quarters. Men shat in a bucket overnight and breathed the fetid reek through their sleep. They dozed above and below one another, as entangled as nesting squirrels, oozing sweat, their raucous gasps whistling and mournful, the air humid with the pong of fusty breath.

The chief was dismayed by his experience with the pale-skins, by their rituals and giant canoe. To sleep aboard such a vessel had been humiliating. Previously, he had slipped away from his berth and, under the stars, slept on deck as the *Émérillon* slowly plied the river waters. How such a fortress floated on its belly without sinking remained incomprehensible to him. How it rode so high above the waves without toppling perplexed him. As it rolled from side to side, death was surely imminent.

Donnacona had sighted the ship the previous year as, ghostlike, it plodded north off the Gaspé coast within the horizon's broad rim. He had brought his people to fish and draw mussels from the ocean's shores, and the men and women had stood in wonderment. Stymied by fear. They looked to the sky as though this weird creation had dropped through a rip there, and finally they sat upon the beach in silence. Donnacona felt the claws of a crow dig into his back. He was being lifted into the sky, in pain—it felt that way. A few women wept. The youngest children danced and occasionally threw stones in the direction of the giant canoe. The lips of an older man trembled, yet soon, everyone's capacity to be surprised or frightened was eclipsed by a true and profound apprehension. They saw the world, the whole of the universe, as different. Who were these sea beings? From what other place had they descended?

As chief, Donnacona accepted the responsibility to act, lest the people squat upon the shore forever. He called upon the tribe to gather old wood from the beach and forest, and by twilight he had ignited a huge fire that stopped the boat's progress and lured the sea beings ashore. As the leader clambered out of his longboat, the chief walked down alone to the rocky waterline to meet Cartier for the first time.

In the firelight of the traveller's torches, he gazed into the eyes of the sea being and conceded that he resembled a man. A stinking man, with a ghost's skin and frightful black fur upon his face. A strange creature in ridiculous clothing, yet this man-like creature possessed a giant canoe, which carried smaller canoes with giant paddles that brought more man-like beings ashore. Ghosts, these men, white-fleshed, whose odd clothing had not been cut from animal pelts. This pale-skinned man indicated that he had come from a land across the sea. An incomprehensible story. Cartier had been shocked to learn that Donnacona and his people had also come to this shore from far away.

The women kept looking for women among the pale-skins, but there were none. Such a strange people. How did they fornicate? With whom? But what women could fornicate with men who stank so foully? Someone deduced, "It's a war party. That's why no women go with them."

Donnacona needed to comprehend the idea that more people lived upon the earth than lived upon the earth. More land rose up from the waters than rose up from the waters. What were the people to understand about these terrible truths?

Cartier had carried on, to explore the shores and islands further north, and when he departed for his land across the waters before the return of winter, he took with him not only Donnacona's gifts but also the man's two sons, Domagaya and Taignoagny. They would fare well across the sea, and in the following year they returned home with wild stories of villages as large as forests, and of a house as huge as a mountain, made primarily of gold, in which the white chief dwelled. They spoke of other wonders so astounding that the chief had threatened to punish his sons if they did not stop uttering such terrible lies. In the land of the pale-skins, massive four-legged creatures taller than moose pulled land canoes in which they carried a man's belongings, the man himself, and his wife and children. These giant beasts obeyed the white man's words and allowed the white man to ride upon their backs.

"I will drown you!" Donnacona had cried out.

In the land of the snow-skins, the women sang like birds in the morning.

"I will slice open your bellies and feed you to the crows!"

In the land of the limestone-skins, trees gave beautiful, sweet-tasting berries the size of a man's fists to eat.

Perhaps they *were* gods, these cloud-skinned, black-furred strangers.

That other world had changed his boys. They had adapted to the vessel and to the white man's oily seal-stink and now laughed at their father's dismay. As a matter of honour, then, Donnacona had had to demonstrate a modicum of courage, yet he chose to wait until the ship merely bobbed at anchor before sleeping below. Throughout the long night, the chief fretted that he'd go mad from the stench. He slept little and under duress, yet endured until dawn without fleeing to the mercy of an open deck and the rebuke of his sons. Life inside a whale, Donnacona believed, might be more pleasant.

He observed sailors in their rapt state. They looked as though they had never seen geese as they watched the flight patterns overhead, all of them curiously silent under the belligerent honking. Had they never seen forests so charged with colour? His sons were right about one thing: the pale-skins were fascinating—their canoe was pushed and pulled by the wind, no man paddled!—they possessed magic, but they behaved in curious ways and seemed to possess little useful knowledge.

Donnacona climbed higher and stood on deck. Sailors gazed upon him now as attentively as they had stared at the ducks. He wore different clothing today—a deerskin laced by coloured caribou thread and decorated by beads— for he had stripped off the contaminated skins in which he'd slept and applied a ceremonial paint. He was expecting to meet his own people soon, another tribe, and was dressed for the occasion. Looking back across the deck at him,

Cartier determined to take his cue, to don ceremonial dress himself. Better to look as though he expected to be welcomed than to wear the garb of a soldier gearing for a fight. He called over his cabin boy, Petit Gilles, and commanded that he prepare his formal attire. If he was going to meet the Indians of Hochelaga, these men and women who held the key to the riches of this land, he would do so properly.

Domagaya, fresh, eager, and his younger brother, Taignoagny, generally taciturn, heaved themselves up onto the deck as well, and were also surprised by the silent, stiff stillness of the sailors. They were in a strange mood. The men only began to stir when Gastineau, the king's man, rumbled up the main companionway. His presence broke a spell.

"Jacques! Good morning to you!" Even ducks peaceably paddling near the *Émérillon* took flight, quacking madly, in response to his loud greeting.

"Gastincau," Cartier replied, sighing. Secretly, the men loved the way their captain put him in his place.

"Today's the day!"

"*Enh?* What day is that, Gastineau?"

"Hochelaga!"

Cartier shook his head. "If you can row that far that fast, you're a better man than me." Cartier habitually kept Gastineau in the dark about the details of any excursion. "We shall embark by longboat. We will not complete our journey before nightfall."

"But the fires—I saw them last night!" the king's man protested.

"You thought they were campfires?" Cartier asked as he headed to the lower deck before re-entering his aft cabin. "They were large fires at a great distance. Wind and current are against us. Look for yourself: the channel narrows. Time to row, and row hard. Two days yet. Unless you can fly with the birds."

Gastineau fumed. Cartier could have explained all this to him last night. He would not have looked like such a fool. "When do we embark?" he demanded.

"Is your belly full? When it is, we'll go. I've never seen you in such a rush. Finally, an adventure that appeals to you."

"Our adventure," Gastineau called back, "will cost us our lives if we freeze here for the winter. We have to be on our way soon, Jacques."

"I've decided to winter over," Cartier announced.

"What!" Gastineau was outraged, and speechless.

"At Stadacona."

The captain of the *Émérillon* disappeared while the king's man, and the crew, absorbed this shock. Winter over? Experienced sailors knew how cold the weather had turned the previous autumn, and the Indian lads had told stories of frigid temperatures and great mountains of snow. The men had seen for themselves how a multitude of waterfowl eagerly fled this climate as the cold season advanced. Yet, a few sailors breathed easier and proffered a different thought. Spending the winter in the New World meant not having to brave the north Atlantic in the late season. Tomorrow was the first day of October. Even if they set sail immediately, they would not make France before the beginning of the new year, which meant a frightful time at sea in nasty weather. Holing up for the winter seemed a lesser ordeal.

Gastineau was bounding across the deck to pursue Cartier into his cabin when Petit Gilles blocked the path. "The captain is changing his attire, sir," the lad proclaimed. The king's man promptly seized him by an arm and hauled him aside for a private word.

"You didn't warn me about this!" Gastineau hissed under his breath. He partially bent the boy over the ship's gunwales.

"Pardon me, sir?" the boy asked, frightful. "About what, sir?"

"We may spend the winter here!"

"The captain never mentioned it, sir! Not to me!"

"Then find these things out using your own devices! Remember, Petit Gilles, you work for your king. That means you work for *me*!"

"I cannot see into the captain's mind, sir!" protested the boy.

"Take my advice! Learn how!" The king's man gave him a rough push, and the tall, skinny boy caught himself as he grasped a ratline.

Some men commenced loading longboats while others went below for the morning meal and to prepare themselves for a tedious row. Donnacona strolled forward to the bow, where his sons joined him. The three gazed across the waters. Observing them, Gastineau wondered what they might be plotting. For his liking, the Indians were too close to Cartier.

Belowdecks, the captain was fitting himself into a frilly shirt with a multi-layered stiff gorget, similar to a beehive's comb, that ran higher than his ears, and an embroidered vest and jacket with lengthy tails. He tried on his wide-brimmed hat with its elegant, flowing plume, and asked himself if he did not strike a dashing figure. While seeing to such preparations, and like the king's man, he was also wondering what was going through the mind of Donnacona.

The previous summer, on his sail up the Atlantic coast, Cartier had encountered Micmacs. They did not know what to make of one another. Sailing farther north along the Baie de Chaleur, the *Émérillon* intersected a second band. They called themselves Iroquois and had come from a place far inland, travelling to the sea by a great river. That interested Cartier, for as a sailor he was not inclined to explore dry land. When the Frenchman erected a thirty-foot cross overlooking the bay and claimed the continent in the name of France, Donnacona took an interest, demanding to know the meaning of the structure. Cartier fibbed. He conveyed that the cross was a navigational aid, to assist him upon his return to the region.

After that encounter, they considered the grave issue of Donnacona's sons returning with Cartier to France. The pair could provide convincing stories for the king. As well, the time in France would allow Cartier to learn a portion of their language, and the boys themselves could learn French. A difficult discussion. Cartier had visited Donnacona in the evening and sat across a fire. He vowed to find the great river and return the boys to Stadacona the following year. He might never have convinced the father were it not for the boys' intervention, for they sat by the fire also, the flames flickering in the darkness of their pupils. Their minds were burning. Their souls were in flames. They wanted to climb aboard the giant canoe and travel across the great waters to another world. They could become great chiefs one day, they argued, with knowledge learned across the water. In the end it was the youthful conviction of Domagaya and Taignoagny that allowed the transfer to happen.

Although he lied about the meaning attached to the cross, and although the outcome was precarious, the captain managed to keep this one promise, returning the young men to Stadacona. *Les sauvages,* a term that meant "people who live in the woods," made a profound impression in court and particularly upon the king. Making use of the king's affection for the lads, Cartier persuaded Francis I to finance his next voyage to assure the safe return of the two boys.

Now they were home, and their own father did not know them.

†††

The land they called France assaulted the young men with such an array of wonders that neither Domagaya nor Taignoagny was certain he'd survive. One more chateau's garden, one more trip in a golden carriage behind beasts called horses, one more long-table with seats for an entire village and food for a month's festivity, one more king's ball, one more blue- or green- or brown-eyed glance from a blonde- or red- or brown-haired lovely young woman, her body heaving out of a cinched dress, and both young men might collapse and cease to walk again. They felt immortal. They could not die because they were already dead, for they'd entered a new state of being where they no longer existed in the world as they had experienced it, for the world they'd known was forever gone.

At the feasts for the king, his court and his friends, so many beasts would be placed upon the table that they didn't know which one to eat. Often they sampled a bite of each. Cartier sat next to Domagaya one night. On the voyage to France, during fair days upon the sea, Cartier had learned to speak a smattering of Iroquois from him, as he seemed less shy than his brother, while both young men had learned French in the company of the cabin boy, Petit Gilles. Domagaya commented to Cartier at the long-table, where ninety men and ladies of the court were nibbling, that the hunt must have been a good one.

"Sorry?" Cartier asked him back. "What hunt?"

"Many animals." Domagaya indicated the array of dead beasts.

Cartier promised to take the two young men on a French hunt.

The boys didn't believe what their eyes were seeing. In small enclosures and in tall houses, the white men kept beasts, animals and fowl that Cartier called cows, pigs, goats and chickens, and when they wanted to eat one they did not go away on a hunt. Instead, they walked from their house across to the animals' tall house and selected a beast to be slaughtered. They raised their animals like the Hochelaga Iroquois back home raised corn! Other animals, similar to wolves and foxes, were not for eating, but ran with the men in the woods and walked beside them across the grassland and lived with the men in their homes, curled up by the fire. Sometimes they misbehaved, and a man would swat what he called his dog and the dog, which had big teeth and could snarl and bark frightening sounds, whimpered like a child. At first, they were frightened when they came across a beast in the house, but Taignoagny learned to play with one of the smaller dogs, and the beast would lick Taignoagny's face until the young man laughed like a pale-skinned girl while Domagaya ran from the room to the pissing room clutching his belly in terror.

Taignoagny was helped onto the back of a beast the Frenchmen called a horse, and the horse went walking around its enclosure as Domagaya fell to his knees, not knowing if his brother was still a brother or a four-legged, two-headed wild beast with a penis the size of a small pine. Domagaya was usually the more daring of the two, but the sight of his brother attached to an animal caused his teeth to chatter uncontrollably. A servant was summoned to carry him back to bed.

More wonders. In pails, the French collected milk from the teats of beasts called cows and goats—and drank it! And gave it to their children! Taignoagny, who was always thinking, said, "That is why! The white milk of cows. That is why they have white skins!"

"That is why," Domagaya agreed. "They are raised on the milk of cows and goats. They are not half-gods. They are half-animals!"

Hens gave eggs for the nourishment of the pale-skins, and young women gathered the eggs every morning and brought them to the table, and the Indian men ate the eggs and marvelled at this food freely provided by the animals. They had such wonderful animals in France! They were not like the irritable bears or the shy and sprightly deer. They were nothing like moose. The birds of this place called France were not like the seabirds who deposited their eggs in the walls of cliffs that, if a young Indian boy wanted to fetch one, he had to risk his life. These birds were much more generous. The pale-skins had birds who refused to fly! Domagaya was determined that, when he got back to his land, he would make the animals behave. He would put the deer in enclosures and tell them not to jump over the fence, to wait there until he was ready to come and kill them. And he would put the bears in big bear houses and tell them to be still, to go out only when they were willing to fish for him in the stream. And he would tell the ducks not to fly away from him, just as the chickens did not fly away from the men and women of France. He would milk the moose and become a half-animal, too. All he had to do was to learn this language, this animal language that the beasts understood and obeyed.

So Domagaya studied French in great earnest.

One day, they did go on a real hunt, for quail. The men of the court took *les sauvages* along with them, and the boys talked about the experience between themselves that night into the following morning. A man would aim a long spear at a bird, and with one finger pull a small tooth. Fire and noise burst from the arrow, so fiercely that both Taignoagny and Domagaya landed on their bottoms with the first blast. Out of the sky, after the spears had barked, birds fell down. These were the birds not willing to listen to the language. But the dogs did! The dogs raced away to find the fallen quail, and when they did, they brought them back in their teeth to their men. Oh, how Taigno-agny wanted to have beasts like these when he went home to his land, while Domagaya wanted an invisible arrow that talked with a voice of fire and made plump, tasty, flying birds land on their backs.

On a cool, misty morning, the Indian men were taken to hunt deer on the king's land. They were astonished to finally find a familiar animal: deer! In France! Domagaya was invited to slaughter one, so walked toward the animal, silently and quickly at times, and the Frenchmen watched from a low hill, fascinated by his movement. He stole through the bushes, although this was a forest unlike any he had known, as it suffered from an absence of trees and underbrush and, from time to time, sprouts of water rose into the air out of circular stones on the ground. Domagaya moved towards the deer, creeping forward now. The deer studied him. The Indian man crept forward. The deer stared into his eyes. Domagaya's heart sank. He had been spotted. He had been smelled. The deer continued to sniff and stare. Then resumed a calm graze. Domagaya walked up to the deer and slit its throat.

Across the lawn, where the courtiers were watching, men and women collectively gasped. Then suddenly burst into cheering. That night, the conversation around the king's table was all about the *sauvage* who had used a knife—a *knife!*—to kill the deer they were eating.

Taignoagny and Domagaya discussed why a deer in France would let him do that. "She saw you," Taignoagny repeated. "She smelled you."

"She does not know how an Iroquois smells."

"This is true."

"It's like with pigs? They wait until the king wants to eat one, then they die."

"Deer are not pigs," Taignoagny pointed out. "Pigs are fat . . . pigs are slow. Pigs make strange noises."

"The hoof of a deer and the hoof of a pig are alike."

"The mind of a deer and the mind of a pig are unalike."

"The deer knew I had come to kill her, Taig. I looked into her eyes. I saw her thinking. She thought to herself, I am on the king's land. This red man has come to kill me so that he can eat me. I will let him do that, because I love the king."

"Is that what she was thinking, Dom?"

"I saw in her eyes what she was thinking."

If Domagaya could comprehend the thoughts of the pale-skins' deer, then Taignoagny considered that he might be able to comprehend the thoughts of their women. They stared into his eyes so often, virtually compelling him to interpret their thoughts. They'd lift their startling, half-bare chests, and giggle, and twirl their dresses, then scurry away laughing. How would it ever be possible to understand them? And yet, he believed that he had begun to discern patterns in this strange world. The gardens demonstrated that the trees, plants and flowers of France were willing to live according to the pleasure of their keepers' vision, just as animals lived and died according to the whims of their keepers' hunger. The chickens laid their eggs purely for the sake of the pale-skins' morning diet. Taignoagny had begun to suspect that the women of the king's court might similarly be in favour of offering themselves for the sake of their men, although whether they would do so for one they called a *sauvage*, he was not sure. From the way they looked at him, he was beginning to wonder, so for reasons quite different than his brother's, Taignoagny also vigorously applied himself to the study of French.

††

That winter, while the brothers were being initiated into court life at Fontaine-bleau, the seafarer Jacques Cartier took a Mediterranean trip to Sicily. Aboard an Italian vessel as a passenger, he spent long, uneventful days preparing his supply list, for the king had consented to provide three vessels for his next voyage, the largest undertaking of his career, which made an obsessive review of his requirements necessary. In the back of his mind he was already musing about the possibility of wintering in the New World. Of this notion, he would not whisper a word in case it slipped back to the king's ears, yet he had vividly imagined the triumph of his return a year later than expected. He'd be assumed dead, together with the ship's company. To commemorate the drama of his arrival home, and to be properly forgiven for the delay, he'd need a significant gift to appease the king. A renowned patron of the arts and a Renaissance man, King Francis I had sponsored Raphael and Titian. His favourite, Leonardo Da Vinci, had died in his arms. That passion for the arts eclipsed any fervour he might have nurtured for transoceanic escapades. The king gave only the lowest priority to New World exploration.

Cartier needed to find a way to startle him, to fire his imagination as did the artists. His voyage to Sicily, then, was intended to guarantee that a proper present from the New World be found. To locate it, he would rummage around the old.

Often windless, the voyage was quiet. Time dragged as slowly as the rising sun and setting moon for the ambitious captain. He longed to be in command of his own vessel again, and regretted in his darkest hours that he had not chosen a land to explore that offered a more forgiving climate, one that might allow him to stay abroad longer. He missed the wildness of those distant shores, the daily challenge to navigate and survive, the exhilaration of unravelling an uncharted coastline. The journey across the Mediterranean bored him.

Given that he had much to prepare, many were surprised that he'd chosen to indulge in the sojourn. Cardinal Ippolito de' Medici de Monreale was an old friend of Cartier's, but surely the cardinal could afford to travel to him, or the journey could wait. The captain insisted that he needed to speak to his spiritual counsellor before he could properly embark, and explained himself no further. Cloaked in mystery, he bided his time on the small ship sailing east, and endlessly prepared his lists.

†††

To Taignoagny's eyes, the new woman who had arrived at court, the elegant, haughty and superior Francine Tousignant de Tocqueville, seemed so staggeringly beautiful that, in her company, all contact with the language of the French he'd learned vanished from his lips. She flagrantly burst from her dress, for, unlike the other women, she was neither a flimsy twig of a girl nor a sapling, but a fine stout maple of a woman, with large hips and robust arms—a woman who looked as though she could carry water up from a shore with a child on her hip, or pull a sled in winter—and yet, similar to other French girls in court, she possessed a smile as chaotic as a gale, her black hair heaped above her head in twists and twirls, while her wide eyes, if somewhat unfocused, were as green as a summer forest. He was saying all this to her in Iroquois, and she was twittering into her hands and exchanging quick asides with her gathered friends.

Domagaya could not believe the audacity of his brother, to be telling this girl that she was as beautiful as a sunset and that her eyes were the colour of a mountain lake and that her cheeks were as brightly speckled as the trout they caught there! He had never heard him be so gregarious, and it took a while before he realized that the woman understood not a word of what was being said.

Promptly, he joined the act as well. He told the ladies present that he'd cut off their dresses and plunge his fingers between their legs and kiss their breasts until they hollered. He'd bring them the shank of a king's stag to munch upon, the balls from one of the king's bull-cows to admire.

Taignoagny was furious at his brother's rude incursion and told him so, raising his voice, but his brother carried on as the women giggled, becoming more daring and explicit with every line. He wanted to press the women against the wall of his bedroom at Fontainebleau, and told them so. He wanted to wrestle them on the floor of the pigs' barn, and splash with them in the fountain where the water flowed upward towards the sky in defiance of nature before it spilled back down to earth, and he wanted to press their bodies to him while they rode in the back of a carriage through the streets of Paris.

Incensed, Taignoagny warned his brother to mind his tongue or he would cut it out. Domagaya reiterated that the women did not understand a word. They could speak as they pleased as long as the language remained Iroquois.

Taignoagny took the initiative to speak French, the language understood by animals, and perhaps, as he'd recently thought, the language understood by women in need of a man. His gentle words escaped his lips in a halting, tentative style the women found endearing. He asked the girl with the flashing green eyes and the great bundles of black hair if she would come with him back to his room.

This time, Domagaya's eyes went wide. His mouth fell open. He seemed to stop breathing. He sat down in the chair behind him, and trembled.

The young women continued giggling, their faces pale as they furiously fanned themselves and looked at one another, wondering whether they ought to break into hysterics or run. The large woman who was new to court, Francine Tousignant de Tocqueville, did not take her eyes off Taignoagny's. When the giggling around them had ceased, everyone present—with the exception of the still-quaking Domagaya—remained motionless, and the woman said, "*Monsieur le Sauvage, comme te veut.*"

The two went off alone to Taignoagny's chambers, and Domagaya, gripping himself in a fierce hug, fell upon the floor, quivering. The other women mopped his brow with silk handkerchiefs and called for wine and warmed him with their hands and soothing words. They counselled the servants to take him to his room while they traipsed along behind, all atwitter.

†††

At the port of Palermo, Cartier was greeted by three odd-looking, black-robed monks dispatched by the cardinal to escort him to the nearby village of Monreale. One short, another tall. One smiled, another frowned. Two bowed often, one did not—he of average height and moderate disposition. The four men travelled in a pair of open carts pulled along by donkeys, the dusty journey drawing them through a cool day into a sweeping valley before they ascended, by late afternoon, towards Santa Maria Nuova and the immense cathedral of Monreale. The donkey carts came to a halt before the extraordinary Romanesque bronze doors, with their inlaid carving that depicted Biblical scenes across its forty-two panels. Cartier nodded approval, hoping that this sudden stop marked the limit of his sightseeing for the day. The monks jumped down from the carts and to his dismay led their visitor through the imposing doors.

The Frenchman was guided to a central spot in the nave from which he could properly view the cathedral's mosaics, created in an extravagant, grandiose sprawl across the vast walls of the interior. The monks stepped back. Two bowed slightly, while the third turned and walked out, probably to water the donkeys. The distinguished captain was left alone to experience the artwork in the fullness of its glory.

Jacques Cartier understood that his appreciation was being solicited. Disconcerted by this tangent after the lengthy journey, he nevertheless accepted that he remained at the mercy of his hosts and shook off the road grit. He turned in circles—at first fairly quickly, glancing around at random, then slowly, as he gazed upon the walls' murals and those on the heights above. The mosaics were brilliantly coloured, exquisitely detailed. As he relaxed, they instilled in him a sense of tranquility, even of solemnity, and he felt the comforting motion of being on a ship at sea. Virtually the complete surface of the walls was covered by the artwork, from two metres above ground to the ceiling vault, each one set upon a background of gold tiles. The full length of the interior ran a hundred metres. Gazing out upon the astonishing glitter of storied mosaics from above the chancel was the Christ Pantocrator, a portrait of Jesus more than forty metres wide and thirteen metres high, stunning in its impact. The seafarer, who had impatiently entered the church suffering from the undesired delay, now stood still, transfixed.

Eventually, the monks came for him and, in silence, guided him away. Their travels continued.

He assumed his destination to be the Castellaccio, atop Mount Caputo, about five kilometres farther north, but really was too exhausted to care. Accustomed to command, the captain did not ask questions of lowly monks. The donkey carts headed off in the direction of the fortress castle, yet when they took a circling trail around it, Cartier was not dismayed. Finally, he understood their objective. His friend had chosen to meet him within the safety and privacy of San Martino delle Scale, the Benedictine monastery a few kilometres along.

Night had fallen before they arrived. Weary, disgruntled, Cartier was greeted with surprising warmth by the monks there, shown to his quarters and advised that a meal would presently be served.

After a modest feast, he was led into a small chamber lit by a torch on each of the four walls. He sat before an olivewood table on a monk's long bench, and waited only a few minutes before his friend, Cardinal Medici, entered alone. Cartier knelt before him, kissed the honoured ring, then was pulled to his feet and the two men kissed each other's cheeks. They cordially held one another's elbows to express their pleasure at the reunion. The diminutive but muscular cardinal, who possessed the body of a peasant, barrel-chested and thick-necked, took a seat on the bench opposite Cartier. A monk stepped into the room with port, a bottle and two glasses, served a portion for each man and quietly departed.

The cardinal smiled a moment before his expression turned sombre. He reached under his robes and removed a small leather pouch. Upon the table he spilled out the contents: a half-dozen diamonds and twenty small nuggets of gold.

"As requested," the cardinal intoned.

"As agreed," Cartier acknowledged. "Thank you, Your Grace."

Although he was not an expert with respect to gems, Cartier picked up each of the small pieces and nodded appreciatively.

"You understand . . ." the cardinal commenced.

"I do," Cartier assured him.

"My family is large and famous."

"The name Medici is renowned throughout time and Christendom. I understand the situation."

"My name, of itself—"

"I understand," Cartier repeated.

"—might misconstrue—"

"I do understand."

Medici knit his hands together. "Did you enjoy the cathedral today, Jacques?"

"I have not seen its equal."

"Sofia, so they say, in Constantinople. Honestly, it's difficult for me to imagine the possibility, although each in its way, I'm sure, offers its magnificence to God."

"Magnificence," Cartier remarked, curious about the conversation's direction.

"One feels a sense of history, Jacques, here, and in the cathedral. A sense of awe, as though we find ourselves in the presence of our Lord's majesty. In your explorations, you are privileged to create a history, are you not? Surely you must feel the presence of God's glory in the New World." He leaned forward and whispered, "Tell me once more about this island."

Cartier nodded. The terms of the transaction were yet again being negotiated.

"Hochelaga, the name the Iroquois give to their village, is set upon an island in the middle of a most magnificent river, Your Grace, truly the most immense river yet discovered by man. It has no equal. No corresponding Sofia. The river is navigable into the heart of the continent, until it reaches an island—"

"An island with a mountain!" the cardinal burst out with rare enthusiasm.

"A mountain, such as this one here, at Monreale, yes! There, rivers meet, and the riches of a continent are guarded by this mountain island."

"Yet you have not yet been there yourself. You have not yet found this river."

"Savages speak only truths. They have no purpose to lie. The mountain on an island in the middle of the greatest river in the world lies in wait of my voyage. This time I will find it."

"The mountain island awaits its destiny."

As the cardinal shifted on his bench, the wood squeaked. Torches flared in a draft, and the shadows cast by the two men's bodies shook upon the walls of this cool, damp chamber.

"I've had a vision," the cardinal revealed in a soft voice, as if even within these stone walls he might be overheard.

"Your Grace?"

"A great city shall rise upon this island."

"I understand."

"A city of churches. I have seen this with my own eyes."

"Perhaps, one day, a cathedral as magnificent—"

The cardinal held up a hand to caution Cartier before he overstepped a bound. To imagine outdoing the cathedral at Monreale would be impudent, even sacrilegious, which might cause an ill wind to blow across a ship's course.

"Therefore, the name given to the city will be vital," the cardinal stressed.

"A name honoured by God, I should say," Cartier attested.

"In your circumstances, under the stress of your position . . . other persons of influence . . . of influence greater than that of my humble station—"

The seafarer, this time, was the one to raise a hand of caution. "I understand explicitly, Your Grace. These matters are to be accomplished with discretion, with care. The power is now in my hands, thanks to you and to the grace of Our Lord."

"Not without risk, Jacques," Cardinal Medici de Monreale noted.

"I understand, Your Grace. May God be with us in this affair."

The cardinal nodded. Then grunted. "Jacques, adieu! And Godspeed."

The mariner carefully picked up the diamonds and gold nuggets and gave the stones another examination, as though committing their facets to memory, then returned them to the pouch. He placed the pouch in the inner pocket of his vest, and rose, only to kneel as the cardinal came around the table. He bowed, and kissed the ring of his host. As he stood again, the two friends embraced and departed for the night. Cartier was led away by a monk holding a torch, then was released to the moonlit darkness of his chamber, and to the light of his dreams.

By mid-morning, Jacques Cartier was on a different ship, returning to France, his mission completed to his fullest expectation.

†††

Upon entering Domagaya's rooms at Fontainebleau, Cartier was surprised to find a bevy of young women scurrying into flight. They were fully clothed, so he could not categorically pronounce their activities illicit, but the savage was wearing very little while seated upon his bed, and apparently had been showing his muscles to the young ladies of France.

"White-skinned women like Domagaya," the lad said in Iroquois.

"Domagaya likes white women," Cartier candidly observed. The Indians had been brought over specifically to create a stir, to arouse widespread interest in his explorations so that the king might feel obliged to finance his trips. If that attention included winning the affections, or merely the idle curiosity, of women at court, then so be it. "I need to speak with you," Cartier told him, switching to French.

"You go long time away, Jacques."

"Far, yes. To another tribe in the white man's world."

"Someday Domagaya go with you."

"First, I need you to do something for me."

"For you, I do what you want Domagaya do."

"Most important, never speak of this matter we discuss today to another man or woman—not here, in France, nor to any white man or white woman, here or in your land. This will be an accord between me and you."

Domagaya looked curiously at him, for he did not understand the French word *accord*. This required a time spent working through both languages, trying to find a word that would be understood in the bargain being struck. Eventually, after a lengthy pantomime, the two men shook hands, pressed them to their chests to imply the swearing of oaths and settled on the word *treaty*. Each spoke the word in the other's language.

Then Cartier broached the issue that concerned him. From the hidden depths of his garments he brought out the dagger that Domagaya and Taignoagny's father had given him on the Gaspé shore the summer past.

"Knife, my father," Domagaya said, curious.

Cartier removed a small sack from under his coat. From it dropped stones that sparkled like starlight on a wave and more stones that seemed to reflect sunlight. "Diamonds, gold," Cartier said in a hushed tone. He'd taught Domagaya the words before, but now they gazed upon their meaning.

Domagaya remained still, quiet, watching.

"I want you, Domagaya, to attach these stones to your father's knife, and speak of this to no one. Use only the materials of your world, and only the tools of your world. Deer hide, beaver skin, the thread from a moose tail, and your own knives. We have the materials with us from our last voyage. Your father told me with great pride when he gave me this knife, that it was made for him by his first son, Domagaya. Now I want you to make it a very special knife that will have great magic. Will you do this for me?"

Domagaya looked from the weapon to the captain's eyes, back to the dagger, and asked, "Why?"

"Domagaya, never ask this question."

The Indian thought of the women who had recently departed his room, of the marble halls and the golden ceilings of Fontainebleau, of the gardens where the waters danced in peculiar ways and the plants grew in strange designs, and he thought of the animals who lived to die on the white man's plate and others who lived to pull the white man's possessions, including his children and his wife, and he considered the many wonders he had seen. "Domagaya make knife, great magic, to give his friend Jacques," he said. "I will not talk of this."

Cartier leaned in closer, to whisper. "I have enemies. They must not know that I hold a magic dagger. With this knife I will protect the Iroquois of your world in strong friendship with the Great White King. But I have enemies. Every man of daring does. So you must never speak of this, not even to the young women who share your pillow at night. I know you love your pillow."

"Domagaya love a pillow."

"We must remember to take it with you, to Stadacona. Imagine how the women there will want to sleep in the bed of a man with such a pillow."

The two men smiled. Then a worry crept across Domagaya's visage.

"What is it?"

"Why," the Indian began, then paused a moment, "does my brother have wings? Is he to become a bird in the white man's world?"

"Taignoagny has wings?"

"The man they call Italian man makes the soul of Taignoagny on wall. Soft wall. It moves when he carry it in his hands."

"A painting. A canvas."

"On this wall that moves, my brother has wings."

Cartier smiled again. "You speak of Michelangelo. It is an honour to be drawn by the great artist. Don't worry, Domagaya. Your brother has wings because Michelangelo can see with his great vision that Taignoagny is loved by God. Someday, when he dies, he will fly to the heaven of our God."

"Domagaya like wings, too."

Cartier understood. "I'll see what I can do. But no word of our treaty. Do a good job on the knife and Michelangelo will draw wings on your back, too."

A final chore. Now he'd have to haggle with a pesky artist. *C'est la vie.* At times, there seemed to be no end to his negotiations, and once again he looked forward to being at sea.

†††

Jacques Cartier stood upon his aft deck to survey the final preparations. The provisioning had gone well, although delays were inevitable, and the cause of the latest fiasco had been exasperating. Monsieur Claude Gastineau, the king's man, had insisted on toting along half his boudoir, as if he expected to be attending an autumnal ball among the Iroquois. He had cases and crates and boxes and attendants—who were not coming. Cartier had exercised his authority on them, much to the relief of the servants. The man was even transporting sheaves of paper and charcoal, for drawing, which could prove a useful contribution on such an enterprise, were it not that he freely admitted to being inept at the craft. Rather, he was bringing the materials to occupy his time. "What else will I do," he inquired, "in a land that has nothing but trees and heathens?" A pair of the crates wedged into place belowdecks displaced two equivalent cases of raw vegetables, which Cartier had then seen lashed to the deck. One good storm and they'd be gone, if not consumed first by the night watch.

He signalled Petit Gilles to his side. Not yet fourteen, the lad had already crossed the Atlantic. A gangly youth, on even the stormiest nights he was sure to take a turn in the rigging, an able-bodied seaman despite his sparse years.

"Yes, sir?"

"Gastineau is settled below?"

"Yes, sir."

"Has he spoken, as yet, of certain matters to you?"

"Spoken? He told me where to put his belongings, sir."

"He will address other issues shortly."

"Sir?"

Cartier brought the lad nearer to him and spoke into the breeze, that their voices might go unheard.

"You are close to me, Petit Gilles. For this reason, he will want you as his spy."

"Sir! I would never do that, sir!"

"And betray your king? How could you not spy on me?"

"Sir!"

They were standing side by side, and Cartier pulled him nearer still. "Spy on me, Petit Gilles. I have nothing to hide. If I do, it will encourage his confidence should some indiscreet matter be conveyed to him. Do so with my blessing. The day may come, lad, when I shall involve you in a separate action."

"An action, sir?"

"I know not what. When that day is upon us, I shall indicate to you that the king's man does not merit your private counsel. This will afford you the opportunity, Petit Gilles, to demonstrate your loyalty to your captain. In all other matters, trust in yourself, be loyal to your king and forthcoming with his emissary. Do you understand me, good lad?"

"Yes, sir." He was perplexed as well.

"Fail to comply and you shall fail to see St. Malo again."

"Out of loyalty to you, Captain, not through any threat!"

"You speak well. I count on you, Petit Gilles. You may now shout the order."

"The order, sir?" He was bright-eyed, too astonished to hope that he might be granted such an honour. Below them, the town awaited their departure, loved ones still waving to the men upon the ship, knowing they might never return. The boy's own mother, tears on her cheeks, stood upon the dock. Bobbing on the quiet waters, longboats manned by hefty men awaited the moment they'd pull three ships free of their docking spaces and haul them through the harbour to open water, to raise sail. Up and down the dock, men in the elegance of fine clothing, women brightly adorned in shawls against the chill, and their exuberant children sallied about, fear and excitement commingling, a tangible sense of adventure stirred by a distinct measure of dread.

Cartier smiled. He had no doubt that Petit Gilles would make a fine ship's captain one day. "Give the order, lad, to cast us off upon the sea."

†††

Upon stones covered by a thick fall of coloured leaves, Cartier stepped ashore. Set back from the river's edge amid the trees, Iroquois were observing him, and the crew in the longboats watched also as he tucked his plumed hat under one arm and knelt and kissed the soil. He lifted his head, a smudge of dirt upon his lips. The island had dwelled in his imagination as the door to a magic kingdom. Now that that portal had been attained, his gratitude to God and his appreciation of good fortune had pulled his emotions to the ground. With the aid of his cabin boy he stood again, then waited while his crew hauled the other boats—and themselves—ashore.

First to come down to greet him were Donnacona and his two sons, sent on ahead two hours earlier to alert the people of Hochelaga to the new arrivals, to assure them of the white man's peaceful intent. They had also to prepare the Iroquois for what might soon transpire. Men who dwelled over the ocean beyond the clouds, with black beards and skins the colour of beluga whales, had returned, and this time they were arriving down the river. The world they knew, Donnacona explained, was no longer the world they knew. In giving counsel to his friend, the chief of the Hochelaga people, he advised Kamanesawayga that the cloud-skins were strange creatures who had great powers. He told him also that, for the white-skins, the Iroquois were equally strange and also had great powers.

"Since my sons come back from the land of the pale-skins," Donnacona explained, "they tell many lies, but they know also the white-skins' magic. My son speaks to their animals, and they obey him."

The old chief nodded. "My son," he said, "calls to the ducks."

"Your son calls to the ducks," Donnacona explained, "by quacking like a duck. My son speaks to the white man's animals by speaking like a pale-skinned man, and the animals of the pale-skinned man obey him."

"This troubles me," Kamanesawayga informed him.

"My son will bring to you a French animal," Donnacona said. "Prepare yourself and your people, for you will be afraid."

Taignoagny returned down the trail to the place where he had left an animal fastened to a tree. The white man's beast had been quietly sleeping after another day of hard travel in a longboat, thankful to be on dry land again. It jumped up at the sound of its master and wagged its tail, and the animal and the Indian youth returned to the Iroquois village. As they arrived at the clearing, Indians gasped, the women hid, and a few young men reached for their spears and bows and arrows.

"A wolf!" Kamanesawayga cried out, leaping to his feet.

"Not a wolf," Donnacona scoffed. "A wolf can eat this beast in the morning and still be hungry. It is a white man's wolf, and that's not much of a wolf."

Taignoagny came towards the circle of men, and the wolf-like animal at his feet scarcely noticed the others, wholly intent on looking up at his master's eyes. "Watch this!" Donnacona announced, forgetting entirely that when he had first witnessed the demonstration he had been terrified to the bone and had believed that he no longer understood his own name or the difference between the sky and the sweet earth. "My son will talk the talk of the pale faces. The animal will listen."

The Iroquois looked on, amazed, as the youth removed a string made of stone—*a stone string!*—from the collar around the animal's neck, and the lowly wolf, freed, scampered around the feet of the youth. Taignoagny spoke to the beast in a strange tongue, and the beast lay down on its side and went to sleep. The Iroquois murmured amongst themselves, and a few believed that this would be a good time to slay the wolf-like beast. Taignoagny spoke again, and the animal woke up. The young man spoke and the animal rolled over and over and over, and when it was done it stood up like a man on its two hind legs and placed its front paws on the young man's chest. The foolish young man rubbed his face on the animal's face and on its neck. The animal had big teeth, but it did not bite him. Then Taignoagny bent down and put his hand on Kamanesawayga's moccasin.

"Now you will see what you have not seen before," Donnacona announced.

"Today I see what I have never seen before. A wolf who is not a wolf, who listens to the words of a man and goes to sleep when he is told. Today I have seen a man kiss a wolf and the wolf lick his face. Do they fornicate together?"

"Now you shall see something you will not believe."

"This troubles me," Kamanesawayga confessed. "Your son has his hand upon my foot."

"He wants your moccasin."

"He has his own!"

"Let him have it, Kamanesawayga, if you are a brave chief."

Challenged, the chief allowed Taignoagny to remove his moccasin. The shoe had been decorated with multicoloured beading and caribou hair, a moccasin worthy of a chief's foot. The young man presented the moccasin to the nose of the animal to sniff, then flung it as far as he could into the woods. He spoke sternly in that strange tongue to the animal.

"My moccasin!" Kamanesawayga called out. "How will I walk?"

Donnacona laughed. "Do you want your moccasin back?" he asked.

"Tell your boy to find my moccasin or I will cut off his feet!"

Donnacona kept on laughing. "The beast will find it for you," he said.

The animal had not moved, but stared into the woods where the moccasin had been thrown. Taignoagny held out a finger above him. When he spoke again, the animal ran into the woods as fast as a jackrabbit—as fast as a real wolf—and men and women scattered from his route.

The poor excuse for a wolf rummaged around in the woods, and they could hear the fallen leaves flying about and the branches of bushes snapping when suddenly the animal raced out of the woods again with the moccasin between its teeth, and a great excitement rose up among the Iroquois who had witnessed this magic. The animal ran straight up to Taignoagny.

The young man pointed to the chief of the Hochelaga tribe, and spoke in a quiet voice to the animal in the language called French, saying also the name of Kamanesawayga. The white man's animal turned then and walked towards the chief. Although standing, the chief pulled his shoulders back and turned his head away, afraid to look into the face of the four-legged beast. The animal looked back at Taignoagny, who encouraged him with the white man's words. The lowly wolf put the moccasin down at the feet of Kamanesawayga, then sat on its haunches, staring up at him, panting.

The old chief looked down at his moccasin. Then he stared into the eyes of the panting wolf-like beast and knew that everything he had ever perceived about the land of the living had changed today, even before the white man had appeared. He put his foot into the shoe. The slobber of the poor-wolf was on the moccasin as he stuck his foot into it, but the animal with the big teeth did not bite him.

"Rub his fur . . . his head . . . his neck—he likes that!" Donnacona called out, which caused his two sons to chortle. They knew that their father had himself refused to do so, out of fright.

Kamanesawayga was less reticent than the chief of the Stadacona Iroquois, and slowly, he lowered a hand. Looking into the eyes of the lesser wolf, he touched its head. The fur was long and soft and warm. The eyes of the lowly wolf were moist and friendly, like the eyes of a contented woman. He stared for a long time as the lowly wolf panted, its big tongue lolling out. Then the chief straightened. "This troubles me," he said.

"In the land of the pale skins," Domagaya stated, "animals live in the village. They wait for someone to be hungry, to come and kill them. They wait to die."

Kamanesawayga grunted in a strange way. These stories were difficult.

Donnacona, passing on the knowledge brought to him by his sons, repeated what he knew to be great lies. "In the white man's land, big animals carry the white man on their backs, and go wherever the white man wants to go."

Kamanesawayga glared at him, his eyes full of fear and fury, then looked at Donnacona's sons. "Why do the big animals do this?"

"To make the men with the pale skins happy," Taignoagny said.

"So the white man will not be tired when he goes a long way," added his brother.

"If my sons tell lies, I will drown them in the river!" Donnacona vowed. He did not believe his sons, but he also did not believe that Kamanesawayga would ever to go the land of the pale skins to learn whether they had lied or not.

Taignoagny called his dog to his side and the animal obeyed, standing still even as the youth fastened the stone string to its collar. The chief returned to the perimeter of the fire and squatted down opposite Donnacona again.

"I will tell you something about the white man's animals you will not believe. Do not believe me, Kamanesawayga, for if you do, your dreams will be troubled."

Kamanesawayga was not a man to be tempted this way. "Tell me," he said, "so that I will not believe you."

"The white man has animals like the moose, but smaller. The female small moose gives milk, like a mother gives milk to her children. In the white man's land, they drink the milk of this moose. That is why the white man has white skin."

The chief of the Hochelaga Iroquois lowered his head to think about such strange matters. When he raised his head again, he said, "Men who drink from the milk of animals cannot be men. They talk to animals, they drink animal milk—these men cannot be men. They must be half-men, half-animals."

Those who heard him speak nodded sagely.

"The animals across the sea live in animal lodges—"

"—like the beaver," Kamanesawayga said, approving of this.

"Like the beaver," Domagaya agreed. "Only the white man builds the lodges for the animals, and these lodges are bigger than any longhouse we make for our own people. Some animals live in the white man's longhouse."

The news passed through the gathering like a breeze through falling leaves, creating a rustle and a stir. Kamanesawayga shook his head.

"Do these white men have white women, or do they fornicate with animals the way they suckle at an animal's teat?" the chief inquired.

"Their women live in longhouses as large as mountains with walls of gold and smooth, white stone," Domagaya explained. "These women wear special clothes for fornicating."

Kamanesawayga nodded, as though he had expected such audacious news.

"I have a gift for you," Taignoagny said. He secured his stone string to the lowly wolf again.

"You give to me the listening wolf?" Kamanesawayga inquired, aghast, yet oddly enchanted by the prospect. He remained affected by the soft eyes of the beast.

"I cannot. When an animal is given to a man as a young beast, it belongs to that man. It cannot belong to another man. If it is given away, men may accept this, but the animal will never accept this. The animal was given to me by the Great White Chief of France, King Francis the First. The full name of the beast, he told me, is King Francis the Second." Taignoagny then laughed, and added, "But you must always laugh when you say that. No beast understands a name so long, so I must call the animal King. He answers to that name. I cannot give you King, but to honour the great chief of the Hochelaga Iroquois, I give you this."

Taignoagny handed him the stone string.

Kamanesawayga held it in his hands and examined it, then gazed at the young man's father thoughtfully. "What great powers do we have," he asked, "in the white man's eyes?"

His friend knew how to reply, for he had heard the white men speak of it often. He nodded before he spoke, for this was a vital mystery that he had chosen to impart. "They believe it is a great magic," he said, "that we live here."

Nodding, the chief consented to meet the salt-skinned men who had come down the river, in peace and in curiosity.

†††

Donnacona, greeting Cartier on the banks of the river, declared, "Kamanesawayga waits to meet the great man with skin the colour of sea foam who comes from the clouds across the sea."

Cartier nodded. He was excited, too. The Iroquois village at Stadacona was small, having fewer than two hundred souls. He imagined from his first view from the river that Hochelaga was home to more than two thousand souls, and he had already marvelled that these people had cleared the land and were growing food, which had not been true at Donnacona's village. He believed that he was meeting a man of greater stature than his guide. Together, the Iroquois family and Cartier, along with the king's man, his first mate, his cabin boy and a handful of trusted and adept seamen armed with harquebusiers, knives and spears, commenced the upward journey from the riverbank to the community that dwelled on the side of the mountain.

Iroquois watched from the trees.

The king's man walked alongside Cartier. "You are here now, Jacques. Will you name this place?"

"The village is called Hochelaga by the Iroquois," the captain asserted.

"The village," Gastineau pointed out to him in a harsh tone, for he knew that the captain understood what he meant, "but not the island. Nor the mountain."

"We shall see," Cartier demurred.

"You have not named the river. I know why, Jacques. You must name this island properly. You must name the mountain. It is outrageous if you do not do so! We cannot have every important landmark named Cartier!"

Cartier stopped along the trail. "My dear Gastineau. Of course I shall name the island. I shall name the mountain. Yet it is only fitting that you allow me to experience the place awhile, the better to deduce its potential and meaning. For example, if an Iroquois were to cut off your head this afternoon, I'd name the mountain Gastineau's Head. On the other hand, should we all survive, I might imagine something more in keeping with this auspicious encounter."

"You try my patience, Jacques."

"Look," said Cartier, bothering no more with the man's preoccupations, "the chief."

And so the two divergent peoples met, through the determined and visionary sea captain and the elderly, experienced and thoughtful chief. The Iroquois spoke first. He said, "Welcome."

And Cartier, understanding him, said back in the man's own language, "Thank you. I am glad to meet you here this day. I bring to you the best wishes of the Great White King of France, Francis the First, and of the people of France, the land that dwells beyond the ocean and the clouds."

"I welcome you in the name of the people of the land," Kamanesawayga stated, "who have dwelled in the world from the beginning, who came here to this place from the stars before the stars had light, to live in the forests with the bear and the deer and the wolves and the moose, to live as men and women under the sky and under the sun as long as the sun has light."

Donnacona listened to the speech and wished that he had said all that when he first met Cartier on the Gaspé beach. Instead, he had said only, "You do not wear the fur of animals."

Cartier was affected by the speech also, and wished that he had initially been more eloquent. He now felt himself at a disadvantage, even while he confirmed to himself that his intuition had been correct. Kamanesawayga was a great chief. Donnacona, by comparison, merely a courtier.

"I thank you for your great welcome," Cartier said.

Kamanesawayga, grunting softly, sniffed the foul air. He took a step back. "I have no moose to give you milk," he said. "I have no listening wolves who will chase your moccasins or your ducks. I have no homes of bright stones filled with our young women. Why have you come here from beyond the sea and the clouds to the land of the forest?"

The man spoke quickly, and Cartier, comprehending only a portion, waited for Taignoagny to conclude a stilted translation.

"I have heard of the great island in the middle of the great river," Cartier stated, "for it is a river more great than any revealed to the white man, and I have heard of the great Iroquois nation that lives upon the island and guards the way to the land of gold and diamonds. I have heard these things, and I desired to meet the great chief of the Hochelaga Iroquois."

Domagaya had to explain what gold and diamonds were to the satisfaction of the chief, who nodded.

"You want stones?" the chief asked him.

Cartier concurred. "Stones that shine brightly," he qualified.

Kamanesawayga nodded, and let out a grunt. "I understand," he said. "I enjoy stones that shine as the sun. I have heard stories of your magic. Show me your magic, so I will know for myself if the sons of Donnacona speak truth or lie like the babbling children of a man who is only a fool and farts often."

"I will drown my sons," Donnacona insisted, "if they lie to you."

Domagaya said, "They have magic spears that make the birds fall down."

Cartier removed his plumed cap and placed it under his elbow. "Jean-Marc," he instructed a seaman, who was a crack shot, "fire at will."

To shoot a flying bird with a musket was a tall order, yet Jean-Marc tamped down the gunpowder and prepared to light it with a spark. The spark ignited and the wick caught fire and the two thousand men and women present on the hillside, those in the clearing with the visitors and those who remained amid the trees, responded with sounds of fright and amazement as the wick frizzled and Jean-Marc took aim at a crow stationary in a leafless tree. The bird cawed and stared back at the gathering. The frizzy fire suddenly made a big noise, and the crowd fell back a foot and gazed at the seaman to see if he remained yet alive. Then someone shouted, and everyone looked as the crow fell down through the bare tree limbs.

When the bird hit the ground, Taignoagny gave a command and his animal ran into the woods to fetch the crow. King came back with the crow between his teeth, and this was a magic greater than the death of the crow: the willingness of an animal to help a man.

Kamanesawayga observed this magic and was troubled and impressed. "We will eat," he said to Cartier. "I have venison and corn."

"Corn?" Cartier asked Taignoagny, not understanding the Iroquois word.

"Indian food," Domagaya explained.

"It is the plant that grows in the fields," Donnacona revealed.

"We shall eat," Cartier confirmed. "You shall show me your island. I have many gifts to give to the great chief of the Hochelaga Iroquois."

Kamanesawayga wondered what gift he might receive from the white men who possessed such strange magic. He wondered also what gift he might impart that would not humble him, nor disgrace his people. Perhaps he would offer the white man many raccoon hides and beaver pelts to help him with his bad stink. Perhaps that would make for a worthy gift.

†††

After the visitors were fed, having consumed with great delight the Iroquois corn and venison, and despite the French sniffing themselves—for they had begun to fart incessantly, although in general their farts were congenial—Kamanesawayga took Cartier on the long hike to the top of the mountain. He gazed out across a great plateau to the rolling hills, an unimaginable, improbable distance. Only Cartier's cabin boy walked alongside him to the final lookout, and Kamanesawayga, taking note of this choice, brought along only a grandson of similar age. The larger entourages for both men were bidden to stand back.

The wind was bitter late in the day, winter approaching.

"I thank you for the animal furs, Kamanesawayga," Cartier said, "for the pelts of ermine and fox, the beaver and the raccoon. The Great White King of France will be honoured to receive them."

"They give a man a good smell," the chief said. "I thank you for the smelling waters and the cutting tool, for the blankets and the coat."

The scissors had been a last-minute inspiration on Cartier's part. They were small, but when the Iroquois saw how neatly they trimmed fingernails, the men were amazed and the women abuzz as they took turns cutting each other's hair. The perfume, on the other hand, confused the Indians, and Cartier had to be very stern in making sure that nobody drank it. Taignoagny spoke for a long time about perfume, and often the Indians had laughed as he told them that they could wear it to help them bear the stench of the pale-skins, but Cartier was never clear on what was meant.

He and Kamanesawayga had been getting along, and they had learned to speak Iroquois very slowly to one another, so that each grasped the other's meaning. Before them, beyond the river island, beyond the rapids, stretching west to the setting sun, the magic kingdom awaited Cartier's exploration.

"I have one more gift to ask of you," Cartier noted. "I seek one more trade between us."

Kamanesawayga concurred with a grunt. "I also want one more trade."

"I will give you my dagger with the blade of steel, forged in a hot fire, which cuts well. You will give me yours made of stone."

Kamanesawayga agreed to the trade, which seemed like a good one to him, and the two men exchanged knives. Cartier looked at the Indian's knife, and smiled, and handed it to Petit Gilles for his safekeeping. Kamanesawayga then made a request of his own: "You will give me your hat with the long feather."

Cartier gave away his plumed hat. In exchange, he requested and received the chief's beaded "small-coat"—his vest. He gazed longingly at the distant kingdom one last time, then commenced the trek downward through the trees as the sun was setting.

When finally they were at the bottom, in the near dark, Gastineau reminded the captain of his obligations. "I still have my head."

"I have seen the mountain," Cartier replied. "I will name this mountain after our great king."

"Mount Francis," Gastineau said. "Good."

"No. This is a great and royal mountain. I will name this mountain Mount Royal, to commemorate the royal house of France."

This was not what Gastineau had expected, yet he could not refute the name, as it sufficiently adhered to the king's interests. "The island?" he asked.

"Montreal," Cartier stipulated. Gastineau detected no difference to the word, and only when he saw it written upon a chart did he note the discrepancy in the spelling. He did not grasp that the island had been named after the Sicilian royal mountain, Monreale, and more specifically after Cartier's private benefactor, Cardinal de' Medici de Monreale. The island could not be called Medici, as that would honour more famous members of the cardinal's family. So the French spelling of the Italian word was struck by Cartier: *Montréal*. Neither Gastineau nor King Francis I himself would know that the island's name intended no homage to the king, but to a poor Medici cousin, a cardinal of trivial import.

"Look what I have received in trade," Cartier stated to the king's man, and motioned for Petit Gilles to produce the dagger. The cabin boy did not pull from his clothing the one that Kamanesawayga had recently traded. Instead, he pulled out the knife that had once belonged to Donnacona and had been improved upon by his son in France. Gastineau studied the wondrous weapon. Embedded in the handle, knotted tightly by moose hair and deer hide and fitted with a soft and supple beaver skin, were diamonds and gold nuggets. "Look what else I have received today," Cartier said. From the pocket of the decorative vest he'd obtained from Kamanesawayga in exchange for his hat, he showed the king's man the remaining gold nuggets given to him by Cardinal de' Medici. Gastineau studied the items by the light of a torch, enchanted.

"Do you know what this means?" he asked, excited.

"Diamonds, gold," Cartier whispered. "This is the land of diamonds and gold."

Deftly, he took the knife back from Gastineau, and the nuggets. "I will give this dagger to our king," he vowed. "He will see the true promise of this land. He spends more on his precious painters than he does on these voyages to New France. This must change."

Gastineau could now see the promise as well. If mere farmers of corn, and eaters of wild venison and squirrel, carried with them knives made of gold and diamonds, and had gold nuggets in their pockets they freely gave away, then all that Cartier had promised, and more, would surely hold true. This was indeed the magic kingdom, and he would recommend to King Francis I that treasure ought to be invested to support future expeditions.

Inwardly, Cartier felt aglow, transported somehow. The island and the mountain had been named. Whatever difficulty Gastineau might have had with either choice, whatever disappointment the king might yet express, such doubts amounted to nothing weighed against the promise of riches forecast by the knife.

Both men briefly separated along the trail, taking time for multiple farts and to sniff themselves, catching the enriched scents of venison and corn on the air.

†††

An early winter that year. By November, the wooden ships were captured in ice. The *Émérillon* was shoved onto its beam ends at a twenty-five-degree angle, so that in his cabin Cartier slept against a wall sheeted in ice rather than risk sliding out of his bunk. The warmth of his body created a perfect shape in the ice for his comfort. Food was rationed, and scurvy broke out among the crew. Lives were being lost.

After the first deaths, Cartier ordered the ship's barber and surgeon to perform the first autopsy in the New World. As the sailor was cut open, great amounts of poisoned blood flowed from his heart, then the barber and the ship's captain gazed upon the body of Phillipe Rougemont rent asunder.

"The heart," the barber said.

The organ was white, evidently rotten, awash in a sink of water, more than a quart.

"The lungs," Cartier muttered. Black. Mortified. "Now let us bury him properly. We shall give our friend back to God. Do not show him to the others, Pierre. Record the evidence in your diary, but never speak of this to our crew or they shall lose the last of their precious hope."

"Pray mercy," the barber added, "for our own souls."

Twenty-five died that winter.

When the scouting party had first returned to Stadacona from the adventure at Hochelaga, Cartier had been distraught to discover that, in his absence, relations between the French he'd left behind there and the Iroquois had not remained amicable. The Indians had grown nettlesome, and as the winter seized the visitors, they withheld a potion that would have saved the dying men. Cartier wept the morning he carried out the body of his cabin boy, Petit Gilles, onto the river's ice. So apparent was his grieving that an Iroquois hunting party on shore noticed him and spoke of his travail to Donnacona, who then sent a group of women to the icebound ships with a cedar extract they called *anedda*.

They were surprised, the women, to discover that ice had formed inside the hulls of the ships, that the French were living inside a giant house of ice. The white men were shivering through their long nights, and during the day were ill and in despair. The appearance of the Iroquois women, while distrusted initially, proved a blessing. Those struck down by scurvy recovered, and for the new arrivals, *anedda*—which in their delirium, and unaccustomed to the native tongue, they pronounced as *canada*—became their salvation.

In the spring, the ice broke with such great roaring cracks in the night that the men believed their ships would be destroyed. The ships' timbers cried out as though snapping. The holds flooded with the melt of interior ice. Cartier did not need to be persuaded by Gastineau, who raged and fumed, adamant that they return to France. Gazing upon his crews, he knew that the trip to the magic kingdom beyond the rapids of Montreal would have to be postponed. His men were depleted. Many of those alive were walking skeletons.

One ship had been severely damaged by ice, so Cartier departed with only two, taking with him—against their will—ten Indians, including Donnacona, his two sons and a young girl.

"You will see the Great White King, tell him your stories," he told the Iroquois chief when they were first at sea. "You will see animals who talk to the white men. You will drink the milk of cows, and see a village as large as a forest."

"I want to go home," Donnacona insisted.

"Why did you take so long to give us the *canada* tea?"

"Why did you take our women?"

"I did not know about that. I did not approve when I learned these stories."

"Better I not give to you *anedda*. Now I know."

Sailing back to France, the situation remained dire, but all was not lost. In his possession he carried what the crew called the Cartier Dagger. They were excited by it. The handle's gold and diamonds would impress the king. What pleased Cartier as much, the island of Montreal had been properly named, in keeping his promise to the cardinal.

Only in one circumstance did Cartier find himself thwarted. Gastineau saw to it that the river was anointed the St. Lawrence. The ship's captain would not have his name inscribed upon the great river he had sailed, and because he had held out for this one substantial tribute to himself, he had neglected to attach his own name to any lesser landmark. Gastineau was pleased by this. The captain, a man of irritable habits and peculiar mind, who had placed him in mortal peril by staying over a winter, had successfully kept the name of King

Francis I off the charts, nor had he thought to name any promontory after Gastineau. At least the name Cartier itself would also remain invisible in the new land.

As he sailed into St. Malo, Jacques Cartier felt distinctly proud. Crowds formed to cheer his triumphant return. The Indians stood on deck alongside him, marvelling at the activity of a seaport, with so many ships and big buildings and animals that lived among the people. Donnacona nodded. His sons were not liars. He believed now that it was a good thing that he had arrived in the land of the pale-skins. He stood on the deck and observed their ships, and the smoke from their lodges, and the beasts like moose, called horses, and the beasts like wolves, called dogs, and he was glad he had come to the land beyond the clouds because now he could say to his people when he returned home, "More people live upon the land than live upon the land. More land stands up from the sea than has ever stood up from the sea in this world. We are a people who lived in the old time, when only the people and the animals walked in the forest, and no man was a half-animal. Our children will live in the new time, when other creatures walk in the woods among them." He had learned from Kamanesawayga to speak with great eloquence. Unlike Kamanesawayga, and unlike his fathers before him, he had met the people beyond the clouds, the men who did not, and could not, exist. He was seeing what his fathers had not seen, and therefore he was a great chief, and the people of his time were blessed.

"Show me," he said to the captain of the *Émérillon,* "a room which is only for shitting. My sons have seen this thing. I think they lie."

Cartier clutched the splendid knife in his belt and dropped a hand upon Donnacona's shoulder. He accepted the cheers of the crowd, even as he searched among the well-wishers for the mother of Petit Gilles. He did not know that meeting her would be the first of many sad moments that year, for of the Indians, only the young girl aboard the ship would survive, and she would not return across the sea because she had not enjoyed the voyage, choosing instead to live out her life in France. Donnacona, Domagaya and Taignoagny, along with the others who had been captured and brought across the sea to the land on the other side of the clouds, would remain forever beyond the clouds.

In his final moments, through parched lips, Taignoagny, the man who had been drawn by Michelangelo as a model for the flying angel at the top of *The Last Judgment*, begged Cartier for *anedda*, but there was nothing the sea captain could bring to him, and nowhere he could take him in the winter of that year.

CHAPTER 5

1955

CAPTAIN ARMAND TOUTON DROVE EAST, AWAY FROM THE ONGOING riot. Delivering bad news had to be done promptly. Procrastination did no one any good, the cop least of all, and usually indicated that the detective was worrying more about his own discomfort than the pending time of sorrow for the family. "The loved ones," he had lectured his squad of irascible detectives, "got a right to be told. It's your job to tell them. Nobody says you have to put on a happy face—we got assholes in this room who wouldn't know how to say a kind word if a dog licked their balls, and if they ever cracked a smile they'd look like shit warmed over." The remarks earned a muffled round of chuckling, for in these late-night sessions Touton was expected to be profane, and the men laughed at anything irreverent. "But give them that much. Deliver the fucking news. Go in. Get it over with. Quietly leave."

The policy was not an easy one to implement, as Touton was discovering for himself. The death of Roger Clément affected him more deeply than he might have expected. He was experiencing an acute regret, and while he would not delay his mission, he was not driving swiftly to his destination, either.

He had delegated the task of informing the coroner's family to Detective Sloan, while Clément's would be his own obligation. A few cops found it odd that he chose to speak to the wife of the dead thief rather than the dead coroner, but he refused to explain himself.

He did not know the thief's family, although anytime they were together, Roger Clément wanted to talk about little else. From the outset, the man's love for his wife and daughter informed the nature of their interactions, setting them both on a course to become better acquainted and appreciative of one another's lives. Just as Touton lived an exceptional life for a cop, so had Clément lived an atypical life for a small-time hood. In the choices they made and the experiences they encountered, the two unearthed a rare friendship.

Now Clément had been killed, a priceless dagger thrust into his chest. He had died amid chaos and intrigue, true to the violent world in which he'd lived.

Shocked. Perhaps for the first time in his career, Touton could apply the word to a perpetrator's story. He was *shocked,* years ago, to learn that while he bullied himself to survive a German concentration camp, Roger Clément was also interned. Not as a POW, which might have been merely surprising. Nor had he been incarcerated in a domestic prison for petty crime, which might have been expected. Roger Clément, the family man, the enforcer and a former battling left winger in the National Hockey League, had served time in a Canadian internment camp, one set aside specifically for political malcontents. To attach political motives to a petty thief and a back-alley bruiser had altered Touton's perceptions of him, especially as Clément's political views contradicted his understanding of the man. What the alley ruffian stood for took time for Touton to unravel. Eventually he deduced that, as in the beginning of their acquaintanceship, the man really believed in nothing in particular except his love of family.

Now Touton had to tell his wife and daughter that their beloved husband and father was dead.

†††

To become a cop had been no snap accomplishment after the war, despite a hiring boom. Armand Touton did not resemble the barrel-chested tough nut he was repudiated to be. The man had worked on railway extra gangs in western Canada as a teenager, in a hardscrabble environment, and defended himself against all comers. His fists had kept him alive. After joining the army as a volunteer, never a popular choice in Quebec, he had given an impressive account of himself both in battle and while imprisoned. Yet the man standing in line at a police recruitment centre failed to live up to his press clippings. Half-starved in the POW camp, further wracked by hunger, dysentery and cold in the dead of winter on the long march out of Poland back to Germany, he'd passed close to the brink of death. Before being demobilized, he remained wan and undernourished. Neither his body nor his mind had fully recuperated.

Then, suddenly, he was returned to Montreal.

A large number of soldiers found work in the construction industry, which was starting to move with the spurt of immigration from a war-ravaged Europe, while others chased opportunities in the gaming business. The city was expanding, and with it the police department, so soldiers were also being given a nod to become cops. Touton desperately wanted to be one of them.

Once his war record had been reviewed, he'd been a shoo-in, but first he had to pass a medical. Although depleted, he seemed to be breezing through the exam until the last moment, when the physician informed him he had varicose veins.

"Excuse me?"

He knew that the war had damaged him physically, but he associated that particular condition with robust old ladies in support stockings. He may have aged prematurely, but he was quite certain that his gender had not been altered.

"Varicose veins," the doctor stated flatly, offering no note of sympathy. "The condition makes it impossible for you to enter the police academy."

"Men get that?"

"All the time."

"Where? Show me one of those veins!" he implored the doctor.

"Your legs are hairy, sir. Trust me. Under all that cover . . . varicose veins."

Touton didn't trust him. When he'd been examined before being demobilized, no one had mentioned it. He submitted to a physical by an army surgeon. "Do I have varicose veins?"

The army physician laughed heartily, as if he'd heard a good joke. "Ask the doctor," he advised, "how much it costs to be cured. Then come back and see me."

He walked into the office of the civilian practitioner a second time, asked his question and received a firm price. "Fifty dollars a year. It's not expensive. A buck a week. Not even."

A lot of money for a working man in those days. "Every year?"

The doctor shrugged. "If you're promoted, the treatments might become more costly for you. I'm just trying to give you a break. If I report that you have varicose veins, your days as an officer of the law are over."

"I look at my legs every night. I still don't see them."

The man shrugged. "I do," he said. "I'm the doctor."

Touton returned to the military, where he was greeted by a phalanx of seventeen physicians. Each examined the war hero, and each signed a document proclaiming that not only did he not have varicose veins, he was exceptionally fit for a man who had endured ordeals fatal to most mortals. They allowed that his body had been compromised in the service of his country, but affirmed that he was returning to full health at a rapid pace. Furthermore, the seventeen physicians declared, they would join forces with the military bureaucracy to assure that any civilian doctor who declared otherwise would be both sued and brought before the College of Surgeons to have his licence revoked for both incompetence and graft.

That day, Touton became a cop for free. Every other policeman who joined the force that year was apparently suffering from varicose veins and would annually pay a physician a fee to adjust the medical record. The recruit had been initiated into a corrupt regime, borne into the culture as its enemy.

†††

As a young cop in an openly dishonest department, Armand Touton took a risk, hitching his wagon to the political reformers of his day. In war and in captivity, he had learned to be true to himself—as a policeman he could do no less. In that period, Roger Clément, who was about seven years older than him, had been hiring out his fists at election time to anyone who needed a polling booth wrecked, or voters and scrutineers pummelled. One of the reformers, Jean Drapeau, had received police protection during his run for mayor, but the cop assigned to him was conveniently down the block buying a coffee when goons arrived to rough up the campaign workers and vandalize the offices. Touton surveyed the damage, then took the absentee cop into a nearby alley and rather vigorously used his cap to thrash him until the officer told him who the visitors had been.

He then drove off to pick up Clément.

He tracked him to a tavern and sat down at a small circular table before a cluster of glasses, both full and empty. In the style of the day, drafts were rarely dropped one at a time, but in batches according to the patron's level of thirst, often by the dozen. "We're going for a ride."

Clément checked his watch. "Naw. It's my kid's bedtime. I was heading home to tuck her in."

"Too bad you didn't think of that before trashing that campaign office."

"What campaign office? You got proof?"

"I don't need proof."

"How come?"

"I told you," Touton advised him, his voice flat and uncompromising, "I'm not arresting you. I'm not putting you on trial. We're just going for a ride, me and you."

"Yeah? Me, you and what army?" Clément's friends were hanging close by.

Touton lowered his voice so that his warning remained between them. "If my pistol accidentally discharges at this moment, the bullet blows off your left little toe. I been in the war. Believe me, it hurts. I seen tough guys bawl because they lost their littlest toe."

"Are you threatening me?" Clément carried weight, including in his neck and jowls, but his head seemed carved from granite. His jaw and chin might have been forged in a smelter. He had heard about Touton's threat to shoot off people's toes, but he also knew that the man hadn't done it yet. On the other hand, no one had called his bluff yet, either.

"I'm just apologizing in advance in case there's an accidental discharge. I'm sorry, I want to say, for the pain and the suffering that might cause you."

Clément nodded. "You're a big man behind that pistol and badge."

"We should go a few rounds, but your friends here might interfere. I don't have enough room in my squad car for everyone."

"Yeah? You'd go with me?"

Touton sat back in the small wooden armchair. The chairs were comfortable, built to keep a patron happily sedentary through an evening. "I wouldn't want to hurt you, but sure, I'd go with you."

"So I'm curious. You took who? Bremen, Talbot . . . those guys I heard about."

"Yeah, they wanted to try their luck. Both those guys I knocked out cold."

"Me, too. I took them out."

"Yeah?" Touton asked him, interested now. "Who else?"

"Lafarge . . . Gabriel Blais. Okay, those weren't knockouts, but I took them. Bloodied them up."

"Anton LeBrun?"

"I fought him," Clément boasted. Immediately, he raised his beer glass to his lips.

"You take him?"

Clément shrugged. "We had a battle. It's hard to say who won."

A couple of friends chuckled. For them, the victor had been more apparent.

"I took LeBrun," Touton told him.

"You did?"

"One punch."

"Sucker punch, I bet," Clément rallied.

"He gave me two good shots to the ribs, I fell to one knee, then I dropped him with a right uppercut. I hit him in a sweet spot, I'll concede that much."

Clément clucked his tongue. "He gave me two shots to the ribs. I couldn't breathe after that. That's how come he took me."

"You're brittle—that's good to know. Now, what are we going to do here?"

The thug took another sip, and considered his options. "I'm serious," he decided. "It's my daughter's bedtime. Let me give her a call at least."

In the interest of making this easy, Touton let him do that. After the call, they went for a ride.

Touton drove out of the East End towards downtown along Notre Dame Street, past the shipyards, the locomotive maintenance facility and Molson's brewery. After the war, the neighbourhood had swelled with working men who toiled in the tough places, where strength and fortitude were prerequisites to survival. The workers went home to small houses populated with streams of children, and on the weekends the streets and lanes were shrill with their bawling and brawling, so that the men usually looked forward to the end of their leisure period and another week of hard labour.

"Where we going?" Clément asked the policeman.

"You'll find out," Touton told him.

"Who do you work for anyways?" the thug asked further along. He had a few scars from his travails. A thick one cut through his left eyebrow, matched by another just under the same eye. He must have looked a royal mess after that adventure. Those marks could have been caused by pucks or sticks, but the line beneath his right jaw suggested he'd been sliced by a stiletto, although again, it could have been the blade of a skate.

"I'm a cop," Touton answered. "I work for the police department."

"Yeah, right, tell me another one."

The cop looked over at him. He had his reasons to let him sit up front. "I'll ask the questions, if you don't mind."

The man shrugged. "Why not? You're an officer of the law."

"Who do you work for?"

"That I can't say."

"Why not?"

"We'd be in trouble then, wouldn't we?"

"Let's find out."

"I work for my bosses and I don't rat them out. That's how I support my family. Hey. Where are we going?"

"You're a tough nut," Touton determined.

"Yeah. So?"

"There's only one thing to do with a tough nut."

"Yeah? What? Take him for a swim?" Clément asked.

"You've heard?"

"Yeah, I heard, all right? I ain't going to talk just because . . . I'm not like those other guys. I ain't going to talk. Forget about it. I don't sing to cops. I just don't."

Touton turned and headed for the docks. Roger Clément had heard this story, that the policeman would park high above the river where the rapids were fast, open the passenger-side door, and invite the poor sap in the car to either talk freely or step off the pier.

"You don't understand," Clément said, and for the first time, his voice sounded uneasy.

"What's that?"

"I can't swim."

The cop quickly sucked in his breath and shook his head with mock compassion. "That kind of limits your options, doesn't it? I don't have a life jacket with me."

"You don't understand!" the thug shot back.

"What's that?"

"I won't talk. I can't! It's not in my nature!"

"Try me."

"You'd piss your pants if I told you."

"Tell me anyway. It's my car. You don't have to worry about that."

"It's not in my nature. That's what everybody knows. That's how I support my family. I'm no squealer. I don't squeal. It's how I earn my living."

"You don't squeal and you don't swim. Jesus. We're at a crossroads here. Have you ever been at a crossroads before? It could be interesting."

"Very funny."

"I'm not laughing. Are you?"

The man didn't say. He was holding onto the dash and the door as the car sped up and swooped over and around bumps and onto the timber pier, where it shook like a freight train on rough track. The cop was driving like a madman, and the passenger was already more afraid than he had been for a while, believing the car was nearly out of the crazy cop's control, and with the river so near.

Worried the man might leap from the vehicle, Touton kept his speed up and drove with reckless intent. They reached the pier over the fast-moving water and he drove hard along the lip. A timber protected the edge, but he knew a place where a big ship had crashed hard and the bulwark had broken away. He scooted into the spot so that the first step out the passenger side of his car was into open air, then water, and he jammed on the brakes.

The thug had to fend himself off the dash. Before he had time to recover, Touton pressed his pistol against the man's knee. "Out!" he commanded.

"You've got to understand this," the man insisted, but he didn't sound fearful or intimidated. He sounded resigned to the worst that this day might bring.

"No, *you* do. Open the door." When the man did not respond, Touton jabbed him with his pistol and demanded again, fiercely this time, "Open the fucking door!"

"This is against the fucking law!" Clément shot back.

"What fucking law? What fucking town do you think you're living in? It's thanks to people like you there is no fucking law. Now open the fucking door!"

Clément opened it.

"Now step outside, Roger. You've got sixty miles to stay afloat before the current runs you into shore. Can you stay afloat that long?"

"I'm reaching into my pocket for my wallet," Clément told him.

"I'll shoot! Step outside or sing to me! Those are your two choices."

"Go ahead and shoot. But I'm going to show you pictures of my daughter, Anik. Do you have children?"

"I don't want to see a picture of your daughter!"

Clément shrugged again. "I don't want you to shoot me in the leg. So there, we're even. Here, look. Look at her. Isn't she sweet?"

The girl in the photograph was indeed sweet, a bright smile with black hair in a pageboy bob. She had smiling dark eyes.

"I don't care," Touton declared. "Talk to me or step out of the car."

"If I step out, I'll die. Who cares? You won't. All right, I understand that. You're the tough guy. You convinced me already. But my daughter will care." He kept the snapshot before Touton's eyes. "Did you think of that? What will she do without me? I want to know. Tell me, what will she do without her papa? How will she live? My wife. Let me show you a picture of my wife."

"I don't want to see. Will you put the pictures away?"

"Just look at her."

The two men looked at the woman together.

Touton toughened up. "If you want to see your wife and daughter again, talk to me. That's all you have to do." A cooler breeze was flowing in through the open window next to him and through the open passenger door, but it was still a warm night.

Clément answered him with silence.

"Before you go for a swim, tell me something," Touton asked, for he needed to be convincing in his menace. A cop could never back down in this situation, because the word would get around and he'd never have the upper hand again. "I looked at your rap sheet. How come you did time in that internment camp? What are you, a fascist? Communist? Spy? What?"

"I love my wife," Clément told him.

"You've made that point already."

"That's why I did time."

"They don't put you in jail for that."

"Yeah, they do," Clément said. "In my case, they did. My wife, she's a unionist. An agitator, they call her. A commie, they call her, but she's only looking out for the working people, in particular for the seamstresses. I took the blame for something that came out of my house. Pamphlets. That's all. Had to do with a strike at a munitions factory. It was considered unpatriotic, borderline treasonous, but you don't know what they made those poor girls do. I'm talking to you about sexual favours. And worse—rape. So they went on strike, those girls did, and my wife, she supported them, because that's what she does. She knows about strikes. So I did the time for her. I told them I printed the pamphlets. I was happy to do it. To me, it didn't matter much. I don't know what your camp was like—in my camp, I got to play hockey in the wintertime. All summer I played ball. The mayor—you know, Camillien Houde, the *ex*-mayor*—he was in my camp, too, doing his time. At night, we talked politics, him and me."

The mayor of Montreal had declared that the French should fight on the side of Mussolini. He'd also driven the city into bankruptcy by supporting the poor with work projects during the Great Depression, and fought against conscription, as did most Quebec politicians. What had finally done him in was his statement that he would disobey the law and not register for the draft, and he urged everyone else to defy the law as well, and for that he was rounded up and, without trial, dispatched to an internment camp, serving four years.

"I didn't get to play hockey in my camp," Touton admitted. "Are you telling me that you work for Houde?"

"I'm telling you no such thing. If I told you that, I'd be lying most days— maybe not every day. If I told you who I was working for today, you'd piss your pants. Trust me on this one thing."

"Pull that door closed," Touton instructed him, "but not all the way."

Clément did as he was told, not comprehending what might be in store for him. "Now what?" he asked.

"Put your hands through either side of the window and hang on to the door."

He looked at the door, at the open window, then back at the detective. "Wait a minute, my wife, my daughter—"

"I'm thinking about them—now hang on to that door!"

Clément hung on.

"Hold tight. Now step out."

"I can't swim! You bastard! You're killing me here!"

"I'm not asking you to swim. I'm asking you to hang on to that door and don't let go! Don't let go, Roger!"

Prodded by the gun, Clément gripped the doorframe through the open window, and, stepping out of the car, swung out above the water as the door yawned open. His feet dangled forty feet above the river darkly fomenting below him, thrashing the air as if trying to find something solid on which to land his shoes. "You bastard!" he shouted out.

"Let's not get personal here, Roger." Touton slid down the bench seat and sat on the passenger side, holding the door open with his right foot. "I'm not asking you to jump or fall. I'm just asking you not to let go while you think about your daughter. That's all. Just think about your family, Roger."

"I can't swim, I told you. I wasn't lying!"

"Then don't swim. Whatever you do, don't let go of that door. Just think about your daughter."

The two men fell silent awhile, the one dangling above the river, the other propped in the front seat of his sedan, keeping the door open.

After a long ten minutes, the thug deduced, "I can't stay out here forever."

"I can't either," Touton admitted. "But I've got ten, maybe twelve hours in me. How many you got in you?"

Clément waited about five minutes to answer. "Not that many," he said.

"Who do you work for, Roger?"

"You're one mean motherfuck, you know that?"

"Who do you work for?"

"Duplessis," Clément told him. What was the point in haggling forever?

Touton released his leg and foot and the door crashed closed. Clément hollered as he took the blow on the shoulder and upper thigh. Getting him back into the vehicle was awkward, and risky, but in the end both men were strong enough and managed it. Then Clément was sitting in the front seat again.

"Stay here," Touton told him.

"Where you going?"

"I gotta piss."

Armand Touton stepped behind his car and pissed into the river. What kind of a world did he live in, he wondered, when the premier of the province used low-level hoods to smash the offices of mayoral candidates? Smashing the offices of his political rivals was bad enough, but now he was sending goons out to disrupt municipal elections—which, on the surface of things, were none of his business. What kind of a world was this?

"I told you you'd piss yourself," Clément said as the cop got back into the car. "Can we go now?"

"There's something you should understand," Touton advised him.

"What's that?"

"You work for *me* now. Do what you have to do for the people you work for—Houde, Duplessis, the mob guys . . . exactly who doesn't really matter. But you work for me now. We can't clean this town up unless people like you help out people like me."

Clément sat quietly in the car awhile. He didn't want to be a stool pigeon, and couldn't think of himself in those terms, but the cop's words had made it sound different than that. As though this was a special mission and a worthy cause. In any case, they wouldn't be driving away soon unless he agreed to do it, and, given the alternatives—jail, the river—he had no reason not to agree.

"All right," he said. "We'll clean this place up. Maybe my wife and daughter, someday, they'll be proud of me for that."

"Now you're thinking with your brain," Touton said.

They drove off the docks, back to Clément's neighbourhood.

"Did you really take out LeBrun?" the thug asked.

"One punch," Touton confirmed, but conceded, "I got lucky. Right up under the chin, and he dropped. Took him more than twelve minutes to wake up, and when he did, his pride was gone. He wept. Something to see, LeBrun wiping tears off his cheeks. You never know how somebody will react. You think you're invincible, and *poof*! You're not. LeBrun never thought he'd be looking up from the floor at another man while his body felt like yellow mush. It's tough to be a legend in your own time, I guess, when your time as a legend is over."

†††

Touton arrived at the address he'd lifted from Roger Clément's wallet. The single-level dwelling hunkered down between a duplex on one side, a triplex on the other. The brown clapboard home had seen better days, and in another time had overseen a backyard of hogs and chickens, perhaps a corn crop and rows of beans and lettuce. Now it would be a patch of weeds, worn to dirt where children played, fenced in, sunless by day, leading onto a lane. The roof sagged. The stoop sloped dramatically forward and crumpled to the left. Visitors quickly assessed that the stairs were booby traps for the unwary. A low, black wrought-iron fence segregated the rather sparse front patch of yard from the sidewalk, and Touton bent at the waist to find the latch and unfasten it. He stepped over the rickety stairs onto the porch, then rang the buzzer by the door.

The house remained unlit, soundless.

He could hear his own breathing.

A streetlamp allowed him to read the sign in the door's glass: PADLOCK YOUR ASS. Meant for cops, it carried more than a single connotation. The first reference was to the Padlock Law, which had permitted the homes of communists and union sympathizers—and, by extension, Jews—to be barricaded by the police while the inhabitants were briefly away. The second referred to the police procedure of padlocking brothels and gambling dens after a raid. Everyone knew the scam. A brothel might have its broom closet bolted shut. One famous whorehouse had a door specially built on the street for the purpose. The door went nowhere—it opened onto a wall. After first alerting the madam, so that she could depart the premises and install her janitor to remain behind specifically to endure the arrest and pay the trivial fine, the police would ceremoniously snap a lock on the door to nowhere. In doing so, they discharged the letter of the law, while the spirit of the whorehouse remained cocky and the daily cash receipts continued unabated. The greatest inconvenience to most brothels might be to discover that their mops and buckets had been locked up, temporarily placed under house arrest.

He rang the buzzer again. This time, a light inside snapped on. Then the porch light came on, and the curtain in the door's glass was pulled aside an inch.

He displayed his badge.

A petite, attractive woman, although not at her best in nightdress and housecoat, applied a sliding chain lock and, once secured, opened the door a crack.

"Mrs. Clément?"

"Who wants to know at this fucking hour?"

"May I come in?" Touton asked gently. "I'm Captain Armand Touton of the Montreal Police Department. I have news about Roger."

Clearly, the woman had been geared for a more confrontational tone from a police officer. She closed the door only to unlock the chain, then let it fall wide open. Turning her back, she led Touton into the living room, where she glared at him, arms crossed. Despite the severe posture, she appeared to be shivering. "So, you're Touton," she stated.

A little voice piped up behind the policeman. "Mommy?"

"Anik. Come here, honey."

Rubbing sleep from her eyes, a girl, about eight years old in pink Bambi pyjamas, moved towards her mother. She rested her head on the woman's hip and wrapped her little arms around her, snuggling in as her mom held a hand around her shoulder. The child looked up at Touton with dark eyes.

"Perhaps Anik should wait in her room," Touton suggested, suddenly unsure of himself.

"She stays." She eyed him up and down. "What do you want?"

"I have bad news."

"No," she said. Her face, that quickly, went pale, and the woman stepped back and found the chair behind her. She managed to pull her olive-green housecoat more tightly around herself, then gathered the child closely to her side. "Did you kill him? Were you the one?"

The cop was momentarily stunned. "No." Then he realized that the question had probably been justified. "It had nothing to do with the police. But I'm sorry to report, Madame—"

"No—"

"That your husband is deceased."

She said "No" twice more, yet something in her manner indicated to Touton that she was not a woman to deny the truth for long. Her body began to quake. She had to heave to catch a breath. Her chin and lips quivered a moment before she tightly clamped her jaw. The child held on to her, and he could tell by the way the woman's head slumped forward and the pain rose up in her eyes that this day had not been entirely unexpected. She had anticipated the moment. Knowing what her husband did for a living, that he took large risks, she had lain awake through many long nights, awaiting the sound of his footsteps and a key in the lock, her heart clamped tight with dread. Only after he had fumbled with his clothing in the dark and his weight had eased down beside her would her thorax begin to unclench. This time, his footsteps would not arrive on their ramshackle stoop. This time, her fears had been confirmed.

"I'm sorry for your loss," the detective murmured.

Madame Clément pushed her child away from herself gently to dab her eyes on the sleeve of her housecoat. She gazed upon her daughter, her eyes filling with tears again, her anguish apparent. At the sight of her mom in such distress, the girl also wept, although she did not know why. For her, "deceased" held no meaning.

"Your papa . . . ," the woman said, then could go no further.

Confused and distressed now, the daughter, Anik, placed her small head against her mom's and held her tightly, as if to squeeze the tears and the obvious pain right out of her.

Touton sat down opposite the mother and child. He had felt uncomfortable looming above them, unable to approach.

"What happened?" the woman managed to ask. Her voice was barely audible.

The captain of the Night Patrol explained what he could, letting her know that her husband had been stabbed and that the case would be given the full attention of the police. He described the murder weapon, but refrained from suggesting that Roger himself might have been the thief who took the knife from the Sun Life Building. He had no evidence of that, and this was not the time to be accusing her dead husband of criminal activity.

Instead, he asked the most routine of investigative questions. "Do you know anyone, Madame, who might want to do such a thing to your husband?"

She had further difficulty breathing a moment, but commenced to pull herself together. As she spoke, she absently combed her child's hair with her fingers, an unconscious habit, and the girl faced Touton while sitting in the chair alongside her mom.

"You, or any cop, that's my first choice. Second choice, goons from this or that mob . . . take your pick. Politicians—municipal, provincial, federal— they'd be next on my list. You should investigate any businessman who has it in for unionists, even if he's hired Roger to bust up strikes in the past. So, yeah, cops, goons, politicians, businessmen. More or less in that order. I don't think the Church had anything against him, so I'll rule out priests, but you never know, and working people were on his side. Every friend he's ever had would die for him, so it was none of them. Does that narrow it down, Captain?"

Touton knew a few things about Carole Clément. Roger had talked about her often, his love for her clearly impassioned and devoted. As well, the cop had culled information from her police record. She had been in jail for organizing strikes among seamstresses. The trade offered the lowest-paying jobs for women, in the most difficult conditions, and usually only immigrants took the work. The sweatshops were primitive, the labour physically debilitating, the threat of dismissal for the slightest fault ever-present. After she had become a mom, Carole had taken on piecework at home, partly to be close to her daughter, Roger had said, but also because no one in the industry would knowingly hire her. Friends had seen to it that she found work without the bosses being aware of who actually performed the labour.

"Piecework's no better," Roger had told him. "You get paid for what you do dead perfect, not for your time. The bosses? They know a woman's got to be home to look after her kids, that they don't got options in life. The good part is, no boss is looking over her shoulder now, checking a stitch, or feeling up her tits—if anybody does that now, it's me—but at the same time, she's got to work fast and accurate or she won't earn a dime. Rights? Hunh? What rights? Carole's organizing pieceworkers now, but in secret. Everything's secret or the work gets cut off. It'll be one mean, long fight."

"As you know, Madame," Touton spoke in a low, gentle voice, "your husband had a tough job. He made enemies. That's what I'm asking about. Who carried a grudge? Anyone? Also, his business partners, shall we say, they might have gone against him. Was he worried about anything like that?"

"You mean, was he worried that his business partners—what you call them—maybe found out he was a stool pigeon working for you? Yeah, he worried about that. Did anybody find out? How would I know? The first clue for something like that would be Roger gets a knife stuck in his chest." The words had come out defiantly, but once they were spoken she collapsed into tears. This time, the daughter was alert to a dire possibility. "Is Daddy coming?" she asked.

Carole responded with tears and hugs, and Armand Touton steeled himself so that a surprising tremor wouldn't trouble him as well. The daughter's presence—prompting him to remember all that Roger had said about her—broke his heart.

Eventually, he offered, "I admired your husband, Madame."

"You admired him," she repeated back sarcastically.

"I thought he was a fine man."

"A fine punk! A goon! A thug!" Carole shot back. "Are we talking about the same guy?"

"He had a way of going about his job—"

"He only beat up the assholes. You don't have to tell me. I've heard that story before. It's a crock of shit. He's a liar, my husband. He makes up stories. He breaks some poor bastard's nose and says the shit deserved it. But . . . he tried to get proper work. Who would let him? Would *you* let him? You didn't want him off the streets. You didn't want him going straight. You wanted him to stay with the bastards. He tried to work in factories—by noon, somebody would find out that he was Roger Clément, who once played a year with the Rangers, a few games over three years with the fucking Blackhawks."

"Mommy, don't say that word," Anik censored.

"I know, sweetie. Mommy's sorry." She turned back to the detective. "Roger Clément, who spent most of his career in the penalty box. Roger Clément, who got beat up by the really tough guys on the other teams, but at least he kept swinging. Okay, so he was never a great fighter on skates. Off skates, in shoes, nobody could outpunch him."

"Except me, maybe," Touton said. "We had that between us, him and me. We wondered who could take the other guy if it came down to it. Maybe I could outpunch him, but we never found that out. It's one reason we were friends. We could both punch."

"Write it on his grave: 'Here lies Roger Clément. He could punch.'" The woman wiped her nose on her sleeve. "Every time Roger got a factory job, every fucking time—oh sorry, sweetie, Mommy won't say that bad word again. His first day on the job, no matter how hard he tried to get out of it, at lunch somebody wanted to take him on, try his luck. So what's he going to do, lose? He'd fight the guy, then get fired, or fight the guy and get arrested, or fight the guy and six other guys would line up to try their luck. Every time, it ended up with him realizing that if he had to fight anyway, he might as well get paid for it without doing all the shit labour and being pushed around by bosses and foremen."

Repeatedly, the policeman turned his hat over in his hand. What she said was valid. When he'd worked on the railroad, and later in the army, his reputation as a man who could use his fists was frequently challenged. There was always somebody who wanted to prove his status false. He didn't know if he could have taken Roger in a brawl. He had taken LeBrun, but he had always believed that that had been a lucky punch. And Roger had a soft middle. Between the two of them, the question was held in suspension—who could take the other guy out?—yet for both of them, the issue would only remain a curiosity. Neither man had an interest in that ultimate test.

Only the rest of the world cared.

"So he's not been particularly worried lately? No new problems with his job?"

"You're so holier-than-thou, aren't you?" Carole fired out.

Touton was now glad that Anik was there. Her presence obliged her mother to mind her tongue. "Did Roger think that way? I don't think he did."

"Roger was confused by a lot of people. Look who he's working for."

"Roger," Touton stated, "taught me that I had no right to look down on him. He worked for the mob, guys in the rackets, I worked for the police department."

"Who are also in the rackets," Carole taunted him.

"That was your husband's point. As he used to tell me, with the gamblers and the pimps you knew what you were buying. With a cop, if you expect one thing, you could get something else."

"We don't have a police department in this town," the woman complained. "The strong arm of the law is nothing more than the strong arm of the mob."

"Some of us are trying to change all that. Roger was helping."

"Yeah, well, some of us dedicate our lives to changing the system."

"We're making progress."

"Speak for yourself," she told him. "My husband is dead."

Her little girl looked up at her. "Is Daddy dead, Mommy?"

For a long time, the woman wept in the arms of her child, while the policeman stared at the floor.

He did not leave before receiving assurances that she would contact a neighbour, to have someone be with her. And he vowed to pursue the case, to bring her husband's killers to justice.

"You don't know where that might lead you," she cautioned him.

"I will take it where it leads me. That's the promise I'm making here tonight. To you and your daughter. That's a promise I'll keep."

She pressed her lips tightly to stop them from quivering.

At the door, with her child against her, she called the detective's name before he stepped off the porch.

Touton turned. He felt captured by the wide, dark eyes of the child.

"Roger and me, we had an understanding. I wouldn't ask him about his work and he wouldn't tell me anything. But we always talked about finding a way out."

"I see." The detective returned his hat to his head and pulled in his coat against the chill. The woman was shivering now in her grief.

"Lately, he's been talking. I don't know how far things got. But he's had some idea about a big score on his mind. I didn't stop him. I didn't discourage him. We needed to change our lives."

"Did he mention anything about this big score? Who he's been seeing lately?"

She shook her head, and Touton knew that he could believe her, that she was not withholding information. Perhaps she didn't know that her husband had also been working for him in recent days.

"Has he ever mentioned something called the Cartier Dagger to you?"

Again, she shook her head.

"Thank you, Madame. Please accept my condolences on your loss. I liked Roger a lot. Him and me, with twists of fate, we could have traded places."

"Detective." Her new reality was taking hold, and through her heartache, practical matters had presented themselves. "I hope I won't be reading in the papers that my husband was a police informant."

Touton gazed at her, then at Anik, and back at the mother.

"No, Madame, you won't be reading that. But I can't control how the papers will describe him. He has a past."

"You understand, don't you? It's not possible. You can't attend the funeral."

She desired to hold her head up over the next little while, and that would include holding her head high among the families of friends who had worked with Roger in nefarious activity. Touton nodded, sadly expressing his understanding. He felt a pang, for he realized that he had both wanted and expected to be paying his respects in a proper manner.

His last image of the evening would remain the most haunting: the dark, doleful eyes of the child gazing at him. Questioning him. He drove home, knowing that he'd be awake early in the morning to confront a city in the midst of its devastation. Yet he was going to feel more troubled, he knew, by these two forlorn hearts.

CHAPTER 6

1608–09 ~ 1611 ~ 1628

NEVER AN EXPLORER BOUND TO HIS SHIPS, ALTHOUGH HE CLAIMED great happiness at sea, Samuel de Champlain was foremost a soldier, a geographer and a diarist. An avid adventurer, he was also devoted to sitting still for hours, imagining or writing. He appreciated the birchbark canoe and valued secrets discerned by a discourse with rivers, yet this daydreamer would become a political strategist whose actions determined the course of nations in the New World. To all appearances a peaceable man, on his own initiative he chose to commence the Indian wars.

His predecessor, Jacques Cartier, on a third and final voyage, had failed to progress beyond the rapids at Montreal. Thwarted in a quest for diamonds and gold, the French abandoned the vast lands of forest and snow for decades. Among the Indians, stories of white men with beards and giant canoes would become half-forgotten rumours, myths passed along by batty elders that were difficult to decipher or believe when, after seventy years, the fabled French returned. Henri IV had been gazing upon the Cartier Dagger, ruminating over reports that the English had plans to explore, and perhaps annex, the New World. The Dutch, those villains, were also up to something, and the Spanish had ambitions brewing. Henri IV always had to second-guess the Spanish. So he chose to dispatch Champlain across the sea, and obliged him to introduce sixty families a year into New France to gain a proper foothold there. Champlain was also expected to explore and map the river system, initiate commerce, and, while he was there, pursue the search for the fabled swift route to the Orient.

A man who had been at sea on his twentieth birthday, and now a handsome, charismatic sea captain in his thirties, Champlain conned the coastline north from the lands called Cape Cod and Maine before attempting an east coast community in the basin of an inlet off the Bay of Fundy, which he named Port Royale. Starvation and illness stymied that fledging effort, but like Cartier before him, he would grow more impressed by the spectacle and promise of the St. Lawrence River. In 1608, having forsaken the initial settlement, he established a second where the river narrowed at Cape Diamond, a place the Indians called Quebec.

The following summer, in the company of two French and sixty Algonquin, Champlain canoed south up the River of the Iroquois to an immense waterway, where he proved to be more pragmatic than his forbearer at naming landmarks. An island in the St. Lawrence had cleverly been called Île Ste. Hélène, for he had landed there on that saint's day. Yet he noted in his diary that naming the island after a saint was really a coy subterfuge, for he had had in mind, as he so often did, his bride back in France, the pretty twelve-year-old Hélène. Now appreciative of the majesty of a long and narrow body of water bounded by mountains on either side, he promptly named the lake Champlain. Unlike Cartier, he would not depend upon others to christen an impressive waterway after himself, and his party canoed the lake that bore his name, south toward the Iroquois settlement at Ticonderoga.

Where they encountered more than two hundred warriors.

For Champlain, the New World had to exist not on the idle dreams of wealth promoted by Cartier, but on sound business practice. That meant trade with the Indians. The Algonquin had convinced him that they could not engage in trade while defending themselves against Iroquois raiders, for they and the Huron clearly feared the ferocious, adept fighters to the south. Needing a strategy, Champlain foresaw a dramatic way to win their favour. With a bold stroke, he could gain the allegiance of the Algonquin, the Montagnais and the Huron, bolstering their confidence and delivering them from constant attrition in fights with the Iroquois. In doing so, he'd establish trading partnerships that could last for generations. In effect, by declaring to the Iroquois that they had to remain far south, that any incursion north would be met by deadly counterattack, he would establish trade with the northern natives and launch New France as a viable commercial entity independent of funding from any king reluctant to untie the drawstrings on his purse.

If the Dutch and the English were planning forays across the sea, it would be only a matter of time before they attempted colonies. He had to move quickly. He had already explored the lands of the Atlantic coast, but the river gave the French excellent inland access, where he could claim massive territory in the name of France. What he needed was military might, and that could only be achieved through a powerful alliance with loyal tribes.

Champlain spent considerable time just sitting, stewing, working out ideas. That he was creating the nascent border between future countries in the New World had occurred to him in a moment of visionary insight. The continent might not be too vast for France to claim, but to hold it all without greater help from the king seemed unlikely. And yet, using only limited resources, the opportunity was before him to create space for his own enterprise while decreeing to all opposing forces that they had to stay away. The New World could change quickly. Move quickly was his plan—stake a claim, and be properly allied.

He had enjoyed the hard paddle south. The surrounding mountains, the waters as clear as the king's own crystal, invigorated him. Extraordinary physical specimens, the Algonquin paddled with great effort hour upon continuing hour, soundless and straining. As winds whipped down from mountains to the west, Champlain himself took up a paddle and did his best to keep up with their rhythm, until the labour exhausted him and the Indians carried on. Late in the afternoon, they made camp, a dapple of sunlight reddening through the leaves while he touched a quill into his ink and wrote in his diary. Soon he'd smell sweet venison roasting on the fire. The Indians were nervous, he knew, but he had promised them an impressive display of power wrought by their alliance, and as the days passed and they approached their destination, his heart quickened with the prospect of war.

Three French, sixty Algonquians. Two hundred Iroquois fighters.

When the scouts arrived with news of the band at Ticonderoga, Champlain smiled. Good. He had hoped to be outnumbered. He told his less-confident new friends, "Tomorrow you will see our power. Together we shall attack."

The French carried with them three harquebusiers.

In the morning, the raiders from the north amassed across a cornfield farmed by the Iroquois. Surprised by the incursion, the proprietors were not dismayed. They raised their voices in ecstatic war whoops and lifted their tomahawks to the enemy and armed their bows with deadly arrows. This would be a wondrous fight, the inferior band killed and scalped. This would be a momentous event for the Iroquois, one worth many stories.

Then the three harquebusiers fired.

Three Iroquois fell.

One man was struck in the eye, killed instantly. Another gurgled on his knees for breath, blood spurting from his throat. The third man moaned in his misery as blood erupted from his belly, the pain more than he could endure as a man. His own brother slit his throat to spare him further shame.

Three more Iroquois fell in a torment of blood and suffering.

The sound of the three harquebusiers firing reached the survivors' ears.

What was that sound? How did noise and smoke kill their brothers?

Another two Iroquois clutched themselves in agony and collapsed upon the ground. Then the sound that charged their nerves with fright followed.

They could fire no arrow upon their enemy, who was too far away. The Iroquois fled and the invaders gave chase. The rout was on, and the day belonged to the French and the Algonquin. That night, they ate from the stores of Iroquois food. Iroquois women aimlessly roaming in the forest were taken to be their slaves, and in the morning their canoes were made heavy with produce and meat and furs and women to take back to their people, and upon the bow of each canoe hung bloody Iroquois scalps.

Champlain did not paddle, not even when the winds whipped up. He had much to think about and dwell upon. He indulged in pleasant thoughts of his child-bride back home in France. He maintained a grip on the handle of the knife given to him by King Henri IV, the same knife bequeathed to successive kings, and initially acquired by Cartier. Champlain had examined the knives in the hands and belts of every dead Iroquois. None had handles of gold and diamonds, as did this one. That puzzled him. Nonetheless, the dagger had brought him good fortune, and the future of his enterprise, he believed, was now assured.

†††

Champlain paid little more than cursory attention to the seafaring hands who had crossed the ocean with him. Seamen were adept in the rigging, brave and energetic in an ocean's tempest, but nothing less had been expected. While he knew the name of every Frenchman in New France, including the few feral trappers who had settled way north on the river, at Tadoussac, before his own arrival, the youth who stood before him three years after his voyage was a puzzle. He recognized the name, but a thick beard, wild hair and an increase in muscle mass had changed him. Three years in New France had not only matured Étienne Brulé, but had also kindled in him a passionate spirit.

Onboard, the boy had been surly, unsure that he wanted to be cast upon the rolling waters on a voyage to the New World. Three years later, he bore little resemblance to that reluctant sailor. The New World had ignited his senses. He had despised only the dull grey ocean. He was now pleading with Champlain to grant him permission to take a canoe west with the Huron, to explore that unknown region where the lakes, they were told, were as broad as the sea. Determined to be the first European to map the waterways there, to discover the mines, he wanted to learn the Huron language and—or so he claimed, because he had studied Champlain's ambitions and interpreted his actions—he would help to draw *les sauvages* into a closer military and trading partnership.

Champlain recognized in the youthful Brulé a version of himself at twenty. While the lad did not share his love for the sea, he did crave the indomitable quest. Whereas the older man had had his nature revealed to him on stormy waters, this young man had found his soul in the woods and on the rivers of New France. Still, Champlain needed to know that the youth could be entrusted with a task demanding so much fortitude, acumen and raw courage.

"The rapids around Montreal and around the Hochelaga islands," Champlain proposed, then paused.

"The rapids, Captain?" Étienne Brulé inquired, curious.

"Let's find our way through. Me and you, with our best men. If we survive, I will commission your journey to the land of the Huron."

Brulé was so excited he clicked his heels and saluted.

Provoked to laughter, Champlain shooed him on his way.

†††

Brulé took the stern of one canoe, Champlain the centre position in another, from which he could make quick navigational choices, and the slender vessels slipped onto the river. The Indians knew nothing of swimming, and so had declined to accompany the foolish white men on their escapade. After all, to reach their destination, they could simply walk. The canoes were manned by the strongest and most fearless of the French, for they would not be travelling down the rapids, but paddling upstream, against that relentless force.

Initially, they stuck to the shore where the current was weakest. Even here, they would be captured by a swirling eddy and one canoe would have to make it ashore and toss a rope to the other spinning craft and pull it from the spiral. In these surging waters, their boats felt fragile and small. Often, the canoes were turned back by the water's propulsion, and the men portaged to a new location to try again. Still, they had not encountered the roughest water.

As the river intensified, Champlain coordinated the advance. He would select short jaunts, moving the boats from rock to rock, or from a promontory to a tree bending over the current, and the men, eight to each side of the canoe, would rest, then shout, then paddle with superhuman strength against the water's force, and strap themselves tight to their destination, and rest again. Both canoes capsized often, Champlain's once in front of Brulé, and it was the youth who dove into the current—not to rescue his flailing captain, but to save the canoe, swimming with it down the current until he could snag it to a rock. Then he intercepted the floating paddles and other rampant debris, and finally the men themselves as they whooshed down the current pell-mell and drunk on frenzy. Champlain stretched out a hand to an unknown arm, pulled to the safety of a midstream rock, and only after he'd coughed up gallons of river water did he see that it was Brulé who had snared him.

"Your help might have been more useful upstream," Champlain carped, stranded and exhausted.

"First the canoe," Brulé told him. "You can find another paddler. A good canoe in the wilderness is not so easy to find."

"I am not," Champlain informed him tersely, "just an ordinary paddler."

But he was already thinking that the lad was up for the task he had set for himself, although he doubted that this first mission would be completed successfully, so it didn't particularly matter. He wondered what his pretty wife might be doing back in France. Baking bread with women, skipping rope with girls?

The boy proved right. Canoes made survival possible. Having gathered their strength, the crew set out again, this time with both Brulé and Champlain in the same vessel. They eventually made it back to the first craft, and there, in the middle of the roaring river, strapped to rocks, they napped among their comrades.

And still, they had not reached the fiercest water.

At night, they made a fire on the rocks from driftwood and cooked perch trapped in a net.

"How much farther?" the young man asked.

"We'll know that when we arrive there," the older man responded.

"Tomorrow," suggested the youth, "shorter advances. Longer rests. Rock by rock. Not only paddles. We must use the ropes. Some water we'll traverse on foot, crawl along the shore if we have to, pull the canoes behind us."

Champlain nodded. He said nothing further, but the young man's advice, and his leadership qualities, were duly noted.

The river the next day had to be attacked. Often, they did as Brulé commanded, with men in the water pulling themselves towards rocks they'd lassoed, then stretching the rope for others to follow. Often, the canoes came last, and slowly, brutally, they struggled against the river and the river fought against their trespass. So loud was the raging torrent that they rarely spoke, and the company of men moved with an empirical grace, as though each step might be their last, one hand before the other, short, rhythmic paddle strokes, hanging on for their lives, then staggering forward. Wet and cold and beyond exhaustion, they were eventually victorious, for Champlain discerned a route somewhat free from the torrent, and from there only quiet water lay ahead.

"For this," Champlain noted, lying on his back on a patch of sand beach, "you will visit the land of the Huron. Live among them. Become as they are—a *sauvage*, a man of the woods. Speak as they speak, do as they do, think as they think, but do not forget who you are. Do not forget your mission. Bring back to us the knowledge of the Huron's lands and great lakes."

"Yes, Captain." Too tired to be happy, the boy's celebration would wait.

"In the late autumn of this year, I will hold a trading fair at Hochelaga."

"Captain?"

"As you travel, tell the Indians you meet to bring their furs in trade. If they come, then I will know you remain alive. That will tell me how far you've journeyed."

"I might travel," the boy said, turning only his head to face Champlain, unable to move any part of himself below his neck, "too far for the Huron to canoe to Hochelaga to trade."

"Good," Champlain said. "Then I will know that, too." Slowly, he dragged a hand from where it had rested on the ground above his head down to his side. He pulled his other hand across his body to meet it. "Étienne, you will travel with the Cartier Dagger, for your good fortune."

"But," the boy objected, "I might die. The knife will be lost."

"If you lose it, do not bother to come back. If you are killed, then the man who possesses the knife condemns himself—someday we will avenge your loss. But I believe the knife will see you safely home. As long as it is in your possession, expect to see us again. Make certain, Étienne, that you return Cartier's dagger to me."

He untied the sheath and the knife from his side. Though it demanded the last of his strength, he passed it across to Brulé. The young man knew what Champlain was really doing. He was commanding him to stay alive.

He received the dagger into his hands, then slept.

††††

Tepees were erected on a waterfront clearing where Champlain waited for the Huron to arrive, canoes laden with furs. This was the first fur fair in the New World. Although Samuel de Champlain was not a particularly religious man, he went down to his knees to pray for its success. He needed to demonstrate the colony's viability. Since the collapse of the first settlement at Port Royale, selling the idea of the New World to the king and to the French people had been difficult. He needed to prove that life could be prosperous here. Yet October had arrived, and still there were no Indians, only disenchanted French and empty tepees awaiting visitors.

Champlain was alone in believing that young Étienne Brulé might somehow survive. When the French spoke his name, they'd genuflect, as if over his grave, while Indians remained mute. He'll never be heard from again, was the gist of general opinion, killed by distant Huron who had never heard of white men, or killed by the rough waters, or animals, or spirits, or starvation. If he survived all that, winter would consume him. He was a boy doing a man's job, and Champlain had dispatched him to his death.

Champlain waited, and believed, and the days went by, without contact and with lessening hope.

They were now a week into October. An early winter howled in the night air. The French milled about during the day and discussed passage home to France on the ship Champlain had waiting upriver at Quebec. He had considered the name Cape Diamond ironic, and discouraged its use. Cartier's men had received gold and diamonds there, yet upon reaching France they learned that the diamonds were quartz, and that the yellow metal they'd lugged along on their passage held no value—mere coloured rock. A disappointment, unlike the Cartier Dagger. Forevermore, that rock would be disparaged as fool's gold. So Champlain brought the Indian name of the place, Quebec, into use, to dispel Cartier's obsession with diamonds and to forget that sad comeuppance.

Now it was the second week of October, and the leaves were vivid in their dance of colours, while the winds carried cold air down from the north.

"They will arrive," he told the traders.

"On the first canoe, look for Brulé's scalp," one replied.

"And hang on to your own," suggested another.

The third week of October came and went. A few traders were beginning to pack their supplies to make the return trip to Quebec and passage home. One of these, up early to prepare his canoe, noticed movement on the river at first light.

He sounded the alarm, and the French reached for their harquebusiers. Champlain broke from his tent and scrambled down to the riverbank.

"Indians!" a man shouted.

"Are they Iroquois?" another asked.

"Not likely, from that direction," Champlain noted quietly.

"Iroquois can come from anywhere."

"That's a lot of canoes."

And Champlain smiled and said, "That's a lot of furs. They're loaded down to the gunwales. Gentlemen! Today, we trade. Tonight, we celebrate like kings!"

The fair became a party, with much food and no small amount of wine and brandy enjoyed by the Hurons, and the next day the Algonquians showed up with their canoes heavy-laden as well. The party continued for days with feasting and exchange and barter, and the French traders loaded their canoes for the journey north and each man mentioned that he'd never forget these five festive days, for they were the wonder of their lives.

Champlain was the last to leave, waving his hand from shore as the Indians departed. None had carried with him the Cartier Dagger, which would have signalled Brulé's death. Champlain had listened to their stories and learned that his protégé had travelled deep into Huron territory. Brulé moved in the company of the young Hurons he'd befriended, and they had made it to the great inland waters and were bound south, exploring rivers below the Iroquois lands.

The inaugural fur fair had been a significant success. Traders were delighted with the furs they'd collected and would ship back to France, but they would also be returning to the maternal nation with words of enthusiasm and praise. Through them, an opinion would progress that the colony could be economically viable, that in New France, the courageous might find their fortune.

†††

Even for the three Huron travelling with him—two his own age and one younger—the beauty of the Allegheny River, as it flowed south through rolling mountains in the majesty of their autumnal colours, moved the young men in ways that altered their appreciation of the world and their attitude towards themselves. In commencing their southbound trek, they'd been excited by the adventure. They had expected to fight, to be beset by wonders and to return with astonishing tales. They had not expected to be apprehended by nature's lore. The rising, falling hills laced by the meandering stream. The wafting mists at dawn. Clear light on a crisp day. Songbirds gathering for the migration south. The soft gibber of water along the stony shore. They felt themselves becoming a part of the forest and the river and sky, as though their paddles could no more fail to break the surface of the water than the wind could refuse to create its ripples, as though they could no more avoid canoeing south than the birds could decline to fly in advance of their passage. So the four young men were united in a different communion than they had expected as they achieved the place where the Allegheny met the Monongahela River to form the Ohio, a place foretold by friendly natives upstream, and they were not in the proper frame of mind to respond quickly enough or wisely enough when they fell into the view of a party of wandering Iroquois who were also distant from their usual lands. Knowing that he had lost the advantage of time and surprise, Étienne Brulé slipped his harquebusier into the stream, to keep it out of Iroquois hands.

They tore at his flesh with knives and hammered his bones with tomahawks and burned his skin with stones roasted in the campfire. They scowled in his face and threatened worse: to tear out his eyes, to slice off his genitals, to roll boulders off an outcropping onto him spread-eagled below. This they did to each of his good friends, and made them suffer before slicing their throats.

The youngest was the last to die, crying out as huge rocks fell upon him. In the end, his body was buried under a pile of rocks with only his head visible, and, dead or still alive, they scalped him.

They waved the three scalps before Brulé's eyes.

What to do with the Frenchman? How to kill Brulé? This was a dilemma for the Iroquois. His death had to be fitting, for all the Iroquois had heard the story of Ticonderoga, of how the white man's magic had slaughtered their brothers. When they told the story of this Frenchman's death, they would need to satisfy the rage of all their brothers.

They cut three slices of flesh from above each nipple, using his own knife—an extraordinary instrument with bright stones in the handle and sharp bone for the blade—and, with his hands tied, they burned his feet, then made him run. They rammed his head into tree trunks, and he bled, and he wobbled on his burnt feet as the Iroquois laughed and discussed how they might choose to kill him.

They made him run along the rocky beach while they threw stones at him and talked about their predicament, and he ran this way and that to avoid the warriors who could throw best. The man who had rammed his head into trees grabbed him and pulled him up onto a low cliff and made him jump off into deep water, and the Iroquois laughed at this, and rushed to the ledge to see him thrash about and sink. They planned to catch him like a fish in their nets downstream, then humiliate him further while they devised their best killing method.

The Frenchman sank, but when his head popped back to the surface, they were confused. No Iroquois had ever swum in water—no native knew that that trick could be managed. The man whose hands were tied was kicking his feet and floating on his back like a tree, and then he would rest—he would appear to be resting!—in the middle of the stream, and he was speaking Huron to the Iroquois.

They all raced back down to the beach, each man frantically exclaiming about the wonders he had witnessed.

One man knew the language, but he was away with the others contemplating the best death for the white man. When he was summoned and returned on the run down to the shore, the white man still swam in the water, with his head up, and when he chose to do so, he'd kick his feet. This was a great magic the white man possessed, that he did not sink.

Did this mean that he could not die?

Was it true, then, that the white men were really only ghosts?

This was debated and discussed.

"What does he say?" the Iroquois chief wanted to know.

The man who spoke Huron asked that everyone be quiet, and he listened to what the Frenchman had to say in the Indian tongue.

"The white man who talks like a stupid Huron," the Iroquois elder stated, "says to us that he is the only man on the earth who can save our people."

This started up a great conflagration among the elders and the young men who wanted to kill him instantly, but they could not catch him without getting into their canoes. A few climbed into a canoe and pursued him in the river.

The white man dove below the surface of the water to avoid the canoe, and the Indians knew then that he was dead, for no man could live under the surface of the water, and this man had disappeared. The canoeists paddled back to shore. The people were disappointed, for they had not killed him very well. The death had been ordinary and did not make for a good story. Then Brulé stuck his head up and breathed the clear air, and the Iroquois were amazed, yet concerned, and the canoe turned back to catch the Frenchman.

While he had been underwater, Brulé had been sawing his restraints against a sharp rock, and with further struggle he was able to slip his hands free. As the canoe approached a second time, he dove beneath the surface and the men stopped paddling, not knowing where he had gone. The young man came up under the canoe and made it rock, then pulled it down hard so that the men panicked. One slipped over the side, trying to get at the man under the canoe, and the vessel tipped over. The four Iroquois hung on for their lives while Brulé swam in the stream and harangued the Iroquois on shore.

He had caused a grave consternation to ripple through the men, who disapproved of his magic and feared his ability to live where any Iroquois would die. The chief gave the order to pierce him with arrows and so the warriors retrieved their bows, but when they fired their arrows, Brulé dove to the bottom of the river again.

He had much to think about down there. He could swim to the opposite shore, although the Iroquois could cross the river quickly in their canoes. His predicament would remain dire if he chose to float downriver, and down the Ohio, for even if he eluded his enemies he would be left in the wilderness with neither weapons nor food, nor clothes, nor companions, nor a canoe. The Iroquois had clearly demonstrated their zeal to kill him properly. He had to negotiate a truce with them. Only in this strategy did hope lie. He was about to resurface when he became the world's luckiest Frenchman at the bottom of a river.

Breaking the surface of the water, he held his right hand straight aloft, and in it his harquebusier. The Indians were suitably astounded, and two men fell over one another in their fright while several of the others stepped back.

"See what I have made from the stones of this river!" Brulé called out. His interpreter let his words be understood by the others, and the Iroquois were both suitably impressed and warily skeptical.

"Do I kill you today, and your children tomorrow, and all Iroquois people? Or do I save you and make a pact between the French and the Iroquois? Speak now!"

Trembling, the translator needed Brulé to repeat himself a few times before he could get the full message across, but once he had done so, the chief moved him aside to fully examine the youth floating freely in the water where any Iroquois man would drown, having devised a fire-spear out of the river's stones. The chief considered carefully what his eyes did see before he spoke. The man possessed magic, and whether he could kill them and their children was a consideration but perhaps not the most important. For him, this white boy who could live like a fish, who could make weapons at the bottom of a river, who was brave and did not flee, but taunted the men who would kill him—such a boy deserved to have his life preserved. More than any white man, he deserved to live awhile.

"Tell the fish-man, who does not die in a river where a man should die," he told the elder who could speak the language of the Huron, "to come to me. He will not be harmed this day or tomorrow."

Hearing the message, Brulé put his rifle between his knees and swam ashore, his smooth, sure strokes an extraordinary spectacle to the Indians.

On the stone-covered beach, Étienne Brulé stood upon his burnt feet, his heaving chest bleeding, his stomach bloody as well, his joints bruised purple. His skin was goose-bumped from the cold water and his teeth chattered. He said, "The man who holds my knife will be killed by every Frenchmen who is alive today and by every Frenchmen who will ever be alive tomorrow, and his children and his children's children will die also."

The dagger was returned to him by the man who had bashed his head into trees. He received the knife and stuck it into its sheath, and although he knew that it could not fire, for he'd need a dry wick and he carried no gunpowder on his person, having been stripped of all his possessions, Brulé cradled his magic spear across his chest. "Now let us talk," he said. "Let us make a great peace between the white man and the red."

"Can you fly?" the Iroquois chief asked him first.

"What?" Brulé thought he had misunderstood the translation.

"You can live in the water like a fish. Can you live in the sky like a bird?"

The man was asking if he was a god. For Brulé, it was difficult to judge what his best tactical answer might be. He chose to be honest.

"I am a man like you," he said.

In their prodigious labour, the centuries would pass, one time folded into another, and a city would rise in that place where the waters of the Allegheny flowed together with those of the Monongahela to cast the Ohio River upon its journey, but in that place on that day, only a camp of Iroquois and a single Frenchman sat still, and three Huron lay dead nearby. A small fire crackled where the men talked, and on the autumnal winds their voices were heard to speak in solemn tones.

Bound north the next day in the company of two Iroquois, including the man who had bashed his head against trees, Brulé paddled his own canoe, and he would cross safely through the Iroquois lands on his long winter's journey home, taking shelter in Iroquois villages and learning their ways. After winter had slipped into spring and spring had yielded to summer, he taught his guides how to do the dog paddle. The young men loved to show the fellow

Iroquois they met during their travels that a man could swim like a fish if he pretended to be a dog.

"What's a dog?" those Indians asked. The travellers did their best to explain that a dog was a white man's shabby wolf.

They had an inkling of what it must feel like to be gods, to be like fish, the young warriors did, afloat on the rivers.

Shortly before reaching the island of Montreal, the place the Iroquois called Hochelaga, Étienne Brulé swam with his guides in the morning, laughing with them as they emerged from the pool by a waterfall, then passed behind them as they squatted to evacuate their bowels, and, in memory of his Huron friends, slit their throats. So that the white man would not be blamed, he took both their scalps, for he was a man of the woods now, a *sauvage,* and paddled on home alone.

†††

Samuel de Champlain received the Cartier Dagger back from Étienne Brulé with a sense of solemn occasion. The young man's return had presaged a burst of optimism throughout the community, for he had proven that a man could endure in this country, travel the uncharted rivers in the company of Indians and come back alive. Their own survival now seemed remotely possible. The two men kneeled in a small, makeshift tent, a swath of canvas fitted between pine trees on one side and a boulder on the other. Here they were sheltered from wind and rain and from the eyes of the other French. Brulé bowed, holding the dagger before him with both hands. Champlain balanced it upon two fingers and lifted it away from the young man's possession. He then kissed the centre diamond on the hilt and placed the knife in a small box alongside his right knee.

"I looked for this in the hands of others. When I did not see it, I believed that you remained alive. It gave us all hope. For you, and for ourselves."

"With respect, sir, I'd rather not travel with that knife again. A man could get killed for that knife."

"Ah. Yes. I see."

Brulé had returned as an apparition emerging from the woods and yet, seemingly, a part of the woods, and for a second time Champlain had scarcely recognized the young adventurer. Wilderness life had changed him—his appearance, the way he carried himself, even the way he spoke, and perhaps not all the changes were for the better. An inner determination had supplanted the youth's earlier impetuousness, and the romantic eagerness with which he had embarked had been augmented along the way by a seasoned fatalism. He no longer possessed the demeanour of a dislocated youth. In idle hours, Champlain had imagined that he would welcome the lad home in a manner befitting the return of a beloved son from a war, and he had done so. And yet, similar to any son arriving back from a conflict, the warrior was no longer the rambunctious, grinning boy who had departed, and the relationship between the two men had also been altered.

Champlain understood the change, gleaning insight as he listened to Brulé's accounts of his escapades. He remained the leader of this mission, but no longer was Brulé a mere foot soldier at his command. The youth was the only one among them who possessed true and generous knowledge of the territory, the only one who had proven himself and developed the capacity to survive on his own in the wild woods, and he alone among the French comprehended the language and strategies of their friends and enemies both. Brulé understood Indian ways, and consequently the ways of this land. While he was much too young to be a rival to Champlain's leadership, he nonetheless had become a person of influence and standing. He was considered courageous and insightful. The people revered and trusted him, so that it was now prudent for Champlain to consult him regarding a variety of crucial decisions. Laughing one night, meaning to make a joke, he dubbed Brulé the first Quebec man.

"What?" Brulé, somewhat inebriated with the last of the ship's wine, responded.

"You were not born here," Champlain expounded, and clamped an arm around the lad's shoulders, "but you are the first Frenchman to belong to this land. You are, Étienne, the first Frenchman of the New World, for you are no longer a Frenchman of the old."

"France," Brulé muttered, taking his final swig, "can kiss my ass."

Given the late hour, and their general state of drunkenness, the French around the campfire that night chuckled.

The next morning, Champlain was still thinking about Brulé as he pondered a new scheme, letting it settle into his head. Eternally at odds with powers guiding him from France, Champlain allowed himself to imagine a new man, a new people. One day, a few years later, he would take his ideas to the Algonquin, and suggest that they and the French form a new race. Indian and French would intermarry, binding their alliance through shared offspring and a unified purpose. The proposal was not without interest to the natives, and they considered the possibility at length, deciding in the end to respectfully decline. The French had brought over too few women to tempt their young men, and they feared that their young men might want for wives while Indian girls merrily ran off with the randy French. Yet both sides agreed, in the face of the idea's defeat, that although intermarriage would not become a requirement, neither would it be discouraged in their communities. Love, then, would be permitted to take its course, wherever it might arise.

Love, for Champlain, who was bereft in the New World while his child-bride awaited his return to the old, had proven difficult to negotiate. While his sweet Hélène might be little more than a girl, she was strong-willed, and had defiantly proclaimed that she would never cross the Atlantic to the land of the Indians and of the bear and moose. "I'm such a small woman," she had pointed out to her husband, "the mosquitoes you speak about might suck my blood dry." Hoping to persuade her otherwise, Champlain had a home constructed at Quebec, a log cabin large enough not only for a wife but for the expansion of a family, and on voyages back to Paris he would again petition her to join him. She would have none of that idea, preferring to pine for him by the Seine than lie by his side, fearing that at any moment they might both be eaten by monstrous bears. Each time he returned to his beloved Quebec, Champlain remained alone.

"Sam," Brulé whispered to him around the campfire one night, as he had done previously from time to time, "if you want a Huron or an Algonquin for your evening, inquire of me. I will speak to the young women. I know a few who are curious, even for someone like yourself."

"Like myself?"

"Old."

Brulé was initiating him into life beyond the island of Montreal. Champlain had seen Lake Huron, and like any European was astounded that such a body of fresh water could exist. An ocean! Of fresh water! With his help, Champlain further developed the fur trade, and Jesuit priests now dwelled among the Huron, converting them to Christianity and to the benefits of commerce. This was Brulé's world, Champlain saw, and his excursions there confirmed that he himself was not the man for the task. The men, Indians and French both, were too rugged for him. They'd fight and debauch and paddle for days, kill a deer, cook it, eat it and paddle for days again, as though the physical effort was no more troublesome than breathing. The wilderness impressed the younger men, with their tempestuous natures, and also the serene priests, with their sage resolve and solitary devotion. Champlain, once the mariner, and warrior, and adventurer, would satisfy himself with building a community and developing the fiscal and social infrastructure to make the colony viable. The great adventuring, the fighting, the boundless exploring of a land that seemed only to grow the more it was mapped, all of that would be left to this new breed of man, the wild ones who were calling themselves *coureurs de bois*—runners of the woods—while he brought over men and women from France and saw that, while some joined the wild men of the woods, others formed the basis for a civilized community, devoted to the Church, to the planting of crops, to the raising of French families in the New World. The years went by in this way, and Champlain took pride in his success, and the small outposts at Montreal, Trois-Rivières and Quebec—and the northerly fur-trading post where so many of the woodsmen congregated, Tadoussac—prospered in their way.

Until the world abruptly changed.

Out of the mists on a chilly morning, while the campfires of Quebec quietly exhaled gentle smoke, a shipload of bold men from England, on their own initiative and in the service of no nation—pirates—sailed into the port and disembarked in a fury. They demanded the surrender of the hamlet. Brulé was not present, for he had gone north to carouse with the wild men of Tadoussac, as was his wont, and neither was Champlain, who was down at Montreal trading with the Indians, his usual habit. Not in the practice of defending themselves, the inhabitants saw no option other than to surrender, so Quebec fell to the group led by the notorious Kirke brothers. The brothers themselves moved into Champlain's home and confiscated the remarkably valuable dagger they found there, a treasure unexpected in this frontier, embedded as it was with diamonds and gold.

Hearing the news, Champlain sailed from Montreal to Quebec, fearing that all was lost, but secretly hoping that Brulé and the Huron could mount an attack and chase the pirates off. When he arrived and walked the muddy track up to his home, he opened the door to find Thomas Kirke with his feet up on his dinner table. "This is my home!" the Frenchman insisted.

"Once. Not now. Everything belongs to me. Thanks for taking good care of it before I got here. Now, shove off back to France and take your pissed-over peasants with you. I've had enough of them."

Champlain's dream had reached its end. He fumed, he raged, but the counsel that he received from friends reiterated the same point of view. All he might do for the good of New France was to return to Paris and beseech the king to send an army. Otherwise, the Kirke brothers now ruled.

Champlain sailed north, first to Tadoussac to pick up Brulé.

"We must return to France, to speak to the king."

"France?" Brulé responded. "King?"

"Yes! France. The king. Quebec has fallen to the pirates!"

The younger man pulled at his beard and threw the blade of his knife into the soil between his feet. He picked it up and tossed it into the ground again.

"Étienne," Champlain implored him, dismayed by the man's reluctance. "We must return to France. Most families from Quebec are with me. The others we'll collect on a second voyage if we don't return with an army. We're going home."

"Home?" Brulé inquired.

"Yes! Home. To France."

The woodsman pulled at his beard again. Around him were the trappers and traders who travelled the rivers and lived most of their lives in the forests among the Indians, or alone among the animals.

"In France, who will the king blame for this defeat?"

"I have my responsibilities here—"

"And I have mine. Who will be blamed?"

Champlain did not respond.

"I will not hang in France, Samuel. I will live out my days here. *This* is my country now. This is my world. Not France."

Champlain stared at his old friend, who returned the gaze without relenting.

"You betray me."

"The king will say that, too. Why should I owe the king the satisfaction of hanging me for not defending Quebec? I don't know the king. I'm staying here."

As though equal in consequence to the fall of Quebec to the brothers Kirke, Brulé's betrayal tormented him on the anguishing voyage home. He was met in Paris by his long-suffering wife, who cheerfully showed him the country home she would now appreciate that he provide for them. In due course, he had an audience with the king. Champlain did not blame Brulé for the state of affairs, but the king himself asked about "our French woodsmen? Where were they when these English *pirates* sailed into our French harbour?"

"Absent," Champlain admitted. "As was I." He wanted to explain that the distances were great in the New World, that neighbours lived days, and often weeks, apart. He held his tongue, not knowing whether his own neck would be stretched as a result of this circumstance. In the end, he did survive to settle with Hélène, who was not so young now in 1629, for in the end the king just didn't care so much that New France had been lost.

"One less problem," the king had determined. "At least I'll save money."

Three years after that conversation, Champlain was planting his back garden when Réal de Montfort, an old friend who had been with him for five years in New France as a fur trader, rode a horse up to his country estate. "What news?" Champlain asked, for clearly the man was agitated.

"The dagger! Cartier's! The king's dowry!" Montfort cried, then slipped down from his nag.

"Make sense, monsieur. What are you saying?"

Montfort caught his breath, and did his best to calm himself. "The Kirke Brothers—!"

"Are they dead? Tell me they are dead! The Huron have their scalps!"

"No."

"No?"

"No! The brothers, they gave the Cartier Dagger to Charles I of England. I have only learned of this now, but they did it, apparently, years ago, to curry the king's favour, to ask for his protection in case you returned with soldiers."

"I heard that rumour. It's of no consequence. I'd rather have it in a king's hands then in the grip of those pirates."

"Well, it's in a king's hands now! The king of France!"

"What? How can this be?"

"The dowry, Sam! The dowry!"

Champlain was infuriated with the slow pace of information. He dropped his gardening spade to the earth and threatened to extract shears lying on a cart. "Explain yourself, man, or I'll demonstrate how Iroquois take scalps!"

Montfort took a deep breath. "Charles I still owes half his wife's dowry to our king. To pay the dowry, he returned the Cartier Dagger."

"This is good news," Champlain conceded. He would travel no more across the seas, but this exchange of gifts among royalty seemed to turn a page on his life.

"It was not the only payment made."

"What else?"

"Charles I—"

"Yes."

"—king of England—"

"Montfort, I know who he is! Go on!"

"Has bequeathed all of New France—Canada—"

"Yes?"

"—back to France. Canada belongs to France once more."

Champlain reeled. This was a joy he had not expected in his impending old age. His friend caught him, and helped him sit upon the edge of the cart, to catch his balance. All his days in the New World seemed to run through his mind, the smell of the woods and the drift of the clouds upon mountainsides, the surge of the spring run-off on the rivers, a light fall of snow, the snapping cold in the dark of winter. He remembered so well the men and women there, native and French alike, and he knew the names of every man and woman who had remained behind, the scant few, most of them still waiting to be evacuated, yet they had been abandoned by their king. He remembered Étienne Brulé also, who would be hearing this news in a few months' time, who would stand on the rock overlooking Quebec as the Kirke brothers departed with their last cache of furs, to sail away, back to England. He imagined that sight. Brulé had betrayed him, but he was glad now that Brulé was there to see that sight, to be his eyes.

Not for the first time, a wedding between royal families had altered the course of history. While one king did not comprehend what he had given away, and the other did not value what he had received, Samuel de Champlain, having never been an especially devout man, grasped that the hand of God had intervened on behalf of the French, on behalf of those who would struggle for the viability of the New World.

He made two fists, and pounded his chest, fiercely, three times, as if to beat the breath out of himself. "Yes," he said quietly, intently, and he looked to the heavens, although his eyes were tightly closed. "Yes. Thank God."

CHAPTER 7

1955

WITH A HEAD FULL OF DETAILS AND WORRIES, CAPTAIN Armand Touton assumed he would automatically wake up early. He set no alarm. His body possessed an alternative plan, and so, on the morning after the riot, he slept in late, unable to rouse himself until five minutes before noon.

He took out his upset on his wife. When she had finally had enough of his sleepy grumpiness, she slapped down a breakfast plate of fried eggs and beans in front of him on the kitchen table and warned, "Oaf. Be quiet. Do I look like a mind reader? Why would I wake you up early if you don't ask me?"

Touton settled into his food, then kicked the dog out of the house for panting.

"What's the matter with you? We're not the ones rioting! But keep it up, Armand. Soon, we might be."

Grunting token concurrence, he swept up the runny yolk of his eggs onto a slice of whole-wheat bread, then piled beans onto that. The food revived him, and Marie-Céleste returned to the table with her coffee. She was a handsome woman, with green eyes and wavy black hair that crossed her forehead and fell almost to her shoulders in curls. Although slight, she had shoulders that were broad for her size and a strong, upright posture he'd admired from the moment of their first encounter.

"Sorry," he demurred. "A coroner was killed last night. Gunned down. I've mentioned Roger Clément to you? I have? Also dead."

"So it's not only the riot," she noted sadly.

"You see? I haven't mentioned the Richard riot yet! Already I forgot! For all I know, downtown Montreal has burnt to the ground!"

"The Rocket was on the radio," she told him. "He made an appeal."

"What did he say?"

She sipped her noon tea while waiting for her soup to warm. "He asked people to stop rioting, what else? He wants people to be nice."

The Rocket on the radio was the best possible strategy, but Touton was impressed that someone had seen to it. For an official to have taken the initiative proved that the situation was dire.

"Probably Drapeau put him up to it. How did he sound?"

"Shaken."

He raised an eyebrow.

"Aren't we all? I'm sure he didn't sleep last night. His words will have an effect. People will listen."

Sipping coffee, the detective considered this development. "I'll have to go in."

"This is why I let you sleep. I've ironed a clean shirt. So you see, the rumour is not true."

Confused, Touton asked, "What rumour?"

"The one that says I'm the worst wife east of St. Laurent."

Touton smiled, rose and took her into his arms. They kissed. They had been married only two years, and both were delighted with their union, despite the policeman's all-night hours and a frustrating failure to procreate.

Outside, the puppy was yapping.

"May Toot please come back inside? He has no clue what he's done wrong."

As he dressed, the poodle jumped around Touton's heels and bit into his discarded slippers, trying to convince him that playtime had arrived. The detective laughed at him and fell into an all-out tug-of-war, fighting to get his slipper back. He growled as loudly, but only half as happily, as the dog.

†††

His office set up the meeting, and Touton went straight downtown, to the Sherbrooke Street apartment of Clarence Campbell.

On the way, he surveyed damage from the night before and tried to assess the mood of those herding together. Windows were boarded up, some because they'd been smashed and the premises looted, others because the proprietors feared that their businesses might be next. Banks were patrolled by armed guards. At most busy intersections, policemen put on a show of force. Quite a number of cops had been out all night and had not gone home yet, which was also true of roving bands of youths and men. The rioting had stopped, a combination of weariness, dawn and the Rocket's radio directive. A number of rowdies still hung around in case something started up again.

They wanted to be in on the action.

The situation remained volatile, citizens were tense, and Touton suspected that this might be the most hopeful scenario over the next few days. The worst case would involve men looking for trouble who would discover a flashpoint, and the city would descend into violence once more. A second eruption, he was convinced, could do more damage.

A stretch of Sherbrooke had been part of Montreal's famed Golden Square Mile, an area of magnificent homes and buildings, each graced with an aristocratic air. The push of a burgeoning downtown, the advent of income tax and the inability of successive generations to continue living at that heightened level of prosperity had caused the properties, one by one, to be bulldozed for office towers or hotels, or else remodelled for shops at street level with tenants above. The president of the National Hockey League lived in a fine Old World apartment building with darkened hallways, staunch doors and high ceilings. The stone frame had been constructed so thickly that visitors wondered if the dominance of the automobile had not been anticipated, for the walls silenced traffic's thrum while successfully muting sirens. The elevator's whir accompanied him up to the seventh floor, and after a sojourn down a long corridor he located the Campbell residence, to be admitted by a maid.

For a man living virtually under siege, Clarence Campbell was found to be in good spirits. He greeted the policeman warmly and coaxed him into accepting a coffee, which his helper discreetly disappeared to prepare. The Queen Anne wing chairs into which they settled were not particularly comfortable, at least not for Captain Touton. Perhaps, he thought, Campbell's short, round body suited them better. He seemed to have odd tastes for a bachelor, including a maid with long black hairs growing from her pasty, pointy chin, and the policeman suspected that somewhere a woman of influence lurked, a curmudgeonly aunt or dour sister.

"It's a disgrace," Mr. Campbell decreed. "If people want to direct a grievance at me, they don't need to wreck the city."

"Perhaps if they were able to find you, sir—"

"I was at the Forum," the former war prosecutor pointed out. "I caught a tomato in the eye. The papers didn't report that one. It bounced off without bursting. Another one caught me on the shoulder. I suppose it's civilized to throw tomatoes."

"Rather than rocks, say?"

"Exactly. Or Molotov cocktails. But I suppose those came later."

"A lot of fires," Touton concurred. "They're worrisome."

"A city in flames." Mr. Campbell folded his hands in his lap. "I'd call that worrisome. Ah! Your coffee, my tea. As long as we have tea, we have civilization, Captain. Tell me, did you have tea in your POW camp?"

Touton shook his head. "Brit pilots did. They had privileges. These days, I prefer my wake-up coffee."

"No wonder. You're captain of the Night Patrol—it must be a narcotic. Cream and sugar?"

"Black, thanks."

"Ah."

Touton sipped, found the coffee to his liking but very hot, and put the cup and saucer down on the credenza next to him. He would have preferred a mug. Suddenly, he was aware of the quiet moment passing between them. Observing Campbell, he realized that he was a shy individual.

Touton began by taking a moderately deep breath. "I bring unpleasant news."

"*More* unpleasant news?" Mr. Campbell asked, flashing a grim smile. Having stirred his tea, he moved the cup from his lips to the saucer captive on his lap. "How much can a man take, Captain?"

"The Jacques Cartier Dagger, sir, has been stolen again."

The executive, who had received his guest into his home as though they had been at the office, was wearing a jacket and tie. He placed the teacup and saucer on the side table to his left and removed a handkerchief from his right jacket pocket. He glanced at Armand Touton, then seemed to cast his reflections upon the carpet. He dabbed his mouth with the handkerchief, carefully creased the folds again and returned it to his pocket. "I see," he said quietly.

"It's an unfortunate situation."

"Would it be correct to say that the dagger had been entrusted to your care, Captain Touton? I recall arguing for its return and being rebuffed."

The officer nodded. He rubbed his hands slowly. "You wouldn't be out of line to mention it. I considered the knife to be in my care."

"Any other officer, you understand, and my suspicions would quickly rest on police corruption. Tell me what happened, Captain."

The policeman took another deep breath and exhaled. "Sir, two men have been killed. Perhaps you heard about it on the news. Driving over here, I was listening to the radio myself. All the talk is about the riot, and the Rocket's statement. But a pair of deaths in Dominion Square—"

"I heard. A coroner, wasn't it? That's awful."

"He had possession of your knife, sir. The men who killed him stole it."

Mr. Campbell's head remained still, his expression blank, but his eyes moved back and forth repeatedly. Then he blinked. What he said next caught his guest off guard. "I'd rather that you not refer to it as my knife, Captain. I only had it on loan."

"I understand, sir."

"So this is a deeper tragedy, then, and not of your doing. I see. Villainy, not police negligence." He tugged his trouser legs up ever so slightly.

"That would be my personal view, sir. Obviously, we had no clue that a second murder would take place. About the first death, I should tell you, the Cartier Dagger was the murder weapon."

Mr. Campbell flexed backwards at the news, and this time he was the one to exhale. "Unbelievable," he murmured, and shook his head. Early in his life, his hair had thinned, so that he looked older than a man set to turn fifty in a few months. "Captain, I have something I need to ask."

"Go ahead."

"Have you ever heard of the Order of Jacques Cartier?"

"Can't say that I have. A bunch of guys in funny hats, it sounds like."

The league president rubbed his eyes before speaking. Given all that had transpired the previous evening, Touton doubted he'd had much sleep.

"If only that's who they were. Check police records. They will show that I once brought the name to the attention of the authorities. I didn't expect any serious danger to be imminent, but at the time it seemed prudent. I'm a lawyer, so naturally I try to follow the precepts of the law."

Touton leaned forward, interested. He had come here hoping to explore a number of avenues, but had expected only to close down a few lines of inquiry. He had not expected to discover a fresh lead.

"Months ago, I received a letter. I'll have to check my records to provide a more precise date."

"Do you still have this letter?"

"I surrendered it to the police. To my knowledge, it's not been returned."

"What did it say?"

Mr. Campbell cleared his throat. "At the office, we receive threats on rare occasion. We don't pay them much heed. Nevertheless, it is appropriate to take at least cautionary notice."

"You were threatened?"

"Me personally? No. My office. 'A Molotov cocktail through the window' was how they put it. If you allow for the fact that the bottom floor has an immensely high ceiling, we're about twelve flights up. Who can throw a Molotov that high? So I don't think they knew where the offices were. The address on the envelope wasn't complete. Just 'National Hockey League, Montreal.' In French. That's how they addressed it, and by some fluke it arrived on our doorstep."

"The post office would find you. Did the letter say anything else?"

"Something to the effect that the Order of Jacques Cartier demands the return of the supreme symbol of the Order, the venerable dagger of Jacques Cartier. Not terribly particular. It didn't provide us with anyone to return it to, for example."

This, at least, was something. "They still sound like men in funny hats to me. After our officers took the report, did you hear back from the department?"

"No, sir."

"Nor from the Order of Jacques Cartier?"

"Not unless I did last night."

Touton stood. Enough issues were churning through his head that at this point he'd rather pace. He was in no position to be confrontational. Campbell was a respected man, relied upon for his integrity, but Touton wished that he had the freedom to push him a little. The man had not owned the knife, but he would see it every day when he stepped into his office. He was aware of the object's value. Was there no residual wish to personally possess the knife? Was there no interest in selling an object worth that much? As a relic, it either sat on his desk or slept in his vault. Millions of dollars would be considered more tempting by many. As for the Order of Jacques Cartier, the lead was interesting, but to a suspicious or inquiring mind, the mention of an "Order" struck him as convenient. As a beat cop, he had answered calls about jimmied doors and broken windows when nothing had been taken, yet a few weeks later the house would be properly burglarized. Coincidence or not, the homeowners had a police report from an earlier attempted break-in to show a skeptical insurance company that might otherwise suspect the occupants of indulging in fraud. In this instance, had there been a conspiracy—one that involved Campbell, or even one that did not—the letter from an "Order" might well have been sent in advance to divert a police investigation later on. He saw no reason to credit an obviously skilled thief with the decency to first announce his intention to commit the crime.

Besides, he had to assume that Roger Clément had committed the crime, not some "Order."

"About the letter, there's another aspect," Mr. Campbell mentioned. His guest had turned his back to him and was examining a large painting from an earlier century of children clustered around a rather vivacious mother.

"What would that be?" Touton asked, without facing him.

"At the bottom of the letter—"

Touton turned. "Yes?"

"—they had stamped a swastika."

Touton's only response was to cock his head slightly and gaze at the other man more intently, indicating his interest and a subtle demand for more.

Mr. Campbell sipped his tea first, then put it down again. "It's something I live with, Captain. From time to time, residual pro-fascist elements choose to disparage my work at Nuremberg. I thought I'd mention it, in case the item assists you. I read an article on you one time, so I feel secure in assuming where you stand on the matter."

Thrusting his hands into his pockets, Touton conferred a pensive nod. "Thank you. Yes. We both served. We've that in common." He left unsaid that the military lawyer had very different war experiences than the foot soldier and POW, yet he knew that the conflict altered the course of both their lives. Both had believed in what they were doing, and both had seen and learned matters about humanity that only a war will divulge. Without making a conscious decision to do so, they subtly segregated themselves from those who had not participated—never fully trusting them, never being comfortable when conversations included the home front during the war. In an odd way, then, the experience did bind them. "Mr. Campbell, do you know Roger Clément?"

"The name rings a bell, but I don't believe I do."

"A former NHLer. Before your time." Touton resumed his seat. "A cup of coffee with the Blackhawks, lunch with the Rangers."

"Then I've heard the name. I don't believe I know him. Why?"

"He was the other man killed last night, with the Cartier Dagger."

"Oh dear." Mr. Campbell sighed heavily and repeated himself. "Oh dear. I don't like the sound of this. A former hockey player? Killed with a dagger from my office? The papers will have a field day."

"Perhaps we won't put it all together for them. They don't need to hear about the murder weapon. Clément, whom I knew quite well, had a criminal record. He spent the war in an internment camp for politicos."

The president of the National Hockey League nodded, content that his organization might elude media scrutiny on the matter. "I hate when a player falls on hard times."

Touton waited to learn whether Campbell had anything to add, and, when the man remained quiet, took his leave. They shook hands at the door. Touton put on his hat, buttoned up his coat and departed the building, intent on a closer inspection of the riot's aftermath. Most of the devastation had occurred on Ste. Catherine Street, parallel to Sherbrooke, two short blocks down. He chose to walk.

†††

One hour later, at police headquarters, his arrival may have been unexpected, for rarely did the famous captain of the Night Patrol show up during daylight, but no one registered even token surprise. The riot had altered the landscape, the times were volatile. Half the department was working a double shift anyway. Under the circumstances, his subsequent activity did raise a few curious eyebrows among the ranks. From Records, Touton wanted to know which officers had responded to a call months earlier at National Hockey League headquarters, and from Archives he requested a report on whatever had been determined about the Order of Jacques Cartier.

For his part, Armand Touton was explaining nothing—not a shock either.

He sat at his desk and placidly drank more coffee while the tumult around him rose, and fell, and rose again. Intermittently, he smiled. The day shift, uninitiated to his habits, felt intimidated, as though under indictment themselves.

Which they were. Touton gently chastised them. On his own internal scale, the riot hadn't been so bad. They didn't know how mad chaos could be. They didn't know what it meant to be on a beach in hell, and so they spoke excitedly of recent events and they related experiences at a feverish pitch.

When Armand Touton had heard the ping of machine-gun fire on the hull of his landing craft at Dieppe, he and the others understood that death was imminent. Only a few dared look each other in the eye, for they shared the shameful truth that they were about to die. They finished up their notes home, tucked photos of their loved ones away, said their final prayers and heard the landing gate creak down, admitting bullets. They weren't far enough in. The first to get out dropped into water over their heads. Touton splashed down, then was pushed down deeper by the men jumping out behind him, and pushed down again by the next, the feet above him kicking him below the water. Looking up, he saw bullets penetrate the surface, like rain, with blood already pooling. He swam underwater and crawled ashore with his comrades. Within two minutes, twenty-four were dead, and the three remaining survivors had been shot. Touton bled from the wrist. He had tucked himself down behind two dead soldiers, and, with the help of another survivor, piled a third and then a fourth corpse onto their wall. Bullets never stopped snapping at the sand around them and ripping into the flesh of those who were dead. *That* was chaos. *That* was fear. Not this exuberant, charged madness in the streets.

Rescue craft arrived after a few hours of the continuing carnage, but, in an infuriating repetition of the landing, stayed out in deeper water. He made a run for it, and was shot for the second time, high on the arm, yet he managed to swim to the craft, but there he helped the comrade ahead of him and was trampled under again. He was confused now. As though no time had passed, he was underwater again—was this a dream? nothing felt real—and when he bobbed to the surface again, the rescue craft had saved a few souls, but it had also moved on without him.

He kept diving to avoid the bullets.

Surfacing one time and spotting a British destroyer offshore, he chose to swim for it. Dying in the water or dying by a bullet on the beach seemed the only options. He swam three miles in the rolling waves and was making good progress. He could see rope ladders dangling over the side and other swimmers clamouring aboard. He would be safe. He would live. As he closed on the vessel, it ignited with explosives from stem to stern, and those on the ladders leaped back into the sea. Touton himself turned and swam back to shore.

Only after the war would he learn that the explosions were a ruse, a trick to make German aircraft believe the vessel had been hit and destroyed. A good ruse. Most swimmers returned to shore because they were convinced the ship would sink, and a few swimmers stopped swimming with the hopelessness of it all, and let themselves drown.

Touton choreographed his landing so that he'd have the protection of burned-out equipment and a litter of bodies as he crawled from the water and, exhausted, collapsed on the beach. He suffered a third bullet wound, a flesh wound to the side, but he hardly felt it. He could hardly feel anything anymore. No fight was left in him. He knew that he had participated in a great defeat. What he had left to face was either death or capture.

That was chaos. That was excitement. And having survived all that and what came later, a gunman's paltry bullets or the hostile rage of a gang would always fail to impress him, and certainly fail to keep him from his duty. Indeed, the one thing he could not tolerate was cowering behind cars or walls as if behind a fort of bodies, waiting for reinforcements. To hell with reinforcements. They could be an illusion or a complete waste of time. They could be an exploding ship. Instead, as a cop, he'd always attack. Attack, attack, attack. And somehow get through it, and survive.

In a foul mood, he thought *the hell with superior officers,* just as he'd said *the hell with generals* who led their men into unrelenting slaughters. He had decided back then that, if he were permitted to enjoy a future, he'd make his own choices. He was willing to put his life on the line, repeatedly and not always wisely, but no fat tub slumped behind a desk would have the privilege of doing so on his behalf. In the future, he would lead, and decline to be led by fools.

While he was waiting, starting on another cup, a plainclothes officer he did not know knocked on his office door and waited politely to be invited in.

"What?" Cops often dropped by, hoping they could be taken onto his squad, but he was fussy about who worked for him. "Who're you?"

"Detective Fleury, sir." The man looked intelligent. He could easily pass as an academic, perhaps an effect of the tiny, wire-rimmed glasses he wore. In an era of tough, physically imposing cops, the man's lanky frame and pinched face struck Touton as odd. He was small. "You were asking about the Order of Jacques Cartier."

The captain sat back in his chair, putting an elbow on the armrest as he touched the back of his jaw with two fingers. "You should not know that," he advised his visitor.

"There's a good reason why I do. If I may explain." Oddly, the man did not hold his hands at his side, but crossed them over his chest, one folded in the other. The fingers seemed especially long and feminine.

"Have a seat, Detective."

Doing so, the man demonstrated a peculiar habit of sitting on the very lip of the chair, as though he might pitch forward at any moment. The posture of his back was arrow straight, and he fastened his hands to his knees in a tight grip.

"What squad are you in?" Touton inquired.

Between clenched teeth, the man drew in a breath as though to suggest he was being asked a touchy question. "I'm not in any squad exactly."

"Which department?"

"Policy."

Despite himself, for he was usually respectful of strangers, Touton released a little laugh. "What do you do in Policy?"

"I *am* a real detective," Fleury tried to assure him, but he was less confident of his bearings than a moment ago. Touton had jangled a nerve.

"That's your rank, but what do you investigate in Policy?"

Fleury rocked his head from side to side, an indication that he was into many things. In the end, he conceded, "My work is administrative. I work on budgets. Assignments. The allocation of resources."

"That's important work." He tried to be serious, without fully succeeding. "Somebody has to do it, right?"

"Somebody does. Isn't it better if a detective does that sort of work?"

"As opposed to—"

"A civilian. An accountant, let's say. I'm trained in accountancy—"

"Are you now?"

"I didn't graduate—the war was on. I had my mother to look after—"

Touton laughed aloud. "Your mother! Ha."

"Sir!" Fleury protested. "I am a detective. Maybe I don't do the same work as you do—"

"Apparently not."

"—but that is my rank." With earnest conviction, he shook his head as he spoke. "I was brought into the department to be an administrator. To represent the interests of policemen on the beat and in the squads. I believe it's important work."

"Sorry, Fleury. I'm sure it's important. But a detective who never gets to investigate anything, not ever . . . I've never met one before."

"Nobody wants to talk to me . . . *until* he wants his pension benefits explained."

"Pension benefits?" Actually, he was interested in the subject.

"*Then* I'm in big demand. But that's not all. Last summer, for instance, when you wanted two more detectives on your squad—"

"Yes?" He remembered that request, and had been expecting to raise holy hell if the issue had been decided against him.

"I'm the one who argued—successfully—on your behalf. Other squads wanted more detectives. They didn't get them, did they? That was not an easy fight. But I fought. And won. You got both your detectives while other squads got none."

Suddenly, Touton could see the virtue of a detective in the Policy branch. He could also see the virtue of being friendly with a man who understood budgets and could explain pension plans. "Thank you," he said, and he meant it.

"You're welcome."

The captain scraped his chair across the floor an inch or two and reconfigured his body language. He slipped one leg over the other, set for a conversation. "So. You were going to tell me why you know my business."

Although it was only by an inch, Fleury moved his posterior back in his seat. "I know nothing of your business, sir. I can assure you of that. But I left my name on the file, asking that anyone interested in the file contact me. The clerk called me to let me know of your inquiry."

"What file?"

"The Order of Jacques Cartier. I know something about it."

"How much do you know?"

"Sir? Well . . . everything and nothing, if you take my meaning."

"I don't."

"More than anyone else on the outside."

"Really." Touton stuck a finger in his ear. "I bet you don't get out much, do you?"

"Ah . . . no, sir. Not much."

"If you're a real detective, you'll have a drink with me. I'm not on duty, so it's no skin off my nose, but you, sir, you'll be contravening the code of the Policy branch. You'll probably cause a scandal. A superior might . . . I don't know . . . *frown*. That would be devastating. What about it? Are you a real detective? Is that hair on your chest or bird shit? Will you have a drink with me?"

Fleury surprised him. He seemed nonplussed. "I enjoy my beer," he said. "I wouldn't mind one. Anyway, it's my day off."

"Your day off?" Touton was thoroughly flummoxed by the guy. "Then what are you doing here?"

Standing, the diminutive detective shrugged. "The riot. All detectives have been called in for extra duty. I presumed that that meant me, too."

"Oh yeah," Touton stated as he grabbed his hat and coat, "we'll need to work out the budget for the riot, that's for sure."

"Actually," Fleury agreed, "we will."

†††

Entering an out-of-the-way establishment on St. Antoine Street, the two men settled into hardy wooden chairs. Montreal taverns served only beer and refused admission to women. As a consequence, workingmen felt free to open their shirts down to their underwear to expel the heat from factories, and talk boisterously, routinely gushing in expletives. Crooks used the tavern to hatch their schemes, the politicos their strikes, and the workingman could address whatever worried him to sympathetic ears. In and out of season, everyone talked hockey.

Typically, the rooms were large, with a glut of round tables and scant decoration or adornment other than the portraits of hockey heroes hanging on the walls and the advertisements of a beer company. Each tavern could choose only one supplier for draft beer, a system that allowed for non-verbal communication between patron and waiter. As the pair were seating themselves close to one corner, Touton held up four fingers. The waiter nodded to confirm the order, and the men shed their winter clothing before speaking. The captain took a long swig of the piss-yellow drink when it arrived, and released a satisfying sigh.

"The reason you know nothing about the Order of Jacques Cartier is because you were a soldier," the detective from Policy informed him.

Touton looked across at Fleury and tried to moderate his response, for the smaller man appeared to be as crushable as a grasshopper. "You're saying to me that soldiers are stupid?"

"No!" Fleury almost spilled his beer as he threw up his hands in his own defence. "I'm not. I'm saying the reason you don't know about the Order is because the Order became famous here when you were over there, in the POW camp."

Another surprise. "So it's been around that long."

"Pre-war. But the war helped the Order expand and gain influence."

Draft glasses were small, and Touton quaffed down the remainder of his as if it were only a taste. The thin man's story already had the earmarks of a longer tale, so he put up his fingers for four more.

"I like my beer, but I do have to be home for dinner," Fleury protested. "I can't arrive drunk. My wife would swat me."

Touton looked at him as though he was gazing upon a Martian. He relented before levelling any insult. "We won't count. Drink what you like, and I'll drink what I like. Now walk me through this."

Again teetering upon the lip of his chair, Detective Fleury leaned in. "If only I *could* walk you through it, sir. Nothing is clear. This is a secret society, circumspect in its affairs. It knows how to keep secrets. Rumour has it that even a man's wife will not know of her husband's involvement. Can you imagine such a thing?" A man's failure to allow his wife to keep close tabs on him was obviously beyond Detective Fleury's ken. "If it's not improper, sir, may I ask where your interests lie in all of this?"

The captain gave him a brief summary of the break-in at NHL headquarters and the murders. At the mention of the Cartier Dagger, Touton noticed, Fleury's eyes lit up.

"So this is a real group? They have members?" Touton encouraged him.

"At one point, it was reported in the Senate that they have eighteen thousand members."

Meeting Fleury had led from one surprise to another, and now he'd been hit with two at once. He didn't know which had shocked him more. So he inquired about both. "The Senate? Eighteen thousand?"

"In 1944," the thin man explained, "you were still in Poland, I guess. Télesphore-Damien Bouchard, a senator, made his maiden speech in the Senate chamber. He rose to denounce the Order of Jacques Cartier. For his trouble, the senator was condemned in every corner of Quebec society—in every tavern also, I'm sure—and fired from his job as president of Hydro-Québec."

To Touton's mind, to be president of a government agency, a hydro company especially, lent credibility to the man's opinion. More so than being a politically appointed senator. "Who fired him?" He would have thought that presidents could never be fired.

"The premier of Quebec," Fleury snapped back.

"Duplessis?"

"Godbout, I think it was, in '44. Duplessis was out of office for a term."

"Ah, I wasn't around for that either. You miss a lot living behind barbed wire. So what did he say that got him fired?"

Fleury took a swig of his beer and wet his lips. He was excited to tell his story and Touton did not hold that against him. The general disposition of plainclothes cops was world-weariness, a seen-it-all, done-it-all attitude that Touton figured was nothing more than a prelude to inertia. The excitable nature of the pencil-pusher from Policy was a welcome change.

"The senator was speaking to a motion on education. A standard textbook was being proposed for Canadian history. Bouchard decried the interpretation of history as it was being applied in schools in Quebec. He considered the history to be a fabrication, a form of propaganda, its purpose subversive. Disrupt the Confederation, overthrow the democracy, that was the idea. Every ill any Quebecer had ever experienced was being blamed on the English, in the schools, and any benefit to being part of Canada was either ridiculed or ignored. At least, that's what Bouchard said."

Touton nodded. Fighting in the war had made him less than a hero to most Quebecers. People left him alone because they were afraid of him, but many still held his war record against him. Thousands of Quebec men had fought bravely, and many had died. Yet the majority had stayed home.

"The Order of Jacques Cartier," Fleury continued, satisfied that he was making an impression on a superior officer, "is anti-English, anti-Jewish. That's not so surprising, maybe, here in Quebec, where most of the people who are anti-Jewish have never met a Jew, and being anti-English is considered to be part of the French soul. But Senator Bouchard went far beyond that. He implied that the Order of Jacques Cartier espoused dictatorship as the ideal form of government. In itself, who cares, right? Why worry about a few hare-brained fascists talking gibberish?"

"But eighteen thousand members . . . " Touton put in.

"Exactly. Plus, the tacit support of the Church, even though, officially, they stand against secret organizations. Plus, members of the Jean-Baptiste Society. Plus, when Bouchard spoke, politicians, academics and journalists all created a storm against him. As I said, he was condemned from every corner of Quebec. Did you know, Captain, that while you were away, the majority of our people supported Pétain? That when France fell, we sided with the Germans, we praised their victory? De Gaulle sent an emissary, a woman, to raise money and support the cause of France. The poor lady found herself among French-men who were unsympathetic. That talk about the Germans, the people here recited to her, as if they knew more about it than she did, amounted to nothing more than British propaganda! 'But I'm part of the Resistance!' she'd argue, and she explained that a week before she'd been planting bombs. 'More British propaganda,' she was told."

"So my incarceration in Poland," Touton put forward, "my march across Europe without boots in the dead of winter—"

"British propaganda," Fleury informed him from his birdlike perch on the edge of his chair, and gave the captain a few moments to absorb this news.

Hard to fathom. Touton had stepped ashore from a landing craft, and over the next few minutes only he and two others would survive. Back home, a large portion of the people they were fighting and dying for actually supported the enemy. He'd heard rumours to that effect before, but after the Allied victory nobody wanted to talk about whom they'd supported. Touton drank his beer with sadness. He felt alone despite the chatter of men around him.

He could hear them, these tavern voices, rehashing their bad days and going over last night's game, and their talk would turn to the war across the sea. What did they say, these men with their beer bellies and families and jobs, while he ate his slice of black bread and scoop of foul porridge, his only food for the day? What did they say? Did they clink their glasses at the prospect of a German victory? Had they cheered the news from Dieppe, that the Canadians had had their asses kicked, that the infantry had been all but wiped out?

Eventually, the source of his new knowledge started in again. "Lionel Groulx, the intellectual, do you know him?" Touton shook his head. "Very influential. Well respected. He glorified Mussolini. He considered Italy and Germany to be among the most fortunate nations on earth because they were being led by strong men. By dictators. He prayed for a man like that to arise here. When Mussolini was killed, he railed against Italians for their ignorance. Now it's true, sir, that when de Gaulle came back, he found support in Quebec again. Victory will do that, but I'm sure some of it was genuine. But the support for Marshal Pétain, for the collaborators, for the notion of a dictatorship, that did not disappear. It just went underground. I believe it exists to this day, inside a secret order to which many prominent citizens have pledged an oath."

"The Order of Jacques Cartier," Touton recited. "So it's real, you believe?"

"Without a doubt, sir."

Armand Touton polished off one glass and downed half of another, then erupted into a smile. "So," he said, chuckling lightly, "we know the truth. A detective in Policy is still a detective!"

At that, the thin man beamed, and together the two hoisted their glasses, clinked and drank. In time, after polite discussion of the riot and of the coming campaign against speakeasies, Fleury announced that he had to head home and the two men split the bill. Touton was intent on his next task, one that he was not looking forward to. The time had come to pay his respects to the wife of the deceased coroner. In the end, he left two full glasses on the table—a sin in some quarters, but he was bent on rearranging his priorities.

On his way out, he muttered under his breath, "One for you, Roger, for the road. One for you, Claude. Drink up."

†††

Night found the city uneasy in its calm, yet at peace. Armand Touton juggled the assignments of three dozen detectives. Which crimes from the night before would have to be ignored, a consequence of the chaos? Which demanded an investigation? His men would be run mad covering assignments, and the quality of their work would suffer. Once they'd been dispatched to the streets, Touton succeeded in finagling a meeting with the director—not an easy accomplishment for most officers, but he and the boss had an understanding. Each man commonly made himself available to the other.

He found Pacifique Plante in his office, munching on a sandwich. The director had already enjoyed a dramatic career, despite being the most poorly qualified of men for the job. He'd never been a cop himself. Two events had brought him to power in 1946, but only temporarily. A grenade had been lobbed into a gambling den. Suddenly, public pressure intensified to do something about gambling. Then, just six days later, Harry Davis, the mob boss in charge of the gambling scene, was gunned down in his barber's chair while having a trim. The public outcry over the violence grew shrill.

Although the mayor wanted to legalize gambling, the Church—the real authority in the province—condemned the pastime as evil. Protestations forced the mayor to retreat from his plans, and now the chief of police was on the hot seat to respond to the new crisis. The usual practice, to give matters time to calm down and fire the head of the morality squad, might yet work. In the previous ten years, the head of the squad had already been fired seven times. Usually, the move undercut any public outcry, everything went back to normal, and when the next chorus of disapproval occurred, the most recent head of the morality squad would be fired once more. This time, though, the matter was more complicated, as the one person who honestly did keep the peace, who made the crooks behave, the mobster Harry Davis, had been the one gunned down.

Now, no one was in charge of anything.

The police chief was approached by a diminutive lawyer, Pacifique "Pax" Plante, who had been working in the municipal court system, in what was identified as the Recorder's Court. He asked if the chief was serious about eradicating gambling. The chief had no choice but to agree that he was, and to deliver a pompous speech. "Then hire me to lead the morality squad," the twig of a lawyer proposed.

The chief was reluctant, for the man wasn't one of his guys. On the other hand, bringing in an outsider would make it look like he really meant business, and the fact that the man had no police experience meant he was likely to fail. Once the mob boys got a hold of him and yanked him around on a chain, everything would go back to being normal and the public would be hushed until the next unfortunate incident.

"Fine," the chief agreed. "But don't come bawling to me if you get run over in traffic."

Plante was a man on a mission. He revered Elliott Ness, and like Ness, who had taken on Al Capone and the Chicago mobs, he wanted to clean up his own time and place. He started by closing down the gambling dens, then went after the brothels. He did his job so well that the mayor had to get rid of him, and Plante was fired. Only when the reformers took power in 1954 was he returned to the police department—this time, having first abolished the title of chief, as its director.

Plante knew that corruption was not merely tolerated in his department but part of the natural order. In Armand Touton, he found a cop he could trust, someone with ideals, integrity and boundless courage. He made the young man a captain while he was still in his early thirties. As Touton stepped into his boss's office, it hit him who had brought Detective Fleury onto the force: the cop from Policy physically resembled the director so closely that he could be his kid brother. He'd check, but if Fleury turned out to be the director's man, he'd know that he had found another cop to trust.

"Armand, how's it going?" Plante indicated that he should have a seat.

"Shit's hit the fan," Touton told him as he shifted his weight in the chair. He was wondering what it was about small guys that made them secretly so fierce.

"The riot?" Plante assumed.

"That, too."

Plante finished chewing a bite of his egg sandwich, then said, "The coroner."

Touton sketched the details of the two murders and the missing dagger, and summarized his meeting with Fleury. "He one of yours?"

Plante brushed crumbs from his fingers onto the paper wrapper, then smashing the wrapper into a ball he tossed expertly into a corner waste bin. "It's my prerogative to hire him if I want to."

"Actually, I was impressed."

The director cleaned his teeth with his tongue. "He's here to look after the books. I don't know what he's doing fiddling around with something like this."

"Maybe he takes after you more than you realize."

That notion seemed to please the director, and he offered a slight smile. "What do you need, Armand?"

"Two daytime track dogs."

His boss surprised him by declining the request. "I'll tell you why," he said.

"Why?" Touton covered his shock, but he was shocked.

"If you're going to examine something called the Order of Jacques Cartier, prepare yourself for where it could lead. This is not a job you can farm out. Handle the investigation yourself and play it close to your buttons. Understand? Nothing can be leaked to any sector of the department. So no, you can't have two track dogs who'll probably pass information to the same people you might find yourself pursuing. Do it on your own, Armand, or forget about it."

He took the man's point, but he still needed help. "I can't work night and day. As it is, I work extra shifts and extra days—that's almost routine."

"Tell you what," Plante considered, and offered a compromise. "We both know someone who's trustworthy, who won't arouse attention if he's away from the office running errands for you."

"Fleury," Touton said.

"Not exactly a regulation track dog."

"I'll take him. I met a uniform last night, on site. Miron was his name. It's normal for the captain of the Night Patrol to get a uniform to work a daytime detail—"

"All right. You can have him. Anything else?"

"Let me try to trace the car, at least, with day uniforms. That kind of detail can feed into other ongoing investigations. Anyway, it's a murder case."

"Don't turn it into anything more. Not in public. That's it?"

"I'm good, Pax. Thanks."

"One more thing." Plante poured himself a coffee from a thermos. With the riot, he was probably working around the clock, and already his eyes looked grey and old. "I don't think I've ever said this to a cop before. This time, I think it's warranted. I want it to sink inside that thick head of yours, Armand."

"Sir?" He felt he was being reprimanded.

"You might find yourself tracking people who have resources and connections. Be careful. Never underestimate the power of power."

"So you've heard of the Order."

Pax Plante nodded. "Worrisome old rumours—the kind that stick."

"How high do you think it goes?" Touton tested him.

"Higher," the man said, and stared back at him.

"What do you mean?"

"No matter how high you go," he said, and he paused to sip his steaming coffee, "remind yourself that you can probably still go higher."

Both men gazed at one another. An impression of understanding passed between them, a puzzling acceptance that what might soon transpire could not be fathomed. Not dissimilar, it occurred to Touton in a trice, to glances shared among the men landing at Dieppe. Pax Plante and Armand Touton each sought to comprehend how time and circumstance had brought them to this moment, and whether they would each stand true if overtaken by dread.

Standing, Touton nodded solemnly, departed and quietly walked through police headquarters back to his office. All along the corridors, the word was being whispered that the city had remained quiet.

CHAPTER 8

1640–42

I N THE COUNTRYSIDE NEAR CHAMPAGNE, FRANCE, HEAVY-SET, BALD, white-whiskered Father Charles Lalemant passed his days amid a galli-maufry of memories, flowers and bees, augmenting a meagre pension through the production of honey. From time to time, whenever the local parish priest had cause to travel or perhaps took ill, as he was a frail man, Father Lalemant would accept the opportunity to partially replace him and again say mass. If the resident priest tarried awhile or his infirmity lingered, Lalemant would consent as well to hear confession and engage in administrative chores. Deferential to his age and position, his neighbours knew nothing of his background. They assumed that, somewhere in France, he had enjoyed a quiet parish and had faithfully passed his days in humble servitude to his Lord. On rare occasion—welcome hours for him, as he favoured company and conversation—he'd receive visitors from Paris or from towns farther afield, men or priests who had learned of his experiences and sought knowledge of his early days. For Father Lalemant, Jesuit and beekeeper, had not lived a docile life. Father Lalemant had preached among the Huron.

His neighbours would be shocked to know that, in his day, he had retrieved the bodies of his fellow priests from the stakes on which they'd been tortured and slain, and that in modest numbers—some would say unsuccessfully—he had converted warring Huron.

A story told about him, one he forever declined to repeat, maintained that he had, on one occasion, converted an Indian who had been torturing him, thus sparing both his own life and the immortal soul of the native.

News had arrived by dispatch a week earlier, so that Lalemant was not surprised when a horseman approached his cottage, which was painted the colour of a daffodil freshly in bloom. He put out an array of cheese upon the pear-wood table, sliced cooked bull's liver and duck's breast, and decanted a bottle of red wine into a jug before stepping outside to greet his guest.

The traveller, arriving all the way from the northwest seaport of La Rochelle, represented the Order of St. Sacrament, a secret society to which Lalemant himself adhered. Members held social and political position, they might be men of commerce or belong to the Church, but they were uniformly pious, and held in contempt Cardinal Richelieu's policies of the day. As first minister, Richelieu conducted the European wars and sought the enrichment of France. Piety was a word he might speak on public occasion, but a personal discipline he had failed to undertake. Hence the need for a society, independent of Church and king, devoted to the propagation of the faith. The need for secrecy, a nuisance, had been determined by the cardinal's spies, who were everywhere as he sought to consolidate power. Peacefully, diligently, members of the Order of St. Sacrament undertook what they considered to be the true work of France, to herald the spiritual sovereignty of their Lord.

The visitor slid down from his horse, doffed his plumed hat to bow formally, and introduced himself as Jérôme le Royer de la Dauversière.

"Welcome, welcome!" Lalemant greeted him. He clutched onto him and clasped his hand, eager, in the manner of lonely men, for the company. "Please. Come inside. We shall break bread. You must be weary, famished from your journey."

After they had feasted, and were indulging their second carafe of wine, the guest revealed himself.

Six years earlier, he had experienced a vision. Lalemant shifted around in his chair. From experience, he knew that visions had a tendency to be compelling, but were difficult to accommodate. A man's own visions were a sufficient hardship with which to contend or validate—another's, more so.

"In my vision, I learned that I was to help establish a settlement on the island of Montreal, from where the faithful might convert *les sauvages*, and where a hospital might be constructed to attend equally to Indian and French patients."

A good vision, and Lalemant was intrigued. Not knowing Dauversière, neither through personal experience nor reputation, he did not encourage him with any facial expression other than restrained respect. His visitor did not strike him as one fit for the wilderness. His hair flowed in great waves, finishing in tight brown curls near his shoulders. Hours had been invested to keep his white moustache and miniature goatee trimmed to such perfection. His clothing was ornamental in the style of a nobleman, rendered in a forest green the priest found pleasing. Capes and waistcoat, collars and pantaloons all bulged and hung about him with the excess of the day, and his boots flopped forward just below the knees. The shining brace for his sword highlighted his chest, a parade of bright stones and intricate designs embedded in the fabric, and the sheath for his sword was embossed with finely wrought filigrees in steel. The man's skin—the softness of his right hand when Father Lalemant had shaken it—and bearing spoke well of a man in court or in commerce, yet such skin was indicative of men ill suited to the hair-raising, demanding wildness of the New World. How would this man respond, for instance, to butchery? How would he adapt to air so cold it burned the skin and stiffened the joints? And why was he here? If all he sought was priestly advice, then this he could freely dispense, for surely Dauversière could see that he was an old, old man now, too decrepit to undertake another mission to New France. At least, on most days, he thought so.

"A few years later," Dauversière stated, "I knelt at prayer at La Rochelle."

"I know the cathedral there well," Lalemant recalled. "I prayed there before embarking to the New World for the last time. Did you experience another vision?"

Dauversière smiled, lowering his eyes a moment. Even among pious men, he knew, suspicions would encroach upon the conversation. Lalemant, in effect, was inquiring if he was a man of feeble mind, who at random would gaze upon the unseen, or in a moment's wonder concoct a scattering of angels in the midst of dancing flames. He was here, of course, to convince Lalemant that his great vision belonged to God, not to himself and certainly not to a man of frail character, and that he was a practical individual who lived to serve others and had already done so with some success, according to God's will.

"Emerging from my prayer, which had been fervent in its moment, I met another man, quite by accident, who had also been upon his knees at prayer beside me. We engaged one another in conversation. I believe you know him, Father. Jean-Jacques Olier, the founder of the Order of St. Sulpice."

Lalemant knew Olier to be a man of piety and substance.

"Through that grand accident," Dauversière pressed on, "although I might suggest that our meeting had been preordained by the grace of God, he and I have formed a company, an association that works through the good graces of the Order of St. Sacrement."

"Its name?" the priest inquired. Dauversière's friendship with Olier obliged him to hear the visitor out.

"The Association of Gentlemen for the Conversion of Savages in New France on the Island of Montreal."

Father Charles Lalemant rubbed his chin. "That's a long breath," he stated.

"For a shorter version, we call ourselves the Society of Our Lady of Montreal."

Lalemant was impressed, and duly excited. That New France had been so neglected by the French grieved him, and often he had prayed for the few who had remained behind, prayed that they might be joined by their countrymen to create a new nation under God. Yet a question remained to be broached in the discussion at hand, for still he did not know why this man had chosen to address him. If the visitor wished to be informed on the ways of the Indians, on the nature of the challenge, he would enjoy sharing whatever expertise his memories might divulge. If, on the other hand, Dauversière intended that he personally participate in an association of gentlemen and embark for the island of Montreal himself, then he would have no option but to denounce him as a raving lunatic. He asked the pertinent question: "What would you have of me, sir?"

Dauversière leaned forward and spoke in a quiet, sure voice. "God gave me a vision. God guided me into the Order of St. Sacrement and into the company of Jean-Jacques Olier. And God has led me here, Father, to the last surviving priest to have converted the tribes in Huronia. My question is this: given your expertise and your experience in New France, do you know of anyone who possesses the remarkable capability, the soldierly aspect, the qualities of leadership, and above all the appropriate piety, to successfully conduct this mission on our behalf?"

Lalemant remained quiet, his eyes askance. After a long pause, Dauversière noticed that the right hand of his host appeared to tremble, and when he looked up he saw that a tear had formed and soon dribbled upon his right cheek. The old man rubbed it from his rough whiskers. Then he, too, looked up, and gazed into the eyes of Dauversière. The old priest knew, at that moment, that God had sanctioned this mission, for he, Lalemant, happened to know the one man in France more capable of the task than any. He believed that no one to whom Dauversière might speak could produce a man better suited. What made the situation more remarkable was that, as a retired priest, he had few friends, and yet he had just happened to have made the acquaintance of a soldier retired from the army, close to forty, who lived now in Champagne. Pious, brilliant, a leader, fearless, and above all an adventurer, for no man could go to the New World and survive without possessing the apposite adventuring spirit, he was the one man for the task. Indeed, this soldier had also sought him out, and had visited him in this house, so intrigued had he been to hear the stories of life among the Indians, so disappointed had he been, in his marrow, to have lacked similar opportunity to have been there himself.

"Yes," Lalemant announced, ending the suspense for his guest in a scratchy, God-fearing voice, "surely God has sent you here. I do know the gentleman you seek, for I have met the very man whom God has set upon this earth to conduct your enterprise."

†††

In the dark of late evening, Dauversière arrived at an inn on the main street of the town of Champagne. He unsaddled his horse, then passed the reins to a liveryman to tend to the animal's feeding and watering before he entered the vine-covered stone house to arrange for his own nourishment and rest. A lively place, he saw, with men and women and restrained merriment about the room, yet it did not seem a dwelling for drunkards, nor did the premises invite licentious behaviour. As a pious man, he was unlikely to be compromised by the establishment, and having taken a rest from his dusty travels and bathed in the communal tub, he returned downstairs for a repast by the light of the moon.

In the time that had lapsed, merrymakers had gone on their way and only the inn's residents remained. Road weary, Dauversière ordered pork loin and the region's most celebrated red wine.

Couples were present, relaxing in the midst of their journeys. Men of court on their way to or from Paris quietly sipped wine. Three tax collectors huddled by the fire, separated only by the masses of cloth that hung upon each of them. Their conversation was hushed, as though conspiratorial. Dauversière recognized them at a glance, for their profession was his own. He collected the king's taxes from the wealthy landowners of his region, funds to sustain the wars and Richelieu's gambits. Funds to seal cracks in the king's palaces with gold. While he laboured as a tax collector in the king's service, in his own estimation he was also a visionary who travelled from town to town in the service of his Lord. A misspent youth long behind him, he had done much work to create hospitals and to assist the endeavours of nuns administering to the poor. Among friends, he liked to say that while his right hand collected the king's tax, his left begged on behalf of the poor. He accomplished both tasks well.

On this evening, he eschewed the company of his fellow tribe, preferring to tip his glass in the direction of a man who also drank and ate alone, for they were united as fellow travellers upon the road. The man nodded politely in return, but offered no further courtesy.

Dauversière noticed the lone gentleman again the next morning, strolling in the gardens before breakfast, at times lifting the petals of a blossom to admire it more closely. The man patted the noses of curious horses whose heads jutted from their stalls and stroked the snout of Dauversière's pale mare. He examined her flanks and haunches and sad sway-back before he moved along to the next animal. *Like a thief,* thought Dauversière, as he secretly observed from his bedroom aerie. He next spotted the man after breakfast as he moved through a riverside market in crisp air, speaking to farmers and patrons alike. They deferred to him—perhaps to his intelligence, perhaps according to his reputation, perhaps because he was a swarthy, handsome man adorned in the extravagant clothing of a nobleman. Cheerfully, he moved along to subsequent encounters after a few minutes' respite. When the stranger stooped to present alms to a beggar, he doffed his cap and bowed.

The gentleman from the inn passed a portion of his morning in prayer, first in the damp parish church, again back at the inn's gardens. Following lunch, consumed quietly, he saddled up and rode into the countryside. Seeing him go, and bereft of ambition for the day, Dauversière chose to mount his own mare and follow along at a secure distance.

The rider ambled through the fragrant orchards, then dug in his heels upon gaining a slope and galloped over the ridge, vanishing from Dauversière's view. Dust hung in the air, and the visitor from La Rochelle wandered through it, wondering where the path might lead, what indiscretion he might idly traipse upon. More than an hour later, he pulled in his reins, dismounted and let his horse water by a stream. He listened. The brook's babble. An exchange of birdsong. A breeze momentarily rustled leaves. Then he heard a horse snort, and spun in surprise. The equestrian he had trailed had apparently been trailing him, and had dismounted also, standing now before him with one hand crossed over his body to grip his sheathed sword, a bold, warlike stance.

"Your sword, sir," the stranger commanded quietly, firmly.

"Pardon me, sir?" Dauversière inquired.

"Surely a Richelieu spy is prepared for the consequence of his occupation."

Dauversière knew he had indeed located his man, and found him as Lalemant had promised. "I am not a Richelieu spy, sir, although I do exist in his employ and I am, undoubtedly, a spy."

"Then, sir, your sword."

"For I am a spy sent by God." As though to seal the proclamation, he removed his plumed hat and provided a deep bow, the right hand, with the *chapeau*, fully extended outward, the left above his heart in a gesture of trust and humility. He held his left leg forward and rigid, waiting.

"Blasphemy, sir. Your sword!"

Dauversière stood, smiled and failed to clasp his sword. "If you prefer, sir, let us say that I have been sent to you by Father Charles Lalemant. I have come to collect you for your next mission. From among the pious, you are to gather worthy Frenchmen, farmers and soldiers, carpenters and priests, and lead them to settle upon the island of Montreal in New France, from where your company shall convert our Indian brothers. Paul de Chomedey, Sieur de Maisonneuve, I am Jérôme le Royer de la Dauversière, and I ask a question: are you prepared today to accept your destiny, and undertake this valiant service in the name of Almighty God?"

In the full regalia of amazement and wonder, Maisonneuve stood stock-still a moment before permitting his hand to fall from his sword. He gazed upon the elegant, yet peculiar man by the stream, then he too doffed his hat and struck a deep bow. When he arose, the strangers closed the short distance between themselves and, as though as friends, heartily embraced.

††††

Three ships were destined to embark from La Rochelle and Dieppe. Supplying the vessels with everything the migrants might possibly require—yet manage to afford—had been an all-consuming project for the leadership. The ocean was unforgiving and they had to travel by summer, so the arrivals would have no time to put in a crop their first year. Arriving late in the season, they would have to struggle through a winter at Quebec, then make for Montreal early the following spring. Anything left behind now could not be recovered in less than a year, so every contingency had to be foreseen.

In the midst of the hectic preparations, where it seemed that any problem solved led directly to another, Maisonneuve had set aside a morning for urgent discussions with Dauversière. Entering the makeshift enclave, his new friend greeted him with unrestrained enthusiasm, perhaps glad for the respite. "Jérôme!"

"Paul! How are you? You look so weary."

"What is weariness? Time enough on the voyage to rest. What news?"

The two settled onto chairs on opposite sides of a table that Maisonneuve utilized as his headquarters. Bags of seed and boxes of carpentry tools and farming implements were stacked as tall walls around them.

"I've brought along a young woman I'd like you to meet. She heard about us in Paris and made her way here on her own. She waits outside. I've decided, Paul, that she must go with you. Sent by God, I should say."

"To do what service?" Maisonneuve was skeptical. He felt that he had his full complement in place, and while women were unquestionably necessary to a new colony, for the time being he'd prefer those who accompanied their husbands.

"She's a nurse. Experienced. She's been on the battlefield, Paul, perhaps as often as yourself. She comes from Langres, a town stricken by plague, and she nursed the sick there, and the dying."

Maisonneuve was impressed. Anyone who could offer the twin virtues of youth and experience might prove essential to the enterprise. "Show her in."

"One thing you should know first—"

"Let me meet her, Jérôme, before you divulge her liabilities," he instructed, for he could tell that his friend had left something unspoken. "Let me see for myself."

The woman who sat before him tendered a slight smile, and a casual jut to her chin that Maisonneuve admired. She was a proud woman, forthright, and fervent in her love of God. After a few minutes in her company, Maisonneuve knew that she could be more than a nurse in their work together, for she also possessed the ability to administrate. She could organize and direct many projects when not busy at the hospital, and thereby ameliorate his own burdens. He saw that he could immediately use her help with the current preparations. He also noticed the issue that Dauversière had been intent on raising.

"Mademoiselle Jeanne Mance," he stated, "the voyage, and life on the island of Montreal, will require great fortitude. A hearty constitution. I am afraid that I must decline your gracious offer to accompany us. Yours is a frail nature, is it not?"

"Sieur de Maisonneuve," the young woman replied, "have you never been struck by a blow, or received a wound in battle?"

He was surprised by this riposte. "Yes, of course. I've been in many battles."

"Did the infliction of wounds cause you to be less of a soldier? Once wounded, some men remain fearful evermore, while others, the wiser, hone their skills."

Put in such a way, Maisonneuve had no choice but to suggest that the worst of his experiences had aided him to become a more adroit soldier.

"As have I, as a nurse, been made more effective, more caring and more diligent in my calling, thanks to my infirmities. My fragile nature is a great blessing bestowed upon me, I daresay, by God. My frailty, as you call it, sir, will never be cause for your concern. Better that you mind the ways of the strong, for they may turn fearful when first attacked, or surrender when first weakened by hunger or fatigue. They. Not I."

Dauversière returned upon the departure of Jeanne Mance. "Well?" he asked.

Maisonneuve felt that he had been in the presence of an extraordinary being. He breathed out heavily, which Dauversière interpreted as rejection.

"Paul, please, I didn't want to bring this up. But she comes here under the sponsorship of Madame de Bullion—"

"Who might that be?"

"A woman who will undertake the cost of the hospital. Please, reconsider—"

"I will not reconsider," Maisonneuve informed him bluntly. "Jeanne Mance will be our company nurse, and she will also serve as my second-in-command. You cannot persuade me otherwise."

Recognizing that he'd been duped, Dauversière clapped his hands once and smiled broadly. "Madame de la Peltrie!" he announced.

"Now who's this?"

"She will also be joining you on the voyage."

"Another angel? How many can there be? What does she do?"

"Nothing." Dauversière shrugged. He had the upper hand now.

"Excuse me?"

"I don't think she'll get in the way. I'm sure of it."

"That is the woman's only virtue, that she won't get in the way?" He was about to rant about the task at hand, the dangers, the deprivation, the toil.

"She has money," Dauversière mentioned. "She's paying the voyage for the entire company. The least we can do is accede to her request to go along."

"That's it? She has money?"

Dauversière offered his palms in a gesture of conciliation. "And she is a most pious woman. Therefore, she goes. All I can promise is that she won't get in the way. She will be accompanied by Mademoiselle Charlotte Barré."

"What? Who is she?"

"Her servant."

"What does she do for our mission?" He had rigorously selected candidates based on their piety and capabilities. Now it seemed that women without appreciable worth were appearing out of thin air.

"She serves Madame de la Peltrie. Who has money. Trouble yourself no further, Paul. What's done is done."

Maisonneuve capitulated. He complimented Dauversière on being sly, for had he arranged an interview with Madame de la Peltrie and her servant before he had met Jeanne Mance, he would not have stood for these unnecessary developments. Heartened by the arrival of Mademoiselle Mance, his colleague had taken advantage of his accommodating mood.

"What's next?" he asked his friend. He had little time for idle chat.

"Jean-Jacques is here, with news from across the sea. Prepare yourself. His disposition seemed grave."

Olier, a short-haired man with a sharply receding hairline—in contrast to the flowing locks of the other two—did indeed appear before them in a sombre mood. Sitting beside Dauversière, he faced Maisonneuve, and such was the nature of his communication that he chose to clasp a hand of the other man in both of his.

"What news? From whom?" Maisonneuve pressed him.

"Montmagny." The governor at Quebec. Maisonneuve already knew that the governor did not welcome his arrival, largely because the new colony would exist outside his immediate control. For services rendered to the king, title to the island of Montreal and been vested in Jean de Lauzon, who, unknown to the king, was a member of St. Sacrement. He had passed on the title to Dauversière's company of gentlemen, and so the colonists were not crossing the ocean under the governance of France, but under the governance of God, to do God's work. The number of French who had survived or been born into the New World or had travelled there since the time of Champlain was about 340, with about 150 at Quebec, 60 at Trois-Rivières, less than that number each at the communities of Beauport and Beaupré, while the rest had scattered along the St. Lawrence, clinging to the land and the river while managing a scant trade in furs. Of these, it was said, many ran with the Indians and had surrendered the Frenchman's natural attributes for civilized life. They were thought to be in greater need of redemption than any Indian. Lalemant had warned Maisonneuve of this occurrence, for the New World could compel a man to live on the rivers and in the woods where he might lose his moral and spiritual compass. No one lived on the island of Montreal anymore, Indian or French, and Montmagny had already stated that he saw no value to the project there. He preferred that all new arrivals settle in Quebec, where he could observe them personally.

"What does the good governor have to say now?" Maisonneuve inquired.

"The Iroquois have broken the eternal peace that they made with Champlain. They've attacked."

Sobering news indeed.

"Montmagny has been strengthening the fortifications at Quebec," Olier continued, "and at the mouth of the River of the Iroquois. He states that he is fearful for all those who dwell along the St. Lawrence or in isolation. These men and women he cannot protect."

"Montreal?" Dauversière asked, although he suspected he knew the answer.

"He cannot, and perhaps I should say he *will* not, protect Montreal," Olier confirmed. "Of course, no one is there at the moment, but his opinion will not change with your arrival."

Maisonneuve received the news and let it settle with him. This was not good. Their mission was exceptionally difficult, pitting a few stubborn French against the wilderness. Add to their woes the prospect of war, and the magnitude of their struggle had just been increased tenfold.

Olier limited the volume of his voice to a conspiratorial whisper. "It's possible," he suggested, "that Montmagny instigated the war with the Iroquois to coax new funds for fortifications and other projects. It's a rumour that arrived on the same ship as the messenger to the king."

Troubling news. If the governor at Quebec was willing to compromise the security of his people as a political gambit, then the new colony would be more vulnerable than Maisonneuve had imagined. He could envisage the possibility that Montmagny would benefit from seeing them sacrificed.

"We can withhold . . . delay . . . the voyage," Dauversière whispered.

Maisonneuve gazed upon both men before speaking, and measured his tone so that there could be no doubting his resolve. "If all the trees on the island of Montreal turn into Iroquois warriors, my duty and honour require that I establish a colony there. I will speak these same words to Montmagny before I sail from Quebec to our island home."

They were quiet at the table awhile, as though the words echoed among them.

"Well and good," Olier concurred, although the gravity of his mood had not been displaced.

Dauversière, fearfully, for this mission had begun with his vision while he himself would be staying home, nodded his consent.

Just then, a lad burst around the corner of grain sacks, full of unabashed excitement. "Monsieur! Monsieur! It's the cardinal! The cardinal is here!"

"What cardinal?" Olier chastised him. He held spiritual sway in this region, and was unimpressed by the interferences of Church officials.

"Richelieu!" the boy exclaimed.

For a man perhaps more powerful than the king to visit their endeavour so close to departure caused Olier to stand immediately and press his garments with both hands. Dauversière's eyes went round and panicky, for he envisioned the entire project imperilled, if not doomed. Maisonneuve alone exercised guidance, cautioning his colleagues to relax.

"The court does not favour our enterprise!" Dauversière complained.

"Nor does the court fear it," Maisonneuve pointed out. "Richelieu and the king are agreed on one salient point: they believe we are crossing the sea to our imminent demise. That being so, they perceive no reason to impede our progress. Our peril is of no concern to the king, and he may welcome it as much as Montmagny."

Olier agreed. "You're right, Paul. But then why is he here?"

"To wish us bon voyage, what else?"

Richelieu sought to do exactly that. Jeanne Mance had shown him into a further chamber in the warehouse where the group was stocking supplies, and she made him reasonably comfortable upon a chair. He wore the vestments of his office, appearing in a red and black cape. Obliged to remain standing, each of the courtiers in his entourage made it obvious that the quaint, humble surroundings remained unappreciated, even odious. The cardinal adjusted his arms to indicate the irritation of his hard and narrow seat.

Olier led his group in, kneeled and kissed the cardinal's ring. Dauversière followed. Both men had met with him before, Olier as a religious leader, Dauversière as a tax collector. Maisonneuve, now, was the man Richelieu had come to see, and he accepted the humility of the soldier's bow as he proffered his ring to be kissed. Maisonneuve attended to the obligation, then rose before the power of France.

"Sieur de Maisonneuve. So. You are the man for this task."

"With God's favour, Your Grace. We expect to embark in a week's time, when wind and tide are favourable."

"May you enjoy fair winds. Godspeed, Maisonneuve, to your destination."

"Thank you, Your Grace. Your words are most heartening."

Richelieu nodded, never removing his eyes from the man. "Yes. Yes," he said. "I bring, gentlemen, greetings from the king. Everyone accepts that your . . . excursion . . . is born of religious zeal, and the king honours your fervour and wishes you well."

"Thank you, Your Grace," the three men repeated, almost in unison.

The cardinal lowered his voice a notch. "So that no misunderstanding should arise, the king has sent a gift to commemorate your voyage, to sanctify your travels with a token of his generosity."

Raising a hand to draw the attention of an assistant, Richelieu received a wooden box onto his lap. The three pious men shared glances among themselves, curious that the cardinal had raised the issue of the king's generosity when they had previously encountered only his parsimony with respect to this project. Richelieu opened the box, and before them lay a knife.

"This is the Dagger of Cartier," he explained. "Given to Jacques Cartier by the Iroquois, and carried back to New France by Champlain. He lost the weapon to English pirates, but it was returned as part of a dowry paid by the king of England to the Holy Monarchy of France. Now it is the king's wish that you receive the dagger from New France and carry it back with you to the New World, and he would bid you go in God's grace."

Their visitor resisted all requests that he remain to dine with his petitioners, or that they be permitted to see to his accommodation. While he protested that he had other men to visit in La Rochelle, that he was expected at the cathedral shortly, it was clear that he feared that the cuisine might not be to his standard and that any bed offered might prove insufficient for his rest.

"There is one more matter we should discuss," Richelieu intimated. He was looking at Paul de Chomedey, Sieur de Maisonneuve, in particular.

"Yes, Your Grace?"

"Montmagny. He has built fortifications at the head of River of the Iroquois."

"So I understand, Your Grace."

"This name, River of the Iroquois, strikes me as inappropriate, given that the Indians have turned against us and instituted a war. Have you heard of this peril?"

"I have, Your Grace," Maisonneuve admitted.

"Are you not deterred?"

"With the love of God, and the blessing of our king, we are each of us the more determined, Your Grace."

"Well spoken." He extended a hand for Dauversière, then Olier, to kiss his ring, not taking his eyes from Maisonneuve's. "I will have you inform Montmagny that the River of the Iroquois shall be renamed. Do you have a suggestion?" Although he continued to gaze upon Maisonneuve, he asked, "Anyone?"

The others were flummoxed, but Maisonneuve, knowing that he required the acquiescence of this man if his party was to embark without impediment, suggested, "I believe, Your Grace, that the river shall be called, henceforth, the Richelieu."

In surprise, the cardinal placed a hand upon his chest. "You do me greater honour than I deserve."

"Not at all."

In humility, Richelieu bent his head slightly. "Very well, then," he concurred.

Once he had departed, Dauversière and Olier looked to Maisonneuve to explain the remarkable encounter.

"We have the king's blessing, and carry with us tangible proof, Cartier's dagger. Should we fail, we shall be remembered as religious zealots ill prepared for our undertaking. The king will have lost no treasure—merely a knife he does not value, sent back from whence it came. If we do not fail . . ."

Maisonneuve allowed his voice to trail off.

Close by, Jeanne Mance picked up his thought. " . . . If we do not fail, the king will claim a credit for our success. Such is the supremacy of his blessing, and the power of the Cartier Dagger."

"The knife gave Richelieu his excuse to come here," Maisonneuve noted, and frowned. "Really, it's nothing more than a payment for the perpetuation of his name."

Olier nodded. "Richelieu thinks of everything."

"Which is what we must do," Maisonneuve reminded them. "Come, let's leave the cardinal to his politics. The rest of us must attend to lowly, practical affairs."

In its case, he held the knife to his bosom. Whatever Richelieu's cunning motive, he was glad to have received the dagger into his possession, his first contact with the New World, delivered now to the service of their endeavour.

†††

Over the course of two days in 1642, May 17 and 18, the colonists landed on the island of Montreal, having wintered in grave discomfort at Quebec. Maisonneuve was the first to come ashore, bounding from his longboat and splashing through the water to fall upon his knees on the hallowed ground. They were alone, save for the ship's crew, who followed them ashore, and the governor's attendants. Each man and woman repeated Maisonneuve's example and kissed the benevolent earth.

While the men worked diligently to unload their armaments and stores, tents, personal effects, seed bags and tools, three women, Jeanne Mance, Charlotte Barré and her mistress, Madame de la Peltrie, created an altar for evening prayers. The decorations, cut from wildflowers and undergrowth, earned the awe of the company as the people gathered in the evening light. In glass jars, Jeanne Mance had collected fireflies, and as the first mass on the island was conducted, the little bugs from the New World shone radiant light from the altar. Each man and woman knew they were being welcomed by God.

That night, they slept in their tents. In the morning, they set about creating a new village, scarcely looking up as the ships that had carried them from across the sea departed, leaving them alone in the wilderness with the trees and the animals and the persistent rumours of war.

CHAPTER 9

1955

A S A PRELIMINARY STEP IN HIS INVESTIGATION, CAPTAIN ARMAND Touton asked his officers to examine all Cadillacs registered in the province of Quebec. A mainstay among the rich of New York or Beverly Hills, the make of vehicle was not so ubiquitous on his home turf that the task appeared either too daunting or costly. That the rich were accommodating surprised him, initially. They opened up their garage doors or sent his officers to their country estates to examine these emblems of extravagance. Soon enough, he realized that owners who chose to advertise their station in life by driving an ostentatious vehicle would rarely deny themselves an opportunity to show it off, not even to the police. Of those Touton interviewed personally, a dozen had offered to take him for a ride, and he could not stop another twenty drivers from turning the key to "listen to her purr." He listened to Cadillacs purr. To Touton, one car sounded pretty much like any other, whereas proud Cadillac owners responded as though enraptured by an evening at the symphony.

"Named after a Frenchman," a diminutive lady in her eighties informed him from the aerie of her Outremont home, high above her street. Touton was still puffing from the climb, as the front stairs were built into the side of a cliff. He wondered how she made it up and down more than once a week, and presumed she had an elevator that descended through rock to the garage. He hoped she had a chauffeur. He couldn't imagine that, shrunken by age, she could see above the steering wheel.

"You've given your car a name?"

"No, silly." Osteoporosis had made her feeble and stooped, although in his judgment the weight of jewellery around her neck didn't help. This tiny woman was calling him silly. He liked that. He liked her. "The car. Cadillac. It's named after Antoine de la Mothe, Sieur de Cadillac, who founded Detroit. Did you know that?"

"I did not."

"You should know the history of your people. He was one of us, a French-man. He called Detroit 'Pontchartrain,' at first. These days, you can find that name down in Louisiana. Cadillac went there after Detroit. He became the governor of French Louisiana in 1713. Did you know that?"

"I didn't know that."

"You should."

"Now I do."

"Thanks to me."

"Thanks to you. What colour is your car, Madame?"

"Black. All cars should be black. Or, as Henry Ford said of the Model T, the colour doesn't matter as long as it's black."

"I didn't know that," he said.

"What else don't you know?"

Now that was a complicated question. A good one. He was thinking that she could have been a cop. "Do you have a chauffeur, Madame?"

"You think I'm too old to drive." She seemed ready to spit.

"I just wondered if—"

"You think I'm too incompetent to drive."

"—if someone besides yourself had access to your car."

"Jim does."

Touton gave her a look, inviting her to continue.

"That's right. I have an English driver. But I call him Jim. Not James. Pretty good, don't you think? An old French dame like me with an English driver. Turns the world on its ear, don't you think?"

"I think you're very capable of turning the world on its ear."

She enjoyed that. She had a good laugh, although her voice was frail and the way her body quaked frightened the policeman, who feared she might lose her balance. If he didn't catch her, she could tumble down a hundred and one steps. She continued to laugh, and Touton kept an eye on her, ready to break her fall.

"Has the car been in any accidents? Has it suffered damage over the last couple of months?"

"You think I'm a hit-and-run driver? I'll hit and run you! Listen, one tiny dent and I'll wring Jim's neck. I'll call him James for that. That's his name, after all. It's on his licence."

"Is James around?"

"James?"

"Jim."

She thought that over, and her complexion turned paler. "Oh no, no. Jim's dead. Who did you say you were again?"

"Ma'am, your chauffeur is dead?"

"Thoroughly. Poor lad. He was only seventy-three. Seventy-four in August, if he'd made it."

"And your Cadillac?"

"It's five or six. Sits in the garage. It hasn't moved since last fall, since Jim passed on. I'm too old to drive, and besides that, I can't reach the pedals. I suppose I'll have to sell, but it seems a bother. Do you have a good job, young man?"

"I'm a policeman."

"You were saying. What is it you wanted, dear?"

Cautiously, he took his leave. The walk down was as precarious as the climb up, and more strenuous on his thighs. Gazing back skyward, he saw that the lady was gazing down upon him from a window. Perched like an eagle in her nest, she waved, and he moved on.

Perhaps, he regretted, he should have asked about the Order of Jacques Cartier. She was rich enough to belong, and daffy enough to have talked about it, but he wasn't going to climb those stairs again, not on his wounded knees.

As the process went along, he discovered that most times when he was denied prompt access to a vehicle, he had latched onto a bad guy.

"So your name is Marcello Gaspriani, is that right?"

"Maybe yes. Maybe no. What do you want with my car?" The man was short and almost fully bald, although he paid considerable attention to the wisps of hair that remained, tacking them into place with Brylcreem. He wore a suit and tie, and his neck bulged from a collar at least a size tight. The two men stood indoors in a parking garage, with Touton standing between him and his vehicle. Perspiration had formed at the Caddy owner's temples. From time to time he mopped his brow with a handkerchief, and they'd only gotten started.

"I asked my question first, sir."

"What do you guys want with my car?" He yelled. He was a yeller.

"We're checking a few things out." Two uniforms were examining opposite sides of the vehicle, which was pristine, with polished chrome hubcaps and gleaming side accents. The white car's upholstery was a bright red leather.

"Tell your fookin' guys to take their fookin' grubby hands off my Cadillac right this fookin' minute, and I mean right now."

"We need to check whether it's been painted recently."

"It's never been painted. Hey! Don't chip my paint job! That's original!"

"It's never been black?"

"Are you insane? Look at me. Do I look like a man who drives a black car? I won't drive no fookin' hearse. I only drive white. Hey! Tell your fookin' guys—"

"Easy, Mr. Gaspriani." Touton planted his big mitt on the shorter man to restrain him. A uniform signalled across that they had their confirmation. This was not a suspect car. "We're going now."

"Yeah, you're going? Wipe off your dirty pawprints first, before you go. I'll get a rag for that."

"Don't bother. We won't be wiping off any prints."

"No? You got your own nerve, did you know that?"

"That makes two of us, then. Because you have yours, Mr. Gaspriani. Here you are, driving a big white Cadillac, owning a tiny ice cream parlour on 16th Avenue. Does that make sense to you? We'll have to watch over you from now on. Keep an eye out. See what else you got going on."

He raised a threatening finger. "Nobody's informed you properly. I own that part of town, me. I'll have my people talk to your superiors."

"Do that, Mr. Gaspriani. Maybe they'll have lunch."

"It's Gaspria*nini.* Gaspria*nini*, you asshole."

"Yeah, I know. Don't worry about it. When we send you away, we'll be sure to do the paperwork properly. The press though . . . you can never count on those guys. For the workingman they got no respect. They'll probably get it wrong."

Two problems were working against Touton: time and bureaucracy. At least half the body shops in town were crooked for half their business, and another quarter were crooked for all their business. Somebody wanting a tail light fixed or even a quick paint job could have that done without much fuss, and long before a policeman had inspected the vehicle. As well, visiting these people was daytime work, and aside from being captain of the Night Patrol and well liked by his handpicked team, Touton was exceptionally unpopular with other captains and district commanders. In their eyes, he was a goddamned choirboy, a reformer who wanted to remove their legitimate right to tax the crooks for their sins, and if that weren't bad enough he also wanted to take away their right to enjoy their own sins in the gambling dens and whorehouses of an open city. For him, cooperation with other departments on a daytime investigation would not come easily.

Making matters worse, Homicide justifiably claimed jurisdiction over the crimes, and didn't appreciate him meddling in their progress. They were certainly not prepared to share information. Then again, he wasn't prepared to divulge a smidgen of news either. As the police director had stated, he would have to do this pretty much on his own, and he'd have to keep everything under wraps.

Which made things almost impossible.

An advantage he did have was the zeal of Detective Gaston Fleury, the accountant from Policy. The gaunt man visited him one night while he was at his desk dispensing orders, although Touton was planning to put himself on the streets once that job was done.

"What's up?" Touton asked. The visitor wore a grin on his face as if he'd swallowed not only the canary but a tropical rainforest.

"You forgot something," he said.

"What'd I forget?" Detectives loved catching him on a detail.

"Government vehicles."

"I didn't forget."

Fleury's face fell. "You didn't check them," he protested. "They're off the list."

"First of all, if I did check them, they'd still be off the list. I don't want the wrong people to know I checked government vehicles. They can't appear on *any* list. But it's true, I didn't check them out. That's because I couldn't find a way to do it without the wrong people noticing. If the Order of Jacques Cartier has all these upper-level mucky-mucks as members who are in government, I can't afford to tip them off that I'm looking into their affairs. Keep that in mind, Gaston."

Fleury nodded to indicate that he would bear his counsel. He was secretly pleased that the captain had called him by his first name. He volunteered, "I know a way to check city cars without arousing suspicion."

"You've thought about this." Touton sat back, twirling a pencil in his fingers.

The accountant shrugged, to deflect credit. "I happened to be going by one day, that's all."

"By what?"

"The municipal garage. Where the limos get washed up and waxed. I was tempted, I got to tell you, to see if I could have my own car polished up. But I figured that would be some kind of graft."

"That would be some kind of graft. A garage?"

"Municipal. We could find out who works there, maybe create a retainer for someone, pay a guy to check every tail light, see which ones have been damaged or repaired in the past, then check them out. Find out who was driving them when."

This was actually proper police procedure, something he should have figured out on his own. Touton was impressed. "Only one thing wrong with that scenario. But I like it, don't misunderstand me."

"What's wrong with it?"

"No retainer. A retainer means a paper trail. Any money that passes hands has to be under the table. You're an accountant. Figure that one out without landing in jail. The other thing that's all wrong with your plan is your use of the word 'we.'"

Fleury stood up. "I'll see to it personally," he said.

"Now you're catching on."

Five weeks later, he was back again, looking grim.

"What's the matter?" Touton inquired. The guy looked as though both his parents had died, and perhaps his dog.

"I made a mistake."

"That happens." He didn't tell him that he expected as much. Fleury was not, after all, a properly trained policeman. "What did you do wrong?"

"I made arrangements with this guy who washes cars."

"That's what you were supposed to do," Touton recalled.

"I got a list of twenty-nine vehicles with possible rear-end repair jobs."

"Twenty-nine? Do limo drivers brake too quickly around here?"

"Not exactly." Fleury sighed, then straightened up, flexing his shoulders back, as though to face the music. "I was paying the guy per car. For every suspect limo, he got another fifteen bucks."

"Oh, Gaston." Putting a hand to his forehead he closed his eyes.

"Yeah. Yeah. I finally started to get suspicious, but, I know, I was slow to catch on. Anyhow, I went down there yesterday and looked at the cars for myself, to see if they really did have damage."

"And?"

"The guy I hired? I saw him take a baseball bat to a tail light, then he drove the car into the garage for a wash."

"So they're all tainted. They're all spoiled." Apologies weren't useful at that point. Fleury merely rose and was leaving the office. Touton called him back. "You were looking at city cars, right?"

"That's right."

"Okay. So if you come up with an idea on how to look at provincial and federal cars—if you find some better method—then we can try that, too."

"All right. I will."

"And Gaston," Armand Touton said as the man tried to leave again.

"Yes, sir?"

"You realize that this incident places you under suspicion."

"Sir?"

"If the killer's car had been a city car, you just found the way to scuttle that evidence. That places you under suspicion. It's not personal. I'm just letting you know. You might be the director's man in Policy, but if you're going to do street work for me you have to prove yourself, day in, day out. I'm putting a black mark beside your name. It's only a question mark. But I want you to know it's there."

He was enjoying a little sport with the fellow, but Fleury didn't seem to catch on. Touton figured if this man was going to work with him, he'd have to develop his internal toughness.

"I'll make it up to you, sir."

"Government cars. Provincial. Federal. Find a way."

"Yes, sir."

Touton figured there'd be no way he could do that, but at least the guy was out of his hair for another week or two.

†††

He didn't know how the homicide squad was doing with the deaths of Roger Clément and the coroner, but he did know that his own side investigation had stalled terribly. Throughout the country, and internationally, he'd posted a description of the missing knife—which, not surprisingly, had not turned up. That the knife had been stolen for its symbolic power rather than for its retail value remained a credible theory and an angle he wanted to explore. How could he make inroads into an upper strata of society where members of the Order of Jacques Cartier might dwell? He had no experience in that realm. He came from the poor districts, had been a beat cop among the poor, and most of his working hours were spent among cops and criminals, all of whom had emerged from the same tough streets. Even the people he could trust, the mayor and the police director, did not come from money, for they were hard-nosed lawyers from the middle classes, perceived as being such fanatical reformers by the rich that they were deeply distrusted. How could he find a way into that mysterious upper echelon?

At a meeting with the mayor and the police director in the director's office, he asked that very question. From time to time, the three of them would do

Yorkville 416-393-7660

Toronto Public Library

User ID: 2 ********** 2602

Date Format: DD/MM/YYYY

Number of Items: 1

Item ID:37131123140162
 Title:River city : a novel
 Date due:03/06/2019

Telephone Renewal# 416-395-5505
www.torontopubliclibrary.ca
 Monday, May 13, 2019   1:53 PM

this—conduct a meeting in Pax Plante's office to remind other cops just who held sway in the new era of reform. Being invited in for a few minutes tabbed an officer as someone who enjoyed the support of the new administration, while any senior cop who was never invited into a meeting with the mayor was considered to be under suspicion. The method kept crooked officers nervous, and good cops trying harder to demonstrate their worthiness. The meetings also proved to the department that a power in the city greater than the police now existed, that the good old days when cops ruled were finished.

Armand Touton explained his dilemma, and Mayor Jean Drapeau and his good friend Pacifique Plante tossed a few names back and forth. Problems surfaced around each person they mentioned, and on rare occasion, when they did not have a specific difficulty with someone, they were also not enthusiastic. Then the mayor came up with a suggestion. Stacked in a corner of his office, the police director kept old copies of *Le Devoir*. These contained yellowing articles from a few years back, when he and the future mayor had changed the city forever. Booted from the police department by a corrupt chief, Plante had absconded with his files. He then conscripted a journalist, Gérard Pelletier, to ghostwrite articles for him based on this trove of information. At the time, the newspaper and Plante were expecting hundreds of lawsuits, for Plante named names and provided addresses of the bawdy houses and gambling dens, citizens with honest reputations were being brought low and those who were known to be shady saw their stature in the criminal world clarified. The articles were so blistering in their attacks on crime and criminals, and on the failure of the justice system as a whole, that a public inquiry became necessary, which led to the dismissal of the police chief, while the mayor at the time decided to retire gracefully. Two audacious young men had led the public inquiry, Drapeau and Plante, and they followed up their success by being whooshed into power.

Drapeau pulled an old article off the stack, plunked it down on the desk and rapped his knuckles across the page. "There's our man," he said. "The one who wrote these pieces for Pax."

"Pelletier?" Plante wondered skeptically. "He's not that high up in life, is he?"

"High enough. His friends go higher. Him and that other fellow . . . what's his name, the one publishing *Cité Libre*? They're upper crust."

"What's his name?" Touton asked.

"Pierre Elliott Trudeau," Plante said. "But these guys are communists," he told the mayor.

Drapeau shrugged. "Are we asking them to run the country? Who better to provide information about fascists than communists?"

"He's rich?"

"Trudeau's from money. Pelletier's not exactly off a pig farm," Plante said.

"Harvard graduates," Drapeau put in. "London School of Economics. Silver spoons. They move in those circles, yet they're unionists. Maybe communists. They're young. Foolish. Smart, though. They have integrity, I have to give them that. I read *Cité Libre*. They want to change the city, so we have that in common even though we disagree on a lot. Talk to Trudeau, he's at the centre of that clique. Call your friend Pelletier. Clear the way for Armand."

As it turned out, the meeting would be with both Trudeau and Pelletier. Trudeau insisted that his friend accompany him, thwarting Touton's desire to wheedle him out. Trudeau seemed to understand the premise that it's infinitely easier to recruit someone as a police informant when he's in isolation. Involve another person and the second-guessing commences. Since two were coming, Touton brought along Gaston Fleury to even the odds as well as to tap his expertise on the Order. Should something with the two men actually develop, he planned to set him up as a liaison.

Touton couldn't imagine meeting these sons of the wealthy in a tavern, so he invited them for lunch instead, at Ben's Deli, for smoked meat.

Both seemed amused to be talking to police officers, as though this was a lark they'd be recounting over cocktails that evening, but just as Touton was beginning to feel irritated, Trudeau calmed the waters. He seemed gracious for a rich man's son.

"Captain Touton, you're quite famous," Trudeau began. "Courageous, it's said. Moral, I've heard. Gérard and me, we've been battling Duplessis's shock troops, so it's unusual for us to be breaking bread with a cop. This is odd for us."

Touton appreciated the candour. He knew what Trudeau meant. Provincial police had a rough reputation, as they were routinely deployed by Duplessis to break up strikes. The premier of the province would announce that the cops were being dispatched to help workers cross picket lines. When no worker chose to cross, they'd beat their truncheons over strikers' heads until at least a few of them changed their minds. At the instigation of the premier, in another example of power run amok, the provincial cops had arrested more than a thousand Jehovah's Witnesses for handing out pamphlets to French Catholics. While making the arrests, they smashed the furniture in the homes of the accused. Are they cops, the young men were asking in their little magazine, or political goon squads? The more they lent support to the aspirations of Quebec workers and to the powerless, the more experience Trudeau and Pelletier were gaining with police tactics.

Touton shrugged. "I work closely with Pacifique Plante. Mr. Pelletier knows him well. He understands his work. We're not that kind of cop."

"I think we both understand that," Trudeau said. "But the police, the intellectuals, even when both entities have goodwill, we're not likely to be on the same side of too many issues."

"This is why I've brought along my good friend here, Detective Fleury. Gaston is one of Plante's handpicked men. He knows more about the politics of this situation than me."

"What situation is that?" Trudeau asked.

He let Fleury explain about the Order, and he could tell by the way that the men shot glances at one another that the discussion interested them. Probably they already possessed information they could impart. Never had they expected anyone representing authority to broach the rumour of a powerful fascist club in Quebec.

At the end of Fleury's summary, Trudeau asked, "Why are you telling us?"

Touton explained that he needed access to the affluent classes. He needed to know who might be a member of the Order, which others might offer information.

Trudeau chuckled and glanced discreetly at his friend. "You want me to be a spy. I can't do that. I won't do that. I'm not a spy."

Anticipating exactly that response, the policeman had prepared an alternative way to look at this. "You run a little magazine."

"I do."

"You could print an article on the Order. I could read it, and that way acquire my information, the same as anyone else."

Pelletier stepped in. "I'd advise Pierre against any plot that results in the magazine being sued. With all due respect, sir, to you and Pax Plante, this could be a huge set-up to bring us down."

"I tend to listen to his counsel," Trudeau remarked.

"That's the trouble," Touton pointed out. "The suing. So try this. You prepare the article, but you don't publish it, and since you're interested in having your facts confirmed, you pass your notes around to others, for their comments. For instance, you pass your notes along to me. That's not spying. That's preparing an article for publication that happens to not get published."

"You'd make a good recruiter of spies, Captain."

"Thank you. I guess."

The pair of intellectuals again shared a glance. Trudeau shrugged. "Fascists, right?"

"Possibly they've committed a double murder. Possibly they've stolen a relic that rightfully belongs to the people of Quebec. You're unionists. You're not on the same page with them. I'm sure they want to break up every strike going. It'll surprise no one that they support Duplessis."

"We don't exactly have access into that crowd."

"You have a social access I don't. If you heard some things, you could guide me through the maze, advise me who can be trusted or who might be involved in such a group."

Trudeau shook his head. "That could quickly turn into a witch hunt, Captain, the power you're giving me. A man gives me a hard time for dating his daughter, do I denounce him as a member of the Order?"

"You might get more dates," Pelletier pointed out. "What father would dare stand up to you?"

"You see, Captain, the power you're placing in my hands?"

"I'm relying on your integrity," Touton pressed on, "that's true. But who says that you won't date a fascist's daughter? Not by design, but it could happen, no? The daughter, in her unhappiness, she tells you something about sweet Papa—something not so flattering to him, you understand, about his habits, his friends, his beliefs. She'll never tell any of that to me, but to you, Mr. Trudeau, when you are holding her in your arms, she might tell you everything she knows."

Trudeau again showed that cocky little smile of his. "So now you want me to spy on my girlfriends."

"Spy! Must we use this word? Eat your smoked meat. Think about it, that's all. You move in certain circles. You will make certain arguments, shall we say, in those circles. People will disagree with you. Sometimes, in a great rage, pissed off with you, they might say something they shouldn't."

"Like what?" He was wolfing down his sandwich, trying not to let the mustard dribble.

"Like, someday," Touton began, and he deliberately slowed his pace so that his words might mean more than what he was saying, "when things change, when Quebec finally has a great man to lead them—a great man, you understand what I mean by that?—and, you know, the Jews are gone, and the English are expelled—"

"Many people want the English out. That doesn't make them fascists."

"But one or two might be. The ones who want the Jews out first, for example. In your circles. Among the rich. I cannot move in that world. Where would I begin? Surely, you two aren't opposed to fighting fascists. In your magazine, you talk plenty tough about it."

The four men ate quietly awhile. The restaurant provided a large, bright space, with spartan decor. A popular late-night haunt among the entertainment crowd, in the daytime it served working people and businessmen, bankers in need of a quick bite and students on a budget. Looking around as he ate, Trudeau realized that this was the one place in town where a couple of hip intellectuals could sit down with a couple of cops and nobody would bat an eye. So even the meal's location had been carefully choreographed. That impressed him.

"My ears," he said, as the waiter hovered over him expecting a dessert order, "are always open. I'll have the strawberry cheesecake," he told the man—dressed like all the others in black pants, white shirt and apron—who thanked him and toddled off. To Armand Touton and his sidekick, he added, "After that, we shall see."

†††

Touton waited in his car on Ontario Street for the man to come out. Reconnaissance by one of his detectives suggested that the guy liked to enjoy a few beers before he went out on the town to make his rounds. He stationed a car a third of a block down from the tavern, then waited with a partner beyond that. Two more detectives guarded the opposite direction, in case the thug got wind of their presence. The stakeout took two hours, longer than the captain of the Night Patrol had intended, but when his man appeared the situation looked easy, a walk in the park, as the man was alone.

Touton's partner climbed out of the car, somewhat awkwardly, accidentally knocking his fedora onto the sidewalk. Stooping to pick it up, he dusted it off, then adjusted the hat as if amending his attitude as he moved towards the bad guy. The bad guy didn't like the car or the clumsy oaf who'd pulled himself out of it, or perhaps he recognized the cop from a previous encounter. In any case, intuition made him take a sharp turn off the sidewalk onto the street, still heading for his own vehicle, a scrunched Pontiac. When Touton opened his car door, the man panicked and ran, crossing the street, darting between two cars—one honked in anger—and Touton was already running and knew he had a good angle on his target.

The culprit knew it, too. He tried to run the opposite way, but spotted the other two detectives charging towards him. The clumsy cop he had first noticed was crossing the street, and he decided to take a chance on his initial plan and run away from Touton, but that didn't work out. Touton heaved him against a brick wall.

"You fucking cop asshole!" He wasn't going to fight. He knew he was badly outnumbered and he knew Touton. He couldn't lick him one on one, and definitely not with these reinforcements.

"Cuff him. Take him in your car. I don't want to breathe the same air as this bastard."

"You got nothing on me, you fucker! You got no proof! No fucker in this town will testify!"

"You've got a point," Touton acknowledged. "You prefer chickenshit clients."

"You got no proof!"

"Get him out of my sight," Touton said, but his voice was calm.

†††

Touton considered himself a freelance cop. Which meant that a reputable citizen could approach him with a problem that required his attention without any strict compliance to procedure, or even to the law. A successful restaurateur whose establishment was a hot spot for athletes, entertainers and businesspeople had called him in a number of times. The restaurant's location was out of the way, west and north of downtown, but adjacent to the racetrack and central to an industrial park. Being Chinese, the owner provided an extravagant Peking cuisine with a serving style that included considerable theatrical panache. Clearly nervous, he had called recently and asked that Touton drive him away for a chat, as he didn't want to be seen in his company.

Touton drove him over to the racetrack parking lot. Fans on a warm summer night were cheering a close finish. He turned off the engine.

"What's up, Lu?"

"Captain, I don't like to bother you."

"If you have trouble, that's my job."

"I understand my business. Always somebody wants a piece. Sometimes, it's the easy thing to make accommodation, you understand?"

"You know I don't like that, Lu."

"I have a wife, three children, a house, a car—it's my situation."

"I understand."

"But this one guy, Captain. He's not reasonable. He's new. He wants to make big rep, to please his boss. Always he wants more money, more money. It's not possible no more—always more money, more money. Not once a month, now every three weeks, this is crazy, crazy—"

"Calm down, Lu. I took care of somebody for you a couple of months ago—"

"That's him! He's back. Same guy. Only now I have to pay him, to start, twice what I pay him before because he had trouble with you. Only that much go up every month, higher, always more, now it's three weeks—"

"The same guy?"

"That's him. He's the one."

This was serious. That a new thug had appeared in town, trying to make a reputation by being a scarier collector than the next guy, was nothing new. It happened regularly. That Touton would take it upon himself to help out a businessman like Lu Lee was also typical. Once the sun went down, this was his city, and in Touton's mind honest businessmen should be allowed to work without fear while the crooks should labour in a contrary atmosphere. That he had instructed the newcomer to leave Lu Lee alone and had been ignored was a drastic breach of police–crook protocol. He sincerely believed that he had to be the most feared man in the city, for when that was not true, the bad guys took the city back from him.

"Lu, I'll take care of this again. This time, I will ask you for a favour."

"You come my restaurant, bring your wife, any time, every night you want, have good dinner."

"Lu, it doesn't work that way, but thanks. I have a different favour to ask."

"What you want, I will give you," Lu repeated. "It's crazy, crazy."

†††

Just south of downtown, busy highways carried traffic to and from the west and south. Under an overpass, Touton pulled in with his squad car. He got out of the car and waited. The slums of St. Henri, Pointe St. Charles and Verdun spread out below this slope. At his back stood a cliff, a high step on the way up the mountain. This was a dark, austere location where he would not be disturbed. He had been here before.

The second car showed up and the plainclothes detectives stepped out and they left their passenger in the back seat. Both men were smoking. Putting on their fedoras, they joined Touton and his partner by his car, but the men didn't speak. They gazed out over the lights of the slum and beyond to the black swath of the St. Lawrence River, ever flowing to the sea.

The two cops finished their cigarettes.

"All right," Touton commanded. "Get him out here."

The ruffian was cuffed behind his back. He wasn't big. The two men had little trouble bringing him over. He had his sleeves rolled up to show off his biceps and appeared to be a man who lifted weights. His forearms were tattooed with black and red inks, a serpent uncoiling on one, an eagle baring its claws on another.

"Oo-oooo," the man said. "Oo-oooo. I'm so scared."

"I've talked to you before," Touton said.

"You gonna talk tough to me again? Read me the riot act?"

"You promised to stay away from Lu Lee. You gave me your word."

"Oo-oooo," the man said, grinning and feinting his head around while held on both sides by the two detectives. "Did I lie? Is my word not good now?"

"Hold him up straight," Touton decreed, and his men took a firmer grasp of their captive.

"Oo-oooo, I'm so scared," the man said.

Touton hit him.

The punch was devastating. Simultaneously, it broke the man's jaw and his will to live. He crumpled and looked totally dazed, and his two handlers had to prop him up to receive Touton's next blow. This one broke his nose, and blood spurted and was suddenly all over his chest. Touton hit his mouth, and the other cops turned away as teeth snapped and the man bit through his tongue. He was moaning now as though from a distance. They let him moan on the ground awhile, then the two cops hoisted him back up. Touton hit him three more times in the same rib, until he felt it crack. The man cried out, and they let him fall to the ground. Touton gave him a minute, then indicated that he was to be brought to his feet again. The man could not believe that his ordeal would continue. Touton drove his right hand into the man's stomach and the culprit lost his breath. This time, he curled up on the ground and gasped and swallowed his own blood and vomit.

"Take him for a drive," Touton instructed. "Put him in the trunk—don't mess up your back seat. Dump him in a cornfield outside of town, somewhere close to a hospital." He crouched down beside the man. "This is what *you* do to good people. How do you like it? Not so much, huh? We're taking you out of town. No matter what, never set foot on the island of Montreal again. Is that clear to you?"

The man possessed sufficient faculties to nod his head.

"Good." Touton put his hand on the man's shoulder. "Good luck to you."

He got back in his car, and was soon joined by his partner for the night. They drove out from under the overpass, up Décarie to Lu Lee's Chinese Restaurant and Buffet. Touton found a booth for himself and his partner and told the waiter who approached him—brandishing knives and a grin—that he wanted to speak to Lu Lee. A minute later, the proprietor slid onto the bench seat beside him.

"You won't have a problem anymore," he said. "I'm sorry that this guy didn't understand the message the first time. I got through to him the second time, I'm pretty sure."

"Thank you, Captain. What can I do for you?"

"We had to miss dinner, so we're going to eat. You can choose for us, okay, your specialities. But we're on duty, so we won't have alcohol—well, one beer each, that's it—and we will pay for the meal, Lu. That's not negotiable."

"You're not like other cops who come here over the years."

"Isn't that the point, Lu? That's why you should not wait so long to call me in the future." He looked across the table at his partner, who, like him, was a war veteran. He was the guy he brought along on nocturnal excursions, such as this one, that might require a certain kind of activity. His name was Michel Desbiens, a nervous type, but he usually didn't have to do much, and the Captain knew that he'd be a good backup should that ever be required. He also knew that he would keep his mouth shut. "Would you excuse us just a minute, Michel?" Touton asked him.

"Sure, Captain. Need a leak anyways."

Alone with Lu Lee, he told him, "You got rich guys coming in here all the time. Big spenders. You also got politicians in here, and lawyers—high rollers."

"Yeah, sure," Lu agreed. "Big part of my business."

"People drink a lot. They talk. They say things they might regret later."

"Yeah, sure," Lu confirmed.

"If people like that ever talk about—listen now, remember this—if they ever talk about Jacques Cartier, or 'the Order,' or an ancient, valuable knife, or if they ever talk about getting rid of Asians like yourself, or getting rid of the Jews—"

"Yes, sir?" Lu Lee spoke softly, but he never broke off his gaze. He was intent.

"—then I want to know who those people are. And Lu, this isn't just for now, or this summer, or this year. This is for as long as you're alive and for as long as I am. I want to know who those people are. Understood?"

"Yes, Captain. No problem."

"No problem. Good." He waved the waiter back. "Now serve us up your best food, all right? I'm willing to spend a little tonight."

The two cops enjoyed a feast, and at the end of the meal Touton wagged his finger at his host, for the bill seemed rather slight to him.

††

Sooner than he had expected, a message was passed along from Detective Fleury to Captain Touton. Pierre Elliott Trudeau wanted to meet him, and alone. Touton agreed to pick him up at midnight that same day.

The man had flair, he had to give him that, although it was hard to take him seriously. Trudeau was waiting for him under a streetlamp on a darkened corner, dressed to look like the spitting image of Sherlock Holmes. Deerstalker cap, stovepipe and a lapelled coat that resembled a cape. Life was an act to this young man, and he was treating the world as his stage.

The pipe, at least, wasn't lit.

"I've created a monster," Touton acknowledged.

"You've only recruited one," Trudeau said. "I have my answer, Captain."

"What is it?" They drove down Sherbrooke Street. People were out on the town, enjoying the warm July air.

"I will not spy for you, sir. Perhaps if we were at war, the right war, I could be inspired. But it's not in my nature and the circumstances don't suit me."

"I'm sorry to hear that."

"I wanted to tell you in person."

"Thanks. I'm still disappointed."

"Will you drive me up to the Westmount Lookout?"

Something more might be on the man's mind, so Touton acquiesced.

The road wound upward among the mansions of the rich. Near the top of one of Mount Royal's multiple peaks, Summit Circle took in the views. They passed the old Van Horne mansion, built by the man who had constructed the first railway across the continent. The house was so large that, when it came time to be resold, it had been cut into two separate sections. Thirty feet of width was removed from the multiple storeys. Farther along, they arrived at the lookout, where lovers had parked and tourists scanned the city's lights.

"So you won't work for me," Touton repeated.

"I have secret ambitions, Captain. If it ever came out that I was a stool pigeon for the cops, it could crush me."

"That sounds like the counsel of your friend Pelletier."

"That's what impresses me about you, Captain. You're astute. Do you know the name de Bernonville?"

He did, although it wasn't on the tip of his tongue. "He was in the papers. Years ago." Then it came to him. "A collaborator with the Germans in France, no?"

"That's right. Tried in absentia in France and sentenced to death. He had tortured and killed his fellow countrymen in the Resistance. And Jews. After the war, he slipped through France and Spain and landed in New York. He came up to Quebec under an alias, disguised as a priest."

Touton nodded. "Someone found him out?"

"Dozens of French collaborators found their way to Quebec after the war. They discovered they had friends here who would look after their welfare. But a few Resistance fighters emigrated here as well. Count Jacques Dugé de Bernonville was recognized, his exploits publicly recounted."

"He'd been well received here?" Good to know by whom.

"With aplomb, Captain. Brought into Montreal society. After being recognized, he threw himself upon the mercy of Canada. He even admitted his deception but begged permission to stay. Canada investigated, and ordered him deported. But the outcry within Quebec was intense. His crimes were brought forward. Supporters declared that they constituted the propaganda of Jews and Freemasons. As if those two groups had ever consulted each other. They claimed he'd been following orders, that the rush to return him to France smacked of a communist plot. He managed a stay while his case was being reviewed, and he hung on for another three years. But his past crimes became indisputable, his support eroded, and eventually the count deciphered the writing on the wall. They say he escaped to Brazil, where he hooked up with another infamous man from the period, Klaus Barbie. Rumour has it that he doesn't always stay away, that he makes return trips."

"Mmm," Touton murmured. "You say that when he arrived here originally, he had a network of supporters in place?"

"Ready and waiting, yes. This is where it gets interesting. In the course of the attempts to keep him here, a petition was signed. Doctors, lawyers, businessmen, students, academics from the University of Montreal, in particular, and politicians, including our Mayor Houde. The student society at the university also voted to keep the count. One hundred and forty-three names are on that petition."

"I'll track down the petition, Mr. Trudeau."

"Call me Pierre."

"Call me Armand. I'll take it from here. I want to thank you."

"Please understand, Armand, that this is not spying. I'm only directing you to a public document. Petitions to the federal government are never destroyed."

Touton started up the engine. He had names! Precious names! He wanted to get on this right away. "I get it. Where can I drop you?"

"In this costume? Best if you take me straight home."

††††

He had phoned ahead, and now drove up to visit the widow of Roger Clément. Having names in his pocket made him feel rich, although he was going to try them out first in this, the poorest of communities, and at the poorest door. A connection between the powerful and the desperately impoverished was one he would love to establish.

Properly dressed this time in a simple grey smock, her hair pinned up, Carole Clément continued in mourning. Her daughter, Anik, remained pinned to her side, as if the life of one flowed through the other and sustained them both. Often, Madame Clément slid a hand over the girl's skinny shoulder as unconsciously as another woman might wear a bracelet.

"I've talked to officers in Homicide," she told her visitor.

"Roger was a friend of mine," Touton explained. "The homicide detectives will do the best job they can with the resources they've been given. But I will pursue your husband's killers to the end of my days, if necessary."

The woman let the words settle over the room, like dust motes drifting in the sunlight, becoming invisible as they moved into shadow. "Would you like a cup of tea?" she offered.

Touton hesitated. He realized that he'd love a cup of coffee. His wife drank tea, Clarence Campbell preferred tea, he expected that the people on his list drank tea, although that was thoroughly illogical. Perhaps he should learn to also drink tea again. The widow had suffered greatly and he did not want to impose by requesting coffee, nor did he want to decline her simple offer of hospitality. "Thank you, Mrs. Clément. That would be nice," he said.

"What did you call my husband?" she asked him. "By what name?"

"Roger."

"And what did he call you?"

"Armand, usually. Sometimes he called me an—well, I can't say in front of the little one."

She smiled, briefly. "All right then. Please, call me Carole. I hate calling someone according to their rank, so I shall call you Armand. It's a small problem I have with authority—I don't respect it." When Touton acquiesced with a nod, she asked, "Perhaps you'd prefer a coffee?"

He was never like this, never cautious to state a simple preference, but he checked himself once again. "Tea will be fine," he reiterated.

When it arrived, she asked what he took in it. He didn't know. In the POW camp, he'd taken it clear because there was no choice. Drinking tea made from teabags already used repeatedly by British pilots turned him off the drink. He could smell and taste his confinement again as he brought the hot drink to his lips. In prison, tea tasted like incarceration, and he'd wished he could add a dollop of milk, a splash of hope. He drank only the warmth. Now tea tasted like a memory, and the coldness that inhabited this house also resided in him.

"I have a list of names. Some of these men you may recognize from public life. I'm looking to find out if Roger ever mentioned any of these people—not from reading about them in the papers, but from personal experience, from his line of work."

She scanned the list of names. "Mayor Houde," she said.

Touton nodded. "He mentioned him to me . . . that he worked for him from time to time. Duplessis, as well. Any others?"

"Who are all these men?"

"They supported keeping that fascist in Canada, de Bernonville."

"The count," Carole said.

"That's him."

"Yeah, it's just like Houde to support him. He and Roger would argue politics in the internment camp. Houde would say one thing, and Roger would write to me and I'd suggest a counterargument, then he'd speak it and Houde would say something else. On it went. I felt that Roger was finally being educated in the ways of the world—and in other ways, too. But I worried that I was only easing my conscience to think that way. It's because of me that he was there."

She had to busy herself with Anik a moment, as the child was growing restless. The compromise was to lift her up into her lap, and the girl placed her head against her mother's shoulder. Her eyes never left the face of the man in the room.

"They read poetry together, did you know?"

The policeman had to laugh. "I can't imagine either man reading poetry."

"I couldn't either. But they had to entertain themselves, do something with their evenings." She grew wistful as a precious memory returned. She had difficulty, and the officer gave her time to regain composure. "After he returned, he'd entertain me—me and Anik—with his Scots poetry."

"Scots?" Something clicked.

"The library in the prison was small. Nothing in French. Not much in English. So the mayor and Clément, with help from a Scottish guard, read Robbie Burns. He could quote long passages in a ridiculous accent. Remember, Anik?"

The little girl nodded that she did, and Touton smiled even as he felt sadness for her well in his heart. He also had something to think about now.

Although pedestrians had trundled past the statue over the years, few Montrealers knew what the Burns monument looked like, nor could they name its location. If the figure were pointed out to them, most citizens would be hard pressed to identify whom it commemorated. The edifice was a refuge for pigeons up high and for the weary and shade-seekers down below. Those who took the time to read the inscription would soon discard the information. Clément and Houde, on the other hand, would have reason to recall the landmark, as it brought them back to their evenings in the internment camp. If they had chosen to meet somewhere, one might well have said to the other, "I'll meet you at the Burns monument." There, under the boot of the poet, Roger Clément had been murdered.

"Did he mention Duplessis in the weeks or months before his death?"

Carole said no. "He became more quiet than usual. What was conspicuous to me is that he *stopped* talking about Duplessis and Houde in the weeks prior to his death. He just closed down on them. If they were in the news, if one of them had his picture in the paper, usually Roger would say something—something nasty about Duplessis—or remember a funny incident from the camp, about Houde. He liked Houde. But prior to his death? Nothing. He just turned away. Clammed up."

"Do other names on the list ring a bell?"

Holding the paper in her left hand, she tapped it with her right index finger. "This name I know. I don't think Roger did, though. A real right winger. He hated strikes. He used to write letters to the editor. He didn't like my strikes in particular, maybe because so many seamstresses are immigrants. And women."

"What's the name?"

"Dr. Camille Laurin. I'm not saying Roger had anything to do with him. Look, you should also know that Roger crossed paths with de Bernonville."

A surprise. "How so?"

"Houde hired him to protect de Bernonville. Just for a couple of days. Straightforward bodyguard stuff."

Interesting.

Touton sipped the last of the tea, the flavour so potent to him, so mixed with memory and tragedy, then reached across and took the child's hand in his. The girl let her hand be held as she continued to stare at him. Holding the hand, he spoke to the mother. "Thank you for all this."

At that moment, the doorbell rang, and Carole Clément rose to answer it. Touton continued to hold the girl's hand, then finally let go and stood to take his leave, smiling at her. She stared up without expression. A man had arrived, and, given the late hour, he wondered if the mourning widow had already found a new companion. He was a rather heavy man, in working clothes, the buttons of his shirt undone to the middle of his chest in consideration of the heat. He seemed out of breath. The fellow looked upon him with prompt suspicion. "Hello?"

He held out his hand. "I'm with the police. Captain Armand Touton."

"Ah," the man said, happy for the explanation. "I'm with the Church."

"This is Father François Legault," Carole said.

The little girl had run into the priest's arms and he hoisted her up to his shoulders.

"Then we are both working for the welfare of this family," Touton said.

"Let's hope so," the priest said.

Touton took his leave. He expected the night air to have cooled, but this was not the case. He looked back briefly, then moved on. A priest without his collar. In the heat, after hours, not so surprising. Something about his demeanour, though, had seemed out of the ordinary. His attire had been anticlerical right down to his sneakers. Touton gathered that in the world in which Carole Clément moved, where she did not respect authority, such a priest might be of greater interest to her, and perhaps of more use.

†††

Touton wanted to make a final call that night before knuckling down to more pressing police affairs. He stopped by the flat where Pacifique Plante lived and interrupted the man's evening. The two took a walk around the block in a middle-class section of the neighbourhood of Outremont. A little to the west, homes became ostentatious. A little to the east, immigrants lived in three-storey walk-ups, contending for scant space. The night was warm, but the two men still wore their hats, although from time to time they'd remove them to let the heat of their brows escape. Plante smoked.

"Sir, I've read all the articles that Pelletier wrote on your behalf."

Plante asked, "Are you investigating me now?"

"No, sir. But I will, if I need to."

The police director gazed at him, curious.

"If something in my investigation comes back to you, I'll investigate. You've told me to always think higher on this case, so I'm already thinking high. But I'm puzzled. When you and Pelletier wrote those articles, and when you and Mayor Drapeau conducted the inquiry—four years of exhaustive investigation—"

"What's troubling you, Armand?"

"You never touched the old mayor. You left Houde alone. Don't tell me he wasn't involved. But you left him alone. I will investigate you if I need to. No one is outside my scope. But you allowed one person to remain outside your scope. Why?"

The pair walked on in silence awhile. Plante was forming his words carefully, smoking and enjoying their easy pace. He was also waiting, Touton noticed, for others on the sidewalk to travel out of earshot before he'd confide an answer.

"Not an easy decision," he said at last. "Not my first choice, either. I was the one advocating that we attack him front and centre, make him our principal target. But Jean Drapeau was leading the investigation, and others on our team convinced me to let him off the hook. We were to attack everyone close to him and destroy their credibility. That way, Houde would be isolated. He'd have no choice but to retire, and if he didn't, he'd be severely hobbled in an election."

"So it was political."

"You make it sound like a bad word, Armand. But we understood from the beginning that there could be no justice without a shift in power. We could create a power vacuum, but who would fill it? From the outset, we wanted not only to bring down Mayor Houde and his cronies, but also to replace that whole gang with ourselves. We had to do both."

Touton let that news settle. He was right, of course. Why cut away the corrupt forces only to depart, job done? The proper, tough course was to assume power, prove that a better path could be developed. That the newspaper articles and the public commission had all been part of a political strategy was still hard to digest. He was in league with smart men, and he was realizing that they were more devious than he'd understood.

"You're disappointed in me, Armand. Politics can be dirty, but we were only being smart, not dirty, and we kept everything above board. Our opponents could see what we were doing, but they couldn't stop us. We gave Houde a free pass because he was popular. If we attacked him personally, the populace might have lost interest in our project. Houde might then have used his charismatic nature to reduce us to sewer water." He took a long drag on his smoke. Above them, gnats circled the street lamps in the humid summer air. "Let's face it, I'm not a charismatic character. The new mayor? On a good day, he looks like everyone's foolish uncle. Even I tried to get him to shave off that silly moustache, but he's stubborn. The point is, we're not the kind of people who win the popular vote thanks to our personalities. Instead, we showed Camillien Houde the writing on the wall. That allowed him to retire with his reputation relatively untarnished, although he still gets depressed about it. I mean, here's a man who spent the war in an internment camp for activities deemed detrimental to the country, and when he was released at the end of the war, ten thousand people came out to meet his train! Not to lynch him, which would have made sense, but to cheer him on! After that, he roared right back into power. How could we hope to defeat such an individual?"

They were turning a corner and had to step back as boys on bicycles flew by. Touton cast a policeman's glance their way, knowing that if he were a beat cop he'd keep an eye on youths out long after a proper bedtime. He'd find out about their home life, check how they were doing in school, and if things were as bad as he expected, try to steer them into baseball and hockey. But he was a beat cop no more. He was also seeing Pax Plante's point, appreciating the genius of the reformers' scheme.

"So you took apart his apparatus—"

"We isolated him. Demoralized him. Retirement looked good to the man. That meant we never had to take him on directly."

"I may have to," Touton revealed.

The pair carried on in silence, and when they had completed the circle back to their starting point, the director spoke his last words of caution.

"You're a popular figure yourself, Armand. What they call a folk hero. But Houde, he's a god. If you take him on, be convincing. Otherwise, don't. If he feels under attack, he'll make the populace feel that they are under attack, and he'll use that impetus to march right back into power and chase us all out. Everything we've accomplished will be blunted. The crooks, the whorehouses, the gambling dens—the works—all will be back in business before the sun rises on his victory."

"You fear him that much?"

"We haven't proven ourselves yet. We're hanging on by a thread, and we've got Duplessis plotting to get rid of us."

"I wondered why you didn't touch him. That nagged at me. Now I know."

"Good night, Armand."

"Sir. Please, pardon the intrusion. My best to your wife."

Driving back to the office, Touton felt apprehensive. The appearance of hunting down Houde would stir up the city. People would characterize even the slightest insinuation as a witch hunt, and he'd be mocked as a lackey in the service of his political superiors, doing their dirty work to rout the opposition and to kick a great man when he was down. He preferred to operate the way he had been trained as a commando: attack quickly, with devastating fury. This action, it seemed, required the opposite approach, and he wasn't sure how to be effective that way.

As he cleared the rise on the eastern slope of the mountain and continued along Park Avenue down to the city's centre, he heard the summer sounds of the city, the radio music and shouts, cars squealing their tires, and he could see the dance of bright lights. He made a mental note to himself, he didn't know why, to check out this Father François Legault, Carole Clément's friend. And then he was idly wondering where the men in the black Cadillac might be hanging out tonight, what they were thinking about, how they were managing to beat the heat.

CHAPTER 10

1642–65

THEY NAMED THEIR FORT PERILOUS.

The first summer passed in peace. Although chosen for their combat experience, brave men, in meadows that, decades earlier, had been Iroquois cornfields, admired the dulcet tones of warblers and wrote poetic letters home. They thanked God for bequeathing such a warm, tranquil garden for their endeavours. The Iroquois had not yet discovered their presence, although accounts from other districts concerning the atrocities of war reached their ears, gumming the hearts of even the most valiant. Outside their stockade composed of flimsy palings, wandering Huron and Algonquin encamped. The French fed them, and spoke of their Lord, and Jeanne Mance tended to the sick or injured among them. Whenever the men applied the paint of battle and went off, she and the other women at Fort Perilous cared for the Indian children and guarded the women the warriors left behind.

To the south, the Dutch had established Fort Orange, where they urged the Iroquois to assail the Indians of the northern woodlands and confiscate their harvests of furs.

Guns, the Dutch offered. More guns for more furs.

"We need guns, our brothers!" the embattled Huron decreed to the French.

The Algonquin pressed the same position. "We bring beaver pelts to trade for harquebusiers."

At Fort Perilous, no one was suffering from an interest in pelts. They were a religious sect. The colony existed through the generosity of the pious in France, and it survived through a fledgling effort to grow food, hunt animals and fish. Their sole devotion remained to convert the Indian soul. Not money, nor fur.

"Will you save the souls from the bones of our dead brothers," inquired a Huron chief, "after the Iroquois kill us? We need guns, our brothers."

As their first winter befell them at Perilous, a crisis ensued.

They had constructed their fortification at the apex of the mighty St. Lawrence and tawdry St. Pierre rivers. A December thaw and an ice dam caused the waters to rise. The moat at the foot of the palisades had filled, and the powder magazine was now in jeopardy. Food supplies would be imperilled next. Should the waters continue to rise unabated, the settlement would be swept away in the deluge, and those who escaped abandoned to the desperate cold soon to return. Those frail few would be left without protection, food or weapons, without contact and bereft of hope. Each man, woman and child would die—huddled, stiffened lumps upon a frozen earth. If the most resilient among them miraculously survived, in their misery depleted, they'd have their scalps razed come spring, upon being discovered by the Iroquois.

The leader of the French, Paul de Chomedey, Sieur de Maisonneuve, a soldier of considerable battle experience, had but one last defence to save Fort Perilous.

He fell upon his knees in prayer.

Between his clasped palms he clenched the Cartier Dagger, its blade pointed to the earth, the diamond-and-gold grip upright to the pale winter sun. In the intensity of his prayer, Maisonneuve felt his hands fuse with the knife, his life's blood radiate with its history. Cartier, Champlain, Brulé . . . these remarkable, if impious, men stirred his blood with their own.

"If the waters recede," Maisonneuve vowed, "as God is my witness, I will carry a cross to the top of the mountain and erect it there, to forever stand as testament to our Lord's majesty and grace."

On Christmas Day, the waters receded. The colony was saved.

The cross Maisonneuve constructed was large and heavy, and through the forest, over rocks and ice, through the snows of winter, to the brink of exhaustion, he carried it upon his back. Upon a crest of the mountain, he erected it to stand as testament above the island of Montreal forevermore. To the cross, under guard, the women and men would go to pray for long hours. No matter what other labours might compel them, or that Iroquois might await in ambush to kill them, they would put aside such material matters to renew their spiritual zeal.

Winter found its slow way to spring, spring raced quickly to summer, and they endured, that first year, before they were discovered.

A year after their arrival, the colonists were betrayed.

A Huron war party led Iroquois to the settlement.

Five Frenchmen bowed their backs in fields outside the walls of Fort Perilous, fighting back the ravages of weeds among their patches of paltry vegetables. They were attuned to a choir of birdsong when unseen Iroquois emitted war cries from both sides of the clearing. They looked up. Then they stood. They neglected to run. Indians bounded upon them, leaping high through the grass, stamping through the lettuce and carrots, tomahawks raised, knives glinting in the sunlight, and the three French who finally ran were quickly snared, their throats slit, the tops of their heads sheared off. A man who remained frozen in his fright was scalped while he remained upright, and he was still on his feet as they pulled him away. The one man who attempted to reach his weapon was snapped up from the ground a foot from his destination, and he was also scalped alive. Like the other, he survived, and was hauled into the dark woods within earshot of the fort, where he and his companion were lashed upright to stakes.

The Iroquois feasted with their Huron brothers that night. They told stories and danced in the pale light of the moon in the smoke of twin fires that burned the feet and blackened the calves of the two French. They tossed sticks upon the fire to keep it smouldering, but not too hot, and as the French cried out in their agony and dismay, the Indians, content in their victory, slept.

In the dark of night, while the moon descended below cloud, as the French mewed in their anguish upon hot coals, only Iroquois warriors awoke, to butcher their Huron informants in their sleep, leaving only one Huron child alive.

Then they ripped the skins from the chests of the French, severed their penises and tore off their testicles, and stoked the fires to make them truly blaze. While they heard the final screams of their captives, they sang and danced in the chorus of their spree and washed themselves in the blood of their eviscerated Huron enemies. The bodies of the white men slid down the stakes as they were consumed by flame, and as their heads fell into the coals and the nostrils, ears and mouths burned orange and blue, fire licked through the sockets of the eyes, staring out upon the festivities.

They roasted the Huron child captured alive, and at the rising of the sun, they ate him.

Inside Fort Perilous, men and women held their children as their bodies shook. Maisonneuve fell again upon his knees. Jeanne Mance, his loyal aid, had already been upon her own knees for hours, and remained there until the distant screaming, and the dancing and the singing, ceased. She arose as the sun achieved its zenith, to deal with the burial of the dead, Huron and French alike.

As one, the people grieved.

†††

Maisonneuve brought out a carpenter and soldier from France, Louis d'Ailleboust, who undertook to rebuild the fortifications. Fort Perilous was bolstered to become seemingly impenetrable, using earth-filled bastions. The Iroquois had attempted a full-scale attack on a fort at the mouth of the Richelieu River, and there three hundred warriors had been forced to retreat, so they had learned the power of the French fort and returned to a tactic where they waited for white people to wander outside the safety of their walls.

D'Ailleboust became not only the builder of the fort, but the community's architect. He constructed the hospital outside the walls of Fort Perilous, and included strong fortifications in his plans. Attacked, his ramparts withstood the first test, as Lambert Closse, with his sixteen men, held off two hundred Iroquois. Arrows rained from the sky, tomahawks turned end over end through the air and harquebusiers fired from the woods, yet with each return volley only Iroquois lay fallen. Jeanne Mance, within her hospital throughout the battle, ministered to those French who were ill with fevers, and to a Huron brought to her after being mauled by a bear, but no wounded.

As safe as the forts proved to be, life continued outside the walls. Crops were planted, worked and harvested. Trees were felled, the wood cut. Rabbit and deer and quail were hunted, the carcasses trimmed and dragged back to the fort. Fish were caught in nets and drawn from the river, and hung to dry in the hot summer sun. Pilgrimages to the cross remained another necessity. Nothing was accomplished without great hazard.

Jean Bédard and his wife, Catherine Mercier, created the largest of the new farms. A good soaking rain was followed by a bright sunny day, and they were happily tending their precious field as Iroquois descended. The man was struck down in combat, the woman carried off and scalped alive. An Iroquois, hideous in his war paint, bared his teeth at her and she cried and turned her head away. He laughed at her fright, then lunged and cut off her nose. Another warrior sliced off her ears. A third chopped off her breasts, and under the light of the moon, while she still breathed and screamed, they burned her alive as her flesh blackened and her screams sang in their ears until her blood boiled and burst from her skin.

"Maisonneuve!" men cried out in their rage. Lambert Closse, the hero of the battle against the attack on the hospital, was unrelenting in pressing his opinion. "Maisonneuve! Sir! Listen to us! Our knees are bleeding! We cannot crawl on them another inch!"

"What would you have me do, Lambert? Kill us all?"

"Sir! We cannot be cowards! The Iroquois will kill us all, one by one, if we don't fight back!"

Initially, Maisonneuve was adamant. "The forest is their home. We have no ability in the woods, where they outnumber us. Inside the fort, we are safe. Alive, we can persevere. Dead, we are good to no one. Reduce our numbers much further and we won't be able to defend the fort. Do you want to die and leave the women and children to the mercy of our enemies?"

His arguments could not sustain his people for long. The men wanted to attack. They challenged his courage and derided the choices he made. Men murmured amongst themselves, and even the women discussed the possibility that Maisonneuve lacked courage, until finally he relented. He was a solider. He would demonstrate that he was a soldier, for otherwise his leadership would end.

He led a war party outside the walls.

In the woods close to the fort, the fight was swift and furious. Six French were promptly dead with arrows through their gullets and eyes and tomahawks splitting their skulls, the wounds from harquebusiers the Dutch had sold to the Iroquois evident on their bloody chests. A fallback was called. Maisonneuve covered the retreat himself and suffered a fierce stabbing, yet fought on. The Iroquois chief sought him out and attacked, howling like a wolf as he bore down upon him. Maisonneuve fired one pistol, which did not discharge, and the chief's tomahawk was raised to crush his skull when the second pistol fired and the warrior, surprised by death, gasped and fell still. The French executed their retreat, firing behind them as they fled, and as the Iroquois came upon their dead chief they lost interest in the pursuit.

Inside the walls of Fort Perilous, the French lost interest in further forays.

†††

"Paul, in their own way," Jeanne Mance attested, "the people are right."

They were speaking in Maisonneuve's small hut as cooler air and the evening light entered through a series of windows that had been cut tall and narrow in case, one day, he had to fire a harquebusier from inside the stockade. Exhaustion seeped through the soldier's veins, for he had spent the day clearing more land and hauling timber back to the fort. The attrition caused by the Iroquois wars required that each man at Fort Perilous perform a variety of tasks, and the leader's position did not make him exempt. On the contrary, he felt it necessary to outwork everyone else, and did so despite not being fully recovered from his chest wound and the subsequent loss of blood.

Maisonneuve could not mount a spirited defence, although he tried. "Iroquois fight a war of attrition. They pick us off one by one. We *must* hunker down inside our walls."

Jeanne Mance had brought her knitting, a sure sign that she planned to stay awhile. "I agree. We cannot attack the Iroquois. Yet the men are also correct. We cannot hide behind our walls, only to die when we step outside the gate to fetch a carrot!"

She was right, of course, as usual. "What do you propose?"

"Our purpose is to convert the savages. Their purpose is to kill us before we do. They are more likely to succeed than we are. We must change their purpose, and to do that we must first change ours."

Such words spoken by a woman of her rare piety left Paul de Chomedey, Sieur de Maisonneuve, perplexed. "How?" he asked.

"Become useful to the Huron. To do that, we must be permitted to trade with them. We must barter for their furs as well as their souls. That will make us useful to the king, who cares not a whit for their souls, and that may encourage him to send soldiers to Fort Perilous." Her knitting needles flashed in her hands, and it was difficult for Maisonneuve to ascertain where her primary attention lay: in their conversation, or with the nascent scarf. "You, Paul, must persuade the governor on these matters."

How to do so would be the more difficult affair, but now that she had outlined the necessary trajectory, he supposed that something could be accomplished in that regard. At the very least, negotiations ought to begin.

Maisonneuve grew annoyed by a nearby dog barking. With a soldier's instinct, he looked up towards the sound, and checked that his harquebusier stood in its allotted slot. In sympathy, other dogs within Fort Perilous took up the bray, which he ignored even as the racket irritated him.

"Iroquois raiders," he said. "These small bands. They come here with a lust for blood. Somehow they must be taught that to attack us on a whim is folly. If they want to attack us, they must do so on *our* terms, in large numbers. In that situation, we will be able to defend ourselves from within the stockade."

"The military aspect I leave to you."

"Why is that dog incessantly barking?" he snapped.

Jeanne Mance glanced up from her knitting, listened and observed her friend closely. Understanding that he was weary, frayed from the aggravations and trauma of recent days, she quietly returned to her primary point, to make sure that he understood its necessity. "Montmagny's army must serve Montreal as well as Quebec, but that will not occur unless we become important to the commercial enterprise of New France."

A knock resounded sharply upon the door. Maisonneuve stood and crossed the short distance to raise the latch. Before him stood a presence he did not recognize—a shock, given his everyday association with all those living within the fort. He had grown estranged from the notion that someone from abroad might someday visit. The young man before him merely smiled from under his broad-brimmed black hat, with its rounded top, and extended his hand. Behind him, a dog yapped and growled.

Then the visitor turned grave. "You've been wounded!"

"My God!" Maisonneuve gasped, backing into the room. "We've met! I know you!"

"You do not know me, sir, but we have met. What a memory!"

"You're Father Lalemant's nephew! Your name, sir, I've forgotten."

"Father Gabriel Lalemant. We spoke only briefly, before you embarked."

Maisonneuve ushered him in, then stepped around him and departed the house himself, even before he had introduced one guest to another.

"Lad!" Maisonneuve cried out. "That darn dog!"

"Sorry, sir," a youth exclaimed.

"What's his name?"

"Pilote, sir. She's a bitch, sir. Please don't shoot her, sir."

"Shoot her? Why would I shoot her? If she barks at strangers—or the arrival of a priest from France—then she will also bark at Iroquois, don't you think? Pilote! Come here!"

He had rubbed the snout of this mutt before, but taken only a nominal interest. "Are you prepared to defend us as we perform our chores?" he asked her.

A few citizens paused to take in what they were seeing.

"Friends! Bring your dogs and puppies to this place! Bring anything that makes noise like a bell when struck and bring great lengths of twine! The Iroquois will not sneak up on us again! Not without sounding alarms and raising the hackles of Pilote and her good friends! See to it now!"

He returned inside, where he warmly embraced his guest. "Father! Father. Your sweet arrival gives us cause to be hopeful! Why are you here?"

"Your wound, Paul."

"It's nothing. I am in Jeanne's care, and God's." Discovering his manners, which in the New World had suffered somewhat, he introduced his guests to one another. Still somewhat shocked, he asked Lalemant once more, "Why in the name of God are you here?"

"To die, of course," Father Lalemant laughed. He seated himself, and mopped perspiration from his brow. "Perhaps before I do, I can be of service. Don't look at me like that! I'm of clear mind. With this enterprise underway, and the encouragement of my uncle, I understood that I could not live my life in a quiet village parish in France. I want to live and die here, in the New World."

"You've chosen well, Father," Jeanne Mance attested quietly. "Many men are dying here."

The priest laughed, expressing the full joy of a man at peace with himself. "Then I have come to the right place! Paul, what did I hear you call this hamlet of mud and sticks?"

"The fort is named Perilous. Within the fort, we call this place Ville-Marie."

"'City of Mary'? *City!* I have visited cathedrals that had more priests than you have people, and you call this a *city*?"

"We know it will rise here, Father. One day."

They talked that evening, the three of them, and it was good for the hosts to speak of what they had accomplished to an outsider, for they could see in his eyes and hear in his words a wonder expressed for their triumphs. Through the visitor's perspective, they understood that they had progressed. Together, by candlelight, the three imagined a new political shape for their community. Father Lalemant believed, as he took to his pallet upon Maisonneuve's floor, that he had been guided here by the hand of God. Maisonneuve required an adept political advisor, which happened to be his particular bailiwick, and why his uncle had, rather than encouraged, *commanded* him to travel here.

In the waning summer months, Pilote became the new heroine of the community, leaping high above the grass in a barking rage at her first sniff of Iroquois, then dashing back at the call of her youthful master as the men prepared their harquebusiers and the women retreated to the fort. Next, they'd hear the clatter in the woods as Iroquois struck the settlers' trip lines, and as the warriors emerged from the trees, whooping and in a fury, they were met by sustained volleys of gunfire. Repeatedly, the small raiding parties were chased off, as occurred the very day that Father Gabriel Lalemant and Maisonneuve were travelling down the river to negotiate for their economic and military salvation with Montmagny, the governor of Quebec.

†††

He dreamed of his uncle's bees. They flitted among a selvage of wildflowers at the edge of the clearing as his Lord stepped down to greet him, extending a comforting hand and the radiant touch of ecstasy.

Father Gabriel Lalemant proved to be exceptionally adept as a political emissary, a busy bee himself. Not all actions were accomplished smoothly, nor did they gain a desired effect. In the creation of a new society, no one could lay claim to the expertise that anticipated every problem. Yet Lalemant carried influence among the Huron, who thought well of him because they thought well of his uncle before him, who had cared for their fathers and mothers in times of need. The younger priest earned their respect and learned to speak their language well. Whenever the governor frustrated the aspirations of Ville-Marie, Father Gabriel murmured in an offhand manner that the fur trade might suffer as a consequence, that the Company of One Hundred Associates who held a monopoly over furs might soon be driven to bankruptcy.

Thinking out loud in this way, he pondered the result if the Huron should decide to dispatch their furs south to the Dutch at Fort Orange, and enter into a treaty with the Iroquois. Given that their association with the French did little for them except to get them killed, the development could readily be imagined. Lalemant did not issue threats. He did not suggest that he might himself cause these dire predictions to come true. He merely postulated various scenarios and allowed Montmagny to infer the consequences. He was fortunate. He was unaware that the company was teetering on the verge of bankruptcy, and so did not grasp the fullness of the fear his words caused Montmagny and the businessmen of Quebec. Those in power understood that any prolonged disruption to the flow of beaver pelts would conclude the French experience in the New World.

Father Gabriel Lalemant gazed across the meadow where his uncle had been tortured before him and where so many Indians had gathered. Fires flared in the distance. The beating of the drums had commenced behind him, and in his fatigue he looked to the skies and felt the warmth of the sun upon his brow. In gazing across time, he had many triumphs to consider, and many difficulties also, some of which had proven insurmountable.

The Jesuit influence among the Indians became an advantage the priest pressed to alter political and economic conventions. New France would come to be ruled by a Superior Council of three men: Maisonneuve, who would be given the title of governor of Montreal; Father Lalemant himself; and the governor of Quebec, Montmagny. The Community of Habitants was formed, a commercial enterprise charged with rescuing the fur trade. The new company would pay a levy to the senior firm for each fur sold, fund the garrison at Ville-Marie and undertake the maintenance of the Jesuit priests there. In exchange, the enterprise received a trading monopoly extending west from the St. Lawrence River. At the same time, in France, Dauversière forged an agreement with the Community of Habitants so that Ville-Marie would be allowed a trading store, a move that promised to make the nascent city a commercial centre. The future of the besieged band seemed bright.

Within a year of the new alliance taking effect, Ville-Marie's future appeared grim again. The new company was interested only in drawing money out as quickly as possible, neglecting the communities it pretended to serve, and everywhere the Iroquois had intensified their raids. The Huron began to buckle under relentless attacks. The number of furs they delivered in 1646 was sharply depleted from previous seasons, and in 1647 that supply dried up entirely. Profits for the Community of Habitants vanished. Lalemant and Maisonneuve took action again, and this time their petitions reached the table of the Royal Council in France. Three commissioners were named to straighten out the affairs in New France, and Lalemant and Maisonneuve, upon hearing the news, grinned like children at Christmas. That night, they drank French brandy, for each of the three commissioners selected turned out to be, secretly, members of the Society of Our Lady of Montreal, their very own group, and with that stroke of a quill, power in the region shifted away from Quebec and Montmagny to Ville-Marie and Maisonneuve.

In the clear air, a small rogue cloud blotted the sun. Father Lalemant was grateful for the respite. He felt cooler, and closed his eyes, and prayed. He considered many things.

Perhaps his most crucial advice came later. Maisonneuve used his new power and the influence of friends in France to retire Montmagny. He was then asked to be governor of all New France himself, which seemed to be a great blessing, an advantage, yet his friend and advisor Lalemant shook his head no. The priest's position was reinforced by Jeanne Mance, who adamantly said no. The offer was a ploy. Should he accept, his energies would be diverted elsewhere, his responsibilities would become more widespread, and eventually his power, seemingly enhanced, would be depleted as he sought to satisfy diverse demands. Maisonneuve accepted his friends' counsel and turned down the position, but managed to have the builder and architect of Fort Perilous and Ville-Marie, his friend Louis d'Ailleboust, made governor instead. At the same time, he had the commissioners address the shortcomings of the Community of Habitants, which led to yet another division of powers. Under the new regime, he was removed from the Superior Council, which was not a concern, given that he had already installed his man in the top post.

Father Lalemant made one more critical suggestion that altered the future of the colony. He developed a network of volunteers, men for whom he revived the name *coureurs de bois*, runners of the woods. These wild men of the forest would continue to develop the skills necessary to live and fight in the wilderness, and they would become close to the Indians, following in the footsteps of Étienne Brulé. Such men would give the French an advantage over the Dutch, and the English, too, whose communities were growing dramatically around Boston and Manhattan. The Dutch stayed in their forts, and the English were not active in the fur trade, except as merchants. As well, these bold, young men would be attached to particular villages—and Lalemant would ensure that many made Ville-Marie their home—bringing back furs to be sold through the merchants in their home communities. As well, he envisioned these *coureurs de bois* travelling farther into the continent, to the west, north and south, to claim ever-greater expanses for the king.

The wise and experienced priest, now thirty-eight years old, reflected upon these matters in the long minutes he had before his captors returned their attentions to him and sliced out his tongue and clawed his nipples off his chest. His testicles were torn away after that and force-fed to Huron captives, men he had converted. In his agony, he may have screamed, but he believed only that he called out to his God and Lord for mercy and forgiveness as blood filled his mouth, throat and lungs. From the hillock where he stood lashed to a stake, he could see the fires where whole villages lay pillaged and burning, and his heart swelled with the anguish of their demise. He moaned for all the Huron people. Voiceless now, he called to God to forgive the Iroquois even as they stoked the fire that scorched his feet and ankles.

Slowly, the flames scaled his legs. His loss of blood helped him fall into a stupor. He would awaken to his own body raging against him, and he cried out, yet made no sound. Angels descended from a cloud, and he was dreaming of bees, flitting among the trim flowers outside his uncle's home in France and also amid the wildflowers of the Huron lands. His heart burst with a new passion, with love and a deep longing as Father Gabriel Lalemant was stripped clean of his body.

†††

In the fall of 1650, one Father Paul Ragueneau and a handful of Huron survivors passed through Ville-Marie by canoe, paddling downriver to the greater security of Quebec. Maisonneuve brought Ragueneau into his hut, where he fed him beans and pork and bread, and they sat together, with Jeanne Mance also in attendance, listening. He told them of Father Brébeuf's martyrdom, and Father Lalemant's, then detailed the more devastating news. He counselled, "In this place, you are about sixty Frenchmen, twenty Huron, a few Algonquin and two of our Fathers."

Maisonneuve nodded. The correct number of French was fifty-nine.

"Thirty thousand Huron have been massacred, or captured and brought into slavery, or routed," he reported. "Corpses darken fields as far as an eagle's eye can see. Villages have been razed, the fires without end. Huron children were cooked on spits, their parents delivered to hideous deaths. Paul, our Fathers were subjected to unspeakable cruelties. How will you, a band of sixty, hold out when thirty thousand Huron could not? Thirty . . . thousand. For the love of God, save yourselves. For the time of your martyrdom will be ordained according to the pleasure of the Iroquois."

They fell to a silence, grieving over the news. Only when the stove fire dimmed and the evening cooled did Jeanne Mance speak, wrapping her shawl around her. "Forgive me, Father," she said, her voice grave, "but the hour of our deaths will be chosen by God, not by Iroquois."

The guest did not argue against her point of view, but he wondered if he had not fully transcribed the horror he had witnessed. Some moments later, though, her voice resumed in the candlelight.

"What have we done?" she inquired, a question Father Ragueneau felt was not asked of him, but rather was directed inwardly, to herself. "We came here to convert the Indians, and now the Huron have been massacred and we are at war with the Iroquois."

The weight of her words fell upon the shoulders of Maisonneuve.

That night, Jeanne Mance gathered the people of Ville-Marie together before the communal altar and asked that they pray the whole night through. Thousands of souls had flown to heaven, and they were to ask the Heavenly Father to receive His Huron children. They would also light candles for the souls of Father Brébeuf and Father Lalemant, trusted friends of their community who had been martyred.

The men and women of Ville-Marie looked to one another, and held one another, and wept, for the lives of those who had been lost and for the tribulation of that hour. Never had a time been so perilous. "We shall carry on," Jeanne Mance declared simply, and she knelt before the altar. Maisonneuve knelt beside her, and in his hands upraised the Cartier Dagger as a symbol of their perseverance, their resilience and their good hope.

The men and women of Fort Perilous prayed, their fervour ignited all the more by the prospect of annihilation.

✝✝✝

The restoration of the mountain cross remained on a list of projects for the community at Ville-Marie, but practical matters had a habit of taking precedence. Devotees still made the trek up the mountainside to pray where the cross had been erected before the Iroquois had committed their desecration, toppling it and gouging it with their axes and partially burning it before the fire was doused by a downpour. Maisonneuve had not arranged to meet Jeanne Mance there—nevertheless they chanced upon one another at the sacred spot. Each had come with an escort of three armed men in case of attack.

"I've been thinking," Maisonneuve admitted.

"Have you?"

"Of the matter we've discussed."

"It bears hard thought. And prayer."

Winter, as seen in the leaden sky, was imminent. The leaves were down, the breeze cool and brisk. The waterfowl had departed. Following the first fall of snow, this pilgrimage would become more difficult.

"I've decided," Maisonneuve said.

"Yes?" Jeanne Mance knew the import of this decision. If he chose to execute their plan, he would be gone awhile, and the survival of the colony would rest in her hands. If he decided to stay, she'd be spared that considerable burden, yet they would be obliged to persevere on hope alone, without any real expectations.

"I'm returning to France," Maisonneuve revealed.

Although the idea had begun with her, moving it towards reality was difficult to bear. Already strained, in her frailty, from the hike up the mountain, Jeanne Mance partially seated herself upon a boulder, absorbing the news. "It must be done," she said. "We cannot go it alone."

Over time, he had come to agree with her. Although the idea of crossing the Atlantic at this difficult time in the colony's life filled him with foreboding, they desperately needed new and skilled recruits, men who could use a gun

but also an axe or a hoe, women who could plant corn one day and weave garments the next. A few of their people had died or been killed, and others had
fled home. In any case, they needed to do much more than merely recoup their
losses. The time had come to either dramatically expand or perish.

"There's a problem about costs. Right now, I don't have the money to
travel to France and recruit new settlers. It'll take time and persuasion."

Clearly, he was broaching the issue to see if she could propose a solution.
In her usual efficient manner, she had long anticipated the question and had
devised a financial scheme.

"The hospital fund has money. Madame de Bullion set aside the original
donation when we first arrived, for our expansion. I have corresponded with
her. She is in complete agreement. We have no need to enlarge the hospital at
this time, so the money can be put to another use. In order to secure it, I have
proposed that we offer land to the hospital to hold the loan, until such time as
the funds can be reimbursed."

"How much?"

"Twenty thousand livres."

That would be sufficient, and Maisonneuve took heart. "Let's do that,
then. We'll let the citizens know the plan."

"The financing remains our compact," Jeanne Mance corrected him.
"Madame de Bullion insists that her generosity remain a secret."

Maisonneuve often chose to work this way. "Agreed," he declared.

"When do you go?" she asked.

"A ship is at Quebec right now. If my paddlers are in good form, I can
make it before departure."

"I see." She lowered her head. This was sounding quite real. "Well, then."

Maisonneuve took a deep breath. He looked over the countryside from
the mountain's aerie. The St. Lawrence, never bothered, plodded on. In the distance, south, the lumbering hills from which the Iroquois faithfully emerged
were smudged by cloud. "Jeanne. Something else requires our agreement. I am
leaving with the expectation of finding one hundred new settlers. Should I fail,
I shall not return. I will only send word. You must promise me, on your honour under God, on your oath, that if I cannot find one hundred new men and

women, you will dissolve Ville-Marie and return everyone, including yourself, to France."

There it was.

While they had often debated the colony's survival, never had matters come down to a simple premise: we cross this line, or we accept our failure. The next few years would be arduous, the risk of being annihilated ever-present. With the Huron nation decimated, the prospects for the fur trade were abysmal, and with the Iroquois likely to be on the warpath, the risks in gathering a harvest were extreme. Life would be strenuous, and, with their commander gone, precarious. Two prospects were nagging her. Maisonneuve might fail. He might not be able to persuade enough daring souls to travel across the ocean to a land of hardship and harrowing terror. Or he might succeed, and return, only to find his beloved village razed to the ground, each of its citizens charred on a stake or, God willing, buried.

"If you hear that we have been destroyed," she told him, "then you, too, must abandon the mission. At least I will know, as I turn into flames, that my death will have spared those who have not yet arrived a similar fate."

"You will vow to come home, should I fail?" he pressed her again.

"Home?" she asked. "This is home. But I shall do as you say. If you are unable to provide us with a minimum of one hundred new citizens, then I shall abolish the community here and return us all to France."

For that one moment, they stepped away from their solitary lives. Jeanne Mance stretched her hand forward, and Maisonneuve clasped it, not to shake it in any formal way, but to hold her palm and entwine their fingers, a momentous act of intimacy neither would forget. Then he signalled to their guards, and cautiously the group made its way down the rocky mountainside.

††††

The years proved unbearably hard while Maisonneuve tramped through France, trying to recruit immigrants. The Iroquois, having vanquished the Huron, travelled the St. Lawrence River, marauding at will. Excursions beyond the walls of Fort Perilous became rare for the residents there. Confined, they danced to fiddlers' tunes and sang the music they'd learned in France. And they began to sing new songs, too. They prayed and worked hard and maintained their weapons in fighting trim. Young boys were taught to shoot before they could handle a gardening implement, and young girls, if allowed beyond the gates at all, carried extra gunpowder upon their backs in case a prolonged fight ensued before they made it back.

Along the river, no man stepped from his door without a rifle, pistols, knives and a sword, and, if he could help it, he never walked alone. A mother sent the dogs out first and armed her children as point guards before she dared hang a laundry. Jeanne Mance would only walk from Fort Perilous to her hospital, now called Hôtel-Dieu, the Hospital of God, with dogs and a heavily armed escort, and she was prepared to stay at the hospital for weeks on end if Iroquois harried the path home.

The struggle was greater than merely surviving. They also needed to make the colony viable. That role fell to the *coureurs de bois,* and in particular to Médard Chouart des Groseilliers and Pierre-Esprit Radisson.

"Des Gros," as he had become known, had arrived in New France in 1641, at twenty-three. For the next five years he worked as a servant among the Jesuits, travelling with them deep into the Huron territories. In 1647 he married, and in 1653, already a widower, he married again. His second bride was a half-sister to Radisson, a young man who begged to join him in the quest for furs. Radisson had never been to the Great Lakes, but his enthusiasm and evident experience—as a youth, he had been captured and enslaved by the Iroquois— impressed the somewhat older man, and he brought him along.

This was a dangerous time to canoe the waterways. Yet Des Gros spoke Iroquois, Huron and Algonquin and had heard from conversations among the Indians of the existence of tribes further north and west. Such news validated the risk. These distant tribes, who had yet to encounter the white man and lived far beyond the territorial incursions of the Iroquois, could supply the French with a greater abundance of furs than anyone had imagined possible.

His ambition, then, was to lead an expedition deeper into the continent's wilderness. Huron who had arrived at Trois-Rivières told of an immense fur cache along the banks of a great salt bay. With that information, Des Gros travelled to Boston and induced merchants there to finance an excursion north by ship, for he believed that he could sail down into the saltwater bay from the Atlantic to secure the furs. The project interested the Boston English, as it would give them access to the northern half of the continent denied them by the French. The trip failed, ice choked the vessel off from its route, but the Frenchman did not surrender his ambition. Des Gros waited for the right circumstance to try again.

†††

In 1654, Maisonneuve returned.

At Fort Perilous, the people were jubilant. Not only did he bring with him a hundred new recruits, he returned with one hundred and fifty-four! Bakers and a brewer, a cooper and a coppersmith, three millers and a pastry chef, a shoemaker, a few weavers and masons. He brought a stonecutter and a nail maker, drain makers and stove makers, carpenters and joiners, a saw maker and a hatter, a cutler and a pair of rifle makers, a road-builder, a blacksmith to shoe horses—and he brought horses!—and gardeners and even sixty plain tillers of the soil. He even brought along a few more priests. Every one of them was prepared to fire a weapon, and each man stood well armed and eager.

The population had suddenly more than doubled. In the exultation of those days, men and women quickly married, and Jeanne Mance prepared herself to begin delivering babies. They had a community! Life! Hope and aspiration! They had good work to do. Dangers persisted, yet they could begin to believe that their defences just might prove adequate.

Also, now, Marguerite Bourgeoys lived among them. In the thirty-three-year-old recruit, Jeanne Mance instantly discovered a sure and devoted friend, while the colony discovered a schoolmistress who would never waver from an undertaking. She began teaching Indian children in the hospital and French children wherever she could find them hiding inside the fort. Before long, she was building a schoolhouse, and in due course she would become the mother superior of the Congregation of Notre Dame de Ville-Marie. Saintly and determined, she created projects and saw them through to conclusion, taking the pressure off Maisonneuve and Jeanne Mance and giving the colony much of its stability and drive.

And Marguerite Bourgeoys found the energy and time to do what others had let slip. She reconstructed the cross upon the mountain. Pilgrimages there soon became frequent. To climb the mountain, kneel at the cross and pray and return alive indicated that the cause was not lost, that the project on the island of Montreal persevered.

Suddenly, good fortune nestled among the trees. In the following few years, the Iroquois became distracted by their natural enemies to the south, the Mohican and Andaste tribes. These tribes fretted over the massacre of the Huron and did not want the same fate to befall them, so they chose to engage the battle early and on their own terms. This gave the French a few years that were remarkably peaceful, and in 1656, when Groseilliers and Radisson canoed from the great saltwater bay after an absence of twenty-five months, they arrived unimpeded with fifty canoes heavily laden with furs. In the ensuing days, both men grew furious when they were not properly paid for their endeavours, yet aside from that poor bargain the colony felt rich again, for it seemed that nothing could stop them now.

Only Maisonneuve, the old soldier, seemed to understand that he still had a war to fight, that the absence of the Iroquois did not mean they'd never return. Indeed, a few years later, after they had annihilated their enemies to the south, they turned their aspirations north once more, as though this was the confrontation they desired the most, as though they were itching to get on with slaughtering the French again. As they returned to the valley of the great river, they appeared to be in a particularly bloodthirsty mood.

††††

As the few good years ended, Maisonneuve could only reflect upon the glory of those days in wonder. The times had not been bereft of an assortment of challenges, which seemed no more than nuisances now. The Sulpicians, the new order formed by Jean-Jacques Olier, entered into rancorous political disputes with the Jesuits, and there had been times when the governor of the Montrealers wanted to throw up his hands and ask God to smite them all. The conflict had flared up first in France, and only when the issues were solved there could the two sides come together in New France and manage a tacit peace. Eventually, they did, and Maisonneuve shook his head, dismayed by all the puffery and upset. *Priests!*

Yet, in forging an alliance, the orders of priests had also manoeuvred to maintain and increase their power in the New World. Governors in Quebec were coming and going, and that vacuum of experienced political leadership was happily filled by knowledgeable Jesuits and Sulpicians. Spiritually, materially and politically, they had a better grasp of life in the cold, cruel north than did courtiers dispatched from France.

Once the Iroquois wars were blazing again, such issues seemed vaguely comical in comparison, and once again the pressure was mounting on Maisonneuve to act. The economy again lay in peril, entirely dependent on the *coureurs de bois* making it through from the north and from more distant travels west, as well as on farmers planting a crop in spring and harvesting it during Indian summer—that window of warm fall weather when the crops were ready and the Iroquois chose to raid. Again Maisonneuve determined that hunkering behind a stout stockade was the best defence, and again he had young men, a different generation this time, anxious to burst outside the walls to fight.

In April of that year, 1660, Maisonneuve was informed of a secret plan, and while he was initially enraged to have his authority usurped by a pack of restless young men, their approach began to simmer in his head. Garrison soldiers devised an idea to venture onto the Ottawa River right at the time—after the breakup of the river's ice—when the fur traders were likely to return. The soldiers would ambush Iroquois raiding parties before they could intercept the fur traders. Everyone knew that Groseilliers and Radisson had travelled deep into the Cree lands. They had not returned the previous spring, so they could easily be dead. The colony believed—the residents prayed—that their travels had been so distant, and that their canoes were now so heavily laden, that their return had required an additional year. This would be the spring of their return, all hoped, and the prospect became a great longing among the people of Fort Perilous. Yet the youthful soldiers were right: the Iroquois would surely be waiting for the *coureurs de bois* along the Ottawa River. Intercept the Iroquois before they intercepted the fur traders—in this way, the pelts might be brought safely through to market.

The plan was audacious enough that it might just work.

Maisonneuve secretly summoned the leader of the group. He did not advise Jeanne Mance or Marguerite Bourgeoys of the meeting, knowing they'd counsel against it. The youths were inexperienced, yet brave and determined. Under the current regime, Maisonneuve no longer possessed the authority to sanction such a raid, so he cautioned the young man standing nervously before him, Adam Dollard des Ormeaux, that their meeting was confidential. If anyone ever asked him about it, the governor would deny that it had taken place or that he had any knowledge of the plan.

"Plan, sir?" the twenty-five year-old responded.

"History will never hear of this conversation."

"Sir?"

"Don't insult me, Adam. This is a very small community and I've been here since you were a child. I know what goes on within these walls. You're planning to ambush the Iroquois."

"Sir," Dollard des Ormeaux said. He felt foolish to have been caught, and expected a sour punishment—a demotion at the very least, and perhaps a few weeks confined to his barracks on depleted rations. Instead, Maisonneuve rose up and crossed the small room to a bureau, where he opened a drawer. He pulled out a wooden case, which he brought back to the table. He sat across from the young soldier with the blondish hair and whiffs of cheek fuzz.

He opened the case.

Inside shone the Cartier Dagger.

"This knife was given to me by Cardinal Richelieu," Maisonneuve informed him, "and handed to him by the king of France. The instrument brings good fortune. When I went to France to find new recruits, I brought along the knife, both for its own security and to help secure the success of my endeavours. As you can see, it contains diamonds and gold. More importantly—and you must understand, young man, I am speaking symbolically—

the knife, through God's grace, grants to the man who possesses it the trust of God and the divine strength of the French people."

"Yes, sir," young Adam Dollard des Ormeaux whispered, in awe.

"And I, Paul de Chomedey, Sieur de Maisonneuve, lend this dagger to you, Adam, as you undertake your mission."

"But, sir. I cannot be worthy." The lad was genuinely aghast. The ceremony felt akin to being knighted, when only a moment ago he expected to be discredited.

Maisonneuve remained severe in his expression and deportment. "I'm sure that Étienne Brulé felt exactly the same way when he was granted the care of the knife as he travelled through Indian lands. He returned it to Champlain safe and sound. If you do not return, and the dagger appears in an Indian's hands, we will know your killer. But it is more important that you go with my blessing, and that you go with the spirit of the French people, and with God."

Solemnly, Dollard accepted the weapon into his care.

"Now you must keep it hidden. Your mission must always remain secret. Understand that I will not take credit for your achievement when you succeed. I may even be obliged to publicly rebuke you. Similarly, should you fail, or not return, I will confess no prior knowledge of your intentions. To do so would imperil my position here, and if my position is compromised, the fate of this community will also be challenged. So, officially, for the sake of Ville-Marie, I know nothing of your plans. Perhaps in your old age, after I am long gone, you can state otherwise—that is up to you. For now, you will reveal to no one that I endorse your actions. Neither shall I for all time. Do I have your sworn oath on this matter?"

"You do, sir."

"Then Godspeed, Adam. Return the knife safely to me. May our Lord be with you always. I have arranged for forty Huron to join you. You will meet them at the rapids where the Ottawa joins the St. Lawrence, and they will carry on with you and fight beside you from there."

The young Adam Dollard des Ormeaux was overwhelmed. His plan had been accepted, reinforcements provided, and he had effectively been knighted. Departing, he was exultant, and eager, as only an impetuous youth can be, for battle.

Alone in his small cabin that night, Maisonneuve prayed fervently. He knew that he was sending a pack of naïve youths off to fight vicious, highly skilled warriors. He also knew that something had had to be done to protect the settlement's trading routes. Perhaps this wild scheme might actually work, although success would undoubtedly require God's grace and the intercession of the saints.

He also prayed for forgiveness, should time prove that he had just dispatched sixteen reckless young men to their deaths.

†††

A pious man's prayers might have been more earnest that night had he been forewarned that two hundred Iroquois were amassing to attack the canoes coming down the Ottawa River towards Montreal. More passionate still had he gleaned that a second gathering of Iroquois, five hundred strong, was paddling down the Richelieu River from Lake Champlain, intent on joining the first group and burn the entire seed crop before it was put into the ground at Fort Perilous. An assault on the stout fort would be futile, but to deny the colony any hope of growing food that year would cause the wretched white people to starve inside their walls. Come winter, anyone who might linger on would face a stern reality, that the sustaining commerce of the region—food from the soil and furs off the backs of animals—had both been ruined for a season. The Iroquois were confident in their plan. In a year's time, they believed, or even less, no white person would be living on the island of Montreal. After that, they would concentrate their attacks further north, until all the French were either dead or driven out to sea.

Had the Iroquois known that a mere sixteen soldiers were paddling to intersect their forces, they might have danced and sang and readied themselves, for to have so few French pitted against so many Iroquois in a forest battle would create a great competition for their scalps. As they did not know that the soldiers were there—any more than the young French knew that they would be fighting two hundred Iroquois in the woods, any more than Maisonneuve knew that a formidable contingent of Iroquois advanced on his colony, intent on its final ruination—the Iroquois paddled on in anticipation of encountering the fur traders Groseilliers and Radisson. They wanted those men dead, for they had penetrated the Cree territory. At the same time, Des Gros and Radisson paddled south and east, satisfied with their one hundred canoes heavy with furs, the largest cache in history, but also leery of the dangers ahead. The garrison lads paddled on as well, with apparent glee, for the time had come in their lives to assume the mantle of heroes, and they were not able to yet appreciate what might be required of them.

All three forces—Iroquois, young soldiers with forty Huron, and seasoned *coureurs de bois*—threatened to converge.

††††

They were not trained Indian-fighters. They were trained only to defend their garrison. And so, coming upon the rapids at Long Sault, the garrison soldiers commenced constructing a fort. The Huron worked beside them, although they were soon bickering, distrustful of the plan. The young fighters had found a convenient semicircle of boulders, which they used to form the skeletal frame of a fortification. They cut trees and set them across the gaps in multiple layers, lashing it all together and packing the gaps with stones and sand. Dollard's plan was to use the fort as a place to return at night after he and the others spent the days searching the river for Indians. As well, *coureurs de bois* would have to portage across this beach, where the waters were too treacherous for a canoe, and certainly one laden with valuable furs. That aspect made the area a critical one to defend, for Iroquois might appreciate the portage as an ideal neck to attack.

The concept of daily scouting trips never materialized. Having spent two days building their defences, they planned to depart at dawn. In the morning, the French and the Huron had no sooner carried their canoes to clear water and dropped them onto the river than they were hauling them out again and hurrying back to their stronghold. Iroquois had turned the bend in the river ahead, and the French had sighted five canoes. They positioned their own fourteen canoes atop the fort to use as cover from arrows.

The pals were excited. They had the Iroquois where they wanted them. This should be a good battle. They could defend their position, for they had ample food and gunshot, as Maisonneuve had secretly augmented what they'd been able to stow. He had also surprised the lads with additional rifles. Inside their low ramparts, the French adventurers and the Huron loaded their weapons and waited.

The five Iroquois canoes slumped onto the sandy beach. The water ahead was too treacherous, and the next portion of the journey would have to be on foot. "Keep down. Stay hidden. They don't know we're here. Wait until they're so close you can't miss, then kill them. We need them close, so the ones who don't die on the first volley will die on the second."

The Iroquois, though, seemed in no hurry to continue their progress, and inside the makeshift fort, the soldiers grew agitated.

"What are they waiting for?" one lad demanded of another.

"We were wrong," Adam Dollard des Ormeaux said. "They know we're here."

"Then what are they waiting for?" the same soldier asked.

"Their friends," the leader replied, for he spotted another six canoes.

The garrison soldiers, inexperienced with any fight in the open, stared out upon the water. "All right. Eleven canoes. That's all right. We have our fort."

"It's a good fort."

Another eight canoes appeared. The French said nothing. Then four more. They remained silent. Then canoes appeared to be coming around the bend without end, and Dollard carefully counted fifty-two.

For twenty minutes, no one spoke a word. Then their leader said, "There's more of them than I thought."

"Maybe they don't see us," a twenty-year-old replied.

"We're going to die here," his friend said. Words that were not fearful so much as a statement of what he assumed to be fact.

Adam Dollard des Ormeaux nodded. "I will die with my hair on. What they do to my scalp after I'm dead, that's their business. But nobody's taking me alive."

They knew the gruesome stories. Of scalping, of men having their limbs removed and, legless and armless, made to drink their own blood. Each soldier feared his fate, but no one was remotely willing to choose surrender over death. They feared surrender more.

"We're French," Dollard declared. "Look." From inside his coat, he took out the Cartier Dagger. "With this, we will fight with the spirit of the French people and the power of God."

"Where'd you get that?"

He had sworn never to tell. But he did not believe that anyone here would survive to reveal his indiscretion. "Maisonneuve," the youth said.

"Maisonneuve knows we're here?"

"Where do you think we got the extra knives and swords and guns? Who else gave us the Huron? He told me that the future of New France depends upon us." He was their leader now, and had suddenly to assume that role. A simple lie couldn't hurt, he figured, not when it might remedy their fright.

"The knife will see us through," a youth with a thick growth of beard said. "We'll beat them back."

"The longer we hold out," Dollard declared, for the cloak of leadership fit him well and he was rising to the task at hand, "the closer the fur traders will come. Sooner or later, they will reinforce us. Radisson. Groseilliers. They will help us rout the Iroquois."

That seemed plausible, and the lads were encouraged.

"Look," one of their number said.

More canoes. Would they never end? Dollard ceased his counting and checked his rifles to make certain they were ready to fire. His friends faithfully followed his example, as did the Huron, who readied their rifles and tested the moose hair on their bows.

Then, when they were ready, most of the Huron fled.

Leaving the young men and four loyal Huron to stand alone.

Twenty, now, against more than two hundred.

††††

The Iroquois moved through the woods to gain position on the rubble of rocks where the white fighters had hunkered down. They allowed the French access to the river, as it would be easy to pick them off if they crossed the beach, and the rapids were no refuge for any man. From the security of the woods, they unleashed a rain of arrows, then stopped to listen. They did not hear the moans of the wounded in their death throes. Hundreds of arrows appeared to be stuck in the air, as though the circle of rocks had a roof. This puzzled the chief who had been given responsibility to conduct the attack.

The Frenchmen looked up. Their canoes had been pierced countless times by arrowheads, but none of their number had suffered a wound. One whooped, and the remaining Huron started to join in, but Dollard hushed them.

"Why can't I give a yell?" the soldier complained. "The Iroquois yell. They're always yelling."

"They don't know how many we are. Yelling lets them count us. So don't yell."

Dollard was not experienced, although he had fought in defence of the fort alongside Lambert Closse, the bravest of the officers. He had blindly fired into the woods as the dogs howled in warning, but he had never waged a battle, having only assisted in retreats.

From here, there could be no retreat.

"The time may come," Dollard added, "when only one of us is left alive, but the Iroquois won't know that because they won't know how many we are."

The others nodded, understanding.

In the trees that lined the beach, the Iroquois leader was unsure of his next move. Not so many French could fit behind the rocks, but he needed to do more than win this battle—he needed to protect his forces. The greater battles lay upon this waterway when the fur traders arrived, and ahead at the island of Montreal. He was confused by this contingent, fearing a trap. Why would the French send out a war party unless they had greater plans than this?

Donaagatai, the young war chief, ordered that rifles be fired at the cairn, and for seven minutes the Iroquois guns barked across the beach along the riverbank, chasing ducks into the air in contemptuous flight. Then the guns fell silent, and the Iroquois listened.

No man moaned.

"Everybody all right?" Adam Dollard des Ormeaux inquired.

"What fools. Do they think they can shoot through rock?"

"Maybe they were hoping we'd stick our heads up."

A few of them laughed nervously.

"They just wanted to see if we would fire back," Dollard said.

"When do we?"

"When they're easy to kill," the leader said, and around the rock embankment the young men nodded their consent.

Then one of their number announced, "Here they come."

They did not begin with the usual war whoops, but came silently, running at great speed across the sand and stones. As the young men put their heads up, they were protected from arrows fired from the trees. They pulled their canoes forward to better cover their heads and opened fire. The four Huron released their arrows, also, then fired their guns. Iroquois fell. They still came running, and now their cries seemed demonic to the Catholic youth, and fierce and invincible, and each soldier continued to fire his rifle, then grab another and fire again and again. They reloaded, and while one lad did so, another fired, and they met the Iroquois onslaught with deadly force. Only a few warriors flew up and over their rock-and-tree walls, and landing, they did not fall upon Frenchmen, as they had hoped, or upon Huron, their second choice, but upon upturned canoes. They'd slip off the canoes awkwardly, a foot coming down first, only to be pierced with a sword. Or an arm would dangle down, soon stabbed, or they'd slide down headfirst so that they'd land at the lads' feet, where they were quickly slaughtered, a Huron knife slitting their throats.

The Iroquois retreated, and the French shot at them some more.

"Don't shout!" Dollard warned when they were done, although his own heart was pounding in his chest as loudly and chaotically as any Iroquois war whoop.

From the forest, Donaagatai stared across the battlefield.

The makeshift guard post remained eerily quiet. What strange white man's war was this? Across the short stretch of beach, he counted eleven Iroquois dead, but he had seen men go over the walls of the fort never to return again. Fourteen dead, then, by his count. Of the wounded, two more would have to be killed, and one or two more might prefer to take their own lives. Ten more might recover, but they would not fight again that day. What was the meaning of this? How was it possible? Why did these French not attack or run as any French, or Huron, would do? Their confidence must surely derive from a more elaborate plan. Were his warriors being led into a trap?

Valiant fighters, the Iroquois were also superb strategists in the conduct of battle. No chief wanted to lose lives, and no warrior wanted to die by surprise. The Iroquois kept looking at one another, and talking to one another, unable to comprehend what had transpired here. How could this odd defence be defeated without further losses?

One of the wounded talked to his war chief. "They squat down. They shoot. Their canoes stand over their heads, so our arrows do not kill them."

These French were smart, Donaagatai surmised. He organized a party to prepare twenty torches. Thrown into the fortress, they might burn the canoes or ignite their powder supplies. If the French wanted to fight the Indians from small forts, they could only do so with great powder supplies.

The French were readying themselves for combat when the torches began to land over their heads. They tilted the canoes up and let the torches fall harmlessly at their feet, then created a collection of them and, from the rear, began to toss them back into the woods. As Donaagatai saw ten, then twenty, torches hurl back at them from the rocks, he shouted in a fury, for nothing he directed had turned out well.

One torch landed an arm's length from his head.

The Iroquois took pride in their organization. They were a confederacy of six nations, and in a future epoch, as yet unimagined, Benjamin Franklin would borrow from their constitution to formulate his own for a country to be called the United States of America. Even in the chaos of war, they followed sophisticated strategies, and during the winter months they worked out solutions to logistical problems concerning supply movements and attack coordination. They were now confronted with a battle they had not anticipated—they had been alone in instigating attacks for decades—and they were stymied as to how to proceed. The warriors looked to their leaders to devise an appropriate response.

For the next foray, the Iroquois made it appear they were attacking from the woods again, but in the heat of battle they slipped dozens of warriors around to the water side and crept up from there. Unseen to them, Dollard des Ormeaux had assigned his youngest and smallest fighter to creep between rocks and keep an eye peeled on their rear. When he saw what was happening and communicated the word back to his leader, five soldiers carried a canoe over their heads for protection and moved to the rear of their fort, where they fired at will upon the exposed Iroquois.

This was the final defeat for Donaagatai as war chief. He was a younger man and was removed from his position by an older one. The war chief who replaced him, Nomotigneega, advised that they wait until dark to stage the next skirmish.

Dollard des Ormeaux, expecting as much, planned his countermove.

To pass the time, the French slept, or cut branches from the trees that lined their fort and fashioned their tips to use as spears. They had seen the way the Iroquois had hurled themselves over the boulders. The next time they did that, they would be impaled. The lads were in full battle attitude now, learning skills quickly, and each one reminded the other that they would die with their hair on or they would not die. When they looked out around them, they viewed the lumps of dead Iroquois. Hard to grasp that they had done all that killing themselves. And still they were quiet, revealing nothing to their enemies.

The moon concealed behind scudding clouds, the Indians crept forward, inching towards the beach ramparts. They were surprised when, from their left and their right, warriors suddenly came running, upsetting their careful strategy of stealth, and they were further surprised when those runners swiped at them with swords, killing a few and causing others to cry out with their sudden afflictions. These four who had betrayed them carried on to the fort and were welcomed there, for they were not Iroquois at all, but French, sent out beforehand in the dark to hide in the bushes, and suddenly the ramparts were lit with the explosion of rifle shot and the Indians cried out upon the ground and bled. Many died, and those who saw that they were trapped arose to attack the fort and swiftly died on their feet.

When the Iroquois retreated, they were incredulous. They bemoaned their failure and raged against one another, and against the French, who fought without being seen and killed without suffering similar tribulation.

Nomotigneega assessed his situation. Down to a hundred and sixty men, he guessed his enemy had fifty or sixty, probably seventy, hidden behind the barricades. He still outnumbered his foe by about three to one. Nevertheless, their trouble here would not be well received in the Iroquois nations. Their Mohawk brothers would rail against them if they accepted defeat now. Honour was at stake. They had to fight this battle and they had to win. As a precaution, the white-haired war chief summoned a runner and told him to carry the news to the Iroquois who were coming up the Richelieu River that their brothers on the Ottawa were engaged in a fierce battle and might not be able to join them in the conquest of the place the French sometimes called Ville-Marie, although on the old maps it was known as Montreal. The runner took four paddlers with him and headed off downstream. Next, the war chief brought his warriors together. He reminded them that the Iroquois would hold them in contempt if they did not win this battle. If they lost here, the French would fight the Iroquois in this way more and more. He told them that the people of the Iroquois depended upon them to vanquish these French. They had fought with courage, but now the time had come to be victorious.

A great cry rose up among the men.

The French fighters heard it.

"They're coming," one lad said.

"Soon," agreed another.

"We'll be ready," said a third.

Dollard spoke last. "We'll die with our hair on," he said.

That morning, they did not die. They fought hard. The Iroquois tried to kill them from the safety of the tree line, firing arrows and spears and shot. Occasionally, even a tomahawk came sailing through the air. The Iroquois had reverted to their favourite tactic, a war of attrition, and the garrison boys knew then that they'd have to endure days of battle. They began to suffer their first casualties, but even the wounded fought on.

At all hours of the day, at all times of night, the attacks came. Sometimes, the skirmishes were meant to upset their sleep, while at other times they were full-on assaults. The Iroquois were rolling boulders closer to the fort, allowing them to aim their arrows and fire their Dutch rifles from closer range. The French were exhausted, scared and rationing food, and still they fought on and continued to kill Iroquois.

They suffered their first death.

A youth named Claude took an arrow through a lung, and for an hour he squirmed in anguish. They cooled his brow, but his torment only increased the closer he came to death. Lads wept at the moment that he expired, then resumed their places behind rocks.

The next day brought another death. A soldier put his head up and was shot through the temple.

Two days later, a third comrade fell. They didn't know how. Six of them were sitting around their little campfire eating a ration of beans when he suddenly gagged and moaned, blood streaming from his neck. In four hours, he was gone. Somehow, a stray chunk of metal shot had ricocheted through an imperceptible channel in their defences. That bad luck demoralized everyone.

Seven days had passed. Exhausted, deprived and injured, the French awaited the final assault. They knew it was coming. They had tried to preserve their shot, but not much was left. Where were the *coureurs de bois*? Radisson and Groseilliers would be voyaging with seasoned Indian fighters and Huron and Cree loyal to them. Every day must be bringing them closer, but could they not arrive sooner? Perhaps they were not coming at all, and their battle was not only hopeless but without purpose as well.

The next full raid also came at dawn. Dollard repeated the phrase that had energized them and become their secret battle cry.

"We'll die with our hair on!" he shouted, as the next fight commenced.

The other riflemen shouted back, "Hair on!"

The refrain rang along the ramparts.

"Hair on!"

"We'll die with our hair on!"

They did, that day—all but one. In the dawn's false light, the attack was ferocious and sustained and unrelenting. Iroquois died in numbers, but the soldiers could not load their rifles quickly enough, and the fort was overrun. Iroquois vaulting the ramparts impaled themselves on the makeshift spears, but the next men to come over landed safely upon their bodies, and with their flailing tomahawks and slashing knives and superior numbers, they battled the twelve remaining French and four Huron, and one by one the sixteen fell.

Adam Dollard des Ormeaux was not the last to die, but he fought as fiercely as any, his sword ripping through the flesh of the Iroquois around him even as his hunting knife repelled the hands and knives of others. He died with his hair intact, a tomahawk shattering his breastbone and blasting his heart apart. Only after he fell was his hair removed by the Iroquois he had wounded.

The youngest among them hid amid a clutch of boulders and stabbed at the hands reaching in to grab him. Finally, an Indian stuck a rifle into his cubbyhole and shot him through the rectum. Wriggling in his great torment, he was pulled from his lair and was the only one among them to be scalped alive, the knife itching across the top of his head, his spirit rising in the torment of his ordeal, before he fell silent, his skull cracked open by a tomahawk, the last to die.

As light came up over the trees, Iroquois whooped and cried out in the glory of their victory, yet only for a few moments. Someone noticed the eyes and expression of Nomotigneega. He was looking around at the Iroquois dead, lumped like driftwood and castaway boulders upon the beach. A stunning array of Iroquois lay dead, including Donaagatai, a skilled fighter who had commenced the battle as the war chief and had been one of the most promising young leaders. Inside the fort, Iroquois formed a floor of dead, their lives lost in hand-to-hand combat. Everyone still alive looked around them and went quiet. Each man saw the same sight. So many of their brothers dead, or beseeching to be killed, delivered from their agonies. Even those who remained standing began to notice, as the fury of war eased in their bloodstreams, that they also bled.

The Iroquois gazed around the pile of rocks and trees that had formed the fort. The white men who lay dead were so few. They looked like sleeping adolescents, but with bloodied heads. The chief kept looking and looking, trying to understand this. He could not believe that he could count only sixteen. Sixteen young men and four Huron had killed scores of warriors.

Inland, they found a cavern they could hurl their dead down. They covered the grave with stones and tree limbs to protect the bodies from the humiliation of animals. They let the French lie where they had fallen, for the carrion. Then they paddled on and veered onto a tributary south, homeward bound, for they'd done enough fighting for a season.

The sun rose and set and rose again, and Groseilliers and Radisson and their substantial party of *coureurs de bois* and Indians passed by. They came across the dead Frenchmen. They did not see the masses of Indian dead, but noticed the blood upon the stones. They did not know what the lads had been doing in that place, what they could have been thinking.

"Idiots," Radisson murmured.

"Maybe," Des Gros acknowledged. "But if they weren't lying here, dead, we'd be fighting Iroquois now. We'd be lying here dead soon enough."

They had to move on as a delay could imperil their lives. A party from Ville-Marie could be sent back later, with priests, to either bury the dead or transport the bodies home to the colony. They had no room in their canoes for brave dead young men and no time to bury them. Instead, they adjusted the bodies into respectful rows upon the ground and covered their heads to preserve their dignity awhile.

Over their bodies, Groseilliers would stammer a prayer remembered from his days as a Jesuit servant.

Radisson overturned the body of Adam Dollard des Ormeaux to drag it away. He discovered, under the lad's belly, the Cartier Dagger. He recognized it, for he had seen it in the hands of Maisonneuve, though he had never been allowed to touch the artifact. He wondered what circumstance had brought the knife here, if these few weren't merely thieves. But no, they had fought too hard to be thieves. They had not been hacked up, a sign of their vanquishers' respect. He tucked the knife inside his deerskin jacket and dragged the fallen hero off.

The contingent of one hundred canoes then completed its portage and paddled safely on towards Fort Perilous.

Farther away, a runner located his Iroquois friends on the Richelieu River. He told of a great battle that would still be raging. During his trip, the fight had only grown in the mind of the runner, and the story he told was one of dreadful conditions and stark surprise. Hearing these facts, the chief decided to countermand the attack on Montreal, for he feared that their foray had been revealed, that an ambush awaited him as well, and he returned his forces to Lake Champlain.

Through misfortune, then accident, folly and bravery, the colony once again was spared.

†††

Passing by Ville-Marie, the *coureurs de bois* were celebrated for their return and for the astonishing array of furs they were carrying. Then they told their sad news. Missing the young soldiers, the colonists had prepared themselves for such a report, yet they were much aggrieved. Maisonneuve pressed Radisson to tell him what he had seen, and the young man repeatedly told a tale of courage and much blood upon the stones. The Iroquois, Groseilliers had emphasized, were no longer on the river, and for that he believed they had the dead Frenchmen to thank.

Radisson kept the Cartier Dagger to himself. He intended to return it, but only if he and his partner were properly paid for their furs. If they were robbed blind, like the last time, he would keep the knife as his reward.

At Quebec, the sounds of one hundred cannon greeted the arrival of the hundred canoes, a grand sight. The people cheered, and a ship on the verge of returning empty to France delayed its departure. The sale in furs was brisk, and the woodsmen expected a handsome payout. They were enjoying a well-deserved beer in a local tavern, waiting for the final negotiation, when the new governor arrived with armed guards and asked to speak to Groseilliers.

Pierre de Voyer d'Argenson congratulated him on his success, and spoke of the significant contribution he'd made to New France.

"Thank you, Your Excellency."

"Nevertheless, Groseilliers, you did not seek permission to embark upon this expedition. You were trapping without a license. Sir, you are under arrest."

Radisson had to be restrained by friends as his partner was dragged off. After the shock, he was less surprised when he learned that his furs had been seized and his compensation established as a pittance. The moment Des Gros was released months later, the two men commenced plotting their next expedition. Within the plan, they embedded the seeds of their revenge.

†††

As Maisonneuve journeyed to a meeting with the bishop of Quebec, Laval, ostensibly to be introduced to the newly arrived lieutenant-governor of New France, the Marquis de Tracy, he felt trepidatious. The politics had changed once more, as New France had become a royal province. The news had been welcomed, for now the full participation of the mother country would come to the aid of the struggling communities. This required a further consolidation of power, and the bishop seemed to be holding sway over the new men in charge. Yet Laval and the others were being persistently thwarted in their ambition by the popularity and power of Maisonneuve. Those at Ville-Marie seemed to rule themselves with a sense of divine autonomy, as though to inflict a decision upon them demanded the consent of Maisonneuve, the pope, the king and God Himself. The trinity formed by the pope, the king, and God he could do nothing about, but Maisonneuve was a problem Bishop Laval might presume to master, and now he believed he had found the occasion.

Laval spoke to him over brandy. "In 1652, you travelled back to France."

Maisonneuve nodded, remembering those days. The conversation with the new authority was going well, he thought. The new man, Tracy, was keen to understand the colony's history. Laval and Maisonneuve were filling him in. "Desperate years. We needed fresh and able recruits or we might have succumbed."

"An ambitious undertaking. How did you finance that journey, I wonder?" Laval inquired.

An innocent question. "More than a dozen years ago now, Your Excellency."

"Ah," the bishop remarked, "may I refresh your brandy?"

Maisonneuve smiled, although he was suddenly feeling leery. His senses were alert as he held out his glass for a refill.

After he had poured the glass and returned to his seat, Laval eyed him closely. "You took twenty thousand livres from the hospital purse, did you not? I've checked the records. Why deny it?"

Maisonneuve finally deduced that the conversation was a trap. He looked first at Tracy, to gauge his reaction, and deduced that the man had been expecting the question. "Your Grace, Madame de Bullion created the fund. Jeanne Mance and myself entered into an agreement to borrow the money against the promise of land. She approved the transaction."

"Paul," Laval said, although they did not know one another well enough for him to address his guest by his Christian name, "you embezzled twenty thousand livres for your own purposes, for your enrichment, so that you could spend two years indulging yourself back in France. I understand. A life of hardship here. What could it hurt to eat and drink lavishly and comport yourself with the ladies?"

"Meanwhile," Tracy added, "the colony at Montreal struggled on in near-starvation. Now that I am lieutenant-governor of New France, it is my duty to call you to account."

"This is preposterous!" Maisonneuve forgot himself and jumped to his feet. "Madame de Bullion will attest to the agreement! As will Jeanne Mance! We did not keep records because our benefactor insisted on anonymity—"

"Enough with these false stories!" Tracy stormed back at him, while Bishop Laval sipped his brandy. "You stole the money. You ought to confess for the sake of your own immortal soul! In any case, pending the judgment of God, the people shall be informed and you shall be removed from office. I have explained the circumstances to the king and he agrees. You are to be recalled to France."

"I will not go!"

"You are a subject of your king, sir. You will follow his commands!"

The two men glared at one another.

"Or do I command my guards to ship you back in chains?" Tracy asked him.

"You pompous ass!" Maisonneuve declared. He'd been outmanoeuvred for the moment. "I'll go to France. But I will clear my name. And I will return."

He did not know that of these three vows, he'd manage only the first— that he would die, still trying to clear his name, in a country he now despised, dreaming of his island home on the St. Lawrence among the trees and the Iroquois.

"A ship departs in three days for St. Malo," Laval informed him. "You shall be a passenger on it. I bid you *adieu*. I wish you a *bon voyage*, Paul de Cho- medey, Sieur de Maisonneuve."

Three days. He would never see Montreal again.

CHAPTER 11

1955

AN ESPECIALLY TRYING DAY, THANKS TO AN ILL-TIMED CONFLU-
ence of professional and domestic upsets, had failed to guide Detective Gaston Fleury towards much-needed restful slumber. August's sweltering temperatures and close humidity didn't help. Collapsed on his bed, under the warm breeze of a creaky fan, he lay there, helpless, tossing, contorted. Sweat slickened his skin.

Somehow, his wife was managing to ignore the heat. While she was lost to the world beside him, Fleury had been out of bed three times to attend to his son, Guy. The boy's tonsils had been extracted and, home from the hospital just that afternoon, he was playing upon parental sympathy. As the clock slipped past 3 A.M., the policeman acknowledged that he would not be sleeping anytime soon. He'd be going to work in a surly mood, again, coaxed upright by caffeine. He propped himself higher on the pillows, partially sitting, to await morning and another day of blistering sun. In deference to the heat wave, he lay in the nude, on top of the sheets, his legs apart, even his fingers splayed to catch every possible particle of cooler air.

"The humidity," Montrealers were found of saying. "It's the humidity." Only later would he recall that he had heard a few telltale nocturnal sounds. A car's motor idling. A door being opened, then slammed. Footsteps hurrying along the sidewalk in one direction, then hurrying back. Tire squeals. In the city, such noises were irritating but commonplace, and had registered neither alarm nor curiosity in the tetchy detective from Policy.

The bomb blast, though, shot him out of bed.

He fell back as quickly, disoriented and stunned. Fleury was sliding off the damp sheets as the walls continued to convulse and the windows rattled. He braced himself to keep from catapulting onto the floor, and his wife glommed onto his wrist, awakening in a panic.

From his room, his son's wail flared up.

He didn't bother with clothes as he fled to the balcony to see what on earth had occurred. Wide open to the air, the door had admitted the full concussive blast. That noise. The impact. Had an apartment blown up? A gas leak?

Parked on the sidewalk two doors down, a vehicle had had its windows blown out, and its interior was now engulfed in flames. As bombs go, this had probably been a small one, although he'd never experienced a blast before. Glass littered the street and sidewalk, reflecting firelight, and he heard the fission of the blaze and worried that the gas tank would be next. He shouted to an old lady on her balcony fifteen feet from the car, "Go back! The gas tank!" She retreated instantly, either heeding his warning or propelled by the sight of a nude, skinny man madly exhorting her to flee. Fleury returned inside to put on clothes, then stopped, rushing back out again. He was looking at the car afire while a different neighbour on the next balcony stubbornly glared at his naked form.

A thought, bursting from the back of his mind, proved true—the burning car belonged to him. That was his Chevrolet! Lillian, his wife, having the presence of mind to first throw on a robe, joined him outside.

"It's our car," he said, still shocked. "They blew it up."

"Who's they?" she asked, stunned also. He seemed to know. "Why?"

Their son was calling for his dad. Both parents reacted and returned indoors, but Fleury headed straight for the phone. He put a call through to Armand Touton, captain of the Night Patrol.

"They blew up my car!" he shouted the moment the man answered.

Behind him, sheltering her son's head against her thigh, his wife demanded again, angrily this time, "Who's 'they'?"

"Who's this?" asked the brusque voice at the other end of the line.

"Captain Touton! It's me! Gaston!"

Perhaps his excited expression had made his voice unrecognizable.

"Gaston who?" Touton asked.

"Fleury! Gaston Fleury! From Policy! Captain, it's me!"

"Somebody blew up your car?" Touton asked.

"My Bel Air! It's on fire! I need the fire department! Send the Night Patrol!"

Touton took charge then, jotting down the particulars and telling him to settle down and stay away from the windows.

"Why?" Fleury inquired.

"In case someone's trying to kill you."

Fleury dropped the phone and ran out to the balcony to usher his wife and child inside, for they'd wandered out to survey the commotion. He closed the door and heaved the drapes across it and the windows. Then he returned to the phone and heard Touton calling his name.

"I'm back," he said. "I'm here."

"Don't do that to me again," Touton told him, irritated that he had suddenly vanished from the line. "Now stay put and stay calm. I'll be right over."

Fleury felt the concussive surge of a second blast.

"What was that?" Touton demanded.

"The gas tank?" Fleury suggested.

†††

Upon arriving at the scene, Touton confessed to being perplexed. This sort of thing did not happen. He knew of no organization or criminal who specialized in making bombs. Cops rarely were targeted for serious intimidation or violence.

Everyone knew why.

When cops were challenged in the heat of the moment—fired upon during a bank holdup, or shot at attempting to arrest a fugitive—the department reacted with deadly force. Anyone committing violence against an officer would be tracked down by every other cop, and, if he didn't surrender upon first warning, shot dead.

Everyone understood the rules.

A cop posed for photographers over a slain suspect, a pool of blood seeping into a gutter. "Around here," he said, "we don't tolerate no monkey business."

The comment made Captain Armand Touton wince. If cops tolerated anything, it was monkey business. The comment implied that minor as well as serious infractions would be answered by bullets. Such was the culture of the times. In Montreal, cops aided and abetted the crime syndicates, but when it came to dealing with freelance hoodlums, they meted out their own justice, and the tough guys knew it and accepted it as the code of the streets.

In this environment, that a cop had had his car blown apart established a precedent.

A chilling event.

"What've you been up to?" Touton asked the officer from Policy.

"Nothing!" Fleury objected. He assumed that the captain was questioning his integrity, asking if he'd played a few poker hands with the bad guys and lost. "Just . . . you know."

"What do I know?"

"I've been investigating government cars."

Touton grunted. "I thought you'd given that up months ago."

"I don't quit," Fleury proclaimed.

The captain considered this. "Maybe you're closer to something than you realize. We'll track what you've been doing. Maybe your investigation's made somebody nervous. Federal or provincial?"

"Both. And private—on the side."

"Figures," Touton grunted. "Why make it easy on ourselves? How's your family doing?"

Fleury took a deep breath. "Lillian started out okay. Now she's getting scared. My son started out scared, but now he's just cranky."

The captain nodded. "See to them. We'll let the so-called experts go to work, but don't expect much. Nobody knows nothing about bombers. This is something new. Something new is always difficult to trace."

Fleury's wife appeared on the front stoop. "Captain? Telephone."

He took the call inside and a moment later was striding quickly out of the apartment, taking the stairs in awkward bounds.

"What's wrong?" Fleury called to him from his balcony.

"They went after my house, too!"

"Who did?" Fleury's wife wanted to know as Touton's car raced off.

†††

Cruisers had made it to Armand Touton's flat ahead of him, and his heart beat high in his throat as he charged up the stairs. His wife was in the kitchen, dressed in a robe, surrounded by perspiring uniformed officers.

"Marie-Céleste!" Smiling up at him, she made a motion Touton misinterpreted. He thought she was going to faint, when in fact she was seeking his kiss. "My God! Easy! Are you all right?"

"I'm fine, Armand. A little shaken."

"Is she all right?" he demanded to know of the officers.

They all answered at once, saying that his wife was unhurt. Finally, Marie-Céleste cupped his cheek to command his attention and told him, "Armand. I'm fine. I'm not hurt at all. Nobody's been hurt. There's no damage."

Getting that one point straight, he was finally able to ask, "What happened?"

Vandals had smeared black paint across the front door to the triplex that contained his flat, then they'd pounded on the door and rung the bell until Marie-Céleste had awakened. The culprits ran off the moment she'd turned on the lights. She had called the police—Armand, at first, but he hadn't been in. The first cops arriving on the scene were the ones to discover the artwork.

"Did they write any words? Any threats?" He was hoping that the act had been random—a bunch of kids, impatient for Halloween. He was hoping that the vandalism was unrelated to Fleury's burnt-out Chevy.

"Sir, not really," the senior of the uniforms in the kitchen said, "but there is something I want to show you."

Touton followed him outside. Streetlights illuminated the white steel door well enough, but an officer passed the detective a flashlight. Not a great deal of time or imagination had been deployed to create the mess. Black paint only, arbitrarily slapped on with a three-inch brush. Nothing could be discerned from the design except to assume that there was no design.

"Look here," the officer said. In his distracted state of mind, Touton couldn't put his finger on what was unusual about the man. He was grey-haired, yet not old. Around forty, in decent physical shape. Touton's initial impression told him he was probably a father and an honourable guy. As the man pointed to a spot on the door, he noticed the man's wedding band, perhaps because he didn't know what else he was meant to be observing. Then he noticed the spot being indicated. Small enough to be barely discernible, probably etched by a stick dipped in paint—a swastika.

Not for another moment would Touton think the act had been happenstance. This was indeed an attack directed upon his home.

"Thanks," he murmured to the cop.

"Sure thing."

Touton comprehended at that moment the odd aspect to the cop that he had missed: he was English. Among older cops, he knew a few detectives who were English, but he didn't know any English cops who made a career on the beat.

He went back inside, and this time wrapped his wife in his arms and held her tightly. He dismissed the other officers from inside the premises and ordered two cars to patrol the neighbourhood to see what, if anything, moved. Touton assigned the senior English patrolman to guard his home until the end of his shift and commanded other officers to report back to their duty sergeant.

"You're going back to work?" Marie-Céleste asked him once they were alone. She thought that he might make an exception on this one night.

He told her about Detective Fleury. "We got off lucky."

"You were at work. Your car wasn't here. That's why we were luckier."

"I have to stay on top of things. The homes of cops are being attacked. We can't have that."

"For sure. Go, Armand. I'll see you in the morning."

She was trying to be agreeable, but her lack of enthusiasm for his departure remained apparent.

"I'll tuck you in," he said. "Stay awhile. Until you sleep."

"In this heat? After all this? I won't be sleeping. I certainly don't need tucking in. I'll be lying on top of the sheets."

Despite her protest, he saw her to bed, and kissed her good night before returning to work. The kiss was lovely. He wanted to stay.

†††

In a drearier part of town, where hookers knelt to do their business in alleys next to pissing drunks, Detective Andrew Sloan was having to deal with a grisly mess. A murder victim had not died easily, having put up a fight. Judging by the bloodied Louisville Slugger left behind at the scene, a baseball bat had been the principal murder weapon, although punctures along the spine and through the man's hand suggested that a thin spike had also been deployed—probably an ice pick. Electrical refrigeration was rapidly becoming universal, yet ice was still used in thousands of homes. The ice pick remained a common household utensil on the tougher streets.

"Know him well?" Sloan asked the beat cop, Lajolie, a surly character with a dark reputation. He usually came in from his shifts with his knuckles bloodied. He liked it that way, relished getting physical with garbage scroungers and young toughs. He wasn't into talking to the riffraff much, preferring instead to shove guys into a wall to get them moving. Nobody suggested that he wasn't a ballsy scraper, somebody to have on your side if negotiations got feisty. But some bad talk went on around him, that he preferred to work the Main because he made the whores pay a toll in kind. Others suggested that he seemed to spend more money than the average beat cop earned. So far, the department had let it go.

Lajolie shrugged. He didn't like this detective. Sloan worked on the Night Patrol, and those guys were serious about cleaning up the city. A wacko squad. The way Lajolie looked at it, a dirty city was good for business. Besides, nobody trusted Armand Touton, the head of that bunch. He was a reformer, and reformers were suspected of selling their own kin down the St. Lawrence River.

The joke that went around the locker room suggested that the reformers even sold out their own, but at a discount.

"Don't know him?" Sloan persisted. He couldn't accept that Lajolie wasn't on a first-name basis with everyone down here.

"I know him a bit. Used to be a doorman at the Copa. Doorman—call it what you want. Different name, same shit. He's a leg-breaker. He's got a record, but something's odd in his story. In some strange way, it's like he's connected to the Church. Some people called him 'The Bishop.' He hasn't caused any trouble in a while that we know about, but he hangs out with the same guys we spot around polling booths at election time. If he was voting, he wasn't doing it only once."

"He's got a name?"

"Michel Vimont."

"Seen him around lately?" Sloan asked.

"Not so much. One time. Outside some club. Leaning on a car. Some limo. I told him not to scratch the paint. He laughed. Said it was his new profession."

"What profession?"

"Driver. Chauffeur. Different name, same job, you know what I mean?"

This time, Sloan wasn't sure. "What do you mean?"

"Once a thug, always a thug. 'Chauffeur,' it's another word for body-guard . . . an arm-breaker."

Sloan got it. "Who for?"

Lajolie shook his head. "Never waited around for the fat-ass to come out. Assholes who can't drive their own cars, they're all the same to me."

"The limo . . . was it black?"

Lajolie thought the question was stupid. What did it matter? "Yeah. Black. Think so. Probably black. Just don't bet the paycheque on that, okay?"

Sloan nudged his fedora higher on his head. "Okay," he said. "Ask around. Work your contacts on the street. I'd like to know who his boss was. Keep on it until you find out."

"You bet."

The alley was a good place for muggings and murder. Garbage cans rattled around at night, fed by the greasy-spoon restaurants or knocked over by drunks. Roughhouse noise rarely alerted anyone. He'd canvass the neighbour-hood, but finding a witness did not look promising. As well, the incident had occurred around closing time—the blood on the pavement hadn't fully coagulated—so the street had been noisy, the pedestrians drunk—a good time for a bloody brawl to the death.

Sloan walked over to a second uniform—Lajolie's partner for the night, a rookie by the name of Leduc who was filling in for the regular guy on his summer vacation. Just that short walk was messy, the slime of rotten vegetables underfoot and the stink of piss and vomit and cat spray. Old newsprint was stuck to the pavement, pressed down under organic compost that may have included human excrement as well as dog feces.

"Who the hell found the body way back here?"

"Blow-job Granny. We let her go."

"Who?"

"She blows old guys for draft beer. Lajolie told me that anyway. She's old. Seventy, maybe. Looks a hundred and two. Her johns must be totally smashed."

"So she took some guy back here?"

"That's the story. She had no reason to lie."

"You let her go before she talked to a detective?"

"Lajolie says she won't go far. She never does. She's real loony, Detective. And a little disgusting. We didn't exactly want her around."

"What about the guy she was with?"

"Lost his cookies and beat it. Lajolie paid Granny a buck for giving us a call."

"Okay. Is there a telephone around some place?"

Over the phone, Sloan was informed that his boss wasn't available, that he'd gone off on a pursuit of his own. He then asked to have the victim's record run down. "Michel Vimont, that's the name." He also wanted to know who the coroner was going to be, which was not usually his business, and when he wasn't satisfied with the answer he requested a replacement.

"A fight on the Main got out of hand—what's the big deal?" the dispatcher asked him.

Probably it was no big deal, he replied, but he had a hunch. He wanted a more experienced coroner. Sloan got his wish. He then asked to have a message delivered to Touton's desk, a question: "Interested in a dead chauffeur?"

"That's all it says?" the dispatcher asked, his curiosity piqued.

"Just say that. I'm going to see the body gets into the morgue truck, then beat it home. I'm bushed. Put the stiff's rap sheet on my desk."

Sometimes it took awhile to sweep a body off a street. The morgue guys were never too swift in the middle of the night. They usually stopped for a drink along the way. A coroner had to be fetched out of bed, and that could require more than one call to make sure he'd stayed awake. Then he might drop himself off at a strip club first, to acquire a taste for the evening air and to make the outing more worth his while. Dawn had arisen before Sloan finally departed the scene, and the soft light of morning had not improved the alley's disposition. If anything, the space seemed to stink more once the detritus of city waste had become fully visible.

†††

Light of day sprinkled gasoline on the fire of Armand Touton's rage. By the time the Night Patrol convened the following evening, his emotions were in an uproar. His commentary to his fellow officers lacked his usual insouciance.

"If these motherfucks think they can . . . Mother of God, they better shit in their own soup . . . *maudit câlice* . . . we're going to vomit down their throats and tape their mouths shut . . . make them blow puke out their nostrils, these fucks!"

He'd had a few drinks, which didn't help, but a day of dwelling on the audacity of punks slathering paint on his stoop and awakening his wife from her slumber, not to mention blowing up Fleury's Chevy, had him in a lather.

"Dynamite, that's the word. Three sticks—three too many! I want to know where those sticks came from. Lean on every shit-eating dung hole in this town. I want to know where those sticks came from, who bought them off who for how much, and I want to know *exactly* how much change the motherfuck got back! I want to know every fucking detail about that transaction. This city is not going to rest until it comes across with that information. You got that? Does everybody in this room understand what we're doing tonight?"

No one did. None of them had shaken down a city looking for information about dynamite, but no one would confess to their ignorance either, not with their leader in that mood.

"They made a mistake, the shit-eating skunks," Touton confided in a quieter, intense voice. "*Two* mistakes, if you want to know the truth. They painted a swastika on my door, and that tells me they think they can hold my military career in disrepute. Do you understand what I'm saying? If they think they can fuck with me, they'll shit their pants before I'm done with them! Second, they blew up Gaston Fleury's Chevrolet. His fucking Bel Air. Know why that's a mistake? Because it pins the two events together. It lets me know that they believe they can shit on my porch. They can't shit on my porch! They can't mess with my officers! Not with any one of you! They want to scare our *wives*? I'll scare the dicks right off their balls! They want to mess with a policeman's property? They'll wish they were sleeping on a cot in Siberia before we're done. You got me?" He scanned the roomful of still, scarcely breathing officers, daring any one of them to twitch. Then he spoke in a deep, growly voice. "Who sells dynamite in this town? Find that out for me. Who steals it? Who offers it up for sale? Who buys it? Pull out fingernails if you have to, but find that out." After scowling over his crew, he finished by asking, "Any questions?"

Everyone had questions, but no one dared voice them, the exception being Detective Andrew Sloan, who raised his hand slowly.

"What?" Touton snarled at him.

The others in the room held their breath. They hadn't wanted any questions. They wanted to get on the job, not because they were particularly enthusiastic about getting started, but because they wanted out from under the furious eyes of their leader. They immediately wished that Sloan had not raised his hand, and when he spoke off topic, the room, as one, wanted to shoot him.

"I had a murder last night," he stated.

Touton glowered at him. "Deal with it. We got more important shit to scoop right now."

"You didn't get my message? This could be important in other ways."

"Deal with it, I said! Don't bother me with your little problems off the street!"

Sloan was surprisingly petulant. "Nobody got hurt," he murmured.

"What?" Touton fired back at him. "What did you say?"

"I've got a chauffeur shot dead in an alley. You've got paint on your doorknob. I say my case is more important."

Both men could feel the entire room silently groaning. Historically, Sloan was the one man willing to stand up to Armand Touton anytime the captain got wild. Touton had noticed the trait himself, and for that reason alone he valued his colleague, even though he made life difficult for him from time to time.

"Investigate," Touton hammered back at him. "Report. Don't bother me. You got that? Is that too much to ask? If it's too much to ask, I can have you transferred to bicycle theft. I'm sure they could use your expertise."

Warily, a few detectives chuckled. When Touton wanted to ridicule a member of his squad, he always used the same threat, which apparently he found amusing. They felt the need to laugh along.

"Some detective pissed somebody off," Sloan objected, "so they blew up his car when he wasn't in it. They knew he wasn't in it. The car was empty, sitting by the curb in the middle of the night. It's a big deal—I agree with you on that, it is a really big deal, but I'm just saying—"

"I don't really care what you're just saying—"

"No kidding. I think that's my point."

"Sloan."

"What?" the detective asked.

"My office," the captain replied. "Now."

"Fine."

That's what he wanted anyway. A chance to have it out with Touton, and if that meant going toe to toe in private, so be it. Sloan followed about ten strides behind his boss as the captain departed the room and headed down the hall. The others in the room, finally free to broach their duties, were relieved, and a few were delighted that Touton had caught a sacrificial minnow to munch upon.

†††

Back in his office, Touton was surprisingly conciliatory.

"What's your problem?" he asked Sloan, having moderated his voice.

"You're not seeing the forest for the trees," Sloan said. Then he toned himself down also, adding, "As I see it."

"So you like this chauffeur to be the limo driver the night the coroner was killed? The night Roger Clément went down?"

"He's a punk limo driver. He's dead. That's all I know. But that's enough to check him out, don't you think? That's all I'm saying."

Touton sat down. "You are aware that we're not officially investigating that case? Speaking about it out loud before the entire squad doesn't help us at all. You're aware of that, right?"

If he'd heard that, he'd forgotten. "Sorry," Sloan said.

"So what's the bee in your bonnet?"

Sloan had thought that this was going to be a tougher point to get across to his superior officer, and he wanted now to deliver his opinion with the appropriate emphasis. He realized that he might actually have preferred the opportunity to sting the captain in a verbal fight, something that might have given his point a heightened credibility. Unfortunately, he would have to stake out his position without the lustre of passionate engagement.

"Everybody's going on about the car-bombing and the paint job on your door last night. Okay, I'll concede that those are nasty things. But why would anyone do that? That's what I keep asking myself. If the goal was intimidation, that's one thing, but if we don't actually know who did it, how is anyone being intimidated? Just because your door—"

"This is not about my door," Touton said tersely. "This is about my wife being terrified."

Sloan backtracked a little. He would have to compromise his attitude. "I understand. That's bad, that people would target a man's wife like that." He breathed in deeply. "Armand. I have a theory, all right? Let me just spit it out."

Touton nodded to give him at least slight encouragement.

"Everybody's going on about those events, but maybe that's the idea. Those things were distractions, maybe. If so, the bad guys sure as hell succeeded in what they're doing—"

"Distractions?"

Sloan could feel Touton's anger rising again. "Let's say somebody wanted to kill another man, that that killing was involved in a case you were working on. The killers knew you'd take an interest and they wouldn't want that. Absolutely, they would not want that. So they give you something else to think about instead, and that way they get to walk away from a murder without you ever taking notice."

Touton leaned back in his chair. He was tired, fuelled by caffeine and alcohol, but what his detective was saying made sense. He leaned forward, checked information off a sheet, and wrote down an address for Sloan like a physician jotting a prescription. He tore the sheet off his pad.

Sloan accepted the paper and read it. "Who's Carole Clément?"

"Roger's wife," Touton explained. "She called today. She was listening to the radio."

"And . . . ?"

"She heard your dead man's name. She wants to talk about him. We'll go see her together, all right? Keep it quiet. Meet me there, ten-thirty. I might be late."

Sloan stood up. For a while that evening, he thought his boss was off his rocker. Now he realized that he was a step ahead of him, again. If the affairs of the previous evening were indeed a ploy, whether by accident or design, Touton had made it look as though he'd swallowed the bait whole. The performance in the squad room had been for show. Sloan understood that he had nearly screwed it up.

"Sloanie, take a meandering route to get there."

"I will," the detective promised. "I'll be—what's the word?—circumspect." He paused on his way out. "So getting everybody to hunt down dynamite, that's about the Sun Life as well, right? Or Fleury's car *and* the Sun Life."

Touton grunted, stood also, and the men went their separate ways.

†††

Touton headed off on a quest for different quarry. He'd arranged an evening rendezvous with a Montreal psychiatrist, one who had inscribed his name on the infamous petition requesting sanctuary for a French war criminal. The man's name was Camille Laurin. Carole Clément had labelled him as a man who hated strikes, and given that her husband had disrupted a few picket lines in his day, the possibility lingered that the two of them might have had recent contact.

The meeting was set up for the working-class north end of the city, close to where the physician conducted a private practice. Touton had argued for the odd hour as he was a late-night detective, and the doctor had grudgingly agreed. At the restaurant door, the captain slipped off his hat and checked his watch: 8:46 P.M. Civilized.

Surprisingly, the doctor had ordered a meal, so the hour could not have been disorienting for him, either. His pasta arrived at the same time Touton did, and the policeman asked the waitress for a coffee. Cops on the night shift congenially joked with one another that they bled caffeine, to pour them a cup of joe if they ever got shot—that way, they'd never bleed out. Close in age, the two men sat across from one another in a high-backed, red vinyl booth.

"The famous captain," Dr. Laurin said, his voice annoyingly quiet, restrained. His handshake felt like holding a fillet of halibut. "I salute your achievements, sir."

"Thanks, Doc. I'm afraid I don't know about your work. I can't—what's the word?—reciprocate."

"I maintain a modest practice—nothing fancy. How may I help you?"

Touton didn't say so, but the question was a particularly good one. In truth, he had no idea.

The doctor had a way of lifting his chin that made him appear to be gazing down his nose. His hair was wavy and black, which emphasized the full height of a broad, impressive forehead. His eyes were unusually small.

"I guess my question is . . . psychological? Is that the word?"

"Psychological, yes." Laurin seemed pleased, and reached for his cigarettes. Judging by the ashtray off to the side, already filling up, he was a chain-smoker. Nicotine stains were noticeable on the fingers of his right hand, so this smoke was neither a sudden nor nervous reaction. "Depending on the question, of course. Which is?" His smile was thin, and once the cigarette was lit his face remained implacable behind a veil of smoke.

Shifting around in his seat, as though the discussion had already ascended above his head, Touton suggested, "It's the psychology I'm wondering about, Doctor—the way the mind works. Why are some people, do you think, left wingers, while others are right wingers? Psychologically speaking, I mean."

In taverns across the city, drinkers with draft glasses barricaded in front of them might assume he was talking hockey. But Laurin knew what he meant.

"Why do some people live in the real world, while others dwell in a land of fantasy, dreaming utopian dreams? Is that what you really mean by your question? . . . A big issue, Captain. I'd be interested to learn how it pertains to police work." He chose to stare high to his right, rather than upon his visitor. "Offhand, the answer is likely to be different in every case. But we can acknowledge that some minds have a predisposition to grasp the potential of the individual, the potential for the race, while other minds, regrettably, prefer to whine about insignificant matters." His eyes met Touton's again. "The universe of the left is based upon materialism. It's a Marxist tenet. The chaos of the imagination, the divine promise of human experience, exquisite achievements of art, man's cherished divinity . . . all these matters are lost on the left, which is primarily concerned with wages and with what can be acquired without being earned. The left wants to know what can be picked from the pockets of the enterprising and the visionary—then wasted."

Touton nodded, as though in agreement. "I see. Do they—the unionists, let's say—have a differing opinion? What would they say about you?"

"Does somebody care?" The restaurant lighting was bright, harsh. Along the counter, pies and cakes that might tempt a patron were on display, the shiny plates reflecting light repeated in a mirror running along one wall.

"If they know your politics—I have no idea of that myself. But if the unionists discussed your politics, how would they describe you, as a person, as a thinker?"

"As some kind of asshole, no doubt." The doctor let the cigarette waft while he returned to his meal. Apparently, he was revelling in the conversation. "They see matters in shades of greed. Wealth must be divvied up, split into such tiny morsels that nothing is accomplished but the feeding of church mice for a minute or two while the elites are impoverished. Without compensation, the elites recoil from their enterprises—we have economic ruin, the collapse of social, economic and political structure. Justice is flummoxed. Chaos or tyranny result, and between the two, the masses inevitably choose tyranny. They'd rather be flogged than enlightened." Laurin sipped his own steaming coffee, looking at his interrogator over the cup. "You smile, you're amused, but history proves my opinion."

Touton tempered his smile, regretting that he had given himself away.

"Yet I draw the rebuke of the left," Dr. Laurin forged on, "who assume that I'm the tyrant for having an opinion, that I'm the one responsible for their measly wages, when all logic suggests that they are the cause of their own situation. You see, sir, I *presume* to express my opinion. I *presume* to have one. I do not allow my opinions to be subservient to the mob. I am not interested in *public* opinion. I am interested in *thoughtful, reasoned, informed* opinion, while the left, I'm afraid, detests both thought *and* reason. The left views thoughtful reason, or reasonable thought, as tyrannical, because its own so-called *intellectualism* cannot measure up alongside. What we saw a while ago, during the Richard riot—*that* constituted an expression of public opinion, did it not? Was it thoughtful? Reasonable? Of course not. Did it represent the left, the unions, the communists—were they involved? Were they enjoying themselves? Of course they were. You'd have to be an idiot not to agree, and the left, if I may say so, is largely populated by idiots."

"I don't know too many intellectuals myself. I don't run in those circles."

Laurin shrugged, as though to indicate that that was apparent.

"Pierre Elliott Trudeau . . . I've met him. Do you call him an idiot?"

The doctor's smile was quick, although anything but sincere. "The biggest idiot of the lot," he insisted, but he was also conceding, "who happens to be smart."

Partially amused by the physician's spree, Armand Touton also sensed that Dr. Laurin took licence to speak to him so freely from another source. This was not a typical splurge. The policeman suspected that he had been found out. In saying that he knew nothing of Laurin's politics he had lied, and the doctor had probably caught that. For the moment, the psychiatrist in Dr. Laurin was not doing the talking. The person who usually kept his own counsel while allowing precious little of his thinking to emerge had been displaced by the man who enjoyed competitive discourse. The fellow was doing what he himself had attempted to do as a policeman, which was to bait the other man. This, then, was a game of cat and mouse, and Touton believed that, in Laurin's mind, he was the mouse.

He wasn't altogether sure that he wasn't the mouse in his own mind, either.

The doctor was grinning at him, proud of himself to have turned the tables. The spiel had been intended to irk, to provoke an agitated reaction, and Touton knew that he wasn't far from a sarcastic reply. He nodded, although he guessed that if he could see himself in a mirror, he'd judge his performance to be an implausible portrayal of thoughtfulness. He dared not look, for there was a mirror to his right. Instead, he chose to change the atmosphere in the room.

"Dr. Laurin, some time ago, you signed a petition asking the government to grant asylum to a reputed fascist criminal. Why did you do that?"

Laurin stopped eating and reached for his smoke, and through that haze squinted, keeping his small, black eyes on Touton.

When the man failed to respond further, the policeman exorcized a few inner rages and asked, "I suppose you were expressing a thoughtful, reasoned opinion."

The doctor returned to his food. He concentrated on cutting up his lasagna and chewing behind the drifting smoke. He appeared to be waiting for an apology.

"Are you thinking about it, sir? Or are you choosing not to reply?"

"War," Laurin declared, "stigmatizes societies with prejudice. These days, we're asked to hate the Russians. During the war, we were expected to detest Germans, Italians, Japanese. Should I investigate my Italian gardener? See what he was up to while the battles raged?"

"Count Jacques Dugé de Bernonville never fought a day under his country's flag. He tortured Resistance fighters, slaughtered his own people. A collaborator."

Dr. Laurin was waving a hand in the air as though to dismiss the discussion as irrelevant. "Understand, many things have come out as time goes by. When I signed that petition, every detail was not known. De Bernonville's detractors struck many of us as being hysterical. Some of us, I would say, were influenced by the personality of the man, which was quite jovial. We may not have been in possession of every fact. But allow me to add, neither may every fact have been at the disposal of his detractors. Certain aspects may yet remain concealed."

"Concealed? He was a collaborator."

"I know you suffered in the war, Captain. You're not inclined to be sympathetic. But de Bernonville helped save France from the communists. If you had suffered under the Russians, you might be singing a different tune."

What did Laurin know of war? If he had paid attention to the war at all, it had been from the safe side of the sea. "Would you sign that petition today?" Touton pressed.

"Why? Are you circulating a new one?" Laurin smiled in a way that did not include the other person in his humour.

"No, sir. I am asking you a question."

Laurin shrugged. "A man has a right to keep his opinions to himself. I don't see what any of this has to do with police affairs."

"Do you know the name Roger Clément?"

Another indifferent shrug. "Should I?"

"He was a union buster."

"Good man," Laurin speculated. He moved his plate away and returned his attention to his cigarette and intermittently to his coffee.

"Do you know his wife, Carole Clément?"

"How is this related to police work?"

"Do you?"

"Rings a bell. I think I know several. I'll have to check if she's a patient, and if so, say no more."

"This Carole Clément is not a patient."

"You say, but you don't know that for a fact, do you? Is she another union buster?"

"An organizer in the rag trade. After the death of her husband, I believe she quit. It's hard enough eking out a living with her sewing machine."

"Her husband was a union buster and she was an organizer? There's a happy couple. I wouldn't want to be invited to their dinner table."

"They got along. Do you know Michel Vimont?"

"Who? No."

Touton felt that this answer had been defensive, too quick, probably a lie. Laurin lit a new smoke off the old one.

"What's this about, Captain? Do I look like a man who keeps the company of riffraff? Are you going to mention every criminal on file to see if I can help you somehow? What's the purpose of this?"

"I didn't say he was a criminal," Touton pointed out. He lowered his head a little and touched his forehead lightly. This time, the posture of thoughtfulness was sincere, as he was trying to formulate a question in such a way that Dr. Laurin might feel trapped, feel under investigation without that actually being the case.

"Sir," the detective began, "there's a matter you can clarify for me. In regards to that petition—"

Laurin turned out the palm of his hand holding the cigarette. "Water under the bridge. No one was in possession of all the facts. The war was a long time ago—"

"Your devotion to Marshal Pétain, you mean? Not that long ago, really."

"Excuse me? Devotion? My politics, which are beyond your comprehension, are none of your business, sir."

"You supported the French fascists!"

"I will not respond to insinuations, to unfounded rumours. Do you have a question? Because I have to get going."

"You're not finished your meal."

"Then you may leave first if you have no serious question."

"This is my question, sir."

Laurin inhaled angrily, as through drawing the smoke down to his toes.

"The petition," Touton said, "no matter the circumstances or the times . . . the petition was not present on street corners for anyone to just walk by and sign. Certain people, the authors of that document, knew whom to contact, they knew—*in advance*—who the willing signatories might be. So my question is this, sir—" and Touton paused, both for effect, to keep his opponent in this discussion off balance and anxious, and also to move the talk to a new phase, "—are you, or are you not, a member of the Order of Jacques Cartier?"

The doctor was partially hidden behind his hands, which he held folded in front of his mouth as he smoked, his elbows on the table. He continued squinting in that irritating, insufferable manner, ostensibly from the smoke but also, Touton believed, because he understood that a line was being invisibly carved on the table between them.

"I know nothing of what you speak," he said finally.

Perhaps he was being impetuous, but Touton felt agitated by Laurin's responses. During the war, the man had probably mocked his comrades for fighting the Nazis. He asked the doctor, "Sir, did you murder, or cause to have murdered, Roger Clément?"

"This is a fucking outrage. I once had respect for you."

"Did you murder, or cause to have murdered, Claude Racine, a coroner?"

"Unspeakable, sir. I'm leaving. Our discussion has concluded. Rest assured, a report to your superiors will be filed."

"Did you murder, or cause to have murdered, Michel Vimont?"

Dr. Camille Laurin did not bother with a final reply. He marched straight to the cashier, paid his bill and, without looking back again, departed the restaurant. Touton gestured for another coffee, and he sat there awhile, feeling somewhat ashamed of himself. He checked his watch. He was meeting Detective Sloan soon, at Carole Clément's house. In the meantime, a respite. He needed to pull himself together. Perhaps the events of the night before, the upset at his home, had put him off his oats. Definitely, he needed to calm down. Coffee might not do that for him, but this cup, his second, felt good, and he could not imagine leaving the restaurant without a third.

His activity would now be confirmed and revealed. His specific interest in the Order of Jacques Cartier stood exposed. If graffiti upon his door had been a decoy, meant to detract him from closely examining the death of a chauffeur, then the culprits now knew that the ploy hadn't worked. His outing with Laurin had confirmed that, and calling out the Order by name would only alert, and probably incense, its members. Then again, if official word went through to his adversaries that his attention had not been deflected, that his visit to Laurin had revealed that he was closer to them than they thought, that he knew the name of the Order and what their business might be, and if they made a mistake and reacted, he would know he had found a conduit into their society. An entry point had been forged, through which water might seep, creating rot, through which fear might wick, creating fright and causing the occasional lapse in judgment. Just as well, perhaps, that he made that gaffe. To his enemies it might come across as confidence, even arrogance, sufficient to unnerve their precious, secret group.

Yet, in his heart he knew he'd made a mistake. He'd been unsteady, agitated by the disrespect shown to his own house.

†††

Carole Clément served strong coffee to men who came around at night talking about nefarious matters, even if the air remained warm. In anticipation of their arrival, a pot was perking. Around the dinner hour, a thunderstorm eased the humidity considerably, and everyone felt more comfortable, although the expectation remained that the heat wave would continue and another storm, probably by the following afternoon, would roll across the city. Standing on her back porch, rapt, she watched the day go black and the storm excite itself with thunderclaps and lightning bolts and heat lightning over the rooftops as the whole of the western sky flashed. She missed her man. Missed his company at a time like this, when he could hold her and she'd enjoy the safe tuck of his body, feel calm and happy as another great storm tried to frighten her, failing. Now storms scared her. What if a tree fell on her roof? What if the power failed and she lost the contents of her fridge? What if a window blew out? How would she make ends meet then?

She didn't want to admit it to herself, but the prospect of having two grown men in her house, as opposed to her only daughter or her daughter's friends, comforted her. They were on their way, the coffee was perking— already she felt less alone and a little excited. Then the doorbell rang. She had to slow herself down to keep herself from scampering to the door.

She opened it to Captain Touton. The other detective, Sloan, was coming up the walk.

"How've you been?" Touton asked.

The inherent kindness of the question nudged her to the brink of tears.

"Excuse me," she said, as though distracted by another matter, and fled to her kitchen to compose herself. She returned with a smile on her face, shoulders back, hips swinging as she walked in with the coffee mugs and fixings. "Sorry about that. I'm fine, Captain, how've you been keeping?"

Somehow he knew not to be disinterested. He told her about the affront to his home the night before, that he was doing well except that the heat and humidity were wearing him down. "Thank goodness I work nights, it's cooler. But try to sleep through noon in this heat. Why do we live here? If we're not boiling in the summer, we're freezing our—"

He stopped short, but that made her laugh.

"I was going to say, before I got religion, that in the winter we freeze our butts off."

"You were going to say nuts. And that's only the half of it," Carole agreed.

"How's Anik?" Touton asked.

"She's fine. She has the same complaints. It's too hot, she tells me, about twenty-five times a day. Does that mean she plays in the shade, or has a nap when the sun is highest? Nope. Turns out it's a plea for more ice cream."

Detective Andrew Sloan grew impatient with the drift in the conversation. Just about the last thing he could tolerate was someone chatting about their kids. "You said, Madame Clément, that you knew the man who got killed last night?"

Touton put his coffee down and explained. "Detective Sloan is assigned to the case. He was on the scene last night. He told me that the dead man, this Michel Vimont, has been working as a chauffeur. Is he the man you know?"

"Michel? Yeah, he drives mob bosses around. Roger got him the job."

"So they were friends."

"Roger thought he was a lonely guy. He looked out for him."

Nodding, Sloan took out his notebook. Her answer had given him hope. She seemed to be a knowledgeable witness, someone with an insider's view. "They knew each other as associates, then, would you say?"

Madame Clément looked at the captain, wondering why he was not asking the questions. Resigned, she looked back at the detective. "They were pals."

"You knew him as well."

She curled a ringlet at the back of her neck over a finger. "Michel's been here a few times, maybe two dozen times over the years. He wasn't exactly sociable. Not like a lot of hoods. Roger's friends—his 'associates,' if you want to call them that—they lived to drink and tell stories. Michel would rather go home after his work was done. Roger was one of the few guys who knew him away from work. He invited him over to listen to a game, shoot the breeze, have a beer."

"So you liked him?" Touton assumed.

"Not so much. I could tolerate him. He never caused me any trouble and I can't say that about all of Roger's pals. Michel was too quiet for me. Spooky quiet. Maybe he was shy, maybe he had nothing to say, but all that silence, along with what I think he did for a living—I found him too scary. Sinister, in a way. I wasn't afraid of him, but I always felt . . . I don't know . . . as though he might not be a guy who could set limits. He could break out of that silence one day and go nuts, I had that feeling. If somebody wanted somebody rubbed out, he was the kind of guy who might get asked to do it."

"Was he the kind of guy who'd agree to do it?"

"That I can't say. Roger's loud friends talked tough, they could act up, lose their temper in the blink of an eye. Among those guys, I always knew who had their limits, who would walk away if they were asked to do something they didn't like. Michel . . . I don't know how he'd respond."

The officers nodded. Everything she said amounted to very little, a flurry of hearsay and unsubstantiated opinion, yet it was always good to know what people close to a murder victim thought about him.

"Do you know who he worked for yet?" Carole Clément put to the cops.

Touton looked across at Sloan, who said, "I've got my feelers on the street."

"I'll tell you right now if you want," she said.

"Who?" Touton asked.

Sloan leaned forward, notebook in hand.

The woman looked from one cop to the other. "It's a good thing you're both sitting down," she said.

"Who was it?" Sloan asked.

"The mayor."

"Drapeau?" Touton was too startled to believe it.

"No . . . sorry. The old mayor. Camillien Houde."

Now this was news. Mussolini's champion in North America, and Roger Clément's old bunkmate at the wartime internment camp in New Brunswick, had been the dead man's employer.

"Roger got him the job," she added. "It wasn't full time. A job with some big hood, but anytime the old mayor needed a driver for a special occasion, Michel got sent. I guess the old mayor and the hood had a deal going, or the hood was doing it for old time's sake, some old payoff."

"I don't recall the old mayor speaking up today," Sloan mentioned, "to express his regrets."

Touton smiled slightly. "When's the funeral? He might show up there."

"Monday morning," Carole Clément said. "I'm going. Sometimes it's hard to believe that men like Michel were my husband's cronies, but I should believe it—get it fixed in my head. It's a way to keep his memory in perspective. I'm a mother. I want to honour my husband's memory, for myself, for my daughter, and that means being honest. The bad and the good both. So it's important to go, for me."

The police captain put his coffee aside and rubbed his hands together, leaning forward, both elbows on his knees. He seemed to be chewing something over. "Carole—" he began, then stopped. With his right hand, he scratched his left jaw, as if digging out a thought long buried in his subconscious. His brow was furled in concentration.

She offered a slight nod. She didn't want to say it, but to hear another person speak her name helped wash away long days of loneliness.

"The funeral for this man is bound to be small. A man like that . . . a few old friends, that's it. If I go, or Detective Sloan here, or any police officer, we'll stick out like Rudolph's red nose on Christmas Eve. No matter how we dress, we won't be able to hide ourselves in that small crowd." He paused, and felt Sloan's eyes on him, for his partner had already caught the drift of this suggestion and probably had conceived of the longer-range impact. Perhaps Carole

Clément also had an inkling of the chance about to be presented to her, for she was looking down at the carpet, as though afraid to look up. "If, on the other hand, you were to go—as you say, you're going anyway—excuse me, Carole, but if you go to the funeral and be our eyes and ears, tell us who's there, repeat what might get said—"

"You're recruiting me? To be a stoolie?" she asked. Her tone was not friendly. "Just like you recruited my husband?" she accused.

Wringing his hands again, Touton thought about her question, then nodded affirmatively and without regret. "One of the good things your husband did in his life," he declared, "was his work with the police department, doing what was right—"

"You forced him to work for you!" the widow objected.

"He was a stubborn man, your husband. A man of honour. That's a tough combination for someone in my position to crack. Eventually, I cracked him by reminding him that he had a family to look after."

The woman was staring at the floor again, which Captain Touton did not consider to be an outright rejection of his proposal.

"Carole, I'd say that my purpose is the same as yours when you invited us here tonight. We're pursuing your husband's killers. Our purpose is the same as yours when you take on the bosses on behalf of seamstresses. We're pursuing the bosses, calling their decisions into question, you and me, and when they act as criminals, we're hunting them down. That's all."

He gave her time to process his remarks, to make an informed decision. She stood before answering, and crossed the floor, then came back to her chair and sat again. When she spoke, she pulled her shoulders back. She lifted her chin. If she was going to do this work, she would do it as her husband had, with pride.

"One time," she began, "Roger wanted to know where the phrase came from—stool pigeon. I helped him look it up. Turns out, somewhere, people would tie a pigeon to a stool, which would attract other pigeons, and then people would be able to either poison them all or shoot most of them." She paused. When Touton and Sloan followed her glance, they saw that she was gazing upon a photograph of her husband. He was a young man in the snapshot, wearing his Chicago Blackhawks sweater. "He said that that was what he used to do when he was a hockey player. He'd step on the ice and the other team's bad guy would be sent out to fight him. That way, the star players, the skilled players, they'd be left alone, because the bad guys were too busy fighting each other. 'That's why they kept me around,' he said. 'I couldn't fight on skates very well, but I was willing to get the shit kicked out of me.' He was using his body as a decoy, so the good players on his teams would be left alone. He knew it was a hell of a way to earn a living, but he was proud of it."

"He had a right to be proud," Sloan put in.

"Detective Sloan's a fan," Touton explained. "He loves his hockey."

Carole Clément smiled slightly. "Like Roger. My husband, he took note that the pigeon they tied to the stool would also get blown away once the shot-guns started firing. Or if they'd spread poisoned corn, he'd eat it and suffer and die, too. But in the end, he said that some poor bird had to do it if the people wanted the pigeons dead. I'll be your poor bird, Captain Touton. Why not?"

Given her description, thanking her was difficult, but he got the words out. "Thanks," the policeman said. "Sincerely."

"I'm a unionist, don't forget."

The captain was confused. "Ah . . . I won't forget that."

"Being a unionist means I don't work for nothing. Five dollars an hour, from when I leave home until I return. I get paid whether you approve of my work or not."

Touton smiled. "What union worker makes five bucks an hour? I'll pay you three, which is fair."

"Hazard pay," she argued back. "Plus, you're not offering benefits. No pension, no unemployment insurance, no security, no vacation pay, no regular hours. Five'll do, thanks."

"Five it is," Touton consented. He glanced over at Sloan, who was grinning to see his boss beaten down in a negotiation. "What're you looking at?" he said. "Do you want to bargain with her?"

The three of them laughed, and the cops returned to the warm night air, hopeful that their expensive new recruit might prove invaluable.

†††

The few who showed up for the funeral blamed the threat of a thunderstorm, a harbinger of cooler, drier air, for keeping people away. They were speaking well of the dead. Only six men, in addition to Carole Clément and her daughter, Anik, attended Michel Vimont's funeral.

The service in the chapel of the funeral home was over in less than ten minutes, so that two of the men arriving late only had time to genuflect before the coffin was wheeled down the aisle and to cross themselves a second time as the body went by. So quick that, when invited to go out to the gravesite with the others, Carole accepted.

No one knew who she was, and could not believe that Vimont had had a secret girlfriend. "Are you his sister? His cousin? From his family?" No other option made sense. When she explained in the car that she was Roger Clément's widow, the men welcomed her and made a fuss over Anik. Roger they had known, and liked. They had attended his funeral also, but that one had drawn a crowd, and she had been hidden behind sunglasses, her face a wreck. What a shame about Roger, they said. Michel? Well, nobody knew him. The quiet guys were the ones you had to worry about. Always, sooner or later, something goes wrong with those guys.

"He had enemies?"

Two men shrugged. The third in their vehicle nodded.

"Did Roger have enemies?"

None, they agreed. "Roger, he was a great guy, you know? The best."

"And Michel? Roger used to bring him home for dinner, once in a while."

"That's Roger. You see? Looking after the lost souls."

"That's Michel," the man in the front seat said. "A lost soul."

The other men did the sign of the cross.

"I hope he had a good time at your house," the man beside her said. He was English, and just finished playing an English rhyme game with Anik, which made her giggle: *Paddy-cake, paddy-cake, baker's man!* "Because I never knew him to relax no place else."

By the time they reached the cemetery, Carole confirmed that it was right for her to attend the funeral. She had not taken to the deceased, but she and her husband had probably spent as much social time with him as anyone alive.

As the thunderstorm was rapidly approaching, the priest had no plans to dawdle here, either. This one would be shipped to heaven—or environs—posthaste. The wind was kicking up his cloak and Carole's and Anik's dresses, and men kept their hats in their hands to keep them from blowing off. That allowed her a good look at the others. They all possessed the fake sobriety of hoods. No bosses stood here.

A man who had arrived at the site in the second car whispered with the English guy, and he came over. "Madame Clément," he said. He looked Italian. He spoke French well, with an accent. "My name is Roméro. Me, I was a really good friend of your husband's, may he rest in peace."

She was thinking that when Roger was alive he'd be pleased to discover so many good friends.

"Me, I'm the bartender at the Copacabana. Been there for years. Roger, he used to come by sometimes. I remember, you came with him once or twice."

She was impressed that he remembered. Roger had taken her there for a night out exactly twice.

"We're going back to the club now. It's not open daytimes, but we'll go today, have a little wake. He didn't have so many friends, but he deserves a send-off. Respectful like. Something better than what I seen so far. That priest, I can't believe that guy. You'd think he had to get to the track before the first race, like he couldn't wait to lose his money on that first bet."

The priest had vanished, whisked away in the funeral director's hearse.

"So I'm asking, would you like to come by? At night, it's no place for your daughter, but in the daytime, she could run around—it'd be like a treat for her. She can break anything she wants, I don't mind. We'll have a drink, say goodbye to one of our own, proper like. Maybe some guys will get out of bed finally and come down."

The man was around fifty, with thin hair that he slicked flat to his scalp. He hadn't shaved, probably because he'd had to wake up earlier than usual. He had a broad chest, big neck and jowls, and for funerals he dressed well. His black suit might be typical of his day-to-day wear, Carole was guessing, but that was all right. She knew she didn't make much of a fashion statement herself. She wanted to ask, "How can a girl on a spy mission refuse?" But instead, she said, "Maybe for an hour or so. It might be fun for Anik. I can't afford to take her many places."

"That's good. I'm pleased to make the acquaintance of Roger's wife. He has my respect. Did he ever mention me? Roméro?"

"To be honest, Roméro, I'm sorry, I don't believe he did."

"There you go! You see? That's my man! That's Roger! Very discreet, Roger was, you could trust that guy. He's been dead, God rest his soul, all this time, and he still won't rat a man out. They don't make them like that anymore, you know, not like Roger. But why am I telling you? You know!"

Nodding, Carole felt happy and sad at the same moment. She collected Anik and started on the walk back to the cars. This time, she would travel in Roméro's vehicle, which she thought was a nice enough car, which he drove himself, and all the way he chatted to Anik, and Carole liked that—she liked the way she was trusted here and aroused no suspicion.

The fun part was that Anik really did have a good time. Once she overcame her shyness and understood that she really could run around anywhere, except behind the bar, she had fun at the Copacabana. One hood or another was always pleased to try to catch her—failing always, her mother noted—and the little girl particularly enjoyed romping on the stage. Roméro put the stage lights on for her and plugged in the mike, and while she refused to sing a song as the men requested, she loved running by, stopping suddenly and making silly sounds. She then ran off, as if trying to hear the sounds she'd made.

The hoods each spoke to Carole in turn, and she accepted a beer despite the early-afternoon hour, and in a way the wake became one in honour of Roger, one that she had missed due to her shattered condition at the time. No one really wanted to talk about Michel Vimont, but they were glad to tell stories about Roger, and she was on her second beer before she noticed that the place had become more populated than the funeral home had been.

With the party in full swing, three well-dressed men entered and removed their hats and cast their eyes around. Each nodded to the other and one went outside, and when he returned, he stood in the company of a huge individual whom Carole and even Anik recognized immediately. Camillien Houde proved to be more imposing in real life than he had been in the newspaper photos or on the movie newsreels, and the legendary way in which he commanded the attention of a room held true in this company. Men lined up to shake his hand, and soon they were ordering more drinks for him than he could possibly consume in a day. Apparently, he was ailing somewhat. He was working his way through the well-wishers to a seat, where, huffing, he mopped his brow and accepted his first gin and tonic gladly. The rapidity with which he downed the glass had Carole changing her mind. Perhaps he really could make it through the alcohol ordered on his behalf. When he saw the woman in the room, then the little girl, he made discreet inquiries. Carole knew that he was asking about her, and out of a feigned politeness, she turned her head away.

In a moment, she felt a tap on the shoulder, and she was asked by Roméro if she'd like to bring her daughter to meet the mayor.

Houde bounced the wee one on his knee while Anik seemed mesmerized to be in the grasp of a man so vast. He was a giant, and terribly ugly, and Carole laughed to see her daughter look baby-sized again. She seemed so shy and sweet, as if being introduced to a mythical beast. They'd met once before, after the war, and Houde reminded her that he'd been a roommate of her husband's in the internment camp, which she well knew, and together they told stories back and forth, Carole reciting her husband's memories and Houde providing his own version of events. He shook his finger at her one time.

"What?" she asked.

"You mailed him his opinions! You gave him his politics! You're the one!"

She nodded. "I was supposed to be imprisoned, did you know that? Roger went instead of me."

A hush encircled the tables where they were speaking and the others were listening. Houde was gazing upon her with such solemn attention that he appeared as though he might cry. "Roger," he said, "was a great man. We will miss him always. A round on the house!" he cried out, his first initiative to buy a drink. "We shall drink to Roger!"

Drink they did, to Roger. Carole was thinking as she sipped her beer, *Are you here? Roger's killer, are you here? Because if you're here, I'll find you out, then I'll hang your balls from the top of the Sun Life Building for the pigeons to peck on.*

She had sat across from many tough men in her day, bosses and steely-eyed foremen. She had stared them down and forced them to negotiate through the sheer will of her resolve. She knew what it meant to play your hand too soon. Observing her daughter on the ex-mayor's knee, she knew that she had gained the confidence of an inner circle. She could hardly wait to tell Armand Touton of her good fortune, yet she did wait, staying on at the party, having dinner with a bunch of men after the mayor had left and they had pizzas delivered. After being driven home by Roméro, she waited until Anik was tucked in and had fallen asleep before she made the call. She dialled the number for the captain of the Night Patrol.

First he chastised her, warning her to never call him from her home again. Then he praised her, and told her that she was a brave woman, that Roger would be proud. Although she knew that that was true, she also knew that Roger would never have allowed any of this to happen. But he was gone now, things had changed, and the work she was doing had to be done. She had to find his killer.

"In the future, when I take my daughter with me," she told Touton, "that's an extra two bucks an hour."

Touton consented, wondering if he now held the record for the youngest informant in the history of the force. He would never find that out, of course, as no one kept that kind of information on file.

CHAPTER 12

1684 ~ 1714

A ND SO THE VOYAGE TO END HIS LONG SUFFERING COMMENCED.
Earlier journeys had begun with equally keen prospects, for
on diverse occasions Pierre-Esprit Radisson and Médard Chouart des Groseilliers had embarked upon grand quests to right their fortunes and defeat
the improbable fates that ailed them. From the moment he'd laid claim to
his manhood, the determination had been borne in Des Gros to locate the
Northwest Passage—not the one fools sought to China, rather, the one to the
Rupert and Nelson rivers, inside the Great Salt Bay where Cree gathered fur
by the canoe-full. So rampant and consistent had been their misfortune that
he finally quit, way back in 1682, and Radisson, always the honourable friend,
agreed to relinquish the gambit also. Des Gros built a log cabin for himself
near Trois-Rivières. Purchased a rooster and a dozen hens. Yet, even in that
comparatively peaceful glen, adversity found him. A fox nabbed a few of the
hens, and the fearful rooster ran off. On four consecutive mornings, he sat
listening on his stoop to the cock crow, awakening the dawn with its lecherous
screech from a woodland refuge before a fox got him as well, or mere hunger
despoiled him.

"No more for us, that's what we swore," Radisson was recounting to a
cabin boy, the first person in a while to take an interest in his tales. Shy in
the beginning, the lad was drawn to the legendary figure. Now that the ship
moved upon the waters and the days passed, grey and rainy, the waves rhythmic, the winds steady on the starboard quarter, the lad wanted to know the
truth behind the fables he'd heard in London and Southampton, tales related

to Radisson and Des Gros. He believed every word that fell from the lips of this weathered, scarred man, his visage craggy and punitive under a rampage of overgrown beard and hair. He had been discovering that the truth eclipsed even the legends recited in their daring and raw adventure, and wished that he could live such a life as had this man, this Radisson.

The *Happy Return* plodded on, old timbers creaking, sails full and by.

"A sadder day," Radisson reflected. Along the leeward rail they sat amidships, the frothy sea skimming past them, their feet comfortably wedged against the bulwarks to keep them safely onboard. "Aye," he said, for he was speaking English to the lad somewhat as an Englishman might, although he blended the diction of soldiers and sailors and the language of various provinces. He further vexed his speech with accents both French and Iroquois. "The guv'ner hauled Des Gros to prison off, that wretched hour, stealing our furs after what we had done for him and his lot! Saved Ville-Marie! Saved New France! What we received in return was a *merci beaucoup*—and prison time. Our furs stolen out of our canoes. A wonder he left us our canoes, that man, that guv'ner!"

"I'd be so pissed!" the lad decried.

"I *was* so pissed!" Radisson concurred. "In more ways than one, and stayed that way—pissed!—for months. I would've stayed pissed longer, but money ran dry. Ah, lad, that was a sadder day."

"What did you do after that?" The lad knew well that Radisson had never stayed put for long.

The *coureur de bois* sucked his pipe, savouring the smoke that helped to carry his mind back in time. "I waited for Des Gros to conclude his time in the stockade. When he got out, we hauled down to Boston. We talked to merchants, and Groseilliers, aye, he repeated one point, always whispering so when he spoke it, the Boston men had to cock an ear. He'd whisper that he had never told the French of our discovery. In his heart, he believed that the Boston men should be the ones to take advantage of the knowledge only we knew, if they'd but loan us a ship."

"Did they?"

"The Boston men did, yes. They loaned us a ship, and it was our intention to sail north, to find the entrance to what we called the Great Salt Bay.

We had been there, from the south, by canoe. A hard paddle, lad, dangerous when we turned back. Iroquois marauding the rapids and anywhere we might portage. One time, we'd set out with a hundred canoes, but forty turned back, giving up—for the diligence required, lad, the courage, I would say, could not be found in the marrow of every man, in French or Huron or Cree. Now, we thought, what if we could fill the hold of a ship with the furs of a thousand canoes? That's what we told the Boston men. Their ears tipped down, their greedy eyes preening up, and they loaned us a ship."

"And you went there, didn't you?" the boy asked, his hair tousled by the wind, his shyness gone, enveloped by the spirit of the tale. "Where we're bound to? The Great Salt Bay?"

"Not that year," Radisson recalled, bobbing his head. "Ice turned us back. Ice as tall as mountains, as broad as Ireland, but sailing just as ships do upon the sea, pushed by the wind and tide. We could sail around those mountains, we thought in our zeal, and so we did, only to come upon ice that locked the sea for as far as any man could see. We had to turn back that year. We were defeated then."

"That's too bad." In his mind's eye, the boy witnessed ice cast upon endless horizons, heaving, yawing, as a flow of lava upon the earth, mauling vessels.

"Defeated," Radisson assured the youth, "but never fully disheartened. We knew—Groseilliers, now there's a man, he knew for a certainty, he had the idea fixed in his head as definitely as the North Star lies fixed in the heavens, he knew that we might yet find a way through the ice. But we could tell, upon our return, that the Boston men were displeased with us, they were dispirited." Radisson puffed upon his pipe, reflecting. He shrugged. "So we sailed, me and Des Gros, for England. That would be in 1665. Four years after that, we sailed from England, with two ships, for the Great Salt Sea."

The wind whistled in the rigging, indicating a gale's approach, half a day on.

"This time you made it?" the boy assumed.

"Des Gros made it aboard his ship, the *Nonsuch*, with that good Captain Henry Hudson. I did not. My vessel floundered. The *Eaglet*, she was called. A brave craft, but myself and all aboard were lucky to survive. We had to head back, so damaged we were. But the *Nonsuch*, stout and true like this fair lass, weathered the storms and made the journey, and when she returned to England's shore, I saw her from a distance. I held my spyglass upon the horizon every morning and each afternoon for an hour at a time. I spied the *Nonsuch,* lad, weighed down by beaver pelts to the brim! The hold packed tight to the brim!"

"You must have made a fortune!"

Radisson considered this, then shrugged, then shook his head. "Fortunes are not so easily earned. That is the one thing I will draw from my life, if nothing else. This journey, now, *this* journey will make my fortune. That is guaranteed! Back then, we were compensated, that is true. I will not judge it unfair. We had incurred the expense of two ships, with only one returned home filled with furs. Add on the king's commission. The price of furs that year was paltry—I don't know why. I would say I suffered a greater disappointment than our poor reward, to hear the name of Henry Hudson attached now to the Great Salt Bay, rather than the name Groseilliers! It had been his dream and purpose, his vision, and he got there with Hudson, but Hudson would never have arrived without Médard!" He shrugged again and smacked his lips regretfully. "That's how it goes sometimes. Glory lands in the laps of others. All in all, we added enough to our wallets to know that a second journey from England would be worth the while. On that second voyage, my ship succeeded as well, and we sailed much deeper into the bay, all the way to the mouth of the Nelson River! That was the year that the Hudson's Bay Company was formed, once we had made it through the Northwest Passage inside the bay, and there we conducted the first grand transaction for furs in the life of the company."

"Blimey!" the boy complained. Bells had sounded.

Radisson smiled. "Your watch begins," he noted. "We shall pick up the story again when time allows."

†††

Radisson lingered on the deck awhile, breathing the cool salt air, savouring the last of his pipe. When done, he knocked out the ashes and cleaned the bowl with care and ceremony, then deposited the pipe, still warm, in his pocket, fastened the button and returned below. The air was not so foul as it would be by journey's end, neither was it sweet-smelling, but damp and close, rife with human sweat. Radisson took to his hammock, located in the hold among the soldiers and sailors aboard, although he had been given the privilege of a segregated corner against a centre bulkhead, where the motion of the ship was least and the hatches that received air close by. He lay upon his back, his body swaying to the vessel's gentle yaw as his thoughts fell to a lull.

The boy had done this to him, provoked this bittersweet remembering.

At times, he felt as though he had never possessed his own life. He was not even positive that he had been born in Paris, although he said so when asked, as his first memories had formed there. He had arrived in Trois-Rivières from Paris, the equivalent, he thought now, of sailing upon the *Happy Return* from England and landing on the moon. As a youngster, he had been abducted by the Iroquois and treated as one of their own, learning their language perfectly, their customs, their woodland savvy and arts of war. He was one of them, and yet a separate part of him had remained French. He had continued to dream in that language. He could not share his red brothers' bloodthirstiness for his own people. So he'd fled.

He had left the Iroquois at Schenectady and run all the way to Trois-Rivières through the woods afoot. Yet Mohawk warriors pursued him. At Trois-Rivières they captured him again before he'd placed a foot inside his father's front door. This time, they did not treat him well, and never again as one of their own. They ripped at his skin, burned hot coals into his armpits, his chest and his arse. They smashed his fingers and broke his toes. They rubbed his testicles with poison ivy, and in the days ahead laughed in the glee of his anguish. They made him their slave. What was he then? He was not a Frenchman anymore, at least not one who could raise a pig and harvest cabbages and take communion on a Sunday and, within the hour, shoot marauding Iroquois off his back porch. He was more Iroquois than Frenchman, but the Iroquois did not agree. They made him haul the heavy loads and shackled him to a birch at night. They fed him old corn and ferns while they gnawed upon the thighs of tender deer. They never let him eat the berries they made him pick as the women did. He fled again, a more difficult task this time, yet he was wiser, knowing better than to suffer a third capture.

So he had knocked around, and visited Nieuw Amsterdam, the place the English were calling New York, and he had become a hero among the Jesuits that same summer, rescuing them from attack and destruction by leading an evacuation from danger. He had joined his brother-in-law and a lowly priest, Father Charles Albanel, on a voyage around the Great Lakes deep into the Huron, Cree and Saulteur territories. Yet, was he an explorer, like La Salle, Marquette or Joliet? Apparently not, for the king of France had grown more interested in the explorations that went west and south than those that travelled north. The north frightened the king—that land of snow and ice and darkness for months of the year. Talk of the north sounded like the coldest and darkest hell to him—not even the fiery furnace of his imagination, but worse, a place where there was no life, no movement, no colour. A place where he would freeze and die should ever he visit. So the explorers who went west and south, down the Mississippi to Louisiana, or out onto the plains to the Salt Lake, these were the true explorers in the king's eye. Radisson and Groseilliers, who dared go north to expand the land of the furs, to wander where even the Iroquois feared to paddle, and who worked for the French one year and the English the next, could not be considered explorers in a true sense.

Which was one reason why he sailed upon an English ship again.

Who was he, then? French? English? Iroquois? A woodsman? A Londoner? A sailor? A *coureur de bois*? A soldier? A naval officer? He had been all these things, and still his fortune had alluded him. Nor could he indicate who Pierre-Esprit Radisson might possibly become. Perhaps he was finding himself in the boy's eyes, believing that he was the very man the youth espied. The adventurer. The misfit. The wild, reckless and courageous man of dreams.

The myth.

††#

"On that second voyage, lad, I had the good sense to take along Cartier's dagger."

"Then it's true," the youth confirmed. They were sailing under the stars, a half-moon five degrees above the horizon, setting. Spindrift lifted off the caps of waves and blew across the sea. White spumes in the moonlight flew up from the bow wave, necessitating that Radisson, along with his new young friend, move farther aft from their favoured spot. "It exists."

"The dagger exists, lad. That's true."

"Do you have it with you, on this voyage?"

Radisson knew what the boy's next question would be: *Can I see it?* He smiled. "On this voyage, no. For I have given it to the safekeeping of my true love. She holds it in ransom for my safe return."

"That's what I heard."

"Have you also heard of the knife's great powers? I have married into the family that formed the Hudson's Bay Company, and is it not the greatest company on the face of the earth today? There's your proof. I took it with me on that voyage to the bay, and that's when we formed the company. I gave it to my love as a wedding gift, and my marriage and the company's fortunes have only prospered since."

The lad craned his neck, studying the stars. He had a sextant in his kit, a gift from a sailing uncle. Developing a facility with celestial navigation formed an aspect of his education on this, his first distant voyage. Radisson looked up also. He adored these times upon the ocean the most: at night, the seas whipped up, the skies still clear, the firmament so bright and salutary that no distinction seemed to exist between air and water.

"There's an aspect to the knife that's not been considered. For at one time it had fallen into the hands of the Kirke brothers, when they raided Quebec, before they bequeathed it to their king. Now it remains in the care of my true love, who is a Kirke herself, and it is another generation of Kirkes that has formed 'The Governor and Company of Adventurers of England, Trading into Hudson's Bay.' Now, for short, we call it the Hudson's Bay Company. Don't you see? The fate of the family appears blended to the northern part of North America, despite the fact that that part is considered French. English merchants don't countenance my people, except for me and Des Gros. So their fate is also married to the Cartier Dagger. Interesting, isn't it, the fates the stars decree?"

The boy considered this tale, yet it only whetted his thirst for another. "After that?" he asked.

"After that, me and Des Gros made our voyages, year after year, to the land of the Great Salt Bay—Hudson's Bay, they are calling it now—and the years were good to us. We prospered from our furs. Prices were paltry, commissions paid to the king's court too great, but we prospered. I have no lasting complaint."

"Then what happened?" the insatiable boy inquired.

Radisson continued to gaze high, to the stars, as though he might find the answer there. "This brings us to 1674, does it not?" he asked the boy. "What turn of fortune would cause us, deep in Hudson's Bay, to come across a Frenchman there, a man we knew from the old days, a Jesuit, an Assiniboine captive, one Charles Albanel? What bend of starlight, lad, could cause a meeting with an old friend to occur in that far-flung place?"

He paused, as though his own question had so snagged his attention that further progress to his tales might be delayed that night. The boy did not press him, and yawned, and watched as the man took up his pipe and filled the bowl, tamping the tobacco down with his thumb, curving his hands over the match to light his pipe in the wind. For sure, the man was a mariner who could light his bowl with a single match in gusty conditions yet think nothing of the skill. The boy observed the ritual, awaiting the day when he might enjoy his own smoke this way.

"Charles Albanel," Radisson repeated, as though summoning a spirit from the deep of the night as the moon behind a cloud bled orange, "a prisoner, a slave, prevailed upon Médard and me to return to the love of France, to work in the service of the king of France again."

"Did you?" the boy asked, rapt.

Radisson nodded. "We did."

"Why?" the youth inquired, for this seemed an odd disclosure to him.

Again, Radisson paused, to mull his words.

"Am I not French?" he asked. When the boy shrugged his skinny shoulders, Radisson gazed up at the stars again, as if to make the same inquiry, as if to revisit that question.

†††

"Are you not French?" Charles Albanel demanded to know.

These Jesuits. You had to admire them, even though, as Médard would say, they were the scourge of the earth. Tortured, maimed, enslaved, horribly slaughtered and never particularly successful in their missions, they continued to come back to the wilderness, to what they called their Indian children, whom they so adored even as these same *sauvages* burned their toes or yanked out their tongues or before their eyes consumed captive infants from another tribe. Always so intent on the welfare of a man's soul, the Jesuits would forgo the welfare of their own lives. "A praying Jesuit," Groseilliers had said one time, "is like a canoe."

They had been paddling on the Rupert River, through that hardscrabble land of scruff jack pine and worn rock, where the animals and birds they'd encountered had likely never spied a two-legged before, certainly not one with a white skin and a full black beard, and whenever the pair stepped ashore their footprints were likely the first upon that soil in all the human account. Radisson brought his canoe alongside Groseilliers's so that they might enjoy a few moments' respite while merely running the river's flow.

"Tell me, why is a praying Jesuit like a canoe?"

"The time comes when we must carry both on our backs."

Radisson took his friend's meaning. At Long Sault, three Jesuits had been kneeling in prayer just as the hour had come to portage. They refused to respond to the voyageurs' requests to keep moving. So he and Groseilliers and another man each picked up a praying Jesuit, slung him over his shoulder and carried him across the portage, and the Jesuits never stopped murmuring prayers all the way across, not until they were dropped down into their canoes again and the paddling recommenced.

"This is what I don't understand about Jesuits," Radisson continued in a similar vein. Apparently, for their morning entertainment, they were going to make fun of priests. "Always there's more, but they're celibate. How do they procreate so well?"

They were the scourge of the earth, but the woodsmen and the Indians admired them. Here, at the mouth of the Rupert River, a Jesuit priest, Charles Albanel—a slave to Indians, a man with burn marks on his arms, his fingers gnarled where they'd been broken and blackened where they had frozen, with each of the long nails missing, for they'd been extracted by the Iroquois just so they could watch him wince—was presuming to rail at Groseilliers and Radisson for failing to be properly French.

"I'm as French as you!" Radisson shot back. He had a few days' ration of the Englishman's rum in him. "Maybe more French!"

"I'm Frenchier than both of you," Groseilliers maintained.

"What flag do I see on the stern of your ship? Is it Spanish? Is it Dutch? Is it Portuguese? Hmm. That looks like an English flag to me."

The flag was English, the two conceded, yet Radisson remained undeterred. "The flag—what does it matter? Me, I'm still French."

"Your wife—tell me, is she an English girl or French? Your children, Radisson, English or French? Do they ever speak a word of French? Where do they live—in London, or in the English countryside?"

"Stop pestering me," the fur trader complained.

"Pestering you? When will *you* stop pestering *me*? When will you stop pestering every Frenchman in the world? Stop pestering your king! Your French king, I'm talking about. I don't know if you pester your English king, though you probably do that, too."

Radisson was becoming more furious while Groseilliers chuckled lightly to himself, getting a kick out of the exchange. They knew the man from the old days, from Radisson's first voyage to Lake Superior, when Albanel had taken leave of his mission at Tadoussac and come along, as he had said then, "for the experience." Not a priest who had distinguished himself, he was poorly considered by his superiors. But the governor had called upon him to investigate the Great Salt Bay and a report of English ships guided there by Groseilliers. Albanel had come to the bay and told the Indians that he had pretty much singlehandedly dispatched the Iroquois from their trading routes. He'd been under the misapprehension that the Indians were living so far north out of fear of the Iroquois, but few of them had actually seen a member of that southern tribe. Albanel returned to Quebec and hand-delivered a report, but the governor had to conclude that he had not exacted any promise from the Indians to desist from trading with the English, and his Jesuit superiors had clucked their tongues as though to suggest that they'd forewarned the governor that Albanel had been the wrong man for the job. He'd come back to make amends, but this time the journey had exhausted him. As he had arrived at the Great Salt Bay near death, and not knowing what else to do with him, the Cree gave him to the Assiniboines to be their slave, and, by extension, their problem.

The largest of the three, Groseilliers, was sitting on a log, whittling a maple branch he intended to implant in a wobbly boot. He continued to chuckle.

"What are you talking about?" Radisson complained. "I pester nobody! I don't even pester you, although I should, the way you pester me with crazy talk. Are you crazy, Father?"

"Are you?" He was a dour-looking priest, as though he'd never had a proper meal or a decent laugh in his life. Yet no one could doubt his wiry strength or the resolve of his frail constitution. Exhaustion and slavery had not broken his spirit.

"I'm fine. At least I'm not some Indian chief's cook, like you are now."

"You've noticed. That surprises me." He was picking at an aching molar, and on occasion spitting.

"What's so hard not to notice? How'd you get to be a priest, Father—a lame fool like you? I'm surprised any chief would take you as a slave. You're lucky you didn't have your throat slit."

Albanel folded his arms across his chest, as though he was a burly man when he was not, and glared with his rather large grey eyes at Radisson. "You notice that I'm a slave. Have you noticed how you've enslaved your own people?"

"Huh? What?"

His eyes had that grey tint to them, and as he grew more intense they'd widen like an owl's. "You two villains brought the English to the north country, almost completing the circle around us French. All this land should be French land, so that our brothers are secure to create a great nation for France. But now, we have to fight, and persevere, and worry what calamity the English will bring upon us next, what alliances they will form. We're enslaved by our fears and the treachery of the English and their puppets, the Iroquois. Every summer, the Indians attack, murder us in our beds and in our fields and slay our children. Does the king of France send more men at arms for our protection?"

"He does not," Radisson concurred. "That's the king of France for you! Aha!"

"It's all your fault," Albanel declared.

"What? *My* fault? You just said it's the king's fault. You can't change your mind like that. You're not too bright for a Jesuit, are you?"

Albanel shook his head in dismay and spoke as though he was speaking a basic truth to a child. "Thanks to you, the English take the furs out of Hudson's Bay on their big ships. With all that wealth going to England, why should the king of France care about his subjects who die uselessly over here? Now, if the king of France, and not of England, were benefiting from all those furs out of the bay, do you not think he'd be interested in protecting his subjects, in securing that source of new wealth? Today, when a French women dies horribly at the hands of the Iroquois, and her husband buries the mother of his children, he says over her grave, 'Radisson and Groseilliers, this is on your souls!'"

"He does not!" Radisson jumped to his feet and drew his dagger, set to stab the priest through his gizzard. "I'll slice open your lying black heart!" he cried.

"He says exactly that." Albanel shrugged at the sight of the dagger. "Whether the husbands or the wives believe it these days matters not. They say it under their breath anyway. It's like a curse. If a child, at play, running in the woods, trips over a root, he says, 'Damn Radisson!'"

"He does not!"

"He does, she does—boys and girls both! And when we French fall ill with a fever—I have heard it many times, my friend, I know of what I speak, for the feverish call me to their beds so that I might console them in their misery—we French say, 'The grippe! Des Gros is in my blood today. My body is wracked by Radisson!'"

"No!" Radisson exclaimed, panicky.

Groseilliers was listening to this, not laughing anymore either. "We're hated?" he asked.

"You're despised. We French, we bring up our children to despise you more than the devil's own. To the devil we'd show compassion, if only he would come to us on a penitent knee. To Groseilliers, to Radisson, we'd lock our doors even if winter were at its coldest and you were naked upon your bellies, beseeching your God with prayer. If you were to arrive at the fur fair in Montreal . . ." The priest let his voice trail off, shaking his head forlornly.

"What?" Radisson begged to know. "What would happen?"

The priest screwed up his face, not wanting to imagine the result.

"Tell me!" Radisson insisted.

"Put away your knife and I will tell you," bargained the priest. "I don't want you cutting my heart out in a fit of temper." When Radisson dutifully sheathed his dagger, Albanel whispered, "The people, I fear, would stone you."

Groseilliers and Radisson considered these things. They didn't know quite what to believe, but they had been out of touch with the French for so many years, and had discussed in the past what their own people might think of them, working for the English.

"Don't they know we were robbed?" Radisson lamented. "Over and over again, they stole our furs. Médard was thrown in prison when all he did was save the colony! We've been treated with contempt, with disdain—that's the French for you!"

Albanel chided him with a clucking sound.

"Why are you talking to me like a duck?" Radisson asked.

"Never have you been treated badly by the French. Only by the governor. The French revered you. They adored you. At one time, every Frenchman in New France would have been honoured to have you sleep in his cabin and feast at his table. Every French soul would have slaughtered a pig to show you a proper welcome. My God, it's true! At one time, any true Frenchman, any one at all, would have paraded his daughters before you for your close inspection, and had you chosen his loveliest, he'd have doubled the dowry on the spot. It's too bad. A shame, is it not? I wonder . . . No, it's impossible now. The two of you, you're too English to ever be French again."

"What's he talking about?" Radisson said to his friend. He slapped a mosquito on his neck.

Groseilliers expressed an interest. "Say what you mean, priest."

"All right . . . dwell on this . . . think of it in that tiny corner of your souls the devil hasn't yet seized . . ." Crouched, he dragged himself closer to the men, to the limits of his rope restraint. "If you were to take a few canoes of furs and paddle back to Montreal with me, if you were to vow to deliver the bay back to the French, then would you not be heroes again? Never mind what the governor thinks. The king of France himself would honour you. He'd ply you with riches. You could probably choose whatever estate you prefer in France. But—" The priest shook his head again, as though downtrodden, defeated, then smacked a mosquito on his wrist.

"But what?" Radisson asked quietly, gravely.

"I suppose the English pay you astonishing livres for your furs. I suppose you are great lords of London now. The king of England has given you lands and riches, it's rumoured. I've heard it said that Groseilliers is a knight. Is that true?"

"A Knight of the Garter!" Radisson cried out. "It's the greatest English honour."

"And you, I suppose, his squire. You must be much endowed, with estates, with many servants."

Groseilliers and Radisson glanced quickly at one another. They had been discussing their status in recent months. While Groseilliers had been honoured for bringing the English into the bay, their sailors knew the route now, and their sea captains had formed their own good alliances with the Cree and Assiniboines. In truth, Groseilliers and Radisson were needed no more—they had surrendered the whole of their knowledge to the English. Their new situation was reflected in the diminishment of their sinecure from the sale of furs brought back to England. They had begun to understand that they served no function anymore, and with a stroke of a pen could be denied even the most meagre portion of the profits. Both men, in recent months, had had a sense that they had left themselves vulnerable.

Whispering still, for the men had unconsciously crept closer to the chained priest, his voice clear in the salient night air, Father Charles Albanel decreed, "And if you take furs and canoes south to Montreal, then, of course, you will also take me."

"We could also leave you here, Father. Radisson will tell you. I prefer my own cooking upon the trail," Groseilliers warned.

"You need me to intercede. Without me, the moment you step foot upon the island of Montreal you'll be stoned to death. Cursed first, then stoned by a mob."

"We have a shipload of furs already," Radisson pointed out.

"Then take the furs back to England aboard the ship," Albanel conspired. "But take me with you. Together we shall cross the channel to France, where on your behalf I will make an intercession before the king."

On that starry night, on the shores of the Great Salt Bay, they hatched their scheme to restore the northern portion of the continent to the French. Once again, they would save the colony, and this time, they believed, they'd be rewarded greatly. At long last the riches they deserved would be bestowed upon them, and they would enter into the glory of France, to be honoured among their people.

"What will the English think?" Radisson whispered to Groseilliers as the two lay themselves down to sleep on an earth floor under a canopy of cedar boughs.

"I fear the loss of my knighthood," the older man admitted.

"I fear the loss of my wife," Radisson confessed.

They listened to the wind in the high tops of the trees as it blew across the stark, silent bay and whisked upon their shore like the animal ghosts of this latitude, timeless and grim, perpetually lurking.

††††

"The French king received you well?" the cabin boy inquired. They sat below, taking their evening meal. Above them, a lamp swayed with the ship's motion, and around them, others ate at this late hour or snored in the slump of their hammocks.

"He wanted to know why my wife had not joined me. 'Will she be coming across the Channel?' That was a question that vexed him, and my replies, I fear, did not allay his concerns."

The cabin boy found this aspect confusing. He consumed two spoonfuls of his stew, mulling the matter over, hesitant to make a further inquiry lest he appear dumb. Finally, he had to say, "I don't understand. Why did the king care about your wife?"

Radisson shook his head as though to suggest that he, too, was mystified by this development, but that was not true. What bothered him was that he had been incapable of doing anything about the problem. "He cared about my loyalty. If my wife remained in England—the king's advisors, those are the rascals who made him think this way—then the way was kept clear for me to return across the Channel. I was viewed with suspicion. But the king grasped the significance of our presence, and he sent Groseilliers and me back across the Atlantic. We were to introduce ourselves to the guv'ner of New France, and he, Frontenac, would see to it that we were properly supplied and encouraged before our search. We were back in Quebec, back in Montreal, and the people kept their distance. They regarded us with suspicion, as Albanel had foretold, but we told them of our plans, to bring the north back into the service of the king. Men supported us, relieved to have us with them again. Many wished us a good result as we awaited Frontenac's disposition and his dispatch."

As though he was one of those citizens himself, the boy awaited the man's further account.

"We were summoned back to Frontenac's chateau, where he inquired if we were willing to take an expedition down the Mississippi. He had been educated on Quebec by his king, and he didn't want to counter the king's preferences. We told him, we pleaded with him to believe us, for we were back in Quebec under the king's letter—and yet, he asked, if we did not want to paddle down the Mississippi, would we then lead a warring party against the Iroquois at Ticonderoga? Frontenac had next to no interest in Hudson's Bay! He would not provide us with ships and men for us to take back the bay in the name of France."

The boy shook his head sadly. Although an English lad, in this conflict between the powers of the two neighbours he sided not with his own king or the one from France, but with the ragamuffin from the woods, Radisson. "What did you do?" the boy asked.

"Groseilliers returned to Trois-Rivières to plant corn and raise children, and me, I joined the French navy."

"You didn't!" The boy was genuinely astonished, that the man of the woods would enlist for a life at sea.

"I did. I sailed to the Antilles, and along the coast of Africa. It's a good life for seeing the world, and I commend it to you, lad. You've chosen well."

Still, the boy appeared confused. "The French took back the bay. I'm quite sure of that," he postulated.

"Patience, lad. Patience. Allow love to take its course."

"Love?"

Radisson gathered up his cutlery and plate. "Step lively, lad. We'll take a walk around the deck, stretch our sea legs. I shall like to breathe the night air before I sleep."

They watched dolphins prance in the bow wave. The air was much cooler now, as they had journeyed north, where light lingered almost to midnight.

"I love my wife, lad. It's a tribulation, love is, between a man and a woman when she is of a merchant class, and English, and the man is French and a *coureur de bois*. Our two countries have been warring as long as I've been alive, and I would guess they'll still be on the battlefield after my death. To make matters worse, I'm a rough man, a man who has lived among the Iroquois and was considered their equal by them, so to the merchants of London I'm half-Indian myself. Not exactly the choice that a leader of the mercantile class intends for his daughter."

"That's something I can imagine," the cabin boy acknowledged. Wild Radisson in the home of an English lady—he had to smile just thinking about it. And yet, the woodsman had married the girl, and despite distance and dangers and war between their countries, they had persevered as man and wife.

"You can imagine a part of it, I don't doubt, but never the whole. To this day, my wife lives under the influence of her father more than under mine. Whenever I invite her to France, or to North America, she declines. She remains at home, awaiting the day my adventuring concludes. Awaiting the day, I should say, when I, like Des Gros, will satisfy myself raising chickens."

"Is that why you sail under an English flag again?" the young sailor inquired.

Radisson watched a dolphin skim below the surface, then break into the air a moment. "One, I suppose," he agreed. "After five years in the navy, I was yearning for grander adventures again. I counted my life a failure, and I wanted to be at my wife's side awhile. I begged her—I begged her, lad, although I'm ashamed to admit it—to come to France with me, to be my proper wife. This was in '81. Yet she declined, which surely broke my heart. Live or die, I didn't much care, so I beseeched the king one more time. 'Don't send me to Quebec,' I told him, 'where I'm despised.' In Quebec, I knew, I'd only be asked to shoot Indians, in the hope that an Indian would shoot me. This time, the king undertook the project himself. Frustrated, he was, with Frontenac. I sent for Groseilliers, who was frustrated himself with the growth of his corn, and together, we took two ships into the Great Salt Bay, and did we not take it back from the English, lad? We did! And seized a Boston ship for good measure!"

"A Boston ship!"

"Loaded with furs, it was! Fully laden, we sailed our three ships back to France. We'd done our duty. We had reclaimed the Great Salt Bay for France and had paid for the cost of the expedition many times over with the bounty of our furs."

"And now you're going back," the boy mentioned, "to reclaim the bay for England. Why? Is that love also?"

Without speaking, Radisson continued his stroll around the deck. Halfway round, he seized the lad by the arm and drew him close for a whisper. "When we got back to France with our cargo and our ships, but more importantly with the news of our conquest, that we had reclaimed the north of the continent for France, Groseilliers and me—we were rebuffed."

"No," the boy decried. "Again?"

"Again! We were not paid properly for our furs, for it was decided that we were indebted to France for leading the English to the bay years before, therefore we had to forfeit our proper portion. That was the year, 1682, that was the time, just two years ago, when me and Groseilliers decided, once and for all, to quit."

They continued their walk, reaching the gangway to the cabin below.

"This time, do you think," the boy yearned to know, "will your fortune be made?" He was less certain now of their intended success, for had not Radisson repeatedly come to the bay? Each time, despite victories, despite acquiring prizes of great value, had he not been, as he said, rebuffed?

"This time I shall seize the bay for England, for this is what my true love wishes me to do. Her father, also. Her father will see to it, if I do this thing, that I will be—at long last—compensated properly. Groseilliers could not be talked into accompanying me this time. He's a defeated man. I'm not. I took the bay for France in the year of our Lord sixteen hundred and eighty-two, and I shall take it back for England again, in this year of our Lord sixteen hundred and eighty-four. Then I shall retire to an estate in England and live out my days with my true love. As God is my witness."

The cabin boy nodded. "That sounds nice," he said. He clambered below. He now felt less confident that a good end to their excursion would come to pass. Why should he trust Radisson to succeed and prosper, which in turn would allow all aboard to prosper, when in truth the adventurer had never known success?

†††

After Radisson had claimed the northern fur trade for France—in 1682, two years before he returned to proclaim the same trade for the English—during that time when the men of Ville-Marie would have again doffed their caps to him had he walked by, while keeping their daughters concealed from his eyes, a beautiful young socialite of fine character and high intelligence remained alone in her room as her mother, under the same roof, gradually passed on. She would not emerge from her chamber to be with her ailing parent, whom she loved, to either gaze upon her or utter a final word. Only when her mother had died did the young woman step from her quarters to visit the corpse. She held the dead woman's hand, kissed her cooling lips, helped prepare the body for burial, then returned to the solitude of her room.

She did not attend the funeral.

Her mother had been one of the King's Girls, and had married well enough to have prospered in the New World. At a time when the colony, reckless with bachelors, remained underpopulated, the king opposed the notion of depopulating France of its able, tax-bearing men who were also suitable, beyond the value of their professions, as soldiers. So he devised a compromise: he'd send women instead. New France would grow through its natural fecundity. In agreeing to the plan, the intendant of New France negotiated to receive only young women of sound character, physical stamina and admirable beauty. He expressly insisted that every girl "be entirely free from any natural blemish or anything personally repulsive," so that the seed of the wild men of the New World might know provident, auspicious wombs in which to create a new nation.

The first group to arrive had been chosen from among the orphaned girls of Paris, as this helped alleviate the significant cost of their care to the king's purse. While lovely, they proved too sickly for the regimen of farm life. Country girls from around Rouen were selected next, and they adapted to the conditions best. Over a span of eight years, a thousand young women, often less than sixteen years of age, made the voyage to New France, into the arms of grinning, excited young men.

The mother of Jeanne Le Ber had been among the first of these, one of the Paris orphans, and had fared well as the wife of an increasingly wealthy fur baron. Yet her constitution had never proven strong. She managed to deliver only two children, and after considerable sickliness, she died. She lived long enough to know that the daughter she'd nurtured to young womanhood, who would not visit her as she lay dying, was singular in her devotions.

As a child, Jeanne Le Ber committed one flagrantly sinful act each year. In April, from the age of five onwards, she would slip away from her home, in disobedience of her parents' wishes, and make her way a few blocks to the old market square. The voyageurs were gathering there, the *coureurs de bois,* fur traders bound for Indian lands. Before embarking, the men would be left alone to drink, to laugh themselves silly and to brawl. Oh, how they loved to brawl! Tucked away behind a sleigh or concealed behind horses' hooves, the little girl could catch as many as a dozen fights at a time. Men slammed their fists into one another's heads and butted their heads into one another's bellies. As their faces were smashed, they'd grunt and bleed and kick and snarl like beasts, and the wee girl would watch them topple, one by one, and collapse upon the snowy pavement and lie still, defeated, unconscious or just dazed, while the victor roared and scanned his peers for the next foolhardy challenger.

After an hour or two of such excitement, or upon being spotted, little Jeanne would scamper home, terrified and thrilled, bursting with an incomprehensible joy.

Yet these excursions were kept secret from her mother, and were not among the attributes that would distinguish her as a child who had been touched by her devotions, either in the minds of her parents, or in the hearts and understanding of the people of Ville-Marie on the island of Montreal.

Having witnessed the brawls, she would sneak away to visit her godmother at the Hôtel-Dieu, the woman after whom she'd been named, Jeanne Mance. The child had already demonstrated a keen interest in the mysteries of the divine, and her comments, at age five, at six, and through her growing years, were original and smart. As a young woman being prepared for marriage, she'd attend the social parties of her set, yet depart early to pay strict adherence to her habits of prayer, for although she was civil and bright and socially adept, she was withdrawing from the world, step by step, moment by moment.

Ribbons were ripped from the gift of a cushion, the adornment offensive to her eyes. She wept when required to wear an ornate robe in a Biblical play, ashamed that her body would ever know such accoutrement. She desired to be locked up, fully segregated from the world, and upon the death of her best friend, a nun, she renounced all attachment to the world.

Uncertain what to do with her, an *abbé* suggested a limited seclusion for a fixed term of five years, to be served inside her own room within her own home. The room was made especially bare, to please her, with every accoutrement or artifact removed, all colour, save for the greyness of her blankets, taken away. Eagerly, Jeanne entered her confinement, declining to emerge either for the death of her mother or to tend to the monstrous injuries her brother suffered in a battle with the Iroquois. For him, as well, she stepped from her room only after his death to help prepare the body for viewing, before she quickly withdrew.

As a recluse, she was similar to ascetics in various times and places, yet with a few distinguishing characteristics. She managed her own economic affairs, as her father had seen to her initial temporal needs and, if she was not to marry, allowed her access to her dowry. She had investments and charitable contributions to supervise. She wore a hairshirt and inflicted the scourge upon herself, yet she maintained a maid and happily ate meat. Naturally, she was chaste, yet in weaker moments, thoughts did wander to the infinite wilderness and the rapacious *coureurs de bois,* and she wondered about Radisson, for she had heard countless tales of his exploits at her father's table. She felt drawn to the legend, even while her fur-baron father had railed against him, perhaps because he was simply the most notorious of the wild men and brawlers and therefore representative of them all, yet also because he was seeking his fortune, while she had renounced hers. While she sought her destiny in the austerity of a cell, he was off plunging into the austere wilderness of the north. She and Radisson were so diametrically opposed, she had imagined—they had never met, although she had seen him in a spring brawl—that they were inextricably linked.

She dreamed of Radisson and she prayed to God, and following her initial five-year experiment, Jeanne Le Ber chose to make her vows perpetual, continuing to live alone in her room in her father's house.

That she could well imagine the universe outside her door, that she acutely envisioned the wilderness and pictured the rowdy men who roamed freely there, gave her confinement its definition, its prerequisite bitterness. In this way, she persevered inside her room.

Jeanne Le Ber had only begun to inhabit her ascetic vision.

Outside her home, fur traders still brawled every spring, and as they returned in late summer, they fought marauding Iroquois, the bands who continued to vex the settlers through the fall and plot with the English, over winter months, to find ways to further harm the French. Peace remained implausible. Would Radisson's return and seizure of the great northern bay help? The governor, some said, had been working towards a truce with the Iroquois. Could that come to pass—peace with an enemy governed neither by remorse nor sanctity, who profited by war? Annihilation remained a prospect. Of these things, Jeanne Le Ber professed no interest, although her father sat outside her door on occasion, and through the grille created for passing food spoke of such matters. The brawling voyageurs remained rambunctious in her dreams, yet during her waking hours she maintained a diligent schedule of prayer, needlepoint and the reading of religious texts to help her limit the world. As was true among the other settlers, fear crept into her consciousness, of Iroquois removing her from her private cell and slicing off the top of her head. She possessed a peculiar premonition, that one day the Indians would come to the island of Montreal and politely wait outside her door. She assumed that the only reason they would come would be to burn her at the stake. Yet she resisted such thoughts, not wanting to indulge in sweet images of affliction that mimicked her Lord's passion. Whenever such images beckoned her attention, she prayed all the more zealously.

Among her daily disciplines—though no one would have guessed, least of all Jeanne Le Ber herself—the quality of her needlepoint as much as the fervour of her prayer would be called upon to save the colony from extinction. Nor could she have guessed that the Indians would indeed come to Ville-Marie, and one would wait politely outside her door, but that a man, a great chief, would take no interest in furthering her suffering, but would arrive to plead only for her counsel.

†††

The cabin boy had been forewarned: he'd be entering another world, another time. Yet no such prophecy could prepare him for the eerie dimension of the immense salt bay. The largest beasts he'd yet imagined—behemoths, great white polar bears—loped along a scraggly beach of sand, rock and pale driftwood deformed into elaborate shapes bleached white by the sun. Small whales blew plumes of vaporous air from their spouts and tagged along behind the ship, patient marauders—or, like them, curiously cautious, too. Brisk air felt just born, as if it were an entity, and the sky, in its unique pale beauty, contributed to his sense that he had not merely entered another world or time, but timelessness, a place where worlds and all their unjust conceits were vanquished.

Upon Radisson's signal, longboats were lowered while the *Happy Return* maintained way on. Soldiers were dispatched into the stunted woods. As the ship eased into the harbour of Port Nelson and dropped anchor, Radisson, standing straight up like an admiral, was rowed ashore. He demanded the surrender of the community. Initially, the French traders chuckled, for they were well armed and sufficiently bored that they'd welcome a fight, but once their eyes had been directed to the surrounding woods, and it dawned on them that Radisson had arrived not merely with merchant sailors but with English soldiers, too, their capitulation was complete. Port Nelson was English again. Given its name, that seemed fitting.

On he sailed to the Hayes River, and there, to his surprise, he encountered his nephew, Médard Chouart, Des Gros's boy. By early dawn, Radisson had persuaded him, and his friends the Assiniboines, to support England. The territory, then, was restored to the care of the Hudson's Bay Company, and he emptied the French storehouses there and loaded a season's furs into the hold of his ship. The *Happy Return* would be making another happy return, this one to England and, he presumed, to his long-overdue grand reward.

"Tell us a story, Radisson," the cabin boy pleaded. Their new recruits, French and Assiniboine, were seated around the campfire, enjoying the shank of a deer.

"What story do you want to hear?" he asked the lad back.

"A new one," the boy suggested.

The voyageur thought a moment. With Indian and French and English ears attentive, he had best make certain that he offended none in this company.

"Let me tell you true tales about The Rat," he told them. "Chief Kondiaronk, of the Huron. For when the story of this land is put to rest, mark the words you hear tonight. The Rat will be one Indian who will have had his say. For he is the wisest of the Indian chiefs, more clever than the French guv'ners. He has more wit in his smallest toe than can be found in the courts of either king, English or French."

The Assiniboines, in particular, were enjoying this account, and nodded, and rocked. Everyone around the campfire had heard of Kondiaronk, but none, save Radisson, had met him.

"Kondiaronk is a sage man, but I know him to be a cruel man also when he needs to be. A determined man. Do you see this scar here?" In the firelight, Radisson opened his shirt and displayed the scar, in the shape of an X, across the centre of his chest. When all had had a good look, he said, "Kondiaronk, The Rat, gave me this. As a warning. For I had cheated him. I had taken two hundred and twenty pelts and told him only two hundred. So he marked my chest with his knife, to show me where he will cut out my heart if I try cheating him again. That, of course, will not happen. For he is too wise a chief, too clever a man, too cruel a warrior, for me to cross him twice.

"This, then," Radisson declared, and poked at the fire with a stick, sending sparks into the night sky as though summoning the spirit of the man of whom he spoke to attend these proceedings, although the man was still very much alive, "is the story of The Rat."

The boy leaned in, his attention rapt, yet no more so than the others.

†††

The French needed allies. The English hemmed them in from every side, and their colonies were growing with rampant immigration, while the French had to grow their community primarily, and diligently, through childbirth. The Iroquois were hideous in their attacks, and the Huron, so often defeated, were reluctant to continue on the French side. Or so The Rat, Chief Kondiaronk, led the governor of New France, the Marquis de Denonville, to believe.

"If we are eliminated," the governor pressed him, "if we either abandon this land or perish with Iroquois tomahawks planted in our skulls—"

"A fortunate way to die," the Huron chief demurred.

"Excuse me?"

"A skull, split by a tomahawk. I have seen many deaths, and this is the best way to die at the hands of the Iroquois. If your people are to die, may they go that way."

The marquis was momentarily taken aback. He had heard that the chief had a knack for repartee, that he should expect both wit and subterfuge from the man. "It's not a picture I care to contemplate," he said.

"You prefer to burn, do you, the little fire at your feet? Slowly, the fire climbs up your calves to your knees, to your thighs, higher. Scorching, blackening. You will cry out—any Frenchman would—as the hot flames lick your balls. That is when even the strongest man who is burning, even a Jesuit priest, pleads for a tomahawk—" Making a hatchet with his fingers, the chief in his raiment used it to divide his skull.

"Quite," Denonville reluctantly concurred.

Kondiaronk wore feathers in his hair and across a highly embroidered breastplate. His moose hide was fashionable, with decorative beads and a leather fringe, right down to his elaborate moccasins, which he'd never wear except to meet the governor of New France, to impress him with his haberdashery. The Rat had been a student of the Jesuit, Daniel Greysolon Dulhut, who had set out in the middle portion of the century on a clandestine mission to gather Indian tribes westward from the Great Lakes, the Saulteurs and the Sioux in particular, into an alliance against the English. With these tribes on the side of the French, the groundwork would be prepared to allow the remainder of the continent, south to Louisiana and west to the sea, to become French. Yet, for the allegiance of the tribes to be meaningful, they had first to make peace with one another. Dulhut succeeded eventually, coming to an agreement in the place that would later bear a scrambled approximation of his name, Duluth, in the land called Minnesota. As a young man in his company, being persuaded by some arguments and taking issue with others, Kondiaronk learned about politics and negotiations, to the point where he would one day supersede his mentor. From Dulhut, Kondiaronk had learned to comprehend—and more fully imagine—the potential power of peace.

"Scalped alive, that's another way to go," The Rat mentioned to the squeamish governor.

"But if we, Chief, are treated to such horrible acts, then what will become of the Huron, after we are gone?"

Kondiaronk knew the answer to that question. He lifted one side of his derrière and pointed to the protuberance. "Our asses," the chief declared, "will look like French heads after they've been scalped."

The marquis chose not to reflect upon that outcome. Why did The Rat have to continually make reference to gruesome details? "Then surely, Kondiaronk, we are agreed. The French and the Huron must fight together, side by side, in our mutual defence against the Iroquois." Except for the bloodiness of certain images, the discussion, Denonville believed, was going well.

"Maybe," Kondiaronk said.

"Maybe?" The marquis expressed dismay.

"Maybe means perhaps. The French and their English brothers have too many words. Why do you have two words to mean the same thing?"

"Why do you say maybe?" Denonville demanded to know, not interested in the Indian's perpetual interest in semantics.

"Rather than perhaps?" the chief asked him.

"No! Why do you say that only *maybe*, only *perhaps*, will the Huron stand side by side with their French brothers?"

"Ah," the chief said, and helped himself to a grape from the plate before them. These foods the French enjoyed, that arrived from time to time on ships, were a marvel on the tongue, well worth the drudgery of these meetings. "It's simple. I need what you call, in your language, guarantees."

"Such as?"

"The French must fight," Kondiaronk insisted. He made a fist and flexed it before the governor, to indicate that the French must not only fight, but that they must fight hard.

Denonville objected to the implication. "We fight!" he claimed.

"You fight when you are attacked," the Huron pointed out to him. He was a strong man with broad shoulders and a stout chest, although shorter than most men of his tribe. In his middle years, he'd grown a paunch he was fond of patting while he ate. "When you have no choice, when it's fight or die, you fight. Usually, you French do both. You fight, then you die."

"So what's the problem? We fight!"

"You do not attack! You rely upon the Huron to attack the Iroquois on their land. The French must also attack. If not, then the Huron, too, we will only wait to be attacked, seeking the enemy no more. Perhaps, maybe, perhaps, maybe, we will run and hide. To protect our asses, you understand."

Now the discussion was not going so well for the governor. He needed to create the semblance of a broad front and a redoubtable force, for he had engaged the Iroquois in secret talks about peace—secret from his visitor, as well—and for those negotiations to succeed, he needed to appear strong. On his part, Kondiaronk needed only one thing: a commitment from the governor to make no separate peace with the Iroquois, but to fight them at every opportunity. Peace between the Iroquois and the French would allow the Iroquois to concentrate on fighting the Huron, and his people, he knew, who had already sustained grievous losses, would be annihilated in any such war.

"If you do this, what I suggest, strike a clever blow against the Iroquois, then we French will also attack. But I need to witness this commitment from you, Chief Kondiaronk, before we proceed."

The agreement pleased both men, and Kondiaronk commenced the long trek back to his lands around the Michigan lake, dreaming strategies of war.

On the way home, he stopped at the French fort that guarded the great river where it flowed out from Lake Ontario. He was welcomed there, as the commandant always enjoyed his company, more than that of any Indian. Over a meal, without being aware of the secrecy that was meant to govern certain information he'd received, the commandant spoke freely to Kondiaronk.

"How did you find the marquis, Chief? Is he well?"

"I left him in good spirits."

The commandant sipped wine. "Wonderful! He's talking to so many Indians these days, it's good news that you got him off to a happy start."

"Yes, yes. Talking to Indians, many Indians. Ah, who's next, did he say?"

"The Iroquois, I suppose."

"That's right, I remember that now. Who exactly—have you heard? I hope it's not Conaymasteeyahgah. He'll make the governor irritable. Or Klow, who will only put a knot in his bowels—he does that every time, to everyone he meets."

Smacking his tongue around his lips to clean them up, the commandant leaned forward to the centre of the table, ripped the last leg off the roasted turkey and blithely waved it in the air. "Whomever they chose to be their ambassadors, they will go. Whatever team they choose to negotiate the peace."

"Yes, the peace between the French and the Iroquois." Kondiaronk spoke as though this was old news to him, while a knot in his own belly began to fester.

"Precipitous, don't you think?" The commandant was always amused that he could use a word like that in front of Kondiaronk and the chief wouldn't blink, wouldn't indicate any lack of comprehension. He was a noble chief, that much was understood by the French and Huron both, and even by most Iroquois and English. Vicious, too, rumours told. They said of Kondiaronk—and the commandant had heard the governor himself say it—that he made his moves in the present in order to influence the future, and no one possessed clearer insight into the future than The Rat. "I don't know who they'll send. Perhaps the sachem, from their ruling council. Probably not chiefs for a first meeting. The Iroquois will be suspicious of a trap, don't you think? It is all great news. Peace!"

The commandant reached for his goblet.

"This is good, this is good." Already defining his next move to counter the white man's never-ending treachery, Kondiaronk feigned passive agreement. After the meal, he headed back the way he'd just come, departing in the dark so the French would not notice his reversal of direction. Following several days of hard paddling, in the Adirondack Mountains well south of Montreal, he ambushed the Iroquois peace delegates, killing a couple and capturing the remainder.

His warriors had been under strict instructions to take most delegates alive and to scalp none.

By the side of the river, the Huron made camp and cooked rabbit from their stores. Kondiaronk threw scraps at the feet of his captives, and slowly, the men bound at their ankles consented to eat also.

"I'm sorry about this," Kondiaronk told them. "It's the French. They made me do it. I had to promise I'd come down here and attack you."

"They did not," the man who would speak for the group protested.

"Why else would I be here, a Huron from Michilimackinac? The governor sent me to massacre you, to roast you over a slow fire. 'Cut off their balls and feed them to the bullfrogs,' he said. 'When I hear the frogs croaking, I want to know that dead Iroquois are moaning in their bellies.' So that's what I will do. I will feed your manhood to the frogs. I want to remain on good terms with the governor."

"We were on our way to see the French governor!" an Iroquois maintained.

Another was equally adamant. "He asked us to go there, to talk about a peace! Does the governor send Huron to kill us when he wants a peace?"

Kondiaronk expressed his astonishment. "A peace? He asked you to come to him to talk peace, then sends me down to feed you to the bullfrogs along the way? What black deed is this? My brothers! I'm sorry. There has been a terrible mistake. How can I be a part of this treachery? Such black and wicked deeds! The white man! Who can understand his animal ways? He is a wolverine on two legs! I shall never be happy, my brothers, until the five tribes of the Iroquois avenge this day! Huron! Cut loose our Iroquois brothers!"

The captives were freed, and Kondiaronk gave them gifts of beads and rabbit meat and delectable deer for the inconvenience and tragedy of the unwarranted attack. He confessed his shame to them and repeated his horror at having been used in such a repulsive scheme. "Ah," he cautioned, just before the Iroquois were about to embark northward again in their canoes, "I do have a slain warrior."

No Iroquois could recollect firing a shot. They'd been outnumbered and taken by surprise in the open, and in that circumstance had been quick to surrender. That any of their own had died had been unfortunate, as there had been no need for the Huron to kill them in order to win the fight. That an attacker had died remained inexplicable, although perhaps a shot had been fired by an Iroquois who was now dead. The dead Huron lay visible, lying at a distance through the trees upon a mound, his body awaiting disposal.

As was the practice, an Iroquois captive would take the place of the dead Huron and remain behind with the invading tribe. Less that one man and their dead, the Iroquois continued on, burdened now by the gifts they'd received.

Once they had disappeared behind a bend downstream, and the lone Iroquois captive was distracted by his slave duties, five Huron climbed the hillock to bury their dead brother. Six men returned from the task. The party then returned to their territory and to the fort at Michilimackinac, by Lake Michigan, where Kondiaronk approached the commandant upon arriving.

"What do we have here?" the Frenchman inquired, for he did not normally see one Indian bound in the company of others.

"Iroquois spy," Kondiaronk bristled, and spat.

"Is that right?" the commandant inquired of the prisoner.

"I am not spy," the Iroquois insisted. "I came to negotiate peace with the French governor."

The Rat shook his head solemnly. "He's crazy," he said. "He's a madman. What should I do with him, Commandant? I can't keep him—he's too crazy."

The military man eyed the Iroquois up and down. He was not from a tribe that came into his area very often, although he was not the first Iroquois prisoner that Kondiaronk had brought to him. He looked like a formidable warrior, taller and more muscular than the majority of Huron men. The Iroquois pleaded again that he had come to talk peace with the governor, which confirmed that he was either a spy or crazy.

"Shoot him," the commandant decided.

"You shoot him," Kondiaronk said. "We Indians, you know, we prefer to roast our prisoners alive."

The commandant nodded, and consented to the arrangement.

The Rat visited him again that night.

"You shot my prisoner," he pointed out to him.

"You wanted me to."

"We have a custom."

"What custom?" He had often negotiated with Kondiaronk, and had learned long ago that he was unlikely to win any advantage over him. He considered himself fortunate if he managed to keep his uniform on.

"You shot my prisoner. You have to give me one back in exchange."

"But you wanted me to deal with him, Kondiaronk. Not only that, you brought me the other prisoners in the first place! They were your prisoners!"

The Rat shrugged. "I'm a poor Indian. I could not afford to feed them. But now you must give me one back."

"Why must I?"

"It's the custom. It's the price you pay for shooting prisoners."

The commandant remained frustrated. He sensed that Kondiaronk was up to something, but he could not comprehend what. "How will you feed him now if you couldn't feed him before?"

"I won't. I'll just send him home."

"What's the good of that?"

"It's the custom." The chief shrugged.

"Oh Jesus, Mary and Joseph. What are you up to, Kondiaronk? They don't call you The Rat for nothing!"

"They call me The Rat because I draw a rat to sign my name. But they don't call you a wise commandant for nothing, either."

The officer thought a moment, trying to imagine how this might hurt him in any unforeseen way. Soon defeated by the train of thought, he nodded. "Go ahead. Take whatever prisoner you want. Just don't—"

Kondiaronk waited politely, then asked his question. "Don't what?"

"Don't burn him alive. Or slice his scalp off. Or eat him, or anything vile."

Enjoying a good laugh, The Rat tapped the Frenchman on the shoulder. "I will send him home. That's all. You will see."

"Yes, yes, I know. It's the custom."

"It's the custom."

Kondiaronk did send him home. He spoke to the man first, who was trembling, wishing that he had been left in the custody of the French and not in the hands of the only Huron the Iroquois feared.

"What did you see here today?" The Rat asked him.

"You returned."

"What else?"

"The French. They shot an Iroquois."

"One of your brothers. Go home. Tell your people this. Tell them what your eyes have seen. That the French shoot Iroquois while they talk of peace."

He made it sound as though he was trying to frighten the prisoner, as if his message would send fear through the Iroquois confederacy. The Indian who was freed mocked him for this when he told his brothers the sad tale of the Iroquois warrior shot by the French. His brothers raised their knives and whooped, and in the firelight each man could see the warring spirit in his brothers' eyes. The French and the Huron would discover that the Iroquois would not be intimidated. And the first lesson would be inflicted upon those who had talked of peace: the French.

†††

August 5, 1689.

Rain had fallen with hard fury through the night, a racket in the leaves, as noisy as a waterfall when it turned to hail and beat upon the settlers' wooden roofs. Thunder boomed low over the hills and rumbled across the plateau, and the farming people at Lachine, on the island of Montreal, slept fitfully as lightning lit up the skies. Soldiers in the three forts by Lachine were driven inside, and they would not budge to go out in such a torrent. Their commanding officers were not around to tell them otherwise, having gone into Montreal to visit Governor Denonville, who was down from Quebec. Under the cover of darkness, as the lightning moved on, under the fury of rain, under the bedlam of brisk wind that chased all sound away from the forts, Iroquois landed by the riverside and beached their canoes.

They laboured diligently and in silence.

Fifteen hundred warriors split up and surrounded each settler's home.

They waited in the rain.

At dawn, upon a signal, they sounded a fierce, calamitous war whoop.

Soldiers remained asleep, or kept watch from their turrets, hearing nothing but the storming wind and rain.

The attack was perfectly executed. The Iroquois burst into homes and bludgeoned the skulls of the settlers in their sleep. In cabins that had been barricaded, the French fought back, only to have the dwellings set ablaze. They ran out from the fires to be slaughtered. Each home had to pitch its own battle. No farmer could come to the aid of another. In a short time, the community was overrun, with all citizens either dead or captive.

The Indians took their time, relishing the victory. Stakes were implanted in the earth, and men and women strapped to them. Small fires were stoked at their feet. Spits over bonfires were created and children roasted. Pregnant women were brought forth to have the fetuses ripped from their wombs. Their dying eyes watched their unborn children being cooked and consumed. The storm continued unabated, suffocating their screams, their outcry before God.

Once word of the attack reached him, Denonville ordered the Marquis de Vaudreuil, who was in charge of the Montreal garrison, to take no chances in quelling the enemy. The integrity of the garrison was more important than revenge. The marquis failed to apply his men to the task of driving off the Iroquois. Soldiers remained hunkered down in their forts while the invaders continued to maraud the island for two more months, pillaging, murdering and taking prisoners. They harvested the crops for themselves and burned seed and winter stores, and as they departed in October they released ninety fierce yells to proclaim that they were taking ninety prisoners home with them, to put to work, then mutilate at their leisure.

They paddled past the forts. Their chief shouted out before each one, "You deceived us! Now we have deceived you!"

In Ville-Marie, the citizens fell to another winter of despair.

In Michigan, the chief who had been named The Rat preached on Sunday mornings, for through his admiration for the Jesuits, and in particular Dulhut, he had come to embrace Christianity. When he spoke in church, his words were received with gravity and thoughtfulness. Learning of the massacre, he grieved for the lives lost, yet also welcomed the safety this would mean for his own community. If the French wanted peace as he wanted peace, he deliberated during the winter months, they would have to learn how to make that peace. Clearly, they did not know how to do it on their own. He, Kondiaronk, the chief of the Huron at Michilimackinac, who signed his name by drawing a rat—he would be the one to teach them.

For there could not be a peace, he preached, if one tribe was left vulnerable to destruction. The peace that was required must exist in a way that all tribes, and the French, and the English in New York and Boston, might prosper. He, Kondiaronk, The Rat, contemplated these things and talked of what he dared to imagine the long winter through, and in the spring he hoed the soil he believed might assist the seed of his vision to finally take root.

†††

On the feast day of Our Lady of the Snows, August 5, 1695, François Dollier de Casson, a mountain of a man and the superior of the Sulpicians in Montreal, concluded the vespers' chants in his parish church. With magisterial élan, he departed down the centre aisle. Clergy fell in behind him. Ville-Marie's administrative officials stepped in behind them, followed by the great spiritual women of the colony, led by Marguerite Bourgeoys and a gathering of nuns from the Congregation of Notre Dame. Representatives of the military came next, marching, then citizens prominent in the fur trade and other mercantile affairs, and finally settlers noted for their devotions. The procession moved outside into the warm night and continued to grow as ordinary folk also traipsed down the centre of Notre Dame Street, bound for the home of the fur baron Jacques Le Ber.

Upon arriving, Dollier de Casson knocked upon the door.

His knock was severe, hard, final, like a judge's gavel. He stood back from the door and waited with an expression that was formally grave. He was a unique man among the Sulpicians, one the Indians especially admired for his exceptional size and strength. He had entered the priesthood after a distinguished career in the military, and loved to tell the story of spotting an enemy igniting the wick of a cannon at short range. The cannonball had been aimed precisely at his head, yet, bound by a French officer's code, he was forbidden to duck. As the wick burned down, Dollier took out his handkerchief and let it drop. As the cannon roared, he was bending over to pick it up. He heard the ball whoosh above him. Then he straightened himself up and carried on the fight.

Such stories were accepted due to the native integrity of the man, as well as to the manner in which he had equipped himself, since his arrival in France, in battle against the Iroquois. A story was told of him at prayer one evening, deep in his beloved forests, which he much preferred to the seminary. A young Indian youth tormented him with obscene gestures. The youth grew too bold, coming too close, and Dollier, still on his knees, dropped him with a single stupendous punch. While the young man moaned and tried to regain his senses, stopping up the blood from his nose, the priest carried on praying.

He was a man who had built the first modest church of Notre Dame, and the Sulpician Seminary, and he had half-dug the Lachine Canal before his superiors in Paris, mindful of the cost, ordered the project halted. For all his physical might and energy, he was a devout man and a careful chronicler of the history of the community, recording stories from out of the mouths of Jeanne Mance and others among the first settlers.

So as he knocked upon the door of Jacques Le Ber, he did so with authority, and with deep appreciation of the occasion.

The merchant emerged. He was sixty-one years old, an ancient age for their community. The people called him Abraham, as a tribute to his years but also in deference to this ceremony, for would he not be leading his daughter to become a victim of sacrifice?

Jeanne Le Ber stepped out from the house behind him. Thirty-three years old, she wore a long, grey woollen gown cinched by a black belt. With her father at her side, she joined the procession, taking her place behind only Dollier de Casson, and the great devout tribe walked back through the streets the way they had come, returning to the chapel.

Where they prayed.

Jacques Le Ber was overcome, his anguish too grave for him to endure any more, and he departed the service before its conclusion. An Abraham, then, who could not bring his sword down upon the neck of his only surviving child. He had become one of the wealthiest fur barons, a man who had broken the rules by not waiting for the return of the *coureurs* in Montreal, but by travelling farther and farther west to intercept them, to garner the best pelts. While he was respected as a pious man, his daughter's passion extended far beyond mere piety and he could not sustain himself through to the ceremony's conclusion. The words that broke his endurance were spoken by his last remaining child's spiritual advisor, who declared, "You are dead. You are enshrouded in your solitude as in a tomb. The dead do not speak, nor are they spoken to."

Following the prayers and dedication, Dollier led Jeanne Le Ber to her new home. According to her precise plans, a cell, composed of three rooms, one above the other, had been constructed behind the altar at the Convent of Notre Dame. Jeanne Le Ber had financed the project through her own impressive dowry, and had donated a large sum to the convent as well and would continue to pay an annual tribute. She had used her influence to have the dwelling built to her exact specifications, and had managed to replicate the chapel at Loretto in Italy, which legend held to be the actual home of the Virgin Mary, transported there by a company of angels. Here, she would be locked inside for the remainder of her life, speaking to rare visitors only through a grille, addressing the convent sisters through it from time to time as though hers was a voice from the grave. She'd take her meals upon the floor, sleep upon a straw mat that would harden over time to the composition of rock and which she would not allow to be replaced, and she'd emerge only after dusk, once the chapel door had been locked, to prostrate herself before the cross.

When not at prayer or reading religious books, Jeanne Le Ber would busy herself with needlepoint, making sacerdotal vestments for the churches in the vicinity. Her silk embroidery, pleasing in design, the details eminent and lovingly rendered, worked against the circumference of her drab solitude and her denial of earthly comfort, giving expression to her love of God. She still kept her maid. Indeed, her contract with the convent demanded a substitute whenever her own lady-in-waiting was absent. While she had a private garden outside her lower door, she would not use it, and many would whisper that she never glanced out a window again. As her spiritual advisor had informed her, "Even the ascetics of old would permit themselves a walk in the woods, to commune with God." But not Jeanne Le Ber.

> . . . and then, at my Lord's bidding, the door is shut, and I am at last more fully alone. No longer in my father's house, but in my cell, a final seclusion from which there can be no release but death, no expectation of life or variance or possibility. I lie prone upon the floor, alone. Dead, yet not dead. Still abject, for my joy surrounds me and overtakes me, and my aloneness—this, too, is a blessing. My very solitude is a pleasure I must defeat, for I must overcome even the slightest attachment to this world. If I am pleased by my suffering, then my suffering becomes my

joy and what is real becomes illusion, and I am defeated. All becomes naught. For I know nothing of the joy of death, only its replication, and I must not be pleased with the artifice. The voyageurs would beat one another before they embarked into the wilderness to prepare themselves for the struggles and the reality of that realm. So must I be dead, but to truly suffer while alive, I must acknowledge that I am not dead, nor can I strain for the glory of death before its time, for I must allow my suffering to linger, yet draw no sweetness from the lingering. I must permit even my glorious solitude intermittently to be broken. For I am dead, but not dead. That is how my life is broken. That is how I will truly suffer for my Lord.

Three historic visits to the little grille through which she spoke gave evidence of her life and spiritual responsibility. The first startled her, yet she was prepared for the task by her days as a small child watching the voyageurs punch one another senseless. When she was told that the Huron chief Kondiaronk had requested an audience with Sister Jeanne Le Ber, the mother superior assumed that she would decline, yet the recluse promptly agreed, for she believed that the meeting had been ordained by God. Wobbly on his feet, accompanied to the Congregation of Notre Dame by sixteen Huron warriors, the chief, in his finery and elegant countenance, was guided to the rear of the chapel alone. He sat on the small stool before the scant opening and adjusted his attire, waiting. He had been informed that the sister would respond to him only when her prayers had properly concluded, that he was not to knock or cough to announce his presence. Yet he was troubled, for a cough had indeed seized his diaphragm, and to suppress it took immense will. Then the port was slid away, and while he could not see her, he was aware of the breathing of Jeanne Le Ber, then he heard her voice, distinct and low, in frail greeting. Rather than say hello, he released his pent-up cough, and the frail woman returned one of her own. The Indian's own breathing proved difficult, and he often had to interrupt himself to cough again, to which Jeanne Le Ber would cough in return, for both were feeling unwell.

"Do you know who I am?" The Rat asked the ascetic.

"I have heard of you. Yet not for some time. News from the outside rarely extends to me. I remember that you are called The Rat. I remember also that you were a Christian. Are you still?"

"I am, Sister." Part of her contract called for her to be admitted to the Order of the Congregation of Notre Dame, and referred to as Sister, although she would never be obliged to participate in the life of the convent. Then the chief surprised her by asking, "Are you?"

"Has my solitude claimed my spirit, you're asking? Chief Kondiaronk, my spirit is ever the more fervently committed to the Blessed Sacrament."

"And are you comfortable in there, are you happy, are you content?"

"I must dissuade you from this discourse. My happiness, my contentment, my comforts, are of no interest to me and should be of no concern to anyone. I will permit no such indulgence. Now, if you have come seeking help for yourself, or for your people, then that is a matter we might discuss."

He had wanted to speak to this saintly creature, this prisoner of God, who had removed her beauty from the world of men and her intelligence from the affairs of her colony to devote herself to life's mysteries and to the command of God. What did she learn from the experience, or was learning in itself an excitement to the senses she had vowed to decline? He had been close to shamans who had delivered themselves to personal cleansing in the forests and a solitude of the spirit, yet they would return and dwell among their people. This refusal to walk under the sky, to be brightened by the sun, this repudiation of human contact, was a fanaticism that he wanted to witness before he died. "There is one thing," The Rat confided.

He told her then of his predicament. Of how he had been working to create a peace among all the Indian tribes, that one thousand and three hundred peace delegates had arrived to represent them. From Wisconsin to the west, and Acadia to the east, the Indians had come, an occasion that was grand and festive. The Montagnais and Assiniboine from the north were there, as were the Sioux, Cree, Saulteurs and his own Huron nation from the west. Indians had arrived even from Florida. The Iroquois had also paddled to the meeting.

"The Iroquois are here, in Ville-Marie, to make peace?" She had difficulty suffocating her enthusiasm, for she forbade herself such interests in any form.

"Yes, the Iroquois are here. If you heard guns firing in recent weeks, they were fired to honour the arrival of delegates. We have a rather new governor in New France, Louis-Hector de Callières. He's been here for a couple of years now. A nice man. Together, with great difficulty, we have fabricated this peace. The Indians agree that we shall never again war with one another. We agree also that if the English and the French make war upon one another, all the Indian tribes shall remain neutral. This will allow the French to control the lands to the west and down the Mississippi. The English will lose their allies, and therefore their power. But they will not be attacked, either—not by the French, who do not have enough warriors. The only difficulty may be that the English have the power to attack the French on their own. This may yet occur, and it disturbs me, Sister."

News of the outside world was not unwelcome. She had to moderate the pleasure this conversation had provided, and terminate it quickly. Still, she needed to know if she could be of service. "Is there something, Chief Kondiaronk, that I may do for you, under the eyes of God?"

The Rat leaned in more closely to the grille. "Sister, part of the agreement requires that each tribe bring its prisoners and its slaves here to the island of Montreal. Here, they will be returned to their tribes, or, if they are French, to the French. If they are English, we will send them home."

The scratchy, coughing voice behind the grille praised him. "You have created a wonderful peace."

"Yet there is a problem. The Iroquois have arrived, and they have not brought their slaves with them, nor have they brought any prisoners. We know they have more than anyone. What shall I do, Sister? I need to be guided on this matter by one so close to God as you."

Jeanne Le Ber pondered the problem awhile. "In this life, I hope that I am the furthest soul from God in all the world. To be close to God is to know His comfort, and I wish no such relief in this life, lest that gift separate me from the Blessed Sacrament."

"I am sorry for my words, Sister," The Rat told her.

"The Iroquois," Jeanne Le Ber continued, "accept that they are the most hated ones. They have given you a reason to hate them more. If you are to break the peace, then break the peace over this issue, Chief Kondiaronk. If you are not to break the peace, then ignore this matter, and the Iroquois will then know that you do not intend to break the peace. For if you do not do it when they give you a reason, they know that you will not do it when they give you none. Now, I must retire. The time has come to recite my prayers."

Kondiaronk thanked her, but the grille plate had already slid shut.

†††

The Rat did as Jeanne Le Ber suggested. He oversaw the transfer of prisoners, including Iroquois prisoners back to the Iroquois, and made no mention to them that their own account was in deficit. Many of the other tribes saw this as a humiliation directed at Kondiaronk, and they wondered how he might respond. If the peace were broken here, each man knew, it would never be regained.

His cough had progressed to a fever, and he felt too weak to stand when the time came for him to address the sacred gathering. Thirteen hundred warriors, delegates from all the tribes, and the French governor and the governors of the largest French towns, were waiting, but he could not stand. The French brought him a stool. He did not have the strength to sit upon it, and swayed in his fever. Out of the home of a merchant, a large and imposing armchair was brought to him, a rich man's extravagance, and this satisfied his posture, his dizziness and his weakened knees. All looked upon the Huron chief in the sumptuous chair and waited for him to speak. Still, his voice was weak, his throat parched. Kondiaronk was offered wine. He stated a preference for the syrup of the maidenhair fern. After considerable delay, this was brought to him, and at last The Rat began to speak.

Though his voice was scarcely audible, so anxious was everyone to hear his words that the silence of the gathering was complete. Everyone leaned in to hear. Would Kondiaronk bring peace or war?

Humbly, yet comprehensively, he described the steps that he had undertaken to bring a lasting peace to the Indian nations. He counselled them on the necessity of peace, and reiterated the prosperity and benefits that it might bring. Then, still in his big armchair, he turned toward Governor Callières. "Act," he told him, "in a manner that no man can accuse you of betraying the trust we place in you today."

At that, his voice failed. He was done. The great throng of French and Indians applauded and whooped. Indians beat their drums. He was carried, still in the armchair, to the Hôtel-Dieu. Early the next morning, having offered his prayers to God and received the sacraments, Kondiaronk died.

The French carried his body from the Hôtel-Dieu to his tepee, where they laid him upon beaver skins. His gun and his sword were placed by his side, and a kettle, for his use in the spirit world. Sixty Iroquois moved in solemn procession towards him, and they, his most vicious enemies in life, paid tribute to him in death. Their chief declared the day to be devoted to grieving, and the Iroquois themselves were the ones who covered the body in sorrow and in dignity.

Not since the procession of Jeanne Le Ber to her chapel had Ville-Marie seen one that matched The Rat's funeral. Sixty military men led the entourage, followed by sixteen Huron warriors, four abreast. Wearing beaver skins, the natives had painted their faces black in mourning, and they held their guns with the barrels pointed down. The clergy followed in their black robes, genuflecting and carrying their Bibles. Six war chiefs from six different tribes bore the body. The corpse was covered in flowers, and upon his stomach The Rat held a plumed hat, a gorget over his throat, and, at his side, a sword. His brothers and children followed immediately behind the body, then the remaining chiefs of the tribes and the leaders of the tribal councils. Then came the wife of the intendant of New France, the governor of Montreal, and the governor of New France, who had worked so closely with him to create the peace. Like a Moses of old, Kondiaronk had been allowed to see the paradise of his vision, but he would not be permitted to inhabit the realm. As his body was buried in the crypt at Notre Dame, muskets—military and Indian—fired in his honour.

In her cell, Jeanne Le Ber permitted herself to smile at the sound of the guns. The Iroquois wars were over. Never again would her people fear being scalped overnight or live with the horror of knowing that their children might be roasted or that they themselves might be slowly burned from the feet up.

Peace with the Iroquois had depended upon the acumen of the governor and the vision of a far-flung Huron chief who lived all the way in Michilimackinac, and she was glad that in his final days they had had a chance to speak. God had arranged that meeting, a knowledge that strengthened her faith. Even from her cell, she might be of use to others.

†††

The second call upon Jeanne Le Ber came in 1711, a decade after the peace with the Iroquois had been signed and Kondiaronk had died. The English, finally realizing that the continent was becoming French, that the Iroquois no longer imposed their will on the people to the north or moved to restrict their movements or commerce, embarked upon a full-scale attack to rout the French once and for all and seize the entire colony for England. They moved an army overland toward Montreal and sent a great fleet up the St. Lawrence to Quebec. The people heard the dire reports and knew that their military was ill prepared. Once again, the colony lay in mortal peril, with scant hope of salvation.

Jeanne Le Ber was told of these perilous circumstances and was exhorted to intercede. To the dismay of the clergy, she turned to her needlepoint.

Normally, she slept only briefly, rising at 4 A.M. between Easter and All Saint's Day, and at four-thirty through the darker, cold months. Now she did not sleep, but embroidered a banner. On one side, she created an exquisite image of the Virgin Mary, and on the other she inscribed the words, "She is as terrible as an army in battle array. She will help us to vanquish our enemies."

When she was done, she called for the *abbé* to visit her again.

The banner was blessed by the Abbé de Belmont, although he feared it might be too little, too late. But that night, in the Gulf of St. Lawrence, a storm ransacked the English fleet. Ships were damaged, a few floundered on rocks, others lost their bearings, and every ship lost contact with the other. One by one, the surviving vessels limped back to Boston. As the commanders in the field were informed of the disaster, their own interest in the expedition quickly faded, and after days of deliberations, the army returned home as well. Once again, Montreal had been spared. This time, Jeanne Le Ber did not indulge herself in a smile, but prostrated herself before the altar of the chapel at night, and pleaded forgiveness for her ongoing involvement in temporal affairs.

She would live three more years, and near the end of her days she received another visit from the Abbé de Belmont. He asked her if she had benefited well and been sustained by her life of devotion. She told him she had received sweetness and tranquility from her life of prayer when she had been at home in her father's house. Since entering her cell, she had experienced no such blessings, but had given herself to the gloom and despair of her days, receiving no divine guidance or consolation, no satisfaction or delight. Yet she persevered, and as she lay dying, she dispatched her nurse to the chapel so that she would be more alone, and she had the curtains drawn to complete the coming shroud of death. At nine o'clock in the morning, on the third day of October, at the age of fifty-three, after twenty years in her crypt, Jeanne Le Ber stepped into the death she had so long cherished, and this time it proved both real and final.

†††

The gentleman who called in 1710 was dressed smartly, if not as a man of royalty, then from a class that had not crossed Radisson's door in many years. He had heard the man give his name—perhaps it had rung a bell, perhaps not—to be sure, his recollections were not what they had once been. "You are, sir, by name?" he asked, perhaps for the fifth time, but he could not be confident of the number of repetitions either.

"Charles Smythe Hamilton, sir," the man replied, smiling, willing to indulge the feeble man his proclivities. "I am waiting for you to recognize me, sir. Perhaps that will be best. If you come to understand that you know me, I think it will be the preferred course for our discussions."

"You confuse me, sir. You are who, did you say, by name?"

Radisson received his visitor from his bed. When the knock had come upon the door, he had barked out the command to enter, twice, three times, before he heard the squeaky hinges on the door respond and heard the announcement of boots upon the floor. A man's. He had shouted out again, so that the visitor would know which way to turn, and soon enough, the smartly attired gentleman in a waistcoat with cummerbund, a tall hat held under one arm, stood to face him squarely in the doorway. If this was Death, he possessed accoutrements superior to those Radisson had expected. If he were the devil, his kingdom could not be so bad.

Seated on a wooden chair he'd pulled up alongside the bed, Charles Smythe Hamilton took hold of the old man's hand, a gesture that startled the invalid for its tenderness and sympathy. Although he flinched briefly, he did not pull back his grip, permitting his palm to rest in the visitor's. In a moment, he mustered a measure of strength to exert a responsive pressure through his fingers.

"You are who, sir, by name?" he asked again. He rocked his head from side to side. "It's no use testing my memory, for it has failed me. You say I know you, sir, but my recollections are feeble. From where do I know you?"

"Do you remember the *Happy Return*? A stout ship, you called her."

Radisson nodded. He gestured for a drink of water, and his guest passed him the ladle. "Surely," he recalled. "A stout ship. We took back Hudson's Bay with her. For the English . . . I *think* it was for the English that one time. Was it for the French?"

"The English. Then you returned, I understand, to the Great Salt Bay."

"I returned, yes. I thought to make it my home."

He bore all the marks of having lived a difficult, yet active, life, one that had succumbed to age, disease and imminent dissolution. His thinned white hair, scraggly and unwashed, fell down the sides of his face upon the filthy pillow. Careless scissors had haphazardly chomped away at his beard, his skin had turned a sallow colour, and the old man frequently coughed, spitting up bloody phlegm. His nose was moist, and the visitor noticed how it had been bent out of shape, this way and that, during the man's lifetime, most probably from the famous fistfights in Ville-Marie each spring before the *voyageurs* embarked for the Indian lands. His nightshirt lay open to expire his internal heat, and Smythe saw the X carved there by Chief Kondiaronk to warn him against cheating. The man must have been born under a lucky star not to have had that incision struck through to the quick.

"I loved the wilderness," Radisson recalled, as though in a reverie now, finding his strength and voice. "My wife in England, here, was not inclined to respect my nature. My own children know not my face. So I procured for myself an end to the marriage, under the Lord. These matters can be arranged, under the Lord, when your wife is the daughter of a powerful man. I went back to the Great Salt Bay to harvest my days. A wilderness, the wildest a man can know, yet with no Iroquois! A paradise to me. I could make a coin there. No fortune—I gave up all promise of that. But I could make a coin for my old age and live beside the icy water."

"So what happened?" the visitor asked. He relished hearing the old man's storytelling voice again, and so posed the question even though he knew the reply.

"I had gone where no man could find me. But the French, they found me. They held some grievance. Louis XIV, silly arse, the king himself, issued a proc-lamation for my arrest and sent a lackey, some sort of chevalier, to fetch me out." Radisson paused, then asked for more water, which he promptly received. "Groseilliers, now he was a knight, a Knight of the Garter."

"I heard that," the man recalled. "A distinguished honour."

"A chevalier—the same as a knight, but of low rank. Chevalier Pierre de Troyes, that's who they sent. Do you know him? Are you French or English, sir?"

"I'm an Englishman, sir, in the merchant marine."

"Oh yes? What do they call you, by name? I was a sailor myself one time."

"I know that. In the French navy—"

"The navy, and in the service of the Hudson's Bay Company, too."

"My employer now," the visitor noted.

Radisson, in his infirmity and frailty, fought through the vagueness of his perceptions to place this man, even to comprehend that he had a visitor at all, one more distinguished than the usual riffraff that filed through his doors.

"Employed by the company, you say?" he asked the man. "On ships? What rank, sir, if I may so inquire of you?"

"That, sir, may depend on you."

"Me?"

"You, sir. Pierre-Esprit Radisson."

Now the ailing man was confused, although not in the same way as before. Instinctively, he believed that a man in full command of his faculties might be no less beguiled. "Even when I lived in toil for the company, I dispensed to no man his rank. Why do you say, sir, that your rank depends on me?"

As though to indicate the delicacy of his mission, the visitor lugged his chair under him a tad closer to the bed. He leaned near enough that his breath could be felt upon the old man's pale, weathered skin.

"Radisson," he whispered, "do you remember the keen blade? The Dagger of Cartier, they call it?"

"Aye," Radisson made known, yet whispering also.

"You had given it to your wife, for safekeeping," the visitor reminded him.

"Aye," suspiciously, Radisson concurred.

"Yet, when you and your wife parted company, you took back the knife."

"Aye," the old man recalled. "Her father had promised me an estate. He did not give me an estate when I sailed back to England on the *Happy Return*. A vow to me, broken—as all men, it seems, do. They may keep their vows between one another, but to me and to Des Gros, we are not worthy of any man's faithful word. That's what I learned in my comings and goings throughout my long life. No king, no chevalier, no wife—and I've had three—no child—and I've had nine, I'm told—no company—though I have toiled only for the one—has stood by a significant vow to me, sir. I took the dagger back from the man who took back the estate that I had most solemnly been promised."

"And where," the man whispered, yet more quietly with each word, and more slowly, "would said knife, the Dagger of Cartier, sir, be now?"

Radisson glared at the man awhile, and a glimmer seemed to register in the darker patches of his mind—a memory, perchance, but he could not be certain or trustful of his own reactions. He was enjoying the company. That's all he really knew. "Who be asking?" he wanted to know. "By name."

"Charles Smy—"

"I know that much!" Radisson spit out. "I'm not clueless yet. Who are you, lad, and be quick about your answer if you know what's good for you!"

"It's been a while," Charles Smythe Hamilton replied, and he grinned broadly, "since you've called me 'lad.'"

The glimmer in the dark patch of his mind began to glow a bit, and the old man could see a light. "Hey, there . . . hey there, now, you're that lad. That cabin boy!"

"Aboard the *Happy Return,* sir. I'm proud to make your acquaintance again."

"Look at you! All grown up! Straight and true! What are you, lad? Speak your rank to me. It's not cabin boy, I can see!"

Hamilton smiled, and told him, "It could be captain, sir. That's up to you. I could have my own commission, if only you would wish it."

"I wish it upon you, lad! But how can this be? What are you saying to me?"

Resorting to a conspiratorial tone of voice again, Hamilton explained. "The company, sir—specifically the younger Mr. Kirke, sir, he knows about our fondness for one another, from the old days. I've spoken of it often enough. Proud, I am to have made your acquaintance, to have shared conversation under starry nights."

"We knew a few rough days at sea, lad!"

"We did, sir. At any rate, Mr. Kirke, sir, knows that you possess the Dagger of Cartier, for you took it back from his aunt—that would be your wife—and rightly so, I must say, when your nuptials failed to endure as you had reason to expect."

Radisson regarded the young man with a cold eye, wondering what villainy had breached his portal this time. "What do you want from me, lad—the knife?"

"Radisson, your time is nearly done for this earth. If you go and the knife remains hidden, the knife is forever gone also. Certainly, it is gone from the hands of the younger Mr. Kirke, sir."

The old *coureur de bois* nodded, comprehending. "His family took everything from me that I delivered to them. My furs by the shipload. Hudson's Bay itself. My true knowledge of the north that did guide the company west. I have been stripped of every sweetness in life, and all good comforts, and the only payment I have received is my citizenship as an Englishman. *Citizenship!* That's what they offered, and that's what I have claimed! A knighthood? No, no, only Groseilliers deserved that. Me, they made a mere citizen, like all the rest. They had to. France would not have me. And now—" A hacking fit interrupted him.

"Sir, I have not knocked upon your door to torment you—"

"Listen! And now, as I lie dying, when I hope that death comes running like a hare, the company desires the one thing I have left. The Cartier Dagger! This, too, your young Mr. Kirke wishes to extract from me. From one generation to the next, do these gentlemen have no depth to their greed, their desire, their endless need to extract from me all that I might possess?"

The visitor had no kind answer to that question, and so kept his peace.

"What's in it for you, lad?" Radisson asked.

Hamilton looked up. He felt dispirited, forlorn, defeated in his mission here. "A commission. I am to be made a captain, if, and only if, I deliver the knife. I will be given my commission so that I can seek my fortune, as you did, sir. Perhaps I shall find it, perhaps not. Perhaps, like you, I will find it many times over, only to have it denied me by those of lofty authority. But I have come here to you, sir, to plead that I be offered the opportunity in my time. That once more we go forth, your spirit in me and upon my ship, once more we go forth to seek our destiny."

Again, Radisson requested water, and this time the visitor held the ladle to his lips himself while the old man drank.

"Of all the bargains I've been offered in my long life," he said, slowly, thoughtfully, "this must surely be the poorest one."

The man's eyes were downcast.

"But you have not come to steal from me, have you, lad?"

"No, sir."

"You have not come to cheat me."

"No, sir."

"You spoke an honest word. No guff. That means something to me. I have nothing. Soon I'll be dead—may the hare be swift. I will give you what I cannot take with me. Make certain, lad, that you gain that commission. Promise me! Have the ship under your feet and your crew about you, have your captain's papers in one hand and your sailing manifest in t'other. Only then, lad, do you hand over the knife to our young Mr. Kirke, the son of a rascal and a rascal himself! Promise me!"

Hamilton grasped the old man's forearm, which still contained the sinew, if not the muscle, of a bygone day. "I promise, sir. I vow it."

"You'll need a pick and shovel."

"I'm capable, sir."

"You'll get yourself more dirty than an Iroquois set for battle!"

"I'm willing, sir."

"Then go forth, young man. Captain Hamilton. Seek your fortune. I ask: do not be cheated of your commission, and take me along, sir, in spirit."

"That I vow, sir."

Taking his leave the next morning, Charles Hamilton was unable to say his final thanks or farewell. All he could do was to close down the lids on the old man's eyes and walk forth, determined to keep his promises. Which he did. He did not deliver the Cartier Dagger into the hands of the Hudson's Bay Company until after his feet stood upon his ship, and the young Mr. Kirke, knife in hand, had to scamper with great urgency to disembark as the bow and spring lines were being tossed.

The following year, Captain Charles Smythe Hamilton carried a cargo of soldiers from Boston for a jolly raid on Quebec, intending to drive the French from North America forever. A banner of the Virgin Mary, created by Jeanne Le Ber, rose up against the stout ship. The doomed sailors and soldiers did not know that, and would have considered it a laughable fortification. Yet they were further entreated by the most violent of storms. Hamilton's ship floundered. Many of the ship's company washed up on shore, alive, to be imprisoned and later returned to the English. A score drowned. Hamilton himself drowned, his body recovered on the beach and buried near Tadoussac. Old men who dug his grave didn't know him or care that he was a captain, although he would have welcomed their acquaintance, for they were all aging *coureurs de bois* of whom he'd heard so many tales.

Slowly, with their old bones and weary muscles, they dug.

A wind whistled up from the river, passing through the trees.

As one, the old men ceased their chore and gazed up a moment, then into the dark forest. As one, they felt the ghost of an old friend pass by, paddling the rivers inland. How had he arrived again, and made his way here, upon this shore? That iron will. Did he paddle again to the Great Salt Bay?

BOOK TWO

CHAPTER 13

1958

THREE YEARS AFTER HER INTRODUCTION TO HER DECEASED FA-ther's erstwhile cronies at the Copacabana, where she babbled silly sayings into the microphone and ran off giggling—once, straight into the arms of the most flamboyant of Montreal's former mayors—eleven-year-old Anik Clément was on her way to visit that illustrious, sage carnival of a man again.

She did so routinely.

Alive, her father segregated his family from his rough work. They lived away from the nightclub scene, and no high rollers hung out on their block. For a while after his death, her mom cut herself off from her father's old pals, but that changed with the funeral for Michel Vimont. Anik never understood the sudden shift, but neither did she regret that her quiet home became a livelier place overnight. Men popped by to fix things. Or dropped in to crack open a six-pack and a monstrous bag of chips to shoot the breeze. Anik loved the chips, which were never allowed in her house otherwise. If her mom had nothing to do on a Friday night, she might make a phone call, and just like that she got to hang out in a crowd while a babysitter with a toothpick between his teeth and a revolver on his hip slouched down on the sofa in her home. He watched the black-and-white TV another of her gun-toting sitters had purchased. Anik didn't dare sneak out on these guys, but as long as she hopped into bed the moment her mom was dropped off, she could stay up as late as she pleased.

She had to educate her sitters, though. One guy, when she was nine, asked if she wanted a beer. She told him that he shouldn't offer young girls beer, that it was his *job* to make certain that she didn't drink beer. That it was his *job*, even, to make sure that she got to bed at a decent hour.

He shrugged and swigged his Molson Ex. After a while, he asked, "So what's a decent hour?"

She wasn't sure how honest she should be. "It depends."

"On what?" He was a thin man with a bald head and a waxed handlebar moustache he constantly shaped. He wore two gold bands through his left earlobe, unheard of at the time.

"On what's on television. *The Honeymooners* starts soon. I should be allowed to watch that. Then I got homework because it's a school night. After that, I should read a little. If a good show's on—I like westerns—I could watch them, too, to keep you company. How late, I dunno for sure—midnight?"

Midnight, then, but no beer.

As a further bonus, Anik had places to go during the day whenever she was not in school and her mother busily sewed. The child was introduced to a world that stimulated her interests beyond the meagre poverty of her district. Carole Clément made certain that the men understood to not expose her daughter to anything shady, but they all pooh-poohed her concerns, reminding her that Anik was Roger's little girl.

"You think I'm gonna risk crawling halfway to heaven—if I'm lucky enough to get that far—on my hands and knees, my knuckles all scraped and bloody, every inch of the way beggin' my Lord and Saviour to gimme a half-assed chance here, only to find out I gotta answer to Roger 'cause I did sumthin' wrong to his kid? Lady, are you plain crazy or just nuts?"

After a time, she trusted Anik to their company. The men enjoyed protecting the fatherless child, taking care of their extended family on behalf of the one who'd been struck down. Apart from her sitters, Anik could depend upon half a dozen of her dad's buddies to keep an eye peeled for her welfare, and among these, no one paid closer attention than the former mayor.

As she walked on her own to his house she was daydreaming and playing with her yo-yo. Working on her sleepers. She needed a new one, she believed, a Master's Series, if she wanted to improve on a minute, but putting her old one away seemed wrong to her and probably unlucky. So she settled for the sixty seconds she could make hers sleep now. Bouncing along, she threw in a Walk the Dog and a Rock the Baby, tricks she could perform without concentrating, and waiting for a red light, she shyly demonstrated her latest moves for a little old lady who seemed nearsighted but quite enthralled. Saddle the Pony. Snake the Ladder. Anik smiled bashfully as the woman bent lower and closer to peer at her showing off, and she received an approving nod before stepping smartly across on the green.

Pat the Monkey—or, as she and her friends called it, Pat the Monkey's Butt.

She took long, bobbing strides.

Anik had sprouted, becoming tall among her peers, skinny and lanky-looking, like a boy. She wore her hair cut similarly to a boy's trim, a tad longer because she adored Elvis Presley's hair. She had a D.A. like his at the back—a duck's ass. Her mom didn't allow her to go totally boyish on the cut. Close enough, though. Some of the men were calling her a tomboy, and they chuckled when they said it, loving the idea. "Eleven's the perfect age," the old mayor said. She didn't know about that. She had big brown eyes and a sprinkle of freckles across her thin dewdrop nose. The first girl in her neighbourhood to routinely wear jeans, she was also the only one to wear a denim jacket on cool days. Her mom had made it for her. Walking to see the mayor, she wore a light-blue sleeveless blouse without a collar, the most feminine top she owned. He'd warned her, "Next year at this time, we'll send a limo to pick you up. A Cadillac! Armed guards, we'll need, to keep the boys away."

She didn't know about that, but guessed that next year would never arrive for the old mayor.

He adored her.

She loved him back. She was going to miss him.

Such a huge man! He made her laugh all the time. On her birthday and at Christmas, he gave her wonderful presents. She'd not been accustomed to that, except from her dad. At Easter, he planned hunts. She scoured his entire house to bring back chocolate eggs tucked under furnishings and collect them in a big bowl. All the while, the fat old mayor would help himself from the bowl, unwrapping and eating up the chocolates almost as quickly as she could gather them, so that she had to go faster, faster, racing around, and only when she had it filled up, despite his best efforts to maintain her pace, would he stop eating, his lips and fingers all smeared with gooey chocolate, and concede, "Yep, I think you've found more than I can eat. You whupped me, fair and square."

She'd stumble home with the big bowl of chocolate Easter eggs in her arms.

Best of all, the old mayor would sometimes talk about her dad. He might say, "I used to go outside to watch him play on the river." Anik would know that he was talking about the rink in the internment camp, because her mother had explained that to her, although the old mayor would hedge on that part of the story. Everything was large about him: his nose, his chin, the way his cheeks expanded as he smiled, which widened his big face, and his voice, immense, filled a room even when he spoke softly. The big voice caused everything he had to say sound more substantial. Especially if he was talking about her dad. "It wasn't fair, him playing in that pickup game. He was better than the rest. In the NHL, okay, maybe he was no All-Star. He was a tough guy, not a skater, not a shooter, but on the river in that pickup game among the pris—" Everything he talked about felt so large that, if he inserted a gap into a story, the space felt cavernous. "On the river in that game, he skated circles around everybody. Scored a few goals, too. I always bet on his team, and me, I never bet dumb."

Her mother had explained to her that the old mayor was dying. If she wanted to see him again, she'd better get cracking.

Yet Anik put off the visit. She was scared of that, someone dying.

She didn't like it that her dad had died. That he'd been killed. She missed his presence in the house—the way his heavy shoes would tromp across the floor and the old, slumping house would rattle. She felt so safe then, and hadn't felt safe since. She missed him tucking her in at night. Although she probably wouldn't let it happen now, after he was gone Anik had missed being tickled. Her dad had been such a great tickler, which remained an easy thing to remember, and sometimes that worried her the most: that someday she wouldn't remember everything important. She might forget him. One thing she wouldn't forget, she knew, was the way he died. A dagger. Stuck in him. She could never get that thought out of her head and it made her feel sad whenever she dwelled on it. She imagined that her dad had felt very lonely, bleeding to death in the park. She liked to imagine that he died thinking of her, but that thought made her even sadder.

The old mayor kept her in stitches with his stories. If he died and stopped telling stories, her dad, she felt, might be further away. He might disappear.

She liked the old mayor's stories about himself, too. He'd had dinner with the king and queen of England! He made the king laugh. Everyone in the banquet hall noticed and wondered what on earth the mayor of Montreal could be saying to cause the king to laugh so hard.

"He was sitting beside me, the king, back before the war," Camillien Houde confided to the girl, "and he said to me, 'Mr. Mayor, what are you reading?' For always, my head was down, reading, even though we were at the dinner table. And I said, 'Your Majesty'—that's what you call a king, you know," the old mayor explained to the girl, whispering. "'Your Majesty,' I said, 'I'm trying to memorize this list. It's a very important list. My advisors worked on it for a day and a half before they gave it to me. It's all the things I'm not supposed to talk to you about.' Then I said, 'Here, Your Majesty, why don't you take the list. If I talk about anything that's on it, remind me to be quiet.' I handed him my list, and the king, he just laughed and laughed. He loved my list! Do you know what?"

"What?" Anik would always ask, although she heard the story often.

"That's what we talked about for the rest of the night. The items on my list. King George, he went down my forbidden list. One by one."

She knew a man who had dined with a king. That made her feel that she, too, was special. Her father, she remembered, used to call her Princess. Hadn't he? Or was it only the old mayor who called her that? Was she already forgetting?

As she approached the house on St. Hubert Street in the *quartier* east of the mountain known as the Plateau, she noticed a heightened level of activity. Comings and goings were common around the home of Camillien Houde, which was one reason she liked being there. She felt at times that she lived at the centre of the world, where all decisions were made, but today the number of vehicles and the solemn huddle of men in their trench coats and fedoras worried her. She slowed down. She'd been Walking the Dog, but the yo-yo spun out of control. She had to catch it and rewind the string after working a knot free.

Anik continued towards the house, yet her pace had slowed so much she was easily overtaken by her mother's best friend, Father François, who clamped an arm around her shoulder, gave her a quick squeeze, and urged her to keep up as he dashed on ahead. He seemed to have an inkling of what troubled her.

"Not to worry. Nothing bad will happen today."

"Why are you running?" Anik asked him, skipping a few steps to catch up. For a large, rather sloppy, man, the priest walked fast.

"Do you call this running? I'm walking briskly." He swung his arms and marched along. Except for his stride, he looked like a priest today, wearing his black cassock. She rarely saw him on the street in a robe.

"Then why are you walking briskly?"

"That's my business, young lady. I'm not telling you."

"Walk by yourself, then." She broke pace, deliberately dragging her heels.

Father François spun around. "I'm trying to lose weight. Or, shall we say, restrict how much I gain. There. Are you satisfied now?"

She had one more critical question to ask before skipping along beside him again. "Why are those people over there just standing?"

"Reporters do that. They stand around," Father François explained, and he returned to his enforced gait. "How they do it yet remain thin is beyond me. They're vultures, Anik. They wait for death so they can gnaw on the bones. Maybe that's why they're so thin. It's their shabby vulture diets."

He cast a glance over his shoulder. The girl appeared to be taking him seriously, so he abruptly changed his tone. He slowed down and clamped an arm around her again. "They want to be the first to praise him. When a man of his stature dies, everyone wants to say what a wonderful man he was. For a while, we forget the bad and talk only about the good."

"Even you?" Anik assessed.

The priest shot her a glance. He considered her question alarmingly adult. "Even me," he said. "We don't speak poorly of the dead in case someone up above is listening while the man's fate is being assessed. Once he's found his place on the other side, what we say won't matter. That's the logic behind it all. Anik, for what it's worth, I share such superstitions. I'm only too human. Come on, let's go in."

First, she wanted to know, "Is he sick today? Will he die?" She grabbed his wrist to keep him from going straight in. The gathering of the press—down the block, a television crew had set up its apparatus—made her apprehensive.

Father François caught the distress in her voice. "He's a tired man," he assured her quietly, "but nothing should be awful today. The end will come soon, the doctor says. Prepare yourself for that. You must. But I've spoken to him on the phone, he's in good spirits. He's himself. He'll be his old self again once he sees you. For a man in his condition, a boost to the spirits is a good thing."

She took a few steps with him before she asked, "Is that what I am? A boost?" She wondered at times why a man who had dined with a king ever bothered with her.

He hesitated. Sometimes the young grew up more quickly than he realized. "We'll go in together, shall we?"

Camillien Houde was delighted to greet Anik, and equally content to spot the priest. As Father François entered the room, a bevy of older women hovered in attendance, a few at prayer, others in full throttle. They had come to attend to the mayor's passing, and Houde was clearly bored by them while detesting the solemnity of their project.

"Ladies! Ladies!" he cried. "As you can plainly see, my spiritual advisor has arrived. Leave us now. A dying man must make time for his spiritual advisor."

The flap of women in their rustling crinolines departed the death chamber. Anik was wondering if she should leave as well when a covert bob of Houde's chin kept her in the room.

"Ah," Houde sighed, once the three of them were alone together, "my spiritual advisor. What advice do you have for me today?"

From under his cassock, Father François pulled out a flask. "Mountain whiskey."

"Oh, it's my good friend Jack! Come to pay me a visit." The old mayor ripped off the cap and helped himself to a long pull. "Aaahhh," he said with exaggerated satisfaction. "That's so good."

A discreet knock on the door caught their attention. Anik opened up while the old mayor hid his bottle under the quilt. One of the little old ladies who'd been shooed outside had something to add. "We realized, after we were gone, that the young lady . . ." she let her voice trail off.

"She may stay," Houde told her. If he'd had the strength, he would have dressed her down for being a busybody. Instead, he told a fib to get rid of her. "She's in training. For the convent. It's good for her to listen to a priest counsel the dying."

The wee grey-headed woman nodded. With some misgiving she gazed at the girl with the yo-yo, who wore blue jeans and didn't look anything like a novitiate. The woman told the old mayor, "You're looking better, Mayor Houde. Your cheeks are flushed. You have your colour back!"

The old mayor shook his left forefinger at her. "Remember that! When your final days come. Always make time for your spiritual advisor."

Father François crossed the floor and, smiling, closed the door on the woman.

"What do they want from me?" Houde carped. "If I close my eyes they mention it and do the sign of the cross. If my eyes blink open again, you should hear them gasp. They thank God, as if they're present at a miracle. Father, if a failing heart and bad blood won't kill me, the sight of those old biddies will."

"We all have our crosses to bear," Father François pointed out to him. "For you, it's your popularity."

"A priest who speaks the truth. You're a rare find, Father. Where's that flask?"

"In your right hand."

Together they comprised an odd coupling—the aging, madcap politician and the youthful, opinionated priest. They were of similar shape, although the older man, taller when upright, was also significantly more rotund. The younger man might match his girth one day, but just as a comparable height was out of the question, so would he never command the attention of a room with the old man's panache. People felt themselves aglow in the former mayor's presence. What made the pair seem odd to others was their political disparity. While it was true that the mayor had initially made his reputation through make-work projects during the Great Depression, creating swimming pools and baths and viaducts that drove the city into bankruptcy while allowing working people to earn a living wage, he had not identified with the left. He had frequently cussed the communists whenever mocking them might charm a vote. His support for Mussolini and the Vichy regime in France attested to a far-right bent that seemed incompatible with his choice of the notorious socialist as his priest for his final days. When Houde had first called Father François to his sickbed, he was weakening but still his old self. He broached the subject with the priest, who expressed his reservations. "Why me?" the younger man asked.

They had met through Carole Clément, but neither man had had many dealings with the other.

"Some people, reaching the end, look around for an appropriate priest," Houde had explained.

"What makes me appropriate?"

"Some people, they don't know too many priests."

"That's true." He remained skeptical. He really only knew Houde through his public image, although they shared some experiences of note. He suspected that the old mayor was Machiavellian at heart—that every decision he made contained hidden manipulations.

"Not true of me, Father. I know more priests than I can count. Anik will tell you I have dined with kings. Well, I've dined with bishops, too, and a cardinal. It's her I asked, you know, to find me a good priest."

Father François found himself increasingly confused. "She orchestrated this?"

"She will confirm it. Father, you may not agree, but I am a religious man. In my way. I need a priest to attend to me. The prelates I know are political men, the lot of them. How can I possibly say my last confession to men I've butted heads with throughout my career? We shared good times, a few laughs . . . once in a blue moon we came to a meeting of the minds. We also enjoyed our share of royal fights. They may keep my secrets, Father, but the sparkle in their eyes, that light, the sense of superiority that would shine upon me in my final hour as I admit to my follies—not to mention confess to my sins—that light would not represent the warm glow of heaven. Father, it might kill me before my heart fails. Besides . . ." he added.

"Besides?" Inwardly, he was agreeing that the man's points made sense. As had happened with many political adversaries of the old mayor, he was being charmed, if not actually duped.

"You and I have seen some things in our time, together and apart, have we not, Father?"

Father François bowed his head, then looked up. "We have."

"And you and I, we know what the other has seen."

The priest wondered who was confessing here. "True," he admitted.

The old mayor allowed that point to shine between them. Then whispered, as the priest bent nearer, "If I asked one of the old priests for a drop, could I trust him to open a flask for a dying man? Out of spite—and I hate to tell you this, but the bishops can be spiteful men, no less than me—they might deny me. They might refuse to sneak a bottle past my nurse, who's a battle-axe and a Temperance Unionist!"

Houde made firm eye contact then, letting it be known that on this one matter he would not broach a compromise.

"I see," Father François noted.

"I'm glad you do. Is it settled, then? All I ask, Father, is that when my time comes you don't get yourself tossed in jail for some union crap."

"If I do, sir, you'll have the connections to get me out."

The old mayor enjoyed a belly laugh, confident that he had chosen wisely.

Father François could decline, or suggest further alternatives, but a dying man was an obligation for a priest, and to say no, to suggest that the man was too rapacious for his blood, or too right-wing, or too amoral in general, struck him as unseemly, not to mention un-Christian. If he really wanted to recuse himself from the duty, he would have to own up to a dent in his own character, for secretly, Father François was interested in what the dying man might confess. Beyond what they had already shared in secret. As well, he knew where Houde was coming from. He uttered his own confessions, and among his peers were many priests with whom he would prefer to remain mute. Rather than acknowledge such a failing, he would see to this man's spiritual needs at the hour of his death.

"How's the young princess of Montreal?" Houde inquired in his failing voice.

- family office : 9M   could have been 12 M
- Founders fonds
- how much equity?
- 45M valuation   45 x .8 x

- reach out people   R|
  recruiter

- file(s) : gets released
  B?

- check out new roles
- Andrew arriving next week

Anik stepped towards the big brass bed where Houde was resting under a sheet and a beautiful patchwork quilt that contained azure and turquoise, with orange piping. She smiled shyly, pleased that he had spoken to her that way.

"I'm all right," she said.

"You don't look all right to me," Houde judged. "You look like a puppy left out in the rain. Maybe that's what you need for yourself—a puppy."

The girl shrugged. She sat at the foot of the bed, as she so often did, and nervously bounced a little. She moved her yo-yo back and forth in her hands.

"Any new tricks?" the old mayor coaxed her.

Again she shrugged.

"The reporters outside," Father François revealed to Houde, "upset her."

"What did they say?" For a moment, the girl felt his spirit, his willingness to defend her.

"Anik is bothered that they're here at all."

The old mayor looked from the girl, back to the priest, then back to the girl again. Slowly, a wide grin began to grow on his visage. He winked at the child. "Come here, you," he said.

When Anik moved up on the bed he pushed himself more upright, which required a considerable outlay of his remaining energy, and drew her close for a hug.

"Now listen up." He held both his hands on her narrow shoulders. "I'm going to give those newspapermen something to write about. But I'm not just a cuddly old bear—I'm a mean one, too. Those newspaper boys will have to be patient. They'll grow frustrated, they'll be fed up and hungry, tired and plumb worn out before I give them what they're looking for. It'll rain on them. Several times! The sun will beat down hot. By the time I'm done, a few of them will wish that they were me and that I was one of them. So bear this in mind, Anik, my pet—us good guys, we don't live to the schedule of the world. The world can wait upon the likes of me and you. Understood? The world can sit back and mind its manners until I'm good and ready. They'll get what they came here for, but not a second too soon. Got that?"

Anik nodded and smiled with him, and when he tried to tickle her she laughed, although she could tell right away that he didn't have much strength left, it was so easy to elude his grasp.

†††

Driving, he inhaled the pungent smell of the street. A sweaty heat. The burnt rubber of fast cars. The oils of haughty, fragrant women who strolled along this boulevard with their suitors. He noticed the relaxed saunter of the ladies' steps, the shimmer of their calves in nylons, the capricious personalities of their white or pastel dresses. Windows lowered, he caught the high timbre of sudden laughter and wished that he could join them, fling himself into whatever sport or seduction the night might bring. This evening confined him to a mission, and the frolic of a warm night in early September had to be ignored, for now.

He hadn't enjoyed a good upper-class romp for a while. Lately, fun had been found in beer parlours and union halls, and in the cramped quarters of friends' flats. Fun had taken serious turns—prolonged, animated discussions supplanting revelry, detailed strategies for strikes or political action displacing, for the moment, his dalliances. The days were tempestuous, and Pierre Elliott Trudeau welcomed the Chinese curse, "May you live in interesting times." He wanted to be wholly immersed in the world, body, mind and—as he was, in private, a religious man—soul.

Jobs of any interest remained difficult to come by. Many believed that his law degree from Harvard went begging as he devoted himself to civil strife and writing for a journal that, in the overall scheme of things, had to be measured as insignificant. Frosh wrote on politics for startup journals, for heaven's sake, not those who could, with a modicum of effort, be senior partners or professors. Yet the enterprise of a law firm could not satisfy his appetite for living, nor even for disputatious talk, and people were wrong that he could easily become a professor in Quebec. Three times he'd applied for a position at the Université de Montreal. Three times he had been rejected. The province's premier, Maurice Duplessis, blocked each attempt—once through an intercession with the rector, once with a word to a dean, and once by putting in a call to the secretary general. In the premier's eyes, Trudeau had studied in communist environments—in Paris and in London—therefore he was deemed unfit.

In the 1950s in Quebec, the heady freedoms of Paris and London were nowhere in evidence.

What to do? He was rich, smart and desired by women. For the time being, he followed his friends Pelletier and Marchand into battle against the regime of Duplessis—since he was being kicked around by the man, he might as well get in a few licks of his own. He also locked horns with American corporations who paid their workers more poorly than elsewhere on the continent. He skewered the political right and took on tough corporations with ideas and logical argument. Nobody could call it a job—it didn't pay—but at least his interest in ideas and action was being stimulated. His choice of weapons—logic, intellectual confrontation—meant that many feared him even as he honed his skills.

By contrast, tonight offered no moment for either argument or agreement.

Tonight was destined for nothing more than a transaction. For him, the most obtuse imaginable.

A base affair. Decidedly illogical. Outside his customary domain.

Yet *exciting*. He had to admit. He was very excited.

I'm travelling as an emissary for the Catholic Church. He laughed as the notion leapt to mind. It wasn't true, just a rationale. *I'm travelling as an emissary for a rogue priest.* Closer to the truth, yet equally amusing. A Dominican. For him, steeped as he was in Jesuit training, the alliance was an unlikely one. *I'm a sucker for adventure.*

He bored easily. Not only was boredom anathema to him, it was also highly dangerous. Boredom pushed him outside his beloved logic, provoked him to be rash. A whisper had been picked up in a conversation, a rumour, so distant it had travelled as a flicker from a far galaxy, passed along out of time from the ears of the upper classes to their lips to fresh ears, so that neither its source nor its veracity could be ascertained. *The Cartier Dagger,* the rumour whirled around, *is up for sale.*

Yet, how could a buyer make contact, when those who possessed the knife, if indeed they existed, craved anonymity? Anyone auctioning the treasure would be suspected of crimes more heinous than mundane possession of stolen property. Buyers had to act covertly. Possession of the dagger itself was a crime, and those who were selling were thieves and killers. The purchase was immoral. Pierre Elliott Trudeau argued such matters with Father François who, having gotten wind of the story about the knife, brought it to the attention of the rich man's son. Apparently, he had wanted to gauge, perhaps pique, his interest.

They discussed the rumour at length. Both men agreed that they should be calling the police, and Trudeau knew whom to call in the department. But they held off. They chose to keep talking, and Father François was developing a different solution. A curious scheme. A proposition. "Purchase the Cartier Dagger yourself, Pierre, why not?" he whispered finally over cognac.

"You buy it."

"Don't be ridiculous. You're the only man I know who can afford it."

"In your dreams, Father. It'll cost millions. I'm not frivolous with money."

"If it's not sold to an honest Quebecer, like yourself, where does it go from here? London again? Paris? It can't appear in the Louvre—it's a murder weapon. To California, perhaps, or to some oil man in Dallas? If so, Quebec loses a measure of its heritage forever. Cartier! Champlain! Maisonneuve! Brulé! Radisson! This is *our* history. No different than if Egypt shipped a pyramid to New York City. Or if the Taj Mahal were reconstructed in Missouri."

"Not quite the same thing," Trudeau said.

"Pierre, if you acquire the dagger—unofficially, of course—the time may come in some future epoch when it can be restored to the populace, no? Enjoyed by a museum, let's say. Or placed in a glass case, let's say, in Notre Dame. Hey, now there's an idea."

"Don't pretend you're entertaining that thought for the first time," Trudeau scoffed.

"Bad enough it should be in the hands of Sun Life or the National Hockey League," the priest went on, ignoring him. "At least in those instances, it's still here, within our borders. Pierre, it belongs to the whole of our family, not to the least worthy of our elements, never to the Order of Jacques Cartier. If they must sell, the people of Quebec must buy. But the people cannot acquire the dagger except—*except*—through secret philanthropy. That's where you come in."

"But how can we do this?" he argued against the priest's spirited ardour.

"That's also where you come in."

Trudeau was flummoxed. "How do you mean?"

"You're smart. I'm not as bright. I'm a priest. You're not. This transaction is beneath my station in life, but you're not even employed. A rich man's folly, we'll call it. Why not? Do it, Pierre. Think of something."

"What rubbish."

The challenge attracted him, he had to concede. Trudeau was also drawn to the project by the priest's desire. How wonderful to do something unique for the people of Quebec, yet in secret, so that no one would find out for decades. As for the moral issues, which stood apparent to both of them, neither man was a stickler for the rules. Leaving the knife in the hands of killers and thieves—as some believed, in the hands of neo-fascists, the Order of Jacques Cartier—did not seem a wholly moral choice either. Father François had another astonishing reason to acquire the murder weapon.

"It's said to hold properties. Those who have possessed it have known great adventures. Imagine, Pierre, someone such as yourself, in possession of the Jacques Cartier Dagger. What a formidable power that union might create."

"You want me to be powerful?"

"The Church can offer the dagger safekeeping. Perhaps you'll bequeath it to us in time. If spiritual properties are at play, perhaps the work of God will benefit."

Magic, then. That, too. Though it belied his logic, and the faith of the Church, it did possess, as an enchanting fragrance of this night, its own seductive allure.

"You're spiritual when it suits your purposes, Father," Trudeau told his friend. "I've noticed that about you."

"I've also noticed something, Pierre. Your Jesuit strain runs deep. You may keep your religion in your hip pocket, yet it's there. It's important to you."

How deep did it run? He had canoed the routes of Radisson, who had carried the knife with him. The spirit of the man seeped into his being during those long hours under the sun, paddle in hand. Those beautiful, endless rivers north. That peace. Radisson had been brutalized by history, working for the British, the French, the Americans—whoever might favour him with a stake. He had allowed the dagger to pass through his hands, sometimes merely to please his wife. With it, his wife's family had prospered. Not the fur trader. That history ran as deeply within Trudeau as did his Jesuit influences. The desire to possess the dagger, to hold the knife once held by Radisson, burned within him. If ever he found it, he would not let go.

He returned to the priest with a calculated scheme. "You heard of the sale from someone—an individual."

Father François buried his hands in his cassock and placed them over his expansive tummy. "I attended a gathering. A lot of ears. Quite a few voices, too."

Trudeau issued an expressive shrug. "Yet, you heard the story from one person in particular. It's not a story that people announce to all and sundry."

"One person, sure. I reiterate, Pierre, he only picked up the rumour from someone else."

"We'll rely on that. Everyone who has repeated the rumour picked it up from someone else. No one speaks too boldly, but confides what he's heard to a few trusted ears. No one knows who initiated the remarks, therefore no one will be afraid to return comments back to their source."

"Perhaps," the priest acknowledged.

They were seated in the quiet of Trudeau's father's library. The house had always been a place for conversation, wine and great debates. From boyhood, when his father had suddenly become wealthy, Pierre Elliott had listened to the best minds of his city argue politics and war, the social contract, the future of the nation. Big ideas had surrounded him during his formative years, and the large canvas of those notions would be tackled in spirited, often inebriated discussion. This room, on the other hand, where mahogany bookcases rose to the ceiling, had been a place for quiet reflection. Trudeau had rarely spoken to his father within this room, and only of matters most solemn. At the age of fifteen he had lost him, a sudden, unexpected death. The pain of absorbing the news had never been extinguished. He now knew why the priest had invited himself over, rather than undertaking this conversation inside a rectory, for theirs was dangerous, subversive talk.

Elbows on his thighs, Trudeau leaned in more closely to his guest. "You must recall who spoke to you, who recited the rumour about the knife going on the black market. Go back. Say to that individual that you repeated the story to a friend, that he repeated it to a friend of his, and so on and so on, you don't know how many times. Say this: that the last person contacted on that chain, an unknown, would like to bid for the Cartier Dagger. He is prepared to pay fair market value."

"What on earth would be its fair market value?" the podgy man in the black cassock inquired.

"Less than its true value, I suppose. Ownership of the relic is dangerous. The market's compressed. If someone is selling, it's either because they need to get rid of it to save their skins, or they require funds. Which also serves to depress its value."

The Dominican-trained priest nodded. For a man who could not hold down a regular job, his friend Trudeau showed business acumen. "Go on."

"Tell the person who had spoken to you to do exactly as you have done. Go back to whoever told *him* the story initially. Pass the message that a buyer has surfaced."

"Ask that everyone ask the next in line to pass along the message?"

"Exactly. No one will know where the chain ended, any more than anyone will discover where it began. If we're lucky, someone will whisper in the ear of the man who possesses the dagger, or the man who started the rumour. That man will only nod and agree to pass along the message, knowing it will be to himself alone."

The scheme seemed plausible, especially if they did not have to travel through too many links. Yet an obstacle remained. "How does the man with the knife, if he's located, communicate back again to the other end of the chain?"

"The same way," Trudeau postulated.

"It might be five people. It might be twenty . . . forty."

"It might become a rumour mill. But communication is still possible. When the time comes to link opposite ends of a rumour mill . . . if and when we get there, we'll figure it out. The point is, we have a chance."

†††

Captain Armand Touton preferred to visit Carole Clément in her home, although his presence could compromise her work as an informant. Yet meeting her outside the home was often difficult as she worked long hours at her sewing machine, and if they were spotted, the rendezvous would be even more awkward to explain. His going to her house gave her the option of saying he'd dropped by to update her on the investigation into her husband's murder. Not that he had anything to update. More than three years had passed without tangible results. In any case, Touton took the preferred risk and used personal time to see her during the day.

"You're getting too close to these people," he told her.

She slaved away at her machine, pins between her lips with which she'd tack a pant cuff. "Is that a fact?" she asked, her mouth closed, voice muffled.

"You spend considerable time with them. Anik, too. You're friends now."

Carole removed the pins from her mouth. "That's the idea, no? I get close. They learn to trust me."

"What happens with all this trust? I haven't heard any great information lately. You're still on the payroll, remember?"

"I'm not in it for the money." She kept her head down, her eyes on her work.

"Maybe. But you take the money and I'm in it for the results."

"Feel free to shove the money up your ass, Captain. If you need help with that, let me know. Maybe your results will fit up there, too."

"There's no need to be vulgar," he said, straightening.

"Who's being vulgar here?" she wanted to know.

He had to think that through. "I'm sorry if I've offended you."

"Are you?" Her machine whirred, a pant leg was completed. She held up the garment for inspection, tossed it aside, then retrieved the next pair off the floor.

"Have you heard anything, to help us out, to justify the budget I spend?"

Pins were between her lips again. She waited until she had her hands free to remove them and speak. "Hypothetically," she said, then put the pins back.

Touton's concern was genuine. His own surveillance had demonstrated how cozy she'd become with gangsters. Other departments, not knowing of their connection to one another, pencilled her in as a gangster's moll. "Go on."

"Let's say I got wind of a bank robbery," she said in a garbled voice. This time, when she took the pins from her lips, she put them down. "What would happen?"

"I'd expect to hear about it."

"*I'd* expect that if the police intervened, they'd make it look like a fluke, not as though they'd been tipped off."

"You've been tipped on a robbery?"

"Several. A few have been carried out. I didn't tell you about those."

Touton wrung his hands, then placed them on his thighs. "Why not?"

"Hey, it's basic. If everything I hear ends up being intercepted by the cops, what does that do to my credibility? I'm doing this to catch my husband's killers, not to foil every little heist."

"But you're willing to tell me about one."

"One. For now."

"Why?"

"To keep you happy. I'm not in this for the money, but . . . I don't say no to the extra bucks. They keep me going. So I'll be good. I'll give you something, Armand."

Touton nodded. As informants went, Carole Clément was unique. She was in with the mob, yet she was not one of them herself. As such, she was not a stoolie who could be intimidated or threatened with incarceration. She actually had more power over him than he did over her, and he was unaccustomed to that. "All right," he said. "Give me what you've got."

"You'll like this." She stuck pins in a pant leg. "It's coming down on your watch. The night shift."

"Do the men involved babysit your daughter?"

"Actually—" she paused to give the machine a whirr. "—they don't."

"This is what bothers me."

"You're right, Captain. You should be bothered. The men I'm closest to get a free pass from me. If you put them in jail, I wouldn't be close to the bad guys anymore, would I? But you're not thinking about that. You're just concerned that I'm willing to squeal on the guys I don't like rather than on the guys I get along with. You think something's wrong with that. Well, Captain, it's a take-it-or-leave-it scenario, know what I mean?"

She had a point. Or several. She couldn't really afford to put away the men who gave her access to the underworld. If she did, she'd lose her value.

"I'll take it," Touton confirmed.

She identified the bank in question, a big one downtown, and provided the date and method. The time would be after hours, as the crooks were planning to drill through a basement wall over the course of a weekend from the building next door. Three false alarms would sound in the downtown area just prior to the robbery, to reduce police capability. "You better respond to those alarms, Armand, otherwise they'll know that you were tipped off. You'd better make it look like you ran into robbers by sheer luck as they were coming out of the building next door with their pockets full of loot."

"Not to worry. Thanks, Carole."

"'Not to worry,' he says."

"I'll take care of everything."

"We'll see. Now why don't you piss off so I can get some real work done here?"

†††

The odd pair put their plan into action. The priest had a drink with a businessman concerning ecclesiastical matters, and in the midst of the conversation revealed the curious, weighty concern on his mind. "The number of people involved so far," he lied, for he knew that he and his friend Trudeau were the only ones, "is impossible to tell. Quite a few, I get that impression. But you told the story to me, and now I'm asking you to speak to whoever spoke to you about it in the first place. Just don't mention my name. That's how this works. No one should know the name of the second person down the line in either direction. Ask him not to mention yours. Then we'll see what transpires."

He departed the meeting muttering a prayer to himself, begging forgiveness for his deceit.

A segment of the community, rich men all, were delighted to be included in the gambit. Before long, the men's clubs were abuzz with the news, and those who were not approached, or not so far, regretted being excluded from a privileged loop. From a friend, Pierre Trudeau learned that word was getting around. His pal had been contacted along the chain not once, but twice.

"How come?" Trudeau asked him.

"I heard the story twice, two weeks apart, from two different people. And after each time, I told a different colleague. And now, first one, then the other, has gotten back to me. So the story's making the rounds. You're not on the chain yourself?"

"Afraid not," Trudeau said. He had been telling a number of lies during this excursion, and saw no reason to quit fibbing now.

He worried that the faddishness of the situation might ruin everything, and told the priest so. "More people are talking about it than should be talking about it."

And yet, word trickled back through the serpentine chain. *Let's make a deal. How?*

He sent a message in return, pretending that he was merely a relay. *Everyone on the chain must maintain discipline and stop talking about this in public.*

The message travelled more quietly, though not with pristine discretion.

A new and difficult query was returned. *Now what?*

A good question. People had puzzled over how the ends of the chain might meet without every link being aware of the encounter, and without the most curious among them, or all of them, discovering a way to listen in. The priest had the same question, and when the query came back to him through the human pipeline, he put it to his point man. "Well? Now what?"

"There's a way," Trudeau said.

He shipped a cryptic message through the pipeline. *Select middleman. Known to you or unknown.*

Whoever purported to be the opposite terminal sent back the news that he'd chosen a former head of the morality squad of the Montreal Police

Department to be the middleman. The title sounded impressive, except that the man had held the position during an era when the job was sacrificial. His responsibility had been to posture as morality's knight one day, then be blamed for police corruption a few months later, thereby taking the heat off the chief of police and the mayor.

"Do you think he's known to the other party?" the priest wondered.

"Of course he's known. Who would choose an impartial third party?"

The idea was both simple and tricky. Each of the men at the ends of the human chain would contact this third party, a man with the imposing name of Réal Guevremont, who would then establish a liaison between them without necessarily knowing to whom he was speaking. When Trudeau called him, from a phone booth on a street nowhere near his home, he told the man to refer to him as *le Noir*, the Black. Sure enough, hearing this, the other entity chose to be known as *le Blanc*, the White.

The chess match had begun.

They had reached their endgame, and Pierre Elliott Trudeau was driving to meet *le Blanc*'s representative. Elsewhere in the city, his friend Gérard Pelletier sat in a café, waiting to be picked up by another envoy from that team. Pierre would drive the man he picked up to a cache of money. Gérard would be taken to the knife. Phone calls would be exchanged, cash viewed and counted, the knife handed over. Gérard would be returned to his café. Safely there, the cash would be removed from its safe and the transaction concluded. Each side would be in control of one environment, and security of that environment remained each side's particular responsibility. That was the idea they had agreed upon, although Trudeau intended to introduce a wrinkle. If all went well, the Cartier Dagger would soon know a different proprietor.

Le Blanc had chosen the Ritz-Carlton as the pickup point for his man, and Trudeau drove his borrowed Jaguar sports convertible, a former lover's wheels, up to the front door. The car was sufficiently unique that his arrival would not be confused with that of any casual visitor, and the man from *le Blanc* was supposed to climb right in. No one did. Trudeau stepped out of the car to speak to the doorman, who wanted him to move along—speak to him cordially and slip him a ten-dollar bill. He continued to wait. Finally, a man emerged from the hotel and nodded. He paused while the doorman opened the door to the Jag, then crouched down and got in.

"What took you so long?" Trudeau asked. "You were supposed to be waiting."

"I wasn't expecting some guy I knew."

Trudeau was merging with traffic. He stepped on the brakes. "We know each other?"

"You're Trudeau. That union fuck."

"So who are you?"

"You don't need to know that."

Cars were honking. Trudeau stayed put. "Maybe I do now."

"Come on, drive. I'll explain."

Reluctantly, Trudeau slipped the car back into gear and escaped the curb. He darted into a faster lane, then cut across traffic and headed up the mountainside on Peel Street. "Fill me in," he said.

"I seen you on TV. In the papers. In person one time. We were on different sides of the line."

"A strike?"

"Don't ask me which one. I've done a bunch."

"I've done a few myself."

He was a big man, this fellow in the passenger seat, legs cramped by the narrow enclosure. Thuggish, in a well-dressed way, with a bull neck, big fists and a diamond ring. Considerable pudginess to the face, as though swollen. Crew cut. Scars around the eyes and a misshapen ear indicated that he'd been a boxer when he was younger. If the two ever had a set-to, Trudeau, who was lean, yet athletic and had done a little street boxing in his youth, would be ridiculously overmatched. He'd expected as much. He and *le Noir* had to manage their way through this transaction with acumen, while the other side could rely upon brawn.

"So I called it in," the man said.

"You called *what* in?"

"When you showed, I phoned my boss. Said I know this guy. I told him it was you. He told me to hang on. When he got back on the line, he said it made sense."

"Why wouldn't it make sense?"

"A union guy? Where do union guys get money?"

"I see your point. I'm not a regular union guy."

"That's what he said—my boss. You got money. Your old man made it for you. You're an *intellectual*."

The disdain apparent in his pronunciation of the word was unmistakable.

"I think, therefore I am."

"Huh?"

"Right now, I'm thinking the deal's off. It's not good that you recognized me. I knew I was taking that risk, but—this is not a development I desire."

He had turned before reaching the top of the hill, going east. Farther along, he'd head north and cross the mountain along Park Avenue.

"Aw, it don't matter. So we know you. Big deal. You hide the dagger, nobody proves nothing, you know what I mean?"

Trudeau shrugged. "I don't like rumours flying around."

"'The union's got romantic ideas'—that's what my boss said. That's why you want the dagger."

"For the union." This was an interesting diversion. If one institution, a union, and not another, the Church, was considered the culprit, the plan might work.

"That's right?"

"Not if you're telling the whole world about it."

"I'll keep my mouth shut."

"Sure you will."

"You think I can't keep quiet? My boss trusts me with this job for a reason."

"You're a stranger to me." He pursed his lips and shook his head. "Tell me who your boss is. I need to know who's selling the knife."

"I won't tell you that."

"You know who *I* am. It's only fair."

"I'm not authorized."

"You're not—all right. Make a phone call. Get authorization. While you're at it, tell them to send somebody in your place, somebody who doesn't have to ask permission to take a leak."

"Hey—it's not that way!"

Going over the mountain, Trudeau sped up, seeing what the car could do. His passenger put one hand on the roof and the other on the door handle to steady himself as his jockey zipped from one lane to another and back again, scaring him.

"Come on, slow down," the man said sheepishly.

"Tell me who you work for."

"I'm not at liberty to say."

"You're not authorized, you're not at liberty. You're not good for much more than nothing, are you? Who owns the knife? Tell me. Go on. I won't tell anyone. Just like you. Who am I going to tell anyway?"

"I don't have permission."

"Are you in Grade Two? That's what I want to know. Who's your teacher?"

"Slow down! Jesus!"

"What's your problem?"

"God, this puny car. You could get squashed in it. Like a bug. Give me a Caddy. Weight. Steel!"

Trudeau slowed, then stopped, for a red light.

"You know who I am. I should know who you're working for."

"No way."

"Then tell me *your* name."

"No fucking way."

As a young man, Pierre Elliott Trudeau had travelled the world. He had begun by retracing the canoe trips of Radisson and Groseilliers. At the start of World War II, when German submarines were reported in Quebec waters, he had walked around the Gaspé and been hassled by the police for potentially being a spy. After studying economics in England after the war, he departed Europe for home, but took the long way around, travelling east, hitchhiking and grabbing trains. He learned tricks in eastern Europe as the Iron Curtain was being lowered, moving through Poland, Czechoslovakia, Hungary and Yugoslavia, forging documents so that he could slip across borders. Every day meant encounters with soldiers and men out of uniform carrying weapons.

Through Turkey to Jordan. Israel had just proclaimed its independence, and Palestinian soldiers were on the roads. Determined, he had carried on from Amman to Jericho, and on to Jerusalem, passing through a crossfire on the city's limits. Often he moved from the company of one priest to another, and one in Beirut had given him the name of a Dominican in Jerusalem. He was returning from a visit to him when he was arrested by Arab soldiers, initially for violating curfew, then for being an Israeli spy. He'd been imprisoned in the Antonia Tower, where Pontius Pilate had washed his hands of the man known as the Messiah.

The Dominican secured his initial release, but freedom was brief. Soldiers, still convinced of his villainy as a spy, shipped him back to the land known then as Transjordan. Repeatedly, they pointed out the ditches they were tempted to leave him in, sprung with bullet holes. Trudeau had learned to maintain a confident air, to show no fear. In Amman, he called upon the British Embassy to negotiate his release. When they did so, he continued wandering east.

In Iraq, he had crossed the desert of al-Hajar by train and disembarked at Ur, the ancient home of Abraham. He wandered alone amid the ruins, where he picked up tiles with Sumerian inscriptions dating back to the time of the great patriarch, artifacts he would never discard. The day was cool, the sun low on the horizon, the air fresh, welcoming. He walked to the ziggurat of Nanna, the best preserved of such temples from antiquity, and, upon reaching it, began the high, steep climb. Ziggurats had been built to house the gods, and in their time only the high priests of the prevailing cults gained entry. He could feel himself ascending to the heavens.

Abraham's old dream. The lights of the angels ascending and descending upon a shape such as this. He could imagine the patriarch asleep upon his stone pillow, his vision as clear as desert stars.

At the top, he surveyed the view and felt the grace of time, the ancient world persevering to this moment. Then he noticed he was no longer alone, that he'd been spotted. A pair of desert ruffians had caught sight of the tourist and were climbing up after him, huffing and puffing along the way.

Drawing near, they made their interests known with an English word.

"Mon-ey!" one demanded.

The other man gestured for his watch.

Trudeau was not going to wait for them to catch their breath. He leapt towards the one who was bent over and the hardest pressed from the climb, seized his knife from his belt and jumped back.

They were not dismayed. "Everything . . . you . . . got. Give me."

Trudeau was holding the weapon. With gestures and rudimentary words, he conveyed the suggestion that they at least descend the ziggurat. They could negotiate on the desert floor.

The ruffians complied, and Trudeau let them start off first. As soon as they were below him and he held that advantage, he shouted, "Come up and get me, you assholes!" and waved the knife.

At that moment, upon that ancient temple, he made his stand, deploying his guile. He began to recite the poems he knew by heart, which were considerable in number and often quite long. He began with Cocteau's rant about antiquity. He rained the poems of the Western world down upon them, gesturing and slobbering at the mouth, and the thieves assumed that this youth was deranged, or at least capable of any vile act. The knife flashed in the setting sun, and the desert boys retreated, climbing down the walls of the temple without him.

Intemperate behaviour had saved him that day, which gave him a thought now. He suddenly burned rubber on Park Avenue. Turning the Jag to face the opposite direction, he stomped his foot to the floor. He raced rapidly through the gears, hitting a hundred and fifty miles an hour with nothing but narrow exits and sharp curves ahead of him.

"What the fuck are you doing!" his passenger cried out.

"This deal is off. You'll take the blame."

"You're crazy."

"I don't give a shit."

Ahead, a concrete median split the lanes of Park Avenue into streets that headed in different directions. Normally, cars slowed down to negotiate their way through the maze. Trudeau sped up.

"All right! Fuck! I'll tell you. Slow down. Fuck!"

Trudeau jammed the brake pedal to the floor, jolting himself and his passenger forward. Before they stopped, he spun the wheel again and they were pointed north once more, southbound traffic heading right at them. He stepped on the gas again.

"Shit!"

"Will you tell me? Don't lie."

"I won't lie! Shit!"

With no room for error he cut into the northbound traffic ahead of a concrete median, startling the driver of a beer truck who was also cavorting too quickly.

"Jesus!"

"What's the problem?" Trudeau asked him calmly.

"What?"

"You seem nervous."

"Fuck you."

"So who do you work for?"

"Slow the fuck down, I'll tell you."

"Tell me first."

"De Bernonville!"

Trudeau downshifted the Jag to a manageable, albeit still fast, speed. Three blocks later, they were again stopped at a red.

"You know him?" the passenger asked.

"That Nazi," Trudeau scoffed.

"That's what a union guy would say."

"He's in town?"

"He's around."

"He needs money?"

"Word on the street says so."

"You don't know him yourself?"

"I said hello once. Look. The word is, after last night, he's desperate."

"Last night?"

"You don't listen to the news?"

Trudeau had. The night before, a bank heist had been interrupted by a number of drunken off-duty police officers who happened to be walking by. The thieves had broken in through the basement and blasted through to the vault. They were apprehended going out the front door of a building next to a bank when one of the cops recognized a man he had once put in jail, and realized simultaneously that it was night, the weekend, that offices were closed. What clinched it, a cop told a reporter, was that each man carried an overcoat slung over a forearm except that one guy carried two overcoats, one over each arm. He had snitched an extra coat from the manager's office to conceal his extra load of money bags.

"All right," Trudeau said. As the light turned green, he drove on with the relaxed ease of a Sunday driver. "Let's get this deal done."

A novice to this level of intrigue, Pierre Elliott Trudeau compensated for his lack of experience not only with wild antics, but also by hatching a scheme with careful attention to detail, in tandem with his considerable resources. Even his accomplice in this crime was impressed when he drove a long way across town and pulled up next to an amusement park. Belmont Park had been owned by Trudeau's deceased father, and the family still maintained a substantial share. He produced a set of keys to a side entrance.

"We're going in here?"

"Don't you like having fun?"

Children screaming on the roller coaster and shouting from the top of the Ferris wheel pierced the evening air.

"What's your name?" he asked the thug.

"I won't tell you that." The man looked at him as if to say he wasn't as dumb as he looked.

"I need to call you something. If I want to know your identity I'll look up pictures of former Golden Gloves heavyweights. That'll tell me who you are."

"It's Barry," the man conceded, trapped.

"Doesn't sound too French to me."

"English mom," the man acknowledged.

"We have something in common, Barry."

They walked from the side gate to a kind of bunker. Inside, they were met by a security guard who had obviously been napping, his head down on a desk, his rump comfortably ensconced in a swivel chair. He stood up quickly, trying to get the sleep out of his eyes. He addressed Trudeau as "sir."

"We're going straight through to the vault, Henri," Trudeau informed him, and the security guard, in his white and navy blue uniform, a pistol in his belt's holster, led the way.

Trudeau dialled the combination, pulled the heavy door open, flicked on a light switch and admitted Barry ahead of himself. The vault was a closet for critical paperwork now—contracts, leases on real estate holdings. These days, the money went elsewhere, but in a pinch this spot would do for a covert transaction. He advised the guard how to shut the door once they were inside.

"Turn the small handle only," Trudeau told him.

"What does that do?" Barry asked.

"Closes the door. We won't be able to open it from the inside. We'll need the guard for that."

"Wait a minute. How do we tell him to open up?"

"Phone him. I have the number. And there," Trudeau nodded to a spot behind Barry's back, "is the phone. Employees used to count receipts in here, all locked up. In the old days, we didn't want thieves walking in, and we didn't want employees walking out with their trousers or bras stuffed with cash."

Barry looked around nervously. He clearly had a problem with the confined quarters. "I don't want to suffocate in here. Is there air? How do we breathe?"

"I'm sure we can last twenty minutes or so, Barry. You're right, though. Maybe less. You're a big man. Big lungs. At least there's a light. Let's do this quickly. Shall I show you the money?"

The suitcase was cheap, with small metal clasps. He had found it in a pawnshop. The bills inside were crisp and neatly bundled, the denominations large, to lighten the load.

Barry whistled. All those thousand-dollar bills.

"One point five million. Take it or leave it."

"That's the deal. I'll take it."

Trudeau closed the suitcase and snapped the clasps in place. "First, we wait. I need the Cartier Dagger before you take this out of here."

Barry shrugged his big shoulders. "I'll phone it in. That's the deal, right? I'll tell my people we got the money."

"That won't be necessary. We changed the deal."

"I didn't change nothing." Barry's natural antagonism was subdued in the confined quarters.

"Not you," Trudeau let him know. "My partner did. He's coming here. We're going to make the exchange right here in this vault."

"This stinks. It was supposed to be separate places."

"Too many ways to screw that up, to take advantage. The two venues shall be made one. It's no skin off your nose, is it?"

"No, but—" the thug protested.

"What?"

"Can't we wait outside?"

"Barry, relax. Shallow breathing, that'll get us through this. Don't excite yourself. I'm sitting down. I suggest you do the same. We'll consume less air."

Barry joined him on the floor. Telltale perspiration leaked from his brow. He waited quietly for ten minutes, carefully monitoring his breathing. Finally, he loosened his tie and unbuttoned his collar, moving his fingers slowly, so as not to exert himself unduly. Then he asked, "What if nobody shows?"

"Good question."

The response worried the pugilist. "How so?"

"If my contact can't convince your people to come in here, you'll be out of luck. They'll fear a trap, of course—we expect that. But they're carrying the Cartier Dagger. Pretty incriminating. So your people have two things on their side. One, our phone number—they can call you, find out from you that the money's here, no cops are around, only one security guard. Two, my contact can walk in carrying the dagger—there's nothing to incriminate your people except being in the pleasure of his company. That should put them at ease. We'll see. If they don't call soon . . ."

"We'll have to get out of here."

"I'll leave first."

"Excuse me?"

"To make sure my contact's safe. Until I find that out, you'll stay behind."

"I'm not staying in here alone."

"I won't be keeping you company, Barry. When I leave, while the door's open, you'll get a burst of fresh air. In here by yourself, you can probably last a half an hour or so."

"You shithead."

"Don't excite yourself. You breathe more air that way. I can't emphasize it enough."

Barry held his head in his hands, trying to calm himself, then thunked his scalp on the shelf above him as the phone rang and his body jerked involuntary.

"That'll be for me," Trudeau said, standing. He answered on the third ring.

Pelletier informed him that everything had gone as expected, that his party was outside, waiting to be admitted. Trudeau confirmed that, inside, everything was going according to plan. They exchanged password phrases to secretly indicate that all was well.

"French toast" was Pelletier's phrase.

"Buddha's smile," Trudeau replied. "There's been a change."

Pelletier asked what that meant.

"*Le Blanc* tried to hold up a bank last night. It didn't go over so well. If they had succeeded, they would have cancelled on me and kept the knife for themselves."

"But we had a deal."

"You see? I don't like doing business that way."

"So what's changed?" Pelletier asked.

"Tell them what I just told you, about the bank. Then tell them that the price is down to one million even. I'm holding half a million back."

"What?" Barry exclaimed. "You can't do that!"

"Just watch me. I don't need the silly thing. *Le Blanc* needs the million."

He waited awhile, then spoke into the phone. "Gérard, how's it going?"

"We have a few excited people out here. Calls are being made. Three lines busy and I hear a lot of shouting. Good thing you're locked in a safe or you'd have a bloody nose by now."

"You're okay?"

"So far."

The word came back five minutes later: a million and a quarter, or *le Blanc* walked. Trudeau consented to the compromise. He depleted the suitcase by $250,000 while Barry checked his math.

"Okay?" Trudeau asked.

"Adds up right to me," Barry said. "For an intellectual, you're a bastard, hey?"

Trudeau phoned the security guard inside the office, telling him to open the exterior door to admit Pelletier and one other person. Then he was to lead them to the vault and shut the door on all four of them while the transaction was processed.

Pierre Elliott Trudeau believed in the bold stroke, the decisive action. His father had imprinted the benefits of action on his young mind. Charles-Émile Trudeau had worked long hours and put together a chain of automobile service stations, selling them for a fortune prior to the crash of 1929 that plunged the world into the Great Depression. With his money he had purchased a gold mine, the Montreal Royals baseball team and the amusement park where Trudeau was conducting business. His purchases proved to be excellent shelters through the Depression, for people still found a way to watch baseball and still wanted to buy candy apples and take a thrilling ride to alleviate the misery of their days. And gold never lost its lustre. Camillien Houde visited the Trudeaus' city house and mountain cottage, and while he was bankrupting the city to keep men working, the men who had those jobs visited the Trudeau family enterprises to spend their wages on a few hours of happiness. His father's timing had been impeccable. His own was proving to be equally savvy. He knew he was waiting for something to happen that would give him something to do with his life, and he was willing to wait—not through any native patience, which he did not possess, but through a conviction that he was blessed by a mysterious quality of good timing, as if bred in the bones, a part of his nature. Sometimes he chose those words, and sometimes he admitted to himself that what he really meant was that God was guiding him. So what if it wasn't logical? He believed it to be true.

"We get locked in here again?" Barry protested. Panic resided close to the surface of his skin.

"I hope you're well paid for your services."

"Not enough for this," the thug admitted.

"Yeah? Are you ever paid well enough?"

"Probably not. I'd say no," Barry agreed.

"There, you see, Barr? You're a union man at heart. You just didn't know it."

The men entered the vault—Pelletier and the second thug representing *le Blanc*. The latter had a cat-like face and a nervous disposition. Pierre Elliott Trudeau demanded to see the Cartier Dagger. The thug had in mind to be shown the money first and to chew out this upper-crust phoney for beating down his boss on price, but he relented, surprising himself, and agreed to show the relic.

He opened the case.

Before Trudeau's eyes, seemingly rather frail and homely, lay the stone-bladed dagger, the bone handle studded with diamonds and gold. He stretched out his hand to pick it up and the man stopped him, placing a thick restraining paw on his wrist, but Trudeau looked him in the eye, saying nothing, and the hand relaxed.

He picked up the dagger. He held it at arm's length, then brought it close to his eyes. This was indeed an artifact, embedded with the power of Iroquois art and Quebec history, or so his senses told him. Gently, he returned it to the velvet-lined case—the thieves had taken good care of their prize—and shut it quietly.

"Take your money and go," Trudeau said.

"I have to count it first."

"Don't be an idiot. You know who I am and where to find me. Take the money and get out. Your friend Barry's on the verge of fainting. Guide him to fresh air."

The thieves took their money and quickly departed. Pelletier and Trudeau remained behind, first in the vault, then in the office. They didn't speak, although from time to time they exchanged smiles. When it seemed safe, in the company of the security guard they crossed to the amusement park's new vault, where they deposited the small box and the extra quarter-million. Trudeau taped the box to make sure no employee could secretly tamper with it, left it in a locked case and made certain that the vault was secured behind them. Then the two departed Belmont Park in the Jag.

"So," Gérard Pelletier asked his friend, "do you feel different, now that you have the dagger?"

He took the question to heart, digesting it. Then he replied, "I can do anything."

"Then let's do it. Don't forget to bring me along for the ride, Pierre."

Pierre Trudeau drove recklessly, earning the ire of other drivers, and turned the radio up full blast to diminish the angry honking of horns.

†††

All this commotion could not be a good thing. Fear turned in her tummy. Anik wanted to flee, cry, shout out, be comforted. Everyone was too busy to notice her.

Outside, the usual slew of reporters appeared to be in a depressed mood. "Bored out of our tree," as one scribe had lamented a day earlier. She could only guess what the English phrase might mean, and she found it funny. The reporters tried to befriend her, hoping that she might give them a tip on what was happening inside the old mayor's house. Anik told them a few snippets, but usually she repeated whatever the nurse had said. "He's resting comfortably."

She sounded so sweet to them. She made their day.

Inside, she was immediately stricken. Older women were weeping. Nurses, generally younger, ran past her, searching for things—fresh water, fresh linen, a fresh pan. Nuns conferred with a doctor, and the doctor made a motion to the priest. Father François, who had himself just arrived—she'd seen him ahead of her—joined a closed, hushed circle. More nurses hurried by. A few older women wept.

No one was noticing her. No one had acknowledged her entry. Ignored, frightened, Anik stole inside the old mayor's bedroom.

She wished he was in a hospital—a place where she'd not be admitted. She wanted him to comfort her, to tell her a story, to make this stop.

He gurgled in his sleep, waking himself. Camillien Houde opened his eyes and tried to focus on the young girl in his room.

"Anik," he murmured. He tried to smile. "Am I in heaven?"

She rubbed a forearm that was covered in goose bumps, and felt herself trembling. *This man's dying! He might die this second!* And she was struck by a thought both self-conscious and self-aware. She knew that she was both terrified and curious.

"Where's my spiritual advisor?" he murmured. He was managing to keep one eye partially open, while the other one, quivering, closed.

The room smelled really bad. The stink came from the bed, and she knew what it was.

Sounds in the hall made her jerk around, and a second later the nurses arrived with a pan and sheets and water and shooed the girl away. Nuns came next, and one caught Anik by the shoulders and gave her a moderate shake. "Don't be here! Who are you? You can't be here."

Father François stepped to her rescue. "I didn't know you were here, Anik."

"Is he going to die, Father?" she whispered.

The priest whispered in return. "We don't like to say those words within earshot of those who are ailing."

She spoke more quietly, although the old mayor couldn't hear her anyway. "Is he going to?"

"We've spoken of this day many times." He held her shoulders as the nun had done, but with infinite tenderness. "We must prepare ourselves."

Nodding, she wiped away a few tears. But more tears flowed.

"When the women are done, I'm going to speak to Camillien. It's time for his last rites, his last confession. If you wait in the living room, we'll leave together, Anik. I'll take you home."

She managed another nod and moved towards the door.

The oldest nun went to the curtains, pulling them shut.

The mayor's great bulk proved difficult for the nurses and the nun, and they beseeched the only male in the room to lend his brawn. They rolled the big man one way, pulled at the sheets and, with eight women heaving, heaving, they rolled him the other way. One set of sheets was opened and another condemned to a heap, all a stinking mess the priest endeavoured to ignore. In the end the dying man was made comfortable again, and the priest was left alone with him.

"Father," Houde whispered.

"Do you wish to say your confession, my son? It's time."

"First," the old mayor whispered.

The priest had to lean in closely to catch the softly spoken words.

"Yes?" he asked.

"Tell me. The dagger."

The priest gazed upon him solemnly, staring into the one eye that battled to remain open. He knew now that this was why the Machiavellian had asked him to be his priest, to conduct a final transaction, a political job. "You did the right thing, Camillien. That young man you admire, the son of your old acquaintance, Pierre Elliott Trudeau, has taken possession. De Bernonville has his grubby hands on his money. Your own estate has been enhanced. The relic will remain here. In Quebec. In Montreal, where you know it belongs."

The priest noted the frail nod of comprehension.

"Now, my son, it is time for your confession."

Father François admired the manner in which the old sinner rallied his strength and spoke, quietly, with a true spirit of contrition. He did not need to coax him. The man had lined up his sins and knew the order in which they ought to be related. When he was done, he could see that the man had emptied his spirit, and now his life had dissipated as well.

The man's hand trembled, trying to reach for his own. Father François took it. He had experienced the remarkable strength of newborn babes and felt a similar pressure on his fingers. The priest bent low to the old man's lips.

He ended his confession as he had begun. "Forgive me, Father, for I have sinned."

Then winked.

Father François gave him absolution. He offered the forgiveness of his Lord, although he knew that his own heart lacked that purity, that love. He administered the last rites, and the man's eyelids quivered, first one, then the other, as though each moment required a fight.

The priest touched the old mayor before he left, surprised by the love within him that sprang for a political foe. Not a great and all-encompassing love, perhaps, yet love, mysterious and corroded, nonetheless. That final wink had conveyed great spirit. He left Houde in peace.

Momentarily, a nurse looked in on him, and fluffed his pillow and adjusted his pyjamas. Then she left the room as well, to allow him to sleep, perhaps to die.

Anik waited for several minutes before she crawled out from the closet, where she had crouched down during the commotion with the sheets. She looked at the old mayor dying. His breath gurgling. Then she got to her feet, opened the door, and walked past everyone and departed the house. A block away, well past the reporters who were calling to her, she began to run.

Tears flew off her cheeks like rain. Then they were gone, and she ran with fury only.

†††

One hundred thousand people turned out for Camillien Houde's funeral procession. Anik Clément declined to attend. Unable to comprehend the child's insistence on remaining home, her mother assumed that her grief was too confusing, perhaps reminiscent of her father's death. In some ways, she supposed, Anik was losing a second dad. Carole attended on her own, and was admitted to the funeral service itself. On the streets, it seemed that the entire city had turned out, sixteen people deep as the coffin drove by, the dignitaries in their finery, the working people in their scuffed shoes and proud, shabby jackets, all the men in hats, the women with their dark bonnets on and so many in black dresses as though they themselves had lost a spouse. The people believed that Montreal had lost a measure of its soul, and a sadness hung upon the city. An era was passing. Goodbye to the all-night clubs, to the dancing ladies, to the girls in fancy lace, and goodbye to the gambling dens where a man might dream of riches and taste the bitterness of further demise. Goodbye to the music palaces and the comedians and the farcical courts of law, where substitute madams paid paltry fines to judges they'd be seeing later in their chambers. Goodbye to the good times, goodbye to the wars and famines, goodbye to the old, weary days, and goodbye to Camillien Houde, the rascal. Goodbye to his comic voice and his broad smile, for he had been a man who could lift a people's spirits even as he confounded them with his logic. He could make a man laugh while picking his pocket. He was a wise old cuss. One of the boys. A grand man and a straw man. Goodbye to all that.

The city mourned.

Four days after the funeral a gentleman showed up at Carole Clément's house carrying a terrier puppy. A last gift from the old mayor. Anik took the animal into her arms and had her face licked, but she did not smile, did not laugh. She hugged the little critter, though, and dashed him through to her room.

Odd behaviour, her mother thought. Yet these were confusing, sad times in a young girl's life.

CHAPTER 14

1728–29 ~ 1734

ERE THE RIVER FLARED, RAN DEEP. NO MAN HAD FOUND ITS depth. Some believed no fish had, either. Perch were plentiful. In spontaneous leaps, cavorting large walleye burst the surface, splashing back into a silty, ale-coloured water neither sweet nor clear, yet deer were drawn down from the hills in the evenings to sip, and in the winter, timber wolves traversed the river's ice.

A good place to camp.

For any weary, wandering people, a good place to make a new home.

From her second-storey bedroom window, Sarah Hanson noticed corn quiver.

A mission existed, inhabited sporadically by assiduous Sulpicians and displaced Indians from various tribes. At intervals along a switchback trail ascending the hillside, priests constructed tall, shallow huts fronted by broad barn doors. In the company of natives, they'd walk through the woods and pull back the doors of each hut to reveal a tapestry, or an artwork, or an example of statuary illustrating the Gospels. Natives were often impressed, and equally dismayed, that anyone would build a house in which only a painting dwelled.

Mohawks were the first to arrive with the intention of settling, long before the men they called the crows. After the signing of the Great Peace, prospects for great wars diminished. Sadly aware that their people had been depleted, bands of roaming native warriors devised a surprising alternative tack. They established themselves as affable neighbours to their habitual enemies, staking a claim along the banks of the Ottawa—*rivière des Outaouais,* in the French tongue, closer to the Indian word—at the place called Oka, a short, energetic canoe trip west from Montreal.

Sarah Hanson had never seen the cornfields quiver this way before, as though the stalks were being born as men and women, learning to stagger forth, to walk. She was drawn to the window and she hobbled across the room, a boot half-on, half-off, to investigate the mystery. Only a slight breeze grazed the curtains.

The fiercest of the Iroquois nations, the Mohawks were a curiosity. Why? Why return to lands they'd inexplicably abandoned after Cartier's arrival two hundred years earlier? Why choose to dwell in proximity to those they'd warred against so intensely, while putting distance between themselves and their usual allies, the English of Boston and New York? For the inhabitants of Ville-Marie, answers to such matters were veiled in mystery, were cloaked also in a familiar, foreboding fear. Citizens murmured amongst themselves. Citing rumours, they repeated the most terrible tales from their history. Men and women fretted that their old foes were lying in wait for them, anticipating a day when the French would sleep unguarded. Zealous Mohawks in their war paint and delirium would then descend, yowling under a full moon to harvest their ripened scalps. Survivors would experience the dreaded slow fires consuming their toes, ankles and shins and rising higher.

As though in fright, songbirds and red-winged blackbirds cried out. Crows cawed in a panic, flitting out of the fields into the trees. Sarah waited, expectant. She anticipated the moment corn would walk.

Fur traders and other woodsmen who dared to make contact with the Iroquois slowly discerned their situation, and over time they gleaned answers to the queries that so vexed the French. To the south, the English were ever-expanding. Shiploads from across the sea arrived daily throughout the summer months. By and large, the French were content to build their nation through the action of their loins, a process familiar to the Iroquois and one that threatened them less.

As well, their habitual enemies, the French, explored the continent west across the Great Plains to the Rockies, and south down the Mississippi to the Gulf of Mexico, activity that offered both remuneration for skilful guides and an opportunity to live traditional lives. Among the French, the Iroquois might remain *sauvage,* in the true meaning of the word—dwellers of the woods. The English, supposedly their old friends and allies, were squeezing them out and moving them on and compressing them throughout their ancient lands.

A sweet morning. Freshened cool air. The horses strangely agitated in their summer stalls. Sarah tried to distinguish the whinny of her own beast.

Having huddled close to their perpetual foes, the Indians tripped over an unexpected benefit. Effective rogue bands were free to raid English settlements to the south. Carting back bounty to the land of the French kept them beyond the reach of English law. To further their economic advantage, they had learned that the capture of rich white girls from New England could grow into a lucrative enterprise. If they treated them fairly, permitting their precious purity to remain unaffected by the ordeal, they could wait for the girls' fathers to journey north to locate them and barter for their freedom. Kidnapping began a fresh venture then, for if the English were tempted to send an army to end the practice, they could not do so into French territory without instigating war. The Iroquois learned to appreciate their new French neighbours, or at least to find them useful.

Aquiver, the corn trembled more violently. Yet it did so only in select places, and now no wind stirred the trees.

In the region known as Massachusetts, on the banks of the Charles River, near the town called Dover, in the year 1728, an Oka raiding party waited amid the corn for first light. The farm formed a small quadrant of a rich man's property, and servants arose to milk cows and peruse the chicken coop for eggs before the man of property had blinked an eye awake. As a rooster crowed and the birds commenced their usual racket, other calls emanated from the fields.

Then she heard a war whoop. As if her body had turned inside itself, she wore her skin twisted and clamped close to her heart.

Sarah Hanson, the rich man's daughter, had been up, struggling as she did every morning to pull on her riding boots. Suddenly, half-naked russet-skinned men bounded from the cornfield outside and ran across the yard. A flaming torch flew up before her and landed on the roof of her dormer window.

"Daddy!" she cried out, running terrified to his room, one foot clopping with a boot still half-on. "Daddy!"

She startled him awake, yet her father did not exhibit a moment's anger, for already he was hearing the manic Iroquois yells. Two decades had passed since that sound had last coursed through him as lightning roaring down his spine. "My God," he murmured, and reached for his bedside rifle. His wife was now whooping beside him, making noises remarkably similar to those of the Indians. With his hand on his weapon, Jeremy Hanson wondered where on earth he had stored his ammunition. Over the kitchen counter? Outside, in the shed? Fending off Indians had not been part of his life since boyhood. In his momentary bewilderment, he scratched his beard ruefully. Three weeks ago, he'd hunted grouse. Had he stored his ammunition in the cellar? He fought off an inclination to shout for the maid.

"Daddy!" Sarah Hanson gasped again, for a pair of Iroquois had burst upon them in the bedroom. Tall, bare-chested, wildly painted, they were grinning.

Indians, she had believed, never grinned.

One shook his tomahawk with a rattle attached to it—as well as feathers and shells—and the terrified family recoiled against the headboard. The warrior, shaking the rattle once more for the pleasure of watching them flinch, laughed. Warring Indians never laughed, Sarah knew. No one had ever mentioned laughing Indians to her. Jeremy Hanson clasped his wife and daughter to him. That he was inwardly pleading for a quick death shocked him, but instinctively he knew it would be preferable to seeing his family burned alive at the stake.

Squeezing between the legs of the natives, his seven-year-old son scrambled up onto the bed to join his parents. The father felt his heart blow open, fearing that these intruders might find his boy appetizing.

Below, they heard an ominous commotion, a rampage of destruction and theft throughout the dwelling, the outcries of servants swiftly muted. Above them, timbers crackled as the fire took hold.

The two Indians in the master bedroom merely stared at them and waited. They smiled. What delayed them, Jeremy Hanson did not know, until he smelled the smoke and heard flames crackle on the roof.

"Please," he whispered. "Mercy." Why were they smiling? What tribe was this?

An Iroquois gestured to the girl on the bed already dressed in riding clothes. "Pull boot on," he commanded. "Come with us."

Sobbing, the mother cried out.

A dawning despair welled up inside Sarah Hanson's bones. She did not know where her skin ended or began, as though the flames on the rooftop had already claimed her as their own. Her fright slammed inside her as she felt her father's grip around her tighten, then, almost imperceptibly, go slack. From their stalls, she still heard the horses whinnying. From the barnyard arose the squeals of pigs as the animals scrambled for cover from Iroquois pursuing them with tomahawks, and the frightful squawk of hens as the raiders systematically wrung their necks.

She waited on the bed in the burning house, feeling glutinous and queer as her father's grip continued to loosen around her and the sound of petrified squealing pigs ended and the hens went silent.

Horses kicked against the stall doors in the barn, distressed by the travesty of sounds, of death to animals.

Her father's grip continued to relax around her. He clasped his young son to his chest, and his wife pressed her weight upon the boy also.

"Surprise comes with me," Sarah Hanson, aged fourteen, announced.

"Is that a dog or a horse?" a Mohawk responded, as though he had negotiated such terms before. He moved a step to his left as the roof above his head was on the verge of burning through.

"Nelly can stay. Surprise, my horse, comes with me." She pulled her boot on.

"I'll come and get you," her father whispered. "It's what they want. We've heard this happens. I'll trade for your release."

"Your father is wise man," the Indian said.

"Treat her well. If you don't treat her well—"

"Hurry," the Indian said to the girl. "Before your family burns up in bed."

Sarah Hanson would pause at the gate to her property as she led her horse down to the river in the company of Iroquois. Blood dripped from the headless pigs strapped to the backs of each horse, including Surprise. Jittery, high-stepping, her horse paused beside her. She waved to her family, who waved back, the house partially in flames behind them. Servants waved also, briefly, then realigned to form a bucket brigade. Sarah turned and guided her captors down the best path to the river, where the Iroquois had ditched their canoes.

They had taken three other horses, and these and Surprise were given over to a pair of young men to guide overland to their new home at Oka, by the *rivière des Outaouais,* either to be used by Iroquois or sold at a street fair in Montreal. Sarah Hanson reluctantly bade her animal goodbye and kissed him on the snout. She told the Indian boy responsible to treat him well.

He glared at her without expression.

Sarah slid down into a canoe and the natives pushed off from shore.

She began to shake all over. Then she quelled herself and bid herself to be strong. A spirited girl who had yearned for adventure, she now understood that the grand adventure of her life had commenced.

†††

They taught her to smoke, these Iroquois.

Sarah Hanson wasn't partial to the taste of tobacco and twigs and the fire on her lips and tongue, but she desired to be treated as a grown person, and a grown person in the woods at night smoked. They sat around campfires and passed clay pipes, and she breathed the smoke and observed the fireflies flitting among the timbers. The Iroquois appreciated that she was not a burden. As they canoed the rivers, she remained still, and when they made a portage she purposefully carried a pack upon her back without needing to be asked. She did not stop until they stopped, nor did she impede their pace. They fed her as well as they fed themselves, with roast pork from her own farm and vegetables from her family's cellar. Her stomach full, her head adrift upon the effects of the twigs and seeds and dried leaf, she slept upon the cedar boughs she'd gathered on her own. Always she hoped for a clear night, for she desired those few moments to herself, spent gazing at the stars as she repeated her prayers. Stars were comforting, familiar signposts. All else stood out as strange, difficult and dark, either perplexing or frightening. Her body ached from the cramped misery of her journey, from the heavy loads she carried at times. Lonely, ravaged by mosquitoes and pesky flies, fearful, her nerves on edge, exhausted, she also felt oddly exhilarated, and each night under the stars or clouds slept soundly following her prayers.

In the morning, Sarah stirred up the breakfast beans.

Sometimes, the young men who travelled overland with the horses made it to the same camp at night as those who canoed north. Then she would hug her animal's neck, water him and brush the dust from his coat with her fingers.

"You're riding him now?" she asked the young Iroquois.

"I teach him ride no saddle. To be a Mohawk horse."

"That shouldn't be so hard. I've ridden him bareback. I ride him bareback all the time."

"White girls lie," the youth proclaimed.

"Do they? I don't know any who do. Anyway, I'm sure you've never met an English girl before, so how would you know?"

"You never before met Mohawk," the young man stately gruffly. He looked to be older than her, yet only eighteen years of age, at the most. While he appeared to be a man, he was usually ordered around by the others.

"So true, I've never met a Mohawk, so I do not know if a Mohawk lies or not. I'll wait, and judge for myself. That's what you should do. Judge for yourself."

"What means 'judge'?"

Sarah Hanson thought a moment. "It means decide for yourself. Think. Don't just believe what others tell you. Do you understand?"

"In old days," he said, "a white girl like you be my slave. You cook for me, come to the bed of Colweenada at night when Colweenada want."

"What old days? You weren't there, so you don't know the first thing about any old days. I would never come to your bed just because you wanted me to. Anyway, you would never have had a chance to make me your slave. One of the warriors would have me, not some *boy.*"

In the light of a campfire built close to the horses, the youth wiped his brow.

"I am warrior," he claimed. "Not boy."

"You're a thief and a kidnapper. You should be ashamed of yourself. But you're a savage, so of course you don't understand what I'm talking about. What do you know of shame?"

"Your father, he come for you. Take you home. Don't worry." From his tone of voice, he sounded as though he'd be relieved when that day arrived.

"What will the Iroquois sell me for, I wonder?"

The Iroquois shrugged. "A walking cow," he said.

"A cow!" Sarah's voice expressed her outrage.

"Two cows still walking, maybe. More pigs still walking. More dead chickens. Sacks of beans. Two more horses. Colweenada would trade you for that, if Colweenada was the man who own you."

"You don't own me. Nobody does. No one can own another person." She sat by the fire and crossed her legs. Using a stick, she poked at the flames, causing sparks to fly up to the branches and leaves.

"A man can own a slave," the boy said.

She had to concede that point. "I'm a captive. I'm not a slave. You shouldn't be allowed to sell me. It's not right. Certainly not for two cows."

"Colweenada pay two cows for you, if Colweenada own two cows."

She looked at him across the fire. "That's a compliment, I suppose."

"Not understand, com-plim-ent."

She continued to look at him, then turned her eyes away.

"Never mind," she said.

"If Colweenada own horse . . ." the Indian boy started to say.

"It's *my* horse," Sarah interrupted him stubbornly.

"If Colweenada own horse, horse stay to me. Colweenada give back horse to you if Colweenada own horse. If Colweenada not own horse, horse go to market in Montreal, a man buy horse, a Frenchman, you do not see horse again."

Sarah curled her legs up so that her chin rested on her knees and wrapped her arms around her folded legs to keep warm. "His name is Surprise."

The Indian boy nodded. He looked at the ground for a long time before he looked up. He was not as handsome as some warriors. He was chubby, his face round and flat with dark pockmarks, as though he'd been frozen during the wintertime as a child. While at first she had considered him ugly, with his red and black warrior stripes and his jaw line emphasized by white paint, she liked his rare, slight smile in a way, and she liked how he talked softly when only the two of them were together by the fire. He told her, "A good name."

"Thanks," the girl said.

"You ride horse tomorrow," the boy said. "With Colweenada you ride."

She immediately straightened up with interest. "I can? Can I?"

"Colweenada ask my chief for you ride."

"Ask. Ask! Go ask!" She was pushing him to go quickly.

"You must promise Colweenada not to escape."

"I can't escape, Colweenada. I don't know how. I don't know where I am."

"English girls lie."

"I don't lie! Now go. Ask him. Hurry!"

The boy would return to their small campfire with the chief standing beside him. The old man had deep furls that ran straight down his cheeks, and black eyebrows, each bisected by tufts of grey. He said nothing, looking from one young person to the other, into their hearts, their minds, before he walked away.

In the morning, Sarah Hanson thought she was saying goodbye to Surprise again, and kissed him on the snout, when her new friend ordered, "Climb on horse. You come ride. My chief, he who is my father, he say okay. If you make escape, Colweenada take your scalp."

"You'd never do that," she said with glee, so delighted at the prospect of riding these deep woods upon her favourite animal.

"Colweenada do what Iroquois warrior do," the boy protested. She never seemed to take him seriously, even when matters were profoundly serious.

"I won't escape and I don't lie," she told him. "Now, come on, let's ride!"

†††

The journey north on horseback became more arduous than Sarah Hanson had expected. She rode long hours with rare stops, the stamina of the boys being extraordinary, and forded fast, rocky rivers against the animals' will. That's when she peed—when she was up to her waist in water. She was too embarrassed otherwise. Trails were Iroquois footpaths beaten down through the ages, often not suitable for horse and rider, although deer, bear and other critters used the routes often. Sarah Hanson's face was slapped by branches and cut and punched by tree limbs, yet she was forbidden to cry out on the chance that bandit Indians were lying in wait. She had to twist her mind to comprehend that she was travelling as a captive in the company of Iroquois raiders, yet should be frightened only of other Iroquois or Indians believed to be bandits. If this bunch was not a concoction of bandits, why was she being held against her will?

Walking the horses down a steep trail, one rebelled and fell, slipping off to the side, and its pack shifted on its back, surprising the animal, which hoisted its four legs into the air and took flight. For Sarah, the fall seemed to last forever. The horse broke its back and neck in the ravine below. She wept. She didn't care if the boys thought little of her—she wept for the animal who had no fault or design in this, brought into the wilderness with no prayer or comprehension and now dead because stones had skidded loose beneath its hoof. She mopped her face dry on her shirtsleeve and forged on.

When they found a good place, the Indian boys tied her to a tree, then went down into the ravine to retrieve the dead pigs off the back of the dead horse. Then they hacked the horse into manageable sections for travel and consumption later.

Sarah stretched her restraints as far as possible from the tree and vomited. Yet she said nothing, and the boys untied her and carried on.

They were descending, and at times she could see the great expanse of a lake. She gathered that they were bound for Lake George and Lake Champlain. In a day, they made it to the French and Iroquois camp at Fort Ticonderoga, where many Indians were sitting in huddled groups. Their dark eyes were upon the girl as she rode her horse among them. She stayed very close to Colweenada after they dismounted. She didn't want him to step into the forest without her, not even to relieve himself.

Within the fort were drunken Indian boys and women and men, and others who never spoke nor smiled, but gazed upon her with a look as indifferent as trees. She could not begin to fathom their intentions. Some Indians wore white man's clothes, including the clothes of soldiers.

"Are they in the army?" Sarah asked.

Colweenada did not answer such a foolish question. Whenever she caught up to him to ask another question, he turned away in a different direction. Finally, she grabbed his arm and said, "Are you mad at me? What's the matter with you?"

He looked over her head when he spoke to her. "You must look like you are the woman of Colweenada. If you do not look like you are the woman of Colweenada, a man will come and make you his woman."

She was unaccustomed to making herself appear to be any man's woman, but she did her best, and only after they had departed Fort Ticonderoga did she ride alongside him, and only then did he let her. They carried on along the edge of the lake, northbound now, their supplies replenished. They had traded a pig and the horsemeat after declining offers for the girl, and they received in exchange a variety of foods and new rifles.

"Bandits were in that camp," she told her guide.

"Colweenada believe this true," he said.

"Now they know we are here. They know *I* am here."

"Are you afraid, Sarah Hanson?"

"I have every right to be worried."

"We ride our horses. We move well. Colweenada not worry about bandits behind. Colweenada worry about bandits not yet seen."

That seemed wise, so Sarah worried about the bandits up ahead as well.

†††

Sarah Hanson was leading three horses down to a gurgling brook for a drink when an attack commenced. An Indian boy saw the arrow that killed him break through leaves before it surged through his throat and he gurgled, dropping to his knees. Colweenada flinched, and an arrowhead passed through his shoulder. He broke the shaft and pulled it out of his back while running for a boulder's shelter. He fell upon the ground and, ignoring his pain, pulled out his dagger.

The whoops and battle cries spooked the horses and she lost control of two. Spinning herself up onto Surprise's back, she bolted off in pursuit of them.

An attacker, the only one among them who possessed a rifle, for these were impoverished bandits, commenced taking potshots at the boulder Colweenada hid behind. The youth hoped they'd soon fight hand to hand. He was determined to be the fiercest fighter in the forest that day, so that his killers might choose to protect his corpse from the appetites of animals.

Colweenada's immediate problem would be the man with the rifle, who was creeping around, trying to find a clear shot. Unable to shoot back at him, he watched the marauder move towards him with impunity. Colweenada peeked and spotted his attacker sliding along a fallen tree trunk suspended above a creek, so he crept slightly to his right to better shield himself. The move exposed his rump to arrows from that side, where other bandits were skulking through the woods. He would have to frustrate their arrows and bullets and tempt them to charge him with knives and tomahawks.

This was going to be a difficult fight.

Then he heard pounding hooves.

Sarah had gone after the other horses to retrieve the rifles slung across their backs, and, having snared the animals and seized a pair of weapons, was galloping back. While in blazing motion, she took a shot at the bandit who sat fully exposed on a tree trunk, missing, although he nearly toppled over from fright, then Sarah reared her horse to a stop and simultaneously fired again. She felled him.

The bandit, wearing a tall and torn straw hat, collapsed through branches to the exposed rock of the meandering creek bed below. His head split open on a rock. Sarah slid off her animal, leaving Surprise to fend for himself, and the beast, in its panic, galloped off. She ducked in behind the boulders, close to her new friend, and tossed him a rifle, and together they fired upon their attackers, driving them off.

Sarah raised her arms and howled as resolutely as any Iroquois.

Her pal, Colweenada, did not join in her celebration.

"Your friend," she said, seeing his sorrow. "I'm so sorry."

"He is my brother."

She assumed that he meant the term in a familiar manner, that all young Iroquois were brothers and sisters.

"My father will be sad to hear of this day," the young man reported.

She understood then that he and the other boy were blood brothers.

"My father will thank you for saving the life of his older son."

"Your father will be welcome," Sarah said. She smiled despite their grief. He did not thank her himself, for she was only a woman, but anticipated the thanks of his father and passed them along.

She helped Colweenada dig the youth's grave. They'd take turns clawing in the dirt, and at one point the young Indian lad went sullen and stiff. She took the branch out of his hands and allowed him to rest while she dug, and at that moment the bandits attacked again. Three arrows pierced the chest of Colweenada, and she heard them pop his skin. One clicked on a bone inside him, and another came out his back, the arrowhead covered in a bloody tuft of tissue. The shock had yet to subside when she looked up and saw herself surrounded. She was holding nothing more than the stick. She'd left her rifle too far away. She was as bad as her father, she thought, who had misplaced his ammunition on the morning she'd been taken, and she swore she'd never be so foolish again. Sarah attacked them with her wood, but easily, laughing, they wrestled her into submission and tied her hands and feet.

Now she was a prisoner for the second time, and this time she felt her heart stagger in her chest with a mortal dread—thumping, thumping.

She gazed upon the corpse of Colweenada—poor, unlucky boy—and knew that his father's grief on this day would be immense.

Sarah had never seen a dead person before, and now she'd seen three, and had killed one of them herself. She longed to be home again. Just the thought of her mother and her house and her brother and the farm caused her to lose all hope, all reason, and she wept and screamed at her accusers and felt out of her mind and cursed them and pulled mightily at her restraints while they only laughed and danced around her and ran their filthy hands over her body and licked her face like dogs. One man tore at her shirt, exposing her left breast, and bit it, causing her to make a rapid series of unearthly sounds. Another man pulled him off her and Sarah, terrified beyond all capacity, raged up at them.

The bandits decided to keep moving. They feared reprisals, discovery. These were unsafe woods. They wanted to sell the girl, but they didn't want her too crazy. She was worth less to them crazy, more if they were the heroes of her rescue. This was explained to the man who had bitten her nipple, and she watched his eyes to see what he might decide.

She feared death less than all manner of upset as they dragged her across the ground, down through the woods to the lake. Her skin was cut and chafed and bruised, and she cursed them. The attackers, who had also lost a friend on this excursion, kicked her quiet.

At the lake's edge, they tied her to a floating log and walked on, pulling Sarah Hanson through the water. The trunk of the tree spun, and her belly was in the water and she had to fight to hold her face up high enough to breathe.

If she possessed the will, she knew, she'd breathe water only and die.

But she survived that portion of her journey.

They made camp after dark, these drunken men unaccustomed to travail in the wilderness. Sarah's log was turned upright, and she was pulled halfway onto the shore and neglected there while the men organized themselves to eat and sleep. They drank whiskey, and the worst of the men who was always pestering her kissed her mouth. His lips tasted of rotted moose flesh, and Sarah Hanson, bound hand and foot, spat at him, and he only laughed as he fondled her vilely. The others told him he had to wait—he had not chosen a straw to be the first to have her, if anyone would have her, because that had not been decided yet. They argued about these matters in English, for they were from different tribes, and their voices echoed off the rocks and trees. One reminded the others that they didn't want her crazy. The vile man declared that the girl wasn't crazy, that she wanted him to touch her, so Sarah Hanson showed how a crazy woman behaves, yelling and gagging and foaming and cursing and kicking—although she could not kick—and the men had to pull the other man off her to settle her down.

Long after the vile man had gone away and stumbled into a stupor, she sensed that she was hearing her own voice, its echo wailing across the desolate waters of Lake Champlain.

But that was the voice of a woman gone crazy.

At dawn, the vilest of the men awoke first and stretched his hands above his head. A tomahawk flew through the air, and Sarah heard the weapon break a thin, dry, dead branch, then crack his skull. The sound was like the snapping of old wood that had a rotted core, and she heard him fall onto his face like the sound of a horse dropping onto its rump with a satisfying sigh. Without a single yell, Iroquois fell upon the three remaining bandits as they slept, and scalped them alive. Two who survived the scalping staggered forth, down to the lake, the tops of their heads sheared off. Blood flowed down their faces. The Indians brayed at them. Strapped to her log, Sarah watched as they stumbled around her and fell into the water as though to conceal their shame and torment, and one rose up again with a yell inhuman in its desolation, a man abandoned even by himself. The other man never turned his face again to the sun, and floated face down in the waterway. The man with the blood in his eyes got to his feet and was pierced by an arrow before he fell upon Sarah Hanson to take the revenge he might have wished, and a second arrow, straight through his mouth, silenced his mournful lament.

Then the Iroquois hacked off the limbs of each corpse and floated the pieces away.

Sarah, strapped to the log, was freed of her restraints by her original band of raiders. She hugged the leader and, weeping, told him that his sons were dead. He nodded, for this calamity was known to him.

Later that morning, as they paddled north, they found the three missing horses, which had located one another and wandered aimlessly together. Surprise did not gallop off as Sarah approached. She asked the band leader who had lost his sons if she might not travel by the overland route again. He wore his hair with the sides of his scalp shaved and feathers hanging downward from a ponytail, and he had blackened his face to show his grief for his sons. He nodded, and gave her another guide for the journey, an older warrior who wore no feathers, but necklaces of beads and stones, who often closed his eyes while riding a horse, as though he could see without looking. He seldom spoke, and only in his own language.

Sarah Hanson carried on to New France on horseback. The day came soon enough when she rode into the village of Oka by the banks of the *rivière des Outaouais,* where the raiding party, having arrived first, waited. The chief greeted her and told her they would wait there for her father to come and set her free.

"I am a free woman now," she said.

He did not know what she meant, or what beguiled this brave girl to utter such strange words.

†††

Sarah was down by the water when news arrived. A tiny, pleasant girl, seven years old, came running calling her name. The little girl looked as though she might burst.

"Sarah! Your father!"

"My father?" Suddenly she realized that she hadn't thought of him in months.

"He's here."

Looking frail and haggard from the trip, he seemed embarrassed that he had taken so long to find her. He had brought pigs in two carts, and chickens, but no cows or horses. He offered, when negotiations intensified, to leave one of the carts and its two horses behind, an offer amenable to the Iroquois. Sarah was informed of the progress of the negotiations.

When the deed was done, she listened to the details of the transaction. The Iroquois would receive forty-four live chickens plus the fourteen they'd already eaten while the talks had transpired. They'd receive eight sows, which particularly pleased them because half the pigs were pregnant. Two horses and a rickety cart. A goat. Four bolts of fabric suitable for ladies' wear or curtains. Nineteen blankets. Twelve bags of onions, twenty-two of potatoes. Sixteen bags of carrots. Ninety-six bottles of rum and a solemn vow—this had been a sticking point, but it was understood that if the promise was not kept, the Indians would have the right to burn the man's house down again—to ship another forty-eight bottles later. Sixteen rifles and twenty large boxes of ammunition. Twelve pistols.

"We will accept this payment," the chief explained, "for our kindness to rescue your daughter who was lost in the woods."

"What do I get?" Sarah was told that Jeremy Hanson had asked.

"Your daughter," the chief replied. He had a man of his village who spoke English very well translate for him.

"You burned my house down."

"Fire is a terrible thing. I am sorry for this accident to you."

"You burned my house down, you imbecile!"

"I heard your roof burned very quickly. Why did it do that, so fast? My men were near that place when we learned your daughter was lost. They went to find her."

"I deserve something for my house."

"What do you want?" the chief asked him.

"Compensation."

"I don't have any of those. I will allow you to take back your carrots."

"I lost my house."

"I lost two sons on the return trip. They were keeping your daughter alive. You get to take your daughter home with you. You can build a new house. Probably you already did that. Why else did you take so long to come here? My two sons cannot come back to me."

That statement sealed their arrangement. Both men had suffered, and this seemed to satisfy Jeremy Hanson.

Sarah was told the details, and then she said, "I'm not going back."

"Of course you go back," an Indian woman responded.

"A deal is a deal," the chief said. "I keep everything in our deal. I only agreed with your father that he is free to take you back. If you don't go back, that's not my problem."

"I'm not going back."

Her father would remain in the Indian camp for eleven days but failed to convince his daughter to return. They would walk along the shore of the Ottawa, and he appreciated that this was a sweet land, with low hills and deep woods and the quietly running river. But what life could exist there for her? Sarah did not seem to know. She had arrived when she was fourteen, and now she was fifteen. She wore her black hair long and tied in braids, and she knotted the braids with beads. While they walked, she smoked and passed her father the pipe, but he always declined. In the end, his resolve was frustrated, and Jeremy Hanson returned home almost empty-handed, carrying only a shawl that Sarah had sewn for her mother, a deerskin vest she had made for her brother, and a few bags of carrots the chief really hadn't wanted anyway.

"Tell my little brother that I shot the deer," she said.

"Is that true?" her father asked.

"I don't lie," she said. "Of course it's true."

He didn't know her anymore.

†††

Following the Great Peace among Indians, natives roamed the streets of Montreal at night. Peace ruined many lives, but Indians were not the only instigators of the brawls. Men of the woods, whose injuries or frailties kept them from paddling the rivers, consumed great quantities of spirits. Destitute farmers who had lost their wives and children as well as their lands, and former soldiers with addled minds, and men who, for no sensible reason, took to drink, all fell to scrapping. A Jesuit priest, now defrocked for having unrepentantly seized Indian women to carry to his bed, often several at once, was the mightiest of the brawlers. Together, the men beat one another over their heads with hammers and sliced off one another's ears and gouged each other's eyes out and bit off the tongues of their attackers. In the worst of the tempests, the victorious relieved the maniacal of their testicles with a sharp, fierce twist and tug, and the caterwauling of the injured awoke Sulpicians in their beds at night. The priests sat bolt upright and prayed desperately, blocking their ears and weeping for the misery upon the streets and for their own gentle fright.

By day, priests discussed what they might do, where they might go.

Talk had centred on the gentle slopes arising from the Ottawa River, west of the rapids where the river tumbled into the St. Lawrence. Iroquois had made camp there at a place called Oka. They were a disciplined tribe, it seemed, not the reckless, inebriated madmen of Montreal streets by night. The Sulpicians longed to be out of the city, in a place where they might commune peaceably with God and pray for the whole of the world, and not just for the eyeless bleeding in the puddles of mud outside their gates.

They paid a visit to a young woman who lived by the Ottawa River, in a cabin on the south bank, her home facing a contingent of Mohawk raiders who dwelled on the opposite shore. She had built a cabin there with her new husband, Jean-Baptiste Sabourin, a wood cutter by trade, and her house was becoming a way station for those travelling the waterways. As the priests arrived, twenty-five strong, Sarah Hanson Sabourin was not surprised to see them steer their four canoes ashore. Once they had arrived, though, she was quickly astonished to learn that they had come specifically to speak to her.

"I'd ask you to come inside, but all of you won't fit," she told them.

The eminent friars laughed, and one alone stepped forward and spoke softly. "You and me, then, just us two. I'm prepared to speak for the rest."

The others nodded, giving their consent to this arrangement, and Sarah Hanson Sabourin and Father Bernard entered her most humble abode.

An irrepressible hostess, Sarah fixed tea and scones for her guest and for the fathers outside.

"Next time," Father Bernard promised, "I'll remember to travel in a smaller group. But each one of us wanted to meet you."

The entire event felt alarming.

"Have I done something wrong, Father?" Although a Protestant, she had married into the Catholic Church and converted to the faith. What more was required to appease these gentlemen?

"Not at all, my child. Forgive us for causing you any unease. We believe that you may be able to help us with a matter of some delicacy, shall we say, and a certain urgency, also. We have sought you out only to plead for your assistance."

The visit was turning increasingly odd. "I don't understand, Father."

The cabin was dark, the windows small to help thwart the cold in winter, and they were shaded by the forest around them. "We want to become your neighbours, Sarah. We covet—I think that's a fair expression—we covet the lands on the opposite shore, east of where the Mohawks now live. We have interceded with the king of France, and he has granted us title. We want to build a monastery there. We would like to have our own farms, establish orchards, raise animals for their produce, not specifically for slaughter—chickens for their eggs, cows and goats for milk and cheese. We've thought this through carefully, and we've come to the conclusion that this is the right place for us."

"I think it's a grand idea," Sarah informed him as she sipped her tea. She did not add that she especially liked the part about them living on the side of the river opposite to her, not on the same side, and farther east.

"Yes. Yes. Thank you. We think so. Ville-Marie—Montreal, people seem to call it now—has grown. After the signing of the Great Peace, it's lost all discipline. The wildest of men aren't killing each other in the woods anymore. They fight in the streets instead. It's become too rambunctious for poor friars."

"How may I help, Father? I'll do what I can. I don't imagine that that can be much. There are so many of you—my husband is fond of saying that there are more priests in Ville-Marie than trees. He and I, we're very busy through the summer, just to make ends meet and feed the horses."

The priest would fold his hands in the lap of his cassock between his spread knees and shake them as he spoke, as though physically coaxing his words out. Grey-haired, physically robust, he was well suited to being an emissary as well as an eminence, as he exuded a natural kindliness while conveying a trusting and a trustworthy disposition.

"You are so very young. Not yet twenty. That I come to you with this prop-osition may strike others as unusual, except that you are so highly regarded by all you've met. We would be encouraged by any welcome that you might pro-vide us, Miss Hanson."

"It's Madame Sabourin now," she corrected him.

"Of course. My age—an oversight. Madame Sabourin, we are anxious to have good relations with all our potential neighbours."

She nodded, beginning to understand. "The Mohawks worry you."

"Don't misunderstand me. As long as we may live together in peace and harmony, we would only delight in having them as our neighbours. But will they delight in us? That's the question."

"And you want me to find that out?"

Father Bernard nodded. "We have heard of your famous connection to them. The story's been told that they helped build this cabin. If you would intercede on our behalf, Madame, we would be most grateful."

Sarah took a walk around her room to consider the situation, and returned to sit opposite the priest.

"Understand, Father, the Iroquois are accustomed to being crowded out of their lands. It's their greatest fear, the greatest agitation in their lives."

"I see," Father Bernard replied, downcast. Prospects appeared gloomy.

"The Sulpicians have had a mission at Oka for some time now. You are the seigneurs for this land . . . it's your right to do with it as you see fit. And yet, obviously, the appearance of a large monastery might trouble the Iroquois. It's true that their worries ought to concern you. A large monastery surrounded by farmland is not as easily defended as a mission within a fort."

"That is our dilemma. Hearing you speak of it in such plain terms, per-haps our plans are for naught."

"There is a way," she said.

The vicar perked up. "Yes?"

"If you were to make it plain to the Mohawk that you pose less of a threat than, say, the settlement of the riverside by new farmers, if you point out to them that you are only men, with no women, that you are therefore unlikely—if you will forgive me, Father—to breed, which would require expansion . . . that you represent, in fact, a safe barrier between the Iroquois and further development of the French settlements, then your project might find favour, and you might indeed be received by amiable neighbours."

Father Bernard sat still longer than he might have realized, staring at the girl. She was not twenty, yet she possessed an intelligent and finely attuned wisdom capable of determining affairs of state. To come to her had been good advice, and the proper choice for the friars to have acted upon. He shook himself from his state of abject admiration, and nodded. "Yes, yes. Of course. We can do that, with your assistance, Madame Sabourin."

"Please, call me Sarah."

He was happy to do so, for it was difficult to think of this child as a married woman. Only a few years ago, she'd been attending school as the daughter of a wealthy man, a society marriage in elegant surrounds in her future. Now she lived in the wilderness, alone on the south shore of the river for scores of miles in either direction, and deftly negotiated deals between the French and Iroquois.

"When we go to see their chief," she advised the priest, "it's best that you not arrive as a flock of crows. Which is what they call you—crows. Better that you come alone, with me, Father. You have one advantage of which you might be unaware, other than your lack of children."

"What would that be, Sarah?" He was helping her clear the dishes from their tea, for priests were unaccustomed to the domestic attention of women except in marginal ways.

"You're Sulpicians. You've had many encounters with the Iroquois, to be sure, but not as many as the Jesuits. A few Iroquois have difficulty looking a Jesuit in the eye these days—they're embarrassed that they tortured so many. They would not want Jesuits moving in beside them, for it would only provoke their shame."

Father Bernard had an inkling that, in her subtle way, Sarah Hanson was seeing to his own education. She was teaching him that *les sauvages* with whom he would negotiate a friendly sharing of land and waterways were a complex and evolved people, not to be treated as children. They had a history. He knew as much from his own experiences among Indians as a young man, yet was grateful for the woman's wise and tactful counsel.

"Sarah, I should tell you also, we have at other missions Iroquois converts, and some Huron and Algonquin. We will seek to relocate them to the north shore of the lake also. They will enhance the Iroquois there now, and also, perhaps, help to show them the way to Christ."

The young woman mulled this over. "That might be all right, Father. But permit me to say that the Iroquois are weary of being divided amongst themselves by their allies. Who will influence who, that will be for fortune to decide. If you were a different sort of man, I might caution you by saying that any plan to divide the Indians amongst themselves will fail, for that's an old tactic and they are on to it. Fortunately, I need not issue such a caution to you, Father."

Yet she had just done so.

Meeting the Iroquois, the priest stressed that the lands the friars sought to inhabit would be substantial for their orchards and crops, but that they would also be fixed. The monastery would contain the dwelling for the priests, and while that dwelling might grow in time, it would never expand to subsequent homes spread across the land. They would not encroach on lands the Iroquois inhabited now, and by being there, the two communities, the Sulpicians and the Mohawks, would successfully dominate that entire shore, preserving it for generations into the future.

The chief of the Mohawk nation of the Iroquois people solemnly nodded.

"We will grant the Iroquois your lands in the white man's laws."

The Mohawk stared back at him, without nodding.

"We will bring chickens with us when we come," Father Bernard said, "which we will not share with you. And cows, which we will not share. And goats."

"You won't share your goats?" The chief moved about on his posterior. This seemed a strange negotiation to him, when the man on the floor of his tepee opposite him informed him only of those things that he would not offer.

"We won't share our goats."

"That's too bad," the chief said.

"But we will share the eggs our chickens lay."

"Ah," said the chief.

"And the milk of our cows and goats, and the butter and the cheeses we will produce from the animals' milk. We will share our apples when our orchards ripen."

"Apples from trees?" the chief said.

"Yes," Father Bernard said.

"Where are these trees?"

"We will grow them from seed."

"Only birds plant trees," the chief stated, "when they shit."

"Birds," Father Bernard revised, "and Sulpicians."

The chief scratched his knee. "You shit trees?"

Father Bernard, sufficiently comfortable on the blanket on the dirt floor of the tepee, attempted a joke. "Like crows," he said.

The chief grunted to the humour, then waited. The priest felt perplexed.

Her legs crossed under her, Sarah Hanson suggested, "Father, would that not be interesting? For the crows to plant apple seeds on Indian land also?"

"Then we have apples, too," the chief said. "We have our own trees from the shit of Sulpician crows."

"Of course! For sure. If you will clear the land, Chief, we will plant as many apple orchards as you want."

"This is good," the chief agreed.

When the agreement appeared to be in order, the chief began to talk about a dagger that had been given to the first white man to come from France to the Iroquois village known as Hochelaga. The dagger had travelled from the hands of kings and voyageurs, eventually into possession of the man who now ruled the Hudson's Bay Company.

Father Bernard was beginning to sweat. How he was supposed to acquire such a dagger went beyond his devising, although it would probably come down to a significant exchange of money or a tribute of lands, more than even the well-to-do Sulpicians would want to manage.

A year earlier, the chief explained, twin girls had become lost in a forest in Boston, in the land known as Massachusetts.

"Lost?" Father Bernard sought to clarify. "In Boston? In the woods?"

"Lost in the forest in Boston, Massachusetts," the chief repeated.

"Boston's a big city," the priest began to protest, but Sarah interrupted him.

"Young girls often wander away from home and become lost," she reminded him. "It happened to me."

"I see," the priest said, and fell silent.

"A Mohawk band from this place found them, and brought them here, so that they would be safe until their father came here to take them back."

"That was," Father Bernard began, hesitated, then continued, "that was very good of you, Chief."

"Their father did not come here. Instead, very soon, the uncle of the twin girls, the man whose sister was their mother, he came here instead."

"Why did the uncle come?" Sarah asked.

"He came because he lived not so far away. This white man, he was the ruler of the Hudson's Bay Company. He took the girls back to Boston himself. He was very happy to have the girls looked after so well. To show his gratitude, he gave to me this magic knife, what he calls the Cartier Dagger."

The chief removed the instrument from a wooden box, and Sarah Hanson and Father Bernard leaned forward to gaze upon it.

"It's beautiful," Sarah said.

"A wonder," the priest agreed.

"As a sign of our friendship, as an agreement that French farmers will stay away from this place because the priests have taken the free land for themselves and leave the rest only to the Mohawk, I give this gift to you, Father Bernard."

The priest was overcome. He had hoped for only the most rudimentary of tacit agreements, and now understood that he was binding his community to generations of trust and fellowship.

"My chief, thank you for your extraordinary gesture of peace. May our peoples know endless days of harmony. As you may know, we priests have taken vows of perpetual poverty—we cannot acquire riches, and your dagger is composed of diamonds and gold."

"Father Bernard—" Sarah tried to interrupt him, concerned where he might be going. The priests may have taken vows of perpetual poverty, but the order itself was not poor. Surely they could accommodate this gift. Yet she stopped, for the priest had raised a hand to silence her.

"I offer a proposal, Chief. Allow me to accept this present in the spirit in which it is given, as a grand tribute of Mohawk friendship for their Sulpician brothers."

The chief nodded, well pleased.

"Then understand that I receive this Cartier Dagger into the heart of my community, and with the blessing and goodwill that is part of this gift, I grant it to our mutual friend, the one who has brought us together and made this possible, Sarah Hanson Sabourin. So that the gift is from you, great chief, to myself and the Sulpicians, and together we are joined as one as we confer it upon Sarah."

The chief was well pleased with this proposal as well, and pleased with the wisdom of his new neighbour.

Sarah Hanson took the dagger back across the river to her cabin, where she showed it to her husband. He had been busy in recent years cutting wood for Ville-Marie, which had an insatiable demand for timber after its old section had burned to the ground. Jean-Baptiste Sabourin, more than a decade older than his wife, tucked her into his side as he admired her present.

"What do you think it means?" she asked him. "Such a knife?"

He had married a woman wiser than himself, and loved her for her acumen. He also knew that, as her husband, he could not always be concerned with harvesting trees and riding them downriver to market. The gold and diamonds embedded in the handle were more than he'd seen of precious stones in his lifetime, yet compared with what had transpired, they were rendered without significant value.

"It means," he said, and kissed her forehead, "that this must be a good place to live."

Sarah hugged him back.

And so the Cartier Dagger remained in the home of Sarah Hanson. As babies were born into the home, the relic was put away, stored deeply and safely in a closet, where it would remain both safe and neglected through the passage of generations.

CHAPTER 15

1968

A CCOMPANIED BY AN EXPLETIVE LOST INSTANTLY UNDER AN ON-slaught of trombones, pipes, drums and a crash of cymbals, the first rock arched gently above the heads of an astonished crowd. The granite chunk cleared the sidewalk before it ricocheted off the fourth step of the broad stairwell to the Municipal Library, where a reviewing stand had been erected. At the bounce, people in all directions ducked, then leaped for cover. The athletic form of the combatant who had darted off the sidewalk into the path of the parade appeared exemplary, the throw adroit, the effect of its relative accuracy electric. Suddenly, a barrage of rocks and bottles flew from the hands of an agitated portion of the throng. Startled dignitaries, including the mayor of Montreal, held up their hands for protection or cowered behind policemen, assistants, chairs and the tall Doric columns.

A security detail sprang forward. The prime minister of Canada, the primary target, did not seek shelter. Defiantly, he stood up for a better view. Young men and women wasted no time in answering the unspoken challenge. On cue, the next volleys rained down upon the reviewing stand, thrown less in anger, perhaps, than in a swift, unbridled release, an enthusiasm for the rambunctious sport of rioting and for the pleasure of endeavouring to strike a foe smack on the noggin.

Yet all their fierce throws missed.

On crowd-control duty that night, a strapping young officer had no specific orders to follow in this circumstance, nor was he experienced at events that deteriorated so swiftly into violence. Insults had been directed his way all evening as the parade moved into the vicinity of his post by the stand. As a rookie cop, he was proud of his blue uniform, and he enjoyed wearing the badge. He stood his ground and let the foul words nick him then fall to the pavement. *Establishment pig!* If absorbing the taunts of young people high on rage, politics and beer was the price of wearing the uniform, he'd pay it, suffering their abuse without being provoked.

Fascist!

The tall, well-built youth was no older than most of them. *Traitor!* Twenty-four. His detractors, long-haired boys and wildly dressed girls, had attempted little in their lives, or so he contended in a private debate with himself, and had accomplished less. "Do something with your life," he whispered under his breath, "before you tell me what to think." Never did he let on that the heckling young women managed to get his goat, especially the more attractive ones. *Redneck!* To stand at his station like a statue and endure rhetoric from pretty girls was not a favourite detail, yet he remained determined to endure it, to not lose his cool.

Power to the people! Fuck the police!

Words. He didn't respond.

Then the first rock was thrown, and instantly he reacted.

Other cops were ducking tomatoes and eggs and bottles, even the ingredients of sandwiches, as people who had intended to enjoy a parade now chose to hurl the contents of their picnic hampers, but Constable Émile Cinq-Mars had caught sight of the one who'd thrown the first missile and he would not permit the miscreant to elude his capture. This arrest would make the abuse he'd endured all evening moderately worthwhile.

He charged after the culprit who had retreated into the apparent safety of the crowd, while on the reviewing stand Pierre Elliott Trudeau, now the prime minister of Canada, who faced an election the very next day, watched him go, disappearing into the impressive mob.

†††

Auspicious times these, Pierre Elliott Trudeau believed.

Rarely was his life his own anymore. In a vague sense, he belonged to the people—words his friends were fond of dispensing—and while he disputed the severity of that limitation, the people clearly held his fate in their hands. Now a contingent loudly brayed that they more properly represented the people than he did, and to drive that point home they were doing their best to stone him. This did not bode well for the next day's election, nor did it augur well for his health if a missile should strike the mark, given that his forehead was their principal target.

He knew what his confreres were thinking, and the security detail in particular. This could be a calculated attack. Trudeau stood upright, calm enough, his weight imperceptibly forward on the balls of his feet, as he had learned to do slipping punches as a boy boxer. He bobbed when he had to and dodged an occasional beer bottle or a chunk of brick clawed out of a building and thrown in anger from the darkness. The fury of the streets convulsed before him, worsening, police and ambulance sirens wailing now, debris clattering around him as though the sky itself caved in before his eyes.

Mounties in plain clothes urged him to come away, but he shoved them aside. He didn't want them blocking his view. Had he not been invited to this parade? He was not going to be driven off by packs of wild ruffians—elections in Quebec had known too much of that. Pierre Elliott Trudeau, the youthful prime minister of Canada, the upper-class drifter, the man who had failed to do much with his life except read and travel a lot and talk to a few people—on occasion, he'd encourage a strike, or scribble an essay, or teach a few classes in constitutional law—had found his true vocation, to represent the pinnacle of power in the land and be prime minister. Now those who would remove him sought to do so through thuggery. He declined to depart the reviewing stand, and permitted the rioters—for the actions on the streets were rapidly escalating to that level of furore—to try to pelt him with hard objects.

He stood fairly still—reserved, defiant—as they continued to miss.

†††

She loved it, and never felt scared. The adrenaline rush was intoxicating. She leapfrogged startled couples who had brought little stools to sit on and spread a picnic of wine and cheese across their knees, and she cut through throngs of people moving towards and away from the commotion of the riot. Other police officers, seeing that she was being chased by one of their own, entered the fray, but she made quick cuts to elude them and they became embroiled with others, who shouted insults or intruded upon their path. She'd brake, shoot a glance around, choose her next destination, and take off. Yet always that one cop pursued her. What was the matter with him? Why was he so obsessed? Because she had thrown the first stone? *Hey, buddy, a thousand bottles are flying through the air right now. Get over it! I'm not the only one out here who's angry.*

He kept running after her.

She thought she could rely upon her youth and endurance, but after a while she supposed that her pursuer was around the same age as her and equally fit, so that wasn't going to work. She pulled her cap off, letting her long hair fly loose. *See, Mr. Policeman? I'm a woman. You're going to all this trouble to catch a woman. What are you, too chickenshit to go after a guy?* Young people in the crowd thought so, and as she cut back through the crowd, a few blocked the cop's access and some tried to trip him. One man succeeded, and the cop went down. The cop picked himself up, grabbed his cap and carried on after the girl.

Jesus, mister. What's with you anyway?

The young constable, Émile Cinq-Mars, controlled his breathing to conserve energy. This was the culprit who had instigated the disturbance, and he wanted him in custody. *Her*, he discovered along the way. That was a revelation. With her long locks flowing behind her, it occurred to him that he was vaguely attracted to the woman—to this arrest, in any case. She was lithe, she could move, she ran like a fawn, with beautiful, long strides and then, when necessary, she eluded him with skittish counter-steps that left him half out of his shoes.

He wanted this girl caught. Too many pretty girls had taunted him, not just insulting the uniform but wounding his feelings. Girls shouldn't be immune from prosecution, especially the one who had started the whole thing. Young men were being rounded up. Paddy wagons had been brought in. He could see two vehicles waiting to be filled. Here and there, cops had their nightsticks out, beating heads. He didn't want to beat heads. But if he could bring this girl in, he'd be doing his job. He wanted to lay claim to the riot's instigator.

Golly, she was lovely, the way she ran. Limber, swift. Vaulting bushes and people, cutting on a dime. She was cheered on, he was booed—reason enough to maintain the pursuit. Failure would only egg everybody on, give the rioters confidence. Success might help subdue them.

Émile Cinq-Mars caught her by the hair, but instantly let go. He could tell that if she didn't stop in her tracks, he might snap her head back more violently than she would expect, and she could be injured. He ran harder, knowing that he was losing his breath, that he had to catch her soon. He was probably half in love with her, he was thinking, almost giddy, laughing to himself, he so admired her form and grit and physical grace. Maybe he would have to just let her go.

The young woman circled behind a cluster of a dozen people, slowing a little to catch her breath. She couldn't run forever. This was nuts. The cop was a maniac. And yet, he had caught her by the hair, briefly, she had felt his grip, and then he'd let go. Thank God for that. She'd thought her neck would snap. Maybe, if she was to be caught, this guy deserved to be the cop to do it. Clearly, he had a conscience. He probably wouldn't drag her to a paddy wagon by the hair, as some cops were doing to both men and women.

Breathe, breathe, she had to breathe and keep running.

Émile Cinq-Mars was thinking the same thing: breathe and keep running.

✝✝✝

The times had changed so rapidly. Friends and foes alike had believed that Pierre Trudeau would find himself with the socialists, but he considered their party to be colossally ignorant of Quebec. Instead, he founded the Union des forces démocratiques, with which he intended to unite opposition groups in advance of the provincial election of 1960. Defeating Duplessis was his priority. Yet *le Chef* outfoxed his brilliant young antagonist with a simple and elegant ruse. He died.

Le Chef was dead.

Which killed Trudeau's party.

Everything changed. Without him, Duplessis's own party disintegrated. The Church, its friend gone, found itself bereft of moral authority as well as power. The ecclesiastical voice became a decayed echo from dusty statuary, the pale words falling upon empty pews. Outspoken political thinkers were brought into the new provincial government, and the fiery, popular René Lévesque accepted a cabinet post. He agitated from within to take the government to a position that favoured independence, and constantly pressed Ottawa to surrender more of its influence and treasure. In short order, Trudeau went from being an out-of-work teacher, to part-time lecturing, to becoming a member of Parliament, to being the minister of justice. With the retirement of the prime minister, he ran for the party's leadership. A rank outsider, yet he won. Such was the shock of his rapid ascent that he had become unbeatable at the polls, yet rocks now rained down upon him and the police were attacking the rioters even as the protesters fought back.

He would not stand down. This was the fight of his lifetime, between those who believed that Quebec rightfully belonged in Canada—the elegant destiny that he believed the country had prepared for itself—and those who vied for an independent state dressed in its full, mythic glory. His astonishing rise to power, his unprecedented popularity, had led to this moment and this conflict. The history of the Quebec nation had moved inexorably towards this quarrel. Trudeau's words and position provoked rocks and bottles, and now he would stand and see if such actions could break him.

On television, the country watched.

†††

She kicked, and flailed her legs. He had her, the bastard, and God, he was strong. Then she was free again. The young rock-thrower didn't know how it had happened. She was running again. She looked back. Bystanders had jumped in, taking the side of the girl against the cop, and now he fought off those who'd jumped him, but instead of arresting the ruffians, he was running after her once more.

He'd catch her, too.

In the end, she didn't want to be caught. So she surrendered. The better option. Her lungs were desperate for air, her whole body was rebelling. She slumped to her knees and waited. Momentarily, the cop was upon her, locking her hands behind her back.

"You got me," she said, breathing heavily.

"Piece of cake," he said, and they both laughed lightly.

Both of them needed a respite, and once she was cuffed, Cinq-Mars put his hands on his knees and caught his breath. He looked at her, and she returned his gaze. Captor and captive, each curious about the other. She seemed stretched to him, her neck elongated, her nose as slender as a knife. Her brown eyes were wide-set, but the face itself seemed pinched, so that her eyes stood out all the more. Her eyebrows, light and gently curved, were the most perfect of angel wings. She was so pretty, he wanted to stop all this and let her go. He wanted to run after her again. To look at her eyes was easier, and more polite, but he wanted to observe her mouth, and, pretending to breathe extra heavily, he looked down between his feet, then back up again, his glance crossing her lips. Slender also, not the full lips of so-called great beauties but he found her lips inviting. Under the left side of her mouth, a quartet of faint spots. A sprinkle of fine freckles across her nose, falling slightly onto the soft rise of her cheeks.

He was the captor, but he knew that he had been disarmed.

She was just so pretty.

"Do you know Captain Armand Touton?" she asked as he pulled her up to her feet.

He was thinking of her legs. They were beautifully long. He was looking forward to the walk in search of a paddy wagon. He reached out to guide her away and was astonished at how easily his fingers encircled her wrist.

"Heard of him." Touton was the most famous and feared cop in the department, yet although both men worked out of downtown headquarters, Cinq-Mars had not been around long enough to make his acquaintance. "You want to tell me a story? How he's your uncle?"

"He's closer to me than any uncle."

"I don't care if he's your father—is he?—you still threw the first rock."

"Eighteen thousand rocks have been thrown so far. I've kept count. Why do you care so much about the first one?" He was leading her towards a paddy wagon down the block. She feared it, for she was mildly claustrophobic and it looked as though they were packing the rioters in tightly. She might not be able to endure that confinement without losing her cool.

"You started it."

"The English started it when they invaded us in 1759. That rock's been waiting to be thrown for over two hundred years."

"Tell it to the judge." He had to wait with her in a line with other cops leading their prisoners to the paddy wagon. Standing beside her, he did not mind the delay.

"You tell it to Armand—Captain Touton," she said. "Treat me badly, and you can kiss your career goodbye."

"There's nothing at all charming about threatening people."

"You haven't treated me badly yet. I'm not asking for special treatment."

"I don't have the energy to treat you badly."

They laughed briefly again, and Cinq-Mars couldn't help but wish that they had met under different circumstances. In the larger scheme of things, throwing a rock might not be the most heinous crime on earth.

"Do me a favour . . . no—two favours." She was still trying to breathe normally.

"You're in a great situation to be asking for favours."

"I'm claustrophobic. Put me in a squad car. Not a paddy wagon. I'll scream. I'll go insane."

Cinq-Mars looked at her. He saw that she was serious. "Sorry, but you should have thought of that before you threw the rock." The response was a tough one, and the woman continued to gaze up at him as though another option might yet occur to the officer. "I don't have a squad car," he went on, "and I don't have the rank to do anything more than put you in that paddy wagon."

"Then promise me this—"

"I can't make any promises."

"Promise me. Get me on *this* paddy wagon. It's nearly full. I'll be at the end, near the window. It'll leave soon. If you put me on the next one, I'll get pushed all the way inside and I'll have to wait. I'll die in there. Please."

Cinq-Mars nodded. Dragging her along with him, he shoved past other officers. "We need this one to go on right now. I can't wait." Other officers didn't mind. The longer they spent in line with their prisoners, the longer they were out of the fray, where no one really wanted to be.

"Thanks," she said. "I'll put in a good word with Armand."

"You do that."

"My second favour . . ."

They were almost at the rear gate, and Cinq-Mars shouted at the guard to hold on, he had one more prisoner to shove in for this trip. The guard argued back, but Cinq-Mars pressed forward with his captive and the door remained ajar.

"What second favour?" he shouted in the young woman's ear.

"Tell Armand I'm under arrest. Get the word to him, all right?"

"I don't have access to the man—"

"Just do it, all right? Trust me. He'll thank you."

"What's your name? I'll have to tell him your name."

He helped hoist her into the back. From inside, an arm reached around her waist and clasped her, pulling her in.

"Get your cuffs back," the guard commanded.

Cinq-Mars helped turn the woman around so that he could reclaim his handcuffs. She spoke to him over her shoulder. "Anik Clément. Got that? Will you remember? Anik. Clément."

He got his cuffs off her. The door closed on the young woman. Cinq-Mars moved off quickly, not really knowing what he should do in the chaos of the street. He noticed that the parade remained in shocked existence, although wildly dispersed, and various segments had lost touch one with the other. Performers, bands and floats were continuing to come down Sherbrooke Street, those at the rear not fully cognizant of what was going on up ahead. He thought that he should at least stop the parade before any baton-twirling teenagers got hurt.

Then he heard a burst of screams and shouts behind him. Twisting around, he saw the tumult of bodies and cops flailing with their sticks close to the paddy wagon. The situation looked rough, but the police had the upper hand. He wasn't needed. Then, in what seemed like slow motion, although it happened in seconds, he spotted a rioter opening the rear door with the keys, and prisoners inside the paddy wagon splurged out. For one quick instant, he caught sight of the girl, and she noticed him, then darted into the mob and into the dark night, away from the bright parade and television lights.

Cinq-Mars took three steps towards her, then let it go.

She was lost to him this time. In any case, she had given him her name. She undoubtedly regretted that now. Just to be safe—who knew what distractions might await him through the night—he wrote her name in his notebook before returning his attention to the streets. When he looked up, he gazed straight across at the prime minister scanning the situation. Interesting. A politician who hadn't run for cover. Cinq-Mars then brought his hand down upon the back of a rioter, opened up the boy's left palm until he dropped his rock, then gave him a shove to send him on his way. The rock he kicked down a storm drain, to keep it out of circulation.

Most of his fellow officers were busy handcuffing their prey and lining them up for transport to crowded overnight lockups, but order had largely been restored in this area and the mopping-up procedures were under control. Cinq-Mars helped out an elderly couple petrified that they might be run down by escapees or policemen. They both walked with canes. Although anxious to avoid any further unexpected adventures, they had enjoyed the spectacle well enough. He clasped the frail, stooped woman around the shoulders and shuffled along with her, while the diminutive old man took hold of his opposite elbow for balance. They made their way through a gap in the crowd towards a quiet side street. From there, they progressed on their own, undeterred by the steep incline. He watched them go, admiring the longevity of their affection for one another.

Before heading back to the bedlam, the young officer again took out his notebook. He had nothing further to jot down. Instead, he read the name inscribed on the page. Anik Clément.

†††

Alone on the reviewing stand, Pierre Elliott Trudeau again took his seat. Momentarily, his good friend Gérard Pelletier, these days a cabinet minister who'd been down at Liberal Party headquarters prior to the fracas, joined him for a preliminary debriefing.

"I'll be blamed for this, I suppose," Trudeau remarked.

"You looked great on TV. The commentary was positive. A few journalists took cheap shots, the people-in-the-street interviews were largely negative. Overall, you looked good. The commentary will be helpful."

Trudeau nodded and moved around as though preparing to leave. The parade was gone now, the big fight over, and only thousands of dazed spectators remained behind. The biggest story they recounted had to do with the rioters—some called them patriots—who'd been tossed into a paddy wagon and then escaped. *That* had been exciting.

"Gérard, this isn't going away. It'll be the fight of our lives."

The tall man beamed. "Interesting times, Pierre. Would you rather be bored?"

The question did not demand an answer. They both knew that a confluence of events and forces had placed them in power in changing times. Two weeks before this riot, Robert F. Kennedy had been gunned down in Los Angeles, two months after the assassination of Martin Luther King Jr. President John F. Kennedy had been dead for less than five years. The potential for attacks on leaders was now part and parcel of the stress of political life, and while the night's foray had been limited to glass and rocks, who knew what the future might hold? He loved to debate. He loved to tangle on the fly with those who brought ideas of their own. He presumed that he'd continue to have that opportunity. Others, though, moved in the shadows and guarded their secrecy. For them, the discussion was closed. Out there, some believed in their own analysis, and while today they had tossed projectiles without much accuracy, no one could predict how their rage might escalate, or their range improve.

"I'm beginning to believe in your Cartier Dagger. The luck you've had."

"Come on," Trudeau said. "Let's go win an election."

Trudeau and Pelletier walked back up the steps to the library, to the relief of the officer assigned to the prime minister's protection, and the two men departed behind curtains erected for this event as though they were moving off a stage. Another performance awaited them as the country went to the polls the following morning, their fate in the hands of the people once again.

†††

She counted this among the best times of her life. No sooner had she broken out of the van with the other prisoners than one had shouted, "This way! Come on!" She had gone with him, running blindly, furious and scared. She was so relieved to be out of that crowded space that she could scream, and she remained utterly terrified that she might be stuffed back into the truck again. Almost immediately, five of them were on the move, running hard, leaping hurdles and sprinting through small openings in the clusters of people. They alerted one another to police sightings—all thrilling, all fun—and headed north, still on the run, where the crowds thinned out, and finally dispersed to being only stragglers. The group slowed to a jog, always glancing behind, then bent, exhausted, they stopped to catch their breath.

"Paul," said one.

Another said his name was Jean-Luc.

"Vincent," said the third.

"Pierre," said the boy nearest her.

"Anik."

"Let's grab a beer," Paul suggested, and they drifted onto St. Denis Street and the bar scene there. They entered a crowded subterranean spot where young people were talking about the night, for most had taken part in the events firsthand and perhaps more were claiming to have thrown rocks than had actually done so. One boy wiggled both his big toes, which poked out from holes in his socks. "I got so mad, I threw my shoes." Everyone was euphoric from the snap of adrenaline.

The five escapees pooled their coins and ordered a pitcher. When the word went around the bar that they were the ones who'd bolted from the paddy wagon, new friends bought them beer into the wee hours. They were the heroes of the escapade, and Anik remained ecstatic. She had been longing for this. Real contact with people like herself, who shared the same ideals. The boys were in school—Paul in photography, Jean-Luc in political science, both Vincent and Pierre studying literature at different universities. They were high on excitement, and after forays to the back alley they were high on marijuana as well. A good night all around.

The conversation ignited her. Anik's own friends had let her down. They had wimped out. She hadn't expected much from them, but definitely something more than retreat. Tonight was the last straw. Time to change her friends. These boys, though, had not only joined in but had come prepared to fight, and one, playfully, was mad at her for beating him to the punch.

"I wanted to throw the first rock," Jean-Luc exclaimed. "I was waiting for the pretty majorettes to pass by, the ones in pink. Why'd they stop right in front of me?"

"I didn't know anybody else would join in."

"I saw you run right out into the street. I couldn't believe it!"

"The people of Quebec joined with you tonight, Anik," Paul said solemnly. "We are rising up."

Finally, she was making friends with those who would not only talk and debate, but with those who understood that actions spoke more loudly than words. Tomorrow, headlines would announce the riot to the world, and the people of Quebec would realize that their cause had been brought forward, that students were willing to denounce the politicians, fight the police and even escape from their custody for the sake of independence. The people of Quebec would know, in their hearts and minds, that their political environment had changed forever.

"Trudeau loses tomorrow, I bet," Vincent opined. "If he does, it's because of us. Quebecers will wake up in the morning and their eyes will be open for the first time in a century. We've exposed him as a traitor—he'll be kicked out of office."

They clinked glasses and waited as expectantly as politicians for the verdict from the polls.

"Are we all members of the RIN?" Jean-Luc inquired.

The boys agreed that they were, but Anik flatly said no.

"You must join," Vincent encouraged her.

"No," she repeated. "I won't."

A shock. "But you must!" Paul insisted. "Why won't you?"

"We need all the help we can find."

"I won't join."

"Why not?" Paul pressed.

"I won't put my name on a membership list. You never know how things will evolve. Someday, we may have to go underground. You don't want to go underground if you've put your name on a list the Mounties have already copied in triplicate."

They were impressed by her foresight, by her commitment. Anik had inherited tactics from her mother's long experience fighting union battles.

Very late that night, exhausted, exhilarated, she slumped home. None of her new friends had cars, and after the last pitcher of beer she didn't have cab fare. The métro had closed for the night, and the bus schedule didn't offer help at that hour. A long walk across downtown, then down the hill into the poor community of Pointe St. Charles, would be welcome anyway. A chance to clear her head and process her thoughts on the night's uproar. To act, to be doing something, felt so great. Yet she doubted the optimism of her new companions. Students had been throwing rocks, that's true, and bottles, which had been foolish, but no general uprising had taken place. For sure, they'd caused a commotion, but nothing more. Among the thousands of spectators, most had turned out for a parade, not a riot, and only a minority had responded favourably to the rampage. Changing people's minds, Anik believed—and again, she drew upon her mother's experiences—could be a slow, discouraging process. At least the contest for the hearts and minds of the population had begun, and that was the value of this night. The sun would come up on election day, and should Pierre Elliott Trudeau be returned to power, he would know, and the whole country would know, that a new contest had indeed begun, one the election itself had not resolved.

Bone tired, she was opening the latch to the knee-high gate outside her house when she heard a step. At this pre-dawn hour, it made her heart jump.

"Hello, Anik," a voice said.

She would not have turned had the intruder not spoken, but now curiosity obliged her to look his way. She recognized the uniform, then him. "You," she said.

"I guess I never introduced myself. Constable Émile Cinq-Mars."

"Curious name. Is this a social call?"

"I'm here to arrest you."

"What's with you, anyway? I met people tonight who threw twenty or thirty rocks, so they say. I threw *one*. I met a guy who threw his shoes—he'd be easy to find. You could do a Cinderella thing—if the shoes fit, arrest him. Why hunt me?"

"You threw the first rock." He stepped closer to her, cognizant that she could still make a run for it, in which case catching her, as he knew, would not be easy.

"Is that a bigger crime? Tell me about this mythical law that says whoever throws the first rock is more guilty than the person who throws the second."

"'Let he who is without sin cast the first stone.' That's from the Bible. So there's an implied dimension of guilt, but I agree, it won't stand up in court. But let's not forget, you also escaped from police custody. That's a bigger crime."

"I'm claustrophobic. I told you. I was going mad in there. I had to get out. When the door burst open, I burst out. When you think about it, nobody actually told me to stay put. Maybe I was being let go."

"You'll have to tell that to the judge, I'm afraid."

"I intend to. He'll be sympathetic, I bet."

They were lit by the porch light her mother had left on, but suddenly the hall light inside the house also snapped on as the door creaked open.

"Anik?" Carole Clément asked sleepily. "Is everything all right?"

Out ran a terrier, bounding frantically around the young woman. She knelt down to calm him by ruffling his ears and giving him a kiss on the snout.

"Yeah, Mommy, don't worry. I'm just being arrested—I think."

"That's nice, dear. Officer, I think you should call it a night. It's 4 A.M."

Anik laughed, and Émile smiled a little himself. "Mommy, I'm serious. He's arresting me."

"He's not your date?"

"I don't date—" she censored herself before uttering the insult on the tip of her tongue. "—cops," she concluded.

"Why don't you both come inside and we'll discuss it," Carole invited, and held the door open.

"Ma'am—" Cinq-Mars was about to issue his objection when Anik snatched the opportunity to skip up the stairs and slip past her mother. He followed her up, where the woman put a hand on his chest.

"Incidentally, Officer," Carole inquired, "do you have a warrant?"

"The arrest commenced outside, ma'am. That gives me the right to continue the pursuit indoors," he informed her. He moderated his ire. "Should such a pursuit become necessary."

Carole removed her hand from the policeman's chest and instead used it to direct him inside with a welcoming, yet sardonic, flourish. "Ranger, stay outside, boy. Have your pee."

The dog welcomed the early-morning romp in the yard.

Inside, the policeman's problems continued. First, the daughter said, "Want a cup of tea, copper?" and then her mother dialled a number on the phone.

Waiting for someone to pick up, Carole Clément asked, "What's this about anyway? What did she—allegedly—do?"

"Allegedly—" Cinq-Mars began, but the woman was holding up a hand to stop him.

Into the phone, she said, "Captain Armand Touton, please."

That name again. Of all the officers above him, Cinq-Mars accorded no one more respect than Touton, albeit by reputation alone. "Is he your brother or something?" he asked the woman, but before she could reply she was talking directly to the captain himself.

"Armand, it's Carole. Sounds as though you've had a busy night."

She nodded to Anik that she would indeed have tea. Cinq-Mars shrugged. Obviously, he was not going to regain control anytime soon. He might as well have a cup, too. He had been through a long night, and had endured a boring wait for Anik outside in the gloomy shadows. "There's a police officer here . . . No, a patrolman. He's come to arrest Anik . . . Allegedly, she was being rambunctious at the parade tonight."

That was one way to put it. Cinq-Mars bobbed his chin to indicate that he'd state matters differently.

"Sorry," Carole said, speaking to him, "what's your name again?"

Her daughter answered first. "Émile Cinq-Mars, Mommy. Where'd you get a name like that anyway, copper?"

He didn't know if she was teasing him.

"Are you from Montreal?" Anik asked.

"I'm from the country. Small town. Saint-Jacques-le-Majeur-de-Wolfestown."

"He's a small-town boy," Carole said into the telephone. "Are you a rookie?" she asked him.

Cinq-Mars nodded that he was.

"Yep, a rookie. Goes by the name of Cinq-Mars."

Waiting for the kettle to boil, Anik had slumped down crossways into an armchair. Having kicked off her running shoes, which had served her well that night, she peeled her socks off and let her bare feet dangle over the side, rocking them a little.

"Is she really talking to Armand Touton?"

"Yep."

"*The* Armand Touton?"

"Scared?"

"That's right," Carole advised the famous captain of the Night Patrol. "He's in the house right now. Set to have a cup of tea like he's the king of England. . . . No, I think he followed Anik home." She paused, then held out the phone to Cinq-Mars. "Your boss wants a word."

The young officer hesitated. This was not going well, and certainly not as expected. "He's not really my boss—not directly," he said.

"Do you truly want to split that hair right now? You've ticked him off enough already."

Cinq-Mars took the phone. "Hello?" he asked, tentatively.

"What the hell's going on?" the voice demanded.

"I'm sorry, but I don't know for sure whom I'm talking to, sir."

"Do you want to find that out?"

He wasn't sure. "Well, sir, no, to be truthful. But you're only a voice on a telephone right now."

"Do you mean to tell me that you followed some girl home for miles?"

"No, sir. I knew her name. I got her address from the station, because she has a driver's licence. Then I went to her house, and I waited for her."

"Why?" the voice demanded to know.

"Sir, I don't know whom I'm talking to—"

"Cinq-Mars, is it? Answer the fucking question."

"Sir, she started the riot tonight. She was the instigator. She threw the first stone."

As he spoke, he realized that his obsession with this one fact carried no legal weight. Throwing the first stone was no more significant than throwing the last one, and Anik had been correct to call him on that. Yet the voice on the other end took a moment to consider this news, and Cinq-Mars took advantage of the pause to add, "And she escaped from police custody, sir."

"What are you talking about? She's never been in police custody."

"Tonight, sir. She was in a paddy wagon. She and the others broke out."

"She was one of those?" The man seemed to imply a certain admiration.

"She would have been the first one out, sir."

"All right, Cinq-Mars. Do you mind staying on until I arrive?"

This sounded suspiciously like appropriate police protocol. "I'll wait, sir. How long, do you think?"

"Quick enough. Just cool your heels," the voice said, and hung up.

The police officer put the phone back in its cradle. He looked from Carole to Anik, then back down at the phone.

"He's coming over," he said.

"Kettle's boiling," Anik announced. "Milk, Cinq-Mars? Sugar? Cyanide?"

Carole Clément, grey-haired with wan skin, flicked on another floor lamp to provide additional light, then pulled her housecoat more snugly around herself as she sat in the chair Anik had vacated.

"How come your daughter's so hard to arrest?" he asked her.

"You've had an exciting night," the woman noted.

"It's been an experience."

"Something new for you, I expect, coming in from the country."

Her reference sounded vaguely derogatory.

"I might be a rookie, I might be new to the city—"

"—and therefore lacking experience in these matters."

"People should not throw rocks and bottles, I don't care where they live."

"My daughter knows to never throw a bottle."

Of all the surprises that had confounded him through the night, that remark topped them all. "Rocks can hurt people, too, ma'am."

"Don't I know it. Twice I've dropped a scab to her knees with a rock."

Cinq-Mars appeared too flabbergasted to respond.

"Strikes," Carole explained. "Sometimes you have to take a side."

Anik returned with the tea.

"What's Anik's side?" the officer inquired as he accepted a cup from her.

"Ask her."

"Trying to humour me, Cinq-Mars?" the young woman asked him back.

"There's an election tomorrow—later today, now. You could express your opinion that way, by voting."

"No candidate in this election is expressing my opinion," she claimed.

"Nor too many of mine, come to think of it," her mother added.

"No one deserves my support," Anik maintained. "I suppose your opinions, and the opinions of the police department, are well represented, Cinq-Mars?"

The tea soothed him, the double whammy of a mother-and-daughter verbal confrontation less so.

"At least none of the candidates run on a platform that the police are pigs. Which seemed to be the main argument I heard expressed tonight."

Both women smiled. "We've touched a nerve," Anik noticed.

"You're right," Carole added. "Not every sentiment overheard tonight—I can guess what you went through—not every insult merited expression."

"Or rocks."

"Or rocks. Now, really, why have you come all this way, expended so much energy, merely to arrest one of thousands of protesters? Before you answer, keep in mind that it's a serious question, one your superior officer will be asking."

"Ma'am," Cinq-Mars began, putting his cup down on the side table by his chair, "if I may ask, what is your relationship to Captain Armand Touton?"

The two women shared a look. "Cinq-Mars," Anik piped up, "that's one issue I wouldn't press if I were you. Partly because . . ." The woman put a hand to the side of her mouth as though to block her voice travelling to her mother's ears, and whispered, " . . . *nobody knows.*" She dropped her hand back down and resumed her normal voice. "And partly because nobody wants to know because the answer might scare the living bejesus out of the person who finds out."

"Anik."

"They might be lovers."

"Anik Clément, stop that this instant!"

"Or maybe my mom has something on him, a blackmail-type thing. Either way, you don't want to know."

"Maybe you *should* arrest her," Carole stated.

"He's got a thing for me, I can tell."

The mother looked across at the policeman again. Suddenly, some things made sense. "Officer Cinq-Mars? Is that true?"

"He's blushing," Anik pointed out. She enjoyed seeing that.

He'd only admitted it to himself, but he now wished he hadn't been so impetuous. Why was he here? He could have had an arrest warrant issued—he didn't need to become personally involved. He also could have not bothered and no one would have cared. Why on earth did this girl and her mother need to be on friendly terms with the most important detective on the force? He figured his career would survive the kerfuffle, but his prospects for advancement—in particular, his hope to join the Night Patrol under Captain Armand Touton himself—had seriously slumped. Cinq-Mars took a lesson to heart: being on the side of the angels, placing himself in a just position, did not automatically constitute being right. He had no business bothering with this arrest, and that understanding fell like a stone dropping down through his gullet as the mythic senior officer climbed the outside stairs.

"Chin up," the young woman told him. "He's come alone. No firing squad."

Her cheery words didn't help.

Carole Clément was already on her way to answer the door when the detective rang the bell. Cinq-Mars jumped in his seat. He then noticed, glumly, that they greeted one another in a familiar manner, that they were indeed good friends. Entering with Touton was the family pet, but he appeared to be quite tuckered out, and after giving the young cop a sniff he plunked himself down on his sleeping cushion under a bench.

Cinq-Mars had chosen to stand upon the detective's entry. Feeling at a loss, he saluted, and then felt exceptionally dumb.

"You military?" Touton asked him. He didn't return the salute.

"Uh. No, sir."

"Just graduated, huh?"

"Four months, sir."

"Four months and you're still saluting?"

"Sorry, sir. I, ah, forgot myself for a moment, sir. It won't happen again."

"It might. Cinq-Mars, is it? You're gung ho, are you?"

Cinq-Mars caught the gist instantly, that there was no way he could respond to that query without appearing to be terribly foolish. He buttoned his lips.

The detective seemed to have made himself right at home. He plunked himself down beside Anik, so closely that she had to squeeze to one side to accommodate his bulk, then rest her weight against him. Cinq-Mars felt doomed. "I expect answers to my questions, Cinq-Mars."

"Yes, sir," he murmured.

"You're gung ho?"

He hated to admit it, and knew how foolish he must sound. "Yes, sir."

"A little more gung-ish than ho-ish," Anik added, then deliberately poked her cheek out with her tongue.

"Anik," her mother censored her.

"I've made an inquiry, Cinq-Mars."

"Yes, sir?"

"You're off duty."

"He's off duty!" Anik shot back. "I told you. He's insane. I know what this is. I'm being stalked."

"You're off duty," Touton repeated, not taking his eyes off the young cop.

"Yes, sir," Cinq-Mars managed to squeak out.

"So what are you doing here?"

"I'm . . . trying to make an arrest, sir."

"Off duty."

"Yes, sir."

"Because you're gung ho."

Cinq-Mars paused. He felt miserable. "Yes, sir."

"How?"

"Sir?"

"I want to know how you're planning to make this arrest, Officer Cinq-Mars. Did you steal a squad car?"

He knew he wouldn't be let off the hook anytime soon.

"No, sir. I don't have a squad car."

"How do you plan to get your suspect downtown?"

"Well, sir, it's a problem. I don't have enough money for a cab—"

Anik interrupted, "A cab? I don't want to be arrested in a cab! I want a squad car—you know, with a siren, flashing lights, all that."

Her mother was chuckling away.

"The métro's not running," Touton pointed out to his officer. "Is it your intention to take a bus?"

"A bus. I won't be taken to jail on a bus. Come on. This is humiliating."

Cinq-Mars and Touton were locked in a visual hold, like a pair of wrestlers. "How?" the older man asked again.

"Sir," Cinq-Mars began, and cleared his throat. "I was planning to walk."

"Walk!" Anik hollered. "Walk?"

"Anik," her mother said, but she was in the midst of a laughing fit herself.

"I'm sorry, but this is an indignity," Anik proclaimed, milking the officer's discomfort. "My first arrest, and I have to walk, for miles, to the police station. Uh-uh. No way. I'm not going."

Cinq-Mars held his head down. He knew that he was at the mercy of his superior officer, who probably had more indignities in store for him.

"So you must admit, Cinq-Mars, that this is a trifle . . ." He hesitated in his search for the appropriate word. " . . . unusual."

"I suppose so, sir. Yes."

"All right." He looked at Anik, then back at the young man in uniform. "Now let's consider what prompted this unusual behaviour."

"There're only two explanations," Anik made known. "He's insane—and man, I've got a lot of evidence to back that up—or—"

"Or?" Touton encouraged her.

"This is the argument I'm inclined to buy into myself," Carole stated.

"Which is?" Touton pressed.

"He has a thing for me," Anik revealed.

"I'm sorry?" Touton asked.

"He has a crush on me. He's taken a tumble. He thinks he's in love. He's obsessed with me. It's the only plausible explanation."

The men shared a glance again. "There is another option," Touton proposed.

Cinq-Mars lifted his head. He was encouraged by Touton's tone, sensing that he might have a modicum of hope in this situation, yet at the same time he prepared himself for further defeats. "What's that, sir?"

"Anik's behaviour this evening may have justified your response."

Swiftly, in a twinkling, the embattled young officer felt that he had finally come home. Life as a policeman had not lived up to his expectations. At the academy, he had found a surprising number of candidates to be dim-witted or sour, while others were susceptible to bullying or an antisocial manner. Still others he was tempted to arrest on the spot, as a precaution, for it was hard, coming from the country, to distinguish these ruffians from the ones he was expected to incarcerate. He had yearned to graduate, and had placed his hope on entry to the police department itself.

Being a cop had its moments. He enjoyed walking a beat, but he was still adjusting to older officers who seemed worn and bedraggled, and to the acrimony between men who wore the uniform and those in plain clothes. Officers often deployed more energy screwing each other up than to investigating crimes, and he'd been deflated by duty officers who weren't the least bit interested in the minor crimes he successfully addressed. Police work, he was discovering, was a bit like fishing. If the catch wasn't big enough, throw it back in.

Suddenly, he was in a room with a real detective. He hadn't had opportunity to be in the company of one before. More importantly, the man had demonstrated a talent for interrogation. He kept everyone on their toes, yet off guard at the same time. He had to watch himself here, track his own progress, but Cinq-Mars didn't care. This man had displayed attributes that defined his notion of quality police work. Explore the possibilities. Get to the bottom of things. Gently allow the truth to surface. Cinq-Mars made a quick mental note to himself to be especially honest here, even if it cost him. He wanted to impress this man. He wanted to work with him someday. He wanted to prove himself worthy of that.

"I didn't do so much," Anik responded, suddenly put on the defensive. "It's not like I was a factor, or anything."

"But what did you do? Let's start with that."

She was saved by the bell, for the phone rang.

"It's probably for me," Armand Touton said quietly to Carole.

After responding, and listening, she held out the receiver to the detective.

He struggled up, feeling the pain from old wounds that had been aggravating him lately, and grunted into the mouthpiece, "Touton." Momentarily, he said, "What?" indicating such surprise that he garnered the attention of those in the room. "Animal husbandry?" He hung up without another word, putting the phone down gently in the cradle, looking as though his mind was far away.

Turning, he gazed at Cinq-Mars and repeated, "Animal husbandry?"

"What?" asked Anik. She was thankful for the reprieve, the attention being taken off her.

Touton returned to the sofa where he'd been sitting and pulled a hand through his thinning hair. Normally, he worked until dawn, so the early-morning hour did not weary him, although the rioting, as always, had been exhausting in its way. Chaos in any form demanded an array of decisions amid a bombardment of surprising information. He enjoyed being at the centre of big events, but after they concluded, an inevitable weariness caught up to him. More so these days, he thought, as he got older.

"Tell me what you did tonight, Anik. How did you break the law? Tell me why I shouldn't allow this man to arrest you and walk you five miles to headquarters."

"It's farther than that. You wouldn't let him—"

"Tell me what you did tonight, please."

She fidgeted. Cinq-Mars noticed, for he'd only seen her as feisty and volatile. She turned sulky.

"I threw the first rock. Okay? Is that such a big deal? I threw it at Trudeau. Yes, the prime minister. So what? I missed, I'm sorry to say. I hit the steps. One rock. Which missed. So arrest me for that, for throwing a rock at a concrete building and causing no damage whatsoever."

"Officer Cinq-Mars will be the one to determine the charges. Why did you throw the rock?"

"Trudeau's a bastard."

"Why is Trudeau a bastard?"

She dropped her jaw as she threw him a look.

"If you're arrested, you'll have to answer these kinds of questions."

She threw up her hands. "He's a bastard."

Touton sighed, and wrung his hands for a brief moment. "What else did you do? What else, that could be of interest to the police?"

"Somebody unlocked the police van. How that happened, I don't know—it just did. Don't blame me for that—I wasn't involved, all right? I just happened to be in the van. Anyway, it was so fucking crowded in there. I'm claustrophobic. I couldn't take it. I told *him* that. He didn't believe me—"

"I believed you, actually."

"You still put me in there, didn't you? You bastard."

"So he's a bastard, too? Is everyone a bastard now, Anik?"

"Fuck you."

Everyone in the room felt a shock and lowered their heads.

They could hear a clock ponderously ticking.

Cinq-Mars shot a glance at the mother, wondering how she felt about her child's antics. She did seem to be in some distress, but she offered no counsel or censure. He thought she might be stunned.

Squirming, Anik wiped away a tear. "Sorry. I didn't mean that," she said.

A more complicated person than he'd first imagined, Cinq-Mars was thinking. Touton was trying to catch his eye. The detective gestured with his chin, and the two men stood and went outside.

"Let Ranger out," Carole Clément directed, so they did.

Touton guided the younger man farther away from the house, to keep their conversation private in the quiet air. "This is a difficult situation," the detective mused. The dog kept tabs on them, staying about fifteen feet ahead, wagging its tail and voraciously sniffing the ground and the tires of parked cars.

"How's that?" Cinq-Mars was already preparing himself for disappointment. He expected that the captain of the Night Patrol wanted him to stand down from this arrest, to let it slide.

"I've been carrying out an investigation for some time."

"Oh?" They were ambling away from the house, more slowly than either man's usual pace. Normally, Cinq-Mars liked to take long strides and travel quickly on foot, while Touton had shortened his gait in recent years, thanks to old injuries that were acting up. The two had nowhere to go, and so made prodigious progress up the block.

"A murder investigation," Touton told him.

"When did this take place?" Just to hear a murder investigation mentioned thrilled the rookie.

"I like how you talk, Cinq-Mars," Touton told him. "You don't say to me, 'When did the guy get drubbed out?' You say, 'When did this take place?' That's very civilized."

Was the older man mocking him? "Thank you, sir," he said. "I guess."

"I should expect nothing less, no?"

He was lost again. Touton had that ability to let him think he knew what was going on, then give him an indiscriminate spin. "Sir?"

"That kind of educated language, let's call it. You're an officer with a university education."

"Yes, sir, I am." Advanced education remained rare in the department, although it was becoming more common. For the older officers, his background was an odd one, and for some of them to have a rookie around who had a degree felt vaguely suspect, as if their own authority and experience were being undermined by the newcomer's apparent intelligence. The old guys resented the development within their familiar culture, and Cinq-Mars had found that the initial reaction to his education usually gave way to curiosity about his choice of program.

"Animal husbandry," Touton stated, proving that he would not be an exception to the rule. "Why would you get a degree in animal husbandry if you wanted to be a cop?"

"I didn't actually do it to become a cop, sir."

"I think I believe you."

"First, I got the degree—my father was pretty adamant that I have an education—and then I decided to become a cop. I didn't make it into veterinary school, you see, which was one of my options, when I was younger."

"I suppose that happens. First choice, I want to be a vet. Second choice, a cop. Either way, you get to spend your life with animals. Or did you want to be a Mountie—join the Musical Ride? Did they turn you down, too?"

"I wanted to work in the city, sir. The job I have now is the job I wanted."

They walked on quietly. Cinq-Mars took out his cigarettes and offered one to Touton. "I don't usually," Touton said, then took one anyway. They lit up and smoked under a street lamp. Walked on a little farther. "So you want to be a cop in this city?" Touton pressed him.

"Yes, sir. For me, it's more than just a job. This is what I want to do."

Touton nodded. He didn't mind the romantic overture, the sense of vocation, as long as the young man knew which side of the world was up. "This is a tough town. The rackets, they're getting worse. We used to crack down on gambling and prostitution. Now we worry about heroin. We get lots of murders here—two a week, about. More banks get robbed in this town than anywhere else in the world. Rough boys with no criminal record are now robbing banks on a whim. There's no defence against that. I had one of those last week. 'Why'd you rob that bank?' I asked the punk. I told him, 'You've got a good job, a family.' What does he say? He was bored. I used to catch criminals. Now I have to hunt down the bored as well. It's difficult."

They walked on, smoking, into a darker portion of the street, so that only the flare of the cigarettes distinguished them. Cinq-Mars knew the older man was exaggerating, but he wasn't going to call him on it.

"Your father was pretty adamant that you get an education—those were the words you used."

"Yes, sir."

"I've never heard a cop use that phrase before—'pretty adamant.' It's a common phrase, just not how a cop talks. Is your father totally pissed with you now?"

"Sir? Ah . . . dismayed, sir, I think is the word. I'm sorry if that's not a cop's word, either."

"Never mind. I understand it. Just like I understand 'pretty adamant.' Which I'm not going to be with you, Cinq-Mars, in this situation. Do you realize the harm you might cause that child if you arrest her like this? Not to mention the loss of a grand opportunity. Do you comprehend—that's not too big a word for you, is it?—do you comprehend the difficult situation you're putting her in?"

Cinq-Mars shrugged. "Didn't she put herself in the situation, sir?"

"Maybe so, if you'd arrested her on the scene. Or arrested her and seen to it that she'd stayed put. That's one thing. The problem is, this is something else. Now you're arresting her after the fact."

"I don't see why that's an issue, sir. What's the difference?"

Touton bobbed his head, as though slipping a punch. "After the jails are full, and the rioters have had their overnight séance with lawyers, and their parents wait for the banks to open to arrange bail—after everybody's had a quick tantrum with the officer-on-duty about bringing us up on charges for false arrest—you'll cart her onto the scene. After the fact. You'll be granting her special status, that's what I'm saying. Anik will be noticed. Conspicuous. She'll be under suspicion from other prisoners. Do you know how this works?"

His moral footing was less secure than he'd thought. When in doubt with a superior, he tried to find the high ground, then do his best to cling to it. Here, he was discovering the high ground to be already submerged. "I guess I don't, sir."

"Cinq-Mars." Touton stopped walking and rested a hand gently on the younger man's forearm a moment. "Big riot. The hotheads are rounded up and incarcerated. Miraculously, hours later, one last rioter is apprehended, one out of tens of thousands who are allowed to walk free." Touton shrugged and flicked his cigarette, only half-smoked, out onto the street. "The more experienced thugs will think she's a snitch. The lawyers will think so, too. Other cops will think that way. The judge, when he hears the story, will think the same way—he'll probably give her extra jail time because he assumes he's making us happy. The judge will accommodate burying our snitch among the other rioters for a longer period of time merely on a hunch created by your actions. Everyone will believe that we arranged to have a stool pigeon dropped into the far end of the cage. That poor girl will then be ruined for life. Not to mention that someone in a situation to assist the police one day will be compromised, under suspicion forever."

"Do you mean that—"

"I mean no such thing, Cinq-Mars. Did you hear me say any such thing?"

"No, sir." He was flummoxed. If Touton didn't want him to think she might already be a police informant, why did he guide him into thinking so? If he didn't want her compromised, why compromise her himself?

"You see, Cinq-Mars, I'm only asking that you consider the possibilities. The opportunities."

The officer looked down the vacant street. If nothing else, this was an education.

"May I suggest a course of action?" Touton asked.

Cinq-Mars nodded. He admitted, "I could use the help." He dropped his smoke and extinguished the butt under the sole of his shoe.

"Go home. Sleep on it. When you come into work in the afternoon, if you still feel that Anik should be jailed, have an arrest warrant issued. Phone her, or her mother. Let them know. At that point, if you've gone forward with the arrest warrant, Anik will come in under her own recognizance, which I can personally guarantee. She'll have a lawyer in tow. He'll do what lawyers do, bail will be set,

Anik will be home in an hour and nobody will think that we tried to drop her into a situation. She won't be noticed. Don't you think that that's fair all around?"

Cinq-Mars nodded. "I do, sir. Thank you. That's how I'll proceed."

"Let's start back." But Touton abruptly placed a restraining hand on his forearm again to impede his progress. "Slowly. There's something else I want to talk to you about along the way. My case."

"Your case, sir?"

"My murder investigation."

Cinq-Mars was again perturbed. "You were saying. When did you say it occurred?"

"I didn't, actually. I deflected the discussion away from that point."

"Sir?" Cinq-Mars liked this old guy, but dealing with him was hard duty.

"You should notice these things for yourself if you want to be a detective. You asked a question. 'When did the crime take place?' That's what you asked me. I didn't answer. We've been all over the map since then, and I'm the one who's reminding you that we were talking about a murder. If you want to become a detective one day, officer, you'll have to learn to never lose the thread of a conversation."

An education, indeed. "I'll remember that, sir. You mentioned that this situation, with Anik, affected your investigation. How so, may I ask?"

Walking on, Touton gently stroked a finger in the air. "The victim, Cinq-Mars, was the girl's father. Carole's husband, you see. He was a petty criminal. Involved in strong-arm tactics, theft, that sort of thing. He spent the war in an internment camp for his politics."

"A communist."

"Good assumption, but it's wrong. Not a fascist, either. He loved his wife, and that got him into trouble with the law. Does that seem right to you? It still doesn't seem right to me."

Hoping to demonstrate that he could keep the threads from unravelling, Cinq-Mars asked, "And when, sir, did this murder take place?"

"Ah. Do you remember the Richard riot? That night."

Cinq-Mars remembered the event—he'd listened to the radio reports. Offhand, he guessed he'd been eleven back then. That imagined world, a big city burning, the fans stampeding and overturning police cars, the images that had been created by the radio voice, stayed with him throughout his adolescence and had probably, in some subliminal way, influenced him to move to the city and forge a career in law enforcement. Some boyhood notion that he was needed here still resided in him.

"I was only a kid. I didn't live in Montreal. But I remember it well."

"That night, Anik's father was killed."

This news came as a shock. "Sir—that was a dozen years ago or more."

"Thirteen, yeah. What are you saying? If someone gets away with a murder for a few years, we should forget about it? Let the killers walk? Is that your attitude?"

"I don't mean that. But . . . I'm just . . . As you said, there's a hundred murders a year in the city. You're still working this one case?"

"Trying to, yeah. May I share a concern with you?"

Although he'd been through different turns on the subject, Cinq-Mars was now glad that he'd found his way out to Anik's house on his time off. "Yes, sir."

"The investigation of this crime may outlive my usefulness on the force. I may, in fact, have to pass it off to someone coming along, to a younger officer. I might pass it on to you, Cinq-Mars."

"Why me? With respect, sir, you don't know me."

"You have a university education. You talk in an odd manner. You are passionate about your job. Apparently, you're willing to work during an off-shift."

"That's all true, I suppose." They had reached the front gate to the Clément home, and they stopped there. "Thank you, I guess. But I get the feeling you're having some fun with me."

"You gotta have fun, Cinq-Mars. Remember that. Now, what are you saying? You don't want the case?" Touton inquired.

"I don't know what to say. I'm not a detective. Not yet."

"You will be. Don't tell me you didn't join the force to become a detective."

"I did, sir, yes. But there are no guarantees."

Touton raised that discriminating finger again, as if it represented the launch of a new idea. "Perhaps you think the case is beneath you, not worthy of your time and effort. Let me give you the gist of what I'm talking about.

A hoodlum was killed. The same night, a coroner, a public servant, was also murdered. The first murder weapon had just been stolen from the offices of the National Hockey—"

"The Cartier Dagger," Cinq-Mars interrupted, suddenly keenly interested in being involved.

"Then you have some background already."

"You have suspects?"

"Hundreds. Names that have merited our consideration include the late premier of Quebec, the late mayor of Montreal, the current prime minister of Canada—"

"Trudeau?"

"He was out for a walk in the vicinity that night. We've had no reason to eliminate him, put it that way. Church bishops. Lowly priests. Persons of high standing in the business community. Doctors. A secret political sect known as the Order of Jacques Cartier, distinguished by their fascist sympathies. We have a roster of interested parties, of possible culprits. We have also had an officer's car bombed, my own home vandalized, the murder of a chauffeur who, on occasion, drove the former mayor around—that's a crime that may or may not be connected. In short, Cinq-Mars, if an officer is going to be involved in an investigation that takes him through most of his career, this is the kind of case it ought to be. In addition to all that, the first victim—the hoodlum, Anik's dad—was my friend, who was working for me that night to secure the Sun Life Building. Now, do you still think the case is beneath you?"

"I never thought that, sir. I don't think it now. I admit, I'm flabbergasted."

"Your language, Cinq-Mars. What kind of a cop are you, anyway?"

"I'm also intrigued. May I use that word?"

"You may. I've been looking for a bright junior officer to do a little under-cover work for me. White-collar crime. A short spell. Someone who can talk like an intelligent man. Are you interested?"

He couldn't contain his smile. "Sir. I'm your man."

Touton tapped him on the elbow. "Good. Before we go back in, be clear. We did not trade anything here tonight. What you do with respect to Anik is up to you."

"Thank you, sir. I appreciate that. I'll sleep on it, then decide."

"Then sleep well, Cinq-Mars. Report to me tomorrow night." With that, the captain whistled softly, and Ranger raced to his side.

†††

When he woke up that afternoon, Cinq-Mars felt his senses alert, his nerve endings tingling. In his excitement, he almost forgot to consider the issue of Anik's arrest. He chose not to proceed, and according to plan phoned her to tell her so.

"Oh, God," she said over the phone. "I got dressed up and everything."

"I'm sorry to disappoint you."

"So, are you admitting to it yet?"

"Sorry?"

"Your crush on me. Why not admit it?"

Good question. "I, ah, have to go to work now, Anik."

"Yeah. Well. You *will* let me know, though, right? I mean, you're not going to just keep it to yourself, right?"

Cinq-Mars got off the phone, wondering. Had Touton put a bug in his ear? Did the captain perhaps want him to be friends with Anik because she had the potential to become a well-placed police informant? The notion confused him. What about friendship? Dating? If he asked her out, would he date out of an obvious attraction, or because she might help him as a cop? Or, the more difficult consideration, could he possibly proceed to do both—be romantic, and recruit?

Later that afternoon, after having voted in the federal election and put in a few hours on his beat, he returned to headquarters and reported to the captain of the Night Patrol.

"Do you own a suit?" Armand Touton demanded to know.

"Yes, sir."

"Go home. Put it on. Report back to me."

Cinq-Mars failed to budge.

"Well, go on."

The junior officer took a deep breath. "I'll look like a farmer, sir."

Touton shot a glance at the young man and nodded. When he had returned from the war, not having proper clothes or footwear had often depressed him.

He suspected that this young man wore his uniform as he had done—proudly, and with élan—because as soon as he changed back into his street clothes he looked ridiculous. He suspected that the fellow had probably improved his wardrobe with his first paycheques, at least with respect to casual clothes, but he hadn't had a chance to extend that to more formal attire.

"I get you, son. That won't work. All right, can you buy yourself a suit with your own money tomorrow? I know a tailor I can send you to. You won't come away looking like a farmer, the price will be reasonable, and I'll ask him to offer monthly terms. Does that seem fair?"

"Sure. Tomorrow is supposed to be my day off, though."

"Forget about it."

Cinq-Mars took the rest of the night off instead. He was too excited to walk his beat. He booked off and strolled uptown from headquarters and visited a small bar, not too crowded, not too bare, and ordered a whiskey. He wasn't supposed to do that in uniform, but who was going to arrest him? This was his first hard liquor since coming to the big city, but he finally had something to celebrate, so he did.

When the television above the bar showed that Pierre Elliott Trudeau had won the election handily, he drank to the prime minister as well. He liked the way the guy stood up to the mob, even if he was a vague and unlikely suspect in Touton's big case. Finally, he called Anik, to see what she thought of the results and to ask if she felt like coming out for a nightcap.

"I don't date cops," she reminded him.

"I'm off duty."

"Yeah, like that makes a difference to you."

"Besides, it's not a date. It's just a drink."

The ensuing silence, he thought, sounded hopeful.

"What's that bit about you and animals?" she asked him.

"I'm something of an expert on horses," he admitted. He didn't usually speak of himself in such glowing terms, but in this instance he had a lot to overcome. Cinq-Mars waited, expectant, almost forgetting to breathe.

"Are you going to admit that you have a crush on me or not?" Obviously, she was determined not to make this easy on him.

"I admit it. Are you coming out or not?"

"Don't get huffy. Just tell me where you are."

He didn't think he'd been getting huffy, but he told her where he was.

CHAPTER 16

1847 ~ 1859

MOTHER McMULLEN ASKED TO BE LET OFF, TO STEP FREE FROM the carriage a fair distance before her return to the Grey Nuns Convent. She needed time for reflection. Pale, stricken Sister Sainte-Croix was instructed to ride on ahead without the mother superior and not to speak of the day's events to a living soul. She acquiesced, wiping a tear from the corner of one eye, a sniffle from a nostril. For both women, their knowledge was nigh unbearable. Their souls felt rent. What they had witnessed that morning had left both too staggered to properly think, let alone speak of the disaster, and holding the reins in her hands felt like a great weight to Sister Sainte-Croix. And yet, upon Mother McMullen's shoulders lay the burdens of responsibility and decision, and while the younger nun wished that she could do more to assist her mentor, she knew to grant her this solitary hour. A stroll through the streets of Montreal on one's own did not constitute proper form for a mother superior. Nevertheless, Sister Sainte-Croix pulled on the reins and quietly called the white mare with the black rump patches to a halt.

The older woman stepped down from the carriage and commenced her walk.

All her life, she had been a student of war. Until that very morning, she had harboured a secret belief that her life would someday be defined by war, that actions undertaken in the grip of battle would mark the measure of her devotion to her Lord and so mark the intersection of her life with its true destiny. Now she knew that she had been prepared for a different battle, one no less valiant, and perhaps more gruesome. She needed time to steel her resolve, to thank her God and to prepare herself to ask others to do as she would, to humbly sacrifice their lives.

Mother McMullen had left herself a hill to climb, and did so with supreme sadness. Still, the act of walking and climbing touched her as a pleasure, one that she was enjoying for the last time, perhaps, as she stepped off the main road onto a footpath. Often she had wandered these woods as a young nun in the company of others, never alone, and always she had adored the carefree splendour of the trees, the dapple of sunlight underfoot. As her sadness weighed upon her, she fell to her knees, prayed, wept for minutes and recovered by giving thanks for the joys of her life in the service of her Lord.

She gave thanks also for this final act of devotion placed before her.

Struggling to her feet again, she walked on, pausing to touch the blossoms of the June wildflowers, to feel speckled sunlight upon her face.

Her visage was lean, longish and pale, the eyes small and seemingly sunken beneath the impressive arch of her brow. Mother McMullen readily smiled. Anyone in her company soon felt at ease, despite her considerable authority. She rose to the disciplinary responsibilities of her position when necessary, but generally her nuns endeavoured to please her, to reward her good graces with humility and friendship. None who knew her were accustomed to the heaviness of her current mood, and they would perhaps be taken aback by the fall of skin around her mouth and the stricken countenance behind her eyes.

Death loomed.

She had studied war. For her, the astonishing movements of peoples into and out of battle portrayed the epic journey of the earth, for it seemed that all the building and planning and commerce of peaceable times would be transformed by the foolishness and accident, terror and spite, of battle, and as often by the absurdity of the Acts and Treaties that followed military conflagrations. Lord Shelburne, for example. Few Canadians were aware of his name, yet he had committed a grave travesty against the whole of the nation. To Mother McMullen's mind, he had committed one of the foremost deceits in history—in all the world's sordid panoply of political deceptions.

After the American War of Independence, Quebec existed under the governance of the Quebec Act, which had expanded the western border to include the lands of the Ohio, the southern shores of the Great Lakes, onward to the Mississippi and southward across the Great Plains. Indeed, the vast expanse of the continent was, essentially, Quebec. After England had ceded the thirteen colonies in its disastrous war, one Lord Shelburne of London drew a line that cut the continent in half, into a north and a south, for no reason other than colossal stupidity, and through a naïve belief that being nice to the Americans would cause the Americans to be nice, in return, to the British. He bequeathed to the thirteen colonies the southern half of North America, land the revolutionaries had never requested. The gift of half a continent was presented to the recent enemy on a whim. Perhaps he feared, when examining the map, that Providence behooved him to restrict the progress of the French language overseas. In any case, the British were obliged to man the western garrisons of Michigan, and down the Mississippi, and further west for thirteen years before the Americans made the trek out from their Atlantic seaboard cubbyholes to visit the land that had been delivered to them with the stroke of pen—a vast commonwealth they had neither earned, nor cared for, nor admired, nor visited, nor desired.

How that edict, the Treaty of 1783, had cost the merchants of Montreal. Their consternation had been immense. Why be loyal to England when England beheaded her devout subjects and cut off their limbs? A preponderance of merchants were English themselves, having moved up from the thirteen colonies to live among the French as a gesture of fidelity to the king. Yet these English loyalists had been equally betrayed, robbed blind by the bewildering buffoonery of Lord Shelburne, a man who had never set foot across the sea. Trading routes traditional to Montreal had been sliced in half. The northern part of the continent had been deprived of its well-earned opportunity to become the dominant of the two fledgling nations, due solely to a civil servant's idiocy. Why fight on the battlefield for anything, when fate could be determined by such louts?

Yet the merchants of Montreal, obliged to develop alternative, imaginative forms of commerce, persevered, egged on by the last fraternity of British merchant adventurers, and the city grew despite its ungainly dependence upon England. Partnerships were developed that exploited both the French ability to trade through the Indian lands and the English acumen for capital investment. The two languages intermingled and intermarried, and the alliances forged a new prosperity despite the restrictions on territory.

Then came war.

What a colossal blunder.

Mother McMullen still became infuriated whenever the American attitude to the War of 1812 reared up. Visiting friars, priests or nuns from the United States might inadvertently extend their condolences to the Canadas for having lost the war, and Mother McMullen would surge onto a verbal rampage, reciting records and illuminating battle scenes. Her audience would eventually disband, amused, for most of these engagements had been staged to playfully provoke her ire and watch her spark. Every so often, she'd catch on, discover for herself that the arguments had been an entertainment enjoyed at her expense. She'd laugh along. Only to continue her tirade with renewed vigour.

President Madison had declared his war, yet unbeknownst to him he was about to receive faint support from New Englanders, and New England formed the adjacent border with what were now being called Upper and Lower Canada. After the American War of Independence, fifty thousand loyalists had left the United States to re-establish themselves in the Canadas, most of these in the newly settled lands of New Brunswick, while a majority of the remainder chose to dwell along the Niagara Peninsula and the St. Lawrence River, creating the beginnings of Upper Canada.

"Madison," Mother McMullen recited, "miscalculated."

"How so, Mother?" a visiting Jesuit from the College of St. John in Fordham, New York, one Father O'Malley, inquired, for he held to the prevailing American view of the war, which dismissed the mother superior's account.

"His own people did not want to fight. The first incursion into Quebec occurred in 1812, and the rascal Americans turned tail without a shot being fired."

"Turned tail?" the visiting theologian inquired. This did not align with his own recollection, although he had to concede that the Americans had advanced, and then retreated, and he had never heard mention of casualties.

"Then in 1813, the American army advanced to Châteauguay, where it was crushed."

"Crushed." Again, his own interpretation of history had not allowed for a crushing American defeat.

"Madison was informed that the British garrisons were absent, which proved true. What he did not count upon was the response of the people. Three thousand volunteers joined the militia from Montreal alone, another three thousand from Quebec. The Eastern Townships sent enough men to fill six battalions, and that knowledge was enough to dampen the enthusiasm of your General Dearborn's advance. His men grew disinterested—and, Father, turned tail."

"I see."

"Then our General Brock defeated the American invasion at Detroit. Your General Hull and his men were paraded through the streets of Montreal. I was on hand to witness the event—they were marched right past our gates. Right under my nose, Father. This is no invention."

"Surely, from your perspective, Mother, it had not all been good news."

"To learn that York had been burned by the Yanks—no, that was not good news. And to learn that the people were being harried up and down the St. Lawrence Valley in Upper Canada proved worrisome. I can tell you, Father, that I and a number of the novitiates visited our Montreal militia while they were waiting for the American advance."

Her eyes gleamed when she revisited the history she so adored, even when she had to relate bad news.

"What did you find, Mother?" He puffed upon his pipe.

"A high morale, Father. I doubt that any army—and I have carefully studied the progress of armies, Father, it is a hobby of mine—has moved towards its destiny in such splendour. I witnessed with my own eyes the long lines of carts carrying the best wines, along with venison, turkey and ham. Cheeses from the countryside in fine array, butters and syrups. Fruit and vegetables, fresh and in colour. The ordinary private, Father, sat down to a table more glorious than did the governor himself. The king of England, I daresay, eats only as well, never better."

This was hard to believe, but she would speak further of the glories of the militia's mess, and the father from Fordham conceded that this had apparently been a military service of a higher order than the norm. "But could they fight, Mother, so well fed as that?"

"Fight they did. Let me tell you about the Voltigeurs Canadiens. They were regulars, raised for wartime home service, and among their numbers were eight hundred French, some English and two hundred Indians. They went against General Hampton's five thousand men and ten cannon. Fifteen miles from Montreal the battled commenced, and there, on the plains of Châteauguay, the future of our city would be decided. The Canadians, though, had only about three hundred of their militia in the field, against that formidable force of five thousand."

"And ten cannon," the priest interjected.

"And ten cannon. One could easily predict our doom."

"The Canadians held?" Father O'Malley of Fordham assumed.

"Held?" Mother McMullen admonished him. "*Held?* Again and again, the Americans returned to the attack, their five thousand against our three hundred, and the battle terminated only with the complete disgrace and defeat of the Americans. They fell back across their border, a testament to Madison's sad folly."

"But, Mother McMullen, surely you are aware of the Canadian attack on Plattsburgh? Or do you call that a victory also?"

"British attack, Father. *British.* You Americans sank a British supply ship, so the British elected to pull back. The Americans had been defeated at Châteauguay, defeated also at Crysler's Farm near Cornwall, defeated by Brock at Detroit. You had been defeated. Consequently, the British considered that perhaps the Americans were now vulnerable to invasion, and foolishly they set forth. Losing a ship, they reconsidered their strategy and retreated to Montreal. Somehow, I don't know how, Americans I meet seem to turn that one rather unimportant event into victory in the overall war. Madison declared war, Madison attacked, the American invasion was repelled, your large army was crushed. How can that possibly be considered an American victory?"

She had a point, and Father O'Malley sucked on his pipe. He might have to alter a portion of his teaching at Fordham to accommodate her viewpoint.

"And yet," Mother McMullen proposed.

"And yet?" the priest asked.

"It would happen again." She sighed. "The war was won by the Canadians, for history shows that when we truly want to win, we win. Nonetheless, instead of giving the victor the spoils—instead of offering us, I don't know, Vermont, let's say—a dimwit in England gave the Americans the state of Maine. Someone in England believed the American claim, that the sinking of a supply ship meant victory in the war. Balderdash! If this is how we are rewarded for winning a war—being stripped of our territory once again—imagine what might have occurred had we lost. On the other hand, I know a merchant who quipped that he hoped we'd be defeated one day, and when I expressed my surprise, and, I might say, my outrage, he laughed, and declared that he wanted to keep our homeland intact. 'Victory,' he claimed, 'has been far too costly.'"

"I suppose," Father O'Malley mused, "that this is why we Americans believe we won. We gained a state. For Maine, we thank you."

She nodded in agreement, then turned philosophical. "War is such silliness, Father. Montrealers, though, did manage to gain something from the adventure. English, French and Indian—everyone fought shoulder to shoulder to achieve victory. We came together as a people. What vestiges of feeling that remained among the French for France, which you might think would only be natural, dissipated. Madison's war was a Napoleonic war—we all felt that way. The Americans were doing what they could to help the French engage the English, and if that meant invading Quebec, so be it. We all lost sympathy for France. And the misjudgments of the British were leading us to understand that perhaps someday we must come together to rule ourselves, notwithstanding our growing fidelity to England. So you see, the war has been a significant part of our maturation process, I would say."

"Not that you advocate war."

"As little as possible. My nuns are expressly forbidden from shooting one another, although on occasion, I'm sure that they'd like to."

He smiled. Father O'Malley concluded that whatever Mother McMullen might wish to say to him would be of interest, for clearly she was a keen and perceptive student of history. She had convinced him long ago to revamp his perspective of the Plains of Abraham, the day that Quebec fell to the British. The cause of the defeat by the French, she had contended, was horsemeat.

"Horsemeat?" Father O'Malley repeated.

"Mother d'Youville, our founder, said so herself. She had gone with Sarah Hanson Sabourin, a wonderful woman from the Ottawa River, who had brought along the Cartier Dagger—a relic said to have mystical powers, Father—to a meeting with the governor of Quebec. This was Pierre de Rigaud de Vaudreuil. We were so proud—our first Quebec-born governor. Madame d'Youville and Sarah Hanson Sabourin, with her dagger—she brought it along to lend authority to their mission—requested that Vaudreuil stop feeding horses to his army. The country was in famine. People were eating whatever they could find, and the army was seizing horses. The governor denied their request. Moreover, he informed the ladies that if they did not leave his presence and cease their petition, they would both be hung."

"So much for the mystical qualities of the dagger," Father O'Malley noted.

Mother McMullen raised her chin. "Not so fast, Father. Vaudreuil would have his comeuppance. First, Quebec fell to the British. The people had no reason to fight for the sake of France. They were uncared for, hungry, dispirited. Their own army ate their horses. Why fight for that? Second, when the British marched on Montreal and the city capitulated, Vaudreuil was banished to France, a country he had never even visited. He should never have gone up against the Cartier Dagger, Father."

"Not to mention Mother d'Youville or Sarah Hanson Sabourin."

"So true."

The next battles for Canadians were amongst themselves.

The time was one of high anxiety for Mother McMullen and the Grey Nuns, for they were close to people on both sides of the *Patriotes* Rebellion of 1837 and 1838. The marshalling of animosity was severe, and she contended against the public displays and private ruminations of hatred.

"Let the arguments be given free expression," she commanded, "while keeping your emotions and the harsh attitudes of your fellow citizens at bay."

The political arguments could only have been expected in a landscape so rapidly changing. Quebec was French, yet had suffered conquest by the British.

The arrival of loyalists from the United States after the War of Independence created a separate political entity growing in size and power. Louis-Joseph Papineau, a man Mother McMullen had had the opportunity to meet on frequent occasion, captured the essence of the challenge to those in Quebec. He determined that French-Canadians, to use a term then coming into common usage, required independence from England to properly fulfill their destiny.

Mother McMullen considered Papineau quite a complicated man. She appreciated his influences, Thomas Jefferson being one. He idealized the small, independent farmer and foresaw a nation built upon an agrarian backbone. The maintenance of French common law was important so that Lower Canada could develop according to its own traditions. On these issues, Mother McMullen was sympathetic. Yet she detected contradictions in the man. He was decidedly anticlerical, no particular friend of the Holy Church. That didn't stop him from supporting the seigneurial system, in which the Church alone dispensed farmland. A great advocate of democracy, he was less interested in the American experiment regarding capital, and so believed the power of the Church to dispense land to be an important check on capitalist speculation. The equal distribution of property among the French protected them from English expansion and from the arrival of disparate foreigners, which buffered Quebec from the new wave of capitalist venture being developed to the south. Papineau's nationalist roots, then, were born both of his conservative underpinnings and the democratic forces of his time. When he proved, in battle, to be unstable, Mother McMullen had not been surprised.

She had been surprised, though, by the rhetoric of his proclamation, by its call to shed blood. Mother McMullen had been searching for some way for her and her order to help the situation—some manner of enlightened intervention that might shed light on the conflicts as they churned through the public mind. British business opposed the French will to remain agricultural. British expansion opposed the French desire to become a nation unto themselves. These were diametrically opposing positions, and when the Church issued an edict to its flock to engage in no activity against the political and legal authorities, priests fled for their lives from those communities where *patriote* fever ran high. Mother McMullen was certain that she had a destiny to embrace as the outbreak of hostilities seemed increasingly inevitable, yet she found the disputes too difficult to forge any form of reconciliation. Pamphlets called upon the French to arm themselves, to count on the support of their fellow French and the Indians. The English formed what they called the Doric Club—a paramilitary group preparing for a fight. The Patriote Party formed a military wing, known as Les Fils de la Liberté. Young men placed their hands on a liberty pole and vowed to keep faith with the fatherland, to conquer or die.

Rebellion was imminent.

Papineau's proclamation included a call to behead Jews. Mother McMullen did not herself know any Jews, yet had often noted a certain discernible loathing towards them among her fellow citizens. A few lived in the city, she'd been told. From time to time, hateful things were mentioned in the papers and repeated in meetings with the bishop, but neither he nor Mother McMullen felt that such a poor reputation warranted beheadings. For all his fiery oratory, she doubted that Louis-Joseph Papineau had met a Jew either. While Jews did not acknowledge her Lord, to imagine their heads being stripped off their bodies seemed the more horrible wrong. In her studies, Mother McMullen had long since decided that grown men were capable of being infatuated with blood, of being riled by blind hatred. Killing begat more killing. Beheadings would only ignite further atrocities.

Her own Lord had been a Jew. The bishop, distraught, brought up the point himself: how could anyone instigate such an affront to the people of their Lord?

She did not trust men at war. She certainly did not trust the conflicted, unstable Papineau to behead Jews in the name of liberty, or in the name of God, or in the name of Quebec.

The fighting commenced humbly, limited to running street battles between Les Fils de la Liberté and the Doric Club, one rabid mob chasing another, only to see the tide turn as the pursuers became the pursued. Even the bloodied found the contests comic. Then fights took to the countryside, and, perhaps due to the rural setting, became brutal and deadly. The English had might on their side, the French their passionate intensity, but the death of an English courier, one Lieutenant Jack Weir, so inflamed the hearts of the

English that they swiftly grew impassioned for the confrontation as well. Their anger instigated pillaging and the burning of whole villages. Repeatedly, the poorly equipped, poorly led *patriotes* suffered devastating losses, in separate battles losing forty men, thirty in another, then seventy more, while English troops lost only a few.

Papineau himself scampered across the border to the United States.

That action demoralized the rebels. Their leadership had not supplied them with proper or sufficient arms, and, when the fight progressed badly, had fled. The rebels' one hope, that the United States would enter the fray on their side, never came to pass.

The rebellion put down, Montrealers were obliged to learn how to live peaceably again, this time wearing the scars of combat and holding within themselves an egregious sentiment, the humiliated and the victorious nursing their hatreds both openly and amongst themselves. Men had killed one another. Men who had killed a husband shopped at the widow's bakery. Men who had killed a son travelled the same roads as the fathers. No talk, no sermons, no quiet counsel by the Grey Nuns did much to alleviate the grievances or the open wounds.

Now, ten years on, Mother McMullen knew that she would be asking her nuns, who were primarily French, to set aside any lingering sense of injustice that they might feel and lay down their lives in the service of others. These others were not French—they were immigrants. She'd ask them to do so for the sake of no cause, only to respond to the spirit of their vows, to follow the charitable instinct of their hearts and to serve their God.

She came upon them at play, for in the spirit of their founder, Mother d'Youville, they continued to enjoy an hour of recreation each afternoon. The sisters stood to honour her presence, and quietly, still composing herself, Mother McMullen sat down and indicated that the others should join her. The nuns gathered chairs and formed a circle. One of their number, Sister Sainte-Croix, who had been with Mother Superior that morning, repeatedly dabbed the corners of her eyes.

"Sisters, today I visited the docks, having heard a most disturbing report. I elected to see for myself the conditions among certain Irish immigrants who have, for the past while, been landing at Montreal by sea. They arrive sick, with what is known to them as ship fever. A physician today told me that the correct name is typhus. Sisters, we have an epidemic in our midst."

The nuns remained silent. A few had already turned inward in prayer, while others waited for Mother Superior's full assessment.

"When they arrived, it became apparent that these Irish—men of all ages, I should tell you, recruited for their labour, and many have brought their families with them, intent on returning to Ireland no more—it became apparent that they must be segregated, not admitted to our city lest the entire population perish. Sheds were constructed for their habitation. These continue to be built upon the docks, for the ships carrying the sick keep coming. This morning, at our peril, yet always in God's hands, Sister Sainte-Croix and I entered the sheds."

Mother McMullen paused. She had been doing fine, she thought, secure in her composure, but the rancid memory of the stench and misery inside the first shed returned to her, and she swayed with an unwelcome dizziness. She took several deep breaths, and those who now felt fearful did so as well, to prepare themselves for what might come.

"Sisters, I have today seen a sight most dire. Hundreds of men, women and children—children, also—sick, dying, huddled together among those who are long dead. The strongest constitution is unfit for the stench that emanates from their foul quarters. The atmosphere is impregnated with the odour, while one hears only the groans of those who suffer so grievously. Death resides there in its most appalling aspect. Sisters, those who thus cry aloud are strangers among us, yet their hands are outstretched—to us—for relief. Lest there be a doubt, I am speaking of a plague most contagious."

The words were all that she could manage for a moment, for the sounds of the men and women, and of children, pleading for a moment's respite, raising hands to beg for death, overcame her once again, and Mother McMullen fell to a momentary fit of sorrow. The nuns watched her, fretful, or kept their heads bowed. They looked up when Mother Superior cleared her throat to speak again.

"In sending you there, Sisters, I am signing your death warrants, but you are free to accept or refuse."

As one, they accepted.

Standing before Mother McMullen, some in unison, others on their own, each woman repeated, "I am ready to serve my Lord. Accept me for this service."

†††

The first task they gave themselves was to drag out the dead.

Bodies were so intricately intertwined, the living among the dead, that no step could be taken in any direction without physical contact with another figure moaning and writhing in the dark, or with a stiffened corpse. Sleeping men bawled as they were pulled free from the entangled clutch of others. The very sound of their murmured complaints secured their release, and they were left to lie among the living. Those who no longer responded were pulled across a floor sodden with excrement, urine and vomit, blood and pus, and deposited outside. There, stinking and rotting, the bodies were lined into tight rows to make room for more.

Only from a safe distance did living men watch the women work.

Mother McMullen had chosen a contingent of eight nuns for the first foray into Pointe St. Charles, and they repeatedly returned inside each shed to locate more dead, to extricate them from those who suffered still, to haul them outside into the sunlight. For those of great weight, three nuns were required to heave the body, their progress difficult and minimal. When they thought they had finished their arduous task, a final tour of the premises revealed that one of the men who had been alive when they began that morning, and with whom they'd shared cogent conversation, had since died, and they pulled him outside to place him at the end of the putrid line of the dead.

"We did him a service," Mother McMullen advised the sisters, for his death seemed the most demoralizing. "He lived long enough to know that his remains would be treated with dignity. In the comfort of that knowledge, he has passed into the arms of our Lord."

They covered their faces with cloths, so foul were the fumes of death, of rot and excrement, increased by the summer heat and the interiors of the dark, airless sheds. Usually, they emerged gasping, clutching their stomachs, their own vomit mingling with the ripened attack of odours, the indictment of death like a gas both inhaled and absorbed through their skins.

The sickest were placed together. Those in the earliest stages of plague were given a respite from the many who moaned with abject abandon, segregated as well from the ones soon to die in silence. Then the quarters were mopped clean. Inches of sordid excretions were shovelled into the river, the floors and walls washed down. The foul clothes of the wretched, in which many had lived for weeks during the passage and ashore, were cut from the infirm, and clean garments were brought in to cover them. The sick would now lie upon the comfort of straw, their faces, backs, chests, bellies, genitals, hands, arms, legs, feet and bottoms washed clean with gentle cloths, their open sores sopped and covered.

As they spread the straw upon the floors of the sheds, the women whispered encouragement to one another in the words of their founder, Mother d'Youville, who, after death, on her way up to heaven, had taken time to admonish a farmer who worked for the order not to waste the hay. "Don't waste the hay!" they'd say softly to one another, and smile, secure in the comfort and purpose of their tradition under God.

The women could not protect the ill from the plague, but they spared them the vile fumes and comforted them with words, and to the less ill they bequeathed an aspect of dignity. They absorbed their sorrow.

They also gave a few of the Irish who were not sick a chance to survive, and a few would do so. Among those who were already suffering the plague, a few would survive also.

"We must have priests," Sister Angélique mentioned. "For their confessions."

Yes. Priests needed to be brought in.

Mother McMullen noted, "Those who come will surely die."

Babies were taken from the nipples of their dying or dead mothers, then isolated to determine whether they had contracted the disease. The number of orphans escalated, and the call went out to the countryside for families willing to adopt them.

Husbands were lost to their wives, wives lost to husbands. Whole families vanished.

"Trenched" became the common word. To say of someone, "He's been trenched," indicated that the man in question had been placed in one of the long common graves dug to receive the dead.

Priests arrived to hear confessions. They had to dip their ears low to a penitent's mouth to catch the last words, at the same time receiving the typhus onto their own skins and into their lungs from the breath of the dying. The disease would lie hidden within a new host for twelve days before symptoms emerged, and those fresh to the sheds worked hard to make the most of their usefulness in the time allotted to them.

The Grey Nuns pulled back for a while to tend to those among them who had fallen ill and, subsequently, to bury their own dead. Thirty of the convent's forty nuns fell ill to the plague, and no one knew how many might die. When they could not answer the matins bell, the Sisters of Providence assumed their places. When these replacements could not continue, Bishop Bourget granted a petition from the Sisters of Hôtel-Dieu to leave their cloister and work among the immigrants. When they fell, the Grey Nuns returned. Only seven of their number had died. The remainder of those ill had recovered, and they resumed their work on the docks.

More ships arrived. The nuns carried the women and children off the vessels, placing them in horse-drawn ambulances to be taken to the sheds. Then they hauled the sick men outside also, pulling them along, inch by inch.

English-speaking clergy were either dead or had succumbed to the plague's ravages, prompting Sister Sainte-Croix to tell Mother McMullen—after both had fallen sick but subsequently recovered—"We need more priests. The few who are left cannot keep up with all those who are dying."

Mother McMullen sent a message to her old friend in Fordham, a call that was promptly answered. A band of Jesuits travelled north from New York State to serve in the sheds of Pointe St. Charles, including Father O'Malley, who in time would die there with the other priests.

Anglican clergy, particularly useful as they spoke English, arrived also. One of these, Reverend Mark Willoughby, the first rector of Trinity Church, mobilized members of his congregation to supply necessary food and materials. The rector himself went from bed to bed, distributing milk and comfort and listening to the last words of the dying. He would contract the disease himself and die.

Citizens of Montreal sought to plow the sheds into the river. They plotted to burn the ships of plague-ridden Irish before the sick came ashore, riled by the report of a sea captain, quoted in the newspaper, who'd admitted that he had knowingly embarked from Ireland with cases of plague aboard. His masters had told him to sail forth or die.

Later, the paper would report that the captain now suffered the disease. Still later, it noted his death.

Local passions were further ignited when a ship sailed into harbour weighed down with the sick tenants of the Irish estates of Lord Palmerston, the British foreign secretary. A riot ensued, for it seemed an act of war, a British lord sending the plague across the sea to wipe out Montreal. Unable to extend their hands to the neck of Lord Palmerston, citizens sought to finally burn the sheds to the ground and drive any survivors into the river, to be rid of the plague once and for all and let the crime rest upon the soul of Palmerston, if he had one.

The new mayor of Montreal, John Easton Mills, an American who had journeyed north from Leland, Massachusetts, under curious circumstances to make a home in the French city, learning the language and becoming a model citizen, appealed to the mobs for restraint and a more caring attitude. He also served the community as president of the immigration commission, and upon first hearing of the plague had had the sheds constructed. Now he stood fast before the rioters, police loyal to him forming a firm line. In so doing, he kept the dying alive. Then he volunteered to be a nurse in the sheds, and on the twelfth day of November, 1847, he died.

Every day, older children tried to escape the sheds, desperate to find the mother or father who had been taken away during the night and trenched. The authorities would corner them, then call for the nuns to fetch them, as the police did not want to touch them or even breathe the same air they breathed. Mother McMullen went along on one such dreadful mission, with her friend, Father O'Malley. Two Irish girls were pinned against a farmer's low stone wall, rifles aimed at their eyes, dogs snarling and barking if they dared flinch. The priest and the nun fell upon the terrified children and swept them into their arms, fully embracing them.

They hugged and kissed the little ones, and assured the girls that their mother dwelled happily in heaven, that she gazed down upon her lovely children.

"Will we be in heaven soon?" one child asked. She was about eight. Her symptoms had only recently commenced.

"Yes, my child, you will be with your mother soon."

Hand in hand, the four returned to the sheds.

Later, the two old friends talked during their supper hour. "Some time ago now, Father, yet less than twenty years, starving English arrived in Montreal by ship. The bishop felt beset by pressures. He didn't know what to do. The French wanted the English moved along. So did he, I might presume. Yet the bishop also suffered from an affliction of conscience, for under the robes of his office he remained a man of faith. The first migrants, he did pass along to Ontario. Many died on the journey, and those who survived were not well received. Others, he transported to your New York State. Alas, the Americans were generous, but they had no intention of receiving them all, for the arrivals were a feeble community in need of great personal care. The bishop did not want to keep them here, for as you know, the Church is responsible for distributing all lands, and it's understood that land is to be distributed only to the French, not to the English. Still, the English were dying and more ships were sailing to our port."

"A tragedy. What did your bishop do?" Father O'Malley inquired. Acquainted with the Church in Canada, he knew it to be unlike any other. In France, the hierarchy of the Church was interested in the high affairs of state, as well as in ecclesiastical issues. In Germany, the Church was a body politic, actively working behind the scenes as an institution of influence. In other European nations, the Church was accustomed to living amid or adjacent to a Protestant authority, whereas in Quebec, the Church had become the dominant power—entrusted, really, with all matters of vital concern to the populace. The power of a bishop was never slight, nor were the consequences of a decision without reverberation and import.

"At first, nothing, although he might prefer to dignify the period as his time of reflection. Then he did something quite extraordinary, Father. He made a deal with an English company—a pact with the devil, some would say, but I am not one of those—an agreement with the Sun Life Assurance Company."

The priest, who taught both American history and New Testament studies, while leading discussion groups among candidates for the priesthood on such esoteric concerns as the nature of the soul and the meaning of free will, original sin and the manifest attributes of the Trinity, inquired in the dim candlelight, "What sort of deal could that have been, Mother?"

"If the company were to undertake the dispersal of certain lands—such as the lands across from the Mohawks at Oka, where no parish had been established—if these lands were to be reserved for starving English settlers, he would bequeath the company the right, and the land, to do so."

The priest nodded, and lightly drew a hand through his beard. "I see. So it is not the Church giving land to the English, but the Sun Life Assurance Company, and only land that does not impinge on the authority of an existing parish. Then it becomes the Sun Life Assurance Company that confers land to the English."

Mother McMullen nodded. "If you are French," she opined, "and you desire land, you must attend to your good relations with the Church. It is the path to God, to a godly life. That will mean, as a rule, that one of your children, preferably the first born, will enter the priesthood, if a boy, or a convent if she's a girl. If your family is large, the Church may anticipate that at least two of your offspring will choose the vocation of the Lord. Often it is more than that, as we know."

Father O'Malley cleared his throat. "Something in what you are saying sounds—how shall I put this, Mother McMullen?—I won't say heretical, but—"

"The proximity of death, Father, causes one to be fearless."

"I understand," he said gravely.

"But my point is not subversive. The English are here and we have given them land. Now the Irish are arriving, and we are giving them a chance to live, or at least to die, with some measure of human sympathy. If circumstances were different, Father, we'd probably be killing one another, firing cannon, engaging in swordplay. Men do that sort of thing, you know."

He agreed. "Men have been known to do that sort of thing."

"And many citizens, if they had the chance today, would drown us all in the river. Nevertheless, if we are willing to die for one another, Father, as so many have shown at the Irish sheds, why are we so less willing to live with one another?"

"Ah. A true question on the mystery of life, Mother McMullen."

"Sadly, Father."

"Sadly?"

"Is it not a question with no known reply? Is that not sad, Father?"

He nodded. He wished his students could be sitting alongside him, listening and absorbing this. Later, they would have so much to discuss. Yet he knew that he would never see his beloved students again.

The next morning, Father O'Malley reported his first symptoms.

†††

Surviving children numbered in the hundreds, cared for by the strapped Grey Nuns, and a renewed appeal to the surrounding parishes brought country-folk into town. Each of these rural families took one, or two, or, if they were bereft of children of their own, many more, and the Irish offspring, allowed to maintain their surnames to honour their dead parents, slipped away into the countryside to live with their new families and become French themselves.

Finally, the ships from Ireland ceased arriving. The dying died. Those who were to recover did so, and knew that they'd been saved.

Almost no one spoke of the horror again. Few could utter its name.

A dozen years later, new Irish immigrants arrived to build a bridge to traverse the St. Lawrence River from the island of Montreal to the mainland, and in their travails the men dug into what appeared to be long trenches of bones. Upon their inquiries, they were informed that the bones belonged to their countrymen, who had died the most terrible of deaths.

Bridge-builders dug a great black boulder, somewhat pear-shaped, out of the muck of the St. Lawrence River, and placed it in the path of the road to the bridge. The workmen commemorated their predecessors and marked their bones with the boulder, which would become known as the Irish Stone. On it, they inscribed:

TO

PRESERVE FROM DESECRATION

THE REMAINS OF 6000 IMMIGRANTS

WHO DIED OF SHIP FEVER

A.D. 1847–48

THIS STONE

IS ERECTED BY THE WORKMEN OF

MESSRS. PETO, BRASSEY AND BETTS

EMPLOYED IN THE CONSTRUCTION

OF THE

VICTORIA BRIDGE

A.D. 1859

Six thousand dead.

Depleted, the Grey Nuns returned to their vocation, and soon enough recruited a full complement of devout women again.

When she heard what the workmen had done, an aging, frail Mother McMullen asked to be taken down to view the Irish Stone for herself. There she knelt in prayer, and in time, despite her resources of will and devotion to God, in apparent indifference to her firm faith in the afterlife, she wept, remembering what she had tried so stubbornly to forget. There, she welcomed to mind the return of the faces of those who had perished in such anguish and incomprehension, and recalled the lives of so many good friends who had died in their faithful service.

The souls of the dead had passed on, yet she felt the spirit of the bones stretching forth to address her. Upon that hallowed ground, Mother McMullen experienced what she would later describe to a friend as "an inestimable grace." Through her tears, although she could not understand it, she felt a joy abide within her that she would call, in her search for a satisfactory language, "a resilient elation. Almost as though," she told the friend, a sister in her convent too young to know of those days, "not that we deserved it, for we were there in God's service, but almost as though we were all, each one of us, being summoned by name and being thanked. I find the measure of that affection and of that grace, Sister, the depth of that bond between the living and the dead, fully all that I can bear, and speak of it now only to gain a corresponding measure of human relief."

CHAPTER 17

1968

CAPTAIN ARMAND TOUTON STUDIED THE YOUNG MAN, FROM HIS well-clipped hair down to his shiny black shoes. He cleaned up well. "This could work," he said.

Émile Cinq-Mars was standing for inspection in his brand new suit, having opted for grey, thinking blue too closely allied to the police. He still didn't know what duty the captain of the Night Patrol had in mind for him, but his fellow officers were envious that he'd arrived in civvies. A few had whistled.

"You look like a man with an education, someone who's prepared to do business," Touton told him. Cinq-Mars had strong features, dominated by a protuberant beak that usually garnered a second glance, or a prolonged gaze, from anyone initially meeting him. His eyes were strong also, and might pose a problem, for somehow they bespoke a gentleman of character, of quiet demeanour. "You look like you've made a buck without working up a sweat."

"Thank you, sir. I guess."

"You also look like a man with secrets. Do you have secrets, Cinq-Mars?"

"Sir?"

"Don't fret. That's a good thing. You aren't expected to be Mr. Good Farmboy. I need you to look like a man accustomed to making sleazy deals. Can you do that—act like a young man who's an ambitious swine?"

Now he was certain that he was being teased, and he sidled up to the occasion. "Anyone who knows me understands that I'm ambitious, and according to the rioters the other night, I'm nothing if not swine."

Touton smiled. "Then you were right in what you said."

He'd forgotten. "What's that, sir?"

"You're my man."

"Thank you, sir." Again he wasn't sure if he was being complimented or insulted.

"Let's meet the crew."

†††

"What's with the suit?" Anik wanted to know.

"Can't I dress up once in a while?" He was proud of his suit, his first decent one, so he wore it on their second date. He was calling it a date, although meeting for a late breakfast, or early lunch, didn't seem wholly romantic. Given the late-night shifts he'd been pulling it seemed the best he could propose. The suit, he realized now, had been the wrong choice.

"Look at yourself. Now look at me. What's wrong with this picture?"

He thought they made a handsome couple, but the question was not difficult to interpret. Anik wore her usual style of duds—patched jeans, a kneecap jutting through a rip, a form-fitting yellow-green top that exposed her navel. Beside her, one elbow on the countertop as they awaited their food, sat her date in a conservative grey suit.

"We clash. We shout out 'cultural divide,'" she answered, when he failed to.

"Sorry."

Their first date had gone remarkably well, surprising them both. They had talked about their childhoods, and Cinq-Mars had gotten onto a tangent about his love of horses, which Anik shared, if only from a distance. That he was a cop and she a rebellious youth got lost in the intimacy of their time together, and they had talked and drunk lightly into the wee hours of the morning. For this second rendezvous, for brunch, Cinq-Mars had had little time to change—it would have taken a quick hustle home to his apartment and a rapid return downtown to meet her on time. He was already regretting that he hadn't incurred the expense of a cab to do so. Secretly, he wanted her to see him in the suit, but now saw himself as the worst stereotypical hayseed the countryside had yet produced.

"This is breakfast for me—an early rising. I can barely keep my eyes open, and look at you. Look. You're dressed like you want to make a deal with the devil, then hail a limo to take you to the airport."

He smiled. He'd already guessed that her flume of insults probably substituted for endearments.

"What're you grinning at?"

If he tried, he could get under her skin. He suspected he could do it to her more effectively than she did it to him. "If you feel underdressed, I could wait here while you go shopping."

She sat with her jaw slack a moment. "Me? Underdressed? You, Mister. You have the problem. You look like—"

"I know what I look like. Handsome. Dashing, even. Debonair."

"Who do you think you are? Cary Grant?"

"So you admit that you have a thing for Cary Grant."

"Hell I do."

"You're not so into radicals with shaggy hair. You appreciate well-dressed, well-groomed men."

"Put a cork in it."

He had not done this before, and the moment did not seem particularly opportune, yet he followed through on the impulse as it popped to mind. Cinq-Mars leaned over and kissed her—emphatically, if briefly—on the lips.

As he retreated, her jaw fell slack again, while her pretty brown eyes opened up saucer-wide.

Their plates arrived, almost tossed down before them in the style of the place. Despite the abrupt service, the fare had a reputation for being exceptional. Cinq-Mars had ordered a mushroom and green pepper omelette, Anik a robust fruit plate with cottage cheese.

"You cocky, belligerent, establishment oink-oink, you suit-and-tie-me-down retrograde, you ignorant lackey of the scurrilous upper classes—"

"Keep it up, Anik, and I'll kiss you again."

She went silent a moment, looking at him, then at her food, then looked at him through the mirror beyond the counter where food was prepared. She said, "You're a worm, a reprobate, a political neophyte, an intellectual aardvark—"

So he kissed her again.

This time, the kiss lasted a while, and she was kissing him back, matching his fervour. They didn't even stop when the waitress came by with their juice, and cleared her throat, and put the glasses down, and went away. They didn't stop even when the occupants of a booth close by applauded.

When they did stop, Anik said, "Jacket off. Tie off. Collar unbuttoned."

"Or what? We don't kiss again?"

"Or—we don't eat."

He removed his jacket and tie, and, smiling, they both ate.

†††

Cinq-Mars remained in the dark about the duty he might be asked to perform. Every night he arrived at headquarters, wearing his suit, to the ever-increasing music of his colleagues' jibes. They'd whistle and straighten his collar for him. He'd stand around anxiously, all dressed up, waiting to learn whether or not he was to change into his humble blues that night or remain proud in his civvies. On two occasions he was sent out to walk his beat, only to be ordered back downtown when he called to check in. He had to take a bus to get back. In the locker room, he peeled off his blue uniform, put on his new suit, then eagerly ascended in the elevator and waited for a further command that never came. His shift ended and he remained seated, waiting, until someone finally came by and told him to go home.

"The situation is fluid," Captain Armand Touton advised him.

"I understand, sir," he said, although he didn't.

"Can't predict when we might need you. The best we can do is signal when you should be ready."

"I understand, sir, but what work am I supposed to be doing exactly?"

"Around here, we don't divulge our operations prematurely."

As Émile explained to Anik, he was being impatiently patient.

On his lucky days, he arrived at headquarters and was advised to report to Touton for duty. He'd check the crease in his trousers and slick his hair back using Brylcreem to look marginally thuggish. Then he'd wait around and twiddle his thumbs for hours, and twice Touton took him for a ride through the streets of Montreal.

"I love this town," the captain told him one time as they wended their way through the tough eastern section of the city, beneath the tall spans of the Jacques Cartier Bridge. "Especially at night. This is my town at night. I'm not saying I'm the proprietor, I don't own it, but I *know* this town. And I protect it."

"Who are we going after?"

"Racketeers. The gambling end."

"Great."

"I want you inside as a gambling man. Detective Gaston Fleury—"

"—the cop from Policy?"

"Don't laugh," Touton admonished him. "He's a real cop. He can be useful and effective in his own way."

"Yes, sir." He acquiesced to Touton's point of view, but continued to think, *The man's an accountant.*

"Detective Fleury will supply you with money. We have an identity for you, a name for you to give at the door, which should get you inside. Have you ever gambled, Cinq-Mars?"

"No, sir."

"Not at all? A little bit? Surely you've placed a bet."

"No, sir."

The captain looked across at him, ignoring the road momentarily. "What are you—not only a farm boy but an altar boy to boot?"

"Yes, sir. I've been an altar boy."

Touton chuckled. "Yeah, this is Quebec. We've all been altar boys. But even they play cards."

"Not me, sir."

"You have no vices?"

"I drink Scotch. Beer, too, a little."

"We'll teach you how to play roulette. It's not exactly a skill game. You put your money down on a number or a colour, or both. You're a smart cookie. You'll figure it out. Nobody's asking you to win. We just want you inside the gambling den. Make it look like you belong there before we come through the roof."

"Ah, the roof, sir?"

The captain nodded. "My favourite. Skylights. Yeah, I've never met a sky-light I didn't enjoy busting through. It's hard to believe so many of these gambling dens have skylights, but I see their problem. They want a place with no windows. They need natural light if the electricity goes out, and they want an extra way out in case cops surround the place. Too bad for them, I never go through the front door if they give me the option of a skylight."

"They haven't figured that out by now?"

"It's a human failing. Nobody thinks anything bad will actually happen to them. At one place, they had a ladder going up to the skylight so they could escape. I used it to climb down and say hello."

Thrilled to be part of the operation, Cinq-Mars retained some residual confusion. "Is this the case where I'm supposed to be an ambitious swine?"

"Here's the plan. Go in. Gamble. Keep an eye peeled for a dirty civil servant who's on the take. Very corrupt guy. It'll shock you who. We'll show you a picture. Then cops bust through the skylight. We'll make it look realistic, you don't have to worry about that."

"You mean it's not realistic?"

"Not exactly. You go out the air vent. Fleury will tell you where it is. But you take our rotten civil servant out with you. There's an escape chute that only insiders know about—and us. Once you make your escape, the bastard will be in your debt—he'll trust you. He'll be grateful. You work that relationship. You tell him you're in the import-export business. When he asks you what kind of merchandise, you tell him you keep that to yourself until the need arises."

Cinq-Mars had another morning date with Anik lined up. He could see where this assignment might make him late for the rendezvous, and he wouldn't be able to make a phone call, either. Sometimes being a cop disrupted his social life.

Touton parked on a dark, forlorn street. They'd made so many turns that Cinq-Mars lost track of where they might be, although he could just make out a section of the bridge to the west of them.

"We wait here."

At first, nothing seemed to be happening. No lights were on anywhere—the neighbourhood seemed asleep. Then a car pulled up behind them and immediately went dark. The driver seemed to be looking through a briefcase when Cinq-Mars shot a glance back at him.

"Don't do that."

"What?"

"Look back."

His first job in plain clothes and already he had screwed up. Two minutes later, the new arrival flashed his lights twice and got out of the car. The small man was Detective Gaston Fleury, and he came up to the driver's side as Touton lowered his window.

"It's off," Fleury said. "He's not playing tonight."

"How come?"

"He met some girl."

"That fucker. All right. It can't be rushed. We wait. We try another night."

Touton drove off, and Cinq-Mars experienced an odd tidal lull, his adrenaline both subsiding and sloshing around, his nerve endings feeling scrubbed.

"Now that you know the plan, don't speak about it," Touton warned him.

"I won't breathe a word, sir."

"If you do, I'll have your nuts in a vice. You'll pardon me if I don't deal in metaphors. I don't have your education. I just mean what I say."

A call that was coded came over the two-way for Touton, and the captain of the Night Patrol sped up until he spotted a phone booth. He came to a sudden stop and fished around in his pockets, but came up empty. "You have a dime, Cinq-Mars?" The rookie cop came through, and Touton went out and made the call. When he came back, he said, "Looks like you might see a little action tonight. Just keep your mouth shut and your head down."

"Yes, sir."

"If you ever feel like you want to puke—don't."

They crossed the city rapidly, heading west and passing north of downtown to avoid traffic. Touton slowed for red lights, then dashed through when the way was clear, and along the broad avenue of Côte Ste. Catherine he put his foot to the floor. When a cop started to chase him, Touton got on the two-way and ordered dispatch to get the keen-bean off his tail, and momentarily the other car turned off its cherries and swerved away. They ended up outside Blue Bonnets Raceway. The horses were quiet in their barns. Bettors had long since departed for home. Cops in plain clothes were milling around, though, and in the centre of the small gathering Cinq-Mars could see a half-naked man tied to a hitching post.

He didn't look so good.

He had his shirt off, but the tail remained tucked into the back of his pants and he'd already suffered a few blows. His lip bled on the right side, and one eye looked puffy, although it blinked as Touton walked closer to him. His forehead appeared lumpy.

Cinq-Mars stood outside the circle, keeping his head down and his mouth shut, as instructed.

When Touton walked right up to him and hit him in the gut, the man keeled over as far as his restraints would allow. Cinq-Mars could see the man's natural arrogance and spunk seep right out of him. He remained slumped over, as though he had no further interest in being upright again.

"That's what I think of you," Touton told him. "Now you know."

The man had nothing to say.

"Now that that part's out of the way, Marcel—that's your name, right? Marcel?"

Although he'd been punched low, his head lolled around.

"Pay attention to me when I'm talking to you, Marcel. If you don't, I'll find a way to get your attention. I asked a question, and if there's one thing I won't do with you, it's repeat myself." In a vague, unfocused way, the man's head came up a notch. Touton took the gesture as an affirmation. "Good. We see eye to eye. I appreciate that. Now, you're going to be moving, Marcel. We've told you this before, but you weren't listening. So we're telling you again, once and for all. Do you see how bad things get when I have to repeat myself?"

Again, that vague nod, as if the man was viewing his own ordeal from a distance. Cinq-Mars noted that he was muscled, and guessed that he pumped iron, probably whenever he was behind bars, yet the punch had disoriented him.

"Where are you moving to, Marcel? That's the question for this happy hour. Do you have any suggestions? Give me your first choice—we'll start with that."

The man said nothing that anyone could hear, and Touton leaned in closer.

"Drummondville. He's moving to Drummondville." For some reason, the other cops found this amusing. Cinq-Mars knew the place, a working-class town on a flat agricultural plain, and wondered why the answer struck the other cops as amusing. "What's that, sixty miles away? I'm sorry, Marcel, but you still don't understand the concept here. Drummondville is way too close. I mean, it's not even off the map. I think you can do better for yourself than relocate there."

Aware now of how the game was played, the captive offered to move to Quebec City.

"You're catching on. Trouble is, I have friends in Quebec City. I won't inflict you on them. They might not forgive me."

The man continued to imagine a life for himself farther down the St. Lawrence River. "Rivière du Loup?" he suggested.

"That's a decent offer," Touton conceded. "I can respect that offer. I mean, since we're shipping you downriver, as the saying goes, I could send you all the way to the Gaspé, where only birds live. They'd shit on you all day long, and frankly, I like that idea, the image of it. But there are a few decent families along the coast, too—you might be a disturbance to them. I expect you're a disturbance wherever you go. So Rivière du Loup is a fair suggestion."

The culprit nodded, as though to indicate that the destination was okay with him, to seal the deal.

"But I'll suggest you get a little farther away from here than that. I will call the chief of police in Rimouski, because that's where you're going. Rimouski. So far down the river you're just about at sea, more than what you deserve. If you don't report to the chief of police and stay in Rimouski under his care and guidance, you will be hunted down, Marcel, I'm sorry to say. We don't have the patience to arrest you or put you back in jail. Anyway, that hasn't reformed you up till now, has it? No, sir. You'll be hunted down, and when we're done hunting you down, we'll make you pay for putting us to the trouble. Now, Marcel, confirm to me that you understand everything I'm talking about, because neither of us wants any further misunderstandings between us."

Marcel managed to stagger up a little higher and nod. "I'll go," he said.

"To Rimouski. Right away. And asshole, listen to me—you get to take no one with you. Hear what I'm saying?"

He nodded to accept that final condition, and Touton walked away from him as the other officers cut him off the hitching post. As the last knot was sliced through, the man slumped heavily to his knees.

"What'd he do?" Cinq-Mars asked his boss as he joined him on the walk back to the car.

"The worst kind of pimp. We got pimps of all kinds around here, but he's an out-of-towner who's too quick to injure his girls. He also has a tendency to pick them too young." Touton got in behind the wheel of his car. Cinq-Mars crawled in on the other side. "A sad state of affairs," he lamented.

"Yeah?"

"We used to have bawdy houses and madams. They ruled the roost. We closed them all down when Drapeau came to power. It seemed like a good thing."

"It wasn't?"

"Don't get me wrong. It was a good thing. But we still have prostitution, and now we have pimps. We can change the landscape, but we can't change the world."

"I guess that's true," Cinq-Mars said.

"I know what's on your mind," Touton said, as he turned the ignition over.

"What's on my mind?" He had a lot to think about, actually.

"I'm too rough. I'm old school. You can't beat people up anymore. It's against the law. That's what you believe."

"Yeah," Cinq-Mars concurred. "That's pretty much what was on my mind."

"I told you so. Well, kid, you're right to think that way."

The opinion came as a surprise. "Why do you beat people up if I'm right to think that way?"

"This is my town. I don't own it, but I keep it secure."

"That justifies beating up pimps?"

"Suits me fine. Leaves a few scrapes on the knuckles, that's all. Nothing I can't live with. You don't like the rough stuff so much?"

Cinq-Mars had no choice. He had to state his position. "No, sir. I believe in the law. I believe it applies to cops the same as it does civilians."

"Good," Touton stated as they drove off. "You have problems with me. Concerns. They're printed on your brow. I haven't lived up to your high ideals for the law, but I'm not apologizing. I was the right cop for my time. I did good work, Cinq-Mars. I kept the citizens safe and the bad guys nervous. That's better than the other way around. Let's see if you do any better. You'll be judged by that standard only—will you be the right cop for your time? Do the citizens feel safe and the bad guys nervous? We'll find out, won't we? Over time."

†††

At headquarters, Cinq-Mars still didn't know whether he should put on his uniform again and return to the streets or call it a night and go home. Touton proposed a third option.

"Find yourself a paper cup, Cinq-Mars, and come to my office."

"What's the cup for?" the younger man asked.

"Don't piss in it," Touton advised him.

When he entered the cramped, untidy office, a clear plastic glass in hand, he showed it to the captain and the man grunted, as if to indicate that it would do. Touton opened a tall green locker stuck between a filing cabinet and a coat rack, and from its base and a congestion of footwear pulled out a bottle of whiskey, half-full.

"Your vice, you said. It's Irish, not Scotch, but a similar effect."

The young man nodded, but he looked more nervous than pleased.

"Relax, kid. We won't get you fired. I want to go over my big case with you. Our sting got postponed—we have time to spare. Besides, since when has someone with more rank than me walked into this office after midnight? Hmmm, what do you know? It hasn't happened yet."

"Yes, sir."

He looked unconvinced as the captain poured to the lip of the glass. "See how that goes down."

Cinq-Mars sipped, then sat, and waited while Touton pulled off his shoes. The captain showed him the cuts on his knuckles under the desk lamp, and smiled. "Everybody has to find respect. Detective Fleury, if he ever hit anybody, his hand would crack. But he has my respect up there in Policy. I'm not saying everybody has to do things the same way. How will you find your way, Cinq-Mars?"

He shrugged. "By doing the best job I can, I guess."

"I have a hunch about you. In wartime, people live at close quarters. I learned from the other soldiers." He sat with one hand on the mug in which he'd poured his Jameson's. The other hand, in which he still clutched the bottle, had fallen by his side. "You're a smart one. The education, that's not the whole of it. You're a smart guy. Admit it."

"Around here, sir? That would be like admitting to leprosy."

Touton laughed, stopped, then laughed again.

"Smart as you are, I've already taught you a few things, haven't I?"

"No question about that, sir."

"Ever notice? A lot of smart guys are too dumb to learn a damn thing."

Now that he thought about it, Émile realized that he had come across the phenomenon quite often. "I know what you mean, sir."

"You can be smarter than the next guy, but still show humility. That's rare."

Cinq-Mars was not certain, but something in the captain's tone seemed melancholy, as though unhappy events moved through his life these days. They drank awhile, with the younger man waiting for his senior to dredge up what was on his mind. In the meantime, he did not want to interrupt his evident preoccupations.

"I want you to revisit the bastards," Touton blurted out.

"Sir?"

"Let them know we haven't forgotten about them. Re-interview. Form your own take on things, establish your own perspective. Mine's old, anyway. We need a new look. The bastards think they've gotten away with it. The motherfuckers. They don't lose much sleep anymore. If they still worry about me, they remind themselves that I'll be out of the picture soon. Pensioned off. Out to fucking pasture. Just for my satisfaction, Cinq-Mars, if nothing else, visit them again, show them it's not over. Show them we will never let them off the hook. Show them they've got a smarter man than me after them now—one who'll pursue them to their motherfucking graves. Maybe not tougher, but a man with brains in his head is after them now. From one generation to the next we will pursue—that's the lesson to impart. We will run them down. Make that point, Cinq-Mars, quietly, discreetly, just by asking the same old questions. Stick a shiv between their ribs. That's not too tough a detail for you?"

As long as the shiv was a metaphor, he liked the idea. "No, sir."

"No different than punching a man in the gut."

"It's different, sir. You know that."

"I want you to hound them, Cinq-Mars. Do you get me?"

"I do. I will."

"Good man."

They drank awhile. The office windows looked across at matching windows on the opposite side of an alley, the frames shrunken by stacks of boxes and cardboard files and sundry debris. At night, the opposing building empty, Touton rarely drew his curtains for privacy, and every evening he'd wave to the office cleaner next door, a ritual carried on for years now. Sadly, he felt that they had been getting older together. The black man appeared to be frail to him that night, and in exchanging their greetings the thin, grey-haired man stretched his sore back, grimacing, indicating his lumbar complaints. Touton put both hands on his left thigh and closed his eyes, communicating the throb his war wounds periodically delivered. The two had never exchanged a single word out loud.

"My daughter's come home to live with me and my wife again. That's good," Touton said, and Cinq-Mars felt an emotional wave cross the desk towards him.

"Where has she been?" the younger man asked quietly.

Touton only blew air out from his mouth and waved the whiskey bottle around to indicate everywhere and nowhere.

Cinq-Mars tried again. "How old is she?"

"Sixteen." Touton sipped his drink. "Pregnant, of course. We'll have a little tyke underfoot."

Cinq-Mars tried to be cheery about what he presumed were difficult matters. "It's been a while, I suppose. You're due."

Touton looked at him as though he might consider delivering a punch to his stomach, just to see how much he'd enjoy it. "I've never had a baby at home. My daughter, we adopted when she was ten. My wife and me, we only had her five years. She ran away. Now she's back—ready to stay, I think. Can't be sure, though. We can give them both a home, mother and child. See how that goes."

The young cop now guessed that there was very little that was cheerful about the captain's home life. "I hope it all works out," he said. That seemed to be safe ground. But he couldn't leave well enough alone—he was prone to asking these sorts of questions. "The father, I suppose, he's out of the picture?"

"He is now," Touton managed to say. He topped up his glass. "Tonight, we sent him downriver to Rimouski."

Cinq-Mars felt the wind get sucked out of him.

Touton gestured to him to pass his glass. The young cop finished off his drink and stretched out his arm and the captain generously filled his cup again.

They sat awhile without speaking, then Touton said, "Men were there tonight, who, if I put that bastard in the river, would have helped me tie chains to his feet. If I decided to break every bone in his face, they would have looked the other way, and they would have made you turn around if you didn't have the good sense to do so on your own. Most men there would not have held me back from anything I chose to do tonight, and whatever I did, they would not have held it against me."

"Except me," Cinq-Mars said.

"Maybe that's why I let you come along. I figured we'd catch up to that guy soon enough. I've been a good cop, Cinq-Mars. A tough cop, I know that. I'll smash a man's face if I think it's required to keep the peace. These days, people have a problem with that. They never used to. Now, if a cop spits on the sidewalk some reporter thinks it's news. City Hall calls for a fucking Royal Commission on Cop Spitting. If a cop takes a punch, then smashes the guy's hand who hit him, guess who's digging himself out of a whole pile of shit? But I only ever do what I believe is right. I never do what I know is wrong."

"So if you'd smashed that guy up tonight—"

"That's where things are strange," the older cop responded, interrupting him. "Odd. He deserves a good smashing up, that bastard. What father wouldn't do it if he could? But I promised my daughter I wouldn't—one of her conditions to return home. Also, I promised my wife I wouldn't lose my badge over this. I should tell you, though, I made a promise to myself, too. Maybe that's the only vow that counts in the end. Maybe. I promised myself I wouldn't be no animal."

Cinq-Mars nodded, and breathed evenly in the confines of the office.

"I want you to know something, Cinq-Mars. Someday, you might hear about some lowlife being fished out of the river near Rimouski. I didn't have nothing to do with that, even though it hasn't happened yet."

"You're just able to predict things, is that it?" He was feeling his stomach clench again.

"I know what kind of fuck-up he is. I know the kind of place Rimouski is. They got bad guys there who defend their turf. I don't expect that bag of shit to survive. I didn't send him to Disneyland to live with Donald Motherfucking Duck. But even though it hasn't happened yet, I didn't have nothing to do with it. That's all I'm saying. I introduced him to friends you don't mess with, and if he's a dumb enough shit to mess with them, that's his lookout. It's not on my head."

Cinq-Mars thought about it awhile. "That true? You're not involved?"

"If I put a rat in among a bunch of cats, I think I can predict how that'll turn out, that's all I'm saying."

"Then what he does, how he gets through it, that's just up to him."

"So, you're not some weenie marshmallow?" Touton asked his protégé.

"I believe in playing by the rules. I don't see where you're breaking any."

Touton seemed grateful for the conversation. After a while, he said, "Do you have any idea how hard it was for me to hit him just the one time, not more? That wasn't even for me. That was just to make sure he'd pay attention."

"I can imagine that was difficult, sir." He felt that the captain needed to get off the subject, away from the obsession of his revenge. "How did you adopt your daughter, sir?" he asked. "Where did you find her?"

Touton shook his head, saddened even by what was supposed to be a happier memory. "A bar fight. An innocent bystander got shot through his right eye. Dead instantly. One second, he's hoisting a beer after work—the next, he's lying on the floor in a pool of blood. So I accept the detail to tell the next of kin, right? I go home to his family. This ten-year-old kid opens the door, big smile on her face, expecting to see her daddy. My whole body just goes to mush. Right away, that breaks my heart. I ask if her mommy's home. She says her mommy's dead, and she's looking around me to see if her dad's coming. Turns out she never knew her mom on account of she died in childbirth. And her father—" and Touton's voice went eerily quiet. "—who raised this girl on his own, and he'd done a great job . . . now her dad was dead, and he was all she'd ever had. Now I get to talk to her real father in my sleep and tell him that, somehow, I let his little girl go bad. Too many nights at work, I guess. Too many days asleep. She got into trouble. Ran with the wrong crowd. I tried. But I failed."

The cop from the countryside had seen men weep at funerals, but quietly, somehow under a restraint. The man who sat across from him was suddenly overcome, and he waited for the emotional slurry to run its course.

"I wanted to kill that motherfucker. Understand me?" Touton burst out.

"He's never going to forget that punch."

The comment seemed to bolster the stricken man, and he pulled himself together, nodding, wiping away the last of his tears. He shook his head, sighed, made a gesture to indicate that this was one helluva night, and downed the whiskey from his mug in a single gulp.

Quietly, intently, Touton said, "You don't mess around with Anik, Cinq-Mars. She's like a daughter to me, too."

The rookie smiled. "I think you should be more concerned that she'll chew me up and spit me out like so many wooden nickels."

The remark helped Touton to revive himself further, and he laughed a little, concurring with a constant bob of his head. "Yeah, she's something," he said.

For their next drink, they touched glasses—the clear plastic to the ceramic mug—and took them down in a couple of swallows.

"I've got twenty years in, kid. I can go another five. Don't know about ten. I've only worked nights. A month can go by in the wintertime when I never see the sun. I'm strong still. But weary. I don't know what it is. I'm tired. I want to find the people who killed Anik's dad. It's a personal crusade, I'll admit that, but it's a good one, it's righteous. Are you on board, Cinq-Mars?" The question seemed a drunken one, as the young man believed he'd confirmed his reply already and had only been waiting around for his marching orders for weeks now.

"Yes, sir."

"Good." Touton stretched, as though his crying jag had assailed his joints, made him sore. "Go home, kid. It all starts up again tomorrow. Maybe you'll be needed, maybe not. We'll play it by ear. But I will want you to go back through the suspects—see if we can't make them sweat."

"I won't let you down, sir."

"Hang on." Touton stepped over to a stack of material on top of the low-level filing cabinets and moved a few items around. He pulled out a file sealed by a pair of thick elastic bands. "This is the history of the Cartier Dagger. Start here. Study it. It's knowledge you should be walking around with."

"Yes, sir. Thanks . . . sir?"

The older man had slumped back down into his chair again.

"What's your daughter's name? You didn't say."

Touton nodded. He stared into his cup, getting his emotions under control. "Patti," he said strongly. "Patti."

They nodded rather than wish each other a good night, and Cinq-Mars departed the office, then the station, and headed home. The sun was almost rising, the false dawn portending a fine, bright day. Having planned a late-morning breakfast with Anik, he had a few hours to kill, so he chose to walk home. She'd appreciate his change of attire—a pair of jeans, which he'd purchased to please her, and a casual shirt. In the meantime he'd enjoy being on these streets as the city awoke to a new day. His boss cherished the city and felt responsible for its safety. Cinq-Mars felt that he was beginning to get that sense, that a mysterious notion of care and resolve was also forming inside him.

†††

So ardent were their discussions, so intense their debates, that Anik sometimes forgot to eat or sleep. She'd find herself woozy on only a glass of beer and realize that, since her orange juice and toast for breakfast, she'd eaten nothing more than an apple and it was now eleven at night. They would change venues, pack away a few burgers in a pub with food, and the talk began again. Ideas were no longer the burning issues. What counted as time moved along were strategies.

Then, at some point in the night, music would spontaneously erupt. Young and old together, and this love for one another and passion for the cause, the harmony of spirit filled her and filled them with a joy for their work. For many, the excitement and bravado, the happiness and spontaneity of those nights could only properly end with a tumult of bodies, and lovers left the closing pubs arm in arm, or kissed against a telephone pole, or reached under one another's clothing to stroke other mysteries. Even those not in love slept with one another, and they waltzed home together on the breeze of happy lust.

Anik would depart the last pub of the night in the company of her new friends, Pierre and Paul, Jean-Luc and Vincent, and she always knew that she could select any one of the four and he'd gladly take her back to his place. But, as she had told them often, "I've got something else going on." They didn't get that—that she could have a boyfriend they never met, who did not come out with her to talk about the future, to plot the next course of action. Yet Anik kept in step with mystery. She still refused to join the party, which now made sense to everyone, as the future would surely know confrontation and rows with the police. She referred to union battles in recent decades as though she'd been there herself, although she would have been five years old for some contests, not yet alive for others. They visited her home once, and listened to her mother talk in the kitchen, her long commitment to social justice humbling their strident convictions. The boys wanted to be like Anik's mother one day, sitting alone in a house with heroic memories to recount. Anik knew that her mom's history made her their leader. But she had a different sense. They thought the political and economic powers of the day were fragile, easily toppled by any sustained demonstration of public will. She knew better. The government was resilient, with the capacity to be unforgiving. The capitalists were unyielding, with the capacity to be cruel and overpowering. All they had on their side was song and the heart's blood of the people.

"Then we'll spill our blood," Paul said.

Vincent declared, "And we'll sing."

"We'll sing a lot," Pierre concurred. "We'll see what that does."

They laughed a lot. Anik was their leader, and she taught them to laugh at themselves. "If we're too earnest, too serious, too one-sided, we'll be defeated. We need to be flexible and visionary. We need to be smart. And if you really want to win, you have to be treacherous."

That all seemed so true.

Yet she walked home alone, thinking of Émile. Why did she encourage him as her boyfriend? He was so lame in some ways. But he wasn't lame as a person. He was full of life, really, and she didn't mind his sweetness—she liked that. She could feel herself being swayed. But a cop—my God. Get serious. *You can't possibly ball a cop.*

But she was thinking that she would, even that she should. She liked him, and while her ideas found a home among her radical buddies, her heart—if not her mind—always swung back towards the tall boy with the big nose and the huge determination. She had never been able to understand how her dad could have worked for the right wing, sacking the offices of the left, then come home to his left-wing wife, sweeping her into his arms. Her mom had so often tried to explain it to her from different angles. "He never really hurt anybody, that's what he always said. He told me that the left was too soft, that he was toughening them up. Oh, Anik. He had his conflicts. He was never clear inside himself, that man. But we loved him anyway, didn't we?"

She was not clear inside herself, she knew. Émile stood for the side she opposed, the established, the entrenched, while she represented an element in society he was bound to fight one day. Maybe it was love, and maybe that was what it had been with her father, too. A rambunctious man who made his living with his fists, and that was perfectly fine except that he fell in love with a girl who wanted to unionize the working poor. And so he had had to accommodate an alternative point of view.

Anik didn't think she could accommodate a different point of view, but she was inclined to accommodate the guy. She liked him. She thought about him all the time. She even got cross with herself at times for liking him too much, but what could a poor girl do? And now, look. Her steps were not taking her home after a long night out with the gang. Her steps, her silly feet—who did they think they were, those stupid dogs?—indisputably guided her in another direction, to a place she'd never been. The address was safely tucked in a jacket pocket, down deep, where she clutched it in her fist. Émile's apartment. *Oh those silly feet!* She could catch a breakfast somewhere, wait for him to come home. Surprise him. And while she was at it, she knew, carry on surprising herself.

††
†

Unaware that Anik Clément had commenced walking to his apartment in the dead of night, Constable Émile Cinq-Mars, on an uneventful beat, checked in with his sergeant by telephone. He kept the fingers of his right hand crossed. "I got a message from Captain Touton for you," the man said, and the young patrolman pumped his fist with glee. "I'll read you what it says here exactly. 'Hurry back. Tonight's the night.' Does that mean something to you, Cinq-Mars? What's up?"

"I can't answer that."

The hell with it. He took a cab back downtown from the north end, despite the cost of half a night's wages.

He dressed in a rush, but this time he never had to ascend the stairs to the offices of the Night Patrol, nor did he have to wait for hours in an anteroom as lively as a morgue. Touton and other detectives hurried downstairs to fetch him. "Car's waiting," the boss called out. "Let's go!"

He ran out to the parking lot and, with a gesture of his impressive chin, Touton directed him into an unmarked car with Detective Fleury. Touton got into another car closer to the exit gate.

"It's a go," Fleury told him as he and Cinq-Mars piled into the car. Thanks to the deodorant strip hanging from the mirror, the interior carried the scent of a pine forest. "Grab that pouch out of the back."

As Cinq-Mars leaned over the bench seat to fetch a small black sack, Fleury stepped on the gas and they flew off in pursuit of the other vehicles in their convoy.

"Should I open it?"

"Open it! Jesus. We don't have all night."

Cinq-Mars knew how far they had to travel to South Central, under the Jacques Cartier Bridge. They had at least four minutes. "Keep your shirt on."

"Mind who you're talking to. Stuff the money into your pockets. Different pockets. Make it look like you got loot from a bank heist squeezing out your rectum."

"How much is there?"

"Doesn't matter. You'll lose it anyway. If you happen to win, don't think you can keep it. I'll frisk you when this operation ends."

"Yeah, yeah." Cinq-Mars didn't like this guy so much. He seemed to be overcompensating for his life as an accountant and taking advantage of the fact that Touton wasn't with them. He doubted that the guy would be so tough on him with the boss around.

"Get that money stuffed away."

"I'm stuffing."

"Now find the picture."

"Excuse me?"

"The photograph in there. Take it out. Look at it."

A separate pocket had its own zipper. Cinq-Mars fished out the snapshot and flicked on the overhead light slightly behind him. "This the guy?" he asked.

"That's the mark. Memorize that face. He won't be the only bald head standing around. I should have you go in there like a dumb-ass rookie and just screw it up, find the wrong guy. But we can't afford to let that happen. We need this guy. We need you to make good contact, okay? This is our best opportunity, understand?"

They swung hard into a curve, and Cinq-Mars was thrown against the door, the tires squealing for mercy.

"Now find the map," Fleury said. "We don't have much time. Study the map."

"Why didn't you show me this weeks ago?"

"Don't get irritable with me, sap. Find the map!"

The schematic, which had been executed with a draftsman's hand, detailed the rooms and their configurations. Superimposed on the sheet had been sketched the design for an escape hatch, ostensibly through a ventilation chamber that led to a modified laundry chute. Cinq-Mars was to make contact with their mark. When all hell broke loose in the room, he'd lead him through the crawl space and down the escape chute apparatus from the third-floor gambling den to the ground.

"What do I land on?" he asked.

"Cement, if I can arrange that on time. But the bad guys keep a bin with pillows and old mattresses in it. It'll be mouldy smelling, but you shouldn't break a leg. But go first. That way, if there's a problem with the landing, you can fix it before the mark flies down."

Cinq-Mars felt queasy about the arrangement. "Bit of an act of faith, don't you think? Dropping down three floors?"

"Not faith. Balls. Either you got 'em or you don't. If you don't, we'll find that out tonight."

"Fine for you to say. All you do is push a pencil."

Fleury braked sharply again, for no reason, then sped up. "Do you have that map memorized? On account of your griping, we're losing time. You've got to get out of the car, Cinq-Mars, find the right door, take the freight elevator up three flights, find the right door again—both doors have three red dots alongside the top hinge. That's what you look for."

"Three red dots."

"Can you handle that? When you're challenged, say that Merlin sent you—"

"You're kidding me." Plenty about this operation seemed half-baked to him, although he'd not step away from it. Put him in charge—when that day came—and a great deal of police procedural guff would vanish.

"*Merlin.* Stop interrupting. Make damn sure you don't choose the wrong man."

Fleury gave him the final details of the operation, then braked.

"Get out," he said.

"Good luck to you, too," Cinq-Mars told him, and took a step out of the car.

"Come back here," Fleury commanded.

"What now?"

"Leave your gun behind . . . your holster, your badge, your wallet. I want nothing in your pockets but cash."

Cinq-Mars still had a ways to walk down the block, then he crossed the street. Other cars had peeled away without them, and now Fleury departed as well, to join the officers on the rooftop to prepare for their descent through a skylight. Cinq-Mars suddenly felt alone, somewhat fearful. He had to pretend to be someone he was not, to act a role and be convincing, or he'd botch the entire operation and, potentially, his career as a detective. Courage, he knew, was not the issue, but concealing his nervousness, feigning bravado, forgetting to be somebody else and suddenly reverting to his true nature—these things worried him. Thinking too much, that was an issue, too. Somehow he had to relax, and Émile Cinq-Mars took ten deep breaths to try to get himself under control.

By the ninth large inhalation, he was at the door.

The bottom exterior door was unlocked, but a bull of a man nodded with his chin, expecting a password. Cinq-Mars took his tenth deep breath.

"Mer—" He lost his voice, his breath, his nerve. He cleared his throat. "Merlin sent me," he said, and the man looked him over from head to foot then nodded, and let him go ahead.

He found the freight elevator and pulled up the large garage-style door. A second, inner set of doors peeled back with a slight tug. He stepped inside. As he punched the button for the third floor, the doors closed and, noisily, painfully slowly, the elevator ascended, coming to a rest with a jolt. The inner doors parted easily, but he had to heave up the outer door on his own again, and this time it didn't run smoothly. He smacked his hands together to shake the grit off them. Only people walking and touching things moved the dirt around in here—the place was never cleaned. Cinq-Mars carried on down the corridor, dark and drab with dusty air. Fortunately, the doors were painted white, and he easily spotted the one with three red dots by the upper hinge.

He knocked.

Nothing.

Knocked again.

Still nothing.

He tried the knob. Somebody opened the door from inside.

"Hold on to your dick," a grizzled, wiry, short old-timer grumbled.

"Merlin sent me," Cinq-Mars declared.

"Who asked you?" the man said back. Unshaven, with white whiskers.

"I was just saying—"

"Who sent you?" the clearly crotchety figure demanded.

"I told you. Merlin."

"What does that make you, you think? Fucking King Kong?"

A subliminal reference, Cinq-Mars deduced, given that he was at least a foot and a half taller than the elfin, irascible doorman. Or perhaps he was expected to know a coded response. He froze.

"You got money? Show me. We're not a fucking bank in here. You want a loan? No sweat. We take your dick as collateral."

"In your dreams," Cinq-Mars quipped, proud of himself. That sounded like a tough, raw response to him, words that wouldn't normally come out of his mouth. Maybe he could get the hang of this detective racket after all.

He chose to be slow, pulling bills from one pocket, then another, and if a few fell on the floor, he left them there.

The doorman rushed him through a set of heavy, dark curtains before the fresh arrival noticed the denominations he'd dropped, and delivered a parting admonishment. "Next time, Prick Face—knock."

Most voices in the room were pitched low—quiet demands to raise a stake, murmured announcements closing a table to further bets. One boisterous fellow let the room know whenever he won or lost, barking out his victories and cursing his defeats. Over the tables, the lights were as low as the gentle murmuring, the smoke intense. Ceiling fans blew warmer, smoky air down upon the gamblers, and Émile Cinq-Mars deliberately coughed.

Good move, he thought. He was coughing to conceal his survey of the room.

About twenty people were present, a quiet night. In the minds of the players, then, a safe night, for a police bust would be more dramatic when the place was packed. The croupiers, at first glance, were dressed for the part, wearing white shirts and black vests, but as Cinq-Mars sidled up to a table next to a bald-headed customer, he noticed that the croupier's vest showed a few dark stains, probably from spaghetti sauce or something similar. His shirt had been due for a cleaning weeks ago. Cinq-Mars was pulling bills out of his inside jacket pockets and shuffling them into some kind of shape. He smacked his tongue over his thumb a few times to moisten it, and decided to put his bills into order by denomination. "I don't know what I got here," he said to no one in particular, then looked up at the bald man.

He was not the guy.

He looked around the room more carefully, and counted. All told, eight bald guys. As if a hair-growth convention was being held in the city.

He went by them all, ostensibly to check the action at the various tables while shooting a glance at each of the suspects. No luck. Then a ninth man, still doing up his fly as he emerged from a washroom, proved to be his mark. He looked exactly like the snapshot.

Cinq-Mars followed him to the roulette wheel and put his money down.

"I feel lucky," Cinq-Mars declared. "You?"

The other man shrugged. He didn't want to talk to the new arrival whose hands were full of cash.

"You're right," Cinq-Mars analyzed. "Luck's got fuck-all to do with it. The wheel is scientific. The right scheme, you come away a fucking winner."

"Everybody's got a scheme," the man philosophized. He was an accountant, Cinq-Mars guessed, and knew the odds on schemes. "Sooner or later, it'll beat you."

"If you let it, it will. Once your scheme goes cold, switch strategies. That's my policy. Stay a step ahead of the game. You watch. Learn. I'll fucking show you how."

He put a hundred dollars down and said, "Red."

"You'll need chips, sir," the croupier told him.

"I'm not hungry," the cop told him.

"Very funny," the man said. "How much do you want to change?"

Cinq-Mars stood confused. "Merlin sent me," he said.

"Great, but you still got to buy your chips."

"Come on, are we playing here or not?" another man called out from the table's end.

"Take your money off the table, sir. I'll sell you chips when you tell me how much you want."

The cop turned to the bald guy beside him. "I'm superstitious. Tell me something. Have you had a lucky night so far?"

"Break-even," the man said with a shrug. He had a dimple on the left side of his chin, and bright blue eyes that made him look like a dog of some kind, Cinq-Mars was thinking, a husky.

"How much did you start out with?"

The man shrugged. "That's your business how?"

"Sir, don't disturb the customers."

"I want to order what he did. He's doing okay. He's break-even. I want some luck, that's all."

"Kid," the bald guy said, "order a couple of grand in chips and stop slow-ing everything down, that's my advice."

"I appreciate that more than you know," Cinq-Mars told him. He was weaving a little, to indicate that he'd had a few. He was wishing he could have a Scotch at that moment and regretted that the barmaid was on the other side of the room. He started counting out two thousand dollars. "You're a gentleman and a fucking scholar, I can tell that. Maybe I can do you a favour some day."

Not being aware of what the coloured chips were worth, Cinq-Mars raised a few eyebrows when he finally placed a bet, depositing eleven hundred dollars on the black.

He lost.

"That's some system," the bald guy said. "Change your mind and lose."

"Hmm," Cinq-Mars said, but he was concentrating on finding the trap-door out of here. "I keep betting until I win." He laughed. "That's my system."

"That's the whole world's system," the man said, and he laughed a lit-tle, too, and a few others around the table chuckled, and then the skylight overhead burst with a nerve-splitting shatter and glass showered down upon them.

The bald guy was scooping chips off the table—not only his own—but was looking around with a dazed expression, as though he could not believe it, but this might be the worst day of his life. Cinq-Mars grabbed the shoulder of his jacket. "Follow me," he whispered in his ear. "I know the secret way out."

"What secret way?"

"I owe you a favour, right? I pay my debts. Come on."

While the croupiers were running for the back exits and the customers were scrambling to get out the front door, a police officer shouted through a bullhorn from the now-open skylight for everyone to stay in place. "We got the building surrounded!" Cinq-Mars got down on his hands and knees behind the roulette wheel and pulled a panel free from the lower wall. A tight crawl space. The owners had to be slim men. He crawled into the dark cavity, receiving a face full of spider web while experiencing the hands of the bald guy shoving his ass through the passage more quickly. He scrambled on his elbows and hips, the darkness severe, the air dank.

After travelling for some twenty feet—which, for all his hurrying, took a while—his eyes had adjusted and he could discern an escape from this purgatory. He fell through the space onto a floor, a drop of three feet, and turned to aid his mark to stand upright again as well.

"Now what?" the bald guy demanded, as though Cinq-Mars had delivered him out of a frying pan into a fire. This section of the building was bordered by floor-to-ceiling windows, and reflections of revolving police-car lights on the street below eerily lit up the space.

"This way," Cinq-Mars told him. He was doing it. He had gotten his mark out of the gambling den and now would rescue them both. The plan was actually working, and he had managed to perform his part well.

They jogged down a corridor, and Cinq-Mars showed him the escape chute, which looked like a fast drop.

"You're kidding me," the mark said. "I'm not going down there."

Cinq-Mars didn't blame him. His own stomach was churning. "Take the chute or face the cops," he warned him. "I'll go first. That way, you'll see it works."

The bald man considered his options. He had none. "All right," he con-ceded. "But I'm not going down there until I see for myself that you come out alive."

"Tell you what. Once I'm down, I'll bang the chute three times. That'll tell you it's safe to follow me down. If you don't hear nothing, stay put."

"Go already. Let's get out of here."

The young officer on his first undercover operation hesitated at the brink of his descent. That was a long way down. Three floors, all of it steep, into the dark, and at the bottom, potentially, oblivion. He sat in the chamber. He straightened out his legs on the slick aluminum slide. He put his hands down by his sides and bent back at the waist. Straightening. The incline was steep enough that he didn't need any help, but the bald man chose to give him a push.

"Go!" he said, and Cinq-Mars descended the ramp like a missile.

The air flew out of him with the rush of the fall. He felt as though he'd exhaled his heart. This was too fast, too extreme, and he uttered involuntarily small cries as he whooshed down towards his destiny.

He yearned to hit soft mattress.

Instead, the chute expelled him, he flew through the open air in the dark, and suddenly his body dove feet first into a fluid.

He was sinking into a pool of molasses-thick darkness, a rheumy sub-stance heavier than water, like oil, and he struggled back up to the surface.

He gasped for breath, and breathed the ghastly scent. He had to act quickly, for his mark might soon follow. Should he knock on the chamber, to demonstrate that he should follow and survive? Or should he spare him the ignominy of this awful bath?

He crawled up and out of the chamber that held him, the air fetid, the slimy texture of the fluid over his clothes quite revolting, when suddenly a bright light shone on him, blinding him. Then he heard a great roar, which he thought for a moment might be an alarm. But that wasn't it. His heart sank. He wanted to shoot himself. That wasn't an alarm going off.

People were cheering.

They started to applaud.

As Émile Cinq-Mars climbed down from the chamber and shielded his eyes against the light, he discerned that he was surrounded by police officers, who were being joined by croupiers and customers from the room above. The man laughing the loudest, almost convulsing, was Detective Fleury. Standing beside him, with a massive grin on his face, stood Captain Armand Touton.

When their eyes met, Touton raised his hands and joined in the applause.

The intense light was turned off, and others that lit the courtyard turned on, so that Émile Cinq-Mars could see that he had fallen into a deep vat, likely of oil, grease, tar and water, and molasses, too, and that his fellow officers were enjoying the prank they'd played on him. He saw also that his brand new suit, the pride of his wardrobe, was ruined. Every pore, every thread, every stitch, had been soaked with smelly grime.

What he could not see, but could readily imagine, and what kept the other cops laughing, was that he looked a sight. When he smiled a little, his white teeth were almost blinding, emerging as they did from his blackened form.

Touton stepped towards him. As he did so, the other men allowed their jeers, laughter and whistles to ebb.

The "mark" came running from the building to join the party. Touton waited before he spoke.

"So we hear you want to be a member of the Night Patrol. To join us. Well, son, you've been initiated now. You're still assigned to your beat, but when we want you, we'll know where to find you."

"Not tonight—" Cinq-Mars started to protest.

"No, son," Touton smiled. He almost placed a hand upon the younger man's shoulder, but wisely pulled it back. "Not tonight."

††††

Cinq-Mars could not take a cab home. No taxi would admit him. No bus driver would appreciate his smelly, oily presence, either, but in any case buses were too public a mode of transportation. Certainly no cop was going to offer him a lift, so he had no option but to walk home, a good distance made longer by his condition.

In an alley, he removed his shoes, then wrung out his socks. That seemed too hopeless a task, so he tossed the socks away and put his shoes back on barefoot. Much better. Less squishy. Next, he peeled off his jacket and did a fitful job of squeezing out the ooze from the fabric and scooping oil from his pockets. The cause was futile, but he needed to improve his mobility.

He wanted to stop dripping as he walked, and leaving footprints marked in oil. Noticing that small portions of his white shirt had been spared, protected by the jacket, he removed it and wiped his face on the bare sections, then threw it away and put on the still-oily jacket over his bare skin. The clothing felt a little better. Looking around, he ducked in behind a telephone pole, opened his trousers and, with his hands, scraped away the residue from his underwear and from around his genitals, then wiped his hand against the brick wall.

Yuck.

And he still had a long walk home.

He stuck to the back streets. At least it was early morning and only a few people were up. Those in cars were too sleepy to notice, or perhaps they habitually drove past weirdoes covered in black oil, their hair plastered against their scalps.

The few incidents that did crop up didn't affect him particularly. The woman who crossed the street to avoid passing him on the sidewalk. The cabbie who slowed down, bolted ahead, then slowed down again. The gawk of a child from a back-seat window, but the child showed no surprise, suggesting he might have gawked at Cinq-Mars in any circumstances. Émile made it to his block, which revived him somewhat, although he was grumpy and determined that, when he was in charge, when he was made a captain, when he had a police force to command, rookies would never be treated this way.

And then he spotted Anik Clément upon the outside steps to his second-storey flat, about halfway up, waiting for him, and his heart sank at the same moment that it floated upward. He felt stretched to the brink of snapping.

His initial instinct was to hide. But she'd been watching him for a while, certain that she recognized the posture, that it had to be him, but how could it be? What in the world had happened? He came closer. She stared with her mouth open, not knowing whether to call an ambulance or run for cover.

Then he was standing at the bottom of the stairs, looking up, grinning in an odd way, his teeth as bright as pearls.

"What the hell—" she began.

"Don't ask," he advised her.

"I'm asking."

"It's a cop thing."

"Cops did that to you?"

"Anik, what are you doing here?"

"Apparently, I'm here to wash you off, although I didn't know that until now. Émile—isn't that . . . ? That's your brand new suit."

"Which your friend Touton made me buy. Knowing that this would happen."

That's when she laughed, uproariously and bent double, and that's when he knew they'd be together.

Cinq-Mars showed off his grimy palms. She was trapped on the stairs, with nowhere to flee. "Hi there, Anik," he said.

She could only run up a half-flight. Which she did. She scrambled on the spiral staircase to reach his door, and there awaited his blackening, smelly, grimy, oily repulsive embrace.

On his doorstep at dawn, she squealed, after a fashion. More a mock scream shared between them. He clamped a gooey black hand over her mouth to shush her, and once he had done so, her fate was sealed. She had to go inside to clean herself up also. He unlocked the door.

††

"I thought you were Catholic," she said. They were lying in the nude on his narrow bed, their bodies cleansed and depleted. Their feet entwined.

"I am *so* Catholic."

"Are you going to confess this sin, then?"

"Don't laugh at me."

"I'm not laughing. I just want to know."

"If I have the courage to do so, I will confess this sin."

No other boy in her general field of vision would ever say such a thing.

"So you feel bad about this?"

"That's the trouble." Cinq-Mars sighed. "I don't. I know I should, though."

"So you're troubled? No—don't sigh and moan to yourself, Émile. I'm trying to understand. We took a shower together and made love—you for the first time, I take it? We had a wonderful time. I did. I know you did. Now . . . you're troubled."

He moaned and sighed despite her admonition. "It's ingrained, Anik."

He wasn't going to allow her to just make fun of him. He'd make sure she discovered that she had gone to bed with a serious man, notwithstanding their sport in the tub, soaping the goop out of his hair and from between the cheeks of his derrière. That had embarrassed him so much. She delighted in making him squirm in his private agony.

Or, perhaps, she was finding out, in his private hell.

"The world is moving on," she pointed out to him.

"Does that mean the universe is, too? The world has never been known for its acumen, its spirituality, its commitment to truth, or wonder, or love, or grace. The world's a wretched place. It's murderous, it's deceitful, arrogant and cunning. The world's judgment does not fill me with great faith, Anik."

She didn't have conversations like these with other friends. Certainly not whenever they lolled around together on a bed. With others, she'd be more likely to talk revolution, and the heat of that expectation would lead them to smoke a joint. Cinq-Mars didn't smoke joints.

"You're weird," she analyzed.

"You're pretty," he said.

"Ah, but does being pretty make me wicked? Have I not seduced a man of God? Therefore, I'm a sinful creature. Bound for hell on a freight."

"That's you, all right."

She poked him in the ribs.

"I'm not passing judgment. What do I know? I'm just happy to be with you. Some things are ingrained, though. I can't pretend they don't affect me."

"But you're willing to grapple with them?"

"Apparently, I'm willing to grapple with you."

"Yeah. Then moan and sigh about it."

"That's about the size of it."

"Speaking about size." She held his penis in her fingers, and he was certain she would say something lewd, so he steeled himself. She moved her lips to his ear. "I'm on the pill. How sinful is that for you?"

He was mortified. He just didn't know how to express it. Anik anticipated his dilemma and, still kneading him as he was rising in her hand again, kissed him.

†††

"This," Émile Cinq-Mars told his new girlfriend, "is the case I'm working on."

"Impressive file. Big," Anik Clément noted.

The pages had been three-hole punched and gathered in a black binder.

"It's the history of the Cartier Dagger—"

"What?" Anik was astounded, frightened, amazed.

"The dagger—" he began.

"—that killed my father," she said. She was perplexed. "You're investigating my father's murder? Why you?"

"I'm not the only one. Captain Touton is bringing me onto the case so that the investigation will not end with his retirement. He wants the hunt for your father's killers to carry on from one generation to the next. Continue on after that even, if necessary. But if Touton doesn't bring the culprits to justice, then I will."

She remained astonished. She had been struck by Touton's faithfulness to the case previously, although always doubtful, lacking full confidence in any official. That his ardour extended beyond his life on the police force did stun her.

"So this file—this is the whole case so far?"

"No. I'm starting with the history of the dagger. I need to know it, backwards and forwards. It's a place for me to begin—my entry point, let's say."

They were less naked. Cinq-Mars had donned underwear and an undershirt, having packed his suit and his other soiled clothes into a garbage bag for disposal. Anik had put on her underwear, but also wore one of Émile's large T-shirts, which hung low on her thighs. They had slept, and woken up timid with one another despite the passion they'd known hours earlier. After showering again, separately this time, they had partially dressed. Then returned to the narrow bed.

"The history of the Cartier Dagger."

"The history," he said.

"A bunch of things I know, but not enough to fill the pages of this file."

Cinq-Mars flipped through the binder and detailed salient points of what was known or surmised of its early history. He highlighted the dagger's movements, as far as researchers had been able to determine.

"It's been an adventure. I can't forget that the dagger was last seen—that it was used to kill your father. A story I like is how the knife came into the hands of the Sun Life Assurance Company."

"Tell me."

He lay on his stomach and went to the pages that gave him the story's chronology. Anik slid over, onto his back, her weight on her knees and sometimes on a hand or an elbow, and on top of him she felt as light as a feather, for he was so large, she so small, and she loved the farmboy strength of him, those massive shoulders. She even adored the immensity of his nose, and had bitten it already and teased him about its prominence.

She hadn't known Sarah Hanson's story, and was interested to hear it, about how the Mohawks had handed the dagger to the Sulpicians, who made a gift of the relic to the brave, wise young woman living by the Ottawa River. She had later deployed the relic to make an impression on the governor of New France, to try to influence him to prevent the army, and the populace, from eating horses, a lobbying effort that had so rudely been rebuffed.

"He threatened to hang her? Jesus."

"Then the history of the dagger takes an odd turn," Cinq-Mars noted. "Not its first strange twist, I'll admit, and not its first tenure of neglect either. But it stayed in the Hanson family for a couple of generations, and they stayed in the same house by the river. The known value of the heirloom decreased with Sarah's death. Apparently, a family member had it appraised, as he was interested in cashing in on the diamonds and the gold, but the appraiser assayed the diamonds as being quartz and the yellow nubs as fool's gold. Not true, and no assayer could possibly reach that conclusion, so it's my guess that the man was either incompetent, which I think is unlikely, or he was really planning to rob a backwoods farmer who might not have a clue."

"You're a cop, so you figure people to be thieves," she whispered in his ear.

"Am I that jaded already? I'm only a *rookie* cop. Come back and see me in a few years."

"I might."

They kissed awhile to commemorate that thought.

"Anyway, instead of buying the relic cheap, which is what I presume the jeweller was hoping to do, he lost out on it entirely. The family chose not to sell it at all, but to keep it as a family heirloom, since it was only a worthless piece of junk."

"Gotcha," Anik said, and kissed him again. "Then what?"

"It gets interesting. The English were dying of starvation in the Lake District."

"Oh, the poor fucking English," Anik piped up.

"Hey. That's not nice. They were dying."

"Yeah, right. Anyway, I've got nothing against dead Englishmen."

"And Englishwomen. And English children."

"Easy. I'm only teasing. Sort of."

Cinq-Mars shifted and bucked her off him. He pinned her under him and kissed her, ceasing only when he discovered that she was poking him in the back.

"The story," she insisted. He'd forgotten for a moment that she had a vested interest in the Cartier Dagger.

He readjusted himself and perused the papers. "Okay. So . . . the English were arriving in Montreal half-dead. To make a long story short, the bishop of Montreal gave them land by present-day Lake of Two Mountains, which is a widening of the Ottawa River. That's where Sarah Hanson lived."

"Why there?"

"Mainly because no parish church existed anywhere around, and because of that, no French would settle in the area."

"Makes sense."

"In a nineteenth-century kind of way, yeah."

"Then what?"

Was she in love? she wondered. Had this happened to her? Had she hooked up with the most unlikely of men—a cop, a practising Catholic, a moralist, a federalist politically—who was not only the most unlikely of men but the worst sort of man for her? His profession seemed almost to belie her family history. Her father had been a crook, a tough guy, a goon at times, although none of those descriptions suited her memory of the man. She preferred to think of him as a former hockey player who had gone to prison to cover her mom's union activity. He had been a beautiful and loving and attentive dad— she still remembered that. No matter how she pictured him, though, goon or daddy, he was not a cop, and he had had a difficult time with cops. On the other hand, she knew that her dad had formed a friendship of sorts with Armand Touton, so perhaps he'd understand, if he were here now, that she was drawing close to this policeman.

And papa, she thought to herself, *he's on your case. He'll catch your killers.*

"The Church had no means to distribute land to the English. So the bishop made a deal with the Sun Life Assurance Company, and here things get interesting, historically speaking."

They had to shift around a bit more. Anik supported her head in one hand with her elbow on the bed, while her boyfriend lay on his back and looked up at the ceiling. She loved the intensity in his eyes, the way he'd absorbed the tales of their history and made them so much a part of his mindset.

"An Englishman, if he wanted land, had to approach Sun Life Assurance on bended knee, and after a lifetime of paying insurance premiums, he might expect a payout for his heirs. A Frenchman had to beg the Church for land, and commit to a lifetime of piety that might get him into heaven. So the cultural divide between the English and French was written in stone."

He might be a cop, she was telling her dad, *but he's not like any kind of cop you ever knew.*

"That still doesn't tell me what happened to the dagger," Anik pointed out.

"The English put in farms along the Ottawa, across the river from Mohawks and Sulpicians. On their side of the river, Sarah Hanson's descendants would be their only pre-existing neighbours. One day, the Sun Life representative came out to visit the landowners, to collect their signatures on policies with his company."

Anik was getting this, nodding. "Sun Life grants them land, then *suggests*, shall we say, that they sign up for life insurance. What the company gives the company takes back."

"Exactly. If a man looks over his brood of sons and wonders where they will go when they're grown, well, he realizes he had better be on the good side of the Sun Life. Every farmer took out a policy. Then the agent, riding home on his buggy, stopped by the Hanson-Sabourin family farm."

"Don't tell me."

Émile kissed her first. He told himself to kiss her without regret, without shame. He was a Catholic, but their lovemaking was done for the day—that sin was behind him. He would have to deal with it later before his maker and his priest. Or perhaps he'd confess in some out-of-the-way parish where nobody knew him. But this kiss would be delivered with the fullness of his love and desire for her, and his clammy doubts and sticky second thoughts would be set aside like his suit of oil and grime. For this kiss, he would give wholly of himself, and he did.

"The agent," he whispered, not stopping kissing her yet, "was the kind of salesman who's a manipulator of human fears. He sold the family on the need for a policy, exactly like the ones their neighbours were acquiring." His mouth moved up and down her neck. "If they didn't take one out, their offspring would be poor when they died, he said, while all around them the offspring of the new arrivals would be made rich by life insurance."

Anik was becoming as interested in the tale as she was with the fluctuations of his lips, and gently eased him away from her a few inches.

"The Hanson-Sabourin family agreed to take out a policy. But they didn't have money to pay for the luxury. A member of the Sabourin-Hanson family brought out the Cartier Dagger and offered it in trade. The agent made a big scene about how he was being generous, but really he knew that he was robbing the family blind. He signed the policy and absconded with the knife. Sun Life had its most cherished possession. Some say it's why the company became so powerful. After the Second World War, the artifact was loaned to the National Hockey League to commemorate the work its president had contributed at Nuremberg, and the league became all-powerful throughout Canada. Some say that's why—because it possessed the knife. So, the question crops up: who owns it now?"

Anik lay back, prone beside him on the bed, gazing at the ceiling. After a minute, she said, "I know who."

"You do?" Cinq-Mars propped himself up.

"Trudeau."

"That's the rumour. But there's no reason to believe it. Just because he's become so powerful—"

"It's not a rumour." She faced him on her side. "I was in a closet when Camillien Houde said his final confession to his priest. I heard it then. Trudeau bought the knife."

He examined her eyes for any trace of doubt or fabrication. "Then help me with this case."

She nodded, then switched and shook her head. "I don't know everything."

"Is that why you're a separatist—because Trudeau has the relic?"

"Don't be silly. But it's why I threw the first stone at him that night. It's why I regret missing."

They did not kiss again on the bed, yet remained facing one another. Cinq-Mars was disturbed—by his love for her, and by a new surge of eroticism that undercut his moral code. He figured he'd have to marry her. He was also troubled by being a policeman who had just discovered a treasure trove of information. Where did his allegiance lie—with the girl, or with his work?

Anik also wondered what he'd do. Love her, or love his investigation more? She had put him on the spot. He'd have a hard time figuring this one out. In the meantime, facing each other, gazing into the other's eyes and longing to determine a place for themselves in the midst of their anarchic world, they'd wait and see. They were both aware that love and passion were involved, but so were certain intellectual convictions. That emotional tempest—electric, it felt, scintillating, inviting—sang between them.

BOOK THREE

CHAPTER 18

1937

SHE KNEW EXACTLY WHAT THIS MEANT. ON THE TWENTY-FOURTH OF March, 1937, a day that turned her life "upside-down, inside-out and backwards, then way inside-out again," Carole Bonsecours arrived home to discover that her front door had been shackled shut. A small pane in the door's window was smashed. A heavy chain ran through it, and out a side window that had been left open a crack for fresh air. A padlock secured the links. Carole wanted to remain strong, but disbelief and torment got the better of her. In a full-blown rage, she kicked the door.

Then slumped down on her stoop.

This was real despair. She wept.

The premier, Duplessis, was cracking down on all those who offended him. Supported by the Church preaching against the red menace, he brought in the Padlock Law. Any communist or unionist, any Jew who might easily be presumed to be a communist or unionist, any unkind journalist or unfortunate jaywalker who also happened to be an immigrant and so was probably a communist sympathizer, a unionist or secretly a Jew, no matter whether he claimed otherwise, could arrive home to discover that he'd been permanently locked out of his house.

The law was now being applied to the woman who possessed the temerity to organize seamstresses, to poor Carole.

She noticed, recovering from her futile tears, that the men responsible for the sabotage were still standing around nearby and enjoying a smoke. A pair of them had had a good laugh as she kicked her house. They weren't even policemen—mere thugs. That galled her. The small, wiry woman did what her instincts and courage demanded. She attacked.

"*Whoa!*" one man cried out, laughing, as she flailed away. The more pathetic her assault, the more angry she became, and she redoubled her efforts. He'd skip away like a prizefighter on the run and easily fended off her blows.

She wanted him to stop laughing. She whacked his arms and shoulders and reared back and tried to punch him in the nose, but these more serious attempts also went for naught. She lost her balance once, and he caught her and propped her up. She was so frustrated that the fight of her life had to be entirely under his control. If only she were a boy, or a very large man. If only she had a gun, she'd kill him.

She was crying, and she didn't know for sure, but perhaps she was hysterical. He had quit laughing, and now was trying to calm her down. So she stopped her useless flailing and screamed bloody murder instead.

"This is my *house!* You can't lock me out of my own house. Who do you think you are, you *punk*?"

The others behaved more badly, taunting her. At least this guy wanted her to calm down and spoke with basic human kindness.

But she couldn't calm down.

"My father, you *goat,* left my mother this house when he died. I took care of this house since I was sixteen. My sick mother, she died—you *asshole*—in this house. Don't tell me you got any right locking me out of my own house."

All of it welled up. The hard life. Her father's tragic death. Her mother's long, sordid, crushing illness. The job that kept her exhausted and penniless, and the endless crusade to improve working conditions for women, which she could never cease because it had become her lifeline, kept her alive. That cause embodied the last dregs of her hope.

"You got no fucking right to do this."

What had allowed her to persevere without succumbing had been ownership of this small, sad, sagging house. Through that gift by her father, and thanks to his life insurance policy, she had enjoyed a half-decent place to live, one that cost her next to nothing to maintain. The house gave her dignity, an advantage that other women in the rag trade could only envy.

"Give me the fucking key, you bastard. I want the key."

Even the snakiest man was feeling less inclined to continue tormenting her. Neighbours were appearing on the sidewalk, including a few burly guys, and everybody knew that men could muster a wild ardour in a woman's defence. If a few more showed up, the situation could worsen. The thugs now felt that their friend was doing the wise thing by trying to calm her down.

"Tough guy! Tough *shit*! So you can lock a woman out of her home, huh? Makes you feel big? Hardens you up? Like you got more than a hose between your legs? What did I ever do to you? You don't even know me."

One of the men, perhaps thinking that he was helping the situation, said something. All anyone heard was the word "communist."

Carole Bonsecours turned on him with her venom throttled up. "You little pipsqueak shit. You think I'm a communist? Well, am I? Am I? Take a good look. Is this what you're so afraid of? I'm half your size. You could snap my neck like a chicken's, it wouldn't be no different. Is this what you're so afraid of? Is this why you wet your bed at night, praying to the Lord to keep you from being swallowed up by the big red monster? If I'm a communist, then I'm the one you're so afraid of. I'm *it*. I'm the *beast*. So take a good look. Now tell me, what exactly are you so afraid of?"

She had a point, and the people gathering on the sidewalk nodded and murmured amongst themselves.

She spun back towards the first man she'd attacked and aimed a forefinger at him. "I work as a seamstress. That's all I do. I sew. We're trying to organize. The International Garment Workers' Union will not be intimidated by these tactics." She swept her eyes across the people in the streets, who were suddenly applauding her tirade, then her sights settled back on the first man again. "Look at my hands. *Look at them!* These are the hands of a seamstress. If I want to make an extra nickel an hour, why do you want to stop me? You stupid fat thug."

"I'm not fat," the man interjected.

A few people chuckled. Everyone could see Carole's bile, already cranked to the limit, rise. She kept her palms raised. "So you admit it. You're a *stupid* thug."

The man shrugged. "I'm a hockey player. Played for the Blackhawks. Before I got hurt."

"He got cut," one of the other men said.

"You got cut. Now you've got nothing better to do than visit a seamstress and lock her out of her house because she wants to organize the impoverished women in her trade." She put her hands on her hips. "Well, you're no fucking player anymore, are you? You're just a stupid, *stupid* thug who some day will be *fat*."

He didn't say anything, although he made a gesture with his head that Carole did not comprehend. She turned to see what the other men were doing. They were getting into their cars and leaving.

"Go. Scram. Home to your nightmares about *communists*. Piss your pants, why don't you? You can't do anything else with your little weenies. Maybe the commies will lock you out of *your* house someday, then we'll see how *you* like it. *Hey!* If that day comes, I hope they melt the keys."

Two cars pulled away from the curb. Carole kicked at the fender of one. She shook a fist at her tormentors, and realized then that the other man, the one she'd been berating all this time, had remained behind.

For a split second, she wondered if she should not be terribly afraid, and then, inexplicably, she didn't think so.

"Let's go for a short walk," the man said. "I want to talk to you."

"Fuck you."

"Take a short walk."

"What for?"

"So we can talk about your problem. I got a solution. I'm carrying it with me."

"Talk about it right here."

"I can't do that, ma'am."

"Why not?" Her question was less contemptuous than she had wanted it to be, more curious than she wished to admit.

"Because I'm standing out here in a public place with everybody watching. I can't help you in a public place. Understand something, all right? I got a job to do here. It's my job. But maybe I can help you in private, you get me?"

She felt swayed. She didn't want to sway. The first rule when accosting an employer or a cop on a picket line: Never let them take you out of public view. Make them answer your questions so that everyone, including the press, hears the response. Yet she felt swayed. This brute of a thug, who wasn't fat and possibly wasn't stupid either, was looking at her with neither contempt nor acrimony.

Anyway, the press wasn't around. "All right," she said.

"All right."

They walked to the end of the block in silence and turned the corner. Now she was growing more interested, because he hadn't said a word.

"If you're going to kill me," she said, "tell me first, all right?"

"Why?" he asked.

"I don't pray much. I guess I could learn in a hurry."

He smiled, and when he looked up, he saw that she was smiling, too.

They had reached the entrance to the lane that ran behind Carole's home. Snow had melted in recent weeks, but the lane didn't receive much sunlight, and it remained two feet deep here.

"Okay," he said, stopping. From his pocket he extracted a key, which he extended to her. "This fits the lock on your back door. Go in and out that way. If you cut through the lock on the front door, somebody—not me, but that won't matter—somebody will put a new one back on. Then they'll lock the back door again as well. So for now, this is the way you can do it."

"Do it?" she asked.

"Get back inside your house, but so my bosses don't know."

She accepted the key.

"Thanks," she said.

"I'm sorry," he said.

"I guess you must be," she said.

"I apologize," he said.

"I heard you the first time," Carole said. "You don't have to go on about it."

"Okay then," he said. "All right."

"What's your name?" she asked him.

"Roger Clément. Yours?"

"Carole. You played for the Blackhawks, you said?"

"Before that, the Rangers. Briefly."

"They're both crummy teams," she pointed out to him.

He shrugged, and hung his head a little. Then looked away.

"I'm sorry you got cut, Roger."

"I got hurt," he blurted out. Then he shrugged again. "Then I got cut."

"That's rough."

"Yeah. I'm sorry. You know. About today."

"Yeah, you said."

"So. I gotta go, I guess."

"I guess you gotta lock up more houses. I gotta go, too. At least I got a place to go to now. Thanks again for that."

"Yeah. That's good. Yeah."

"What?"

"I don't know. Maybe—I was thinking, you know?"

"About what?" She waited. "Yeah? What about?"

"I don't know. Maybe you'd like to go out sometime. You know? I don't know."

"I don't know if you don't."

"I was just asking. We could go out, I mean."

"If I say no, will you lock me out of my house again?"

"I won't—Carole, I won't lock you out of your house no more."

"Okay, then," she said.

"Okay." Then he dared to look her in the eye. "Okay what?" he asked her.

"Okay, I'll go out with you. You mean, like, for a drink?"

"Ah. Yeah, or . . . I've been making some dough for these jobs—I mean, we could go for dinner. If you want, a movie, something like that."

"Wow."

"Wow?"

"Wow. It's been a long time since I've gone out for dinner."

"Yeah? Do you wanna?"

"I guess so. It's too bad it has to be because of these jobs, though. I feel sorry for the other people. Maybe you can help them out, too."

He sighed. "Maybe. I don't know yet. Maybe not."

"Yeah. *Voo!* This is weird. Okay. What the hell. I'll go out to dinner with you."

"That's great."

"Ah—do you carry a gun, Roger?"

"Yeah. Not always. Sometimes, yeah." He lifted one of his big shoulders and let it drop, as though to say that that's what his life was like now. He had put down his hockey stick and picked up a gun.

"Don't, okay?"

"Ah, pardon me?"

"Your gun. When we go out, you and me, don't carry it with you."

"All right," he said. "I won't. I'll do that. I won't carry no gun."

Four months later, on a warm summer afternoon in the parish church just around the corner, Carole Bonsecours and Roger Clément were married.

†††

A weekly luncheon with friends at the Mount Royal Club had been his habit for more than three decades, yet on this occasion Sir Herbert Holt chose to make an unusually flamboyant approach. Slowed by his years, the octogenarian had nonetheless made prodigious progress from his home on Stanley Street in central Montreal to his club, a few blocks west along Sherbrooke. Four soldiers, each with a long rifle slung over his shoulder, protected him. They marched in perfect formation, with Holt shuffling along in the middle. He mounted the forbidding stone stairs, one shaky step at a time, towards the impressive oak door. Once there, he commanded his escorts to stand guard at the entrance, a precipice with a full, clear view of the active street. He promised to have the kitchen prepare a warm bite for each man. Three could form a barricade, he advised, so that the fourth could eat without insulting the vision of members as they, too, chugged up the stairs for lunch or departed. In this way they could then take turns until each man had enjoyed an elegant sufficiency.

The foot soldiers thanked him.

Then the richest, most powerful man in Canada entered his club.

As it happened, a luncheon companion, Sir Edward Beatty, had been approaching from the east in time to witness his friend's arrival, as had Sir Charles Gordon, puffing along about a block behind Sir Herbert. Sir Edward had to stall only a half-minute at the foot of the stairs for Sir Charles to join him, and the two climbed up together, arm in arm for their mutual stability. Inside, they found Sir Herbert at their regular table by the great bay window.

"Let me guess," Sir Edward mused. In his late seventies and considerably less wealthy than Sir Herbert, his position and influence were such that he could rival his friend's power. "You've turned off the electricity on a homicidal maniac."

"He's done it this time," Sir Charles added with a wink. "He's denied heat to the cathedral."

"I've seen it published," Sir Edward continued, "that our friend will turn off the heat on a woman in labour and not lose a moment's rest." A French daily had made expressly that claim.

"But not if she's a proper Englishwoman," Sir Charles countered, as though rising in his friend's defence, but in fact quoting the same derogatory article.

"Right. If she's an Englishwoman, he'll switch off her power and let her freeze," Sir Edward postulated as he pulled back his chair and examined it for dust motes before sitting. "His conscience, however, will cause him to toss and turn for an hour, until he falls into the deep sleep of the damned."

"So the French say." Taking his seat, Sir Charles flashed his serviette to open it fully, then let it glide down upon his amble lap.

"Newspapers may publish what they wish, and the people are free to believe them," Sir Herbert Holt waded in. "I say if a woman cannot pay her electric bill, or her fuel bill, she ought not to be having babies. If she is in labour for perhaps the tenth or fourteenth time, then undoubtedly the Catholic Church put her up to it. Therefore, in my opinion, it is not the responsibility of Montreal Light, Heat and Power to comfort her with warmth or electricity. That charity lies at the footstools of the bishops. Let them pay if she cannot."

"You're a hard man, Sir Herbert," Sir Charles stated, "with a calloused heart." As president of the Bank of Montreal, he was known to possess a calloused heart himself. Throughout the Great Depression he had foreclosed on thousands of families. Neither as rich nor as powerful as the other two, he had nonetheless become their most trusted ally.

"I am a businessman, Sir Charles."

"I'll drink to that," Sir Edward responded.

"I'll drink to anything," Sir Charles acknowledged, "if only our bloody drinks would show up. What's keeping our man?"

In their waning years, the men still ruled much of their visible world. Herbert Holt had come to Canada from Ireland, working as a young engineer on the construction of the Canadian Pacific Railway. He had retained the gaunt, fit physique those days had imposed throughout his life. His particular responsibilities had included the prairie and mountain sections of track, a task in which the young man had exulted as a test of his rough-and-readiness. After the railway had been completed, he considered his next venture carefully. He was determined to gain wealth and advancement in the world. Banking soon became his vocation, and following a brief stint with a fledgling institution, he accepted the presidency of the Royal Bank of Canada. From that august pinnacle, he was able to secure executive positions for himself in numerous enterprises, such as Montreal Light, Heat and Power, Montreal Trust, the Sun Life Assurance Company, Ogilvie Flour Mills and the Dominion Textile Company. Montrealers could not get through a day without using his power or eating his food or wearing his clothes, while his influence held lunar sway across four continents. Though he sat on the boards of directors of more than three hundred corporations, when pressed, Sir Herbert could name but a few. Yet employees of these unknown enterprises were in the nasty habit of going out on strike from time to time—lately, more often than he could stomach—and whenever they did, death threats frequently ensued. They accumulated on his desk alongside invitations to balls and fundraising dinners, and as the threats intensified to both a feverish pitch and manic frequency, overwhelming the social obligations, he'd call upon his friends in the military to protect him, hence the armed guard on this occasion.

A dour man, severe in deportment, intimidating in his personal style, in his old age leaner than ever and scraggy behind a white frosting of beard, Sir

Herbert conveyed a puritanical nature and, both in his private and public lives, remained true to that bearing. He stepped away from his self-imposed bounds only for these luncheons, for his companions viewed life differently than a man of his ilk. He had long ago conceded that they had lived more interesting personal lives than his own, and had been rewarded with superior stories to relate. Indeed, in his dotage he had begun to live his life through these outlandish, often roguish, tales. His friends made him laugh, and he enjoyed a good chuckle more now than he'd ever done as a practical, ambitious youth, or as a middle-aged tycoon.

In this instance, the story told about him by Sir Charles held more than a wicked grain of truth, and did not cause him to laugh. Without hesitation, he *would* cut the power to anyone who had failed to pay a bill. Damn the Great Depression, damn the excuses. If the Church exhorted Catholic women to make babies to advance the population of Quebec and secure the political power of the French, then the Church could bloody well render payment for their unpaid bills. If not, the people could live in the dark and freeze in the cold—that was none of his concern. The French, he knew, would dance on his grave, delighted that he was finally wedged underground, and while he had acquired his wealth during an era void of income tax, they'd ignore that he had voluntarily taxed himself, siphoning significant funds to charities. He knew, if no others did, that he paid particular mind to charities that aided those he let freeze.

Business was business, and charity was charity. The two didn't mix.

A different sort, Sir Edward Beatty had been the subject of whispers that his close friends knew to be true. Witness his support of the Shawbridge Boys' Farm and Training School. Sir Edward, president of the Canadian Pacific Railway, built a rail line onto the farm's property. For a pleasurable weekend outing, he'd tuck himself away in his luxurious coach, then have it pulled north to the farm to deposit him on a private siding. There, he'd regale the delinquent boys from the slums with stories meant to encourage a change in their direction. A number of times, Sir Edward selected a young man for a junior position in one of his companies and indicated the sky as the lad's limit. Several successful Montreal businessmen were indebted to him for being rescued from lives of crime and destitution. Although there were whispers.

Sir Edward was one of the wave of Scotsmen to come to Canada, often driven off their lands and shipped overseas against their will, who had prospered in the new land. They uttered a special prayer: "Lord, we do not ask You for money, we only ask that You show us where it is." As had many of his countrymen, Beatty had discovered where money could be found.

He was homosexual, a situation his close friends tolerated. His success as a businessman, his genuine philanthropy and his fiscal acumen allowed them to forgive the idiosyncrasy even while their society did not. He struck a fine figure, for his stewardship included being the chancellor of McGill University and the president of the Royal Victoria Hospital. For someone in his position to be able to speak of an occasional risqué escapade to pals he knew from business was a fond luxury. These days, he had only the memories of dangerous follies with which to entertain his companions, as his health was frail and the aging process less than kind to his libido.

In contrast to the depleted homosexual, Beatty, and the arch puritan, Holt, Sir Charles Gordon remained an active womanizer. He would not own up to what he actually did with the women he'd debauch these days, in hotel rooms that Sir Edward discreetly supplied from his company's chain, but he insisted that he not only had a good time, but so did his partner for the evening. The other two old men merely smiled and shook their heads. In truth, they didn't want to know more, and Sir Herbert felt that he knew rather too much already.

The three knew themselves to be the very last of their breed.

Prime Minister William Lyon Mackenzie King had seen to it, advising the British that they were no longer to bestow titles upon Canadians. As the nation's colonial past was being washed away, those vestiges that persisted were being given a particularly stiff scrub. Each of the three tycoons had been inaugurated into his knighthood prior to the edict, but now, as they passed on, others would not be replacing them at the knight's table—not in this land—and they found no solace in this sad denouement of regal tradition.

Their drinks arrived. They had not been required to fill out a chit—even that wee chore had been done for them—and Sir Charles affixed his signature to the card.

"War," Sir Herbert ruminated, "approaches."

"Bloody row, I should think," Sir Edward acknowledged. "Messy business."

"Opportunity," Sir Charles suggested, "for men of affairs. Grand opportunity."

Sir Edward picked up on the theme. "At war's end, one needs to find oneself well positioned. History has demonstrated exceptionally strong growth."

"Gentlemen," Sir Herbert pointed out to them, "need I remind you—I daresay that I do—that if this bloody thing proves to be of long duration, two years or three, as some say, no one at table will be around to do his part. No one at table will be partaking in the obvious opportunities, either during the war or after, and neither I nor either of you has a snowball's chance in Bermuda of seeing the thing through to any conclusion, be it victory or defeat."

"Oh, victory, surely," Sir Edward piped up, aghast.

"Rather," Sir Charles concurred.

"Victory, then. Even so, you will not live to see it," Sir Herbert intoned.

Sir Charles sipped his gin. "Rather," he agreed, albeit reluctantly.

"I say," Sir Edward said, "jolly good humour today, old chap. Jolly good."

"Not altogether," Sir Herbert agreed. "Do you know why the military permits me an escort, the four stout lads outside? I don't pay for the privilege."

"It's been my observation, Sir Herbert," Sir Charles chuckled, "that you pay for very little in life."

"Not so. The military, you see, is concerned for my safety, as they desire to keep me alive as long as possible—so that I might requisition things, you see."

"What *things*?" Sir Edward inquired, interested. He himself had worried about the combat-readiness of the Canadian forces. They were deemed to be in dire shape, in poor position for war.

"I've agreed to purchase for the air force a squadron of fighter aircraft. Spitfires. They're quite anxious that I live long enough to sign off on the allocation."

Both men were still. No one really had any idea as to the full extent of Sir Herbert's wealth, yet to be seated with a gentleman, an old friend, wealthy enough to purchase a *squadron* of aircraft, momentarily stunned their senses.

"The least I could do," added Sir Herbert, to fill the pause in conversation, "given that I won't be seeing the nasty business through. I presume you are both making your own plans to offer support, ahead of the game. You're unlikely to be of much good if you wait too long."

"That's jolly good of you," Sir Edward noted. He was duly impressed, and agreed that Sir Herbert's tack was the correct one. If death should seize him in his sleep, his heirs were more likely to hoard their benefits than deposit them in the cause of war. "I'd rather like to purchase a tank or two, help the army along."

"I suppose the navy could use assistance," Sir Charles consented, although he didn't want to get into any fundraising competition with these two gentlemen.

"A ship? A frigate—perhaps a destroyer," Sir Herbert suggested.

"Munitions, I was thinking."

"Think harder, Sir Charles. This is a time of war, and as they say, you can't take it with you. It's our legacy at stake. By that, I do not refer to my reputation or to yours, for I'll be remembered as the dastardly chap who turns off the lights at night and the heat in winter. But our society, the companies we have built, the institutions we have seen take shape—all will be forsaken if the war is lost."

"Quite right, quite right," Sir Edward wholeheartedly agreed, and while he did not thump the table, his resolve was not to be denied. "Two tanks it is."

"I think that I should rather like to buy the tanks," Sir Charles suggested, "to leave you free to purchase a frigate. After all, you *are* in the steamship business."

"By Jove, you might have something there. We'll look into that, Sir Charles."

Their first round had been finished and the next arrived, followed by the soup, a French onion. Sir Herbert seemed preoccupied during the course, failing to hear questions asked of him and failing to respond when they were repeated. As the soup bowls were being taken away and they awaited their succulent roast pork, Sir Herbert broached another issue that had been occupying his mind.

"I have in my possession," he began, then corrected himself. "Not altogether in my possession, you understand. I have under the aegis of one of my companies, Sun Life Assurance, a certain relic, a cultural heirloom from a bygone era. I am at a loss as to what to do with the artifact, as I'm told it has significant historical relevance. I've had it appraised, only to discover that it has significant commercial value as well. The item is said to possess near magical powers, for anyone who has held the relic in his or her possession enjoyed prosperity. Some would argue that this did not bode true for that fellow Radisson, who had it, but kept trading it to his in-laws to help him keep his wife. The in-laws did rather well. When he finally took it back, well, his life was over, but at least he got to die in his sleep. An achievement for a man like him. In any case, prosperity came to Sun Life. By extension, it's also true of me. The artifact was acquired by a Sun Life representative in exchange for an insurance policy, paid in full, for which the representative had to endure a scolding by his supervisor for making a questionable deal, until he managed to bring to his attention the diamond-gold handle. Now the item is worth at least as much as a squadron of Spitfires—"

"No!"

"By Jove, the man's good fortune. You ought to pay for lunch on occasion, Sir Herbert."

Sir Herbert looked across at him, unsmiling, without comment.

"What is the relic?" Sir Edward inquired.

"The Cartier Dagger, it's called. Initially acquired by Jacques Cartier himself from Indians right here on the island of Montreal. Legend has it, in any case."

"That would indeed be of rare value."

"Complete with gold and diamonds in the handle, as I say. Stuffed away in a storage box. The company was clearing room for more office space when it was discovered. Good thing a man didn't just walk off with it. I never would have been aware of the loss, yet it would have been grievous."

"Indeed. Good on you, Sir Herbert, to have found such a thing." Sir Charles made a mental note to send employees scrounging through the archives and storage rooms of his companies, to see what treasures might be lurking there.

Sir Herbert explained how the knife had come to be in the hands of Sun Life Assurance, when once it had been held by the Hudson's Bay Company. As he rarely had opportunity to tell such a tale of high adventure, he relished every turn and nuance. He felt at one moment that the Cartier Dagger must indeed possess magic powers, for suddenly he was seen as the storyteller in the group. His friends were all ears, and delighted in the daring ascribed to Sarah Hanson.

"The dagger remained within her household for a few generations, until a dolt of a great-grandson traded it to Sun Life in exchange for an insurance policy. So it's languished with us to this day."

His companions shook their heads, unable to comprehend the extent of this man's luck.

"But what to do? You see my dilemma. It's not the sort of thing you leave to family. A recalcitrant grandson-in-law of mine will be pawning it before I'm fully comfortable in my grave. Shall I donate? But to whom? That's the issue."

Sir Edward, who valued his title, for it secured his station in society at a time when, if it were more known, his homosexuality would mark him as an outcast, suggested that Sir Herbert consider giving the artifact to the British monarchy. "King George plans a visit, raising spirits for the war effort. It would be a gesture."

Sir Herbert rejected the idea out of hand as he bit into his pork. "I am loyal to the Crown. But I am an Irishman by birth and a Canadian by way of my good fortune. I cannot bestow a relic that remains of monumental importance to my adopted land to the Old Country, which is already stuffed with ancient treasure. Besides, the knife has been in the possession of the British monarchy in the past, apparently. Obviously, they gave it up, the silly, inbred dolts."

"Give the knife to Canada, then," Sir Charles advised.

"With that oaf, Mackenzie King, as our prime minister? I'd rather give it to the man who delivers my coal. King would receive the dagger and make himself the centre of the ceremony—use the event to win more votes. No! He's taken away the possibility of knighthood from our younger peers, and the three of us, we'd be lords by now if not for him. For that reason alone, he cannot receive the relic. Canada's loss, but nothing's to be done."

"King," Sir Edward scoffed, "has declared ten times that we will not go to war in defence of any nation. Did you hear his speech? No foreign wars, he says. We all know he's lying. All to win votes in Quebec, the scoundrel."

"Meanwhile," Sir Charles took note, "the air force is collecting promises for fighter aircraft from our friend over here."

"The government is building the military for the defence of Canadian soil," Sir Herbert pronounced. "The military has been given free rein to prepare for our national defence through private resources. It must be done, but it's all such nonsense, half-measures, and it's all that blackguard King's fault. He tells Hitler he'll fight on the side of Britain, that's fine, but tells the people of Quebec he will not fight at all. Hitler takes solace, I tell you. No one else does."

"I have just the ticket," Sir Edward sparkled. "Oh, this is splendid. Place the dagger in trust, to be given at war's end to a great Canadian hero. Why not? If the military wants to raise private funds, they cannot say no to an honour bestowed by private financiers."

Their discussion, then, became quite animated as they debated the merits and demerits of the notion. Sir Charles was concerned that the knife would be won by a foot soldier who'd then return to his life as a fisherman or a woodsman, only to have his wife use the blade to skin fish or hack apart a moose. That wouldn't do. "Bit of a pickle that," Sir Edward agreed. Sir Herbert could not tolerate the thought that a recipient might sell the relic for its exceptional value, something his heirs would surely do, causing the knife to soon appear in the hands of a Swiss banker or "a miner from Bolivia." That wouldn't do, either. He noted that many genuine heroes in battle would have neither the resources to secure the relic from theft, should it be given to one of them, nor be able to manage the insurance premiums.

Yet the idea evolved, and by the time they had finished their succulent pork they had decided that the Cartier Dagger should be held in perpetual trust by Sun Life, or by trustees the company might appoint should the business fail. The relic could then be presented to a suitable Canadian war hero who had become, after the war—this was Sir Edward's contribution—the president or chief executive officer or chief operating officer of a major corporation. The corporation would then hold the knife in trust until the demise of either the hero or the company, whichever came first, when it would be returned to Sun Life, who would then seek another national hero who was also a business executive to receive the knife on loan. "In this way, the so-called magical powers of the ancient dagger will be put to good use, to the benefit of an enterprise. Nobody will use it for whittling."

"Do you know," Sir Herbert enthused, "receiving the knife could become as significant as receiving a knighthood. Or a lordship. The closest thing to it in our land. Nothing Mackenzie King can do about it either, the oaf."

The idea took hold. Sir Herbert Holt and his companions left the Mount Royal Club that day happier than when they had arrived, believing that they had devised a secret legacy for themselves that, apart from tanks and Spitfires and frigates, would allow them to celebrate the victory of their nation in war. Although they'd likely not be alive to join the festivities, they could now gaze out upon the gathering cloud of battle, and upon the larger parade of eternity, with brighter, more expectant, eyes.

"Good roast pork today," Sir Herbert mentioned upon reaching street level.

"Succulent." Sir Charles smacked his lips.

Sir Edward had a sudden thought. "I say, Sir Herbert, we're going your way."

"That's true, we are," Sir Charles concurred.

"Jolly good, then," Sir Herbert offered. "Fall into step. Look lively now."

The three old men shuffled their way east on Sherbrooke Street, enjoying the escort of the four riflemen. They smiled at their friends, waved to those who gazed from windows, feeling that victory was in the air, even that they were somewhat younger again—stalwart lads, heroes returned from the trenches to commandeer their country's devotion.

††††

Only when she went out with him did she realize how lonely she'd allowed herself to become. Only when she laughed with Roger did she understand that her spirit had cracked, that she'd been living on a fortitude nurtured deep within herself. She did not recognize her reflection, not as she had appeared back then and certainly not now, this fresh smile in her eyes, this sudden jittery laughter in the throat. Who is this dame? She recognized only her fierce determination to neither succumb nor die. Now she was seeing someone else—the person she might become, but also, the person she had always meant herself to be. Only when she kissed him did she realize that she was worn, that in another month without him, or a week, or an hour, she'd have been worn right down, forever. Only when he held her in his arms under the rear porch light to her home—because she still could not enter by the front door—did she grasp that her life these days was dangerous, that anyone entering her life submitted to danger. The only man who could love her had had to be a man with big fists and a brave heart, and maybe even a pistol on his hip. Who else could survive her existence?

So he was perfect.

His imperfections made him perfect.

When she guided him into her bed, she didn't let him up. She let him know that she wasn't going to be padlocked under his great bulk. He was astonished by the force of her desire. She told him what to do and how to behave, and he had never heard of a woman like this. He complied until he was unable to do anything other than move with her. She exhausted him first. Later, she let him hold her, drop that heavy arm around her while she slept. Only then did she accept that she now needed and loved this man. If he had ideas in his head she despised, she'd hate those ideas, but she'd still love *him*. She admitted that she had no choice in the matter. If Roger loved her, too, then she'd be free, and count herself as blessed. If he didn't—but she could not imagine that, so would not allow herself to try.

Roger loved her. He said so often. When she teased that all men spoke foolish things to the women sleeping with them, he was nearly apoplectic. He couldn't stand that she might not believe him. She was still only teasing, just kidding around, when she said, "So prove it."

"How?" He'd climb mountains, learn to swim seas, fix her shingles . . . what?

"What's wrong with my shingles?"

"Don't change the subject. How do I prove it?"

"You don't like my roof?"

"Have you taken a look at it lately? What can I do to prove myself?"

"I dunno. Marry me, I guess."

He didn't hesitate for a second. He immediately dropped to one knee and asked her properly. She then tried to talk him out of it, tickled him and laughed him off and told him to be serious and scolded him for being a big, dumb, well-built thug. She put her hands on her hips and stomped a foot and screamed his name, "Roger!" as if trying to call him back from the land of the clinically insane, but he would not be dissuaded. So she said yes.

"Yes?" he asked.

"Yes," she repeated, very quietly, her well of determination surfacing again.

Why not? She had never claimed ownership of her life before. Now she did.

Problems arose that were not typical of most married couples. Roger led a battalion of goons to a picket line, intending to clear the way for thirty female scabs on a bus. The men piled out of their cars with baseball bats and wire cutters to open a hole in the factory fence away from the entrance where the picketers had gathered, when the strikers spotted them and converged. They were all women. The men put their bats down because they weren't willing to use them on women. Then Roger realized that the voice over the bullhorn was speaking directly to him. "Roger Clément! Get away from that fence!"

The goons thought it strange that their leader was being addressed by name, and they looked at the woman, then back at Roger, who said, "Uh-oh."

"Roger! Get away from the fence!"

He walked up to the woman with the megaphone and tried to speak so that he would not be heard by the others. "Carole, what are you doing here?"

She chose to speak through the bullhorn. "What are you doing here?"

"I'm breaking up this strike," he whispered. "I'm leading the scabs inside."

She shouted into the bullhorn, "He says he's breaking up the strike!"

Eighty women shouted back, "*NO!*"

"He says he's leading the scabs inside."

"*NO!*" the women shouted back as one.

"What do you say to that?" Carole asked the throng.

"*NO!*" the women roared back, and circled closer.

She put the bullhorn right up to his face. "Are you going to use those baseball bats on women?" she asked the strikebreaker. "If you do, mine is the first head you'll have to crack, just so you know. Are you going to drive that scab bus over our bodies?"

One of the thugs behind Roger defiantly called back, "If we have to!"

"Because I'll be first to lie down in the road!" Carole called through the horn.

"That's okay with me!" the thug shouted back.

Roger turned around to face him. "She's my wife," he told him.

"What?" he asked. Then he told the others. "She's his wife."

"Carole, come on, what're you doing here? You don't work here."

She lowered the horn to her side. "This is what I do. Defend striking women."

"Well, this is what *I* do. I bust up strikes."

"Not today. Not this strike."

"Yes, today," he argued back. But then he caught himself. "They'll send other guys if I fail."

"Fine. I'll bust their balls, too."

The standoff was short-lived. Roger turned to lead his men away, and they all expected to be going at that point. After all, a man could not beat up his wife in public, not even when it was his *job*.

Carole called, "Hey."

Roger turned to face her again.

She kissed him on the lips.

Then she picked up her bullhorn and shouted, "Go home!"

The women promptly responded to the cue. "*GO HOME!*"

"GO HOME!"

"*GO HOME!*"

Before that rising chorus, the thugs and the scab bus departed. The women beat their fists upon the cars and the bus and cheered as the vehicles vanished down the road. For Carole, the day was a lovely victory.

Roger, on the other hand, had some explaining to do to his bosses.

The couple tried to find Roger a new profession. He tried factory work first. Men were eager to take on the guy with the fists, with the big reputation. He'd come home bleeding and feeling vilified. Nobody wanted the former hockey lug lifting cement bags or picking out the defects on an assembly line. They wanted him to take on challengers during the noon break, or to crack the boss's nuts, or to come along with a bunch of the guys for a drink after work, and after that—*you know how it is*—they wanted him to work over this one guy who owed this other guy money from an unpaid bet that the first guy said he'd never made. They wouldn't leave him alone, and sometimes Roger talked about it to Carole around the kitchen table.

"When I was paid to use my fists, I never had to. I never hit nobody. Almost never. Hardly ever. I just showed up, and maybe I smashed some tables and chairs, or knocked out a window. I damaged the furniture. The worst I did—"

"The worst you did was lock my front door."

"Right. But the next worst thing, this one guy had a toy train set. He had the Rocky Mountains in there and everything. A little postman delivering the mail, and milk trucks. He had bridges and rivers and a complete village, with tiny dogs and women in fancy clothes, everything just right. The train went around in a circle, into a tunnel for a while—it was really neat—then it came back out, blowing its teensy horn. *Toot-toot!* So anyways, I smashed his toy train set, and I think, afterwards, he'd've preferred it if I crushed his skull. Anyways, that was the next worst thing to locking your door. Okay, the occasional bloody nose—nothing big, you understand me? I intimidate, that's the word for it. That's all I do. I never hurt nobody unless a guy was stupid enough to take the first swing."

"Yeah. So? You're not doing that anymore." They were talking by candlelight and she gently caressed the back of his big right hand. His friends said his right hand could knock out a truck.

"I've already beat up six guys from my factory. Look at my knuckles, they're all cut, bloody. Tomorrow, there's two tough guys coming over from the factory *four blocks down* to see if one of them can take me."

Carole sighed. He did have a problem. The good honest life of the workingman just wasn't up to snuff. "You could lose," she suggested. "Then maybe nobody will care about taking you on anymore."

He looked at her as though she'd lost her mind.

"What?" she asked him.

"You don't understand," he pointed out to her. "Losing means I end up half-dead. Or all dead."

She thought about that. Then the reality of his life occurred to her, why he was feeling so badly.

"Roger, do you mean that, when you fight, you—" She didn't want to say it.

"Usually the other guy ends up in the hospital. Sometimes I knock a guy out with just one punch. He's out cold, but at least that way he's not a bloody mess."

Maybe he should go back to being a goon. Life was more peaceful that way.

"I don't like beating up all these guys," he said. "I didn't like it in hockey, I don't like it now."

"Tell you what," she said. Gently, she placed her fingers on his muscled forearm. "Go earn your living whatever way you know how. Something better will come along. For now, I'll stay out of it."

"You have to tell me what picket lines you're on."

"That's a deal."

She didn't like it though when he smashed up politicians' offices.

"Roger. He's the good guy."

"What makes him so good?"

She'd have to explain it.

"Then he should hire me to smash up the other guy's office."

"Roger, sweetie, that's *why* he's the good guy, because he doesn't hire goons."

She was especially unhappy when he disrupted polling booths and frightened voters away.

"Was that necessary?"

"It's my job."

"To destroy democracy? To stand in the way of the people? To not allow working men and women to exercise their right to vote? Roger, that's wrong."

"But they're voting the wrong way."

She'd have to explain it to him. "Even though I prefer that votes go one way and not another, I accept that people have the right to their own choice. That's why we have a vote—so that everybody can decide who wins, not some pack of goons."

"I don't decide who wins."

"Ah, honey, sweetie, actually, you do. You know nothing about politics, nothing about the issues, nothing about the politicians involved, yet you, sweetie, you and your two big fists and all your ballot-stuffing friends, you decide who wins. Now, do you think that's right?"

He didn't know if it was right, but he thought better of himself somehow.

"No, sweetie, that's not the point."

"Anyways, what's so wrong with ballot stuffing? Nobody gets hurt and we get the right result."

That's when she realized that he was teasing her, and she smacked him on the bicep, then held her sore hand and winced. By the end of the discussion, as they did after so many others, they took one another to bed and enjoyed all that, too.

CHAPTER 19

1968

A S A YOUNG BUCK DEMOBILIZED FROM THE ARMY AND INTENT ON becoming a cop, Armand Touton had tangled with a corrupt physician. He believed, twenty years on, that rather than invent varicose veins, the man should have displayed X-rays of his war wounds. He'd have paid the charlatan's price back then, signed a blank cheque. Today he'd forfeit his pension to any quack offering a night's relief.

Due to the pain, the end of his career was approaching prematurely.

Along the floor at the back of his desk, stacks of old reports formed a staunch barrier. No one could peer below the modesty skirt where he'd positioned worn-out seat cushions—flattened by time and the rotund posteriors of cops—on crates at various heights. Gingerly, he transferred his right foot from one level to another to ease his general discomfort, later bringing it back to the rung of a chair while elevating his left foot to enjoy, for minutes at a time, the pleasure of a fresh setting.

Opposite him, Detective Fleury from Policy knew what the boss was doing, but never let on as the captain scrunched down to raise a foot higher or stretch it forward. Officer Cinq-Mars, sitting up straight in the chair on Fleury's right flank, could not comprehend his superior officer's bizarre posture. He seemed to be slumping down as any drunk might do who'd surpassed his upper limit, and having detected the scent of whiskey in the room, the young cop privately scorned the officer he otherwise so admired.

Fleury took the whiskey to be medicinal.

"If I hear you right," Touton summarized, sliding lower, "you want to march up to Parliament Hill, strut into the prime minister's office and take a seat—maybe straighten your tie, comb your hair, make yourself look present-able—then you want my permission to accuse the PM of being in possession of a murder weapon—"

"Sir—" Constable Émile Cinq-Mars endeavoured to interrupt, cut short by a hand rising from the captain's half-prone body.

The man yawned before speaking again. "—because you had an anony-mous 'tip,' you were saying, from a left-wing radical—"

"I didn't say—" Cinq-Mars began, only to be prevented from speaking further by that authoritative hand.

"—who got her information from a dead man and a priest sworn to secrecy. Oh, that'll go over well on the witness stand. You'll be up on charges for slander and false arrest—they'll have a field day, those government lawyers. Turn the courthouse into a carnival. Know what? I'll sell candy floss on the front steps, make my fortune that way."

Cinq-Mars allowed the captain's perspective on the situation to float in the room awhile, coming to rest upon his shoulders as sadly as grey city dust.

"You can answer now," Fleury advised him.

The constable shifted nervously while trying to get his emotions in check. He didn't want to burst out, all steam and bluster, although he could feel the heat rising inside him. "First," he declared, "I wasn't planning to march up there and I'm not the kind of person who struts."

"Now he's in a pique," Fleury noted.

"Second," Cinq-Mars pressed on, "I don't intend to issue accusations. I'll introduce the subject to the prime minister, listen to what he has to say. Third—"

"Third!" Touton was enjoying the officer's defence.

"—I never said 'left-wing radical'—"

"That's true, you didn't," the captain acknowledged, still with that damned sparkle in his eye. "But she is, isn't she?"

"And fourth—"

"Four already, how high is he going?" Fleury asked. Touton winked at him.

"I never indicated to you that my informant is female."

"Ah!" The ranking officer took time to make another adjustment. "You see my dilemma, though. I need to visualize your informant—it helps me to remember things as I get older. I make her out to be twenty-two, pretty, short brown hair, a cute nose and bright eyes, also brown. I imagine her as a left-wing radical. Maybe her mom's a union agitator? Why deny my mental picture, when it's so clear?"

The young cop recognized that he was growing dangerously annoyed, that he had to watch himself. "Picture him as male, sir. Forty-eight, let's say. Give him a beer belly and bad breath. Snaky eyes. We might as well honour him with a name. Let's call him . . . Alphonse, how's that?"

Touton smacked his lips and rocked his head around skeptically. Wishing to take a slug of whiskey, he knew he ought to hold off, bear another night determined to be rough.

"I got a problem with that," he said.

"I got my own problem with it," contended Fleury.

Cinq-Mars muttered under his breath, "You would."

"You got something against this Alphonse jerk with the stinky armpits?" the captain asked.

"I didn't . . . discuss . . . his armpits," Cinq-Mars rebelled.

Fleury clamped his hands together and leaned forward. "It's obvious to me, sir, from the kind of information the kid's been getting, that he's sleeping with his informant."

"There it is," Touton agreed. "The nail on the head. That's why I have a hard time picturing your ugly slob with the beer breath and the smelly feet, this Alphonse. Are you telling me you're *that way*? Because I'm not your Father Confessor here, my son. About things like that, I want to know nothing."

They had him again.

"That's not what I'm saying, just like I never mentioned smelly feet. But nobody says I'm sleeping with her—him—*whoever*!"

"How do you acquire information of that nature? Gaston, do you know how?"

The diminutive accountant offered a thought. "Maybe we could refer to the boy's informant as an animal. A critter from the barnyard. He comes from a farm. How about it, Cinq-Mars? Are you screwing a pig?"

Fleury had gone too far. The uniform was on his feet, ready to smack him around.

"Hey-hey-hey-*hey*!" Touton called out, progressively raising his voice until Cinq-Mars stopped short. "Kid, sit down. Detective Fleury is going to apologize to you for that remark."

He sat back down, and Fleury said, "It's good you defend your girlfriend's honour. I apologize for any insult. I take it back."

Thinking he could keep Anik out of the discussion had been foolish. "Apology accepted," he muttered, although overall, he was feeling miserable.

"Kid," confided the captain of the Night Patrol as he struggled up to a common posture, "here's the point. Whoever your informant is—man, woman or critter—she smells nice, I bet. Can we agree on that? The stinky feet are out. The smelly armpits, we won't mention them again. Are we agreed on that?"

Grudgingly, Émile nodded his consent.

"She smells nice?"

"She smells nice," Cinq-Mars mumbled.

"Good. Now, this is what bothers me. You think the prime minister of Canada has something to say to you about stolen property. You've got an idea in your head that if you go up there, strutting or not—although I don't know what's so wrong about strutting—"

"Me neither," Fleury interjected.

"—you seem to think that when you go up there for a conversation, Trudeau will say, 'Officer, you're right. It'll ruin my career, cost me an election, I might get jail time, but it's been on my conscience. Tonight, I'll go on television to tell the nation I'm in possession of the Cartier Dagger. I'll beg the people to forgive my damned eternal soul.'"

This time, Cinq-Mars was the one to shift around in his chair.

"You don't like it that I quote the prime minister?" Touton asked.

"I don't expect him to confess," Cinq-Mars conceded.

"Good to hear. What do you expect?"

"I'm not sure . . . I . . ."

They waited, but he had nothing to add.

"Maybe you expect him to be careless with the knife after your conversation?" Touton pushed himself up to press his advantage. "He'll carve the Christmas goose with it, show it off to his best friends. Or maybe he'll let the media into the prime minister's residence to film him *strutting* around with the knife between his teeth?" He took a deep breath and noticed the effect of his words on his protégé. "You're grimacing, but obviously you don't expect he'll hide it more deeply. You don't think—" Touton winced as he shifted his hips. "—that he might worry his career's at stake? You don't imagine he'll sell it on the black market for what you or me make in fifty lifetimes? Because if you expect that, why would you propose this tactic?"

When he considered what he had been expecting, Cinq-Mars accepted that it had probably been as ludicrous: he wanted to defend Anik's honour. He'd been told who possessed the knife that killed her father, and wanted to let that man know he was on the case. In a sense, he anticipated no further benefit than a chance to rattle the man who owned the relic, unnerve him a little. He now grasped that that would be an ineffectual exercise. Counterproductive, perhaps. He also realized, to his dismay, that he had not told the men in the room anything they hadn't already known, or at least postulated. Perhaps he was confirming a rumour, but that confirmation had not advanced the investigation. A dead witness—Houde, the old mayor—and a close-mouthed priest did not open up avenues of exploration. For now, a prime minister with a secret could keep it.

Nodding, Cinq-Mars and Touton made eye contact. Both men gathered that the other's awareness was up to speed.

Yet, as Cinq-Mars stood to leave, Touton asked the young man to stay put.

"This is what we'll do with your information," the captain suggested. "Alerting the most popular prime minister in history that we might know about his alleged secret possession does us no good. About the dead mayor, what can I say? He's dead. I doubt that he'll have much to say if we dig him up. So let's take a closer look at the priest."

"The priest?" Even Fleury was surprised.

"Father François is Anik's mother's priest. He's Anik's priest. He was Camillien Houde's priest. He was a member of that *Cité Libre* crowd back in the fifties, which included . . . ?"

"Pierre Trudeau," Fleury caught on, finishing the other man's conjecture.

"Kid, something in the way you worded it," Touton noted. "You said your informant, the one who smells nice, told you the priest *comforted* the old mayor at the hour of his death. He told Houde that the transaction had been accomplished. This was not a priest listening to a confession, but a man involved in a conspiracy."

Cinq-Mars chewed that over. "I found it curious. But my informant—" He exchanged a glance with Fleury. "—feels that the priest was conveying information, that he wasn't personally involved."

"Conveying information *is* involvement, Cinq-Mars. Who'd he been talking to? What did he know? Was he picking up his facts from deathbed confessions? I doubt it. Besides," he concluded, "I've never liked him. Call me old-fashioned, but he's political. Not like a real priest."

"I'll get on it," Fleury stated.

"Let the young guy do the legwork," Touton instructed, which clearly disappointed Fleury. As usual, he was anxious to slip out from behind his desk and his usual job assessing budgets. "He knows about priests. But he reports to you." Opening a lower drawer, Touton fished around inside, then pulled out a bottle of rye. "Now, scram," he told them. "Some of us have work to do."

In the corridor, Fleury turned to his new charge. "What's this about you and priests?"

"I don't know how he knows."

"He knows everything," the detective declared. Cinq-Mars raised his eyebrows in doubt. "Now tell *me* what I don't know."

With a slight and self-conscious cock of his head, the young cop admitted, "I considered the priesthood. It's what my father wanted. I got interested. But I don't know how he knows. I've kept that to myself around here. I thought I had, anyway."

Fleury shrugged. "Do you think he'd let you on our team without checking you out? He probably knows your shoe size, the colour of your mother's eyes, the names engraved on your great-uncle's tombstone back in France."

"No," Cinq-Mars said. He'd had enough games from this guy for one night.

"If I exaggerate, sue me. But we're going against the flow, Cinq-Mars. What's the one thing that you've got going for yourself that you haven't figured out yet?"

He was expecting another dig.

"You're not from around here," Fleury told him. "You're a small-town boy. Half-farmer. As it turns out, half-priest. That's significant. It's possible to believe that you haven't been corrupted. It's possible to imagine that you don't have some dead uncle's sister's boyfriend's cousin's dad who'll put the squeeze on you to protect the family name. You think we're going after the prime minister on this one? That that's tough? Maybe dig up the dirt on a few dead politicians? We could be going against the *people*—at least more than we care to count. We may be up against a few outstanding mythologies—are you following me on this? Do you have the brains? The balls? We might be setting ourselves up to provoke the grievances of an entire population, not just some big-shot next door or the guy up on Parliament Hill."

Émile had to believe that his new boss was not putting him on this time.

"Not only did he check you out, Cinq-Mars, he put his faith in you. I would say his hope, too. He started with his faith in you, then checked you out. So far, you've passed muster."

"Sounds contradictory," Cinq-Mars noted. "Having faith in me, then checking me out."

"Fuck you. Do you hear me, smart-ass? Fuck you. I saw you in there, the look in your eyes when he pulled out that bottle—"

Cinq-Mars pulled the identical expression a second time, barely disguising his judgmental condemnation, his head and eyes rolling back.

"Hey. If he needs a shot to pull him through—*hey!*"

Cinq-Mars had begun to turn away completely. He rotated to face Fleury again. "Look, you're my superior officer, but you don't need to apologize for him and I don't need to listen to this."

"Maybe you do. That man in there, in the Second World War—"

"Everybody has an excuse." He tried to walk away again, but Fleury caught his arm and came close, under his chin, speaking in a harsh, whispery voice.

"Wounded. Captured. Seventeen days with minimal medical attention. Force-marched. Operated on with no anaesthetic by a French doctor employed by the Germans. After the operation, during which Armand did not cry out— maybe he moaned a little, but he did not cry out—the doctor told him he was the bravest, strongest man he'd ever met, and shook his hand. Years later, he was force-marched back to Germany in the *winter . . .* in the *snow . . .* in *frigid temperatures—with no shoes.* Now, if he needs a shot today to handle the pain after being cut up by that doctor in butcher-like conditions, then you'd better hurry up and respect him for what he's going through. You would've cried out, Cinq-Mars. You would've bawled like a baby. Any man would've. *Every* other man did. On that march, you would've curled up by the roadside, gone to sleep and died. Like so many did. That man in there did not. So if you want to pull a face because he's having a drink, be prepared to fight me outside, because that'll happen sooner rather than later."

Cinq-Mars was looking at a man who had to be sixty to seventy pounds lighter than him and eight to ten inches shorter. A man with a desk job who had never done a day's work on a farm in his life, and if he'd tried, he would not have survived. Any skirmish outside would be brief and one-sided, the younger man knew. Yet, graciously, he backed down.

"That won't be necessary," he told him. He was thinking he might have made it through that long winter's march, although he was grateful for never having been tested that way. Fleury, he imagined, would never have seen the first dawn, but of these things, who really knew?

The older detective from Policy continued to glare at him. Then he issued a fractional smile, an admission, as if to say, "Thank God for that," and walked off.

He was nearing the end of the corridor, about to turn the corner towards his office, when Cinq-Mars called after him. "Sir? What should I do now?"

Without looking back, the smaller man commanded, "Follow me."

So he did.

††††

Travelling up and over the eastern flank of Mount Royal on Park Avenue, Touton was driving through a light rain into breaking sunlight.

Parkland graced the rising slope to his left. Lower to his right, fields for baseball and football occupied a flat plateau, then yielded to congested communities that eventually, way in the distance, gave way to industrial territory dominated by oil refineries and rolling stock.

To be driving in daylight, to be able to see a distance, felt good to the captain of the Night Patrol. He had an appointment. This time, Dr. Camille Laurin had declined to meet him in a public setting. Touton would sit in his waiting room like a manic-depressive hoping for entry, a kind word and a prescription. He'd have to loaf around before hearing his name called.

"Captain," Laurin spoke from the doorway to his office, a privilege he did not extend to other clients who would normally be admitted by an assistant.

Touton endured a painful push up to his feet and limped into the man's untidy chamber.

"Good to see you, sir." Laurin shook his hand, then seated himself and indicated that Touton should do the same. Between them, files in folders of various pastel hues were stacked in squat, leaning towers on his desk. "How've you been these days?" the doctor inquired.

"Like the rest of us, a little older."

"How do you live, sir, seeing the sun only on weekends?"

"Weekends I work. Mondays, Tuesdays, those are my days off to catch a glimpse of light. But I'm not someone who feels any need for a tan."

Cigarette in one hand, eyeglasses dangling in the other, Laurin indicated by the ensuing silence that the time had come to conclude their pleasantries, bear whatever point the cop had journeyed here to make. The day was a Tuesday, so he had now been informed that he was seeing the officer on the man's day off, which troubled him. The doctor flicked his cigarette over a heavy glass ashtray filled with butts, then brought the smoke to his lips. Inhaled deeply. He squinted at his guest.

"Cancer sticks," Touton pointed out. "Nails in the coffin."

Laurin shrugged.

"I'll come to the point."

Laurin stared back, waiting.

"The case continues."

"Case?" Laurin asked.

"The death of Roger Clément. The killing of a coroner. The murder of Michel Vimont, on occasion a driver for the old mayor, Houde. The rest of the time, he drove for a racketeer named Harry Montford. Did you know him?"

He inhaled. "Why would I know a racketeer?"

"You knew Mayor Houde."

"Of course."

"Did you know Harry Montford?"

And exhaled. "I just said—"

"You answered my question with one of your own. I don't know why you'd know Montford, sir. You didn't move in the same circles. He was a mobster. You're a psychiatrist. He was English—we could draw the conclusion that the two of you never met. But I must ask the question. Humour me. Did you know him?"

Laurin shrugged, reluctantly acceding to the protocol. "Was he famous? The name rings a bell. But did I know him? Not to my knowledge, although I meet so many people, including English people."

"Including racketeers?"

That query provoked an honest grin from the doctor. "Not to my knowledge."

"You see, after Mayor Houde was ousted he didn't have a chauffeur—he didn't have a car. Sometimes Vimont would chauffeur him around in Montford's car. I guess Montford owed him a favour or two, from the old days, the heyday of city corruption."

The doctor flicked his cigarette again. "As you say, Captain, we're a little older. Your case cannot be going well. Time's passed by. Mayor Houde is dead, and what about this Montford? Him, too?" He smiled ever so slightly.

"I couldn't have said it better myself," Touton concurred. "We're older. Some from the old days are dead. In the near future, sir, you'll be receiving a visit from a young officer. A strapping young man. Educated. Smart. A good cop. He's being integrated into the investigative team and is presently becoming an expert on the crimes in question. I wanted to notify you, Dr. Laurin, about his presence. Your cooperation is much appreciated, and this new officer—he's younger than us—will inherit the file and carry it through to conclusion."

The spiel provoked a wry grin from Laurin. Without apology, he lit a fresh cigarette off the embers of the old, then crushed the butt in the ashtray.

"Why would he want to speak to me? My so-called youthful indiscretion? In a moment of poor judgment, I signed a petition I failed to fully comprehend. Or are you again going to ask me how many people I killed? Quick answer, none."

"These days, you're involved in politics—"

"It's a responsibility for citizens to be engaged in Quebec independence."

Touton smiled, twirled his hat in both hands. He hadn't been offered the option to hang it up, or his coat either. "Our new religion. I was never fully converted to the old one, Doctor. I suspect I won't easily convert to the new one either."

"The movement will sweep everyone along. Those who won't join us will be left behind."

Touton chuckled aloud. "More threats. If you don't get on the train to heaven you'll be shipped in a handcart to hell. If you don't obey the law, you'll go to jail. We know that's not always true."

Behind the shroud of smoke spewed by the wee furnace of his cigarette, Laurin matched Touton's chuckle with a grin on one side of his mouth. "You paint me as a mindless dupe. That's your prerogative, but I have analyzed the situation from my perspective as a psychiatrist. In my professional opinion, Quebec independence is a necessary *collective*," he paused on the word, "psychotherapy, you understand, a collective psychotherapy, to treat the inferiority complex of the Québécois people."

"I don't feel inferior."

"Captain, that's not the point—"

"Sure it is. You believe that Quebecers suffer from an inferiority complex. I'm a Quebecer. I'm telling you that I don't feel inferior."

"The collective does. Not that anyone wishes to admit to it—"

"I'm not in denial, if that's what you're suggesting. Although I've never understood how anyone can deny being in denial and still be taken seriously."

"It's a problem, yes." Laurin nodded behind his veil of smoke.

"Surely it ought to be voluntary," Touton threw in.

"Excuse me?"

"This treatment of yours. You feel the people are ailing with a condition, this inferiority. Surely the treatment, such as independence, ought to be voluntary and not imposed."

"We're democratic, sir. No one's imposing anything. Our aims are peaceful."

"Ah, but now you're asking the people to treat themselves. Do you ask your patients to treat themselves? If so, then how do you render a bill for your services?"

"I often ask my patients to treat themselves, albeit under guidance."

"Ah, guidance. So you know best, is what you're saying. But you're asking all of us, everyone, to undergo this treatment for our so-called psychological wounds. That strikes me as unfair. I would not want to be committed to an insane asylum, for instance, because my neighbour's nuts."

Delicately, Laurin flicked ash off his shirt. "You don't want to be included in our enterprise. Yet you include the rest of us in yours."

"Mine?"

"Duplessis. Drapeau. The federal government." He inhaled down to his ankles. "We're a conquered people, Captain Touton—"

"Conquered!"

"We behave accordingly."

"Speak for yourself. Nobody's conquered me. I fought—"

"Yes, Captain," the doctor interrupted. "Frankly, I don't believe you should have fought, but since you did, I commend your bravery."

"Don't mock my war record, sir." Touton glared at the man.

"I'm not, sir."

"Men died beside me. I will not have their memory mocked."

"Captain, are you delirious? I'm not mocking your comrades. I commend their bravery. But it does not alter the articles of history. We are a conquered people and we behave accordingly."

Touton collected himself. This was no time to fight the war all over again. He knew that Laurin had been one of those allied against him, a supporter of the Vichy regime, but that time had passed. He bunched his trousers up higher on his thighs, then briefly rubbed his jaw.

"Perhaps that's what we have in common, Dr. Laurin."

The physician squinted through his smoke at him, curious now.

"I keep fighting the battle at Dieppe," Touton continued. "It never leaves me, while the battle that never leaves you took place on the Plains of Abraham."

Laurin nodded, as he might when counselling a patient. "We French fell to the English, Captain. That's a tragic fact of history, an aspect of our mutual collective psychotherapy. Perhaps you dispelled your personal psychosis on the battlefield, or altered it, but the rest of us did not."

"Are you saying that Quebec should have gone to war, too?"

"I'm saying that Quebec ought to become independent, to shake off our inferiority complex once and for all. Only then can we be truly free."

"If Quebecers are stuck in some complex, let's shake it off, and once we've shaken it off, choose our fate then. If you're going to treat the province as a patient, Doctor, we'll have to disagree. I don't think the patient should be doing the surgery. Also, if you want to win independence, you'll be forced to appeal to that sense of inferiority. I don't see how that's healthy."

Laurin smiled, perhaps content that the subject of conversation had run its course, but surprised also that the cop possessed any political awareness. But this was a land where people revelled in their politics as much as they revelled in hockey, or sunshine. "Captain Touton, please tell me what has brought you here on your day off. Not to discuss the war or independence. You could have let your new detective introduce himself. So tell me, how may I help you?"

Touton pursed his lips, returning to a more profound seriousness. The moment he had been hoping to broach had arrived. "Sir, your old cronies were fascists. In your new political life, your cohorts have arrived from the left. A minute ago, you said that the movement sweeps people into its embrace. You're now hugging people you once wanted to bash over the head—"

"Captain Touton, your naïveté is charming to a point—" He was speaking with the cigarette still bobbing up and down in his mouth with each syllable.

"—if I may finish. You find yourself forced to occupy the same space as the left wingers you once ridiculed. In the new group, won't some of the members be dismayed, sir, to discover that you once sought freedom for a Nazi war criminal?"

"The naïveté of my youth—"

"Does that excuse hold water?"

Laurin smiled grimly, looking down at his desk. "I so enjoy our discussions, Captain. To a point. Regrettably, I find myself requesting that we conclude our chat."

"Perhaps your new friends," Touton pressed on, as though the notion had only occurred to him at that moment, "might be more impressed if they discovered that you helped recover the Cartier Dagger for the people of Quebec, that you guided the authorities through the maze of Quebec Nazi sympathizers."

Laurin sucked smoke, and stared at him. "I do not believe that that would be a fruitful exercise."

"Camillien Houde was involved. He helped sell the knife. He's dead, others are dead also. Why won't you help us, sir? Assist the police. The people of Quebec, Dr. Laurin—help them."

Fashioning his skills for a new life in politics, Dr. Laurin let him know that he would take the matter under advisement even while he showed the captain out.

"Émile Cinq-Mars is coming," Touton called back from the doorway. "Remember the name. He's reviewing the entire case, top to bottom, making his own assessment. Before long, he'll drop by to conduct an inquiry. He'll have questions."

Waiting patients assumed he was cracked.

"Good day, Captain Touton."

"So long, Doc."

Reflecting on the quandary into which he had tried to steer the eminent psychiatrist, Touton was generally pleased as he drove home. He did not really expect Dr. Laurin to betray his old friends, although stranger things had happened, and certainly, more ruthless betrayals among thieves had taken place during his tenure as a policeman. If the doctor provided information and proffered identities, he'd be admitting to his own culpability at the same moment that he compromised his right-wing pals. Yet, by betraying the old guard, he'd be ingratiating himself with the left-wing trend within the independence movement, although by doing so he would also be inviting himself to come more deeply under the influence of Touton, subject to his investigation and wily schemes. Spirals revolved within circles.

Touton had left the man little room to manoeuvre.

If Laurin withheld information, he'd be announcing himself as uncooperative, someone requiring Touton's focus. If the doctor failed to be friendly with his enquiry, the policeman would surely sic his new dog on him, the mongrel pup up from the countryside, Émile Cinq-Mars. At the very least, the doctor would deduce that he'd know no peace in his lifetime, that Touton's impending retirement from the force, bound to come early for medical reasons, would not spare him ongoing scrutiny at exactly the time when his political ambitions had begun to foment.

Touton had let something slip. He had told Laurin that Houde had been involved in the sale of the dagger—which Anik had confirmed. In doing so, he was letting Laurin know that the police were closer to a judgment than he might have guessed. That tidbit should settle in the psychiatrist's craw and nettle him.

As he drove, Touton smiled. Between them, he believed, he and Cinq-Mars should be able to smudge the doctor's bright glow.

††††

Like a long, lit fuse leading to a dynamite stack, excitement snapped through the bar scene. Then came the usual denials, bringing people low once more. Partisans grew depressed as the cause seemed lost, when suddenly the key moment was taking place on TV, live. Dishevelled, windblown, smoking while he spoke and looking like a man just down from a mountaintop, René Lévesque announced that he had quit his provincial cabinet post. He was forming a new political party dedicated to the only option he believed to be viable—independence.

The great project of their lives had commenced.

"Finally," Jean-Luc sighed, "we have our leader."

Anik sniffed. The others gave her a look.

"Now what?" Vincent parried. Among them, he had expressed the most telling interest in marriage and career. He didn't want to be a single, out-of-work radical at forty. More than anyone, he was anxious for all the big issues to be resolved soon. "You don't think we have our leader?"

Anik threw up her hands. "I've been telling you since like forever. The point of the exercise is independence. It's not to find a leader. Quebecers are so infatuated with leaders. God! Now that we have a leader everyone's happy, but we're no closer to our goals."

"But we are," Pierre argued. "Lévesque's a populist, he can rally the people. The movement has momentum now. We have that because we have a leader."

She considered her position. Having qualms did not necessarily mean that she was right, and she had to remind herself of that. Her natural tendency to object, to go against the common sentiment, was not a perfect remedy for every ailment.

"Stop being so stubborn," Vincent counselled her.

"Nothing's changed," she grumbled.

"Except that now we have a leader," Jean-Luc insisted, his eyes shining.

Given that he was a political science student, Anik expected more from him. He was cerebral, unlike Paul, who felt his passions viscerally, who felt his love for his people in his bloodstream. For Jean-Luc, everything—the world, his aspirations, his politics—resided solely in his head.

Anik shook hers. "It's fucked. We keep looking for a hero to rise above us."

"What're you objecting to?" Paul bristled.

"I met Lévesque once," Anik told them.

Suddenly, they were very interested in her side of things.

"On a picket line. He'd gone down to support the garment workers. Me and my mom, we were on the line, too. He gave a quick speech."

"How'd he do?" Jean-Luc asked. He envied her the experience, but worried that she'd disparage his hero.

"The seamstresses loved him. I had a problem though. I was wearing jeans. When nobody was looking, he ran his hand up the crack of my ass."

"Lévesque!"

"At the most, I was seventeen. He was a lot older."

The boys nodded solemnly, as though to commiserate with her and a sad experience. But Jean-Luc rethought his position. "René Lévesque," he said, "ran his hand up the crack of Anik's ass. I tell you, boys, that man is a leader of men. A minute ago, I respected him. Now I'm in awe."

In time, with further ribbing, even Anik joined the laughter. She was thinking that it was true—Lévesque was different. Others listened and responded to him, and if he had wandering hands, he also had audacity. For the task ahead, that attribute might be useful.

They raised their glasses. "To independence!" Paul cried out.

They drank to their cause.

"To Anik's ass!" toasted Pierre, and she belted him for that.

Later, along with the entire bar, they sang deep into the night.

†††

Father François had vestments to remove—a cloak, a shawl, an outer robe— which stripped him down to a second, more comfortable cassock for socializing. A helper appeared in his parlour, a matron who kept her grey hair knotted in a bun. She was taller than the priest, yet remarkably thin, and happily accepted the presence of an extra guest for lunch with aplomb. Her employer, as usual, had neglected to mention he had extended the invitation. The two men sat in matching armchairs angled slightly towards one another, a lamp and a serving-table between them in the warm, shadowy room.

Afternoon light fell through lace curtains upon an ochre carpet.

Initially, the discussion touched on Anik, for Constable Émile Cinq-Mars had received the invitation to the luncheon after Sunday Mass by mentioning her name. He now had to assure the inquisitive priest that he had not come to discuss a marriage, and suddenly he wondered if he should retreat and come back another time.

"You're the new boyfriend, so I jumped to a happy conclusion, Émile. Perhaps on another occasion, you will make that announcement." Hot soup

arrived, a cream of broccoli, bordered by a plate of sandwiches cut into quarters, the crusts removed. The helper tarried long enough to receive compli-
ments from both men and collected the resident tabby before departing, as
though disappearing into the woodwork.

Cinq-Mars thanked the priest for his hospitality. Rarely did he eat a
homemade soup these days—only on trips home.

"Truth be told, the company's appreciated," Father François assured him.
"Now tell me, Émile, what has brought you here if not the frightening prospect
of marriage? Neither illness nor death, I trust."

Bluntly, Cinq-Mars stated, "Anik's father." He placed the hot bowl on the
table bedside him, the varnished wood protected by a cloth doily. He noticed a
char mark. "His murder. I'm working the case."

The older of the two stirred his soup slowly, absently, before gazing back
at his young visitor. "I'd have thought that case in mothballs ages ago, or whatever it is policemen do with unsolved crimes. Roger Clément. My."

While he allowed his own soup to cool, Cinq-Mars bit into another sandwich. The morsels were quite tasty despite the bread being stale by a day. He
doubted that having a matron to run his kitchen helped the priest's overt
waistline. "It's my understanding, Father, that the case will never be neglected."

"Why should that be?" He rocked his head from side to side. "I suppose it
has to do with Armand Touton, his friendship with Anik's mom."

Cinq-Mars feigned disinterest in his own response. "Also, his friendship
with Roger Clément. That might have more to do with it. The fact that a coroner
was killed remains important. Let's not forget that the theft of the Cartier Dagger
means a great deal to our society. Whatever the motivation, I'm being brought
up to speed. The investigation will continue through the next generation."

"The perseverance of the police department, Émile—admirable, I must
say."

"Father, could you fill me in on your relationship to the deceased?"

Both men caught the shift in conversation. The young man was no longer being received into the priest's rectory as an act of hospitality. The priest
was being questioned with respect to any involvement he may have had in
heinous crimes.

Despite his inexperience, Cinq-Mars felt strangely confident, as though he had conducted such interviews for years. At one time in his life, he had expected to become a priest. Later, he had pursued an alternative ambition, to involve his love for horses in his life's work and become a veterinarian. Few placements were available in those days, and no university accepted him. With that disappointment, he had seized upon a new vocation, and in proper time he would rise to the rank of detective. Embarking upon his interview with the priest, the sensation that overtook him was not awkwardness, or unease, but rather the shock of familiarity, as though he'd been doing this work for years. More powerfully, the overriding sensation had to do with finally performing the work he was meant to do—investigate crime—and out of that intersection with destiny, he felt his confidence flow.

"Father?" he asked. The man seemed to have dropped into a daydream.

"Roger, yes," the priest acknowledged. "You must understand my hesitation. I am obliged to segregate my sacred relationships from my friendships, and memory can easily confound the two."

"You're saying, then, that you were friends," Cinq-Mars stated. He sensed that the priest was stalling as he gathered himself.

"I suppose, yes. Like me, Carole Clément was active in union affairs, and in the rights and interests of the poor. We found ourselves on the same side of many issues. Through Carole, I got to know Roger, although that wasn't as natural a process as one might suppose."

"How so?" Peculiarly, once he had commenced his digression, Father François had failed to glance his way.

"His politics. I blame his wartime internment for that. Nobody's ever accused Roger of being an intellectual. To be incubated with fascists, like Houde—"

"A strong term, Father," Cinq-Mars pointed out to him.

The priest shrugged. "If you wish that I moderate my language, Émile, I'll do so. If I were speaking from the pulpit, you're right, I'd be more circumspect. But we're only having lunch."

The policeman nodded, encouraging the man to continue.

"Being from the left, I found Houde and Roger to be excessively right wing."

"Yet Carole was on the left—"

"Far left," the priest underscored. "She fought the tough battles. She was the one, remember, who was supposed to have been sent to that internment camp. Roger took the blame in her place."

"Whereas her husband—"

"Broke up strikes. He bashed union men in the face."

Cinq-Mars flexed his shoulders, as if accommodating the contradiction proved physically demanding. "So the woman on the left and the man on the right loved one another. They went home at night and made peace between themselves—is that the general consensus?"

"Perplexing, isn't it?"

"Or, perhaps, that's how Roger Clément wanted it to appear."

"Excuse me?"

Émile Cinq-Mars rarely drew attention to his imposing beak, but in this instance he was fraught by an itch and had no choice but to raise a hand to the bridge and offer it a good scrub. Then it required a second, gentler tweak between his forefinger and thumb. The moment passed with the priest feeling free to stare at the appendage, looking away sharply, somewhat embarrassed, once the rapid ablutions had concluded.

"I've met Anik's mom," the young man explained. "She's formidable. Says what she thinks and does what she pleases. There's no way she'd tolerate her husband walking around town aiding and abetting the enemy."

Father François adjusted a crease in his cassock and nodded. He appeared to be evaluating what Cinq-Mars had said, giving the remarks their due, but he concluded his meditation by dismissing the young man's point of view. "Roger was as wilful as her. The fact is, he aided and abetted the enemy."

"He appeared to be doing so, yes." Cinq-Mars held up a finger, and, finding that this was not a sufficiently distinctive gesture, stood as well. At six foot three, he had physical dominance over the seated cleric, and full command of the room. "And yet," the younger man pointed out to the priest, lowering his voice as though including him in an intimacy, "the moment his wife might have gone to an internment camp, he confessed to being the perpetrator of the crime. Which was not a crime at all, we know, merely the dissemination of ideas. You, for instance, might have been involved in printing a few of those leaflets. A number of political tracts came off Church duplicating machines, thanks to renegade priests. You were a student, involved in the same issues Carole was immersed in. No friend of hers rose up to take the heat when she was in trouble with the authorities. But her husband did, even though he didn't think as she did, not politically."

The priest uncrossed and re-crossed his legs. Cinq-Mars waited, watching. He liked this, being a cop. Ideas seemed to flow through him, and with those ideas, temptations. What lines should he cross? What pitfalls should he avoid? He knew that he had told the priest a few things. He had told him he knew more about him than he might have guessed. The priest was adjusting to his new role on the defensive.

Father François put his top leg down and crossed his ankles.

"She was his wife. That must have been the overriding concern. Love."

"Yes, Father, but why does no one consider that perhaps Roger Clément only pretended to be working for the right? All along, he may have been a spy."

"A spy?"

"An informant."

"For whom?"

Cinq-Mars raised that perceptive finger again. "For the left. Opposition persevered during Duplessis's Great Darkness. Perhaps he might have been a fraudulent informant for the right, who plied Duplessis, and Houde, his roommate in the camp, with lies."

Father François shook his head. "You possess an overactive imagination, Émile. I suppose it'll come in handy in your work as an officer of the law."

He recognized that he was being dismissed, and so Cinq-Mars chose to respond by crossing a line. "I can tell you what I do know for a fact, Father. Roger Clément was an informant for the police."

"The police?" The priest seemed to take the news as being preposterous.

"Specifically, for Armand Touton. Now you know another reason why the captain has never dropped this case into the dustbin, why he never will. One of his own was killed that night, and he takes it personally."

The priest had clearly undergone a sea change, comprehending now what had previously eluded him. "That's why he stayed so close to Carole. And to Anik."

"Out of guilt, perhaps," Cinq-Mars postulated. "Though the answer might be simpler. He's close to the family out of concern for one of his own."

"I see."

Cinq-Mars seated himself again, and continued his meal.

"I'm going to invoke your confidentiality as a priest on this one," he told him. "Over the years, the family has relied upon the good graces of the mob— Anik has entertained me with descriptions of her gun-toting babysitters. For safety reasons, we don't want that relationship to change."

"Of course. I'm wondering, Émile, why you are telling me this."

A fair question. He had never lied to a priest before, and he was going to have to do so with only a modicum of preparation. He folded his hands between his thighs and looked up at his host. "We're keeping the case alive. Time's gone by. New tactics are required. Whatever you can provide for me, secretly or openly, will be appreciated. I'm telling you all this because I want you to understand that when Roger Clément was killed, it's very possible that one of your own died that night."

The man in the black robe nodded, before he caught himself. "My own?"

Cinq-Mars smiled. "Not one of your flock, exactly. One of your political brothers, someone so committed to the cause that he had been willing to live his life pretending to be what he was not."

Now was the time for the priest to reveal what knowledge he possessed. Cinq-Mars already knew that he understood more than he had publicly stated, as Anik had overheard his talk with Houde on the old mayor's deathbed. Touton had been right about that—the priest's remarks had not been locked into a confession. Now was the time for the intellectual priest of the left to disseminate information, or be secretly revealed as an accomplice or culprit.

Father François nodded, somewhat earnestly, and remained mute.

"Father, where were you the night that Roger Clément was murdered?"

The priest looked at him, his eyes level, his expression indicating neither surprise nor concern about the question. "I guess you have your duty to perform."

"Thank you for understanding."

The older man sighed. "I was nearby, relatively. Attending the riot."

An odd choice of word, Cinq-Mars thought—*attending.* "Did anyone see you?"

"Thousands."

"Anyone you might remember? Who might remember you. Corroborate."

"Émile, you're more insulting by the minute. Are you aware of that?"

"Sorry, Father. I have to ask everyone I interview. I'm to build a file."

He sighed again. "I had a conversation three blocks from where Roger was killed, in Phillips Square, during a brawl between the police and demonstrators."

"Do you recall with whom?"

"Pierre Elliott Trudeau. He's somewhat well known now." Once more, he looked squarely at the young man. "At the time, he wasn't our prime minister. I'm convinced that I was one of the first to discern his potential."

Cinq-Mars stood again, this time to leave. "If anything comes to you that may help us, that perhaps you've forgotten for now, please don't hesitate to call."

Father François breathed heavily, and stood as well. "Émile, if you decide to marry the girl, I hope that you'll think of me for the wedding."

Although the remark was intended as a pleasantry, neither took sufficient notice to smile.

†††

Anik was not amused. "You went to see Father François? Why?"

Cinq-Mars enjoyed the sombre, poor, elegance of her mother's place. The patina of the home had acquired what convention termed *character,* but he often experienced an inherent grace. In its every nook and cranny, the house spoke to a sense of perseverance.

"Who told you that?" he asked.

"He did." She and the priest were lifelong friends—he would have to keep that in mind. Anik was cross with him, brittle, and he didn't know why. Her dog, given to her by Mayor Houde and named after one of her father's old teams, collapsed upon her feet, a ruse to encourage her out of the house. "Émile, what are you up to?"

"Doing my job. You know I'm working the case."

"I gave you information from a deathbed confession."

"So? I didn't tell him that. I wouldn't."

"But—it's why you went to him. Admit it!"

"I don't see the problem."

"Émile! Admit it."

"What's to admit? What's the big deal?"

"You're using me. That's the big deal."

"I'm not using you." But he had his own doubts. "How am I using you?"

She released a noisy, frustrated sigh and moved away from him—first to the hall, then down to the kitchen where she collected a beer from the fridge and slammed the door shut with a sharp poke of her hip. Ranger nearly had his nose squished. Émile lazed in behind her and leaned against the jamb, hands in his pants pockets. She cracked off the cap.

"Anik, I'm investigating your dad's death. We're on the same side here." Taking a swig from the bottle, she slightly contorted her body, which seemed to concede the point. "One of the things I'm *assigned* to do is talk to anybody who might have known anything—"

"Father François wasn't in the park," she burst out.

"He was three blocks away."

"What? How do you know that?"

"He told me. That's not very far away."

Upset, she pushed past him and returned to the living room, where she slumped onto the sofa. He reappeared and sat opposite her. "What're you saying?"

"Calm down. I'll explain."

"Just fucking explain it," she told him, and started scratching on the label of her bottle. "I don't have to fucking calm down."

"Father François knows everyone involved. Your dad. Your mom. Houde."

"I know them, too. So interrogate me. Ask *me* where I was that night. Or have you been doing that secretly, you shit? Do you browse through my closets when I'm not looking?"

"I know where you were. You were a kid at home. Will you let me finish?"

"Finish."

He released tension by blowing air out of his lungs, like a whale surfacing. "Father François also knew Pierre Trudeau back then. He still does. He was involved in the de Bernonville affair, as was your mother, working to have the man deported back to France to face war crimes charges. He either worked politically with the people involved or found himself aligned against them. He knew all the players. He also knows, because you told me, that Trudeau acquired the knife. Now, he could have told me that in our conversation the other day, but he chose not to do so."

"He's a priest!" she burst out. "He can't talk about confessions."

"Houde didn't confess that part. Houde wanted to know if a transaction for the dagger had occurred. Father François was in on that part, Anik. Face it."

She held her hands apart, yelling at him as if trying to berate the wall behind him, the beer bottle in one hand as though she might throw it. "He wasn't in on it. He just happened to know about it."

"Knowing about it means he was in on it. In some way."

"Oh, balls!"

"It's my job to ask questions. He's key. It's not because I know you."

"It *is* because you know me! I trusted you, Émile. The only reason I told you about Trudeau and the dagger is because we sleep together."

"Occasionally."

"What? What was that? A complaint?"

"You're out a lot, that's all. It's not a complaint. That's just how it is."

"Hello? Who here works the night shift? Who plays detective on his days off?"

"Okay, okay."

"So, what's your complaint?"

"It's not a complaint. I'm not complaining."

She sighed heavily again. Having lifted the edges of her beer label, she ripped it clean off, dropping the debris beside her on the sofa. "Just spit it out, Émile."

He sighed, too. "You're out a lot, that's all."

"That's not all. Say what's on your mind for once."

He had a notion to do that, but he found the going difficult. "Your friends don't like me much."

"You *are* a cop. It comes with the territory."

"I'm not so crazy about them, either."

That made her think. "True. They talk about overthrowing the government. In that situation, you'd have to shoot them, right? Won't that be fun for you?"

Their quick smiles acknowledged that their differences felt odd, even to them.

Ranger's nails were clicking on the kitchen floor as he paced in circles.

"I wonder," Émile said. "Did your mom and dad have conversations like this?"

Often Anik wondered something similar. According to her mom, Roger didn't often voice contrary opinions. He just made sure that he knew which strike she was supporting that day.

"I'm not very confident," Anik said quietly, slowly, measuring her words, "if I can live with our disparities as well as they did."

"Anik—"

"Let's just . . . I don't know." She inhaled. "Take a breather."

"Anik—come on. It's not that bad. We can work this through."

"Can we?" She sipped her beer, but could scarcely taste it. Her chin quavered. "I'm not so sure. For now, Émile, for today at least, I need room."

"What are you saying?"

"Nothing—definitive. I'm just saying, I'd like to be alone today."

This was hurting. Émile accepted her resolve and crossed the room to kiss her. Their lips touched lightly. When he left the room, and the house, and shut the door behind him, he felt as sad as the rain beginning to fall. She hadn't said so, but this felt terminal. An ache pestered his back. He wanted to turn, to see if she had come out to watch him go, but he could not fully twist himself around. He didn't know what to say that would be new or beneficial, so he walked on.

All day, the part of him that was a policeman wanted to ask why she had cried the day she ran from the old mayor's house after hearing his final confession. She'd made a point of telling him that. She had wept uncontrollably. Was it the old mayor's imminent death causing her to weep? Or had she overheard something she had yet to reveal? Émile would become cross with himself, for always he faced this dilemma. Was he her boyfriend or her inquisitor? He supposed, as he took the corner and looked to see if a bus was in sight, that Anik probably had to struggle with the same issue.

The nature of the question seemed to carry its own response.

From the living-room window, Anik watched him go, stopping herself from rushing out and offering an umbrella. Ranger wanted to dash out, too, but she squeezed him to her side and rubbed behind his ears. "Later," she said. "Soon." This hurt. She felt awash, sad, unable to determine what to do next. She went through to her room and plopped down on the bed. She hugged herself, then her dog. A while later, she napped. Waking, she knew she had somewhere to go, people to see. Time for a quick bath and a change of clothes, a scoot around the block with her pet, then she'd be off. Another late night. Which is what Émile resented—the late nights made him suspicious. As she dressed, her sadness weighing upon her, she wondered if she'd be coming home that night. She'd leave her mother the usual note, advising her not to wait up. Her mom would think she'd be sleeping at Émile's, but she wasn't planning on it. And if she didn't sleep there, or here, that might at least resolve a few matters in her life. Or, if not resolve them, abruptly end the discussion.

"Okay," she told her dog, "we'll do better than around the block." She locked eyes with Ranger. "The park!"

The terrier jumped three feet.

Hours later, her usual bar was lively as she entered. Parallel to a brick wall, a long table was crowded with young people. Others pressed in close, standing with their beers in hand. Anik tried to get near to see the principals, going around to one side and elbowing her way through the throng until she could catch a friend's attention. When she did so, she was signalled to the table. A spot had been held for her. Dozens of young people looked her up and down, wondering why she was important. The older man at the table had seen her coming, and signalled others to move, and after this sport of musical chairs had played out, the free seat that awaited her now appeared, magically, beside his.

Anik squeezed her way through. She smiled at the man. He kissed her on both cheeks before continuing with his general conversation. He was addressing the group, and the young people listened, enchanted, enthralled. This was the second such gathering. At the first one, Anik and the politician had hit it off, unexpectedly for her. She listened, evaluating. Could it be possible? Could they really create an independent country for their people? Could a way be found? And she thought about Émile, wondering how they had come to love one another when that love felt impossible. If Émile were here, he'd be arguing each point. He would not sit in thrall, basking in the glory of the moment. *What's up with me?* Was she destined to inhabit a relationship similar to that of her parents, and shouldn't that be an ugly thought, or at least off-putting? Had she been searching for a man who could attract her, yet whose politics were opposite her own? Wasn't that unfair to everyone? She wondered if she shouldn't go home, or over to Émile's, rather than carry on into the wee hours in this rapt discussion and into the arms, perhaps, of this renegade, magnetic leader, for that was the danger, even now, as his hand delicately touched her knee, her thigh, her wrist, for she had yet to pull away from him. She watched, and listened, and waited, and wondered, and bickered with herself, trying to decide.

CHAPTER 20

1939

O<small>N THE FIRST DAY OF SEPTEMBER IN 1939, THE PREMIER OF THE</small> province of Quebec lay sequestered in mid-debauch. He declined to be distracted by the news that Hitler had invaded Poland. Over the next few days, he maintained his public silence on world events. Not an uncommon tactic. Let others surrender their positions, then see what voids remained for him to wisely inhabit. Prime Minister William Lyon Mackenzie King had backtracked on his longstanding rhetoric and declared that Canada would fight on the side of Great Britain, and the House of Commons was called to address the issue on the fourth.

Duplessis, nonplussed, drank on.

He had retreated to a room in the Château Frontenac, high above the St. Lawrence River. To ease a vexatious spirit, he had invited a series of consorts to pass through his suite. Business and news were periodically brought to him, which he perused while the damsel of the day bathed or took a nap.

Then King invoked the War Measures Act.

Officially, King's premise was the defence of the nation in the aid of France and Great Britain against Germany's aggression, yet the first casualties of his legislation were the premier of Quebec and, by extension, the bombastic mayor of Montreal, Camillien Houde. These were his true political foes. He needed them out of the way to properly conduct a military campaign. He could not rally the nation if two adversaries, each of whom enjoyed strong populist sentiment, were strategically aligned against him. So he went after their Achilles' heel: both men were running their governments into bankruptcy. Houde had the city forty million in debt, and a trio of banks had cut the city off from further advances. Houde had already stated that Quebec should fight on the side of Mussolini, which had helped the banks reach a determination regarding his civic management. Now he was assailing them. "I won't allow the people to die of starvation to please a pack of bankers." The pack hardened their hearts and sealed their vaults against him.

Duplessis felt King's squeeze. He had the option of raising government money in the United States, for Americans were accustomed to many of their own states being in worse fiscal straits than Quebec. The banks had bailed him out in the past, but now the War Measures Act forbade any borrowing by cities or provinces unless approved by the federal government.

All vaults were closed to him. He sent a man to Ottawa to beg funds from the federal government itself, only to be stiffly refused.

The Opposition took heart. Godbout, the Liberal gnat, declared, "With each beat of your heart, Duplessis extends your debt by two bucks!" In the past, the premier could have countered the accusations with wild spending sprees calculated to buy votes. He could have ordered the building of roads or bridges or wharves, but with empty coffers he was stymied, and from his room in his drunken spree he sent notice that he was calling an election for October. When he awoke to sobriety, he discovered that, compounding his dilemma, King had also instituted censorship. Duplessis could not campaign over the radio without first submitting his speech to federal censors, whose red pencils and snipping shears were kept especially sharp for him. His first reaction was to refuse to speak on radio altogether, and to disallow anyone in his party to speak, effectively surrendering the airwaves to the glory of his silent sulk. And to his enemies.

The fresh campaign, which he called to rally support against the federal government, began as a disaster, quickly worsening. For his inaugural speech, his diction was precise, as usual, his oratory robust, as usual, but he was uncommonly drunk. By the night's end, the people were uncertain whether he meant to lead them towards independence or war, or against war, or into the arms of Hitler, or was inviting insurrection. His coalition of forces fell away quickly. The English business community was appalled. Cardinal Villeneuve had recently travelled through France, treated with the élan reserved for a head of state while being educated on the impending peril posed by Germany. He could no longer support Duplessis, and so the crutch of the Church was also withdrawn.

The Liberals fought hard, taking up several positions the premier might have considered his natural ground. They dismissed conscription, declared it would never happen, and effectively vilified Duplessis. A vote for the premier was a vote for Hitler and Stalin, a vote against him a vote for civilization. Intoxicated and feeling absurdly assured of his own power, *le Chef* was losing control over his confederates, who now believed he was marching them towards disaster.

Disaster ensued. He was scorched in the election. His regime of artificial dictatorship, scandals, martinis and attendant ladies buckled.

In his home in Trois-Rivières, his sister, unaccustomed to defeat, quietly wept. He stepped up beside her and sat down. "Why cry? Do not cry," he said. "I will be back. Next time, I will remain in power for fifteen years, or until God takes me. I promise you, never again shall we know defeat. They are saying that my government has been an aberration, but we will rise up again to show them that *this night* is the aberration." He kissed her temple, and her weeping ceased. "I will be back."

In the days ahead, Duplessis stayed home, not drinking so much, remaining contemplative, rearming his energy. On his desk he kept a clipping, in English, culled from *Time* magazine. He read it aloud each morning, and before lunch, and at the end of each business day, permitting the rancour of the separate readings to settle deeply inside him. He returned to his office before retiring for the night and read the clipping to himself once more, to embed the nettlesome comment into his marrow. Centred in the journalist's assessment was an insult he could not abide—one he would correct, but, more important, one he would use to motivate his comeback. He read, "Because he used Hitler's theories of racism, Mussolini's system of corporatist trade-union laws, and Huey Long's finger-wagging, roughshod political tactics, he was called a Fascist . . . But things went badly for pink-cheeked, Hitler-moustached, Bon Vivant M. Duplessis."

Never again, Duplessis vowed, would anyone think to call him "pink-cheeked." Of that, he was profoundly certain.

To the clipping, he'd say each day, "I'll be back."

†††

In Ottawa, Prime Minister William Lyon Mackenzie King was ecstatic with *le Chef's* demise. "One down," he confided to a senior advisor.

"We'll get the other one, soon enough," the confidant replied.

"I want Houde's head on a platter."

†††

Carole and Roger Clément were awakened from their beds.

The cops went straight to the small, hand-cranked printing apparatus in the otherwise empty back bedroom, where a crumpled copy of a pamphlet was mysteriously discovered in the waste bin. They never left copies lying around.

"Get dressed, please, ma'am. You're coming with us."

Under the War Measures Act, some criminal trials had been disbanded.

Roger declared, "I did it. Not her."

An officer held up the offending leaflet. "Says here a woman was raped. In a munitions plant. That's sedition. You printed this?"

Roger said he had. To prove it, he said, the crank had been malfunctioning, stubborn and strenuous to turn.

"Go ahead. Turn the handle yourself."

The officer tested it out, realized that a small woman could not possibly have turned the crank, and ordered that Roger be arrested in Carole's place.

She watched him go.

The man who loved her sacrificed himself. Somehow she knew that was right. What would she do in a prison camp except die? Roger would survive, and he'd return to her. She would help by making airplane wings and trust that her labours shortened the war. Each night she returned alone to her little house, as she had done for so long before she'd been married. Each night, she gazed at a picture of herself and her husband on their wedding day, whispering to him, "Be so very brave. Come back to me, Roger." Each day, she'd check the mail, hoping the censors had let something through from the camp.

Always, before he finished a letter by saying again that he loved her, he would write, "I'll be back."

†††

The justice minister had news. The last time he was this excited, he was reporting Duplessis's defeat. Since then, Paris had fallen. Few around Parliament Hill were feeling chipper.

"What is it?" the prime minister asked.

"Houde!" he exclaimed. "He's come out in public against conscription. He urged the people of Quebec to defy the law."

"Sedition?"

"Sedition," the man proclaimed.

"Off with his head."

"Sir, I don't know—"

"Oh, for heaven's sake, it's a metaphor. Arrest him. I want him interned."

"The mayor of Montreal?"

"The mayor," King confirmed, "of Montreal."

"Just like that?" the man asked.

King paused. "No," he decided, his political brain at work. "Do we know that he said these things for a certainty? Or will he claim that he was misquoted?"

The minister told him that the journalist who overheard the remark had phoned the news to his editor, a man by the name of Ludington, whom King had once met. Ludington advised the reporter to write out the remarks as he had heard them, then take them to Houde to see if he would sign them.

"He signed?"

"With some élan, apparently. You know Houde."

"Call Ludington," King advised. "Tell him we're using the censors to scuttle the story."

"It's already been printed."

"Doesn't matter. He can write no more. When he complains, tell him that if the story had been mentioned in the House of Commons, he'd be free to write about it. As is, we're free to scuttle it."

"Then we don't get Houde," noted the justice minister.

"Oh but we do," King told him. "Ludington will call the Opposition. He'll coax them to air the story in Parliament. Once they do, I'm obliged to discharge my duty and arrest Houde. It won't be because I want him gone, but because my arm has been twisted by the Opposition. Make the call."

†††

Roger Clément watched the big, jovial man arrive at the camp in New Brunswick, along the banks of the Saint John River. He'd heard that he was on his way, and arranged it so that he was among the first to greet him. "Mr. Mayor, remember me? I used to crack heads for you."

The mayor sized him up. "Yes. Roger, isn't it? Roger Clément." True to his reputation, he never forgot a name or a face.

"Do you want to bunk in my cabin? It's not so bad. We've fixed it up."

"Is it amicable? A good group of guys?"

"We distill our own spirits."

"Lead the way, young man. Take my bags, will you?"

So Camillien Houde, a poor man's son who had become a big city's mayor, became an inmate in a wartime interment camp while enjoying the services of his own valet. Some prisoners passed the time by plotting escape, a favourite plan being a hockey game, prisoners against the guards, on a day when the river froze before it was covered in snow. Some prisoners dreamed of outskating the guards on an endless breakaway to the sea. Houde could skate, but he had no intention of being a runaway in the wilderness, or living life on the lam. A man of his bulk and fame, where could he hide? Instead, he plotted his triumphant return. "You watch," he told Roger, and shook a thick finger. "I'll be back. Hell, son. We'll both be back."

CHAPTER 21

1968–69

CONSTABLE ÉMILE CINQ-MARS NEEDED TO TRAVEL BACK IN TIME TO retrace the events of the night an antique dagger was stolen from its safe. He arranged to speak to the investigating officer on the scene, Detective—now Precinct Captain—Andrew Sloan.

"Touton won't let it go, will he?" Sloan muttered, shaking his head.

A blustery day.

Citing cabin fever, the sixty-year-old detective chose to conduct the interview outdoors. He and Cinq-Mars strolled down to the canal locks at Ste. Anne de Bellevue, where small craft could negotiate the roiling junction of two rivers. At intervals, pedestrians were permitted to cross on the locks' gates to a small island park, and the two men traversed the walkway and gazed out at the rapids.

"Sometimes I forget that Montreal's an island," Cinq-Mars mentioned.

"Tell me about it," Sloan grunted. "I used to love it. The stinking city. You wake up in the morning, sniff the night on your clothes. Puke an asshole upchucked down your cuffs. Smell a perpetrator's garlic breath on your shirt. I craved clean air. Now I live off island, in the country. But you can't win in this life. Mornings, I smell pig manure, or some shit like that."

Cinq-Mars smiled, remembering those rural days himself. His own heart remained saddened. At least working a murder case gave him something more to do than mope over losing his girlfriend.

"I live close to pasture. Soon, I'll pension off. It won't be a big change."

"You put in hard time downtown. You must've seen some things."

"Curl your hair. I still go to the barber twice a month to straighten mine out."

Only wisps of hair remained on top, the sides white. His skin possessed a ruddy complexion, toughened by wind and sun, as if he'd been a fisherman or farmer throughout his life. Capillaries lay visible and broken across his rosy cheeks.

Cinq-Mars appreciated the intimacy of the encounter. Sloan was no longer the hard-assed gumshoe his reputation had painted him to be. These days, he administered a small detachment. If a few young fellows came into town and drank too much, got into a brawl with knives, that would be his worst shift of the year. Better than the days when it would've been a typical start to any evening.

"I've heard stories." The visiting cop rested his forearms upon a security bar above a steep embankment and watched the river flow. "A lot's changed since then."

Sloan put his hands in his trench coat and made it flap, warding off a chill. "What can I do for you, Detective? Since we're talking about the good old days."

"I'm not a detective, sir. I'm working for Captain Touton, and he's got me busting my ass on my days off. That's why I'm in civvies."

"For Armand, being a cop is like being a priest. You never take the crucifix off your neck."

"I've learned that. As I said, I'm looking into the murders of Roger Clément and the coroner, Claude Racine. Way back when."

"Armand's favourite hobby." He decided to continue walking along the stone barricade that separated them from the river. Cinq-Mars ambled along after him.

"You were the first detective on the scene. How did you get called up to the hockey offices?"

"How? I don't know. Somebody sent me a telegram."

"Nobody was allowed in the building. So how did anybody find out there'd been a robbery?"

Sloan stopped walking, apparently lost in thought. "Detective, I'm not sure anybody has asked that question before." He resumed his strolling.

"I'm not a detective," Cinq-Mars reminded him again. "But it sounds good when you say it."

"Sorry. I'll call you Émile, since this is your day off. Jesus. How did I get called?" The captain stopped walking to pull his thoughts together. "Armand had given us sectors. He was expecting trouble. We all were. Senior detectives were each given a sector of downtown to watchdog. Not for the riot, so much. For any major crimes that occurred while the riot was going on, if one broke out. I remember now, it's coming back to me."

Cinq-Mars recalled listening to stories of the big city riot over the radio. The city had seemed so far away then, in flames. "So the Sun Life was empty."

"That was our understanding. We went to the company and said, 'Look, we can't protect the NHL offices unless we seal the building.' They were already shaking in their shoes, those guys, the bosses. If they could've *evicted* the National Hockey League at that point, they would've. So they cooperated."

"This is all before the riot?"

"Yeah. We knew it was coming. The mayor's office decided that if we planned too much, it would be like inviting the riot, in a way. Armand had a sense though. He was more worried than I'd seen him. He knew what guys were saying in the taverns. Maybe he got some orders, but mostly he made his own plans, on the quiet."

"You admire him," Cinq-Mars noted.

Grudgingly, the older cop nodded. "I stood up to him more than anybody. Maybe I did it at first because I was ticked off. Here's this young guy passing me by—the first time it happens, it's hard to take—but then I kept on doing it because I found out that he appreciated the input. He didn't want only a squad of yes-men around him." They had reached the tip of the small island, and now turned and began to walk back along the inner shore, towards the canal. "On some jobs, he'd cut me out of things. He wanted guys who'd do what they were told and not say a fucking word. Other jobs, he wanted me around, because he needed somebody who might make him think twice. He kept himself on the ball that way."

Cinq-Mars was enjoying the nostalgic talk. Yet he had learned lessons that Armand Touton had imparted—convoluted conversations were fine, they helped oil the tongue, but his job required that he maintain the thread and guide the speaker back to the main point.

"What's your recollection on the sequence of events that night?"

"It starts at Sun Life. The vault had an alarm on it. A local alarm would've rung in the hallways for nobody to hear, but there was also a remote. Downstairs, security guards saw the alarm go off on their board. Then it went dead, a sign that the line had been cut."

"So they went upstairs," Cinq-Mars surmised.

"Our guys wouldn't let them. That caused a brouhaha, let me tell you. I got a call over my two-way, so I went over to intercede. To keep everybody happy, I went upstairs with security tagging along."

"And?" The east gate was releasing water. A pair of small powerboats inside the lock, one a beautiful wooden Chris-Craft, gently lowered from the level of the Ottawa River to that of the St. Lawrence.

"We saw what we saw. The door to the NHL office smashed in. We were pretty shocked to see the safe blown open. We saw the busted case where the Cartier Dagger used to be, and it's a good thing security was around, because they told me the importance of what was missing."

"You didn't know about the knife before that?"

"Why would I? I thought it was a French thing, but Armand, when I told him, he didn't know about it, either. I guess you had to be a buff."

Cinq-Mars looked at him quizzically.

"Like a history buff."

Voices of the boaters arose from low in the lock, chatting away amiably.

"So, if you're inside Sun Life, how did the murder in the park come to your attention?"

"A citizen—a student, I believe—spotted a man on the ground, and other men abusing him. Cops were hanging around Sun Life, so the witness ran up to them. But the cops weren't allowed to leave their posts. We lost an opportunity there. Finally, a uniform checked things out, and that's when the killers, assuming they were the killers, fled. Then things got interesting."

"Only then?" Cinq-Mars said.

"I was called over. I was busy but it was my sector. I looked at the dead guy in the park, and had a thought, you know? So I asked a security guard what the stolen dagger looked like. He'd seen it on display. When he told me, my bowels felt loose. This is how come there's no doubt about what scene I encountered first—because I brought the guard from Sun Life back across the street to identify the knife, which he did, and then he shocked the hell out of me, because he identified the dead man, too."

A surprise. "How?"

"Said he was a hockey player, or used to be. The guard was a fan. He recognized him." An expression crossed the younger cop's face that Captain Sloan inquired about. "What's wrong with that?"

Cinq-Mars gestured with his chin. "Roger Clément had been a hockey player, but not for almost twenty years. He'd changed over that time. Plus, he was dead, and you were outside at night in bad weather. People don't look so good when they're dead, and they're never easy to recognize in the dark."

Sloan couldn't dispute the logic. "What're you saying? The guard knew him?"

"Could've been an inside job right from the get-go."

"Naw, they came down from the roof. They busted in through the window."

"My job is to look at every aspect and see if anything was missed. You just told me that the guard might've known Roger Clément. I've been up on the roof of the Sun Life—"

"You've been on the fucking roof?"

"I don't think they went down from there. I think they just made it look that way so nobody would think it was an inside job."

"We didn't think along those lines."

"I'm not saying it happened that way. But I've been looking at it from a certain angle, and then you tell me about the guard. It starts to make sense."

Sloan shook his head, impressed with the new guy's smarts. Their route had brought them back to the point where they'd cross the canal again, but the lock was opening and they'd have to wait for the procedure to conclude.

"You'll have to speak to that guard. No way will I remember his name."

"He's dead."

Sloan took a step back to eye his colleague. "How do you know that? From what I told you, you don't even know who he is."

Cinq-Mars shrugged. He was showing off a little, but the man was a captain and he was an ambitious cop in only his second year on the force. "I'm going over the whole trail. I reinterviewed every guard who'd been on duty that night. Captain Touton has those records. He interviewed them all back then, so I knew which one had gone out to the park with you, and he's dead."

"Touton didn't catch this, about the recognition thing?"

"Afraid not. But just because somebody recognized somebody, doesn't mean they were working together. That's only a guess on my part."

"You asked me questions you already know the answers to. Jesus."

"Everything requires corroboration. You know that. I want the facts lined up. I'm really looking to get a feel, you know? As to how things were back then."

"I know cops. You want to spike some guy's ass on a lamppost, Émile. Well, I'm glad my memory didn't fail me. You got what you came here for."

"I appreciate the talk, Captain."

They watched the boats depart the lock. The crews were chilly, but the life seemed idyllic.

"Someday it happens," Sloan said quietly, without being prompted. "You're looking at sixty, see retirement ahead. You never pictured yourself sitting in a goddamn shack on a windy fucking field on a grey fucking day by the side of a fucking highway nobody drives down much anymore that smells of ripe pig stink. The wind howls right through the cracks of your shack, feels like it's through your bones. You never knew that this is what you wanted, but you must've, because this is what you got. This is what you dreamed of. Clean air, minus the stink. But no city punks in gold chains, no creeps in Mercedes fucking Benzes. That's beautiful. Retirement. Yippee. Nothing to fucking do except dream of slaughtering pigs. Or pig farmers. I don't wish it on you, kid, but there it is. Good luck with your life."

Cinq-Mars wasn't sure what to say. "You're not retired yet," he reminded him.

"Six weeks. Hey, if you ever want to come out to my place and bust my balls, feel free. I'll appreciate the diversion." The man held out his hand, indicating that they were separating early. "I'm staying out awhile, breathe the air. You can find your own way back."

Cinq-Mars eyed him closely. He didn't look bad at all. All he had to go on was the man's temperament. "Cancer?" he asked.

"Fucking prostate. Hey, you're some detective."

They shook, and when the gates of the lock closed again, Cinq-Mars walked across, then drove back to the city. Over the car radio he heard news of a bombing. The details were still coming in. A terrorist cell of the FLQ—Le Front de libération du Québec—was mounting a new campaign and threatening to become more violent. They'd been blowing up mailboxes. This time, a shoe store. With somebody in it.

†††

Anik stirred. Roused herself sleepily.

Afternoon liaisons were often the best.

He'd be wired. She'd be sultry. Together, they'd be naughty.

The apartment belonged to neither of them. René had borrowed a key. That alone felt sexy—doing it in someone else's place, in an unknown person's bed. Another couple would come home to their room and probably think to change the sheets, yet echoes of her cries would continue to whisper in the walls, above the tinkle of her laughter and his wry, smoky chuckle. Knowing that he'd come from an important meeting, that another awaited, that felt sexy, too. She'd catch him on the evening news and calculate that two-and-a-half hours before her man stood before the phalanx of microphones he had knelt before her and kissed her thighs, moving to combat her desire with intimacy. The sex would linger over the airwaves, through her bones, her blood, her head, warming her desire again.

Did she love power? The thought vexed her from time to time. Maybe. That could be part of it. He was such a little guy after all, like a gnome—whenever she wanted to get his goat or take him down a peg she'd call him Napoleon. For a while her favourite had been "You stunted Napoleon," which had evolved into "Well, if it isn't Napoleon's stunt double." He never liked that one, so she stuck with it. And if she wanted to be objective about the overall picture, he was not good-looking, either. She'd say he smoked like a chimney, but what chimney smoked that much? Yet his head was always full of ideas and his body a chute of passion, and, as she got to know him better, a fester of doubts and frets also. He often experienced the weight of the nation on his shoulders, and always the weight of the enterprise. Was he making the right choices? Would they work? If they gained independence, would that work? What compromises would have to be negotiated, and how would the rest of Canada react, really? How would Trudeau counter his next move, and what would be his archrival's next ploy? Could he win an election? Bourassa, the new premier, was a grasshopper of a man. Any thought that René couldn't trounce him was inconceivable, yet his vision for the society was difficult to sell across the generations, difficult to project through each segment of the population. His people were inclined to be socialist, but his support, if he wanted to win, had to be broader than that, which meant compromise, and that meant disappointing the expectations of the faithful. He talked to Anik about these matters, and she gave back her counsel. She said he had to follow the pragmatic course. Victory would heal most wounds, she assured him, and he'd nod, he'd agree.

Anik herself hated that the right wingers were involved and carried so much clout within the party, men like Laurin and Parizeau, who were always a threat to René's leadership and forever a pain in the butt. Creating a country was difficult labour, and it seemed most often that that was what they were doing, really, as they twisted and convulsed on borrowed beds, willing a country into being as other couples might lock together to create a child. She loved power, she had to admit it, but the thrill of revolution affected her more, the intoxicating imagination of it all, the sense of being on the cusp of history, of time, of causing the world to bend to your better judgments. So the two of them gyrated in a desire of limbs and blood-flow and irreconcilable lust to create a new land, afraid of success, fearful of failure.

Progress seemed minimal.

More problems supplanted any being resolved.

Still, they could take themselves to bed and believe they'd make it work, that here they could fabricate the new out of the furor of time and place and the long fortitude of their history. And she'd think, *That's why I'm sleeping with him.* For when she was with him, it felt as though she could become an equal partner in creating a nation. When he was not around, that conviction floundered.

But oh, how he'd fume about Trudeau.

With Anik, more than to any other, he'd let his guard down and she'd see how he feared the man, how the prime minister intimidated him. René loved debate and discourse and adversarial confrontation. He was so adept at winning that in most contests he enjoyed the advantage of victory being a foregone conclusion. Observers waited for him to strike, and when the moment for his attack or his proper defence arrived, he'd be beautifully derisive or foul-mouthed, galvanized to his passionate core yet aided by a sense that he spoke out of the heart and suffering of his people. Admirers raved, delirious, forgetting points he may not have properly countered or contradictions of his own he had let drop. Yet he held no such advantage over Trudeau, whose freewheeling, off-the-cuff brilliance perfectly offset Lévesque's folksy, foxy charm. Rather than holding the advantage of an anticipated victory, Lévesque could only debate Trudeau while expecting to lose. Anik could see it in his eyes. René had battled him too many times in too many smoky rooms back when they were friends not to twitch under that dire lack of confidence. As much as he might fret and pout and sneer there was not a bloody thing he could do about it.

René and Anik shared that secret between them, although it remained unspoken. All their grand plans might be for naught, as the breadth and wonder of their vision came affixed with paradox. Lévesque believed he could never defeat Trudeau, and if he could never defeat him, how could he expect to win? Anik had no answer. She could only hope to prop him up, hope that someday he might find his confidence. In that light, she had done her best to detract from Trudeau's glow one time, explaining why the other man was so powerful and wielded such an intellectual aura and spiritual force. She told him, "He has the Cartier Dagger, you know."

She had to explain to him how she knew.

They were in bed then, too. After she spoke, Lévesque placed his hands over his face and turned onto his back in an attitude of abject misery. In trying to demythologize Trudeau, she had inadvertently made him appear invincible. Lévesque writhed in physical agony. If Trudeau possessed the knife, it explained his swift, rather extraordinary ascent to power, not to mention his rampant popularity. What hope now for Napoleon's stunt double? He was not only up against that scintillating intellect and high moral, near-religious, charismatic authority—that sun!—but now he was up against the neo-mythic power purported to be attached to those who possessed the dagger. What hope?

A quandary. Anyone who openly accused Trudeau of possessing the knife would be chastened by the slur of slander, dismissed for being petty and derided for believing in a paltry magic. Credibility lost would never be regained. He'd be lucky not to be laughed into extinction, and rightly so. Yet any man with sufficient superstitious tissue in his gullet to actually believe that the Cartier Dagger possessed mystical qualities that granted one person an advantage over others was doomed to self-defeat if he went up against the knife's proprietor—and Lévesque guessed that that applied to him, too. He felt himself psychologically whipped.

"I'm sorry," Anik said, trying to peel his hands off his face.

"I'm fucked," he lamented.

Trudeau had been born rich, while Lévesque had been hatched poor. His foe was well educated and had travelled the world. Lévesque's own learning was substandard, his travels routine. While Trudeau was brilliant, Lévesque was merely damn smart, full of quips and an arrogance worn as a thin disguise. Trudeau seduced more women than he did, although he didn't do too badly. And Trudeau possessed the coveted dagger, whereas he had a knife at his throat, demanding that he deliver what he probably could not.

Now he stirred beside her, emerging from a post-coital nap dreamy-eyed and content, at least, with their shared time together. She kissed his forehead and drew his head down onto her shoulder as normally he might do with her. "Where are we?" he wondered.

"I don't know. You better give the key back to the right person." Above the bed's headboard rose a wall of bare brick. Floor-to-ceiling shelves on a side wall stood crammed with books.

"Some writer's pad," Lévesque recalled. "Some hack. What time is it?"

"Sixty-five minutes to your next appointment. Senior citizens' centre. Which means you can be late, as usual. Nobody will notice."

On that news, he snuggled up closer to her. A hand idly came up under her breast, and he was leaning down to kiss the opposite nipple when the phone rang.

"Don't bother." He went for the nipple and she closed her eyes, thinking that, yes, she could go again. So could he. He didn't have to be *on* for octogenarians. Most of them would only be there for the hors d'oeuvres anyway.

The phone was connected to an answering machine. A disembodied voice interrupted them. "René. It's me. Pick up."

They didn't know who "me" was, but presumed it to be the man whose bed they were lying on. Lévesque picked up. "Yeah?" He listened a moment. "Oh fuck."

"What now?" Anik asked. His tone seemed ominous.

He hung up. "The fucking FLQ. They bombed a shoe store."

"*What?* Nobody bombs a shoe store."

"Nobody bombs mailboxes, either, except those pricks. They killed a salesgirl."

"Oh my God."

"She's French. I don't know if that makes it any worse. But she's French."

"Those damn fools."

He put his hands over his eyes and rubbed his temples with his thumbs. In opting for independence, in keeping the issue on the front burner, he ran the risk of igniting passions. A few might scatter off beyond his control. This was supposed to be his job, to pull sentiment into one constructive enterprise, but could that be wholly possible? Knowing that he wasn't to blame made it no easier.

"I better go," he said. "The press will be hunting me down. I should make myself findable."

She pulled his hands off his face. "The bombers. They're attacking Trudeau. It's not your fault."

Lévesque nodded, sighed, indicated that he understood. Yet, while dressing, he mentioned, "Apparently, she was young. The salesgirl." He shrugged, and felt to add, "Like you."

†††

Dark, this street she travelled, poorly illuminated by street lamps. People dozed in their beds, although a few lazed before the telltale blue glow of televisions. Sporadic insomniacs persevered. Anik was listening to her steps, taking an arcane pleasure in the rhythm of her heels and toes upon the pavement. She heard a car drive up behind her. Her skin tingled, a premonition of fear. She didn't want to look. Young guys, probably, checking out her ass, too dim or too dumb to do more than stare before uttering some shrill remark as they sped off into the night, tires squealing, not knowing that their laughter failed to conceal a pathetic fright. To look back would only provoke them, so she marched on.

The car continued behind her.

This could be trouble. She should look at the driver. Confront her demons.

Anik shot him a glance.

A single driver. Not young. Middle-aged.

The car sped up, then slowed to draw alongside her. Parking was permitted on the opposite side of the street only, so the vehicle could hug the curb here, stay close.

She bent down as she walked. Looked in. Let her anger show.

Behind the steering wheel, Armand Touton smiled at her.

She stooped to peer through the open window on the passenger's side as he came to a stop. "What are you doing here?" she demanded. Relieved, yet mystified. Angry now for a different reason. At least she wouldn't have to battle a pervert.

"What does it look like?"

"You're following me?"

"I'm keeping the streets safe," Touton declared. "Hop in. I'll give you a lift."

Intuitively, she knew that the meeting was no accident, and although she was content to be walking, and the night was warm and quiet, she also knew that something was up. Opening the door, she crawled into the vehicle, bumping her knee against the police radio, then slammed the door shut behind her.

Like a little girl, she slouched down in the seat. She had half a mind to kick her shoes off and stick her bare feet out the window.

"What's up?"

"You heard about the shoe store?"

She nodded. "It's terrible about the girl."

"We checked her out—the victim. Nothing political in her life. She's an innocent. Dead, blown apart, for what? I don't know how these guys justify that."

"I don't either," Anik murmured. But she did know. She'd overheard the discussions often. *Innocents? There are no innocents.* No one had the right to be a bystander. If you weren't with the movement, or the cause, or the insurrection, you were against it. Innocence was merely a bourgeois disguise to protect the culpable. *We're all damned for our complicity. Condemned by the conceit of being born.* She'd heard similar talk in bars and at house parties and on balconies in the city while holding a beer in one hand, passing a joint with the other. But she'd not repeat any of it to Touton. He was right. Only a damned fool or a butcher could justify killing a shopkeeper, no matter the cause.

"Mailboxes are bad enough. Nobody gets hurt from that. Except it's not true. A postman finds a bomb, the army sends an expert to defuse it—*boom!* It goes off in his hands."

Faint streetlights shone through the mirrored image of his face imprinted on the windshield.

"Can you imagine that? In his hands. *Boom.*"

She didn't want to imagine it. A lot of people made fun of the FLQ planting bombs in mailboxes. So *Canadian*—polite bombers. They didn't want to kill people, just blow up pieces of paper, and bills, to make a point. But that was a better idea than killing people, so why did people make fun? Weren't they proving that they were not mad killers, but revolutionaries exploding an effective statement into the lives of citizens, into the government's fearful mind? Their point? The very existence of the federal government, of federal *mail*, was sufficient to set them off.

Boom! Confetti all over the ground. Media coverage across the land.

But she knew what was coming.

"Mailboxes. Fine. Nobody gets hurt, except a soldier, but who gives a flying fart about him? His family? But who thinks about that? Someday, maybe a cop gets it. What's one soldier, more or less? One less cop? Someday, a poor mailman. Shit. Never mind that the dead guys are fathers—don't think twice about that, it serves them right for being in the army or the police or, heaven help them, the post office. Isn't that what they say?"

"What who says?"

"People who plant these bombs."

"You think I know who plants these bombs?"

Touton looked at her. "It's inevitable, the people you hang out with. I'm going to drive you somewhere, Anik. I want to show you something tonight you haven't seen before."

"I don't know any bombers."

"I'm not saying you're close to them. You may not know that you know them. But where you go, the rooms you're in, the bars, you've shared the same space with them. I'll guarantee you one thing."

"What?" She was feeling grumpy.

"They know you."

He took her down to the docks.

The shock of the grain elevators, defiant, tall in the moonlight, felt moody and forbidding. Bare lamps shone upon dark patches of pavement. Between widely dispersed lights, large, looming shadows deterred any errant trespasser, as if only marauders and deviants lurked here, while nearby, policemen pounded the noses of recalcitrant types. Not an ill-founded impression, as the docks remained home to rogues, and all manner of malfeasance had occurred here. And yet, from night to night, from moment to moment, a sense of industrial slumber remained more prevalent, as the thrum and cough of machines circulated air and fluids, as through the heart and lungs of a wheezing beast.

They breathed the still, expectant air.

The car's tires thumped across the wooden crossings of railway tracks, then back onto paved road and a parking lot, cracked and lumpy from the heaves of winter frosts, intermittently patched but never properly repaired. The ride was jarring, and Anik held one hand against the ceiling of the car's

roof to keep herself pressed down into her seat. Touton slowed over a particularly coarse section of road—they might as well have been crossing a field—
then turned around the corner of a shed and travelled towards the river's
edge. He drove out onto a pier above the St. Lawrence, the water swift and
confused below them in a boil of eddies and whirlpools. He stopped and shut
the engine down.

In the ensuing quiet the motor made small clicking sounds as it cooled.
Time passed in the afterglow of that near-silence by the whoosh of river.
Anik asked, "Why are we here?"

"I drove your dad down here. Right to this spot. The first time we met."

"How come?"

Touton was gazing at her. From the distant lights along a shed's roofline,
and the moon's glow reflecting on the windshield, she could make out his
expression.

"I asked him to open the door," he told her. "I had the car parked right on
the edge. Right over the river. I asked him to open the door and step right out."

"He wouldn't do that." She was feeling nervous. She knew that Touton
had something to say outside the limits of her knowledge. Something about
her dad.

"I pointed my pistol at his kneecap. He opened the door."

She waited, listening to the river. She swallowed. "He really believed you'd
shoot him?"

"He knew I would. I made him get out. I made him hang onto the open
door while he dangled above the river. I wasn't going to let him back in the car.
I didn't care how many days it took. He could either fall in the river—"

"My dad couldn't swim," Anik recalled.

"So he told me. He could either fall into the river—"

"—and drown."

"—and drown—or he could come work for me."

She had to mull that through. She felt so sad for her dad being put in
that position. She wished he was still alive so that she could run into his arms,
weeping, and he could hug her, and she could hug him right back.

"You're a bastard, Captain Touton," she said quietly.

"I am," he agreed. "I never said otherwise and your dad knew it, too. Him and me, we were honest that way. But he understood me, your dad. I had a job to do."

The story struck her as dark and disquieting. "You're telling me my dad was a stool pigeon."

"I never call him that. You won't hear it out of my mouth. I'm saying your dad was a hero. All he cared about in this world was his wife and daughter. Everything else and everybody else, including me—including mayors and premiers, because he worked for them all—we could all go fly a kite in an electrical storm while standing in a puddle."

Touton paused, and tapped the steering wheel a moment as though repeating Morse code from beyond the grave.

"But his family meant everything to him. So he worked for me, yeah, and he told me things that helped me in my job, but he didn't do that because he was so afraid of falling in a river. He would've drowned if it wasn't for you and your mom. He didn't want to leave you two alone. But another reason he worked for me so well, is because he wanted to do good. He didn't want his daughter growing up to find out that her old man was only a thug. He wanted her to grow up and find out that he worked on the side of the law, too, that he was trying to do something good in his life, with the cards he'd been dealt."

Touton breathed easily and thought about lighting up a smoke, except that he only smoked other people's. When they adopted their daughter, his wife wanted him to promise to never smoke again, but during that negotiation they settled on him refusing to buy another pack for himself.

"I guess now's the time," he told Anik, "for you to find that out. Your dad, he was proud of what he did, so don't call him no stool pigeon. If I was you, I'd call him a hero. A man who did a tough job really well."

Anik chose to climb out of the car. She walked down the pier a short distance, and hugged herself against the slight chill in the breeze. Reaching into her jacket pocket, she pulled out her cigarettes. That brought Captain Touton over. He accepted her offer and pulled out a lighter to stoke both smokes.

"I should quit," she said.

"We both should," he said.

They stared out at the river surging below them. In daylight, pleasure boats took tourists on wild rides through the swirling swift currents. Anik had never been down to this spot and seen this view of the islands, the remnants of the World's Fair of 1967, whose theme had been "Man and His World." She stepped away from Touton to stand on the lip of the pier, looking straight down into the fleet river.

"Maybe I'll jump," she said. She thought, *Man and his world.*

"I don't advise it."

"It'll be on your head, for what you did to my father."

"I gave your father what he wanted—good work to do in life."

"I bet."

"It looks cold and fast and deep, doesn't it? But it's colder and faster and deeper than it looks."

She took a step back, still keeping one foot on the rail.

"You would know," she told him. "You've seen men wash away from here."

"Maybe I have," he said.

"What do you want from me?" she asked. "Spit it out."

"Come work for me," he said.

"What? As your stoolie?"

"I don't ever use that word for good people doing good work—the right work."

"Just like my dad, huh? Is that what you're thinking?"

Touton shrugged. He inhaled smoke and held it deep in his lungs, then breathed out. "He did good work, your dad. That's one thing."

"He made sure I knew how to swim, you know."

"Did he?"

"He didn't want me to have the same weakness as him. He was afraid of the water. I can swim. I can jump in here with an even chance of swimming ashore somewhere downstream."

"Sorel," Touton said.

"What?" She knew the town, sixty miles downriver.

"That's where most bodies wash up, the ones that get tossed in from here."

"I'll be swimming. I got an even chance."

"You don't want to jump," he said.

"I don't want to be your stoolie, either."

"Don't get me wrong, Anik. I'm not threatening you. This is a friendly conversation. I want to convince you that you can do something very positive with your life, that's all."

"It'll be symbolic. My jumping. I'll do it for my dad."

"That'll do no good."

"I'm not here just to please you, Captain Touton."

"Your dad wasn't either. But he did good work for me."

She stayed quiet awhile, looking downstream, following the movements of the current in the sporadic light.

"Anik?" Touton asked.

Finished with her smoke, she flicked the butt into the water. She watched the ember fall the long way down, to be extinguished on a wave.

"I don't know any bombers," she said.

"You might. Either you know them, or you know someone who knows them, or you know someone who knows someone who knows them. They can't be any farther away from you than that."

She nodded, as though to concede that that was likely. The city wasn't so big, the huddle of radicals in the various political movements wasn't that extensive.

"I know people who know people. But the people I know are my friends. Who trust me. They know I'd never sell them out. I don't think my dad was selling out his friends. Thieves and punks, guys who worked with him, maybe. But not his friends. Besides, my star has fallen in radical circles. Lately, I've been hanging out in different company."

He knew.

She turned, pulled by his silence.

"Are you trying to tell me that you want me to spy on René?"

Touton shook his head. "He's not a bomber," he said.

"No," Anik emphasized, "he's not."

"I understand what you're saying. You associate with the *establishment* now. But Anik, listen to me. Watch what you say when you're with him."

"Excuse me?"

Touton had smoked his cigarette down a lot lower than she had, and now tossed it into the St. Lawrence as well. Its light was extinguished long before it hit the water. Wearing a sports jacket, he hiked the collar up around his neck and also hugged himself. The river's cool night air was giving him a chill, too, and he wished she'd get back in the car.

"Why does Mr. Lévesque always take you to other people's apartments?"

Before she could answer that, she had to process the bulletin that Touton knew more about her private life than she revealed to anyone. She didn't go around advertising that she was sleeping with the politician, but her closest friends and her mother knew. She never told anyone about the clandestine meetings in strangers' bedrooms. The only people who knew about that part were the strangers who donated their homes, but few among them, if any, knew her.

"He lives in Quebec City," she answered. "He has an apartment here, that's true, but it's always full of people coming by. Journalists are always at the door. We go to other people's places because it's private."

Touton was shaking his head.

"What? You don't believe me? You think he has another woman at his place?" She had thought that herself, so the idea was not outrageous.

"Maybe he does, but I don't care. Lévesque doesn't take you home because he suspects that his own bedroom might be bugged. He knows it's a possibility."

"By you?"

"Why should I care about him? The RCMP, different story. The federal government sees him as a separatist, a subversive, so they'll try to bug his conversations. Your friend René knows that."

She would have suspected as much herself. No big deal.

"What he doesn't know," Touton continued, "is that sometimes he uses an apartment that was offered by someone working for the Mounties. Such as the one you were at today when he got the call about the bomb."

Anik spun, her mouth ajar. Aghast.

"That's why I'm saying, be careful what you say around him. Especially when you think you're alone in somebody's apartment."

"Mounties, you said?"

"I have friends who are Mounties. Sometimes I have access."

She quickly reviewed what others might have overheard. She was not concerned about sensitive political discussions—there'd be nothing new in those talks for curious ears—but she was fearful that the sounds of their intimacy had compromised her privacy. "Oh God," she said, thinking of a few moments during lovemaking. "Oh God."

Touton stepped closer to her, and briefly touched her shoulder.

"You see, it works both ways. I can be helpful to you, too."

She let him tug her back towards the car.

They got in.

Anik felt numb, displaced.

Touton started the engine, and as they moved away from the pier, the headlights scanned the walls of facing sheds. They saw two men moving slowly in tandem, not looking their way. "I should probably arrest them for trespassing," the cop muttered idly to himself.

"Go ahead," Anik told him. "I could use the company."

They smiled at each other, culling some small pleasure from their brief aside, then Anik came back to reality and let her face drop into her hands. The knowledge of what she'd just learned burned through her.

"Come on," Touton encouraged. "It's not that bad."

"No? Then how come I want to go back and jump in the river?"

†††

Touton dropped Anik off at her mother's house.

As she was climbing out of the car, he said, "Anik, do me one favour? Talk to your mom."

She got out and closed the door, then hunched down and looked at him through the open window. "You want me . . . to talk to my mom . . . about what we talked about? Why?" Of all the matters he'd discussed with her that night, this was the most puzzling.

"Talk to her, all right?"

She declined to give her consent even to that, or to anything else, and slowly stepped across the sidewalk, stooping to open the latch on the low metal gate to her home. Knowing she was coming, Ranger was inside, frantically scratching at the door. "Sic him," she wanted to say, but it would be no use. He wasn't that kind of dog, and would only run up and deliriously lick Touton's face.

†††

Ranger was yapping in the backyard while her mother sewed.

Anik Clément didn't awaken until 11 A.M., when she needed to rush to work. Three days a week, she pitched in at a restaurant to help quell the noon rush. She drank her morning coffee and munched on a toasted bagel, then told her mom about her night. As she got to the part where Touton had taken her down to the docks, her mom stopped the machine.

Touton wanted them to talk, she told her mother. "Why, Mom? I don't get it."

Carole went to the fridge and pulled out a beer.

Anik watched her pour the contents into a tall glass.

"Mom, it's not even noon."

Carole took a few swallows anyway. "Captain Touton wants you to know that you come from a family of liars." Her mother's tone felt ominous, and Anik waited, scared and hushed. "Your father, Anik, hasn't been the only police informant in this household."

Carole drank a little more, then began to tell her daughter stories. Anik knew she wouldn't be going to work that day. But that was okay, because she wouldn't need to lie when she called in sick.

†††

Problems cropped up all through his schedule, and the prime minister was giving his office secretary fits by not allowing her to fully rearrange matters to her liking. A bomb going off in a store in Montreal the day before had that effect. Attention paid to the aftermath required cancellations and adjustments.

"We should put back your 11:15," she advised him. A handsome woman in her sixties, she was capable of tangling with his advisors, most of whom were male, and holding her own against their bullying. Although the PM had an assistant who was her superior, she often took charge. "Since the gentleman is travelling, we might fit him in at four, if you come back from the House on time for a change."

Not remembering who the 11:15 might be, Pierre Trudeau cheated a glance at the daily outline on his desk.

"He's scheduled for forty-five minutes, Prime Minister. You'll agree that that's out of the question. Under the circumstances, he'll understand were we to make that twenty-five, which is still being extreme, sir. I'd recommend ten."

"Leave it as it is."

"Sir, we just—"

"The slot and the length of time. I'll see him."

She did not exactly leave the office in a huff, yet whenever the prime minister declined to listen to basic reason, the heels of her shoes managed to thud more loudly on the thick, plush carpet, then echo more sharply as she walked across bare wood. An amazing skill, Trudeau believed. One that never failed to make him smile. What could he say? No explanation was possible concerning his 11:15.

When the time came, he rose to greet his new guest, coming out from behind the majesty of the prime minister's desk. "Father François, how're you doing? It's good to see you again."

"I'm fine, fine. Good to see you, Mr. Prime Minister. Kind of you to find the time. Especially, I would say, with all that's going on."

The secretary's chin rose in agreement as she closed the door.

Trudeau bobbed his chin to indicate that the priest, who had arrived in his cassock, should be seated. He did not return to the far side of his desk, but joined him in the second chair in front of it, all smiles and warmth.

Yet he said, "Sadly, Father, the timing for our meeting is inopportune. I was hoping we'd have pleasant topics to discuss. I even planned to take you to lunch. We'll have to postpone that, I'm sorry to say. I've rebooked. I know how you enjoy good food."

"You never resist poking fun, Mr. Prime Minister."

"Not at all. A serious talk instead. Tell me, what's the word on the street, among your radical pals?"

"My radical pals," the priest repeated, and smiled slightly.

"Also, among the clergy, if you know any. I've never had the impression that you communicate with priests, though. What news, Father?"

Father François settled into the comfort of the guest chair and declared, "Thanks, Pierre, for asking. I'm fine. How have you been?"

With his hands on the arms of his chair, Trudeau put his head back and laughed. "Am I so rude? Are you my priest now, Father? Have you come to take the measure of my soul?"

"I may not be your priest, Mr. Prime Minister, but I am a priest, and we're old friends. An odd pairing, perhaps, but we've been through some times together."

"True enough," Trudeau concurred. "You're astute to call me on my lack of manners. Let's begin again. I shall offer you coffee. I'd like one myself, actually."

"In the old days, when we were putting together an issue of *Cité Libre*, we used to make it ourselves."

"Before we grow too nostalgic, let's remember that the coffee we made tasted like mouthwash."

He laughed. "A couple of times, someone snapped pictures, and it seemed that every time they did I was holding a fist to my esophagus and wincing in pain. I think we considered it necessary—bad coffee for the intelligentsia. Somehow, it seemed appropriate. I bet the coffee in the prime minister's office is outstanding, and I'd love a cup, thanks."

Trudeau called through on the intercom to have it done. While they waited, the conversation turned to casual matters—who had been marrying whom, who was being hounded by scandal. The two were no longer young men with ambitions and moral authority over their elders. Both of them were now weighted by their decisions, which often could never be delineated as right or as wrong, only as being somewhat beneficial or not yet fully conceived. After the coffee had arrived and they were alone again, feeling more comfortable with each other amid the quaint trappings of power in which they found themselves, Father François chose to reply to the prime minister's initial query.

"Mr. Prime Minister," he said, for even their long-term friendship could not override the aura of power associated with this room, nor dismiss the importance of the position, "the times are not so good. The word on the street is worrisome. More and more, ordinary men are expressing a willingness to acquiesce to the violence. 'Justice' is a word bandied about these days to excuse any crime, even the brutal death of a shopkeeper."

"Where's the justice in that?"

"Sir, I'm not the radical I may once have thought myself to be. I cannot find a speck of justice in that. Violence begets violence, love begets love—all contrary positions I find wanting."

Trudeau nodded, smiled a little and offered that telltale twinkle in his eye.

So invited, Father François inquired what he was thinking.

"I heard," Trudeau confided, "that you've come under the influence of hippies and peaceniks."

Father François did not take the remark as an insult, and smiled also. "So have you, in your own way, Mr. Prime Minister. I don't think Trudeaumania would have occurred if the world hadn't first gone half-cocked over the Beatles. If we didn't have love-ins and sit-ins and Martin Luther King, we wouldn't have Pierre Elliott Trudeau wearing a carnation in his lapel and seducing a nation. If there's a man alive who has harnessed flower power, Mr. Prime Minister, that man is you."

Trudeau deflected the comment, for whether the priest's statement was meant to be complimentary or derogatory was difficult to ascertain. He turned his head and pursed his lips knowingly and permitted his eyebrows to dip and rise. His contorted expression scurried around, mouth and cheeks a busy potpourri of nonchalant opinion and indecipherable emotion that flummoxed his adversaries while titillating his friends. Unlike anyone in politics, he could win an argument—or bring to conclusion a great debate—merely by making a face.

"I appreciate the change, Father, that's all I mean to say. You're not siding with the bombers. In the old days, you might have."

"You, too."

Trudeau wasn't going to accept that. He pulled a face again, but this time he was more direct with his comeback. "People might have thought so, I'll grant you. But I've never sided with force over logic. Not ever."

With a nod, the priest conceded the point and backed down. "You're right about me, though. When I was younger, with revolution in the air—or at least, in the smoky air of our lofts and backrooms—violent upheaval seemed an inevitable adjunct to history. Now, it might still seem inevitable, but I can honestly say that I know the process to be a relic of history, one that should never have been allowed to escape the stone age."

"Yet, the man on the street is accommodating violence."

"The man on the street is undecided. That in itself is worrisome. But the man on the picket line, the union man, the man in the tavern, the man whose politics are suddenly moving from prehistoric worship of a king, and when there was no longer a French king, the Church, that man is accommodating the idea of violence. I would say the romance of violence."

"Why romance?"

"Kids today," Father François opined, "not to sound like an old fart, but, I guess I am one now—kids today believe that victory can be won through violence. Mao is telling them so, and some are listening."

"Victory," Trudeau scoffed. "We create new victories every day. As I said a while ago—the press loved this one—the universe is unfolding as it should."

"The flower child in you, Mr. Prime Minister."

"Or the priest in me. Yet it's true. We don't hold the future as a vision in our heads, we create the future through our daily lives, one day and one idea at a time."

"Some more so than others," Father François said.

Trudeau looked at him. "What do you mean?"

"Some of us are able to create the future a day and an idea at a time more than others are able to do."

The prime minister leaned forward a touch, placing his palms down on the narrow armrests. "We've arrived at the nature of your grievance."

"Sir? My grievance?"

"No one enters this office without one."

Although he had run this conversation through in his head countless times already, the priest took a moment to consider his words. "Mr. Prime Minister ..."

"Yes, Father?"

"I've had a visit from an officer of the law."

"I see. I presume you understand that the Mounties sweep my office on a regular basis, searching for listening devices."

"I would presume as much. The Russians have spies everywhere, we're told."

"Never mind the Russians, although they're bad enough. The Americans worry me the most. Well, actually, do you know who worries me the most?"

Father François mouthed the words, *The Mounties?*

"Right you are."

The priest nodded. He understood. "I intend, sir, to be circumspect. You will recall an implement."

"An implement," Trudeau repeated. "You're referring to a certain farmer's shovel?"

"Correct. An officer of the law visited me with respect to a farmer's shovel."

"Why you?"

"I have known a variety of people who have shown an interest in the shovel over time. Including yourself."

"Me?" the prime minister inquired.

"That's correct, sir. Not that anyone, to my knowledge, is pointing that finger. Rumours persist, on the other hand."

"Rumours. Yes." The PM eased back in his chair. "Apparently, I'm homosexual now. Have you heard that one?"

"Khrushchev's your lover, I've been told."

They both laughed. "Nikita's not really my type. Others say I have a thing for Fidel. At least no one's put me in bed with Reagan."

"I'm glad, sir. Some people, however, have said that you have a passion for that farmer's shovel. That story goes around and around."

"Nothing I can do about it. That thought's been on the Ferris wheel. What's new?"

"A new detective is on the case. A young man. He paid me a visit."

"Fresh legs."

"A fresh mind, I'd say, sir. A bright young lad. Also of interest, I've learned that the deceased . . ." Father François paused to allow the PM a moment to catch the reference.

"The first?" the PM asked.

"Yes, sir. Among his, ah, other talents, shall we say—"

"What shall we say?"

"He also worked for the police."

The PM nodded, comprehending. "That explains the unending enthusiasm."

"Correct, sir, among other contributing factors of which we've always known."

"Such as?"

"It's a big case. Monumental, I'd say, in a policeman's career."

"Of course. Yes." Trudeau tapped his fingers on his blotter. "Father, this is why you've come?"

"I've corollary interests, shall we say. A pair. Like bookends."

Trudeau waited. Father François knew the truth, knew for a fact while others were left merely to speculate. Not that the priest could prove anything—it would be one man's word against another's—and the cleric was also culpable, as the entire affair had begun as his idea. Still, he was in the know, and so both trust and suspicion necessarily passed between the two old friends.

"Although I'm a priest, you know me to be a modern man, Mr. Prime Minister. Yet all of us, modern men in particular, are complex, often contradictory. We're an odd species. I'm an advocate for logic, philosophy, theology, symbolism and even, to a guarded degree, magic."

"Magic," echoed Trudeau.

"You have accomplished so much, Pierre. Your success has done nothing to diminish, in my mind, the power of an icon." He shrugged. "I'm in the Catholic Church—"

"Many have wondered how, given your ideas."

Father François smiled, in a way that suggested cunning rather than a happy moment. "The power of an icon," he said. "I have never promised what

I am unable to deliver, but I have always been attached to a certain understanding, a willingness on my part, an accessibility granted to me by God and through my associations."

"An accessibility." Speaking in code took a toll on the prime minister's famous impatience.

"Here I am, after all, seated in this august room."

Trudeau nodded. Smiled. "No one enters this office without a grievance, Father, and no man enters this room without wanting something from me."

"Where will it go, sir, when your work here is done?"

"Our farmer's shovel?" The prime minister gazed across at his visitor. He was not sure yet if he was being judged, courted or threatened, and he realized he might never know that answer. "You have a suggestion?"

"In the past—at the pertinent time, shall we say—the Church was undeserving, in my opinion, of a good man's philanthropy. But the Church has been dissected since then. Torn down. Its prestige and authority and a goodly measure of its wealth—locally, at least—stripped away. We're becoming a different Church. We have a long way to go, and our worldly destination will perhaps forever remain unknown, other than the gates of heaven. So I'm suggesting to you that, given your own faith, given all that you have achieved, and deservedly so, that you might consider an act of philanthropy when that day, in a distant future, arrives."

The man who bore the responsibilities of a nation in a time of increasing and vexatious tension mulled over the conversation. He kept wondering why the priest was making such a proposal now, wondered also if, in future, he shouldn't accept the advice of his office secretary more readily. "Father, you mentioned bookends. You have another thought?"

"You asked what word I've heard amid the clergy. From within and without, Mr. Prime Minister, dark matters have come to my attention. Which, in truth, is what brings me here today."

"Ah." Now, perhaps, they would get somewhere.

"Our old cronies," the priest began.

"Which ones?"

"I'm remembering the Russians, sir, and the Americans."

The potential for hidden microphones, yes. The potential to be betrayed by your friends. Trudeau nodded to indicate that he understood, although he still didn't know what was meant by "cronies."

"As young men, we were aware of them. I'm being facetious. A certain order, sir, an adversarial force."

The Order of Jacques Cartier. All right, he understood the reference now. He felt his skin tighten on his bones, as though an invisible hand was cinching him up.

"They persist, sir. They continue to look for a way to take advantage of the times. They would hope for chaos, revolution, an opportunity to contribute further to the chaos, in the hopes of creating a power vacuum that they might rise to properly fill. I'm here, sir, to make the point that our infamous shovel must be used to dig the proper field. The right trench. It cannot be passed around for any man to dig whatever well he chooses."

Father François feared Trudeau might sell the knife, perhaps as a way of unloading a political liability, either now or in the future, to clean up his legacy. In the wrong hands, Cartier's dagger—whether because it did possess an intriguing magical influence or merely due to its symbolic majesty—might readily encourage retrograde thinkers. The knife had been in the wrong hands when Trudeau had bought it, but it had been too hot for those in charge at that time to handle. Apparently, they had been disorganized then, in desperate need of money, or they had feared what they possessed, or who knows what chaos had existed within that tribe. Perhaps the ascent of an often-unemployed lecturer to the office of prime minister had opened their eyes to the relic's potential properties. In any case, this secret band of adversaries knew to whom they had sold what they had sold, and now a fresh contingent of like-thinking foes wanted the knife back. Father François was here to issue fair warning, and to plead that its line of descent be carefully selected.

"If I respond, would you take the information somewhere?"

"Well, not to the Jesuits, Mr. Prime Minister."

"Neither to the Dominicans."

"My Sulpician friends, on the other hand—"

"—might continue to be friends."

With a slight bow of his head, the celebrant indicated that the PM understood his position.

Trudeau thought about it awhile. Possession of the dagger was a burden. While he could never proclaim its mystic power, he could not deny his extraordinary and improbable rise to power, and so would not dismiss its potential for magical properties, either.

"When that time comes," he told Father François, "your proposition will be fairly considered, and at this moment stands in good stead."

Gobbledygook. They were suggesting a transfer of power back to the Church once Trudeau's political days were done—such was the perceived importance and vitality of the relic. The matter of its illegality, or of Trudeau's questionable ownership, would never be broached between them. Yet Father François had also delivered a more important message—namely, to be circumspect. The array of forces aligning against him might be more diverse, and more concealed, and better organized, than those represented by idiot bombers.

"Thank you, Mr. Prime Minister, for your time. You've been most kind."

"Good to see you, Father. Someday, again, we might bump into each other on the streets of Montreal."

"Hopefully in peaceful times."

After the priest's departure, the PM's secretary reclaimed the room. "Well," she recited, for she had probably been rehearsing her remarks the whole time she'd been gone, "may we return now to affairs of state?"

"I thought it was lunchtime?"

"Your luncheon will be with the commissioner of the RCMP, remember?"

"Ah. The commissioner. Good man. We'll want to discuss that bombing."

"Yes, Prime Minister, you may wish to discuss the bombing, if that does not conflict too much with chatting with your old friends."

She was adjusting the curtains to admit more light, another of her habits that expressed annoyance.

†††

Having spent hours alone during the day, taking a long hike with Ranger and napping in a park bundled in a bulky sweater under a warm sun, Anik Clément had returned home to sequester herself in her bedroom. She left for dinner at a fast-food restaurant, where she'd enjoyed silly banter with a pair of local characters in rags, then back to the house. She still did not speak to her mother. Finally, after she'd heard Carole depart the washroom and enter her own bedroom for the night, she came out from under the covers. She lit a candle in her room, watched the flame awhile, then changed into her pyjamas and crossed the hall to brush her teeth. Done, she tapped lightly on her mother's bedroom door off the kitchen. Anik tiptoed inside and crawled in next to her mom, who was sitting up with the reading light on, a book in her lap.

They lay there, together like that, mother and daughter, silent.

Finally, Anik asked, "Why, Mom?"

She couldn't hate her for life. She was her mother, and they were close.

"Two reasons," Carole said. She'd prepared her explanation.

"The men who came to our house, my babysitters," Anik interrupted. "Did you put them in jail?"

"If I thought somebody was a good guy, I gave him a pass. I wasn't all business. Your babysitters got off scot-free."

"Some of them went to jail."

"Not on account of me."

"I wish I could believe that."

"I'm not lying to you, Anik."

"You've lied to me all this time, Mom. For God's sake."

She closed her book and put it aside. "If it was you, exactly when would you tell your daughter that you were a police informant?"

Anik didn't think she'd ever be in such a position—that was the difference.

"Why?" Anik asked again.

"Two reasons."

"I'm listening."

Carole took a breath. "Primarily, to help the police find who killed your father."

Anik nodded. She liked that answer. "What else?"

"To make money."

"Aw, Mom."

Anik made a move to crawl back out of bed, but Carole restrained her with a gentle hand on her wrist. At that moment, Ranger joined them, but he was weary and he curled up at the foot of the bed.

"I was a woman who had to support a daughter after suddenly losing her husband. Back then, the union busters tried to prevent me from working. Do you understand? Life was hard, Anik. I wasn't sending good men to jail. I was preventing crimes from being committed, seeing that the worst guys got sent up. A killer, once, and some mean guys. Some shithead was going to pull a bank job? Something would go wrong. Cops would accidentally bump into him. Armand was very good at that—he made everything appear like a fluke. Okay, okay, I was a snitch, but I was not a scab. I never squealed on the more decent guys. I just made life hard for the real bastards."

Anik tried to process all that. "You always used to say that Dad had his rationale for doing what he did. He never really hurt people, he just knocked them around a bit. He never really interfered with elections, he just made people appreciate the vote more."

Carole had to chuckle. She had often repeated the line herself, but she'd never not laughed.

"Yeah, and I didn't put bad guys away. I only put the worst guys away. How's that? I needed the money, Anik. And I needed, deep down inside me, I needed to know that I was helping to catch your dad's killers. Talking about it now, I admit that there was something else."

"What?" She was tired, and snuggled in closer to her mom. She had not done this in ten years, but she felt like sleeping with her for a night.

"I wanted a life. I didn't want to just sew and get beat up on picket lines. I wanted a life. Hanging out with your daddy's old pals, I got to live a little. Even—you're a big girl now, right?—I even got to love a little. A teensy bit."

Yeah, she'd sleep next to her that night. Had her mom done anything so different than what she was doing with René? She liked the life, the attractions, the action, the intrigue, the possibilities, even the dinners out and the dinners in. She adored the sex. The company. The conversations. She knew all along that she wasn't making a life with him, that it was just exciting and temporary.

They lay together in silence. Carole reached across and turned off the lamp. Her daughter, it seemed, wasn't going anywhere.

Minutes passed before Anik spoke out of the darkness. "Should I do it, Mom? Do you think?"

Carole sighed, and put her head back. She didn't like any of this. The unanticipated problems, worries that seemed to leak out of your spleen and contaminate your bloodstream, tremors along your bones on the darkest nights, deceit an unhappy companion who never went home. She was on the verge of attempting an answer. Say no, don't do it. The public demands are too great. Nobody wants bombs to go off. The personal cost is too high—the loneliness, the feeling that you have no centre, no core, no place within yourself where you can always go and be who you are for a few minutes. Those consequences were too grave. And yet, before Carole had mustered the resources to talk to her, Anik had fallen sound asleep beside her. Poor child. Why awaken her only to say that she might never be happy, that she might never be safe?

Carole edged down under the sheets herself, and although she did not expect that she'd sleep a wink, before long, before she had a chance to formulate too many frets, she nodded off, feeling her body borne upon waves. The sky was moiling and fiery in an epic dream, touching down upon a seashore of grievous confusion.

They slept together, mother, daughter and, at the foot of the bed, dog. Silent awhile. Still.

CHAPTER 22

1941–47

THE FUNERAL TRAIN MOVED SOUTH ALONG THE EASTERN SHORE of the St. Lawrence, ponderously rattling away from Kamouraska towards Quebec City. The land in that region proved exquisite for farming, flat and fertile, the air moist from the river in summer when the daylight hours were lengthy. At that moment, in November of 1941, upon the commencement of winter in a dreaded time of war, dusk fell early, and in the waning light, the flatlands were already white with snow. Ghostly sculptures of ice haunted the beaches, washed up amid tangles of driftwood.

For Prime Minister William Lyon Mackenzie King, the day had been a sad one, although not unexpected. He welcomed the final end to the slow agony of dying inflicted upon his true friend, and most important minister, Ernest Lapointe. The man had been his Quebec lieutenant, and without a notable replacement, his own political life might soon suffer. On the journey back to Quebec City, where a second train waited to return him to Ottawa, he mulled over the issue of his friend's replacement, and consulted his advisors for their best thoughts.

Of these, Arthur Cardin was a political master and a superb campaigner. Undoubtedly, he was Lapointe's equal, and in many ways his superior, a likely candidate for the very job they discussed. And yet, at the funeral, he had seemed frail to the prime minister, and never had he been well known in English Canada. King had worked long and effectively with him, yet on a personal level they had never clicked. Of these three liabilities, the issue of his health was the most pressing. In a time of war, King required energetic men.

The premier of Quebec, Adélard Godbout, the hero who had defeated Duplessis, also accompanied him on the train. Along with Cardinal Villeneuve, he led the province as a loyal and fierce backer of the Allied cause. Godbout remained adamant that conscription, should it ever be enacted, would be a crime, and yet, in King's assessment, Godbout was his man. He ought to resign as premier and join King's wartime cabinet in Ottawa. Even Cardin agreed with the prime minister on this choice, though he added in the same breath, "Why not Louis St. Laurent? In peacetime, I doubt you could pry him loose from his law practice. So many corporations depend on him. But in wartime? Men are willing in this circumstance to perform a public service. He's sixty, but vigorous, well known, a significant orator, respected in Quebec—I'd consider St. Laurent, Prime Minister."

"I am not only choosing my Quebec lieutenant. In all likelihood, I am also selecting my successor. If I choose St. Laurent and he leaves public service at war's end, the party will be left rudderless."

The choice was worthy of consideration, although King remained certain that Godbout was his man. He found himself, however, gazing across the river that bore the name St. Lawrence— in French, St. Laurent. Could it be that the river was speaking to him, humming the tune of a separate possibility?

Returned to Ottawa, King learned that Godbout had refused him. An October by-election had been held to replace a member of the Quebec Legislative Assembly. Shockingly, Duplessis's candidate had merged victorious in Saint Jean, a riding *le Chef* had never won, a riding that had voted Liberal since Confederation. "I must remain where I am," Godbout informed King. "To leave now would be to allow Duplessis to take hold again."

While Mackenzie King consulted his best advisors and gave weight to their opinions, he also conferred with the dead—in particular, his deceased mom. Always he was attuned to instances of the other world communicating with this one. The name St. Laurent had been suggested to him while he'd been riding alongside the *Fleuve Saint-Laurent*. He had had a sense that the river itself had been speaking. And so, having lost out on Godbout, and having had his mother endorse his second choice, he selected St. Laurent.

Still, what would become of St. Laurent at war's end? King was aging, and if St. Laurent departed, no one would be prepared to succeed him. Since 1880, the party alternated between English and French leaders, and upon his death or retirement, it would be Quebec's turn. Without St. Laurent, who was ready?

The French, for all the grief they caused him, provided King with great solace, friendship and counsel. Lapointe, whom he'd buried with full pomp and splendour, had been his closest friend. Upon his deathbed, each man kissed the other's cheeks and spoke of their undying regard for the other, secure in the knowledge that they would meet again beyond this world. When Cardinal Villeneuve visited, the cagey prelate reminded the prime minister that their souls were linked, that they shared the same system of beliefs. King had to reserve his most intricate political stratagems for dealing with Quebec. This was frustrating and maddening at times, but for him a separate Quebec could be accomplished only by tearing his heart out. And so, he sat dismayed one day, towards the end of the war, and gruffly dismissed his advisors, both those who worked among the living and those who interceded with the dead, to contemplate a sad document that had landed upon his desk.

A letter from the president of the United States, Franklin Delano Roosevelt, had arrived. In it, he suggested the dispersal of all French in North America—from Quebec in particular, but also from the northern United States. He proposed that these millions be scattered across both countries to dilute their political and linguistic concentration. In this way, the language and the culture of the French might swiftly vanish from the continent. An end, the president was suggesting, to King's troubles and payback for Quebecers' anti-war sentiment. The action at war's end would conclude the infernal nuisance of the French presence in North America forever.

William Lyon Mackenzie King sat stunned in his chair.

He laboured under an abject duress.

And prayed for guidance.

At the end of an hour of solitary soul-searching, a scant smile indicated the revival of his spirits. Won't Roosevelt be surprised, he concluded, to learn that he had chosen his replacement as prime minister. His successor would be none other than the man the river had endorsed, Louis St. Laurent.

A Frenchman. A Quebecer.

Try to disperse the French then, Mr. President. Just try to suggest it.

King nodded to himself, satisfied. The French would remain in Quebec. Strong and free. As well, St. Laurent would continue as a politician. If the man had any further thoughts about returning to his lucrative law practice—which he did, for he rarely stopped mentioning it—King would wave Roosevelt's letter under his nose. That's all he'd have to do. St. Laurent would have to stay on then. Duty called. He'd have no choice but to become prime minister.

Roosevelt's letter had backfired on him.

King took a breath. *Thank you, Mr. President.* A giant load off his mind. He took another moment to thank the river for offering up its namesake, as well as to thank his dead mother for confirming the wisdom of the appointment. Then the prime minister returned to the further demands of his day, both fiscal and occult.

✝✝✝

Duplessis took oxygen.

Great gulps of enriched pure air.

In 1942, when the world had been at war, Hitler's move across Europe demoralized the Allies, prompting Cardinal Villeneuve to declare the advent of Armageddon. Even nationalist commentators within Quebec moderated their remarks, knowing how profoundly English-Canadians grieved over each military defeat. Nonetheless, the prodigious movement of Canada towards conscription, imposed finally through a plebiscite, for domestic defence only, fuelled the nationalist engine, and a few orators carried the rhetoric forward. Louis St. Laurent had one man tried for sedition, although he lost that battle in court, and still the aging leader Henri Bourassa had the audacity to unveil his vision for a new world based upon the cornerstones of Marshal Pétain's fascist regime in fallen France, Franco's Spain, Salazar's Portugal and Mussolini's Italy. To keep himself out of prison, he neglected to mention Hitler's Germany, but the cluster of dictatorships left the implication obvious. Support for a new party of the right was growing, to Duplessis's dismay, as he intended to occupy that political terrain himself. Under the grievous concerns of conscription, strange bedfellows were entangled upon the same mattress.

A youthful twenty-six, yet a sharp, impassioned speaker, a lawyer named Jean Drapeau ran for Parliament in a Montreal by-election. He began his political career by lecturing on the evils of apartment dwelling, warning mothers to lock up their daughters in such a licentious environment. His supporters included everyone from the key anti-Semites—the philosopher Abbé Lionel Groulx and the unionist Michel Chartrand—to a young and impressionable Pierre Elliott Trudeau. The new party called itself the *Bloc populaire canadien,* and over the protestations of Duplessis it chose to enter both federal and provincial politics simultaneously. The old monk, Groulx, advised them to do so. Many in their midst had scores to settle with Duplessis and desired that he be erased from the political canvas. Even those with no personal grievance against the man concurred. The question went forth, "Who wants a drunkard as our leader?" On that basis alone, the new right-wing alliance gained strength.

Embattled, Duplessis entered an oxygen tent. Into his lungs he breathed the name of every man opting for the Bloc. Liberals were his natural enemies—what could be expected from them if not contempt? Yet those who chose the new option committed a greater crime, for they were acting in clear defiance of him. He'd never forget their names. One of many, that of Pierre Elliott Trudeau, although he was only a sprig of a young man, was inhaled by Duplessis down into the depths, and silently, deeply, took root there.

He would never forget.

In his tent, he breathed. Outside the tent, he suffered. Consumption, diabetes and alcoholism had left him physically impoverished, often angry and depressed, yet never dispirited or willing to quit. Such an option had not crossed his mind. The contrary. Inside the oxygen tent, he marshalled his resolve and plotted his grand return. He already knew that he had been given an argument to win the next election.

This is Quebec, he'd think. *Quebec is gasping for air. Quebec lives in an oxygen tent, as do I. In here, I am Quebec.*

Remarkably, his most prominent adversary came to see him. Premier Adélard Godbout sat outside his oxygen tent and spoke cheering words of encouragement. Duplessis reminded his guest that he still intended to defeat him, that inevitably the leader of the province would become too cozy with the Liberals in Ottawa. Conscription would yet be his undoing. Godbout argued back on the merits of the war, that civilization itself remained at stake, not merely the comfort of their old colonial master.

For Godbout, to see any man turned onto his back like this, confined and debilitated, moved him to great sympathy, yet he was impressed by *le Chef's* ongoing tenacity, a will not only to live again but to fight again, and to win.

At the end of a long discussion, Godbout declared to journalists that Duplessis, if ever he were freed from alcoholism, would yet make a significant contribution to Quebec public life. Godbout had turned down King's offer to be his Quebec advisor, and by doing so had stepped away from the possibil-ity—indeed, the probability—that he would become the next prime minister of Canada. Now Duplessis, ailing and flat on his back in an oxygen tent, had him where he wanted him—in his sights, ready to take him down in the next election. Just as he would remember those who had betrayed him by joining the new political party, so he would remember Godbout's generosity of spirit and expression. He recognized that he was an outstanding man. All the better. What satisfaction could there be in defeating a nincompoop?

Well, some. But victory over a worthy opponent was all the more joyful.

He breathed the rich air within his tent.

When he emerged, alive, he quit his beloved drink.

From a day in 1943 forward, he would limit himself to orange juice, neat, although his health required no moderation of his continued devotion to women.

He took on a further discipline: the daily injection of insulin.

Strong again, knowing that an election approached, Duplessis surveyed the realm and called to a covert meeting a committee representing a certain secret sect of gentlemen active in the land. They derived from various occu-pations—business and agriculture, mining and academia, one among them was a priest. Above all, they were united in their thinking on crucial matters, supporting Pétain and Hitler. Each man had publicly decried Cardinal Ville-neuve's insistence that Catholics pray for an Allied victory.

Seven men came before him, two of whom represented the society's youth. Each man knew why the committee had been summoned. The issue of which party their group might support remained critical to Duplessis, for they were eighteen thousand strong and, moreover, possessed the ability to penetrate every sector of the society vital to him and draw votes his way, or repel them.

"The Bloc Populaire has many voices," he pointed out to the seven men, "but I am the master of this house. The leaders of the Bloc, that gaggle of quacking ducks, in their lifetimes have known only political defeats. I have known defeat, that's true, but I have also demonstrated that I can win against Liberals, whereas no other man has done so before me for half a century. Mistakes took place in the last election. I should never have stepped away from radio broadcasts. Even the sound of my voice distorted by the federal censor might have soothed voters and permitted them to choose with greater wisdom. Such an error shall not occur again. With your assistance, gentlemen, I will return to power. The Bloc Populaire can make no such claim, except to the gullible, and even then, only in their dreams. The movement demands a leader for our times, and I sit before you as that man. Gentlemen, when I regain power, be advised, I shall not loosen my grip on it again until God calls me to my reward. Now," he directed, and pulled each of his pant legs up an inch and leaned forward to ask, "what say you?"

Prior to the meeting, five of the seven were of a different mind, set to support the cause of the Bloc. Upon hearing Duplessis's appeal, they realized that they were listening to the remarks of a man who would soon be taking his petition out on the stump. They were reminded that he could prove persuasive in that arena, as he was proving to be in this meeting.

"How will you win?" a young man asked. He was a student of medicine, Duplessis had been informed, who had the intention of entering the psychiatric sciences. Due to the secrecy of the society, no man had provided a last name, only a Christian name and general occupation. But Duplessis knew them all by their full names, where they lived, the identities of their parents, wives and children. He knew the names of their friends, also.

"Camille, the Bloc Populaire supports Pétain, but it's confounded by its many voices, and is loathe to come out and condemn the Allies. Those who speak on its behalf would rather stay out of jail, so they make utterances out of one side of their mouths only. I suffer from no such compunction. The Allies, gentlemen, now include Russia. The Allies count among their fraternity the communist beast. When I take this message to the people, that a vote for the Liberals is a vote for the supporters of the devil himself, of communism itself—of Stalin—the election will be won. I can convince the people that the alliance is unholy, that they must mark their ballots for the integrity of Quebec, and for a government that will stand up to the federalists and their infernal conscription. I am the one to do it. Not Jean Drapeau, who worries more that a girl's bloomers might perchance be smudged than he does about the politics of the world. Let him tell Montrealers to live in homes that do not exist rather than in apartments, if that's what he wishes to say, but do not permit that impish young man to go against the likes of Mackenzie King or Louis St. Laurent on behalf of Quebec. He'll be devoured like a morsel of Charlevoix cheese by a waterfront rat."

The other younger man in the room, perhaps not meaning to sound insolent, although he did come across that way, pointed out, "He's not running specifically against King or St. Laurent."

The remark was naïve, for of course the federal politicians would be keenly interested in the provincial election, and in their way endeavour to affect the outcome. Rather than shame the neophyte for thinking so foolishly, Duplessis told him, "Godbout, then, who is a man possessed of greater acumen than I had previously understood. Godbout will spit him out before he's been properly chewed—Drapeau or anyone else they put up against him. I know them all."

"Can we win without Villeneuve? That's the real question," one of the older men stated, and at that moment Duplessis knew he was winning the day.

"It's a question for you if are supporting the Bloc Populaire. It's not a question for me. Villeneuve is incensed with the Bloc, Henri Bourassa and his new civilization, with his new friends, Pétain and Franco and Adolf Hitler. In his misguided apprehension of the world, Villeneuve calls it the devil's alliance. So the cardinal cannot support the Bloc, and if he does not support the Bloc, you cannot win. Now, you are assuming that he will support the Liberals against me, as he did the last time. After all, he supports the Allies, as does Godbout. But your great plans to rule the world are failing to come to pass, gentlemen. The war may not be over, but the outcome is increasingly apparent. The Axis is crumbling. You must prepare for the aftermath, and so must Cardinal Villeneuve. He has seen by now that the Liberals hold enough anticlericals tight to their bosom that it may be wise for him to withdraw his support, and when I have concluded pointing out to the people the obvious links between the Liberals in Ottawa and the communists in Moscow, he will have no choice. He will look to the future. He will see that the future is Maurice Duplessis. In the next election, understand why you will not hear me discuss the Jews, although I know well your position, and you know mine. Mention of the Jews will only torment the cardinal. One must be circumspect in these affairs. You, gentlemen, you and your great fraternity, must also look to the future and see to it that I am returned as premier. For your sake, you must do this, for the sake of your Order, and most of all for the sake of the Fatherland."

Although they were swayed, Duplessis needed to push one last button to achieve their passionate support.

"Your Order," he stated, "the great fraternal Order of Jacques Cartier, has been disgraced in the Senate chamber by one of our own. You have been betrayed. The existence of your Order has been made public and held in disrepute, its secret nature exposed. Your good works to effect that our textbooks record the truth of our history have been stalled. Who did this to you? Not just one man. Who brought that man into the Senate to make that speech? King and the Liberals. Support the Bloc Populaire and see for yourself what will occur. The Liberals will triumph once again. Or support me, Maurice Duplessis, and defeat those who have dragged the great name of your Order through the mud."

That did it. They were behind him now. They were willing to put aside the more extreme aspirations of their society in order to defeat their enemies. When it came to beating Liberals, Duplessis was the man for the job. He had convinced them of that, and the members of the committee from the secret Order of Jacques Cartier solemnly shook his hand, vowing to work for him through their eighteen thousand powerful members, to launch him to victory in the next election.

Duplessis required one more break. He needed Godbout to call an election before the war was won, before that victory celebration took place and became attached to him. Godbout did not fear him enough, and believed that the right wing would be divided between the Bloc and Duplessis's Union Nationale, believing also that Villeneuve would deliver the Church into his hands. The premier dissolved his government and went before the people in a general election.

"The federal government is in league with Stalin!" Duplessis warned across the countryside.

Thousands came out to hear him rant.

Godbout fought back. "Yes, Stalin—and Churchill and Roosevelt, don't forget about them."

The die had been cast. The people did choose to forget about the others. Roosevelt was rumoured to be anti-French. The communists had been allowed to sit at the table, to break bread with the civilized world, and fault lay with the Liberals. Most everyone believed that France was better off under Pétain, yet the Liberals remained devoted to the mother country's so-called liberation, and this business about Hitler being half-mad and against civilization was merely Allied propaganda—British and English-Canadian rhetoric. The Germans had suffered under the Allies, but hadn't the French of Quebec suffered under the English? Conscription was a plot to shed French blood overseas. *Quebec blood for Quebec soil only,* a goodly portion of the population believed, and if ever they forgot it, the Order of Jacques Cartier kept the slogan current. Although Duplessis had never feared the communists himself, and did not believe that they could manage a significant position in Quebec, he rode the fear of communism and of conscription to a narrow upset victory.

"I'm back," he told his sister on election night. "Too bad I can't have a drink to celebrate."

"Have a glass of orange juice instead."

"In the morning, I will content myself with a call from the prime minister of Canada to congratulate me on my victory. I suppose he's stewing over it now."

"King will call," she assured him, although King had delayed matters, for the election was a tight finish. Duplessis's claim to victory had still to await close results before being verified. *Le Chef* was pleased with the work of the Order of Jacques Cartier. As an opposition leader not expected to win, he had more restrictions placed on his funding, and hiring goon squads to oversee certain polling irregularities had proven too expensive. But the Order had taken care of that aspect, seeing to it that ballots were stolen and the appropriate ballot boxes stuffed, intimidating scrutineers so they'd be afraid to show up for work, and generally making sure that close ridings fell his way. They even escorted the nuns to get out to vote for Duplessis, and had themselves voted under the names of men long dead, or still fighting on the fields of France, to make certain that sufficient loyal votes were cast.

Duplessis took a deep breath, inhaling good, clean, northern air, and nodded. "Yes," he agreed. "King will call."

Outside the window, the people were cheering, cheering.

Le Chef was back.

†††

Houde took the train.

He had made the best of his confinement. He became the camp's Chinese checkers champion, and taken an inmate's idea of escaping by skating to freedom and turned it into a winter sport. He won the long-distance skating championship, after bribing Roger Clément not to participate, and had been elected mayor of his hut. Yet the years had been difficult as well. He had had to make it through sixteen months before he was allowed a first visit with his wife and eldest daughter. Even then, he was permitted no more than thirty minutes in their company, while a guard stood close by. A single postcard constituted his monthly ration of outgoing mail, which was censored, although when he realized that Roger Clément was using a guard as a courier to send letters more often, he took advantage of that outlet as well. The guard worried about posting letters from a politician, not wanting to be caught, but out of his sense of Catholic decency—for he was an Irish lad—he eventually agreed to mail letters addressed to Houde's wife.

By the summer of 1944, no one could imagine that he might sabotage a war that was going well, and the demands upon King to release him increased. The prime minister finally acceded, not wishing to further damage his own reputation in the city, and the papers announced that Camillien Houde was coming home.

He told Roger, "When you get out, come see me. We'll work together again."

"Go see my wife. Make sure she's all right."

"I shall. Be of good cheer, Roger. You'll be free soon. The war goes well for your side."

He said goodbye to the inmates, and understood as he was doing so that he had enjoyed the company of the communists far more than that of the fascists. And now that the fascists were confronting defeat abroad, they made for even less of a convivial band.

In Sherbrooke, a few hours east of Montreal, Houde got off the train. He spent the night there before proceeding on. After all, the citizens of his home city had not had ample time to arrange a celebration for his arrival, and he owed it to them to give them that. As well, he much needed to improve the state of his haberdashery, for the finer clothes he'd brought to the camp were now worn and bedraggled.

He decked himself out well. He returned to Montreal wearing a morning coat over an elegant grey vest. Broad suspenders held up his striped trousers, the creases sharp and accentuated. He bought new shoes. Even though they sparkled, he had them buffed until he could peer over his belly and see himself wink in their mirror finish, then protected the shine with grey spats. To complete the effect of his attire, he found in Sherbrooke a Malacca walking stick— a real find, a cane he could twirl as he whistled down any boulevard.

His life had not been easy, despite his successes and the station to which he'd arisen. The first of ten children, each of his siblings had died in childhood, and when he was nine his father had passed away as well. His first election victory, to the Quebec legislature, had saved him from penury. Indeed, he had run for office back then to make a salary, and had won by threatening to flatten the top hat of the premier of the province, the old-money Liberal Taschereau. He then lost the next election. Impoverished again, he ran for mayor, winning despite being destitute and living in a grimy, cold, poor man's flat.

The role of the politician had reminded him of a time in his schooldays when he played Cyrano. He hadn't required a fake nose, as his own had served the purpose. He could drive an audience to a fever pitch, fill them with rage and conviction, then, with his next words, cause them to laugh and dab tears of pleasure from their eyes. His critics called him a clown, yet in considering the insult, an astute writer observed that clowns were the most intelligent characters in Shakespeare's plays, and in that tradition, Houde could play the role of the clown very well. The office of the mayor had been emasculated by the provincial government after Houde escorted the city into bankruptcy. He'd be obliged to serve as a figurehead only, but Houde had set his sights on that prize, and when he stepped off the train in Montreal, he was greeted by more than ten thousand citizens, all come to welcome him home and praise his name.

Working his way through the crowds in Windsor Station was a difficult task. He was glad that he had his cane with him. On the street, a speaker's stand had been erected, with microphones, and from that raised podium he spoke to the enchanted crowd. "I was lonesome for you in the concentration camp," he called out to them.

They cheered, and so many women wept.

"And it looks as though you were lonesome for me, too."

Their shouts became more feverish.

"I am ready to accept my mandate from the people who are crying for me. Your spontaneous ovation should be a warning to all political leaders."

As one, the crowd took up the fight with him.

A reporter asked, upon his announcement that he would again seek the mayor's chair, "Do you not fear that your support for Pétain and Mussolini will be held against you?"

Houde shrugged. "I don't recall speaking of support for Pétain. I was in a concentration camp when he came to power, so that opportunity was denied me. As for Mussolini, the people will say that the war is over, or almost over, and do you know what? They'll be right."

When reminded that he had left the city bankrupt, he repeated his constant theme on the subject. "The banks wanted me to starve the poor. I declined to do so. I know how the bankers have judged me, and I know how the prime minister of Canada has judged me. Now let us see what the people think, and let them be the final judge."

Houde won. He wrote to Roger Clément,

> *Roger,*
> *I need you here to take care of the rough boys, to be their boss.*
> *Things have heated up, gotten out of hand. Seventeen men were shot on*
> *election day. Can you believe it? Do you remember the good old days of*
> *baseball bats and fists? Of course you do. When you return, you'll find*
> *that it's all about guns and knives now, brass knuckles and lead pipes.*
> *Oh, you'll love it, Roger! It's all so exciting. I shall use my new influence*
> *as mayor to do what I can to secure your release. In the meantime, I*
> *have looked in on your beloved Carole. She has managed to sustain*
> *herself, but misses you terribly, as you miss her. I'm afraid that she finds*
> *me a bit of a fascist, to use her word, and so I am limited in what I might*
> *do for her. Rest assured that I shall watch over her from a safe distance*
> *(safe for me from her, you understand), and I have already seen to it*
> *that her house tax has been reduced. She'll never know why unless you*
> *tell her. Don't tell her, Roger. She might pay a higher tax if only to spite*
> *me. Be brave, Roger. See you soon.*
> *Yours truly,*
> *Camillien*
> *P.S. Roger! I'm back. I told you I'd be back.*

††††

The war was over, and the old gang was back.

Duplessis was premier and Houde the mayor. Roger Clément returned also, with a few boys from the internment camp who had won jobs with Houde. He kissed his wife and held her for a full twenty minutes before he managed to release her and introduce her to his friends. Then they all went home to his house to party.

Late in the evening, a knock was heard at the front door and Roger answered. The mayor stood before him, grinning as widely as the mouth of the St. Lawrence and holding up a bottle. "Champagne!" he enthused. "Good for what ails you." The mayor, too, joined the party, which lasted until dawn, long after Roger had walked off to bed with Carole, where they kissed one another and loved one another to sleep. When he briefly awoke to shift his weight, to take in the room that was his own, to pinch himself with the knowledge that he was free and Carole again lay beside him, Roger heard the mayor's voice, boisterous and laughing in the front room—"Did I ever tell you the story of the man it took six years to bury?"—and Roger smiled, for all was well, and he returned to the arms of his wife, and to sleep.

†††

Across town, in his sister's tiny apartment, where he had gone after his return to civilian life and where he slept under her bed, Armand Touton tried on his new uniform. He was a policeman now. He thought he looked mighty sharp in blue.

He did strike a handsome figure.

Before the bathroom mirror, the young veteran smacked his powerful right fist into the opposite palm, and smiled. Hard and fast—that's the kind of cop he would be. Commando style. He vowed that no man would ever be braver.

†††

In New York City, a traveller by the name of Count Jacques Dugé de Bernon-ville tried on a priest's cassock. He was hoping that the disguise would al-low him to cross the border into Quebec, for what would be more familiar in Quebec than a priest's black robes? He had spent the war hunting down Jews in France to hand over to the Nazis, and torturing and shooting resistance fighters. He was now living the opposite life, on the run. A war criminal, they said. He did not know how there could be such a thing. A war was a war—how could any action be considered a crime? And yet, the war was obviously not finished for him. He had found no peace.

He was looking for a home.

Dressed as a priest, de Bernonville entered Quebec, where, he heard, many remained sympathetic, even loyal, to the true cause.

CHAPTER 23

1970

I
N A BORROWED CAB, THEY DROVE UP WINDING STREETS ALONG A RIM
of Mount Royal, through a community of mansions they hadn't even
known existed prior to beginning this operation.

We've tracked you down. On your mountain. You're in our sights.

One man knocked.

Your friends call you Jasper.

They waited on the stoop.

The housekeeper answered. Politely, Jacques asked her to sign for a birthday gift. Yves carried the long, narrow box across his arms. Days earlier, James
"Jasper" Cross had turned forty-nine.

Jacques forgot to hand her the receipt for her signature.

It begins.

Swiftly, he thrust it forward. He didn't have a pen handy—part of the
plan. He dropped his hand into a pocket to fish for one and pulled out a black
.22-calibre Beretta pistol. He thrust the muzzle into the woman's belly and
pushed her inside as he entered.

She put her hands up and talked excitedly in Portuguese.

Yves followed him in and pulled on his gloves. He reached into the gift-
box and retrieved his M1 rifle. Tossed the box on the floor.

Still on the street, Marc saw that they'd made it inside. His cue. He ran
up from the street, trying to conceal his own sawed-off M1. A gardener across
the avenue concerned him, so he kept the stunted rifle tight to his body as he
went inside.

A little girl suddenly appeared in the front room, shocked by the entry of the men and calling to her mother, the housekeeper. The first unexpected occurrence. The second was a dog's bark from upstairs.

"Pick her up," Jacques told the woman. The Portuguese maid plucked her daughter off the floor and bound her into her arms. "Where's Cross?"

The woman pointed upstairs.

The mansion had twenty-two rooms.

Upstairs, Jacques found a short, stout woman in bed and James Richard Cross padding around in his pyjamas. A Dalmatian leaped onto the bed, growling but seeking shelter in the covers. "We're the FLQ," Jacques told them. He pointed his black gun at the man. "Lie down on the floor." He told the woman, "Control your dog or I'll shoot it."

She calmed the animal on the bed. Her eyes shone with fright.

Jacques signalled for the others to come up.

Yves pushed the maid and her child into the room ahead of his M1.

Face down on the floor, Cross asked, "What do you want?"

"Liberation," Jacques told him.

"I can give you money."

"Rich man, you can't buy your way out of this one. Stand up. Get dressed."

Each of the women held onto a smaller life, one a dog's, the other a child's.

Cross had a dressing room. A whole room for storing and putting on his clothes. That alone seemed reason enough for a revolution. Jacques watched him dress, and the two men emerged together.

"Say goodbye."

Wearing grey slacks, a shirt and a green-checked jacket, Jasper Cross stepped shakily towards his wife and kissed her. He patted the head of his dog.

Then Yves handcuffed his wrists in front of him, tugging down the sleeves of the jacket to hide the cuffs. "Let's go," he said.

Jacques gave final orders to the others in the house. "Don't call the police for an hour. If you do, we'll kill your husband."

On the way out, he tossed a raincoat over the man's hands.

He held the pistol against Cross's back as they led him down the walk to the taxi.

When it comes, people aren't ready for the moment. When a man needs his boots and an iron constitution, he's wearing bedroom slippers. He's taken by surprise.

Through the upstairs window, Mrs. Cross waved wildly to the gardener across the street, who was raking leaves.

He stared up at her.

The men and Cross climbed into a taxi.

"Don't make a sound, Jasper."

He was pushed down onto the floorboards of the car's back seat.

They changed cars at the Royal Victoria Hospital, getting into a Chrysler. A man being assisted from a taxi into another car would not be conspicuous around the hospital, where so many required assistance. With Cross on the floor of the Chrysler, Marc put a gas mask over the man's face, the eyes blacked out. Then he straightened up and said, "Shit."

"What?" Jacques asked him.

"Our masks."

They all looked at each other.

"What about them?" asked the woman who'd been waiting for them and who was driving now.

They didn't answer.

Then she understood.

Jacques explained it anyway. "We forgot to wear our masks."

†††

Gaston Fleury understood the question. He just couldn't work his tongue around the answer. He had been disturbed by the answer in the past, putting it aside, letting it fall away from his consciousness. Why had he not pursued the discrepancies?

"Hard to say."

Cinq-Mars continued to wait for a more satisfactory response.

"It was a long time ago."

"Fifteen years," Cinq-Mars said, but his tone suggested that this was not a lifetime. Men could remember important events that were fifteen years old without this jittery impairment. The young officer reviewed the facts for him again—for the fifth time, by his count. "Sir, you were looking into limousines owned and operated by the provincial, federal and municipal governments."

"Right," Fleury agreed. That was the easy part. Cinq-Mars had come to him and said he needed to ask more questions. A nuisance, these years later. Fleury had made captain, responsible for the Department of Research and Strategic Planning. He'd lost interest in Touton's pet case, now passed along to Constable Cinq-Mars.

"You discovered that the logbooks for three levels of government showed discrepancies."

"I did."

"The discrepancies occurred because elected government officials and high-ranking civil servants used the cars in secret. For liaisons, we presume. To visit girlfriends."

"Except for men who visited boyfriends. Those, too."

Cinq-Mars nodded. His stomach remained tense. He loved asking questions, but interrogating a senior officer with whom he often worked felt odd. Risky. "The logbooks were commonly doctored. Actual trips didn't match the records."

"Hundred-mile trips, but only twenty showed on the odometer. Or the opposite. Everyone assumed nobody would ever check, so they were careless." Fleury had been excited when he first penetrated the deception. "It had become routine. Almost everybody who had the right to use a limo used it to conceal his comings and goings. Which made investigating the cars next to impossible."

"But knowing that logbooks, routinely, were improperly maintained . . ." Cinq-Mars let his voice fade away.

In a fog, Fleury acted as though he could not guess the next question, although it had already been posed four times.

"Sir, why did you not reinvestigate the entries for the night of the Richard riot, for the night of the murders, once you'd learned that the information was commonly doctored? At that point, why did you continue to take the entries at face value? Sir, it's a simple question. There must be a simple answer. You must have made a decision not to pursue that particular line of inquiry."

"I don't remember."

"I wish you would. Or try harder. It's important, I think."

They were back to the same impasse.

Fleury bowed his head a little, and was rubbing his chin, for he still seemed perplexed by something. Then he said, "I didn't think it mattered so much."

"Why not?"

"I'll tell you something, all right?"

"I'm listening," Cinq-Mars said. This, at least, felt akin to progress.

"I got a phone call."

"All right."

"Back then."

"Who called?"

"Anonymous."

"What was said?"

Fleury breathed in deeply before continuing. "Next time, you'll find your little boy in it."

Cinq-Mars awaited further explanation, but none was forthcoming. "What did that mean?" he asked. They were getting to the bare bones now, yet he remained mystified by the line.

"My car had blown up."

Cinq-Mars waited.

"I didn't think it was all that important, what I was doing. I thought I was mostly being a nuisance. I was an accountant. I stopped investigating the limos but I didn't know—I never knew—if that's what had pissed people off. I didn't think I was getting anywhere. But if I was, it wasn't worth my only son."

Cinq-Mars nodded solemnly, grasping this. "So first they blew your car up, then they sent you a warning to go along with it."

"Pretty effective threat, if you ask me. I'm just an accountant, really. I'm not like a real detective."

Cinq-Mars stood and crossed to the door as if departing, but he had no intention of leaving yet. "Captain, I appreciate that we're speaking in confidence, and that you're a captain and I'm a uniform. But it makes me wonder. Why tell me this? Why me? Because I asked?"

Fleury uttered a short little laugh, as if to dismiss the gravity of the confession. "You're a priest, Cinq-Mars—at least, you wanted to be. You've got it in you, anyway. I'm a Catholic who just went to confession."

"You're kidding me now? Why?"

The new head of the Department of Research and Strategic Planning sighed and squirmed around in his chair. He loved his new leather swivel seat. "That's not it. What I told you has been on my conscience. I did confess it to my priest, but I received no relief from my remorse. I had to confess it to a cop, don't you think? Or it would be meaningless. So now I've done that, I got a load off." He leaned back in his chair, a man teaching himself to relax. "Like you said, you asked the question. Time's gone by. I don't feel like escaping the answer anymore. You're onto me anyway, right? I don't want to make things hard for you, Cinq-Mars. You think it's strange that I confessed to someone below my rank? Think about it. If I confess to anyone, it won't be to a colleague with higher rank than me. You young Turks, you presume we're corrupt anyway—you think we're a bunch of fuck-ups and has-beens. So maybe I'm proving that point. But see, there's nothing you can do to hurt me. You won't be on a promotions committee with my name in front of you. By the time you get that high up in rank, I'll either be planting roses in front of my retirement home or fertilizing them from six feet down."

Cinq-Mars suddenly felt strangely alert, his fingertips tingling. The captain had been wrong about one thing. He had never thought that Fleury was corrupt, a has-been or a fuck-up, despite the friction between them. Now, he wasn't so sure.

"This helps me," Cinq-Mars told him. "I'm discovering where gaps exist. It helps to know where to keep looking."

"It won't help you so much," Fleury predicted.

"Why not?"

"Do you think the old man doesn't know? That he didn't know back then?" Fleury had a cocky look on his face again, as though he was glad to always be one step ahead of the keen young cop. "Come on, the old man's been around the block. Maybe he didn't want to put my son at risk, either. After that, he kept the investigation going without my input."

Cinq-Mars nodded. Complications persisted in the world. Hitches inevitably derived from the interplay of people's natures, their foibles and fears, flaws and strengths of character, and in particular their envy and greed. None of that had surprised him in his move to the big city, but still he had to learn that he could never underestimate the intricacy of human interplay. Life was not only about avarice and power. Life was also about striving, and the disappointments and quiet failures that attended to the realm. These daily turnings did much to help the world revolve, to cause it to circle on itself and revisit again seemingly innocuous social exchanges.

A detective with a big, black moustache who was not wearing his jacket, his holster and pistol showing, rudely reached his hand inside the open door and rapped it twice.

"FLQ," he said. "The director is calling us in."

"Him or me? Or both?" Fleury asked.

"Senior officers to his desk on the double."

"A bombing?" Cinq-Mars inquired. He was being excluded from the session, and so tried to snatch information on the fly.

"Kidnapping. A British diplomat, I heard."

That sent a chill.

Before dashing out, Fleury paused long enough to exchange a nod with the junior officer. Their pact was sealed. Cinq-Mars had information to go on, but he was not to reveal its source.

†††

Tied to a chair, at times blindfolded, at other times wearing blinkers that restricted his peripheral vision, James "Jasper" Cross listened to the radio. Communiqués from the group holding him, calling itself the Liberation Cell, were being broadcast. If certain people the cell had deemed to be political prisoners were not released, and if other demands concerning the governance of the land were not conceded, he would be executed. A deadline was aired.

The government, Cross's captors believed, was doomed to negotiate. He was baffled by their optimism. He had once read, with only passing interest, that the FLQ had distributed a leaflet titled *The FLQ Will Kill!* He wished now that he'd never seen the article. He might die in this still, airless room. He felt bloated by impotence, and in his worst moments he panicked under the blindfold, desperate for light, air, release. He suffered imagining the pain inflicted upon his family. He could forgive his captors many things, but not the affliction they had brought to bear upon his loved ones.

"I've never harmed you." He spoke to a mute presence he detected in his room in the morning.

A woman answered. She seemed to him the most callous among them. "You're English. What harm could we inflict on you to pay us back for the conquest?"

"Actually," he noted quietly, "I'm Irish."

He could sense, or perhaps was hoping, that he had touched a nerve. The French had long had good relations with the Irish. Down through the centuries, the French had invited forsaken Irish into their homes and adopted orphaned Irish children as their own. Irish surnames had become prominent in Quebec society, and the Irish were generally viewed as confederates, having shared the experience of being colonized by the British.

"Then you're a collaborator," the woman declared. "You work for London. You've betrayed our people and your own."

The admonishment felt severe, yet Jasper Cross was heartened. They had made a mistake! They'd snatched an Irishman. That slight sliver of a doubt might hold him in good stead if ever the value of his life was weighed, if a choice had to be made to determine whether he was to go free or die.

Over the radio from the other room, he learned that the government had declined to negotiate. He also learned that he was still alive. The hostage-takers, it was reported, had postponed their most recent deadline to kill him.

They had set another.

The radio in the other room informed him that he had eleven hours to live.

†††

"Where's Bourassa?"

A shrug. "New York."

"Still? What's he doing there anyway?"

Another shrug. "Farting around. He's reachable. He sent a number."

"Big of him."

The prime minister had pulled his most trusted colleagues together: Marc Lalonde, his finance minister; Gérard Pelletier, his secretary of state; and his labour minister, Jean Marchand. Lalonde had not spoken, but addressed the prime minister now. "Pierre, we've learned of a meeting."

"Tell me."

"Ad hoc, in Montreal, of interested people to discuss the situation. It's taking place at Ryan's office." Claude Ryan, the editor of *Le Devoir*. A leading intellectual and moral figure in the community. "Parizeau's going." A separatist politician of influence, and president of the executive council of the Parti Québécois.

"Not Lévesque?" Trudeau asked.

"Apparently not. It's safe to assume that he's an informed party."

"How do we know this? I take it we're not invited."

"Someone on the guest list is keeping me apprised."

"So we're also an informed party at the meeting?"

Lalonde shook his head. "Our friend would be tossed out on his ear if anyone found out he was talking to us."

Trudeau nodded, getting it. "Lévesque has representatives who keep him informed. We have a spy. I appreciate the dynamic. What's the meeting about?"

"That's not fully understood. Ryan is animating the talk, which is all right, but the list of those attending worries me." Financiers, politicians, academics, journalists, businessmen—a gathering that cross-pollinated the powerful and the merely influential. "It's been suggested," Lalonde went on, "that the agenda will include a discussion on what to do."

"Do?"

Lalonde was austere and cerebral. "If they conclude that Bourassa is unfit to govern, they may choose to govern on their own. It's in the air. Everyone's convinced he's inept. Those who know him don't believe he can handle this crisis."

"Now it's a 'crisis.' I thought it was a kidnapping."

"Prime Minister—"

"I know what you're saying."

Trudeau took a moment to process what was being illustrated. "A palace coup? Already the FLQ has set itself up as a parallel government, presuming to dictate policy. Do these people at the meeting intend to do the same thing? How many governments can there be in Quebec at one time?"

"They haven't met yet," Lalonde pointed out to him.

"They might decide to become the government," Pelletier considered. "It's not out of the question. Fear that Bourassa can't handle this mess is widespread."

Trudeau made a few faces, mulling things over, then opined, "Give him time. He might rise to the challenge if he ever comes home. I think it's possible."

"Do you know what he's doing in New York?" Pelletier asked. If Trudeau had a weakness, he valued ineffectual adversaries. Men who could not perform brilliantly in debate or before a scrum of reporters were his pawns, for he could manipulate them from dawn to dusk. Bourassa was neither a natural adversary nor an ally, but in this circumstance they would have to work in unison, as partners, though not as equals. Trudeau might miss the opportunity to guide the other man where he should be led, and do so through positive encouragement, rather than mockery or intellectual slight. "He's hiding," Pelletier said. "He's in denial."

"Shit."

The news was all bad. If the powerful citizens of Quebec were discussing an overthrow of their own government to fill the vacuum left by a young, timid, and, for the time being, absent premier, then the political authority in Quebec really had become a vacuum. That gave the FLQ infinitely more power with their broadcast manifestos, their bombings, and now, a kidnapping.

"Banana-republic politics," he muttered in disgust. "Gérard, what do we do?"

Pelletier stretched out his long legs. A person entered government for moments such as these, to make decisions that determined the viability of a nation. When they had first come to Ottawa, Trudeau had wanted to delay assuming responsibility until he learned the ropes. Pelletier and Marchand counselled him differently, reminding him that they had not fought an election to sit on their posteriors. Now, a short time later, they were in a political maelstrom beyond their imagining. Yet, this is what they had come here for, and this is how history would judge them—by how they handled pressure.

"When Bourassa calls, Prime Minister, befriend him. He lacks resolve. Show him your own. Permit him to lean on you. Coax him along. Offer comfort."

"Jean?" Trudeau asked of Marchand.

"Sentiment is running against us. Further demonstrations in support of the FLQ are being organized. Public support gives those bastards their courage."

"Who cares about their courage?" Lalonde asked.

Pelletier chose to answer. "The demonstrations are exhausting the police. They're taken away from their primary task, which is to find the kidnappers. If this keeps up, the mayor and probably Bourassa will be asking for the army again."

Trudeau had sent troops a year earlier, to defuse bombs in mailboxes and patrol streets. "If Bourassa asks, I'll have no choice. I'll have to accept the request. It's the law."

"Bourassa will ask," Pelletier said. "Once he flies back from New York and realizes that he can't avoid this, he'll ask. In a crisis, a weak man loves an army."

"As for what we do," Marchand stated, finishing up, "we wait. See what develops. We can't allow ourselves to be caught off-guard again. This is not merely a criminal act, a kidnapping. We have a developing crisis that involves a significant portion of the population."

"Marc?" The prime minister polled the minister of finance a final time.

"Monitor what the people do and say after these power meetings. If they communicate with the outside world, we'll closely examine the language. Their choice of words will show us the nature of their debates. They may have to debate whose side they're on."

"You're not serious."

"Prime Minister, I could not be more serious."

Trudeau acknowledged the sentiment with a nod. The quality of leaders attending the meeting in Montreal promised a lively discussion. He was almost sorry to miss it.

"All right," he summed up, and in so doing excused his counsellors for now, "we'll carry on."

†††

Anik Clément lay in the arms of her lover. She could feel the tension rising through his bloodstream again, the strain of these dire days returning.

The telephone rang and his body jerked spasmodically, a compressed spring suddenly released.

"Easy," she said.

Lévesque reached across and picked up the receiver. "Yeah?" Only one man had this number, and he wouldn't be wasting his time with trivia. He listened, then said, "My God," his voice grave.

Placing a hand on his back, Anik could feel adrenaline inflating him.

"All right," he said. "I'll be there."

He yanked his trousers on so quickly, he forgot he hadn't yet donned his underwear, forcing him to start again.

"What's happened?" Anik asked quietly.

"They've taken Laporte."

"Who?"

"Laporte! Pierre Laporte! The minister of labour. They've taken him."

"Taken? Kidnapped?"

"Right off his front lawn. On the South Shore."

"Oh, Jesus."

"Bourassa will want the army now. We've got to stop him."

"How?"

"Political pressure. Public and private. You'll see. He'll bow. He better. I have to persuade the others. There's to be a meeting."

He was nearly out the door when he remembered that he alone had the keys to lock up this place. He tossed them to her. "Keep them on you. Figure out the exchange later."

"Good luck," she called.

"This is destiny. It's no longer a matter of luck."

If you say so, she was thinking, as he closed the door, but she didn't believe him. His remark reflected his own combative energy, the primitive, involuntary pleasure he took in being thrust into the vortex of chaos. Everyone's destiny was on the line, she knew, René's, Trudeau's, Bourassa's, the FLQ's. Perhaps her own. Somewhere in that mix luck would play a role. Then all these warring men would see what destiny's project really had in store for them.

She didn't know where her sympathies might be rooted. Adrenaline's high, the rhythm of change, the intoxicating momentum that the radicals could feel and she sensed, too—amid all that it was hard to think straight. For a while she was one of them, but she listened to other voices, also. She believed that René could effect real change, without the violence or the shame of it, without the manic, male zeal for bloodletting. Those poor kidnapped men. Their fearful families. Resorting to snatching a Quebecer after the abduction of the Brit meant that one of their own had been taken now, all because some people didn't agree with his politics. And before entering politics, Laporte had been a journalist, one of the brave ones who had stood up against Duplessis.

Her mother's struggles seemed nobler. A woman who had defied the system and demanded simple rights and fair wages. She boycotted, frustrated, flummoxed, barricaded and interfered with the system, with the flow of goods and the easy acquiescence to greed and exploitation. But she did not knowingly imperil another life.

Revolutions put the violent in charge. The FLQ assumed that someday they'd win. "*Nous vaincrons,*" they told each other—we'll conquer. They'd be in charge, but honestly, who ever asked them to lead? And why can't anyone discuss this anymore? René was right—and for that matter, so was Trudeau. If your cause is just, if it's viable, convince the people of its authenticity, carry the whole of the nation, or at least a majority of it, on your back and let them validate your opinion. Win or lose, let that be your legacy.

Change can't happen, some said. But look. Archbishops were once the crown princes of Quebec. Now they were court jesters. Duplessis once controlled the press. Now the press was out of control. The bosses were once exclusively English, but many were French now, and the English were hitting the highway to Toronto. To effect change, you had to believe in it, and if you blew people up it was because you didn't believe in it enough. All you had to do was be convinced of your stance and convince people to think accordingly.

Who would she fight for? Armand Touton had already called, wanting her to help him and the police. Her friends in the movement had called, wanting her to join them in demonstrations. René had called, wanting her to soothe him in his bed and listen to his troubles, even to counsel him. Everybody wanted a piece of her, while what she wanted was a piece of herself—a quiet, true, heartfelt portion so that she might truly examine her own desire.

This is what it was like, her mother had confided, towards the end of her father's life. Everyone wanted a piece of him, too, and all he wanted was a piece of himself for his family. Anik hoped she'd fare better than him, and survive, not only for her own sake, but as homage to him.

She got out of bed, and dressed.

She knew that when she stepped outside, the streets would be animated and tense. She didn't want to visit the bars where her friends would be overexcited and debating all this. She didn't want to go home, where Armand Touton might find her. She just wished that she had somewhere to go, somewhere to be. And she wondered how Émile was doing, how he was making it through all this. As a junior cop, he must be on edge. Fortunately, she had stayed away from the demonstrations, or they'd probably have locked horns again by now.

†††

Captain Touton knew that he was late, and despite having legitimate excuses, he would not be spared the jibes. He hobbled down the corridor within the RCMP's Montreal headquarters as fast as he was able. Barely knocking, he entered the designated boardroom. Old friends, adversaries and a few recent acquaintances glanced up. One man headed for the coffeemaker as though the sight of Touton's face indicated that he suffered a grim need for a cup.

This was a meeting of second-level cops, a slew of captains and lieutenants from the provincial police, the Mounties and his own municipal force. Catching the back of a chair and wheeling it around to sit in, Touton calculated quickly that he would not be the only late arrival.

To be expected. They were all run off their feet lately.

Still, wisecracks commenced. He would have to pay for his tardiness.

"Good of you to join us, Armand. I believe you know everyone. As you're the captain of the Night Patrol, I hope we're not getting you out of bed."

A few men around the table chuckled.

"I was looking forward to seeing you guys in the daytime for a change," the captain struck back. "I thought you might look half-human. I guess I was wrong."

"Four hours of sleep a day—" a Mountie, who was probably secretly in love with his own handsome reflection, commenced to explain.

"Who gets four hours?" Touton interrupted. "Even my dog doesn't get four hours anymore."

He was winning now, and enjoying that.

"Anyway, us city cops, we look like hell because we work like hell. You Mounties, you look like hell because you just do. Maybe if you didn't drink so much, maybe if you didn't spend all your meal money on hookers, you might have better luck with the ladies, live better lives."

"Mounties sleep with hookers, city cops sleep with homely wives, but in the Sûreté," one of the provincial police officers bragged, "we get the honeys. That's the difference between us."

"The difference between us is that we sleep with women who are over sixteen," Touton fired back. "You should try it sometime, if you're man enough."

While cops were smirking and hooting, Touton shot a glance around the room and realized he was the only one there without a moustache. These guys really did care about their appearance, and they cultivated a certain cop look. They looked terrible. Worn. Bedraggled. Overcaffeinated. Poorly fed. Sleep-deprived. A miserable lot.

Someone put a cup down in front of him. Touton took a sip, not bothering with cream or sugar. They were all motoring on coffee now, the stronger the better, and getting each other's goat served as another survival tactic. A few laughs, and they might endure their endless shifts without falling asleep or coming unglued.

Then a Mountie brought them to order. "The brass has been compiling lists," he announced, patting down his moustache. "Maoists, Trotskyites, radical separatists, union guys who make trouble during demonstrations, and so on."

"What do you mean, and so on?" Touton asked.

"Guys like that."

"Guys like what?"

"Excuse me?" The Mountie looked confused. He hadn't expected questions.

"You said union guys and political guys, and guys like that. So who are guys like that?"

"Political guys, and guys like that. What's the problem?"

"I don't know who guys like that are. You say 'guys like that,' and I think you mean everybody you want it to mean. I get nervous. So, anyway—what are these lists for again?"

Another officer tried to help his colleague. "Your mayor told us, Captain Touton, that he's putting pressure on the prime minister to invoke the War Measures Act. So is Bourassa. If the War Measures Act goes through, then we can arrest whomever we want, whenever we want, and put that person away for just about as long as we want. So we're compiling lists, to be ready, so we know who to go after when the time comes. We don't want chaos. We want to be effective."

Cops with infinite power. Politicians with even more. Touton wasn't convinced that he relished either scenario. "That's why I'm asking," he stated, "who you mean by 'guys like that.' I don't want to give orders to my men to go out and arrest radicals and 'guys like that.' Who knows who they'll bring in? Anybody with long hair and a beard? Girls with cute behinds? It has to be clear."

"I agree with you," the older Mountie said. "It has to be clear. Sergeant Leduc is going to modify his statement to exclude phrases such as 'and so on' and 'guys like that.' From now on, he will be more precise in what he says."

Touton didn't know whether the older Mountie was politely calling him an asshole or was actually on his side and advising his colleague to do better. Either way, he had made progress, and words would have to mean what they were meant to mean in this room from this point forward.

"When does this War Measures Act take effect?" Touton wanted to know. "What will it mean?"

The more junior Mountie spoke up again. "We can make arrests without interference from lawyers, judges, the courts or the law. We become the law, essentially."

"I was afraid of that," Touton murmured.

Everyone needed to assess the development. They'd been cops long enough to know that they did not operate within a perfect system, and that their own guys were as imperfect as the public they endeavoured to protect.

"Know why this stinks?" an officer asked, and Touton turned to see that it was a man from his own force speaking, a captain like himself, seated at the far end of the table. This was the man who had brought him coffee.

"Why does it stink, André?" Touton inquired.

The man shook his head and said, "It feels like a fucking war, and that's fine, but we're not the fucking army."

They remained still awhile, mute. Then the senior Mountie told them, "When the War Measures Act is declared, they'll bring in the army to help."

†††

He'd been looking for a way out, an alternative political device to provide the necessary security to the citizens of Montreal and Quebec. Dramatic enough, sending in the army, and he was in favour of doing so, but in truth, he had no other option. The law demanded that if he received a formal request from a provincial justice minister for military support, he was legally compelled to provide it. The War Measures Act, which suspended civil liberties and gave extraordinary powers to the police, was a different matter, and the burden of that extreme tactic pressed upon his conscience.

Drapeau wanted him to do it—the mayor of Montreal.

Back from New York, Premier Bourassa begged him to do it, the man sounding as though he was at the end of a short, frayed tether. On the phone with him each day Trudeau did his best to calm him, yet the request remained persistent. Bourassa wanted civil rights suspended.

Around him, counsellors were convinced that the time had come for drastic action. A violent, clandestine group had set itself up as a parallel government, and with each passing day its popular support increased. Yet the War Measures Act seemed too cumbersome, too draconian, and invoking it might seem like a move made in panic. Like hunting quail with a bazooka. "Let's see what the army can do," he argued. "They'll patrol the streets. Give the police a chance to investigate."

The demonstrations grew. They became better organized.

The police made no headway and were seen to be botching the job.

Then on October 15, 1970, an elite group of persons held a meeting in Montreal. Out of that discussion, they signed a document published in *Le Devoir*. Trudeau read the columns of signatories, an impressive list. René Lévesque, the president of the Parti Québécois; the president of Desjardins Life Assurance; half a dozen union heads; Claude Ryan, the editor of *Le Devoir*, the most prestigious French newspaper in the country; Camille Laurin, the parliamentary secretary of the Parti Québécois; four professors from the upper echelon of academia, representing the major French universities. Together they proclaimed that, in light of "the atmosphere of semi-military rigidity that can be detected in Ottawa," and having expressed the concern that "in certain non-Quebec quarters in particular, the terrible temptation of a policy for the worst, i.e., the illusion that a chaotic and thoroughly ravaged Quebec would be easier to control by whatever means," they espoused the desire to elicit the support of the population to oblige the government of Quebec to negotiate. Trudeau was already in a rage at the mention of a ravaged Quebec, but he reached a feverish moment when he first read that the signatories were offering "our most urgent support in negotiating an exchange between hostages and political prisoners."

In print.

Black and white.

An elite of Quebec society had referred to gunmen, bank robbers and bombers—each individual fairly tried and convicted according to the actions of the judiciary—as political prisoners.

Some of the rhetoric he recognized. The part leading up to "a chaotic and thoroughly ravaged Quebec" was pure Lévesque, his diction and rhythm as readily identified as the chip on his shoulder, and he hadn't been at his best or most biting, either. Probably, Ryan had toned him down a tad. And Ryan had drafted the latter portion, he was sure, except that somebody had slipped him a mickey, then inserted the words "political prisoners." He'd had to have been drugged or inebriated—what other explanation could there be?

He'd been browbeaten. That was it.

Trudeau's rant over the letter had to be brief and short-lived, although he considered it more offensive than the FLQ manifestos, which insulted him and the intelligence of the society more directly. He telephoned Bourassa and Drapeau both, and asked if they were willing to commit to writing that they believed they were under an apprehension of insurrection.

They promptly committed their demands to him in writing.

Trudeau invoked the War Measures Act, then sat by the window in his study. The same law that had landed Mayor Houde in an internment camp had been brought back. Back then, he had personally bellyached against it. Now, he had invoked it himself. The army, its soldiers, its weapons, its troop transports, its Jeeps, its tanks already were rumbling into Quebec and taking up positions on the street corners of Montreal. He felt alone that night, as the army moved under cover of darkness. He knew that, while others had insisted on the manoeuvre, the results of this escapade would forever attach to him.

He stepped across to his private and concealed safe. At knee level, it looked like any other cabinet. He opened the wooden doors, then the double combination lock on the steel door, and pulled out three thick black binders and placed them on the floor. He looked in. Then looked up. Trudeau crossed to the wall switch by the door to his office and dimmed the lights. Only the lamp on his desk shone now. The room was eerily quiet, save for the distant thrum of the building's complex components. Then he clicked the lock on his door, and returned to the safe. He reached inside. The prime minister pulled out the Cartier Dagger and held it in both hands, gazing down upon the knife. Before the relic had come into his possession, the tip had been broken off, but since then only a few moose hairs had unravelled. If the dagger possessed special power, he wanted to receive it now. Winning elections was all very well, but the real test of a life in public service pertained to those irrevocable choices that defined a person's stewardship, which in some way helped define your country and your time.

He stood still. Breathing. Waiting.

Pierre Trudeau held the knife as a man might hold a prayer in the core of his solitary heart.

†††

Cross feared the worst—not merely death, but a lonely, shabby one. His captors possessed what he considered to be a naïve expectation of negotiation. They'd cheered the newspaper ads placed and signed by community leaders, demanding that the government negotiate. Perhaps this crazy place called Quebec behaved differently than the world he'd known. Where else on earth would union leaders and journalists, politicians and business executives exhort the prevailing power to cave in to terrorists? Only in Quebec, apparently. Individuals, even segments of the society, might choose surrender, but surely not leadership from the intelligentsia, business and labour.

But he was wrong.

He thought he heard trucks rumbling on the streets below, but they were on television. The military had been granted the authority to act. Which would probably cost him his life. The army had arrived, and his next deadline approached.

"You see?" carped the woman. She was pacing around his room. He could smell her cigarette and hear her deeply inhale. He despised her.

"What is it I see?" Blindfolded, he saw nothing.

"When the poor of Quebec lie sick and dying, do they send in the troops? When the workers have their skulls cracked by the bosses' goons, do they send the army to defend them? When we sit in our shit, prisoners of misery, do they send soldiers? Never. Not for the nigger French."

She stood behind his back and spoke into his ear, her spit touching him, making him flinch and lean his head away.

"But if one man is taken away from his home high up on the mountain, and if that man is a British trade commissioner, they send in the army. They want to destroy our cause, but their idiot fascist response will make us stronger. It'll bring on the revolution. Before it does, Jasper Cross, we will shoot you through the mouth. Count on that."

The men gave him water when he wanted, and let him urinate and defecate without delay whenever he made the request. The woman made him wait until the pain in his bladder was excruciating. Then she'd pull him up by the hair and shove him towards the bathroom door.

He was hoping that one of the men would bring him his lunch today, and escort him to the loo. He hoped it would not be that dreadful woman.

†††

Few enjoyed the task they were given. Émile Cinq-Mars departed headquarters each night with a team of six in three squad cars. They were handed a short list of names and addresses. If they made an arrest, they took the suspect in, and if they did well they received a new set of names.

Cinq-Mars brought in a guy, an artist, who seemed relaxed about the matter, as he had expected any police crackdown to include him. He admitted to being an anarchist. "I kidnapped nobody," he maintained. "I could never handle the extra mouth to feed. I have enough trouble scraping up food for my pets." Apparently, he thought he would be questioned and released. When he learned that he was to be incarcerated for an indeterminate time, he panicked. "My budgies!" he cried out. "My cats, my goldfish. God," he shouted, "you'll kill them. Who'll feed my animals?"

Cinq-Mars, who for a time had expected to become a veterinarian, wanted to help. He accepted the prisoner's house key and agreed to find someone to care for the menagerie. Shortly after that conversation, still down at Sûreté du Québec headquarters, he encountered Father François hulking along the corridor.

"Father. What brings you here?"

"I haven't been arrested yet, if that's what you're asking. Probably that's imminent, or will you do it right now, mmm? What are *you* doing here, Émile?"

Cinq-Mars was surprised by the priest's curt retort. "Working," he answered.

"Arresting the innocent? You call that work? You cops should be ashamed of yourselves."

"Father—you're in an ornery mood. Look, it's my job, and if you can't understand that—"

"That's what Nazi war criminals maintained, didn't they? Following orders."

"It's not the same thing, Father."

"Isn't it?" The priest was not about to let him off the hook, but nor was Cinq-Mars going to cower from the man's heckling. He didn't like his duty, but that didn't mean he'd knuckle under to someone's ridicule. "How's it different?"

"If I have to explain that to you, Father, then you're not the political thinker I took you to be."

Father François took a breath and calmed himself. "I've heard a few desperate stories tonight, Émile. I'm a little worked up."

"I understand, Father. That's what you're doing? Visiting prisoners?"

"Somebody has to. They're not allowed to see lawyers."

"Frankly, I'm surprised they're allowed to see you."

"They're not." He spoke quietly for the first time. "I made people feel guilty enough that they let me in."

"Good for you. You must be unhappy with your old friend right now."

Father François was momentarily at a disadvantage. "Trudeau, you mean? No, I'm not happy with him." He buttoned up his overcoat. "You'll have to excuse me, Émile. I have people to see."

"A moment, Father. I have a man inside. He has a number of pets and no one to care for them while he's being held. He's given me his house key, but—"

The cleric sighed. "Hand it over. I'll talk to him, get his address. It won't be me, but volunteers are being organized for this sort of thing."

"Thank you, Father."

"Any other such issues, Émile, get in touch. Maybe it's a good thing that I know a cop. It's good of you to be concerned."

After the older man visited the prisoner, Cinq-Mars checked in with headquarters. He waited on the line for over ten minutes before Captain Touton could clear a moment to speak to him. "Kid, what's up?"

"I'm at the SQ jail. Father François was in ahead of me. He has full access."

"That's not right. But does it matter? We don't have to stick to every rule. Most of our arrests are arbitrary, God knows."

"That's not what I was thinking, sir."

"Go on."

"He knows every radical in town. He always has. He could easily be a courier between those locked up and those on the outside. You might want to tail him."

Cinq-Mars listened to silence awhile.

"I suppose you want to be the one to tail him," Touton said, his tone gruff. "I know it's a rough job you guys are doing right now, but it has to be done."

He was taken aback. Did Touton really think that this was a ploy to get himself onto another detail? "I thought it could be a lead, sir. You once told me yourself that you didn't trust Father François."

"Why should I?" Touton asked. "Look, like everybody else, I'm short of man-power, but when I get someone free, I'll try to follow up your lead. It has merit."

"Thank you, sir." He hung up the phone in a rage. Everyone was working with a short fuse these days—he had to bear that in mind. The old man was probably going around the clock and he probably had to deal with officers jockeying for better duty. Success in a crisis stood out, so officers were looking to get the best roles for themselves, but he hadn't been one of them and he was angry that Touton had thought that way.

Still, he said he might follow up on the idea. Maybe, by the end of his call, Touton was already reconsidering. That man could be annoying.

Outside, his squad had acquired a new list of names. Cinq-Mars glanced down it, then told them he still had another call to make. The men were hold-ing hot coffees, so they were in no rush.

He fished another dime from his pocket and dialled.

The phone rang three times before being picked up. "Hello?"

"Anik. It's me. Émile."

"What a surprise."

"It shouldn't be," he told her.

She was quiet a few moments, then said, "I'm on a list."

"Not on mine, but your mother is. She's on my arrest docket."

"Shit."

"Can I talk to her?"

"Hang on."

He didn't have to wait long.

"Émile! Good to hear from you after all this time."

"Thank you, Mrs. Clément. I have bad news tonight though."

"Anik tells me I've been listed. I'm impressed. You'd think that the authorities would have forgotten me by now."

"Afraid not."

"Anik's disappointed. She wanted it to be her."

"I can't say that she's not on someone else's list. She's just not on mine."

"That probably disappoints her the most, Émile. What do you think we should do? Run like frightened rabbits? I'm not a good sprinter. I have nowhere to hide. Will you at least be gentle when you arrest me?"

"You should leave, ma'am."

"Easier said than done, Émile. At a friend's house I'd be endangering the friend. Anyway, most of my buddies are probably on a list, too. I've been through this before. I don't think there's much point—"

"Ma'am, you can go to my apartment. You're welcome to stay there. You and Anik, both."

She paused, then said, "That's generous. Do you have room? We'll be with Ranger, too."

"Ranger, too. I'm just figuring this out as I talk, but I could move into your house, ma'am. Nobody gets arrested that way. You really don't need to spend three or four weeks or months in jail right now. You won't enjoy the experience, trust me."

"Hang on a sec, Émile, okay?"

He could hear her discussing matters with Anik, who was next to come back on the line.

"Listen, Émile, it's a good idea. Thanks. I don't want Mom in jail. But if you walk in and out of this house all day wearing your uniform," she continued, "you could cause us more trouble than this is worth."

"Anik—" Cinq-Mars started to protest, but she already possessed the solution.

"So all four of us have to stay at your place. You included. We'll just squeeze in and make the best of it."

That suited him just fine.

"That's what we'll do," he said, then let a bitterness slip. "As long as the fourth is Ranger and not René. I don't want him sleeping over."

Silence.

Finally, she said, "How the hell did you know that?"

"You're a watched woman. He's a watched man."

Neither of them understood why she said what she said next, but Anik apologized. "I'm sorry, Émile." The words struck them both as odd. They remained mute awhile.

He broke the tension. He knew that he should apologize, but instead he said, "I'm not sure how to get my keys to you. You've got to pack and go now."

"I still have a key," she told him. "I remember where I left it, too."

That surprised him.

"You two take the bed."

Cinq-Mars still wasn't ready to go back to work, although his cohorts were antsy now. He possessed prestige among their group, so he was able to coax them into waiting a while longer. Going back inside, he talked to the sergeant on duty.

"That priest who comes in here," he said. The sergeant looked sleepy, done in, but he carried more rank than Cinq-Mars and put up a brave front.

"What about him?" the sergeant asked.

Cinq-Mars was interested in learning if his hunch was right, that Father François might be working the jail for reasons beyond the bounds of the purely pastoral.

†††

Fewer men guarded him, he knew. One had been sent away. Perhaps two. The one who'd spoken kindly to him was gone. Punishment for letting him get free, when he'd flung himself at the window, cutting himself up. Or banishment for no longer having the stomach for this action. Whatever the cause, Pierre Laporte now had fewer captors, yet he believed that reduced his chances.

Those who were left behind were the more difficult individuals.

After the window, he'd pleaded for a doctor, a hospital.

They denied him.

Now two men, as far as he was able to discern, entered his room.

They were quiet. Saying nothing to one another. Nothing to him.

"What?" he said.

They did not reply.

"Water, please," he said. Still they did not reply.

Then he pleaded, saying only, "*S'il vous plait. Messieurs. Messieurs! S'il vous plait.*"

And he felt the cord around his neck like a hangman's noose around his soul as his whole body rebelled and fought to live. Great, horrendous bellows bore out of him as the cord squeezed tighter and his limbs, constrained and depleted, flailed as if set upon by an electric charge. He roared in his anguish and heard his attacker yell out also—once, twice, goading himself on, and before he called out a third time, the cord suddenly relaxed and was unwound and the feet of the two men rapidly retreated from the room. He was still alive, he believed. *I'm alive!*

His heart was smashing through his ribcage like a locomotive screaming through a night forest.

They had tried, and failed, to kill him.

Pierre Laporte felt alive and dead at the same time, all his body roaring, each atom, nerve ending, corpuscle, droplet of blood in his veins, roaring, all his bones and tendons a single collapsed scream as he listened with the power of ten wild animals for the footsteps to return or to stay gone.

He was still alive, but he could not breathe or think and dared not imagine anything. Dared not even hope, for hope was too painful for him now, too infested with the torment of this hour. He was still alive, yet he felt now the first inkling of a contagious despair.

††††

Carole and Anik had changed the sheets, made up the bed and slept together, their terrier between them. They thought it might be fun, mother and daughter, living on the lam. Anik had second thoughts, though, once they were done. The room looked tidy, the bed neat and quietly expectant.

Her mother noticed. "What's wrong?"

She screwed up her face. "Mmm. Nothing really. It's a little weird, that's all."

"Sleeping with your mom is a little weird?"

"That's a *lot* weird. But I've rolled around on this mattress before. That makes it a little weird."

That's when Carole said something she regretted even as the words were slipping across her lips. "Child, if we tramped around the city looking for a mattress you *haven't* slept on, we might go sleepless awhile."

Not since Anik was sixteen had her mother poked her nose into her sexual business. "Excuse me?"

"Sorry. Forget it."

"You think I'm a whore?"

"Did I say that?"

"You implied it."

"My mistake. I'm sorry. Forget it, all right?"

They couldn't really forget it, and both fumed quietly to themselves. Carole pulled out a novel she'd brought from home and did her best to read, while Anik went to the living room and eventually flicked on the black-and-white TV. Regular programming had been interrupted to show the foot soldiers on the streets of Montreal. She watched for a while, but had to click it off.

She went back to see her mom.

"Sorry," she said. "I didn't mean to flip out."

"I'm sorry, too. I was mean."

Anik lay on her tummy with her feet up, the soles facing the ceiling, her head on her hands while her mom played with her hair. This was nice actually, being this close, under at least the illusion of exile.

"Talk to me, Anik," Carole said eventually. The different environment and their tiff had had that effect, of breaking the mould of their routine interactions and drawing them closer to intimacy. "Tell me what's happening with you."

The daughter was quiet awhile, perhaps tempted to formulate her troubles and detail them, but eventually she only replied, "What do you mean?"

"You know. Why are you sleeping with an old man who smokes like a bus? Do you love him? If you do, then please explain to me why you're so unhappy."

"I'm not unhappy."

"You're not yourself."

Mothers. You can't live with them, but just when you most want them to disappear, you can't live without them, either. Still, Anik wasn't ready to talk.

"You told Émile that you were coming here because you didn't want me to go to jail. Thank you very much. But I know what the inside of a jail looks like. I could survive another spell. I'm here because I don't want *you* going to jail. If you're not on a list right now, you know you will be soon."

"Why? So they can interrogate me to find out what René's thinking?"

Carole nodded. "Make fun. But probably people in high places would love to see you arrested just for spite. Then what will René do? Demand that his woman-child girlfriend be released?"

"I'm not a fucking child." She wasn't angry. Merely petulant.

"I know that. So does René, I presume. Do the newspapers? How do you think you'll be portrayed? Anyway, René would have to keep his mouth shut, even pretend he doesn't know you. You're not the only girlfriend he has—only the youngest, I hope. He can't publicly protect you."

She put her head up and brushed her mother's hand out of her hair. "How do you know how many girlfriends he has?"

Carole sighed and put her book down. This looked to be a night where things would get said. They were probably overdue.

"I heard you on the phone," she told her daughter. "You were telling a friend that René has different love nests around the city so the media can't keep tabs on him, or on you. Okay. I buy that. I do. But he also has love nests around the city so that one lover won't walk in on him while he's in bed with a different one. And I'll lay odds it's not only this city."

Angry, Anik came up to her knees. "You don't know that. You just think that because—"

"Has he ever invited you to Quebec City?"

Anik hesitated.

"Of course not. You'd only be in the way up there. He gives you some other reason, but who're you kidding, child?"

Anik fell onto her side and did a pantomime of agony, writhing around, but came up, like a mermaid surfacing, beside her mom and gave her a squeeze. Her mom kissed her forehead and she snuggled in tighter.

"What to do what to do what to do," she said.

"You know what to do, Anik. If you can leave a great boy like Émile—"

"Oh, stop it. You don't get to choose my boyfriends for me—"

"It's strictly hands-off, okay? But I'm saying, if you have the moxie to leave someone you like, who's hurt by what you do, then it can't be that difficult to leave a man who'll give you one of his famous shrugs and his wicked little smile, then make a phone call to your replacement."

"You're such a bitch," Anik complained, but not too hard.

"Hey, sweetie. I'm sure it's been fun and educational. But when you're done, don't beat yourself up. Be the one who jumps ship first. Remember the phrase 'women and children first.' Stick to it. Don't get hurt by some guy who combs his hair from all the way over on the other side of the moon."

That made them both laugh. He had the worst haircut on earth.

"How'd you know I was with him, anyway? Oh, right. You eavesdrop on my phone calls."

"My first clue? Your incredibly smoky clothes."

They laughed, then Anik once again fell silent. "Are there any secrets?"

"In this town?" Carole put her arm around her daughter. They were having a good time now. "Apparently, only one. Make that two. Who kidnapped James Cross? And who kidnapped Pierre Laporte?"

Carole could feel, subtly, a tremor, a slight stiffening of her daughter's spine and a flex to her biceps. She relaxed her hold.

"Or perhaps," she whispered quietly, "there are no secrets at all."

††††

Finding two women and a dog in his bed upon his return home, Émile Cinq-Mars wiggled Anik's big toe. She got up then, groggy a bit, and followed him out to the living room, still dressed except for shoes and socks. They did not know how to properly behave with one another, and at first stood awkwardly. Then Émile made a move and they held one another, perhaps as a measure of their old affection, or as ballast to the unsteady times they each endured.

They talked, then later slept in different rooms. In the morning, Cinq-Mars was awakened by a phone call, and he turned on his television. The sounds returned Anik to his living room to join him on the couch. By a fence that guarded a small airport on the outskirts of Montreal, off the island, the body of Pierre Laporte had been found in the trunk of an old car. On television, they watched the police arrive.

"Okay," Anik said.

"Okay what?"

"It's time to do something."

††††

After his shift that night, Émile Cinq-Mars strolled into Captain Touton's office.

"What are you doing here? Why aren't you out arresting men with beards?"

"I'm pulling double shifts, not triples. Sir. Let's take a walk."

Something in the young man's demeanour commanded Touton's attention. The two walked out into the dawn light together and strode silently in step for a block. Too many policemen were milling past them for Cinq-Mars to begin. Touton indicated that they should step onto the construction site at the end of the street, where they found a spot for themselves amid debris and stacks of building material. Now that it was his turn to declare himself, Cinq-Mars felt himself go reticent. He moved a few pebbles around with the toe of his shoe.

Waiting, Touton pulled out a pack of cigarettes and offered him one.

"You're buying your own now?"

"It's the fucking crisis, all right? If you tell my wife, I'll kill you dead. Now tell me what's up."

"Sad day," Cinq-Mars said, stating the obvious. As a Canadian, he never expected to be living in a country where politicians were strangled to death and dumped in a car's trunk. He had to think differently about his world.

"With Laporte dead, I fear for Cross," Touton said. Something about the moment solicited his patience. He smoked, waited, glanced at the scaffolding.

"Anik might help us," the young man said.

Touton nodded and flicked his cigarette. "What does she know?"

"Before she tells us that she needs some guarantees."

"Like what?"

"Her mother's name taken off an arrest warrant."

"I didn't know it was on one."

"If her own name happens to be on a list, it should be removed as well."

"Is that her demand or yours? Anyway, it can probably be arranged," Touton told him.

"I don't think the word 'probably' is useful at this point."

Touton aggressively sucked on his smoke. "She's bargaining with us? Cabinet ministers are being strangled and she wants to strike a deal? She should be introduced to the facts of life as they pertain to her right now."

"She's under a lot of stress herself, that's my impression. She's taking risks."

Touton flexed his shoulders, trying to slough off the strain. "We're working across different jurisdictions here. Nothing is easy anymore. I can't make promises I might not be able to keep."

"We can't operate on 'probably.'"

"If Anik knows something, she has to tell us. If I have to bring her in and strap her to a chair and zap her with a thousand volts, she's going to tell us."

"That won't work," Cinq-Mars maintained.

"I don't care how stubborn she is."

He knew the captain was serious, in his way, that he had to be careful. "It's not a question of what she knows. It's a question of what we can figure out together. She's been talking to people. After a demonstration, she makes a few phone calls. She asks who was there, picks up the local gossip. Through a process of elimination, she's been finding out who might be conspicuously missing."

Touton was catching on. "People you expect to be there aren't. Is it because they're preoccupied by holding someone prisoner?"

"We need to run our arrest lists past her. Show film on the demonstrations, see who she can identify and so eliminate, then see who's left. Also—"

"What?" Touton liked this line of inquiry. He could see that it at least held the potential to produce results, which was more than he could say for their other operations lately.

"She's stubborn, as you know. She's not sure whose side she's on. Strapping her to a chair might have the wrong effect. She'll choose a side and it won't be ours. Besides, there's no way in hell you'd harm her. On top of all that, she's gone into hiding with her mom. You have to cooperate or you'll never find her to talk to her."

Touton's expression conceded ground. "What do you need?"

"Complete arrest lists, with Carole Clément's name removed, and Anik's, if it's on. But we need the full lists to check through them. Film on the demonstrations from every jurisdiction. I also need the tip of the Cartier Dagger, the piece that broke off in Roger Clément's chest—"

"What?"

"I need the tip of the knife."

"Why?"

"She wants it."

"Why?"

"She wants it. You possess it, don't you?"

"It's evidence. I'm protecting it. It wouldn't be safe in police custody, not after all these years. So I keep it myself."

"She knows that. But now she wants it."

"I don't understand—"

Cinq-Mars remained adamant, knowing how intransigent Anik had been on this one issue. "The tip of the knife had been in her father's chest. If anyone should have possession of it for safekeeping, it's her and her mom. There's no use arguing. She wants the tip of the blade."

Touton shrugged. Desperate times. People could make extreme requests at such moments and get what they wanted. He had to accede to her wishes. "All right," he said. "What else?" He knew there had to be more.

"There's two ways we can do this. You can give me a leave of absence—"

"What?"

"Or . . . you can temporarily promote me to detective so I can at least get paid. If you move me up, then you have to turn me loose. I can follow up on some things. That'll include running down the information with Anik. Although I can do that in uniform, I'll have to be in a suit for a few side investigations, and for those I'll need a detective's gold shield. I'm not looking for anything for my own sake—I don't give a shit what you think. But I need that gold shield to do what has to be done, to talk to the people I have to talk to."

He hated to do it, to press for a better position at a time when so many people were doing so for their own selfish reasons.

"Explain it to me," Touton demanded.

"I can't do that. But I'll warn you about one thing. I might have to go up to Parliament Hill—and I won't strut, and I won't ask the prime minister to confess to anything, but it's possible that he knows something, but doesn't know that he knows. At least, he doesn't have a clue that it might help us—"

"This is coming from Anik—"

"Yes, sir."

"Then explain it to me."

"I can't."

"Why not?"

"It's confidential. Look. I'm getting information we need. But it comes with a price. We both have to live with that."

Reluctantly, Touton was willing to do so.

"What else does she want—anything?"

Cinq-Mars sighed. "Well, sir," he began, then stopped and breathed in deeply.

"Come on. Out with it."

"Well, sir, she wants the Cartier Dagger."

"Excuse me?"

"That's her price. That's why she wants the tip from you, so she can put it back together again, whole. She's not being greedy about this. She's not in it for the money—at least I don't think so. For her, it has to do with her father's legacy."

"The Cartier Dagger."

"Yes, sir."

"But I don't have it."

"Trudeau does. That's one reason why I have to go see him."

Touton searched into his eyes and tried to discern the depths of this. "She's trading," he said.

"Yes, sir," Cinq-Mars agreed.

"The dagger—"

"Yes, sir."

"—for the FLQ cells?"

"Yes, sir. She's not sure that she can deliver. But if she can, she will. In that case, we have to deliver, too. She feels that the knife has to do with our people and that our people—look, do you want to hear this or not?" Touton had turned away, but now looked back at him. "According to Anik, Quebecers need to get something out of this beyond a few individuals being put in jail. If she's going to inform on friends who have trusted her, she expects something in return, and what she wants is to make the past right. Maybe that's just her conscience, I don't know, but I wouldn't waste a single breath trying to argue with her."

"Yeah, and like you say, she's in hiding. Will she give the knife to that fucker, Lévesque? Quebec becomes independent that way, that's her idea?"

"Does the knife have power like that? Do you believe in magic like that?"

"Yeah. Well. All right. That's true. If you believe in that shit."

At their backs, a crane commenced raising materials skyward.

"I don't know what she's going to do with it, sir. It's worth millions. She might sell it. But she has her ideals. She's a complex girl. She wants the knife and if she can get the information we need—which she tells me she doesn't have yet—she'll trade. One for the other. The knife in exchange for bringing these murderers to justice, maybe. Maybe finding Cross for us. A life is at stake here, and we don't have time to bicker about it."

Touton stomped around. He didn't like huge portions of this exchange. He especially didn't know if Cinq-Mars was the right man for the job, to be in the middle of this affair. He might become overly sympathetic to the girl's position, too inclined to take her side whatever her cause might be.

He turned back to face Cinq-Mars. "Desperate times," he said.

"Yes, sir."

"Desperate measures."

"That's my thought, sir."

"Have it your way. But deliver. If you don't, you can kiss your career good-bye. Am I making myself pretty damn clear?"

"Pretty much. Sir," Cinq-Mars objected, "there are no guarantees—"

"You don't think so?" Touton asked him. He came in closer, breathing on his face. "You're making me a guarantee. We can proceed on that basis, or you can French-kiss your ass goodbye. What'll it be, kid? This is your Dieppe. You have to survive, and you have to deliver with zero time to think. Now, what are you going to do, Cinq-Mars? Tell me."

Émile could not bear the rage in his boss's eyes. Yet got the message. He crushed the smoke under the toe of his shoe. "Find me a gold shield," he said.

"Here!" Touton barked, tearing his own from his front pocket. He pressed it into the younger man's chest, and Cinq-Mars reached up and clasped his hand over it. "Now fucking deliver."

Touton turned and strode back towards headquarters. Cinq-Mars remained behind on the job site, gazing at the superstructure in its skeletal form. He had an urge to climb through the maze like a kid, to ascend to the top and there—but he did not know what he could do there, what prayer or vow was in order, or how he could properly respond to a moment of such solitary anticipation and yearning.

Cinq-Mars hoped this would not become his Dieppe. Captain Touton, the resilient survivor, seemed to forget that the good guys had lost that battle, that on that beach they had seen their forces crushed.

CHAPTER 24

1947–49

AS THOUGH QUEBEC HAD BEEN SEGREGATED FROM THE WORLD TO determine its destiny in a vacuum, out from under the influence of foreign wars and tectonic political shifts abroad, Maurice Duplessis had emerged from his oxygen tent and the scullery of alcoholism to resume power as the premier of Quebec, while the oversized bon vivant Camillien Houde, stripped of real power and a figurehead only, was shunted back from an internment camp as the dapper, cane-twirling, jovial mayor of Montreal, his beloved sin city.

Whereas the world at war had merely nicked Quebec society, an issue as mundane as two cents would soon challenge the existing status quo and disrupt the social compact. Over a meagre two pennies, all hell broke loose.

The Church was proving to be a divided house. Talk of Cardinal Villeneuve becoming the next pope dissipated. He had supported the Allies, earning him the approbation of English-Canadians and Europeans alike, but sway over his own people had lessened. Time to recoup. Now that peace had been achieved, he determined that the Liberal Party no longer constituted the lesser evil.

In peacetime, he identified the Liberals as the party of the English, of Protestants, of Jews and immigrants, and contemplated that liberalism was a wave of the future the Church ought to avoid. Duplessis loved to sketch the Libs as communists in three-piece suits—"Look how they adore the colour red! It's on all their banners." Villeneuve allowed that the portraiture amounted to bogus electioneering, yet, similarly, he also knew that Duplessis was not the cartoonish goose-stepping fascist stencilled by his enemies. Although he shared a similar appearance and a birthday with Hitler—Duplessis was his junior by exactly a year—the rogue premier was not cut from the same cloth. The cardinal correctly judged that *le Chef* conducted his government in the same way that he managed Church affairs, and in essence had adopted the administration of the Catholic Church in Quebec as his template. In labelling him a dictator, the premier's detractors missed the more appropriate barb, one that might have defeated him. Duplessis was no dictator. In Quebec, he sat in the premier's chair as a pontificate.

The legitimate pope, the one in Rome, decided that the Church in Quebec required a sharp change of direction. After Cardinal Villeneuve enabled Duplessis to win a second successive election in '47, he died, and under no circumstances did the papacy wish to elevate one of the cryptic, neo-fascist underlings in black robes vying for the position of archbishop of Montreal. Pope Pius XII had had no difficulty deducing that Mussolini and Hitler were unworthy of the accolades bestowed upon them by the likes of Henri Bourassa, the monk Lionel Groulx and other Quebec leaders. Needing an antidote, he ignored those within the fervent ranks looking to crack the fascist whip, and chose instead an outsider, Father Joseph Charbonneau.

The new arrival promptly turned everything the wrong way up. Villeneuve had espoused a haberdashery of pomp and colour, a multitude of robes for every occasion, fit to compete with any cardinal or pontificate. He wore chains and crosses and rings galore. Charbonneau preferred austere attire. He acquired an elegance to his bearing, although his grey cassock was often patched from wear. Being from Ontario, he championed the cause of the French in all of Canada, not Quebecers in particular, and he avowed to be an archbishop to all Montrealers, not only to Roman Catholics. He was inclined to think that the Church ought to be less materialistic, that it should renew itself by first reducing its own wealth. He argued that the state should be socially inclined. He posited his affirmation of a strong united Canada as more important than the strength of any of its components, including Quebec. And as a final indignant heresy, he flew the Union Jack above the archiepiscopal palace.

For some, the Church had fallen from its appointed heaven. For Duplessis, the Antichrist had shown his grim face upon his doorstep.

Other bishops found reason to plot and scheme, and refreshed their skills with respect to Machiavellian strategy.

If the Church was suffering cracks and schisms, unions fared no better. The internationals—regarded as merely American by most Canadians—saw cultural and linguistic differences as minor irritants to their movement. Quebec workers were torn. Some valued the assertive stance of the militant unions. Others believed that the federations ought to remain Catholic, to strike a balance for the sake of a segregated culture. The internationals, as Duplessis broadcast the message successfully, were run by rapacious Jewish lawyers and the sly devil's own—namely, communists. That many had fallen to the grip of American racketeers never tweaked his interest.

The right wing, nebulous to some, proved rambunctious. Barely tarnished by defeat in Europe, the hope of the world for these men now resided within Quebec, to be signalled by the ascent of a new Quebec man who had yet to manifest himself, but whose appearance was presumed to be inevitable. As this soon-to-be-revealed eminence arose, business, academia and politics would claim a high plateau, and a great age for the world would ensue. Such rhetoric drove Duplessis to distraction. He believed that he was all the man that Quebec required, and that he was perched as far to the right of the centre aisle as any sane politician needed to nest. Yet Houde, in Montreal, quietly bused the theories around, knowing how they needled *le Chef,* knowing also that by championing such thinking, the support of the occult right stood squarely behind him. Those striving for the triumph of a zealous faction located a catalyst for their cause in the perceived persecution of a French migrant, one Count Jacques Dugé de Bernonville.

De Bernonville's supporters argued that he had fought the predatory resistance in France and had faithfully dispatched Jews on trains into the hands of German justice, as any enlightened man might do. That he desired to settle in Canada seemed appropriate, even an honour for Quebecers, who brought him into their Montreal homes and north to their cottages as the most significant celebrity within their midst. Dire Canada, ruled by communist sympathizers, Liberal hoaxers and English drivel, sought to deport him back to France to face war crimes charges. The indignity of it all, that a man of such exemplary achievement and character should be reduced to pleading for a place to hang his hat appalled the French elite, particularly those who composed the Order of Jacques Cartier and the Jean-Baptiste Society.

All these groups, the splintered Church and the fractured unions, the hostile elite and the vested interests of American business, the political leader who would not allow his authority to be questioned and a right-wing ortho-doxy that viewed the government as morally impoverished, confronted a situation brewing in the small mining town of Asbestos, about sixty miles east of Montreal. There, twenty-one hundred of five thousand miners had gone out on strike. The workers wanted a fifteen-cent raise. The company proffered a dime. That nickel divided them, so workers manned the picket lines. Further negotiation brought the difference between the two groups down to a glum two cents. Duplessis, though, was not interested in having his authority coun-termanded—he had established an arbitration process to which the miners had not adhered. So he sent in the cops. The night they arrived, they couldn't find anyone to arrest—the miners had departed their barricades and gone home—so the Riot Act was read aloud at dawn before surprised supplicants on the steps of the local church. The miners woke up to cops on their streets, just hanging around with submachine guns slung over their shoulders, smok-ing and acting tough. That night, the miners captured eleven of their visitors, bound them with their own handcuffs and scuffed them up, marched them through the streets and further tormented the officers in a church basement. Priests arriving on the scene, including Father François Legault, advised that the policemen had to be released if the miners desired the continued sup-port of the Church and the archbishop of Montreal, the beloved Father Joe Charbonneau.

So the cops, none seriously harmed, were let go.

The next night, the police sought revenge. Trapped by the imposition of a curfew, a few miners sought refuge in the same church basement. Cops entered the building and hauled the miners out, beat them savagely, pummelled their faces beyond recognition and packed several off to police stations around the countryside for further beatings. When the victims emerged days later, they wobbled, so battered were their legs and bones.

The province of Quebec collapsed into crisis again.

Charbonneau sided with the miners. Duplessis squealed on him to the pope.

The miners warred amongst themselves, particularly the members of the Catholic union against the internationals.

Bishops met in secret, whispering strategies. No one knew what about.

Quebec's upstart intellectuals—Jean Marchand and René Lévesque among them, as well as Pierre Trudeau and Father François Legault—all lent a hand, and a strike in which management and labour found themselves two cents apart at the negotiating table continued for what seemed a violent eternity, but was actually a four-month standoff.

"It's not about the two cents," Marchand said to his younger pal.

"A principle," Trudeau presumed. His first junket into a major dispute. He'd taken sides on political issues in the past, and supported one candidate over another in certain elections, but in those instances nothing more had been asked of him than an intellectual response, a position. This job required that he step into the homes of striking miners and teach them basic economics and the essentials of political action. He also listened to their perspective on the dispute, learning something of what it meant to be a miner of a material that damaged their health.

"It's not even about principles," Marchand instructed him. "This is about the dispersal of power in Quebec. Who has it, who will share it, who will seize it, who will inherit it."

"A lot is at stake," Trudeau determined.

"Everything," Marchand advised, "is at stake." This was his realm. A tough battle against a brutal corporate opponent, complicated by the harsh anti-labour policies of an autocratic government. He was at home in this struggle, and he took up residence in Asbestos among the miners. "When so much is at stake, count on it to be a dirty fight."

Trudeau, also, was loving it, for he was learning, although he never overcame the sensation that he was a salamander out of water, neither fish nor fowl. He bombed around on his motorcycle from home to home, teaching and learning.

The workers knew only that they were sacrificing a lot—half-starving most days—to gain or relinquish those two miserable cents an hour.

"It's not about the two cents," Trudeau tried to advise them.

"People around, they say you're a millionaire's kid," a miner countered once. "But your papa's gone, so now it's you who's got those millions of dollars in a bank just for yourself to spend."

The young man could not deny it.

"So I guess it's not about the two cents for you. For us, maybe it's different."

He could neither deny that assertion nor the catalogue of implications.

†††

On a Saturday night at the El—the fashionable El Morocco, where Lily St. Cyr performed her mesmerizing lock-and-key striptease and attracted lovers such as Orson Welles, Frank Sinatra and champion prizefighters—Roger Clément's greater troubles began.

"He's looking for you."

Roger and Lily were pals. She enjoyed having a big, strong man around who was not actively trying to sleep with her, and who would talk about his child.

"Who?" he asked.

"The boss."

He almost replied, "What boss?" He had several, although he called himself an independent contractor. To advertise that he worked for different people was unwise, so Roger checked his response. "Where is he?"

"Diddling girls backstage."

As he navigated through the thick stage curtains, Roger was caught off guard to come across a bevy of chorus girls, a few wearing less than on stage, surrounding Maurice Duplessis. Lily's reference to the "boss" had perhaps been intended as a poor translation of the man's nickname, *le Chef*. He waited for the portly, diminutive premier to slide free. In the dark, Roger agreed that the man really did look remarkably like Hitler.

Duplessis crooked a finger, then tilted his head. As if on strings, Roger veered to his right and found a nook. Momentarily, the premier joined him there.

"My man phoned your house, Roger. No reply. We guessed you were out on the town."

"Yes, sir."

"I have a small task. It will mean some travel."

"I'm free these days."

Duplessis looked up at him, as though to suggest that his schedule was of no logical interest. As far as he was concerned, Roger would attend to whatever task he directed him to do, regardless of his availability.

Catching the nuance, Roger inquired, "Where am I going?" He realized at that moment that they had both been whispering.

"Asbestos."

Roger felt himself sobering up quickly. He didn't know if it would be wise to point out to the premier that his wife and two-year-old daughter were already in that town—on the picket lines. If she'd been quizzed by reporters, Carole had probably already sullied *le Chef*'s reputation.

"You got a thousand cops out there," Roger brought up. "What do you need me for?"

"I *wish* I had a thousand officers in Asbestos, Roger. In lesser numbers, policemen are on hand, but do I tell them how to do their jobs? I only expect them to maintain the peace." Roger doubted that, but the premier brooked no dispute from underlings. "Should I desire that specific actions be taken, I call on you. We don't want to create a fuss, Roger."

"I understand, sir. Ah," he hesitated, thinking that he might not like the answer, "what actions?"

"The intellectuals," Duplessis hissed. He waved over Roger's shoulder at a pretty chorus girl, nude from the waist down, walking past them in high heels. Roger took a glance, then refocused his eyes where they belonged.

"Sir?" he inquired.

"They think they can run my province. As if they know what's best. Like these girls here, they're wet behind the ears. What do those truants know? How to lace their own shoes? By the time you're finished with a few of them, Roger—"

"Yes, sir?"

"—they'll lace themselves up in corsets. Dance in high heels. One thing's for sure, they won't make any more trouble for me."

The assignment must be vital for the most powerful man in Quebec to give him illicit orders in person. Usually, he sent a man. "Sir? Who do you have in mind?"

"The riffraff," the premier dictated, whispering still. "Marchand. Trudeau. That journalist twit, Pelletier. Also, the priest, Father François."

"A priest?" Roger was shocked. This was crossing a line he'd not trespass.

Duplessis scoffed. "Don't be an altar boy. Father François is a lackey for Monsignor Charbonneau, which makes him no priest worthy of his collar. He deserves an old-fashioned whipping behind the outhouse to preserve the good name of our Church. It's a tradition. If a priest goes astray, not much else can be done. Whip him in private. The pope will be on our side on this, as will God."

"Yes, sir," Roger said. Still, a priest. He recognized the name. He was thinking that Carole might have mentioned him from time to time.

"I don't know who you'll bump into. Maybe Chartrand, the union guy, if you're lucky."

"*Reggie* Chartrand? The boxer?"

"That's the one. You're not afraid of him, are you?"

"Why would I be?"

Duplessis nodded approvingly. "I don't care who it is as long as you come across one of them in a dark alley at night." The premier winked. "When you do, help that man understand that being an intellectual communist is not what it's cracked up to be in Quebec. The others, they'll learn from the good example you deliver."

"Yes, sir."

"If given a choice, find Trudeau and teach him a lesson in high finance. London School of Economics, my ass. Who does he think he is? Communist riffraff. If you find him walking alone at night, make him wish he lived in Moscow."

"I'll do my best, sir."

"On your way, then. Have a good trip, Roger."

Duplessis brushed past him and reconnoitred with the three women he'd chosen for a night's merriment.

†††

They met in the park down the escarpment below City Hall. The mayor was wearing his morning suit and shiny black shoes with spats. Seated on a bench, tossing breadcrumbs to pigeons, Roger's old campmate leaned forward with one hand on his cane for support, his grotesque, ugly face all smiles.

"I need you in Asbestos. A mission of mercy," Houde informed him.

The trip was beginning to look as though it might be profitable, at least.

"Who's giving you trouble there?"

"I said mercy, Roger. What do you take me for, some goon? Oh, who am I kidding? You know me well enough. But this time it's different. A friend of mine arrived there last night. He's doing a survey. He's discerned that people there are hostile to his presence. Go. Protect him. Be his bodyguard. Once people spot you, the rude ones will back off."

"Does he have a name?"

"Count Jacques Dugé de Bernonville." Roger had heard his wife mention him. "He's at the hotel. It's a small town. You'll find him."

Feeling flush with the promise of two paycheques, Roger took a taxi home to pack. While there, the phone rang, and he answered to a high-pitched, secretarial voice inviting him to meet the archbishop of Montreal.

"I was just leaving town," he stated.

The priest repeated, "The archbishop of Montreal." Something in the snooty tone suggested that he'd comply or be directly dispatched to a lower tier of hell.

Roger heard himself acquiesce. "Yes, Father."

For the first time in ages, Roger Clément felt fear. Although he knew the most powerful men around, he had never encountered a prelate of such distinction. A religious man himself, after a fashion, for Roger the encounter was akin to standing two doors down from God. At the archiepiscopal palace, his travel bag—which contained knuckle dusters, a switchblade and a pistol—in hand, he gazed up at the towering ceiling vault and the ornately embossed balustrades and columns, before he was led in to see the city's most authoritative clergyman.

"Roger Clément." The man sprang to his feet as though greeting a distinguished monarch from abroad. "Good of you to come on such short notice."

He didn't know how to conduct himself. Perhaps he should fall to his knees and kiss the floor, or the man's shoes. Flummoxed, he sank to his knees. The man gently guided him back up. "I've been speaking to Father François, a priest from your district. He's in Asbestos as we speak. He's been talking to your wife. Apparently, the two of them have cooked up a plan. They tell me that you're the man to carry it out."

"What plan, ah, Father? Bishop? Ah, Archbishop? Father? Your Grace?"

"We need you to secure the peace in Asbestos. See that the miners remain disciplined, yet strong. We do not want them subjected to further brutality instigated by Duplessis and the police."

"Just me? There's a thousand cops, I heard. With submachine guns."

"You can handle it. Discipline is the answer. A calm disposition."

"Ah, Father, Archbishop, Your Grace, Mon—Mon—"

"Call me Father Joe."

"I'm going to Asbestos."

"Good. You must leave at once. My office will see to the fare. What am I saying? Better yet, we'll send you by car!" Father Joe was smiling at him. He was a tall and distinguished-looking man, reminiscent of a matinee idol if not for his plain grey robe. Roger felt intimidated, although not in any usual way. "Your wife was correct," the monsignor stated.

"Sir? Mon—Mon—excuse me—I mean, Father Joe?"

"You're the man for the job."

"I was going there anyway."

"To see your wife. Grand! We've spared you the expense. We will anticipate your rendering when the work is done, Roger, when the strike has been concluded to everyone's satisfaction. A nasty experience, don't you think?"

"Premier Duplessis—" Roger coughed up. He felt himself teetering on the brink of confession. *Forgive me, Father Joe, for I'm about to go to Asbestos to sin.*

"That runt? Don't be concerned. The tattletale. He telephoned the pope to berate him over my good intentions. The *pope* has given me a lecture on Quebec politics. Quite amusing, actually. In the end, Roger, justice and calmer hearts shall prevail. That is my conviction. As it is yours, I'm sure."

"Yes, Father Joe."

Archbishop Charbonneau took a gander at the muscled man's bag. "You're packed? Have everything you need?"

"Yes, Father Joe."

"Efficient. Off you go, then. I'll call for the car. Godspeed. Blessed be the peacemakers, Roger. That's what you are in this circumstance. A peacemaker."

Roger bowed deeply, kissing the archiepiscopal ring.

He thought he had pulled that off quite well.

Between guarding a fascist war criminal, beating up intellectuals, protecting striking workers from submachine-gun fire, and hanging out with his family, Roger gathered that he was headed for an interesting excursion. One good thing: this would be the first time he'd been driven to a job in a limousine. He only wished that Anik were older. His little girl might be impressed to see her dad chauffeured into town in a limo to greet her and her mom on the picket lines.

†††

On the streets of Montreal, supporters of the strike rang trinket bells, as they had observed the Salvation Army do. Men and women dropped coins and even bills into their buckets to support the miners of Asbestos.

Everyone took a side and held a strong opinion. People knew about the beatings. Brave newspapermen, such as Pierre Laporte, had defied Duplessis and gotten the stories out. Men had been taken out of town to police stations around the countryside and had their faces and bodies smashed.

Everyone knew it. Asbestos had become a battlefield.

†††

As he drove into the dreary town, Roger became increasingly anxious for his daughter's safety. Rough-hewn, dusty, the landscape a litter of boulders and cannibalized old trucks and earthmoving machines, the company town resembled a cross between an outpost from the Wild West and a movie version of gangland Chicago. Barricades constructed of lumber, scrap metal and decrepit furniture determined which streets were accessible. Behind them, he saw cops with high-powered weapons or miners with shovels and bricks, anything they could swing or throw. Another group of men milling around the entrance to a corner store proved to be journalists—he recognized a few of them from the El. Driving in a Cadillac that belonged to the archbishop, with a driver who could prove it, allowed him to finagle his way through the roadblocks, no matter whose. The town was on edge, at war, and while confrontation might suit his job description and be familiar to his wife, he was not happy about his daughter's proximity to the action. Stray bullets, stampeding boots, Molotov cocktails, mysterious fires—amid incendiary emotions, anything could happen, making the town no place for a child.

A set of miners didn't want to let him through, although the driver displayed a letter from the monsignor. One guy in particular was belligerent, and the chauffeur got out of the car to make his point. Roger was ready, thinking a fight would ensue, and noticed for the first time that his driver was a big man, perhaps a good ally in a battle. The chauffeur was also wise. He surmised that the miner confronting him might be illiterate, which made a letter thrust under his nose both useless and an insult, so he read the gist to him aloud without implying that he could not read it himself. Properly informed, the guard permitted the pair in the magnificent vehicle to travel down that dusty street.

"What's your name?" Roger asked him. He'd conducted himself well.

"Michel Vimont."

"Good work back there. I guess you got a good job with the monsignor."

"It's a great job. I love the guy. We'll see how it goes. He's under a lot of fire."

"What do you mean, fire?"

They passed poor homes, narrowly segregated by shabby yards, kids by the dozen at play for every few houses, their voices vibrant, shrill and strangely reassuring. A large number stopped their games to stare at the limousine, while a few chased after the elongated black car, the oddest and most impressive vehicle on wheels they'd seen.

"He confides in me as we drive along."

"What does he say?"

The man chuckled. "That's the point. He *confides.* I can't tell you any of that."

"I understand, yeah."

"But I'll say he's under some fire. Pressure. If he goes, I go."

"Goes?"

"The pope might give him the boot. Send him to Timbuktu. Father Joe let me know that's a possibility. Depends on this strike thing maybe, what happens here."

"Jesus."

"I wouldn't say that in this car."

"Sorry. I didn't know so much—" He nearly added *depends on me.* "You're saying you won't stay with the Church?"

"No different driving a bishop than someone else. The man wants you to be his driver, not the other guy's. The next bishop won't want me. He'll choose his own."

"Michel . . . Vimont, is it?"

"Yes, sir."

"You lose your job here, look me up. I know a few people. Politicians, club owners. We'll get you established. Maybe it won't be as good as you got it now with the monsignor. But if he goes down, we'll take care of you, all right?""

"Sounds good." The man seemed genuinely reassured, as though he expected to be relieved of his duties any day now. Which was ominous.

Disembarking, Roger quickly discovered another reason not to have Anik nearby. As he entered an expanded union local that had set up shop in a church basement, his daughter was abruptly thrust into his arms by a stranger. All at once, he had to cling to her and catch his balance. Told that the babysitter was on her way, but late, that Carole was at such-and-such a barricade and couldn't leave, the woman impressed upon him that he could look after Anik from now on because she had children of her own to corral. Apparently, his arrival had been expected. The woman addressing him dashed out the door before he could counter her decree—or receive directions to his wife's fortifications.

Roger gathered up Anik and her things and played with her, at first on the floor of the strikers' makeshift headquarters. She seemed glad to see him, relaxed, and not at all perturbed by the surrounding strife. She uttered a nickname for everyone who walked by—Nomo or Deeka or Manna or Moze. Later, still no babysitter, he left a message for his wife and took Anik back to his hotel room while he unpacked and got himself organized, then did what he could with a child in tow to learn the lay of the land.

Carole finally broke in on them, only to reveal that there would be no babysitter that day. "My regular burnt her foot. Don't ask—it's too complicated. I had a second babysitter on the way, but I'm afraid that's you. I didn't want to tell the other lady, or she might not have stayed, since we didn't know for sure if you were coming. Roger! You showed up. Kiss me."

"There's no sitter?"

"I knew you were coming."

"You left our child with a complete stranger—"

"Her husband's in the union. She's practically family."

"Carole!"

"Hush-a. Anik was fine, wasn't she? Besides, would you rather she was on the picket line? Roger! She could've been shot. How could you think such a thing?"

How he was getting shit for this confounded him. "That's my point."

"Roger. Anik was fine. I believed you'd be here sooner or later. I had faith in you."

"I don't have time to babysit."

"Sure you do. But don't worry. We have real work for you, too. I'll find someone for tomorrow besides the lady with the burnt foot. Lots of miners' wives are pitching in."

"I was coming anyway."

"Couldn't live without me, huh? That's nice." She kissed him. She looked sexy to him in her tight jeans, loose plaid shirt and yellow bandana, which kept her bangs out of her eyes but also pushed her hair up at the back. A bundle of energy and taut passion. She seemed so lithe and mercurial to him, both strong and soft. He could just hug her and toss her on the bed if she weren't doing six other things while talking, if she wasn't preoccupied with saving the union.

Roger was quick enough not to push his foot down his gullet. "I missed you, too, Toots. Tons. But the reason I was coming anyway, I'm trying to say, is because I got hired to be here. I don't mean by you or the monsignor—do you know, he wants me to call him Father Joe. How can I do that? I tried to call him 'monsignor,' but every time, the word stuck in my throat. I hope I don't get to meet the pope ever. That'll chew me up."

Carole had stopped moving for the first time since coming into the room. She held leaflets and papers she'd been rifling through, and a press release she needed to edit, but she put everything down and placed a hand on her jutting hip. "Who," she asked quietly, "has hired you?"

"Pretty much everybody," Roger Clément admitted. "I'm going to make a good buck this month anyway."

"Roger," she said, and the mere mention of his name seemed to chastise him. "Whose side are you on now?"

He tried to look everywhere but into her eyes. But that could not be helped in the end. "Everybody's," he admitted.

††††

Journalists crowded into a small ballroom in Montreal for a press conference called by the premier to discuss the strike. When any man asked a question he didn't appreciate, Duplessis had him escorted out. One scribe was taken away because *le Chef* didn't approve of how loosely he knotted his tie. Several others were selected for removal because they'd recently offended him in print. Two gentlemen of the press were banished because the newspaper they worked for had failed to pay proper homage. That fate awaited a reporter from *Le Devoir*, Pierre Laporte. Others were kicked out of the room because the premier had gotten the hang of throwing people out. Two other writers who asked questions about the strike were told that he would have them fired. No one doubted that Duplessis would make good on the vow. After that, the only journalists who spoke were men who only ever praised him, and he never did take a question on the strike.

He intended, he swore, to preserve Quebec from outside contamination.

†††

A compromise was worked out. Roger was willing to make himself available for babysitting chores and afford a bit of time to be an attentive husband, but he would not move into a miners' billet with Carole. He'd stay at the hotel, graciously paid for by the archdiocese of Montreal. She was not welcome there, as he never knew when a brick might fly through his window or out-of-town cops might kick down the door. Besides, she was happy enough where she was living. Roger took a glance in. A beehive. Anik had other toddlers to play with, for the cottage had become both a communication centre and a nursery. Dozens of miners' wives made soup for the barricades and coffee for the picket lines. They arranged medical supplies in case the centre suddenly became a hospital. Teenagers painted picket signs.

"I'll stay at the hotel."

"You should stay—see how the other side lives."

"What other side?"

"Mine."

"I've got a job to do."

"For the monsignor."

"For him, and for Duplessis, and—"

She tucked her hands under the lapels of his coat and pulled him in closer to her. "I know about those guys, but don't forget the monsignor. You're working for him, too. Which means, if you think about it, that you're working for me."

"I am?"

"Miners won't take orders from a woman or from a priest. They need a tough guy to be in charge. The young ones are a wild bunch. We can't have them taking potshots at cops with their hunting rifles. They need to know that if they screw up, they will answer to you."

"Tell them they'll get sent straight to hell," Roger suggested, "since we're working for Father Joe."

"You should know. You're going there yourself," Carole teased. "But only for what you do in bed with me."

That made him grin, and he felt better about many things, even as he returned to his room alone.

Journalists and out-of-town union guys were staying at the hotel. Not many sightseers were visiting Asbestos. Roger enlisted the help of the hotel night manager, who for five bucks put a name to the face of each man standing around the downstairs bar. Pierre Trudeau and Gérard Pelletier, Jean March- and, René Lévesque, and Father François, who was billeted with the miners but who'd come over to the hotel for cocktail hour, were part of the mix. Roger took the boisterous, pugilistic-looking man in the corner to be Reggie Char- trand, the union guy. Among the barflies, only Chartrand and Marchand had chins that could take a punch. Marchand looked too distinguished to beat up, and anyway Roger liked the guy right off the bat—he didn't put on airs. Char- trand seemed overly full of himself, and when he and Trudeau began playfully sparring, Roger was surprised that the skinny rich kid did okay against the for- mer prizefighter. The union boss was even embarrassed by the rich kid, who was a little too quick for him, and tried to laugh him off. But Trudeau's nar- row chin—Roger clucked his tongue. He figured if he unloaded a haymaker on him, the fellow might never be called an intellectual again. In his battles, Roger preferred to minimize the damage done, so for this job that would mean a punch-up with Chartrand, the ex-middleweight. He'd meet him alone in an alley to satisfy Duplessis's desire for carnage.

Assessing his foes, Roger quaffed a beer in a corner by himself. He noticed another gentleman glance into the room. The night manager had left, so couldn't help him with the identification, but judging by the way the others had stopped talking to glare at him, he presumed that he had found his count.

The spiffily attired gentleman walked out of the hotel bar, and the hotel, onto the street. Roger padded after him. He could not allow a count to wander these treacherous streets alone at night, not when his safety constituted one of his jobs.

†††

They had trundled into the archiepiscopal palace as chatty bishops, but as the meeting progressed, they turned sullen. They asked Monsignor Charbonneau to provide his rationale for supporting Jews and communists. The archbishop of Montreal asked if they knew what happened to men who breathed asbestos into their lungs day after day. Yes, one remarked. They provided for their families.

Unanimously, the bishops informed Charbonneau that, due to his support for the strike, the fabric of the Holy Church was being rent asunder. Perhaps never to be repaired. The people expected guidance, they maintained, not revolution.

"I support the just cause of the miners," Charbonneau maintained. "Not revolution. But I support their right to a fair wage and to choose their own unions."

"Your Grace, we have a Catholic Union."

"The miners are free to associate with it, or not. They will choose, not the bishops."

"What about Quebec?" he was asked. Charbonneau was distrusted for being a francophone from Ontario.

He answered, "What *about* Quebec?"

The bishops left unhappy.

Monsignor Charbonneau—Father Joe to some—despaired. He felt himself alone against the world.

†††

Probably, nobody cared. Roger surmised that no one in Asbestos had any reason to hurt the count. Miners had their own troubles—what did it matter to them that the guy was an old Nazi? No Jews were around. The cops were working for Duplessis, and the premier didn't mind if ex-Nazis drifted through his province looking for a home. So no one cared that the count was checking out the strike, perhaps taking note of police tactics or evaluating the conviction of communist sympathizers. Although Roger wondered why. He deduced after only a few minutes that his own purpose here was different than what Mayor Houde had suggested. He wasn't the man's bodyguard—he'd been sent along to keep the count company, to see that he wasn't lonely, to be his friend.

That first night, he and de Bernonville walked all over that little town.

"Your name's in the papers," Roger mentioned.

"Journalists," the man scoffed. "They have nothing better to do to occupy their pickled brains. A miner is bruised, they make it sound as though the sky has fallen. Miners live tough lives—of course they're bruised. Besides, they beat each other up, for sport."

"The government wants to deport you, they say," Roger persisted.

"Journalists are the problem," de Bernonville maintained. "I will have to persuade them to think differently. If they can understand my presence here, they will give me some peace. Governments never look for problems. If the problem about me goes away in the press, I won't be deported."

They had reached an edge of town and gazed across a rocky terrain. The moon was nearly full above them, which was good to see, or they might have mistaken the land stretching away from them as being a moonscape, stark and uninhabitable.

"That's why you're here," Roger noted.

"I'm here because I'm here," de Bernonville told him. The man was slightly above average in height, with excellent square shoulders but a plump face that might have foretold future girth. Perhaps he'd not been eating well, and had taken off weight below the neck only. An ascot camouflaged his neck, and a handkerchief was tucked into the breast pocket of his pinstriped suit. The count strolled along with the aid of a stick that had a heavy knob at one end and a pointed brass tip. A weapon, Roger considered. He carried himself as though cinched up, strapped in by a girdle.

"You want to make friends," Roger supposed.

"I would like journalists to receive me more graciously into my new homeland than they have done to date. Where besides right here can I find so many of them in one place? If I can have a word with them, share a drink, a few laughs, they might be persuaded to gaze more kindly upon my stay. If they stop writing about me, or change what they say, I can resolve this situation."

Roger didn't know how he was going to influence men so set against him. "Are you asking me to introduce you? I don't know them myself."

"Sooner or later, they'll stop glowering at me and invite me to debate. When they do, I'll shift the ground beneath their feet. I'll charm them. If that doesn't work, then you can do your job."

"*My* job?"

"Smash their faces in."

"Whoa—journalists? Wait a minute. I didn't sign on for that."

De Bernonville patted him on the back. "I'm having fun with you, Roger. It won't be necessary. The mere sight of you walking with me sends a message. That, together with my famous charm. I know how to handle these people. Before we're done, we'll be sharing our meals with them."

Roger was skeptical of that. The bunch he'd seen at the bar were known to be a feisty breed, and not well disposed towards Nazis. De Bernonville had confidence that he could charm the birds out of the trees, but a journalist out of his convictions might be a more difficult task.

"Now, lead me back to the hotel, Roger. I'm lost in the dark out here. Tomorrow, we'll work on this."

†††

Of his three tasks, two would seem to be a snap. Sooner or later, he could segregate an inebriated Reggie Chartrand from the pack and give him a quick going-over. As long as the man bled, he could exaggerate the damage to Duplessis, keeping him content. Guarding de Bernonville would seem to be easy, as well, as the count had not come here to berate miners or forestall a revolution. Given that his mission was to make friends and influence the province's fifth estate, Roger could keep him safe. He doubted that the man could overcome the animosity among the intellectuals at the hotel bar, but they were unlikely to do more than sneer at him, and perhaps raise their voices in debate. The exception might be Chartrand, who was sufficiently volatile to resort to his fists, but if he did so Roger could kill two birds with a single counterpunch. Overall, his most difficult task would be to do his duty for his wife and the Catholic Church. How could he marshal two thousand striking miners into a disciplined corps when each man, by dint of his labour, probably could match his physical prowess?

As expected, Carole had plenty of suggestions, none of which inspired him.

"I don't see why I can't just go out and have a beer with a bunch of the guys and ask them to behave themselves. If not, I'll say, the monsignor will ship them to hell in a limo."

"Because they'll get drunk and forget about the monsignor and forget about hell. Not everyone's as worried about hell as you are. They'll only laugh."

"They'll get drunk no matter what I say. Why do I have to make a speech? That'll be an excuse to get drunk, if they're forced to listen to me."

"Not a speech. A kitchen chat, we call it. Go into the miners' homes. Don't only talk to the men, but to their wives and kids. Get everybody in the community behind the strategy. Then if the men get drunk, they'll have to answer to their wives and neighbours. They'll think about that first."

"Bloody hell," he said, an English phrase he'd picked up in the internment camp. Once in a while, the English knew how to express themselves.

"You can do it," she encouraged him.

"This is starting to sound like real work to me," he said with a sigh.

When she spun around to chastise him, she discovered him smiling brightly in full tease. They kissed, and let it linger.

"Babysitter?" he asked, as they stepped away from their embrace.

"Anik's coming with us this morning. She's a great icebreaker. Gets everybody gabbing. She's a union girl, our child, right from the get-go."

"Bloody hell," he repeated. Anik was going to be a union girl because she wouldn't have a choice. Her mother would see to that. Someday, he might have to face the two of them across a picket line, and wouldn't that be a picnic.

†††

He awoke thirsty in the night. From the hotel window, Roger Clément spotted fires. He got dressed. Pistol, knife and knuckle dusters were thrust into his jacket pockets and zippered securely. He laced up his boots, for this was no battle for a man in shoes. Leaving his room, he slammed the door behind him.

The thin walls of the shabby hotel shook.

He hollered in the corridor and pounded his fists on doors. "Wake up, you intellectual shitheads! Wake up! You wanna be part of this? Wake up!"

He heard men stirring, but no one dared open a door to investigate. He continued to lumber down the corridor, pounding doors, yelling.

Pelletier was the first to emerge, tall and imposing, holding a towel around his waist, sleepily scowling. "What the hell's going on?"

The door opposite his opened. Trudeau poked his sleepy head out.

Another door yawned ajar, so Marchand was also awake, and across from him, Chartrand, who'd lit up a smoke first, stood forth in speckled shorts.

"A battle's starting up. Unless we stop it."

"What battle? Don't stop it. Join in!" chirped Chartrand. He jumped back into his room to dress.

"Who're you?" Pelletier asked.

"Don't give me that shit. You know who I am by now. A battle's forming. Whether you're a journalist or union, you don't want to miss it. I need your help."

"What kind of help?" Trudeau asked. To him, the thug in the hall didn't sound crazy, he just behaved that way.

"If the union fights the cops, it'll be a slaughter. Is that what you want?"

Chartrand had looked out his window and seen the parade of torches, the miners and cops heading for a confrontation. "He's right. They're gonna brawl. We'll see about who gets slaughtered!" Still pulling on his clothes and carrying his boots, he was off, hobbling down the stairs with his stuff.

"Help me," Roger demanded. "It might start out as fists, but it'll end up as guns against bricks. Is that what you want?"

"Whose side are you on?" Marchand asked, still skeptical. Roger was right—they'd checked him out. His long record as a Duplessis and Houde henchman, as a union buster, wasn't hard to dig up, but he had also done time in an interment camp as a communist sympathizer, and he was hanging out with a known fascist. No one knew what to make of his presence here.

"Monsignor Charbonneau hired me to preserve the peace. That man's faith is in God, but it's also in me. How can I do this by myself?"

"We'll get killed if we're in the middle," Trudeau pointed out. He sounded neither afraid nor reluctant, only prudent. Through the varied contours of his intellectual life he had persevered as a man of faith himself. He respected Monsignor Charbonneau, which might have dictated one course of action, but logic countermanded that response. "What do you expect us to do?"

"Get dressed," Roger suggested, then ran after Chartrand to intersect the brawl.

Fires in empty oil drums delineated a scruffy vacant lot, which yielded to a sloping hillside where the two gangs were intent on hostilities. Miners carried torches to light their way. The cops had lit a couple themselves, which cast long and wavering shadows as they walked down a curving, descending dirt road, but most of them carried flashlights. They were out of uniform. This was a private brawl, supposedly, instigated by the hotheads on both sides jawing at each other all day. No badges, no guns, that was the deal—men against men, twenty to a side. Young men all, looking to settle scores and insults and enjoy a rowdy fight. Roger was no dope, and he guessed that not everyone on both sides was a dope, either. Whatever anyone had agreed to, this would not be a battle in good faith. Both sides made sure that covert reinforcements were ready and nearby. If the fight was fair, they might never be called in, but let one side break the contract, or even lose badly, and the night could succumb to disaster.

He thought he detected a shadow spread out and move along a higher ridge. More cops, snaking down. Towards the gentle valley where the miners lived, he could see nothing, but this was their turf. They knew how to move through this town undetected.

A couple of boys, miners' sons, were responsible for lighting the barrels, and as the two groups moved onto the field Roger jogged there on his own. Only Chartrand had reached the battleground ahead of him.

"We don't want this to happen," Roger told him, hoping the man possessed a modicum of sense.

"I do. Send twenty cops to the hospital and this strike takes a different turn."

"Or twenty dead miners."

"A fight's a fight," Chartrand warned him. "Anyway, it's too late to stop it."

He feared the man was right.

The men from the hotel arrived just as the miners were forming at one end of the square field, their numbers lit by the smoky, flaring barrels. As they lifted their torches, their faces shone as if disembodied, their clothes dark, their forms indistinguishable. A bank of cloud cover eclipsed the moon. At the opposite end, cops spread out into a single line, flashlights held low around their waists, beams daring the darkness. Except for the nervous lamps, they could scarcely be seen.

The so-called intellectuals joined Roger at the edge of the field between the two groups. They stood still as the warring factions moved closer in make-shift battle formation, each of the combatants assuming a stride and, when he stood still, a stance meant to show no fear, to intimidate.

Moving alone to the centre of the field between them, Roger Clément stood as a darkened figure, a stout form, and soon, a voice. Just by standing between them, he secured the brawler's attention and stalled their advance.

"You cannot do this," he called out in the dark.

A cop answered. "Out of the way, whoever the fuck you are."

He turned to face the police. "How come you think so much of these guys, the miners?"

A few scornful laughs. A cop said, "They insulted my mother, the bastards. They insulted my sister, my wife. They insulted my dog, my cat and my nose. Tonight, they pay for that, the cocksuckers."

"Buddy, I can't see your nose in the dark, so I can't say if that was justified, but the rest of it, that's what men say on a picket line. Cops have to live with that."

"I remember that nose," a miner shouted out. "It's an obscene nose! It needs to be flattened against his ugly face!"

"Who are you, anyways?" a cop demanded. "You're one of them, only chicken-livered."

"You think I'm chicken-livered?" Roger shot back.

"And yellow-bellied."

"You think I'm yellow-bellied?"

"Probably. Why not? Is that a yellow line or chicken feathers running up your spine? It's hard to tell in the dark."

Even a few miners laughed at the comment, and a number of cops clucked like chickens.

"You don't want to fight? You're a coward."

"Out of the way, fucker, or both sides will stomp you into the ground!" That was a miner talking. Inwardly, Roger smiled. At least he had gotten both sides to agree on something.

Each line took steps towards the other, then stopped and traded invective.

"Hang on," Roger called out. "Hang on."

"Let him speak!" a voice from the sidelines shouted. A journalist.

"Fuck him! We're here to kick police ass!" This voice also came from the sidelines. Roger recognized it. Reggie Chartrand. *You little bugger.*

"Listen to what he has to say!" the unknown voice from the side called out. "I'm a journalist. You know how angry the public is. Any more cop violence and heads will start to roll. You cops will be the scapegoats. Listen to him, or we'll report you in the papers." Pelletier was pleading for peace, although he had no clue how Roger could finagle his way out of this one.

The presence of journalists gave the cops something to think about, something more than a miner's fist to fear. Like air from a balloon, a portion of the fight went out of them.

"I was saying," Roger called out to the cops. "You must think a lot of these miners if you think this is all who showed up. Think they'll fight fair? Get the upper hand, and the rest will come out of the shadows, ten to a man. And you, miners!" He turned. "Do you really think their buddies with submachine guns aren't far away? I've already seen them on the move. This is not going to work, guys. It's a nice idea, but you guys don't trust each other enough. So it's not going to work."

"I've seen them, too," Trudeau called out. He'd been in the homes of many of these men and knew their families. "More cops are coming down the hill."

"There's just us!" one cop called out, but he didn't sound convincing.

"You're a liar!" another insisted, shouting at Trudeau.

"They got their backups, we got ours," a miner admitted. "Keeps it fair. Us against them."

"It'll be a bloodbath. And that won't be the end of it, either. Think about your wives, your babies. How many of you do they need dead? You think it won't happen? Think again—think! This is a bad situation. It won't work."

"Who the fuck are you, anyway?"

"I represent the Catholic Church," Roger called out at the top of his lungs, which took both gangs by surprise. "I'm here talking for Monsignor Charbonneau. You're all Catholics. Now go home, or I'm telling you, *you'll all be sent to hell*!"

His trump card, and he should have known that Carole was right. They only laughed at him for that. Times had certainly changed in the province of Quebec. At least, the saving grace, both sides were chuckling now, totally amused.

Then Chartrand called out, "Let's get on with it. Beat the crap out of them. Remember what they did to our boys."

In shouting out again, Roger knew he was taking words right out of the mouth of his wife, who often had exhorted strikers and cops to behave. "You're all Quebecers! You're all brothers. All of you, you draw paycheques to feed your kids. You're not fighting the bosses here. You're not fighting the system or the English. You're fighting each other, and that makes no damn sense. Now cut it out!"

"First, we'll beat the crap out of *him*!" Chartrand suggested.

"All right! Do that!" Roger agreed. "If you're man enough!" His voice was powerful in the still night, and the idea sufficiently absurd, that both sides fell silent to await his explanation. "I'll take you both on," he challenged. "I'll take on whatever cop they want to send up against me. Then I'll take you on, Reggie. You're small, but you're a boxer. We'll see how tough you are. Show me how tough you are. You want to fight each other? Prove it. Prove you deserve it. One guy out of two beats me, you'll have your brawl. Okay? The journalists here, they'll keep their mouths shut, they'll close their eyes, they'll walk away.

You can fight in peace. But if I beat whatever cop the police send up against me, then if I beat Reggie, or whatever miner the miners send up, if I'm the last one standing, then you all go back to wherever the fuck you're supposed to be right now."

Every man was pumped with adrenaline, looking for trouble. The offer was a good one, for they couldn't step away from the challenge, nor could either side expect to lose. A miner, though, voiced an objection.

"You can beat up a cop, I don't see no problem. They're lazy, fat fucks. But you want to take on Reggie—he's smaller than you. That's one-sided."

"I can take him," Chartrand sneered, but his tone sounded more like bravado than confidence.

"Like I said, if you want to send somebody else out, that's fine with me. I'll take him on. But he's the one doing most of the talking. I just wanted to shut his yap for an hour or two."

"How about if I take on Reggie instead?" a voice from the sidelines inquired.

People turned, trying to see in the dark. The cops aimed their flashlights, and discovered the determined face of Pierre Elliott Trudeau.

"I'm about the same size," the young man pointed out.

Leaner, though, and he did not possess a pugilist's bulky physique.

"You've been working out, sir?" Roger asked him. He'd seen that he was quick enough, he was probably smart enough, but that didn't make him a likely victor.

"Canoed all summer."

Miners laughed, but to Roger his response sounded promising.

"I'll take on the rich kid," Chartrand declared, suddenly more keen.

Neither the cops nor the miners could turn down the deal. The big guy in the middle might be able to take whomever the police put forward, nobody knew, but the prospects for Chartrand to beat up the upper-class city intellectual who'd been talking to the miners about economics and discipline within the ranks—that was pretty much a foregone conclusion. The cops liked those odds as well. As soon as Chartrand disposed of Trudeau, they could all go at it, kill each other even, while the journalists would be bound to secrecy.

"Do it your way," a cop agreed, "as long as the newspaper rats take a hike."

"We got no problem with that," the miners concurred.

"Me first," Roger announced. He took off his jacket and brought it over to the sidelines to hand to Trudeau. "Don't fuck this up for me. We got a lot at stake here."

"I think I can take him."

"That's not good enough."

"I've got a lot at stake, too. To do my job properly, I need these people to respect me."

"Wanting to win, that's not good enough, either."

"I can box. My dad taught me. All through school I beat bigger guys."

"Okay. Good. But Chartrand fights dirty. I been on picket lines with him."

"Then I'll fight dirty. Hey, I'm impressed with what you've done tonight. But watch your back," Trudeau advised. "Look who they sent out."

A giant.

The shadow he cast from the glow of police flashlights made him look like Goliath and put Roger in darkness. Roger couldn't distinguish his face, which made him seem particularly menacing, but he tried not to overestimate the challenge. He put the man at six-four, maybe an inch more, weighing two-fifty, maybe up to twenty pounds more. Roger was shorter, a fit two hundred and ten, barrel-chested, compact in his muscularity, with iron fists. As they drew closer and the circle of miners with torches and cops closed in around them, he saw that the man did not have a muscled neck, which suggested that the rest of him might be soft as well. The man's first left jab glanced off Roger's forehead. He could hit, he had big hands and power—Clément would have to stay beyond the lengthy range of those fists. But did he have a stomach? Roger feinted a left hook, then went in low to the belly to find that out.

Hearing his opponent's telltale grunt, Roger knew he had him. And in the cop's eyes, he saw that he knew it, too.

Roger walked into a right hand, though, and the shock of it, as much as the blow, drove him to the ground. Then he had to dart around on all fours, fending the man off as he tried to mount him and wrestle in the dirt. Roger panicked—he didn't want that. He scooted around and twisted and kicked and got clear. Back on his feet again, the throng roaring for its favourite, both sides wanting to see him clobbered, he circled warily and waited for an opening.

He had to watch out for shadows in the firelight. A fist could swing at him unseen. He circled. Then he attacked before the cop gained too much confidence. He took short punches to the chin and cheek, but the man didn't have short-punch power, he needed a full swing. Inside on him, Roger worked the body, the tummy, the heart, the gut again, then once more up and down the ladder, and finally that right uppercut across the jaw that drove him back on his heels. The cop almost toppled right there. In on him quickly, Roger again landed half a dozen blows to the head. The guy could take a punch! Then back to the stomach, where he was less able to endure solid blows. When his opponent's guard dropped—and they looked at one another in the light of flame and both men knew that these were the final moments of their contest—Roger came back to the chin three times and the man was down.

The cop had little interest in rising up again.

If this were an alley, Roger would jump him. Boot-fuck him. Bang his head against the pavement. Smash his balls. Finish him. See that he regretted being alive. You had to rupture a man's spirit or he might come back at you. Such conduct would not work here. The giant's fellow officers would enter the fray and his strategy for the evening would fail. So Roger let him paw about on the ground, and when it was obvious to everybody that he was done, that he had no fight left in him, Roger moved back to the sidelines to retrieve his jacket from Trudeau.

"One down," he said.

"Heavy jacket," Trudeau mentioned. The gun.

"You never know what you might be up against."

"Apparently."

Trudeau took his own jacket off and left it with Roger. They moved to the centre of the field. The cops were still attending to their fallen hero, the miners pitching in to enliven the festivities with snide remarks. But in this environment, the police weren't taking any backtalk and the moment was precarious. On the picket lines, they'd been prevented by superior officers from retaliating. Not here. Not now.

"Wait'll this city boy goes down. See what you say then."

Chartrand was cocky and excited, Roger saw. Not a good sign. He was itching for a piece of the intellectual. For him, strikes were for workers—he didn't need any rich kids butting in. Roger came up behind Trudeau and gave him a word of advice.

"Be careful when he's in the dark. You can't see. But when you're in the dark, unload on him. He won't see what's coming."

Trudeau didn't see what was coming, and was down on his knees in seconds. The quality of his chin would now be tested. Chartrand moved in quickly and kicked him in the side of the ribs, and Trudeau, wisely, rolled with the blows and used that momentum to regain his footing. Chartrand moved in on him, but the skinnier man skipped loose, stumbled, then danced away again. He was on the run.

Between the two of them, he was probably the fitter. Backpedalling was not a bad strategy for a minute or two, to tire his opponent.

The miners and cops were swearing for blood, and they shoved Trudeau back into Chartrand's path whenever he ventured too near the circle's rim. Roger was about to warn him that he was going into the crowd again, but the imp had planned it that way. When miners pushed him towards his foe, he put his head down and came up swinging, landing a few and taking the other guy by surprise. Mad now, Chartrand chased him erratically, but the more adept Trudeau skipped free and hit from the side. The pugilist turned even angrier, then stopped briefly, and it was apparent to all that he needed to breathe. He wasn't accustomed to a ring this large.

Then Trudeau stopped leading him. He moved in tighter. He circled. He worked himself into the shadows, and as Chartrand bobbed, he belted him two good ones and the stout boxer backed off. Observing him, Roger had already decided that Chartrand's life in the ring had mainly been mythology. If he'd defeated anyone, the other guys had been stooges. You could do that during a war, when the good fighters were overseas. Yet when Trudeau snapped a couple of good left hooks to the eye, he also left himself open to a right cross that knocked the rich kid to the ground.

He got up in a twinkling. Chartrand knocked him down again, and this time kicked him. Trudeau managed to grab a boot and give him a yank, causing him to tumble. With both men on the ground, a cop helped the union guy up.

Roger stepped in and gave Trudeau a hand up.

"I'm all right," the city boy said.

"You are now," Roger told him. He slipped a knuckle duster over the fingers of his right hand.

Trudeau turned back to his opponent and moved towards the shadows again.

As Chartrand moved in, Trudeau hit him, and the man's head jerked back. The expression on his face in the flickering light showed alarm. Trudeau hit him again, a knee buckled, and the young man moved in and landed a flurry of blows. Chartrand was bleeding now above the eyes, and another shot smashed his nose. Blood gushed. Another blow sent Chartrand back on his heels, fighting for balance, and the so-called intellectual from the city showed that he had great instincts, working in tight and setting up the man's head with a left hook, then coming back with that heavy right hand across the chin. Chartrand snapped like a jack pine.

Trudeau was shaking his fist as though he'd hurt himself against the other man's jaw, but he was slipping the dusters off, secreting them into a pants pocket. He was the victor, yet only his confederates from the hotel were congratulating him.

"We had a deal," Roger Clément spoke up loudly. "I expect you men to honour it. No more fights tonight. If there is, it'll be in the papers tomorrow. You cops know your bosses don't want more shit to flush down on the police. All that does is raise more money for the strikers."

The gangs moved off, and, aside from parting invective, they were done for the night, to meet again on the barricades in the morning. Reggie Chartrand made it up to his knees. He fought off a miner trying to help him and pointed a finger at Pelletier and other reporters who'd been witnesses to his demise. "You're not writing about this. Not ever! We have an agreement."

"Don't worry, Reggie," Pelletier promised. "We have an agreement."

"Not ever."

"Your sterling reputation is safe with us." A reputation that would lie in tatters if the public knew he'd gone down to the womanizing lawyer from Montreal.

Trudeau took back his jacket from Roger. "Thanks," he said.

"For what?" he asked him. "You beat him."

"I cheated."

"In a fight? No such thing."

"I figured that." Trudeau slipped his jacket on. "I've got something that belongs to you," he said. "Now might not be the best time."

"I know what you mean," Roger said, and tapped him on the shoulder. "Clean it up. Wash the blood off. I don't want it back dirty."

"What are you two talking about?" Pelletier asked. Marchand was right beside him, and gave his friend a big hug.

Trudeau looked at Roger. Who turned to Pelletier and told him, "Nothing." He knew better than to tell a journalist that his good friend had cheated. The man could probably use a little mythology in his life. He had a story to tell now, of the night he dropped Reggie Chartrand to his knees. Nobody would believe it, had so many not seen it with their own eyes.

"Do you think we can get the hotelkeeper to open up the bar again?"

"With all these cops around? With the curfew?"

"I know a man with whiskey in his room," Roger piped up.

"Who?"

"A guy I know. You don't like him much. But whiskey's whiskey."

"De Bernonville?" Marchand charged. "I won't drink with him."

"How come you hang around with that guy?" Pelletier inquired. "Don't you know who he is?"

Roger shrugged. "I'm paid to. Mayor Houde was worried that one of you guys might beat him up. I thought that was crazy. After tonight, I'm not so sure."

They laughed. They were so happy. They were young and fighting the war of their lives and glad to be alive, and they were amazed by the evening's progress. Sure, why not, they'd wake up the count and drink his liquor. Talk to the bastard and tell him to go fuck himself, and if he didn't like it, they'd beat the crap out of him. But before that happened, they'd drink his whiskey.

One of the reporters who had joined them on the sidelines, the smallest man among them, moved forward in the procession to walk alongside Trudeau. He said, "Sometimes you surprise me, Pierre."

"I surprise myself sometimes, René."

They went up to the hotel, woke up de Bernonville and piled into his room. Chartrand was the last in, all bloody and in good spirits. He was tough. Holding out a paper cup for whiskey, he kept his hand outstretched until the glass was filled to the rim, then drank it down and let out a holler.

"Woo boy! Didn't we have ourselves a time."

They were laughing, enjoying themselves, only going quiet when Pelletier scratched the back of his head, then turned to de Bernonville and said, "Hey there, Count. I hear you're looking for a new home. You kill Jews for a living. What makes you think we'll let you do that here?"

The night ascended from there.

†††

The striking miners packed it in. They signed a new contract of no particular benefit to them, cutting their extensive losses. Lobbied by Maurice Duplessis and fed a full quota of lies, the pope banished Monsignor Charbonneau to the hinterland of British Columbia, never to be heard from again. As the prelate was on his way out of town, the premier sent him a note of fond farewell. The intellectuals returned to their cities, knowing that *le Chef* had again defeated them and would redouble his dedication to their future demise. The mine bosses praised the premier, and the premier praised himself. Normality returned, and with it a sense of impending gloom, of darkness. Ottawa chose to deport de Bernonville to face war crimes charges in France, but, aided and abetted by associates in Quebec, he fled to the Caribbean. And from there, to Brazil. Carole Clément came away from the Asbestos strike bitter and angry, haunted by defeat. Still in his late twenties, Father François Legault resolved to be more selective in choosing his confrontations in the future—he had to win a few, but he also had to protect himself within a Church no longer orchestrated by Monsignor Charbonneau. He was to be dispatched to serve as a pastor among northern Indians, but a heart attack caused his foes to fear him less, and he was offered the respite of clerical duty while he recuperated. Camillien Houde made peace with Duplessis, vowing to work only for his perpetual re-election. Finally satisfied with his fidelity, Duplessis, having previously denuded the mayor's office of any real power, returned a modicum of responsibility to the position.

Roger Clément would remember with interest the conversation that night between de Bernonville and the journalists. "Yesterday," the Nazi from France had pointed out to them, as a way of vying for sanctuary, "the Cartier Dagger was given to Clarence Campbell, who's a president of hockey, something like that, for being a war hero. He wasn't even in the war. He went to Germany after the fighting was over to prosecute Germans for being German. I know you have your opinions on that subject. I have mine. But this man, this Campbell, has been anointed as if he's a knight, permitted to hold an ancient relic of Quebec heritage in his safekeeping for the remainder of his life. I ask you, as Frenchmen, as patriots, what do you think of an Englishman being in possession of this artifact?"

Roger detected the man's indefatigable confidence in his ability to seduce, to conjoin, to paint what was black a muddy beige.

"Can you not tell, gentlemen," de Bernonville went on, "that you've been fighting the wrong battle? While you're out on the picket lines, worrying if miners will make an extra two cents an hour for digging in the dirt, while you bother yourself about whether or not Count Jacques Dugé de Bernonville, a free man, ought to be deported—although you can plainly see that I've come in peace, and bear no malice towards a soul, including Jews—in the midst of all this, you have allowed your heritage to slip away, to be rudely handed over to an Englishman. Don't tell me that you are such great defenders of your national interest, of the pride of your people, for I will not believe you. I have seen the truth with my own eyes. You have been preoccupied with lesser interests—the miners have a cause, I grant you, but what of me? I deserve to be no one's cause. I am insignificant. Yet you write about me. You condemn me. Meanwhile, gentlemen, a great symbol of Quebec has passed into English hands right under your noses, and you didn't print a word on the subject. Shame on you, is what I say, gentlemen. Shame on your negligence. Shame."

He had wanted to give them another battle to fight, to remove public attention from himself. He failed. Although the others got drunk with him, and made a good night of it, Pelletier would have the final word.

"Count—" he began.

De Bernonville's whiskey was gone. He knew that whatever Pelletier said next would be significant. He smiled. "Yes, my dear, dear Gérard."

"The souls of the dead torment me tonight. In particular, the souls of the resistance fighters you tortured."

His face turned grim. "Are you convicting me without a trial, Gérard?"

"I'm convicting you in lieu of a trial. I will rescind my statement if you agree to return to France to be properly tried as a war criminal."

De Bernonville shook his head. Then looked up. He had one last card in his hand. The time had come to play it. He had not wanted matters to depend on this. He said, "And where were you, my dear Gérard, when the battles raged?"

Pelletier looked him straight him in the eye. Among all of them, he was the least physically active, and the least likely to rise to intemperate rage. But he held the Count's gaze and levelled his words with intent. "I did what I believed to be just. Do not suggest, sir, that the same holds true for you."

He did not articulate his threat, but de Bernonville spoke no more that night.

What impressed Roger the most, as he awakened bleary-eyed the next morning and shunted off to visit his wife and child, was that he had achieved the impossible. People thought him to be a dumb thug, but he had finessed three sides against the middle and back again. Chartrand and Trudeau had each sustained severe blows, which should keep the premier happy. He'd never tell him that they punched each other. De Bernonville had been physically protected and managed to have his midnight party. The count had had an opportunity to press his charm upon the journalists, and so would send a good report back to the mayor. And Roger had served the monsignor well, and his wife, by maintaining order in a time of imminent peril.

Aware of what he had accomplished, he now considered that he had it in him to manipulate various forces, that he could surprise people with his acumen. For he now held an idea in his head, as did perhaps a few others who had been in that room, although among them he was the one most capable when disparate forces would again converge, this time to steal back for the people of Quebec their revered Cartier Dagger.

CHAPTER 25

1970

ARRIVING HOME IN THE WEE HOURS AFTER A DOUBLE SHIFT, CONstable Émile Cinq-Mars slept past noon. He was vaguely aware of the women being up and having breakfast, and remembered them saying something about taking the dog for a walk, but when finally he roused himself, he was alone in his apartment. He awoke to a note, which made him want to just go back to sleep. He felt sad.

Émile needed time to feed himself, shower and shave, and generally prepare himself for the next foray. Yet there was no shaking a sluggish mood. After the double shifts and the deep lows of the job, and now the departure of the Clément women, he felt let down and lethargic. Late in the afternoon he received a call from his watch commander.

"Hey, kid, how's it hanging?" the duty sergeant asked.

"Good. You?"

"Listen up. An SQ sarge called me ten minutes ago. Said he got the number from you. Your man's down at the jailhouse again, he said. What's that about?"

For a few seconds, Émile couldn't recall. Then it hit him—Father François was visiting prisoners.

"A lead I'm following."

"Yeah? So Touton told me you work for him now."

"Special duty, yeah. For a bit."

"Take care, Émile. He didn't seem all that pleased with you. He kept referring to you by your rectum."

That didn't sound good. "He's trying to keep up our morale."

"I also heard you requisitioned a squad car this morning. I'm giving you the benefit of the doubt using that word, 'requisitioned,' instead of saying you stole it."

"I need it, sir."

"We all need something, but you don't need a brand new one. Get your ass down here. I'm also referring to you by your rectum, asshole. Trade the car in. You get to drive some old wreck."

Sometimes life in the police department just seemed so damned trivial.

"I'll be down as soon as I can, Sarge."

"Whatever Touton's got prepared for your arse won't be nothing compared to what I do."

If he ever acquired rank, Cinq-Mars vowed, he'd change a few things. Such as how things worked, even the way people talked to one another. "Sarge, make sure the replacement car is ready. I don't have time to screw around on this." He just had to fight back, snap out of his slump, although, really, he could think of nowhere to go.

"Look who's high and mighty."

"Whatever you say, Sarge, but I got a gold shield in my pocket."

"What?" Cinq-Mars heard the other man sucking air. "Don't shit me, son. You never made sergeant yet. You haven't put in the time."

"Desperate times. Desperate measures. I'll show it to you when I get there."

He listened to the pause at the other end of the line. This was probably a difficult adjustment for his sergeant. "Forget it," he said. "Keep the car. If you got that shield—"

"It's in my pocket."

"Keep the car. Unless you want an unmarked."

The sergeant had changed his tune. Amazing, the difference created by the hue on a badge. "The blue-and-white suits me fine," Cinq-Mars told him. Then he chose to twist the knife deeper. He had nothing against his sergeant, although a few grievances against the department as a whole were brewing. He had logged time as an officer of the law, and his early romanticism was wearing thin. He added, "For now."

He knew he was getting big for his britches as he flicked on the siren and flashed the cherries and drove down to SQ headquarters at blazing speed. At every main intersection, soldiers with automatic weapons watched him whiz by.

He felt his good energy flowing back.

He wasn't really sure what to do once he reached the Sûreté lockup. He chose to park by the curb and sit in the car. His presence was insignificant. Half the other vehicles around were cop cars. Probably the majority of those that were unmarked were official vehicles or owned by cops. They had that aura.

On Parthenais Street, near the northern mouth of the Jacques Cartier Bridge, which rose high above the St. Lawrence, SQ headquarters stood as a narrow, black monolith. When he brought in prisoners, he processed them on the first two floors before they were transferred to penthouse suites via an elevator. Up there, way up the mast, the windows were barred. Prisoners were given rooms with a view. Escape was not impossible. Before the bars had been installed, and several times since, felons had knotted bedsheets together and slid down the external wall to freedom. Twice, fledgling escapees had lost their grip and fallen to their deaths. Another prisoner had miscalculated the distance. Bereft of enough sheets, helpless and exhausted from dangling four storeys up, he waited to be rescued by jailers who deliberately took their time before dialling the fire department. Cinq-Mars wondered how that man felt, dangling above the pavement, knowing that his scary bid for freedom reduced him to pleading for rescue by his captors. He felt vaguely sympathetic, and a bit that way himself, a dangling man. A yob. He didn't know if he'd even be able to saw through the bars, or if his sheets would be long enough, and if he came up short, the man who'd have to save him would be his own boss, who'd probably prefer to watch him dangle for hours, then let him plummet.

Putting his hands behind his neck, he arched his back, and, really for the first time in his life, experienced an unruly duress—pressure. His body required release, his muscles a good stretch, although mentally he believed himself set now. Hadn't he become a cop for this?

Still, what to do about Father François?

Cinq-Mars had no assurance that the cleric would depart through the same door as the last time he'd been there—likely, he'd leave by whatever exit was convenient to where he'd parked, which could be at the other end of the building or even on another street altogether—nor did he have any idea how long he'd be staying or if he was still inside.

But he waited. He called it a hunch.

Father François Legault, he knew, had been involved in every transformative social uprising that had occurred in the province. He'd walked in the big marches, been on the picket lines for the critical strikes, observed every riot. That was his way, his life's blood. His appearance among prisoners during this crisis should have been expected, and had Cinq-Mars been making the bet ahead of time, he'd have assumed that the priest would be incarcerated by now. Of all citizens, his name should have come up on a warrant, and he ought never to walk freely down prison corridors offering pastoral support. His collar alone saved him. In a land where priests were still accorded residual respect, he'd been skipped over for arrest.

He was the prime minister's pal. There was that, too.

Logically, Cinq-Mars believed that he had good reason to monitor the priest's movements. He was here, suffering a potentially fruitless reconnaissance, to serve a hunch. If he was going to be the cop he wanted to be—and, eventually, the detective he intended to be—then he needed to develop a nose—*oh, that magnificent beak of his*—for crime. A nose for investigation.

Like it or not, he was going to have to trust his instincts. He'd wait for Father François and hope he had the right exit covered. He also prayed that the priest was no different than anyone else involved in this affair, busy busy busy, and that he wouldn't be staying inside the building forever.

That aspiration, at least, was soon rewarded.

Father François emerged, large and shuffling, hands stuffed in his pants pockets, emitting both the lethargy of obesity and resolve. When the man checked his watch, Cinq-Mars checked his own. Twelve to five. Five o'clock would be a fitting time for a rendezvous. The man hadn't parked anywhere. Instead, he was travelling by cab and hailed one near the entrance. Luckily for Cinq-Mars, he could tail the vehicle without the passenger becoming aware of him in the rear-view mirror.

They each headed off, first through the military checkpoint protecting the

SQ, then along broad, busy Dorchester Boulevard towards downtown, which commenced a couple of miles to the west. Jeeps occupied by soldiers and other military vehicles were interspersed along the way, standing guard over the intersections to the major cross-streets. The cab, before reaching downtown, veered south as though Old Montreal might be its final destination. This proved to be true, and Cinq-Mars took advantage of being in a blue-and-white to park his vehicle in an alley off narrow St. Paul Street, as parking spots in the district were otherwise scarce. The priest had to be intent on a meeting of some sort, for he piled out of the cab and entered a bar-restaurant just as people were pouring in for their afternoon cocktails.

Cinq-Mars surmised that the priest was not hearing confessions in there.

The English preferred the phrase *happy hour.* In Quebec, the French used the term *cinq à sept*—five to seven. The meaning was specific to the province, for in France the same phrase referred to an illicit romance, as a man typically might meet his mistress between five and seven before heading home to his family after work. In Quebec, the term referred only to the hours for early-evening drinks, though it borrowed from the Europeans a sense of the mischievous.

Cinq-Mars knew how meanings and pronunciations changed as language crossed the Atlantic. His own name literally meant the fifth of March. In researching his family background, he learned that the origins of his name were obscure, that it derived either from antecedents with a name similar to Mars, in which the offspring of the fifth son had prospered while families of the other four sons had petered out, or the pronunciation had drastically altered over time. Likely, the name had begun as Saint-Marc, and he was descended from inhabitants of such a village.

He sequestered himself on a barstool, hoping not to be spotted by the cleric.

Along a far wall, he caught sight of the priest's shiny pate. The identity of the man seated across from him took a moment to determine, due to the congestion of patrons and the inconvenience of a pillar in his line of sight. When he shifted barstools, he could see the man clearly, and immediately the blood vacated his body and shot to his brain.

The priest and his confidant had fallen into a heated exchange.

As he made his exit, it occurred to Cinq-Mars that he was close to his own police headquarters. Father François had essentially travelled from one to the other—from the SQ to the Montreal Police Department—for the man he was talking to was none other than his own boss, Captain Armand Touton.

That gave him a lot to think about.

He had to wonder.

He was in awe that his boss maintained a pipeline into the SQ lockup where revolutionary suspects were being held. At the same time, he felt a rising dismay, for he remained a practising Catholic who felt seriously at odds with the priest's conduct. How long had this liaison been in force? Cinq-Mars rehashed the order Touton had given him some time ago to check out Father François. When had Touton established contact? Before or after that command? In his deliberations and investigations, the neophyte detective could only tap the surface of the alliances, betrayals and deals that intertwined so many diverse people. Dwelling on that, he remembered what Captain Gaston Fleury had once told him: that they could be going up against the *people*—not this or that person or authority or institution, but a gallimaufry of mythologies and allegiances interwoven through the entire population.

Getting into the blue-and-white and creeping out of the alley, Émile Cinq-Mars told himself that he was learning fast. He experienced a sensation of being alone in the world. He had no one to call upon for reliance or favour, no one to signal. He also felt, for the first time when not under an overt threat, scared.

The ride was rough. He had to stop the car to find out why. Kids. Or people sympathetic to terrorists. Someone, in any case, had let the air out of his front tires.

At least they'd not been slashed. He limped off towards headquarters nearby.

†††

Late in the afternoon, Jasper Cross felt queer and dizzy. His testicles went tight, as if shrunken to the size of peas and forcibly inserting themselves back inside his body. He cried out from the pain of it. His captors ran into the room. A young man placed a cool compress on the back of his neck, and the sensation made him jerk as if he'd been stabbed. Suddenly, he realized that he was perspiring. His clothes were soaked. He believed it was over—the world, his life. He'd made it easy on them—he was suffering a heart attack or a stroke and he'd die before they needed to shoot him through the mouth. Yet they were taking the trouble to calm him down, speaking gently, and as he quieted down he began to feel half-normal.

His rapid breathing slowed.

Silently, he spoke the phrase that described what he'd been through—*anxiety attack*. Knowing the name was beneficial, a comfort, but he guessed that another such attack was imminent.

How could he prevent it? Laporte had been killed.

Pierre Laporte was dead. No one could pretend now. They killed the other captive. He'd be next.

His life persevered in precarious balance, and even these men who might have pretended otherwise knew it now, too. They comforted him, in order to keep him alive so that they could kill him.

He was their barnyard animal.

The woman repeated the news for him, in case he hadn't heard the television distinctly through the walls. "The scumbag is dead, gotten rid of. They killed him. Strangled him, they say. With wire, they say. Stuffed him in the trunk of a car. What's the word in England? Merry old England? In the boot. They stuffed him in the boot of a Chevrolet."

"Leave him alone," a man's voice intervened.

"He thinks we'll drop him into a Rolls-Royce, or a Jaguar, this guy."

"Stop it, I said. Enough."

"He thinks we'll do him a favour. Hey, it'll be a Chevrolet. An old wreck."

"Shut up. I'm not going to tell you again."

"I just want to know if he's expecting a limousine. Maybe we can find him an old hearse from the scrapyard."

"Okay. Out. Now."

That was a change. A development. Someone was standing up to the woman. The killing of Laporte had altered the landscape, violated the rules of engagement.

Pierre Laporte. Oh, that poor man. His poor, suffering family.

Instigated by anxiety, or perhaps not, the pain that stemmed from his heart was visceral and real, compressing his chest and suturing his windpipe closed. He coughed and gasped. *That poor man.*

In idle mind, removing himself from the sordid reality of his captivity, he had fantasized about meeting Laporte. He had wanted to sit down and have a drink with him and exchange notes. He had imagined the conversation, the menu, the décor of the restaurant, its cozy fireplace and old stone walls. No man knew what they had gone through, except the other. They were brothers, that way. And now that dinner would not occur, and he felt diminished, reduced to lesser aspirations.

Laporte. And he was named Cross. Were they unaware of the symbolism, these folks? How could they not get it? At a time when the entire population was abandoning the Church, a new wave of political alarmists chose to kidnap a man called "the Door" and another called Cross. Blindfolded, he would run these matters through his head, over and over again. Longing to rant, *This isn't a fight against the political power in the land, as you believe. It's a subversive, scurrilous attack directed against the ancient regimes of Church and cultural upbringing.* He wanted to bring that up with them. Shout it from a podium, give them a lecture. He fantasized about addressing college students, putting things straight. If his captors placed a pistol against his temple, which he imagined repeatedly, he'd say, *Forgive them, Father, for they know not what they do.* Surely, they'd recall the reference. They'd been brought up in the old Church. How could they shoot a man whose name was Cross? Others, others had strangled the man called Laporte. He had to keep that detail in mind. Trust in it. Hope. Others had killed. Not these few.

He rehearsed what might become his final plea.

Remember, I'm Irish.

An anxiety attack. *Don't let it get that far again.* He felt so miserable and woozy going through it. He had to be stronger of mind, less prone to despair and desperation. Be an unemotional diplomat to the end. If only they'd remove his blindfold. If only they'd relax his restraints. If only they'd let him piss and defecate in private, have a bath on his own, revel in the water, recover. If only he could argue with these people. If only they'd let him get inside their heads. If only he weren't so damned *anxious,* then perhaps he could think straight. React. Do something. If only he were a free man again.

They killed Laporte—their friends did. Now they think about killing me. They prepare. It's not right. Hey! It's not right, what you want to do. Scriptures prevail against you. You were Catholics one time. You learned about right and wrong. This is wrong.

He rocked in the chair to which he was strapped. He didn't want another attack, but it was so hard, so difficult, to remain steadfast and calm. To remain a diplomat.

Killing poor Monsieur Laporte, that also was wrong. Don't you know that? Don't you know anything anymore? Have you lost your minds?

†††

In the midst of the various furies that spun around him in his august office, Prime Minister Pierre Elliott Trudeau bore in mind that the FLQ had killed a friend. Perhaps the man had died precisely because he had been his friend—he had that to consider, also. Other considerations were prevalent. The attention grabbers and wild radicals were willing to kill, and while their politics were now less serious than ever, their determination to do evil could no longer be dismissed.

They were killers now.

That changed everything.

Amid the demands upon him as the country's leader, he took a few moments to remember his friend, Pierre Laporte. A good man, a family man, a journalist of integrity, a government minister, but particularly, someone he'd gotten along with, a pal. Murdered. Strangled first, then shot. Stuffed in a trunk. *The bastards.*

He repeated the thought under his breath, aloud. "Bastards."

He had to watch himself. His office demanded much of him at this time, and he could not step away from his duties to cosset grievances or personal pronouncements. He could also not take the death too deeply upon himself. He was obliged to govern, not indulge an inner fury. The country would be second-guessing him right now. Pundits would suggest that his hands had been around Laporte's throat, although the polls indicated that the use of military force and the suspension of rights were supported by the population, equally among English and French. A comfort, to have the people behind him. Yet a man was dead, and his policy had initially been devised to save his life. Initially, then, the policy had failed, and tragically. Still, he said it again, whispered aloud in the sanctuary of the prime minister's office, as though he needed to step away from the trappings of his duty for a moment and just be a man on the street with an opinion. "*Bastards.*"

Then he went back to muddle through his agenda, keeping abreast of police and military developments while his staff prepared for the funeral.

Coming up, the minister of foreign affairs was on tap for a recital, prelude to a duet with the British ambassador. Then the secretary of state would command centre stage for his dull solo, followed by a barbershop quartet of army generals, a choir of police directors, the off-pitch harmony supplied by the leader of the opposition, a deep-based response from the labour secretary, then Marc Lalonde, his finance minister, had been begging time to rehearse an encore. During the concert, he could expect to be interrupted endlessly by stage managers and their production assistants—Bourassa, for one, would call in desperate need of assurance, and probably the mayor of Montreal would plead for another audition. As well, a chorus of walk-ons—presidents, prime ministers and kings—were telephoning to express their regrets that Canada had fallen into the sinkhole of an alternative universe where provincial cabinet ministers were snatched off their front lawns and executed. Life had become an opera, dramatic and large, chaotic, vibrant and ultimately tragic.

He had no time to grieve, he knew, yet grief lodged inside him. Somehow he had to make it through this travail. He had to lead.

†††

Life itself these days—the erotic silk of life, time's living tissue—had become next to impossible to fathom. Once upon a time, she knew a few things. In the United States, an underground radical group, the Weathermen, had taken its name from a line in a Bob Dylan song. *You don't need a weatherman to know which way the wind blows.* From the first time she'd heard the lyric, she had assumed that that was true, actually and metaphorically. Lately, she'd grown less certain. She might need a weatherman to know which way the wind was blowing. She couldn't cross a street without being buffeted by gusts from every sundry direction. Soldiers held their rifles so lovingly in their arms, no differently than young fathers would their newborns. Of friends she had known and trusted for years, some were bitter, others fearful. They didn't want to go to jail for their radical politics, as they were no longer convinced that their politics were radical. They didn't like the idea of French killing French to make a point to French politicians about the English. How did that make sense? And for a few, a notion that the blood stained their hands and clothing also, for past actions, troubled them. Would it wash off? A few, even quite a few, exulted in the tumult and the violence. Yet for most others, the issues were less tidy. Arguing the future of Quebec in a bar or a classroom had been intoxicating, an elixir of life. But declaring with one's being that the proper future of Quebec lay only in following Mao's dictum that power exists in the barrel of a gun was less fascinating than had been surmised. Always confusing, now the idea felt reactionary: *against life.*

Catching hold of the winds of change proved ephemeral, for she heard an argument for one position one night, countervailing reasoning the next, then grasped that the same person had pontificated both points of view. The guy had changed his mind during the day as fresh news had come in and events had been debated. He wasn't the only one. A man she knew had long scoffed at her political interests, and suddenly he was not only keen on current events, but had been radicalized. He suggested while inebriated that they form their own terrorist cell. "Hey, buddy, have you talked this over with your wife yet?"

Many radicals gleefully dug in their heels, and the socialists and separatists happily Krazy-Glued themselves to one position or another, yet the man in the street, the woman in the office tower, the young person on his way to school, the mother with her stroller, the grandparent fretting over the safety of a society—among these, few felt secure or stable or firmly decided on what anyone should do next, if anything at all.

Everyone watched the news though, and followed each rumour and talked it into the ground.

Anik herself felt run to ground.

She had called her friends together, ostensibly to connect, but really to access what they were feeling. These were the four she'd run into in the midst of the Jean-Baptiste Day riot two and a half years earlier. That time seemed different now, only because they had changed. Their dreams for the nation had shone with brilliance, yet now so much seemed tawdry. Recently, she was in touch with each of them, yet they were not coming together as a group. A boy pointed out that they had not come together as a group since Anik had taken up with Lévesque, but she was largely oblivious to that cantankerous opinion. She was floating ideas that she considered to be more immediately vital than any strains on their friendship.

By the time she arrived at their usual subterranean watering hole on St. Denis Street, the two literature students, Vincent and Pierre, had secured a corner nook. The boys had been served their beers, and Anik kissed them on both cheeks and held a finger up to the waiter to indicate that she'd have the same.

"What's happening?" she asked, waving a hand in the air. "Hey. Let's make a deal. For two whole minutes, we won't talk about Laporte."

Vincent had decided to return to school for a master's. In the context of the times—amid the chaos and the uncertainty—his choice struck Anik as political. Pierre had dropped out with no intention of going back, or of doing anything that might seem vaguely adult. His friends felt that he suffered from an odd pride—he accepted life only on his own terms, but Anik believed that he was fundamentally too lazy to make that work.

They asked what she'd been up to lately.

"Hiding," she told them.

"Anik," Vincent parried, wanting to gloat, "you were the one who'd never join anything. No petitions. Your name would never show up on a list that way. Remember? Are you telling me you're on a list?"

"My mom is. I'm hiding out with her to keep her company."

Her experience and background always seemed more stimulating than theirs.

Jean-Luc arrived next. Anik could tell immediately that he was suffering from the airborne virus of the time—paranoia. She'd have to stay clear, or at least be constant in her friendliness while making no demands on him. He entered the bar talking, and hardly a sentence passed without him saying "soldier" or "sell-out" or "pigs" or "Trudeau the fuck" or "Bourassa the little shit." He was wired to the vocabulary of the times—a surprise, for he'd always been the one with his head in books and his ideas had seemed two steps removed from reality. Now he seemed overwhelmed by reality, as though his cerebral world had imploded. The revolution, or at least that bit of it now known as the October Crisis, had buried him alive.

That Paul came in last was another surprise, until he explained himself. Traditionally the most social among them, he was constantly pulling people together for a beer, then coaxing them to stay out as long as possible. By Anik's count, he'd never been late for a get-together *ever*. Yet Paul was finding his element. He studied photography, and dreamed of creating artistic work through a camera's lens. The kidnappings and the army's advance had changed his approach. Now he wanted his camera to record life as it was being experienced in the moment. He wanted his snapshots in the news.

"One way or another, we'll get through this," Anik suggested. "Then you won't have any more big moments."

"Send me to the next crisis, then. War, earthquake, famine, plague, I don't care. I want excitement, you understand? I've acquired a taste for it. I'm hooked."

They believed him. He had discovered his true vocation and glowed with a new enchantment. Anik assessed, at that moment, that among them she'd trust only him, only Paul.

†††

Touton contacted his young protégé through his squad car's two-way radio. The message was to go at full speed to an address in the industrial north end, adjacent to an expressway.

"Full speed?" he inquired back to the switchboard operator. He meant the question to be rhetorical. He was unaccustomed to personal messages being sent over the air to him and replied somewhat dumbly. The woman took his question seriously and got back to him with Touton's response.

"Lights flashing."

He zoomed.

He arrived at a dreary ten-storey warehouse and rag-trade building within seconds of his boss, their front bumpers nearly colliding as they braked severely. Other officers had already arrived and were just lounging around, but when Touton extracted his pistol and dashed into the building, they suddenly did the same. Through the melee, Cinq-Mars caught up to him inside.

"You two," the captain barked. "Guard the elevator. More guys are coming. When they arrive, tell them to start evacuating everybody out of the building. The rest of you, we're taking the stairs."

The old man was puffing by the fifth floor, but he didn't relent. On the sixth, they went into the corridor where two RCMP detectives tried to block their progress.

"Captain," one said, "there's no way around this. It's not legal."

"Ask yourself two questions. You guys are already here. The RCMP does not call in the Montreal police to help them with an illegal task. So. Who called me here? When you answer that question, then ask yourself why."

The Mountie thought it over a second, then stood aside as Touton and his ten men went down the corridor. They stormed through broad doors and Cinq-Mars raised his pistol.

"Police! Don't anybody fucking move!"

The six guys inside had been expecting trouble. They carried semi-automatic weapons leisurely at their sides. The man who answered had a thick Spanish accent, but his French was good.

"We already told those Mounties. This warehouse is under the control of the Cuban Embassy. This is Cuban soil. You must leave. You have no right here. You are in violation of international law."

The man was small, with a snide look on his face, and watching him, Cinq-Mars deduced that he was treacherous and experienced. A soldier.

Touton looked around the room. He saw what he'd been told he would find. His fellow officers were clueless as to the meaning of this raid, and one man visibly went pale as he checked things out. Cinq-Mars took it in at a glance, then knew that this fight was serious. He could easily die here.

"Who are you?" Touton demanded.

The man shrugged, made a gesture as though he was inventing a name, and said, "Miguel."

"Miguel, there's one thing you have to understand. Those other officers left. But we will not leave. The guns you have here, the dynamite, the explosives, the grenades, have no business being on Canadian soil—"

"This is officially Cuban soil—"

"I don't give a shit!" he yelled, and suddenly the Cuban was less arrogant. He understood that he faced a problem now where the rules of diplomacy might not protect him. "You brought explosives and bomb-making material into a country that is combating an insurrection. I was a soldier once. I am speaking to you at this moment as a soldier, not as a cop. You are not going to be permitted to blow up my city and the citizens in my city and I don't give a sweet fuck about your goddamned diplomatic immunity or international-fucking-law. Is that clear to you?"

"My guys are better armed than yours."

"Then some of us will die and some of you will die, but you, Miguel, will be the first. You'll have your international incident then. But no Cuban or terrorist will have access to this material."

The standoff was secure. No one had a next move. Cinq-Mars heard the door open behind him and looked back. Half a dozen Mounties entered, including the two they'd spoken to in the corridor. They now carried semi-automatic rifles, too.

"I told you men before," the Cuban said to them. "You have no right here. This is Cuba!"

"We were cops then," the ranking officer told him. "We've resigned our commissions. Maybe that's temporary—we don't know yet. Now we're just a bunch of hard-assed boys with stolen guns. You got to leave now, or we will help this man blow your heads off."

Miguel didn't budge. His eyes surveyed the officers. Occasionally, he glanced at his own men. He was getting no help here, and seemed to be waiting.

A phone rang and everybody jumped.

One of the Cubans answered. He indicated that it was for Miguel.

"Excuse me," the man said, and went to the phone. He said, "Si," and then only listened. After he hung up, Miguel returned to his position facing the policemen.

"What does Castro say?" Touton asked.

Miguel cleared his throat. "If there is any mention of this in the papers, we will deny it and cause an international incident that will embarrass your government. If you do not agree," and he indicated his own men, "we must die here. Many of you will die also, probably all of you if something explodes."

Touton looked around. None of his men budged. "Well," he said, "we're staying. And I don't see any reporters around, do you?"

"It has to be more official than that."

"I got this," the Mountie who had talked to them earlier said, and he left the room. He was gone for seven minutes, and during that time the men just stared at one another, too fearful to blink, ready to shoot. Each man feared for his life and stared at the man across from him that he might soon kill.

Then the Mountie returned.

"What does Trudeau say?" Touton asked him.

The Mountie raised an eyebrow. Then he said, "It's been taken care of."

They waited, eye to eye.

When the phone rang again, nobody jumped. Miguel answered it himself. "*Si*," he said. Then he listened. Then he said, "*Si*," and hung up.

Miguel did not look at the policemen—not so much as a glance. He left the room, and his confederates followed. As each man arrived at the exit door, he set down his heavy weapon, then left.

When they were gone, the Mountie said, "Gather 'round."

The policemen—city cops and Mounties—formed a circle around him.

"There's enough explosive in this room to bring down a bridge. In a crowded place, thousands would die. There's enough here to do that over and over again. Your country will never know to thank you, but I thank you. And now we're duty bound to keep this among ourselves. It's not going to be in the papers because there'd be more shit to pay than any of us can afford. Captain Touton was right. This comes down from Trudeau himself. If what we did here today gets leaked, I'll arrest every last one of you, and if that doesn't give us the one guy who talked, then you're all fired. I don't care who you are. I can, and I will, deliver on that promise. Plus, that'll be only the beginning of your troubles. Captain Touton—thank you."

The two men shook hands.

"If you don't mind," the Mountie said, "we'll take care of this now."

"I don't want to be around here."

Nobody said another word until they got outside, where Émile Cinq-Mars, who was both a religious man and someone who rarely swore outside of a hectic moment, calmly said, "Holy shit."

Touton exhaled a deep breath.

Cinq-Mars looked at him. "Are we at war?"

Touton was digging for his smokes. "If we are, we're the only ones who know it. Fuck. This is what Trudeau's talking on TV about—his 'apprehended insurrection,' he calls it, what he's telling the people he can't tell them about. Now he still can't tell anybody, not unless Castro dies first." He turned suddenly towards the others and barked a final command for this operation. "Everybody, out of here before somebody wonders what we're doing. Cinq-Mars, come with me for a second."

They moved to a corner of the building, then a little farther to get out of the wind.

"Here," Touton said, and he handed the younger man an envelope. "The arrest lists you wanted. Both names were on it, both have been removed."

"Thanks."

"And here." Another envelope emerged from the man's coat pocket. "Don't lose it."

He did not need to look inside to identify the contents. The envelope carried the weight of a dime. He could feel only a small, thin, hard fragment. The stone chip from the Cartier Dagger.

"Thanks again."

"Stop fucking thanking me," Touton told him, "and do something."

†††

"Can't you climb it?" she asked.

"Not with all my stuff," he said.

"Fuck your stuff," she said back.

"What do you mean? I need my stuff."

"One camera. That's all you need."

Paul had never thought so. He needed his tripod and light meters, assorted lenses and filters, his telephoto for sure, the zoom, a bag of film, the extra camera bags, a flash wand, light reflectors, his—

"Just climb up the fucking tree and take the fucking pictures when somebody fucking shows up. Stop being such a prima-fucking-donna."

A radical idea. Paul climbed with a single camera around his neck. Anik waited nervously below.

"Pssst!" she hissed.

"What?" he asked, curled on a limb.

"Toss me down a smoke."

†††

"What," the prime minister inquired, "do we have?" He sounded hopeful, yet wary.

"Nothing."

"Don't say 'nothing.' Whatever you say, don't say 'nothing.'"

"Sir, we have very little so far."

"Why do people say I'm in power? The press should report, honestly, that I'm now the least powerful man in the country."

"Sir, the army has control of the streets—" the commissioner pointed out.

"—and the kidnappers control me."

"You don't mean that, sir."

He didn't. That was true.

"If I may say so, Mr. Prime Minister, we're making progress on many fronts."

"Progress?"

"We know a few of the kidnappers. Except for one, we can't find them."

"And you call that progress."

"The police are drawing the net closer."

"If they don't know where to look, how can they draw the net closer?"

"It's only a matter of time."

"Who said we have time? A Quebec cabinet minister is dead, and where's James Cross? You're closing *in,* but you don't know where *in* is. What if that cell or another cell kidnaps somebody else? What if Laporte's killers strike again? For that reason alone, I can't have the commissioner of the RCMP come into my office to tell me that matters are at a standstill."

His secretary rang through on the intercom. Someone had arrived to see him who was not on the agenda.

"Who is it?"

"A police detective from Montreal."

"Name?"

"Émile Cinq-Mars. He says he wants to talk to you."

He'd heard that name before. Lately, he'd heard a lot of names. "Ask him to go through channels. Follow protocol, for heaven's sake."

"Yes, sir. Thank you, sir."

"Take down the name of his superior officer before he leaves."

The prime minister returned his attention to the police commissioner. "What are your plans?"

"Mr. Prime Minister, Laporte's body, the car, the discovery of their hide-out, then finding Lortie, that business. What was bungled was bungled, but each clue brings us a step closer."

"Cross was abducted by a different cell," Trudeau reminded him.

"A lead that concerns one cell may help with the other. We are working every lead to its limit."

The prime minister shook his head as the intercom lit up again.

"He's insisting, sir," his secretary said.

"Don't we have a Mountie outside?"

"We do."

"Ask the Mountie to escort him out. If he'd like a direct command from the commissioner, he's with me now."

"Yes, sir."

The voice returned a moment later. "The Mountie is escorting him out, sir, and has acquired help to do so. The officer insists that he has something you must see before you make a final decision."

"I've made my final decision."

"You don't have to see him. So he claims. Only what he has to show you."

A belligerent cop. Even the commissioner was smirking, to decry the lack of discipline in the more primitive forces.

That name. He remembered. He'd heard it from Father François.

The prime minister clicked the button to speak. "Hold on." He looked at the commissioner and shrugged. "Go out and collect whatever it is I'm supposed to look at, will you?"

"Sir—"

"If it's a waste of time, we'll see that the officer is disciplined."

"Yes, sir."

The top officer in the land accomplished the rather modest errand in short order, and returned with an ordinary business envelope marked fragile and folded to a third its size and sealed. Whatever lay inside felt weightless and small.

"Curious. I wonder what it is."

The commissioner stood waiting to find that out himself.

"How'd he strike you, this Cinq-Mars?"

"Young," was the commissioner's first reaction. But he conceded, "Intelligent. It's odd. He's too young to have a gold shield. He says it was given to him by Captain Armand Touton in order to conduct a special line of inquiry on the FLQ. But he's still a Montreal cop. You know what that means."

Trudeau ignored the slur. "We owe Touton for the Cubans."

"It's curious, sir."

"Isn't it."

"We should call Touton and check him out."

"Intelligent-looking, you say? An odd description, Commissioner."

"Sir?"

The prime minister used a letter opener carved by Inuit from a walrus tusk. He looked inside, but did not touch the object there. "What's this?" he said, more to himself than to the man in the room. He continued to stare at it, perplexed initially by the seemingly innocuous contents. He picked it out and held it up to the light between his thumb and middle finger.

From the opposite side of the desk, the commissioner squinted at the pale greyish chip.

Then the prime minister deposited the object back into the envelope and punched the intercom button. "I'll see him," he said.

"Sir," the commissioner protested, "we should contact Touton."

"Don't bother."

"What is it, sir?"

"That will be all, Commissioner. Good luck. We're counting on you."

"Yes, Prime Minister."

Feeling snubbed, the commissioner departed the room.

"Should he come in with an escort?" his secretary was asking.

"No," Trudeau directed. "Send him in on his own."

"Sir, there are more people on your schedule. We have—"

"Ask them to wait."

He got out from behind his desk to greet the mysterious and unknown police officer who had called upon him with the missing chip from the pointy end of the famous dagger. The last he'd heard of that missing chip, it had been lodged inside a poor bastard's heart.

†††

The door was held open for him, and with his knees feeling somewhat slushy and his heart jumping an occasional beat, Émile Cinq-Mars entered. Silently, the door swished shut behind him, and that easily, after all the commotion and argument and pleading down the corridor, when he'd come within a hair of being given the bum's rush, he stood quietly, alone, with the prime minister of Canada.

"Officer Cinq-Mars," Trudeau said in a tone that made his name sound like an accusation.

"Sir," the younger man commenced, and discovered his mouth dry. For some reason he'd been talking English in the outer office, and now stumbled as he reverted to French. "Thank you for seeing me." He caught himself bowing slightly, not sure how to conduct himself.

This was a time of crisis, the circumstances of the meeting unorthodox, so Trudeau had no patience for pleasantries. "I presume you know what this is," he stated, holding up the envelope that Cinq-Mars had sent as his calling card. He wiggled it, as if jingling a bell.

"I do, Mr. Prime Minister." He ventured a few strides across the pale carpet, hoping he wasn't tracking mud in behind him. His eyes shot around the room. "As do you."

"Do I?" Turning, Trudeau moved behind his desk to sit in his high-backed swivel chair, from where he observed the officer intently.

Nervously, Cinq-Mars took in the room with a glance. The old mahogany woodwork impressed him, as did the lush carpet underfoot. Interior shutters had been folded back to reveal windows shaped like elongated spires, the sides closing at the apex like hands at prayer. Over a sofa hung a woven Inuit hanging—figures hunting walrus and tracking wolves. The igloos, Cinq-Mars noted, were a perfect decorative feature for a Canadian leader.

"Have a seat," the prime minister invited. Perhaps a command. "I don't mean to be rude, but I've neither the time nor the patience to digress. As you must know, the Montreal Police Department is not in anybody's good graces these days."

"I thought that perhaps, after the incident with the Cubans—" He stopped as the prime minister scorched him with a look.

"No incident occurred between Cubans and police in this land."

"My mistake, sir."

"So the poor performance of the Montreal police remains our only reference."

The department's name had been sullied. Having found and searched the abandoned house where Laporte had been held captive, they'd located an address on Queen Mary Road. There, they discovered a female college student, who had answered the door, and, hiding behind a chair, Bernard Lortie, one of those wanted for the death of the Quebec labour minister. Montreal cops exulted in their coup. Lortie was willing to sing, was being mocked in the press for doing so, and they had the apartment to scour for clues. The cops were there for more than twenty-four hours, after which they kept a pair of detectives on the premises. Then the two officers went to dinner. When they returned, they discovered that a false wall had been opened in their absence. Through the wall was a compartment with benches, water and food. To further taunt the police, the men who'd been hiding there had smeared their fingerprints all over the freshly dusted apartment. The cops had screwed up by not bringing in dogs and not finding the fake wall, but even those glaring errors might have been forgiven by the other jurisdictions had they not screwed up more seriously again. Embarrassed, they failed to tell the Mounties and the SQ what had happened. While the perpetrators were clearly in Montreal, the Mounties were searching for them on the other side of the continent, continuing to do so because the embarrassed Montreal cops did not share their information. The department would have remained silent altogether were it not for an FLQ communiqué that blew the whistle on them and extolled the virtues of Bernard Lortie for not telling the police about the secret wall, and now no Mountie, and no prime minister, was willing to trust a Montreal cop again.

"Why have you brought this to me?"

"It's connected to the crisis."

The answer appeared to take him aback, and Trudeau, setting the envelope down on the desk, rubbed under his lower lip with the thumb and forefinger of his right hand. He studied the man seated before him, then asked, "How does a sliver of stone relate?"

"Sir, in seeing me, you have, in essence, if not explicitly, admitted—or shall I say, rather, indicated—that you know what this sliver of stone, as you call it, represents. What it means."

"Not true, Detective. This is merely the most curious calling card I've ever seen. And you told the commissioner outside that you're Armand Touton's man. That's what got you in the door. Now, why don't *you* tell *me* how this sliver of stone relates to the current crisis. But—before you do that, just so we're clear—did Captain Touton send you?"

Cinq-Mars cleared his throat before replying. "He knows that I'm here."

"Ah, but does he approve of your being here? You've not entered the room through the usual channels, Detective."

"It's not an authorized visit. Captain Touton has made a conscious decision not to stand in my way, and—" Cinq-Mars said, then paused to take a breath before proceeding with his gambit, "—he did give me the tip of Cartier's dagger—"

Trudeau stared back at him. He spoke quietly. "Is that what this is?"

Cinq-Mars paused again, perhaps to signal his distaste for the prime minister's deception, for they did not need to confirm that detail. The prime minister possessed the knife, and the shape of the missing tip would be well embedded on his consciousness. "By giving me the chip, he facilitated this meeting. Let's say that that's something he and I understood between us."

The prime minister touched both forefingers to his lips. "How did you come upon this sliver?"

"It's evidence. The last known whereabouts of the Cartier Dagger was in the heart of a murder victim. The tip of the dagger remained behind when the knife was removed. It's evidence. Captain Touton has been holding on to it all this time because he's never given up on the case. Shall we conclude, sir, that my possession of this tidbit of evidence validates my presence here?"

Rocking his head one way, then the other, Trudeau demonstrated that he was reluctant to concede the point. "The question still remains, Cinq-Mars. How does any of this relate to our present circumstances?"

"It could lead to the beginning of a negotiation between the terrorists and the government for the release of James Cross."

A silence ensued. In the prime minister's gaze Cinq-Mars detected a modest hope, a genuine willingness to seize any valiant straw that might save the day.

"If you can begin a negotiation to bring an end to this fiasco, Cinq-Mars, then why have we not commenced that task already?"

"We have. It starts here, with me and you."

"You're representing the terrorists?"

"I represent someone who is willing to lead us to the terrorists."

Another pause. The prime minister then spoke slowly, "Shall I not call the commissioner back into the room?"

"Let's keep this between me and you, sir, for now."

"In this room, I outrank you," Trudeau noted.

Cinq-Mars acknowledged that fact with a brief nod, then stood. He reached across the table, his movement deliberate, slow, and pressed the middle finger of his right hand upon the white envelope to slide it back across the desk towards himself. He then picked it up, visually checked that the chip remained inside, and returned the envelope to his jacket pocket once more. Then he sat down again.

The prime minister observed him.

"Explain this to me," Trudeau asked. "For instance, why should I not have you arrested—or at least questioned—immediately? Someone can dream up a charge, I'm sure."

"Under the War Measures Act, no one will have to."

The prime minister smiled so slightly that it was difficult to determine if he had found the riposte amusing.

Cinq-Mars carried on. "Arresting me won't move us forward. The person who knows what we want to know is in hiding, and if we go after that person, we'll be back in our familiar pattern of seeking and not finding. If captured, that person will likely choose silence, or at the very least, fail to divulge what's critical. Time will be lost, and you'll agree, time is of the essence right now. We don't want to obliterate the trust being developed between the police, as represented by myself, and the only person who seems able to help us at this time."

The prime minister's intercom beeped. Pressing a button, he said, "Hold all calls and appointments."

"Premier Bourassa is on line one."

Trudeau pressed the answer button for a moment and did not speak, delivering silence to his secretary. Then he said, "I'll call him back. Hold all calls and delay all appointments."

Cinq-Mars knew then that he had the man's undivided attention.

"What's the deal?" Trudeau asked.

"The dagger in exchange for knowledge of the terrorists' whereabouts. The government must consent to negotiate with them—"

"What curious folktale have you heard that makes you think I know anything about the Cartier Dagger? Aside from that, I do not negotiate with terrorists."

Cinq-Mars had anticipated the response.

"With respect, sir, if we find them, and Cross remains alive, you will negotiate the terms of their arrest. If they want a plane to Algiers, or Cuba, chances are they'll get it. I'm not suggesting that they should get anything more. The proposal being presented to you at this moment, is that the government will negotiate any flight to freedom in good faith."

"A provincial cabinet minister was murdered, Cinq-Mars."

"We're not talking about the people who killed Laporte. Only those who currently hold James Cross alive. Not that kidnapping is a misdemeanour."

"An issue—why are you even talking to me about an ancient relic?"

"It's in your possession, sir."

"Says who? You're supposed to be a police officer, not a rumourmonger."

"In giving his final confession to Father François Legault, who I understand is a friend of yours, Mayor Camillien Houde spoke of the knife's sale to you."

That shocked Trudeau. He pushed himself back in his seat. When he spoke again, he had lowered his voice. "What could Houde possibly have known?"

"He was one of the sellers, sir. Part of that consortium."

Trudeau rolled his chair back a few inches this time, and crossed his legs, an ankle coming to rest just above the opposite knee.

"Near Houde's bed was a closet. Someone was hiding in the closet, a girl, when he made his last confession. She was there when Houde succumbed. She's grown up now, of course. She once threw rocks at you, precipitating the rioting before you won the election. She's come forward to make a deal."

"She's a terrorist?"

"No, sir. But she knows the culture. She's been around the radical element throughout her life."

"And you believe her?" He still appeared ready to dismiss him.

Cinq-Mars felt that he could not yield on any aspect of their discussion. He could not blink without his position unravelling. "Without a doubt, sir."

Trudeau elected to stand, thrusting his hands into his pockets. "Why should *I* trust her? This rock-thrower? Why give her a priceless relic? What is her stake in this, other than to undermine the prime minister of Canada with what sounds suspiciously akin to blackmail? Does she expect to sell it?"

"The tip of the dagger, sir," and Cinq-Mars tapped the pocket containing the envelope, "broke off as it entered her father's heart. She feels that she and her mother have more right to the knife than anyone, including you."

Trudeau processed this news, then jumped ahead. "Don't tell me. She thinks it has magic powers. Some say that nothing else explains my rise to power. Does she not understand what's at stake here?"

"I believe she does. I'm not sure that you do, sir."

"Officer Cinq-Mars—"

"I don't mean to be disrespectful. Not at a time like this and not in this room. Cross's life may depend on us coming to a binding agreement, right here, and very soon. Time is of the essence."

Trudeau went to one of the tall, narrow, church-like windows of his office and looked out. Behind him, Cinq-Mars placed three photographs on his desk. The prime minister returned to look at them.

"A terrorist we're looking for," Cinq-Mars explained, "somewhat disguised, so his identity is not confirmed. Nonetheless, it fits an existing description. He's entering a flat by the rear. The lane is innocuous—we won't find it on the basis of these photographs. If we publish them, the kidnappers will probably change hideouts and the public will overwhelm our switchboards. We need to find the address. Only one person can give it to us, and that's the woman I'm here to tell you about, and she has slipped underground."

Trudeau gazed at the images. He picked up a photo. "Cross is in this house?"

"Probably not. But if we can follow this man . . ."

The two men sustained a period of thoughtful silence.

"She wants the knife," Trudeau said quietly. He held something in his hands, a hope to properly deliver the country from its deepest crisis in modern times.

"If the negotiation with the terrorists does not go well," Cinq-Mars stipulated, "and if that's the government's fault, then she will tell the media how she acquired the knife. She'll have it in her possession. Which will make her story highly credible. I'm merely stating her position, sir."

"Do you understand that she's asking a lot, this radical contact of yours? A thousand organizations and a million individuals crave ownership of this knife. If I possessed such a thing, how could I possibly give it up on a mere gambit?"

"Because the country's at stake."

"Which is why the matter must be turned over to the police, Cinq-Mars. Oh, I know, you're a policeman. But I'm asking the commissioner to take it from here."

"That won't work, sir."

"Cinq-Mars, you're asking me to trust you, a policeman I do not know, a member of a department that has performed abysmally."

"Except with the Cubans."

"The Cubans don't exist."

"Yes they do, sir. You know they do. I saw what was in that room, sir, and the blood, the deaths, the destruction, the chaos that would have resulted had that material been delivered into the wrong hands—"

"I know what you're saying, but we cannot speak of that action. Do *you* understand, Cinq-Mars?"

"My colleagues and I would have died in that room, sir. If necessary. Just between us, don't say the Cubans don't exist. We have to stop this, before we find more Cubans, or Algerians, or who knows who. The idea of a revolution on North American soil right now is very attractive to a lot of people."

"I know that. But you're asking me to trust a friend of yours, not of mine. What else am I to do but ask the *proper* authorities to pursue the matter? No

Cartier Dagger. Even if I possessed such a thing, the situation mirrors that of any kidnapping or blackmail. How do I know that a bargain struck will be kept?"

Cinq-Mars knew he was losing this debate, but he recalled his boss's words. This was his Dieppe. Around him, lives succumbed in a tapestry of horror—had it been him on that beach, would he have valiantly warred on? In this circumstance, he had to forge ahead, with no thought for himself, and see at the end of the day whether he bled on a beach or stitched up his wounds on higher ground.

"You owe it to her."

Trudeau stared back a moment, then exhibited his familiar elegant shrug.

"The man who was killed with the knife—her father—you knew him."

"News to me," Trudeau maintained, stretching his back. "I remember hearing of his death, during the Richard riot. With all that was going on it was almost a footnote. Would have been, too, if not for the fact that an antique dagger had been stolen from the National Hockey League. But I do not recall recognizing the man's name back then. What was the year? Fifty-five?"

The two men were both standing, as though their verbal joust had taken on the manifestation of a physical sparring.

"The town of Asbestos, sir. The strike. Your fight with Reggie Chartrand."

Trudeau rocked his head from side to side a little. "That story's gone around. So what?"

"The real story has never gone around."

"What real story?" the prime minister inquired.

"Of how you defeated Chartrand. The man who slipped a set of brass knuckles over your right hand, that man, he died with the dagger embedded in his chest. His name was Roger Clément. He kept the story to himself, except that he told it to his daughter."

The prime minister spoke quietly, "The same man? I never realized."

"That man's daughter wanted me to remind you that if her father had not helped you out back then, a fight would have occurred between the police and the miners that would have had a fearful effect on our society—at least back then. Lives would have been lost, which might have been the least of it. She asked me to relate the same point to you. Our current straits can be repaired also, by slipping us information on the hiding spot for James Cross. But now, as then, a sleight-of-hand must first occur. Back then, her father was working for the Church, among others, and was determined to secure the peace. He succeeded in Asbestos, but he failed on the night of the Richard riot. She wants the Cartier Dagger in exchange for her father's life, to commemorate his life in some way. What she will do with the knife remains to be seen. Or, it may remain unseen. That's her business. Isn't delivering the country from the abyss in which we find ourselves . . . won't that be worth the price?"

Trudeau pondered his choices. "I admired that man. I'm ashamed that I never came away with his name. Roger, yes, that part I remember. He died during the riot? Did he steal the knife then?"

Cinq-Mars nodded, but only slightly. "That's broadly assumed. I assume it myself. I'm involved in that ongoing investigation. We have not acquired complete knowledge of that night's events, not as yet."

The prime minister first placed one hand, then both, behind his neck, and stretched in that position. Cinq-Mars recognized the gesture as a technique to release stress. It's how he felt also, although, as a guest here, he did not feel sufficiently at ease to put himself through any similar gyration.

"Roger Clément's daughter is someone who wrestles with her beliefs and convictions. I actually arrested her on the night that she threw rocks at you. But she does not condone kidnapping or murder. She's in a fight here, as we all are. In a sense, she's overmatched, as you were against Chartrand. In asking for the knife, in my opinion, she's asking you to slip a set of knuckle dusters onto her right hand, just as her dad did for you." Cinq-Mars looked down and tapped the desk briefly with the ring finger of his right hand. "In a sense, to do what she has to do here requires that she attain the high moral ground. Some will say that she's in the mire. To do that, to get herself up on a higher plane, she needs to make the knife a part of this arrangement, perhaps because the knife represents, not magic, but history. She needs to understand that what she does will have a particular—and, I would say, beneficial—effect, not only with respect to her father's legacy, but on the history that is being made. The history we make. For Quebec."

"History is subject to interpretation, and bias," Trudeau pointed out to him.

"She has her ideals, sir. We have to work with her assumptions."

After a prolonged and deep sigh, the prime minister crossed the room and opened a cabinet drawer to reveal a safe, dialled a combination and opened it fully. He handed the rustic artifact, ensconced in its case, over to Émile Cinq-Mars.

"Sir?"

"Study it. Hold it in your hand. By showing it to you I'm taking a great risk. It is a murder weapon, after all. With knowledge that the knife is here you can probably try to get a court order to retrieve it, but you will fail. Or, you can give me time to check you out, and you can give your trusted friend time to produce the kidnappers. If she does, and if she meets my other criteria, which is an exceptional demand, then you have my word, Cinq-Mars, as she has, that I will surrender the knife to you. My word is my bond, but by placing this object into your hands, if only for a few moments, I am demonstrating that I will honour my word, as I have made myself vulnerable. Politically, if not legally. The terrorists first, you understand. Plus one more—no, two more demands. This is my only offer and it is non-negotiable."

Cinq-Mars held the knife in his hands, finding it heavier than he had imagined, and not so well balanced as a modern instrument might be. The diamonds seemed scuffed and tawdry, the gold a dull yellow. He returned the knife to its case, and the case to Trudeau.

"Your other demands, sir?"

The prime minister took a moment to consider his words, put the case down, and placed his hands on his hips.

"Detective," he said, then looked at him, "are you Catholic?"

"I am."

"Practising? You're under no obligation to answer."

"I consider myself to be a man of faith."

"I detected that in you. Or thought I did."

They both took a moment to consider their odd exchange.

Then Trudeau said, "What Houde revealed on his deathbed interests me. I have often wondered how I was able to acquire this knife—from my enemies, in fact. If she knows something that sheds light on that mystery, then I'd like to hear it. I'm making that part of this arrangement."

Cinq-Mars nodded. "And your last demand?"

"Maintain the knife's security."

He glanced up. "Excuse me?"

"This knife is being entrusted from my care to this young woman's. Don't let me hear about it next after a robbery. I don't want it stolen from her. You're a cop. Help her to keep the knife safe. It means too much, its history is too diverse, to allow it to be hocked in some shabby way among international collectors."

Cinq-Mars continued to observe the prime minister a moment, then looked away at the Inuit wall hanging. "I'll communicate your terms to her."

Pierre Trudeau put the case back into the safe, and closed the doors.

"You keep it close at hand," Cinq-Mars mentioned.

"For its magic powers," Trudeau said, and the policeman could not decide from the man's tone whether or not he was being serious.

"I suppose, if it ends this crisis, it will have done a great magic."

The prime minister nodded again, assessing that statement. "That's actually my own sentiment. It makes the purchase, in another time, a good one. The return on investment was not what I had anticipated, but all in all, it's not bad. You have an unusual name, Mr. Cinq-Mars. Where are you from?"

"Saint-Jacques-le-Majeur-de-Wolfestown. Do you know it?"

Trudeau nodded, as though to say that he did, but he did not reply immediately, and was gazing out the window again. Then he turned back, his face seemingly quite bright, as though he'd been freed from solemn obligations. "You're a small-town boy, Cinq-Mars, and now you're a big-city detective. It's astonishing, is it not? How our lives turn, then turn again."

Cinq-Mars wanted to agree, but stood waiting.

The prime minister looked at the young detective. "You and I never had this conversation."

"Yes, sir," Émile Cinq-Mars assured him, and departed.

CHAPTER 26

1955

H IS MIDDLE NAME WAS MENDELSSOHN.
He lived with it.

Few knew of the appellation. At one time he wanted it expunged from his records, but found the lawyer's fees exorbitant. As a shyster related, "You can pretend it doesn't exist—that'll cost you nothing—or you can pay me four grand and I'll take care of it."

He rarely made that much in a year.

"By the way, for my advice today, the fee is thirty bucks."

He'd taken less than a minute of the man's time.

What had his mother been thinking to call him that? What had she expected of him? It's not as though she went out and bought him a piano. She was a bit batty, she lived in her own world, and her second-born son was called Michel Mendelssohn Vimont. His father had made sure that his first name was Michel, having learned from the experience with Brahms, their first-born.

Michel Vimont had no music in him. If someone were to put a pistol to his kneecap, he couldn't beat a drum to any rhythm. Yet, on his only spell in prison, he felt differently about the tag.

"Last name?" the admitting guard asked him. He had a birthmark under his right eye the shape of Greenland.

"Vimont."

"Spell that."

Six measly letters. He wondered why it was necessary.

"First name?"

"Michel."

"Spell that."

How did this man keep his job? "You can't spell Michel?"

The guard stared back at him coldly until he spelled his name for him.

"Middle name?"

"Mendelssohn." For once, he spoke it proudly. What the hell. He was unlikely to encounter the pencil pusher again. He declared his name as though it was a title, a designation that marked him as different, and for the first time he was proud that his mother had distinguished him from being merely Michel or Jean-Guy or Marc, and had segregated him as well from young thugs named Louis and Pierre and Serge. He was Michel, but he was also Mendelssohn.

The guard waited, but Michel Vimont declined to anticipate his next command. "Spell that."

Very slowly, he spelled his name, forcing the guard to look up after each letter to await the next one. Halfway through, Vimont said, "Tell me what you've got so far."

The guard glared back at him, pulling the skin taut around his eyes, and Vimont looked at the map of Greenland and continued spelling his name.

Then he did his time.

He met Father Joe Charbonneau in prison. The priest had been visiting with a contingent of clergy to evaluate conditions in federal prisons, and they hit it off and enjoyed an affable chat. After Vimont was released, he read in the papers that Father Joe had been brought in from Ontario to be the next archbishop of Montreal. He wrote a letter, reminding Father Joe of their jail-cell chat and asking if he knew of any jobs. He couldn't believe that the man promptly took him on as his personal driver. Then, after the Asbestos strike, Father Joe got into hot water with the pope and was shipped to British Columbia, to an obscure parish there. Michel was not surprised when he was the first person fired after the change of guard.

"You have a criminal record," the new bishop had stated, spreading his hands apart and smiling broadly. Apparently, that explained everything. *In time,* those eyes, those hands, were saying, *you'll steal candlesticks.*

Vimont merely nodded and bugged out.

After three days in a funk, he called Roger Clément.

"You're a big man," Roger observed. "Have you done much bouncing?"

"I held my own in prison."

"I know somebody. We'll start you out. Then, when a big shot needs a driver, we'll get you doing that again. It shouldn't be so hard. You were the bishop's chauffeur. That's practically like being a priest yourself."

"I know how to keep a secret," Vimont admitted.

"That's what I'm saying. You got all the right credentials."

He did some bouncing, and Roger proved true to his word. Michel Mendelssohn Vimont had the proper attributes to be a chauffeur, and he began driving for a club owner and racketeer named Harry S. Montford. His new boss checked his driver's licence before giving him the keys to his Caddy.

"Mendelssohn?" he asked.

Vimont appeared glum.

To cheer him up, his new boss showed him his own licence.

The S stood for Sylvester.

"Tell nobody mine, and I won't tell a soul yours. If somebody starts calling me Sylvester, I'll know it started with you, that you can't be trusted. After that, I'll tell everybody who comes into my place your middle name. I'll paint it in bright letters above the bar."

They shook on a pledge to keep each other's secrets.

"You drove a car for an angel, a man of God," Montford cracked one day. "Now you're driving the devil around. I guess you're on a bit of a downhill plunge, huh?"

Everybody presumed that the job was a great relief for him, not to be driving a bishop around, when he watched his tongue and hid any hint of whiskey on his breath. He never told people that he preferred driving the monsignor. The man of the cloth was more fun, related more interesting stories and confided in him at a trusting level. Vimont also never told anyone that, between the monsignor's appointments, he and Father Joe would often share a nip. Driving the bishop, he felt that he was making something of his life, whereas the job with Montford paid better but offered no satisfaction. He was a big boy, though, and took what life dished out. He soldiered on. That he kept to himself made a few people wary, but he preferred his solitude. Then again, whenever Roger Clément brought him over to his house to spend an evening with his family, he always enjoyed that, too.

When the phone rang, Vimont was cooking bacon and eggs.

"Mendelssohn," his employer said. They kept up their tease in private.

"Sylvester," Vimont answered back.

"What we discussed, that thing is tonight."

That thing. "All right."

"You'll get a call later. You'll be told where to pick this guy up."

"What's his name again?" Vimont knew the man's name. But in his best interests, he chose to feign a lack of knowledge.

"Count Jacques Dugé de Bernonville."

"Right. I'll wait here for a call from the count."

"What he asks for, where he wants you to drive him, take care of that."

"I throw stuff, right? Nothing more. Nobody gets hurt?"

"A little stink. A little smoke. Nobody gets hurt. During the panic, take a hike. Then drive the man where he wants to go. In the meantime, look at it this way, Mendelssohn: you get to enjoy the game."

"A part of the game."

"It'll be the whole game, if things go right. Because the game will be short."

"Okay. I'll wait here by the phone."

He was turning his eggs over as he talked, the receiver cradled between the crook in his neck and his raised shoulder. Then he hung it up and served his breakfast, eating it standing by the kitchen counter. When he finished he put the plate and cutlery in the sink with yesterday's supper dishes and soaked them, then flicked his hands together to slap off the droplets of water, cleared his throat and picked up the telephone receiver once more. He was feeling lethargic and worried. As though he might die. He dialled.

"Hello?"

"Roger," Vimont said, "it's me, Michel."

"How's it going?"

"Good. So I got the word. It's on. Tonight."

"Son of a bitch, hey? What do you know? Yeah. It figures. Had to be tonight. But it's on, nobody's chickening out. Goddamn that Richard, eh? While God's at it, he should damn Campbell, too, eh? That's what I say, anyways. Okay, thanks, Michel. You take care now."

"You, too."

Vimont washed his dishes and set them out to dry on a dishtowel spread across the counter. When he was done, he dried his hands and from the adjoining room collected his personal phone book. He found the number he was searching for, returned to the wall phone in the kitchen, and dialled again.

The man at the other end of the line picked up on the third ring.

"Hello?" A high, chirpy voice.

"Father François?"

"Yes, that's me."

"It's Michel Vimont."

"Michel, how are you, my son?"

"Fine, thanks. Father, I'm calling to let you know that—" He wasn't sure why, but he didn't want to say, as though this action could only work against him.

"Tell me, my son," Father François quietly insisted. "We know how important this is."

"It's going down," Vimont informed him.

"Tonight?" the cleric double-checked.

"Yes, Father."

"That makes sense. Thank you, my son. By the way, I've been talking to Father Joe. We had a long chat on the phone. As always, he sends his best regards."

"Thanks, Father. I appreciate it. I'll see you."

"Thanks again. Have a good day, Michel."

Vimont hung up. Have a good day? A good day? With his lonely Catholic soul imperilled, how was he supposed to have a good day?

††††

Captain Armand Touton woke up earlier than usual, having booked off at a decent hour the night before. Still, he was not particularly well rested as he stepped into his meeting with Mayor Jean Drapeau and Pacifique Plante, the director of the police department. He was grumpy and motoring on caffeine when he caught sight of his two bosses. They'd obviously had less sleep than him.

Fair enough, Touton thought, and he closed the door behind him to receive his marching orders.

"The main thing about a riot is, it's a riot," Touton explained to the men, for they didn't have much experience with the circumstances, either. "Nobody can predict what will happen."

"Something will happen, do you think?" Drapeau asked. Everyone recognized that emotions were running high. They wouldn't be having this meeting if the entire city did not expect trouble. The question, then, was either too naïve or too dumb to be believed, but the mayor had a propensity to do that sometimes—seek a comforting opinion the way a man with a headache reaches for a bottle of Aspirin.

"I'm no fortune-teller, but is the city a powder keg? Is that what you're asking me? Yes, sir. It is."

Plante was the more realistic of the two leaders. "I've put Captain Réal LeClerc in charge of the uniforms. We expect him to contain any outbreaks of violence. What we expect from you, Armand, as captain of the Night Patrol—" He paused, as though to confirm his own assessment first. "—is to protect property. Anticipate the targets that a mob might choose to go after, and keep them safe."

Touton would accept his orders, but first he had to make certain that the proper bases were being covered. He wasn't going to leave that up to the mayor or to the director, and he certainly wouldn't leave it up to LeClerc.

"Sir," Touton began, and briefly coughed, making a fist to cover his mouth, "please, make certain that LeClerc lines his forces up in such a way—"

"It's really his job to make that determination," Plante interrupted, mindful of police protocol.

Touton carried on as though his boss had not spoken. "—as to prevent any mob from leaving the Forum and going up the mountainside. A mob can do a lot of damage downtown, for sure, but it will be to property. If a mob gets up into Westmount, among the English, the rich will get out their guns. If the vandals start to get rough with citizens, we'll be talking about a civilian death toll. I hope you understand me, sir. Don't leave it up to LeClerc. *Order* him to prevent any mob of angry Frenchmen from running loose in the backyards of the English."

His superiors nodded gravely, for they hadn't really considered that before. They knew that Touton had his problems with LeClerc, which could be an undercurrent, but what he said made sense. If a mob formed, what direction it took would be a major concern.

"Also, I wouldn't undertake any display of force before the fact. Mobs don't know how to get started—they don't know how to form. But if you give them an obvious enemy, that'll bring them together. Keep the uniforms out of sight, and don't go through the day as if you're planning for a fight. A fight might be inevitable, but if it isn't, you can avoid it by showing that you don't actually expect it to happen. Pretend that you're not busy preparing for the worst."

The men nodded, accepting his analysis.

Touton had more to say, and his advice went beyond the bounds of his rank, but these two were listening. "I wouldn't bring extra men on shift, either. Keep reinforcements at home. Otherwise, reporters will get wind and it'll be all over the airwaves. That'll provoke more men to get interested in rioting."

Now feeling that his wisdom had been both imparted and received, Touton returned to Pax Plante's earlier command. "Look, of course I'll protect property as best I can, sir. Frankly, I don't care about store windows, but I'll make sure that the fire department is ready to move in the blink of an eye. I'll put fire trucks on side streets during the game, park a few by Eaton's and Morgan's. They're the stores in the most jeopardy. I'm going to shut down the Sun Life Building—nobody goes in, nobody comes out. That'll protect Sun Life Assurance, because who represents the English more than them? But it'll also protect the National Hockey League offices, because they're in the building. Other than that, I've got to keep a few men back to respond to emergencies and track down criminals who, I can promise you, are planning a few heists under cover of any riot. Those are my resources, stretched to the limit."

Plante and Drapeau had not been in office for long. In the past, their foes had been gangsters or corrupt officials. On this occasion, they had no identifiable enemy, unless it was the very people they were sworn to protect.

"Perhaps we'll have a peaceful night," was Drapeau's wish.

"As Captain Touton explained," Plante concurred, "mobs don't know how to form or what to do once they come together. With luck, it might blow over."

"Sir?" Touton asked, addressing himself to Plante, his immediate superior between the two.

"Yes, Armand?" the director answered.

"Is Clarence Campbell going to the game?"

The mayor answered for him. "So far, yes."

"If you can't stop him from going, at least make sure you have cops inside the building with one job to do and one job only—to get him out in a hurry should something go wrong."

Plante made a note of that.

"Thanks, Armand," Plante told him.

"Thanks," the mayor said. "And good luck tonight."

He shook their hands. He could tell that neither man wanted to be in his shoes.

†††

Touton headed down to the Sun Life Building to personally supervise its evacuation, set for 3 P.M., and attend to its ultimate defence. Commonly described as a wedding cake, with its great Doric columns ascending in interrupted stages to the top floors as the higher sections shrunk proportionally in size, the grey-white cement-and-marble edifice seemed impenetrable and stalwart, secure for an eternity. Touton had yet another meeting planned with the executives of Sun Life, all of whom had been remarkably cooperative, and wisely fearful.

The company's internal security force, though, had created a fuss. Feeling that city cops were treating them as dumb cousins, they took umbrage at every instruction. Touton needed to hammer matters through without any further ruffling of feathers. The guards' usual concerns were to protect the premises from typewriter thieves and rid the building of loiterers, so he was not going to trust them to take charge of this assignment.

He wasn't impressed when they declared, "We know the building." If the Sun Life was empty and locked down, all that needed to be defended was the perimeter, and that sidewalk space constituted Touton's turf.

"It's true," he told the executives, with the huffy security chief listening in. "We have to go through the building office by office to clear out stragglers."

"Stragglers?" the security man asked.

"Stowaways. I'm going to bring dogs in."

"Dogs?"

"Listen, I've been assigned responsibility for the security of this building. I will make it airtight. No one can get in, and if somebody slips through our net and hides inside, that person won't get out. So, yeah, dogs. Nobody's going to be left in this building. Your men can help us conduct that search, they know the building. We need you for that, no question."

By the time they were done, the security chief had also won approval to operate a small contingent on the main floor, to man the phones and the fire alarm system, and to be at the disposal of police officers should they require guidance through the maze in an emergency. Touton insisted that they not move around inside without police approval. If they did so they'd be arrested. Grudgingly, the executives upheld his demands over the security chief's objections.

Touton took possession of a set of master keys. The responsibility was his alone.

"Detective Sloan is downstairs as we speak. I'll send him up to introduce himself. He'll be the authority onsite for the remainder of the day."

While the execs were expressing their appreciation and satisfaction with the captain's thoroughness, the security chief adjusted his jacket, which had gotten rather tight in recent months.

††††

Just a year earlier, he had run for his life from politics. Those damned reform-ers and their damned crime commission. He resigned. In the proverbial twin-kling of a jaundiced eye, he was no longer the mayor of Montreal.

A demise that still festered in his bones.

Camillien Houde bowed out to Jean Drapeau, the weak-chinned, bald-headed reformer, a man half his size who possessed a fraction of his personality. Drapeau—"Crapeau," Houde called him—was such an irritating pipsqueak, to be obliged to step aside for *that* prude, then to watch him win the election over his own choice for his replacement, tore at his spirit. He might be depressed forever, and guessed that the acidity of his downfall would escort him to the grave. He'd be scuffed up now, derided, exposed, excoriated, debased. Branded for all time as a corrupt politician. In his waning years, to come to grips with that public drubbing seemed beyond his capacity. Had he been a younger man, he could suck it up, forge on. Not now. Not again.

Crapeau, the reformist moron, was taking his beloved city apart, sending dancing girls to New York and whores to Las Vegas, with the gamblers in tow. One by one, the fun palaces shut down. Corruption, corruption, that's all Cra-peau nattered on about. Didn't he know how the world turned? Was it such a big deal if somebody made a dollar on the side, as long as the revolving doors twirled in full circles?

In political disgrace, Houde felt blindsided by that dour, stick-up-the-ass reformer. His great run had ended. He'd strut as a bon vivant no more.

Two days after the electoral defeat of the man Houde had handpicked to be his successor, Roger Clément stopped by to cheer him up, and to be paid for busting up polling booths for Houde's candidate. In vain, as things turned out. "Roger, we've been though some tough times together. Bury me, Roger, like Guibord. You remember the story? I used to tell it in the camp. One of your favourites. Now I know how his corpse felt."

Undoubtedly, he was still giving himself too much credit, an unerring trait even in the midst of his unbridled depression. To compare himself to a famous, dead liberal seemed especially odd for the living, conservative Houde, but in his state of mind, logic was not a strong component. He referred to Joseph Guibord, whose pals had needed six years to bury him, between 1869, when he died, and 1875, when his casket had finally been sealed, in cement and iron, below ground. So that his remains might never rise again, he was not only buried, but encapsulated.

In his time a free thinker, Guibord had worked as a printer. He joined the Institut Canadien, a club of inquiring minds whose existence had riled the Church, in particular the bishop of Montreal, Father Ignace Bourget. The bishop stood as a staunch proponent of the theory of ultramontanism, which contended that government ought to be subject to the will and wisdom of the Church, whereas Guibord sought to separate Church and state, a heretical thought in Quebec. Guibord published a speech by Horace Greeley, the editor of the *New York Tribune,* who had flaunted ideas similar to those overtaking Europe at the time, including the incredibly radical notion that a man ought to be the principal administrator of his own conscience, rather than, say, his priest or bishop. The text was placed on the Catholic Index as prohibited reading. In Quebec, mere possession of Guibord's *Annuaire,* which printed such speeches, would cost any Catholic the privilege of ecclesiastical sacraments. A majority of the Institut's members capitulated. They publicly recanted, if privately they bristled, but Joseph Guibord alone stuck to his guns, and, as the hour of his death approached, the Church denied him last rites.

His corpse was then rejected for burial in consecrated ground.

Armed with pistols, for they had overheard dire rumours, friends escorted the coffin to the cemetery, only to find that the gates were closed. Falling under a tempest of stones, they retreated. The horse-drawn hearse was forced into a ditch. Later that day, the corpse was brought to a Protestant cemetery and the man's remains temporarily interred in a vault normally used to hold the dead over through winter for spring burial. Friends embarked upon a legal and public harangue that took six years to resolve, when finally they were permitted by the courts to plant the dead man in consecrated ground.

On their second attempt, armed only with a court order, they were again rebuffed by a mob.

On the third try, twelve hundred troops were mustered to escort the body to its final resting place. The mayor of Montreal at the time, who considered himself to be a good Catholic, one Sir William Hingston, rode his horse about town to determine whether there might be an uprising, eventually concluding that the day would find a peaceful resolution. A thousand persons waited at the gravesite, but they were seeking the curiosity of the moment, having no violence in mind.

Representing the bishop, the *curé* of Notre Dame, Reverend Benjamin-Victor Rousselot, rode up in his carriage. He was accompanied and protected by a notable policeman of the era, Detective Cinquemars, and the two men stepped down. Already, the supporters of the Institut Canadien could feel themselves growing spiky, fearing that the priest had arrived to block the ceremony and thwart any court order. That he might have shown up to administer the sign of the cross and a prayer seemed a remote hope.

They were wrong on both expectations.

The *curé* had come to pose two questions.

"Are you certain that the body in this coffin is that of Joseph Guibord?" he asked, and the printer's friends replied that they were positive of the deceased's identity. "Have you dug the grave to the required depth of four feet?" he inquired. Again, the dead man's colleagues responded in the affirmative.

The priest and the detective, satisfied, went on their way.

Concrete was poured into the grave. Before it hardened, the coffin was lowered down. More concrete was shovelled all around the casket. Scrap metal and tin were then thrown onto it and piled up, and workers busily shovelled more cement over that, to create an impassable barrier between the living and this one corpse. Earth was then tamped down above the concrete, and later a great rock was set upon the earth. That first night, police encircled the tomb as the cement hardened, standing guard. Guibord had been dead six years, but the cops maintained a vigil as the liberal thinker, a man who, in his devotion, had yearned for a dimension to Catholic thinking that included tolerance and an interest in scientific and social experiments, concluded his lengthy journey into the black earth.

Bishop Bourget had a plan. He asked his flock not to interfere with the burial on the third attempt. He directed his parishioners to cause no further violence on hallowed ground. The following day, he deconsecrated the burial plot in which Joseph Guibord slept. That space was segregated from the rest of the cemetery and would no longer be considered holy by the Church, but profane. All those who slept around him in their eternal rest, and those who would one day join him beneath the soil, could lie peacefully, without fear that their bones might be contaminated by a heathen's rot. Guibord's grave, armoured by rock and cement and metal and tin, was declared forever outcast, and the bishop noted in a public letter that the men and women of future generations who passed by the spot would likely shudder.

In political disgrace, Camillien Houde felt similarly about himself. As though cast in cement like Guibord, segregated from the world and the heavens both, declared unworthy to receive anything more than a shudder from those who might inadvertently pass the spot where he sat upon a public bench feeding pigeons. And so, he asked of his old friend, "Bury me like Guibord."

Roger knew the story. Drinking gin, Houde had told it several times during their days and nights in the camp together.

A year after making the burial suggestion, Houde was entertaining a revival of his spirits. "Soon, you'll be free to dig me a decent grave," he told Roger. "Full pomp and ceremony. I insist. Let there be a wake in the Irish style, with whiskey and beer and laughing women in every corner of the room. Bounteous bouncing breasts all around the table. Whether I'm in heaven or hell won't matter, so long as I hear the gaiety. Let there be speeches! My God, let there be grand talk. I am ready now to receive many fine tributes."

"You're in a good mood all of a sudden," Roger Clément noted.

"Bound to get better. And you know why."

Yes. On this day, Houde believed, he would possess at least a share of an invaluable and sacred object. How could life become more outstanding than this? Crapeau and his reforming breed could go to hell once his hands gripped that magic, mythic link, for Houde intended to claim possession of the Cartier Dagger in the name of the Order of Jacques Cartier. That one secret and dramatic act restored rhythm to his stride, wit to his wisdom, magic to his legacy—and victory for a new political uprising. Or so he was convinced. Tonight, he would claim the knife, and, having done so, he need not be buried like Guibord.

Possessing the dagger would be no different than being crowned. In rescuing the treasure from out of the hands of the English and their devil, Clarence Campbell, he'd be revered by his people forever. Rumours would travel around the city and through the countryside. He might instigate a few himself—*Houde has saved us! The great Houde! In our plight, when the people of Quebec were being humiliated by the hockey establishment, when the skies were darkest, when our hero, the Rocket, was being subjugated, Houde—what a man!—snatched the sacred symbol from under Campbell's ruddy English nose—the square-head!—and restored pride to every true Quebec heart!* Grand words like that, he'd hear them spoken again—valiant tributes whispered of him and to him, even to his spirit after he was gone. Despite his condition of disgrace, which he could not undo, he'd earn his greatest triumph yet.

†††

As he waited, bitter winds whipped across the roof of the Sun Life Building. During the day, patches of snow had melted upon the asphalt surface and turned icy, and he walked on these areas, slapping his hands to stay warm. He tromped across the snowy sections as well, to create a haphazard design to foil any subsequent interpretation of his activity. All he was doing, though no one tracing his footprints could imagine it, was waiting.

He wished he could look down from his aerie as any city-dwelling pigeon might do, view the specks of people below. He could not risk being spotted. He awaited a signal. One that would arise from the people of Montreal. When they rioted in the streets, he'd begin his formidable chore.

The game against the Red Wings had begun. Keeping the volume low, he turned on the fancy-dancy transistor radio supplied by a confederate. Imagine. Listening to a radio without electricity. The announcer mentioned that Clarence Campbell had not yet arrived at the rink—that, so far, his seat remained vacant.

"Come on now, Clarence," Roger whispered to his marvellous little unit. "Don't be shy. Don't be a sucker. Show up."

†††

Vimont burst into the car. "Holy shit!"

"What happened?" Count Jacques Dugé de Bernonville demanded.

"They started before me. They threw tomatoes at him!"

"Rotten tomatoes?"

"How should I know? I didn't taste any."

"Who threw them?" Dr. Camille Laurin occupied the rear seat with the count.

"People!"

"At whom?" Laurin needed everything to be explained.

"At Campbell! He got hit with a tomato. Smack in the chest. I was close enough to see. Then I threw my stink bombs and got the hell out of there. People panicked. Everybody's gone bananas."

"That was the idea," de Bernonville posited. "Start the car. Let's go."

"No, I mean they've gone insane. It's gonna be a fucking riot!"

"That's the point," de Bernonville replied. "Now drive."

"You heard him. Drive this thing!" Laurin commanded.

Michel Vimont steered the limo towards the vicinity of the Sun Life Building.

†††

Up on the roof, Roger listened to the excited announcers' voices as Campbell was pelted by tomatoes, and their dismay and budding panic when the stink and smoke bombs went off inside the Forum. He could hear the excited roar of the crowd, the angry taunts, the bedlam rising, the screams of women and the raised pitch of the radio commentary. The game was soon cancelled, not least of all for the safety of the visiting team. The crowd, the radio was saying, was spilling out onto the streets and causing a ruckus.

His cue to get busy.

He possessed mountaineering rope for the job, and now spun two opposing loops over a cement outcropping. What appeared to him to be a line of tombstones stood along the roof's edge, although they were really meant to emulate the shields of medieval warriors defending a castle wall. One served well to anchor his line, strong enough to support a man. He gave it a good tug to make sure. Satisfied, he lowered the rope gently, so as not to attract any interest, two flights down to the first landing, twenty-some feet. Taking up the coils of two more ropes, slipping one over each shoulder, he put on his gloves and slid safely down.

A four-second drop. Then a nice, soft landing.

On a balcony, a double railing connected concrete pillars shaped to resemble urns. He tied his next rope to one of these and let it fall slowly. This was a greater descent—one he hoped was less than forty feet, the length of his rope. Under the night shadows and the variegated city lighting, the rope covertly snaked down the side of the Sun Life to conclude its run near the spot he desired, on a broader ledge. The length seemed a bit shy. He would have to come back up this way, so he would need to be able to reach the bitter end of the rope from below. He gave it a good strong tug and, satisfied with the attachment, descended.

He could land a helicopter on the next ledge, or hold a party for four hundred. Again, he was offered good posts for hitching his rope, and he lowered a long one down the face of the building. The next landing looked a long way down to him, and he hated heights. Happily, he had no intention of going farther. Never a second-storey man, he was way above that level now, nineteen flights up. Forget it.

Instead, he used his great strength to climb. Hand over hand, also clutching the rope between his thighs, shins and ankles to take his weight, he ascended to the ledge above him, then pulled himself up the other rope as well to the roof. There he crossed to the rooftop exit, took a glance around to make sure that he had not forgotten anything, opened the door and stepped through to the stairwell. Once inside, he nudged the sliding bolt back into place—he loved working with insiders—and snapped the padlock to seal it shut. Then proceeded down the stairs. At the first corridor, he looked around, listened, then, confident that the building remained vacant, stepped quickly to the stairwell that would take him farther down.

Alone here, he moved as quietly as he could manage without going too slowly, and wound his way down to the twelfth floor, where the offices of the National Hockey League were located. There he listened again, poked his head into the corridor, and, seeing no one, moved to the NHL's door.

He used a skeleton key to open it.

Perfect.

From a coat pocket, he pulled out his flashlight and briefly shone it around. Everything he needed was waiting for him. The operation was going smoothly. No night cleaners to worry about, no after-hours workaholics, no security guards on patrol. His equipment was ready, so he could take his time. He had rehearsed this manoeuvre in the dark. The lights could go out across the city and he'd not miss a well-practised move.

Inside the room where the safe was located, he closed the door and switched on the light. No windows. He could work in the light with impunity.

Three explosions would detonate, two attacking the hinges on the vault's door, the third imploding the lock. One way or another, he'd crack the safe open.

Putty kept each dynamite stick in place, then he cut the fuses to equal lengths. He wiped the blade of his penknife clean on a thigh. He tidied his bit of mess, which he loaded onto a newspaper culled from a stack that he carried to the far reaches of the office. He dumped the entire concoction into a trash bin there. Who would notice? What bomber would ever be this meticulous, this neat?

Next, he got his lighter ready and tested it once. It worked.

He switched off the overhead, breathed deeply, and opened the door behind him. In the hallway, working with light rising from the city below and occasionally from his flashlight, he gathered up what he needed. With a great coil of rope under an arm, he worked his way back into the security room, lit the slow fuses and departed quickly.

In the corridor again, Roger ran to the exit, then down four more flights. Exiting the stairwell at that level, he moved to the window at the end of the corridor and opened it. There he knotted one end of his rope to the long stout radiator that rose to his thighs, then crawled onto the ledge. He didn't like this part. He dared not look down. Already he could hear great roars from a crowd that didn't seem so distant anymore, and when he did look back, once, he saw the glow of fires illuminating the air above a block of Ste. Catherine Street. All around, he heard the choir of sirens. Cops and fire trucks, ambulances and more cops. He saw a quartet of police cruisers rush down Dorchester Boulevard, cherries flashing. He could see a lot from up there, and he just hoped that no one saw him.

He guided the rope out the window. While he was tempted to heave the whole thing out, he commenced lowering it down slowly, again for the sake of keeping it inconspicuous. He was glad he would not be climbing down.

Just then, the safe's door was blown off its hinges.

Roger looked up. He felt the tremor through his toes. He hoped that the men on the first floor, the cops and security guards, didn't feel it also—or if they did, were assuming it to be a trauma of the riot.

Quickly, he was back to his rope, releasing it more rapidly now. Done, he hopped back to the stairwell and ran up to the NHL offices. The closer he got, the louder he heard the ringing of an alarm. Oh, damn. An alarm. He hadn't thought of that, and the sound was incessant as he scooted back inside the offices.

One alarm was inside, and another in the corridor, and both were hammers drilling a bell. With his penknife, he sliced both wires, and the alarms went silent. His heart seemed to stop with the cessation of the racket.

Roger exhaled. He knew it might not be the end of his troubles. He'd broken through alarms before, and often he could count on a remote sensor. Down below, cops and building security could well be mounting a charge to his floor.

He scampered through to the safe.

The room stank of foul burn. Smoke and dust drifted in the air. The door wobbled only partially upright, but he was able to create a space to pass through to the inside.

And there, within the dark and smoky cavity, unharmed, in the beam of his flashlight, lay the mahogany-and-glass case for the treasured artifact.

Diamonds on the handle appeared as eyes, watching him as he gazed upon the dagger.

The final item left for him in his kit was a crowbar. He had to crawl back out with the case to get it, then return to the security room so that he could close the door and switch on the light. Roger placed the case on the floor. He didn't want to damage the knife, so he rapped the case cautiously, gradually increasing the strength of his blow. To no avail. He had only one option—he reared back with the bar and brought it down full force upon the thick glass. Which cracked. Three more blows and he retrieved the knife from the box.

There. He had it. Safely in his hands. The thing that all the fuss was about.

He didn't expect much—a very old knife with a few diamonds embedded in a handle that contained nuggets of gold. Old. He'd assumed it would seem decrepit. He was astonished. The way the diamonds sparkled in the faint light of the room, wee winks, so that he was never certain if he had imagined or actually seen the quick refractions, and the tight weave of moose hair on the handle, and the chipped but elegantly carved blade—Roger was oddly moved, and he took time to get going again. Holding the knife, it did seem magical to him, its plainness but also the sombre patina of the instrument communicating a sense of time and strange, wayward desire, as if he held in his hands the vision of its creator. Suddenly, like a genie, he sprung free.

He wouldn't mind keeping it himself, if that could be allowed.

Quickly, he wrapped the knife in the kerchief he'd brought along in his coat pocket, picked up his crowbar and headed out. He locked the door to the office again, then smashed the door open as if he was entering it for the first time. He tossed the crowbar on the floor. Checking that he had his flashlight and gloves, his transistor radio—which he'd soon be giving to his daughter, for he had no intention of returning it to its rightful owner—and the Cartier Dagger and the last of his rope coils, a small one, he headed back down the stairs. He still had police and security officers to elude, but an escape route had been predetermined that would be available to him—he really did love working with an insider, and he didn't want to labour without one again. The building had three sets of elevators. One that ran between the first and seventh floors, another that ran between the eighth and fifteenth and a third that served the sixteenth to twenty-third floors. If cops were coming up after him, they'd be on that mid-level elevator. He could risk being on one himself, but wouldn't. He'd use the stairs.

The distance seemed interminable, as he ran down, down and down. He concentrated on not falling, and despaired that his progress seemed minimal. Soon enough, he slowed, panted and exhorted his limbs not to seize up now.

†††

Half the north wall of the Sun Life Building abutted its neighbour, a movie theatre that stretched south from Ste. Catherine Street. On the other half, an alley divided the building from a nondescript modern structure used primarily as a parking lot for rental cars. Roger Clément looked over the alley. He entered an office using his skeleton key and, according to plan, placed it in a particular drawer. His trail of evidence was intended to convince investigators that he dropped from the rooftop and slid down the outer face of the building in stages, that his final exit was really the shortest of his forays by rope. Cops would see the evidence on display for them while missing the invisible. All this to protect his insider from suspicion.

He opened the side window.

Here, the building appeared impenetrable—the steel doors had stout locks and no windows. Consequently, no cops guarded the alley. The tricky part now was to close the window behind himself, as he had to dig his nails into the exterior woodwork to gain sufficient purchase. He tamped down a little putty for the window to sink into, catch and hold shut.

He now sat crouched on a small ledge, the drop too great to jump. No handholds were available on the way down over the marble base, but right at his feet stood a design filigree in cement. A lopsided oval, the size of a large sink, was bound on both sides by a pair of curved forms that ended as curlicues. The upper pair fell down over the oval and vaguely represented eyes, while at the bottom they had the appearance of claws. The effect created a highly stylized owl. Roger looped his last rope around the oval and an ear and descended about ten feet, then dropped two more feet onto the pavement.

He was down, he was outside, he was safe.

He then manipulated the rope to free his loop from the owl's ear, and it fell beside him. Quickly, he hauled it down the alley and tossed it in a corner.

As he stepped onto the sidewalk, Roger noticed a change in the weather. He smelled the smoke of fires, heard the uproar of men in the delirium of a rampage. Through the park on the next street over, a rowdy gang had climbed up Peel Street from the poorer neighbourhoods, dancing down the centre line with no vehicle or cop to oppose them. Small clusters of young people moved through the park, howling at the moon and headed for the tumult on Ste. Catherine.

Sirens resounded from all directions and echoed off the buildings. On Dorchester Boulevard emergency vehicles sped past going both ways. Stray cars blared their horns.

Bedlam.

Roger stepped off the curb, headed for the park and Robbie Burns's boot.

His confederates were waiting there. They had spread out in a row like pallbearers marshalled for a funeral. On the left, wrists crossed, chin held high in an attitude of superiority or condemnation—a meaningless pose, as it was his default expression—stood the count. Not since the Asbestos miners' strike had Roger seen him, but instantly he recognized the posture and overall set of the man. He'd put on weight in Brazil, living amidst his Nazi cronies. What Roger had heard, through Michel Vimont—who'd heard it from Harry S. Montford, who'd heard it from Premier Duplessis himself— was that the French count had been treated like a lapdog by his German cohorts. He had no money and constantly begged at their heels. Skeptical of the rumour, Roger figured the count was too proud to ever admit to such a thing. He suspected that the idea probably originated with *le Chef*. The story went that de Bernonville wanted out of South America and would prefer the comfort of Quebec friends again, to stumble through his last days speaking French again rather than Portuguese. The idea of stealing the artifact originated with him. Since Asbestos, when he'd talked about the Cartier Dagger to the elite journalists there, he'd not forgotten about the knife, and remained intrigued by its worth and mythic authority. A man in his situation could benefit by owning a share in an object of such value, given its potential for lucre, or influence, or both.

So he contacted Duplessis, to entice him.

Le Chef knew that the relic held no sway, except symbolically, and yet he believed in symbols. He counted himself as a symbol of the Quebec people, of their destiny. In that sense, the artifact was competitive to his own glory. But if those two suns were conjoined as one, the emblematic, metaphoric power of that union could enshrine him politically throughout his lifetime and continue to buff his legacy after he was gone. He might never be able to admit to being a holder of the dagger, but rumours could travel the countryside, and why would a man of his esteem stoop to refute them?

In daydreaming about the count's enterprise, Duplessis knew with whom to discuss putting a plan into action. He dialled Roger Clément's number.

The stakes were high. Duplessis did not speak only to Roger. He reasoned that the dagger's value was too tempting for one thug on his own. Anyway, Roger would need help. So, the premier met covertly with Montford, a gangster not unaccustomed to elaborate, lucrative gambits.

On such an excursion, Montford would never be out waiting in a park—too risky for his style. He made sure that he had his own man there, choosing his driver, Michel Mendelssohn Vimont, who stood next to the count.

Roger knew Vimont's weakness. The one thing he wanted out of all this was something he did not want—to go to jail. Whatever else occurred mattered little to Michel, as long as he did not wind up in the slammer. To that end, he had made a phone call, for advice, to his old friend and counsellor, Father Joe. The former archbishop, now living in British Columbia, contacted Father François in Montreal, putting him in touch with Michel Vimont. And for their end of the caper, to support the interest of the Church, Father François contacted Roger.

Roger was connected to nearly everyone and no one knew it. So he anticipated schemes within the larger scheme, and understood to be careful. He plotted a scheme of his own.

Next to de Bernonville and Vimont stood a third man Roger did not know, but presumed him to be Dr. Camille Laurin. He was not Roger's insider at Sun Life, but he suspected that the doctor represented him. He represented somebody, that's all he was allowed to know. Roger had no clue how the fourth man in the row fit into all this. Even in the ambient dark, under the canopy of noise and confusion and smoke, no one who knew him could mistake the robust, egg-shaped bulk of Camillien Houde.

The four men stood waiting.

Although he could not see him, Roger presumed that, around the front of the Robbie Burns statue, out of sight for now, Father François was waiting. As arranged. The outside player in his own scheme.

A fateful entourage.

"What news?" the count enquired as he drew close.

"Mission accomplished," he told them. "It's nice to have a rooting section over here."

"Let's see the dagger," Laurin said.

"Not so fast," Roger warned him.

The count took him up on that. "What's the problem? Don't you have it? Show us."

"First, tell me what he's doing here." Roger nodded to his friend and former boss, Houde.

"Roger!" The old mayor put his head back and unleashed that big guffaw of his. He was convincing, for this was their ruse. Roger was not supposed to have known that Houde was part of all this, except that Houde had told him. "This is my town. Do you think I'd be left out on such an occasion? Come on, now. Show us the dagger."

"Who brought you into this? I have a right to know." For the sake of keeping the others in the dark about their alliance, he demonstrated petulance.

Houde raised an eyebrow and touched a finger to his big nose. "*Le Chef,*" he declared, which was the truth. "Who else? For my loyalty at the end of my career, and also, to keep an eye on these guys. Nobody trusts anyone here, but I am the old mayor, and if there is to be deceit on this evening, I will speak of it, and be believed. Now, show us the knife."

Duplessis would never come on his own, nor could he trust the Nazi, who might abscond with the dagger worth unknown millions. Fencing ancient relics and paintings kept Nazis well heeled down south. The relic would be right up their alley. As far as Roger could tell, Duplessis now had at least three representatives on site, four if he counted himself, and five, possibly, because—who knows?—he probably had a hand up Laurin's spine as well.

He removed the Cartier Dagger from his inner coat pocket. He unwrapped it from the kerchief.

Perhaps because he knew him best, Roger first handed the knife to Houde. The light that caught the old mayor's face came from a travelling ambulance, yet he seemed to glow, his smile emerging at the corners of his mouth to become the expansive grin he'd made so famous. The least likely to be at a loss for words, he said only, "Yes. Yes."

He passed the knife to Laurin.

Who said nothing. His evaluation seemed scientific, as though discerning authenticity. He passed the knife to Michel Vimont, who immediately presented it to de Bernonville. But the count refused to receive it, saying, "I can see we've got it."

Roger took the dagger back from Vimont.

More sirens. Fire trucks eastbound on Dorchester, chased by an ambulance. The men awaited the uproar's end, as it was a nuisance to speak above the wail. Roger saw Father François emerge from beyond the Burns statue behind the conspirators.

Suddenly, just as the trucks sped by, a bellow from a crowd on Ste. Catherine echoed off the face of buildings and resonated in the smoky air. "What was that?" Roger asked.

The others had grown accustomed to such outbursts on this night, and did not react. Vimont shrugged. Out of the dark, Father François chose to answer him. "A mob," he declared, "engaged in its idea of fun. Roger, might I not also view the dagger?"

"Who're you?" de Bernonville demanded.

Vimont told him, "He's a priest. You've met before."

"When? What priest?"

"Asbestos," Vimont said, and de Bernonville nodded.

"Father François Legault, sir. Not exactly at your service. But I am here in service of the Cartier Dagger, and in the service of the Holy Mother Church."

"This is no place for a priest, Father," Houde scolded him. "Anyway, you're more communist than cleric."

"This is no place for the former mayor of Montreal," Father François shot back. "Nor is this any place for the eminent Dr. Laurin, or a Nazi already barred from this country."

The last thing anyone wanted here was to be identified.

"What do you want, Father?" Laurin asked him.

"Why," the priest said, as though the news should come as no shock, "the knife. The Cartier Dagger. For the greater glory of the Holy Church. Would you like to show it to me, Roger?"

"Father, I've already promised it to these men."

The priest smiled then. He was standing a little higher than the others, on the monument's base. "Roger, Roger, Roger," he said, and shook his head. "From the time of Maisonneuve, who with Jeanne Mance held this knife in trust, through Étienne Brulé, Dollard des Ormeaux and Radisson, the knife has honoured those blessed with its possession. Such men and women achieved the impossible. Initially, their cause was spiritual. Our duty must be to return the dagger to its true vocation. The greater Church, the one that we have yet to create, ought to be the next recipient, to protect the welfare of the souls of this land."

"Fine words for a priest," Houde remarked. "I say the Church is rich enough, Father. But I'll come to you next time for my confession. I'll sing you an opera."

"You can begin right now, if you like. What are you doing here, Mr. Mayor?"

Houde chortled again. "Father, I was out on a walk to discover what was happening to my beloved city. As so many are doing this evening. From a distance, I spotted Roger here—a man I'd recognize at a thousand paces. We spent years together in an interment camp, did you know? Seeing him, of course, I came up to greet him. Shall I say a rosary, Father, for the impudence of talking to a friend? What kind of priest are you to war against civility and friendship in this way?"

"The picket line boss," de Bernonville said, remembering him from Asbestos. "He's a rioter. Out tonight to smash store windows."

"A Nazi would know," Father François retorted.

"If you want to turn the dagger over to *his* church, Roger," de Bernonville kept up, "you might as well give it to the Communist Party."

"So you suggest that he give it to the old regimes of Houde and Duplessis instead?" the priest parried. "The has-beens? Duplessis's darkness pervades the land. Houde, you've had your day. You're not coming back."

"A has-been? You must be talking about the Church, Father," Houde retaliated in a swift fury. "Roger! Give us the knife! Your compensation is assured!"

"The Church is also capable of compensation—"

"For a stolen object?" Laurin spoke up. "What church is this, Father?"

Father François shrugged. "Whoever owns the object will do so in secrecy. Whoever pays compensation will be cautious doing so. If the relic is to be tied to the spiritual destiny of its people, the Church of Rome will intercede to protect it from being pilfered by fanatics."

"Rome!" de Bernonville burst out. "Now, Rome?"

The portly priest vaguely nodded. "As always, jurisdictions overlap. Yes, you are not dealing with a lowly priest in his cassock. As you can see, I'm not wearing mine. There's a more formidable front than you can imagine that stands against you. The unions, too. It's an alliance, shall we say."

"More commies."

"With cash. Roger, take note. You, de Bernonville, take note: with cash."

De Bernonville took a stride forward and, for the first time that evening, smiled. "You lack imagination, priest. Not only you, but these others."

"How so?" The priest was also smiling, willing to debate.

"Roger, let me see the knife to prove my point. I didn't have a chance to touch it before."

Confident that he could recover it easily, Roger allowed the count to receive the dagger onto the leather gloves of his opened palms. The former torturer handled it delicately.

"Priest," de Bernonville stated, "see this." The count walked over to the monument and passed the knife to Father François, who removed one mitt and stuck it under his arm, to better feel the blade and handle. "You see,

Father? Stone and bone. Animal hair. There's no magic. You have not been transformed. You're still a lowly priest and a pitiful communist."

"And you're still a Nazi."

De Bernonville took the knife back in his gloved hand. "Gestapo, let's not forget. Proud of it, too. By the way, Father," the count mentioned as he walked away from him, returning the knife to Roger, "thanks for gracing the dagger with your fingerprints." He swiftly spun. As he completed the turn, his grip on the knife changed. He reared back and, whirling like a dervish, thrust the blade deep into the chest and heart of Roger Clément, up to the hilt. Roger remained standing, his mouth agape, his hands upraised as if in supplication, one upholding the kerchief as a flag of mercy, and as he staggered forward a few clumsy steps the others, in their shock, fell away. Father François pushed forward and grabbed him. Roger died while still on his feet, and the priest could not hold him up, although, illogically, he tried to do so, as though keeping him on his feet would dispute his death. In falling, the body twisted slightly, a last gesture towards redemption, and Roger collapsed into the arms of his bewildered friend, Michel Vimont, who eased his form to the ground.

He lay below the back of the Scottish poet.

The count's smile slowly broadened. "Pull the knife out of him," he directed Vimont.

As though in a trance, the driver also put his bare hands on the knife, but he could not extract it. The blade seemed stuck, or perhaps he lacked the gumption to do it. "I can't," he declared.

The count cried out, "Squeamish, weak bastards!" and shoved him aside.

"Hey!" bellowed a voice in the park, from towards the Sun Life Building. "What's going on?"

They all glanced up just as the count bent down to extract the blade. The man who'd shouted was running away towards a cluster of cops on the steps of the Sun Life.

"Shit," Houde whispered, his voice sounding distant and hollow, but at least he was emerging from paralysis.

Father François commenced mumbling last rites.

"It's stuck!" the count lamented.

"Why did you do that? You didn't have to kill him," Vimont complained. He implored the count with his hands, pumping them up and down, palms up. "You could've had the knife without doing that."

"He's a fucking communist."

"So what?" Houde argued. "Anyway, he's not. He's just a thug—a friend of mine."

"I saw your friend operate at Asbestos. He would've betrayed us, I have no doubt."

Laurin cried out, "Here comes a cop. Run!" He tucked his political career between his legs and heeded his own advice. Vimont, scarcely involved and terrified of prison, lit out as well.

As though drawn by the vacuum the speed of their flight created, Houde hobbled after them. He had not run in twenty years, but he was still the occasional skater, and his legs gathered momentum, beginning to churn under him. His arms commenced pumping.

Finally, de Bernonville, fearing extradition to France and charges of war crimes if captured, quit trying to extract the knife. He ran, and when the priest looked up from his chore, he saw the policeman approaching fast and realized that he alone remained the object of the cop's charge. He remembered his fingerprints on the weapon and the count's words on the subject, and ran himself. He did not know what else to do. He had been here to procure a stolen object, and the man who was in league with him to foil the others now lay dead. He ran. They all headed for Peel, and the policeman kept pursuing them even after he had passed Roger Clément's body, but each man was soon lost in the rampant, shouting riot, escaping into the frenzy of raring men and boys reducing the city to litter and flames as best as they were able.

The nearest to being captured, Father François threw in his lot with a wildly hooting ragamuffin crew, whose miscreants appeared to have an appetite for flesh. The policemen did not want to chase anyone into that cop-hating mob, so he chose to retreat, not unwisely, to care for the man who lay in a lonely, crumpled heap upon a statue's base.

The cop discovered that the man was surely dead. He shouted to fellow officers for help, and a few idled over. While waiting, not wanting to look at the corpse, the first he'd ever seen, he read the English words on the face of the monument, not certain of what they might mean.

IT´S COMIN´ YET FOR A´ THAT

THAT MAN TO MAN THE WORLD O´ER

SHALL BRITHERS BE FOR A´ THAT

The lines didn't look like any sort of English he knew.

†††

His bowels, his chest, his legs threatened to implode. He was not supposed to exert himself, and Father François Legault did his best to slow down to a pace he might survive. His heart felt crushed. In their floppy boots, his feet keened in abysmal agony. He suspected that he might soon collapse.

Fear of facing his maker in this circumstance kept him alive, kept him running for his life.

What had he done? *What had he done?* What had he gotten himself into? *You idiot.* And not only himself, but Father Joe, too, the former archbishop. If he was caught—they'd check his files. They'd read the letters to Father Joe. His notes. Never had it occurred to him that he'd been incriminating himself—and Father Joe—through his correspondence, but any investigation into his rectory would surrender embarrassing details of their scheme.

His fingerprints. What could be done about his fingerprints? He'd been arrested so often on picket lines or at demonstrations, the cops would find a match. How could he explain this? He'd soon be up on murder charges.

Jogging down Ste. Catherine Street, finally stammering to a stop, he bent over, panting, even as his lungs threatened to tear at the seams. His heart felt like pure, compressed pain unleashed. *Oh dear Lord. I need an alibi now.* What he did not need was for people to see him on the run. Thank God he was not in his cassock. That would have been a sight. The fat priest in flight down the centre of a public riot. Catching his breath, Father François thanked God for that particular leniency. He had gone to the park in civilian clothes not only because they were his preferred proletarian dress, but because he had intended to commit a profane act—taking possession of stolen property. Now those clothes helped him blend in.

He took note of things, and stopped briefly to counsel the wounded, officers and rioters alike, to not beat up their fellow Quebecers. He knew that he was being an ass, yet they might remember him that way. Both sides told him to go . . . and engage in activity unbecoming for a priest. Noticing people milling around a burning car, he did his best to shoo them away, in case it exploded. He didn't want them to kill themselves, but also, who knows, someone might remember him, confirm his innocent presence during the riot.

The grim sight returned to his mind's eye. Roger Clément, dead. What would he say to his widow? To the poor child, the man's daughter? He should have squelched the scheme from the outset, but his damn politics, his ambitions, his desire to effect real change—what had that gotten him but the death of a valiant soul, a man trying to do a good deed for his family, his people and his Church? Roger's adventure had killed him, and his own adventure had made him an accomplice to the murder. Bad enough, but it might have been worse if those fascist bastards had made off with the knife. That it remained stuck in Roger's heart indicated at least a measure of spiritual justice. The knife had refused to be abducted by men of that ilk.

So, truly, it must be magical.

But now it would incriminate him as the killer. A terrible magic, that.

He went on ahead, to calm down, to give his heart a moment's ease, and to place a greater distance between himself and the scene of Roger's murder. There, in a small park, sitting on a bench with his bum up on the ridge of the backrest, the priest spied his alibi. Father François came up behind the man, at first to confirm that he wasn't seeing a mirage, then to speak to his colleague at sufficient length to dispel any doubt that he had been elsewhere that evening. He would have to be calm, complacent, not the sort of man who'd just fled the scene of a murder. "Pierre?" he spoke up. "I thought that might be you."

Pierre Elliott Trudeau turned to him, as if annoyed, but in recognizing the man who approached him, his grimace vanished. He said, "Father François. A surprise. How's it going?"

"Fine, Pierre. Taking in the riot on a midnight stroll?"

"Father, are you blind? I'm sitting here, minding my own business."

Chuckling, the priest sat down at the opposite end of the bench, on the icy seat portion. He thought this was going well. "I see the potential arsonist in you, Pierre. You're in the mood to burn down a building. So don't tell me you're here as a neutral observer."

"Observations are neutral? Since when? We see what we want to see, with the slant we prefer. What about you, Father? Packing snowballs with rocks inside? Burning cop cars?"

"Twenty-five minutes ago—like you, I was minding my own business—I was standing alongside a cop car when it burst into flames."

"Spontaneous combustion?"

"Something similar." The priest leaned forward. "I singed my jacket." He had—a month earlier, when he had put it down too close to an electric heater in a restaurant. "My first thought: what happens if the gas tank explodes? I tried moving people away, but on a night like this, people have minds of their own. They insisted on encircling the car, cheering."

"And you, incognito with no collar on. You could have said Mass."

"I didn't expect to be attending to my flock this evening."

"Didn't you? You usually listen to hockey games, Father?"

"At this time of year, of course. Not you?"

"Tonight for the first time. But I expected tonight to be different—more than just a game." Both men were distracted by a momentary roar from the approaching throng. "Sports fans," Trudeau scoffed. "Their team scored a goal."

"Another cop car's been roasted," the priest surmised.

"An English store window spontaneously shattered."

The priest eyed the other man closely. He knew him from *Cité Libre*, but he'd never forget the time he fought Reggie Chartrand during the Asbestos strike. "You're not curious, Pierre? You'll walk no closer?"

"They'll be here soon enough."

Father François looked around. He wondered if they could not be friends. He knew that Pierre dismissed the harder edges of his political opinion, but he also gauged that he himself was beginning to turn away from those extremes.

He did not like violence, and if you were going to be a revolutionary, you had to expect to see most, if not all, of your best friends die. Why had that never occurred to him before?

To his mind, this other man could be the brightest of the current crop of intellectuals in the city. Perhaps he could learn from him, try out a new direction in his life. "Why be confident, Pierre, of where they'll go? It's a mob." *The knife had refused to be lifted from Roger's heart.* Already a man of religious conviction, Father François felt himself on the verge of a deeper conversion. The knife—was it really possessed by magic, not merely lore, not merely historic and cultural significance? "Without a destination. It could turn off anywhere, slide away in any direction."

"Why trouble myself by finding the riot," Trudeau remarked, a nod indicating Morgan's department store, "when I can sit here in a front-row seat and the riot will find me?"

"Then you'll agree, Pierre, that this evening has nothing to do with hockey." He, for one, had found God. Had he not?

"Hockey is the flashpoint. But there's more to it. This mob will start selecting targets. When it does, it'll discover its *raison d'être.* Watch. Our rioters will educate themselves as they go. That's already happened, or they would never have bypassed the National Hockey League offices."

"They don't know where the offices are."

"Just as well."

"I'm serious," the priest reiterated. "Someone asked me if I knew where the league office was located. He had a brick in one hand, a beer in the other. I almost answered him before I thought better of it. I offered him a smoke."

"Good of you."

"I traded. A smoke for the brick."

"Quick thinking."

"It's hard to get rid of a brick on a night like this. I stuffed it in a mailbox."

The story, a lie, marked him as experienced in the riot, and his companion of the moment might remember it. But he began to relax into the conversation, moving from the world of treachery back to his safer precepts. He could share the experience of the night now with someone else, and he was grateful for that, even as his heart, arrhythmic with the memory of Roger's ecstatic death, beat heavily.

†††

They ran through the muddle and the maze, ran through the dancing teenagers and the car fires and the gauntlet of beer bottles flying over their heads and the spectacle of objects being tossed at store windows, followed by the cheers whenever a huge sheet of glass shattered. A nightmare scenario, and their running caused others to flee, as if they must know something others did not. They did. They knew they'd been complicit in a murder, and even the famous ex-mayor of Montreal ran.

Down Ste. Catherine Street they went, safe in the bosom of the mob, secure amid the tempest. When they turned off the main artery, it was to catch their breath, to gasp, bent over, clasping their bellies, and to look around, to see if they were being chased. They were not being chased. Yet each man felt himself pursued. The eminent young psychiatrist, Dr. Camille Laurin, had not signed on for any such activity, never murder, nothing so blatant and horrific, but his mind raced. He knew that he could not allow the charges to stand. He would not give himself up to face public rebuke. His medical practice and achievements, his political ambitions, his distinguished station in life, all would be lost by any suggestion that he'd participated in the terrible act, and so he ran.

Michel Mendelssohn Vimont also ran hard. After a difficult youth and a sampling of jail time, he followed the straight and narrow, within reason, yet knew that he worked among powerful men. If they needed a fall guy, he'd be the chosen one. The man with the peculiar middle name. He was the one to hang on a cross. The ex-con—snag him! Wasn't he Clément's good friend? Some grievance must have come between them. And so, knowing how the system worked, how the powerful could ally themselves against the weak, Vimont ran. He ran hard.

His heart ached for Roger.

The former mayor kept running, too. If he stopped, people would point at him and say, "It's you! It's Houde! Camillien!" The world would know that he'd been there, at least close by the scene, as they called it, of the crime. He had done this for his legacy, and now he was running for whatever remained of his life. He didn't want anything now—no tributes, no consolations, no apologies from the electorate, no revenge. All he desired was exoneration from this crime, this killing. He did not want that death attached to his good name. He ran.

De Bernonville ran as well, mightily pleased with himself. He was pleased to be killing again. That guy Clément, he'd seen him in Asbestos, working for everybody and nobody. Working for himself, de Bernonville deduced, while everyone assumed him to be their lackey. He didn't care whether Clément had something planned or what it might be. All of them were political dilettantes, safe in their privileged Quebec, whining about this or that. Who had it so good, really? They needed to be taught that life required action, and he was a man of action. He needed them to grasp what it meant to have blood on their hands. They wouldn't be so pompous with him now. Now, when he said "Money," they'd know that he meant *money. Pay up. On the spot. To me.* Their precious knife. They probably secretly wanted to keep it locked in some obscure vault, taking it out for an occasional covert banquet and to bow to its presence, then use it to slaughter a calf. They didn't want to keep it now, did they? If they got it back they'd beg him to sell it, and quickly. They'd want to get rid of it, and that meant converting the relic into money. Brilliant, he thought, congratulating himself. Killing that guy was genius. Despite that one dire quirk of fate. How was he supposed to know the blade would get stuck in his breastplate?

What he had to do now was escape the police on this night, not get caught, and recover the knife. Unlike the others, he was already an unwanted citizen— on the run, an illegal alien, and officially an undesirable. So, first, he had to escape. He ran.

They had preconceived no meeting place, no destination, yet, exhausted and confused, they regrouped at the Caddy. As if each man, following the strains of his particular logic, had determined that they had yet to be together, that they had matters to resolve and restore.

Michel Vimont was the last to show up. Perhaps he only wanted the car, and was not pleased that the others had gathered.

"Good," de Bernonville dispatched. "We have a set of keys."

Vimont unlocked the doors and they all trundled in.

De Bernonville made his case immediately. "We have to go back. We have to get the knife."

"Are you out of your mind? This man's a lunatic." Houde attested. "The place will be crawling with cops. The cops, Count, the cops have the knife! Not us, thanks to you. We had it in our hands. You killed my friend and now you've lost the knife. You shit!"

"Stay with the plan," de Bernonville advised. "We came out tonight to get the knife. We'll get it."

"How do you propose we do that?" asked Laurin, either remarkably calm or in shock.

"Follow the knife. They're only cops. By definition, that means they're sloppy. They won't expect anything to happen, and they're all confused tonight—they have a lot going on. You're right, Mr. Mayor, cops are on the scene. But people don't get to see a dead man every day, they will swarm around, they'll gawk. One of us will be there, pretending to just gawk."

"Not me!" Houde shot in, still sulking. "Oh, you don't mind. You live in some fucking jungle in Brazil with Eichmann and those Nazis. You don't worry about what goes on up here. But I live here. I am *known* here. I am the *mayor of Montreal, for God's sake.*"

"You *used* to be the mayor."

"Fuck you, you fucker!"

"Take it easy."

"You take it easy! You creep. You didn't need to do that. I'm not a murderer like you."

"Oh, but now you are," de Bernonville corrected him.

"Fuck you!"

"Okay. So we follow the knife," Laurin interjected.

"Camille, don't listen to the bastard," Houde pressed him. "You saw what he did. He's a fucking maniac."

"My fingerprints are on that knife," Laurin reminded him.

"Oh God," Houde moaned. "So are mine."

"That's what I wanted," de Bernonville let them know. "A sense of liability. A commitment to the cause."

Houde punched the dash and rocked in the front seat. He'd gotten into the front with Vimont because he couldn't stand the idea of sitting beside de Bernonville. Now he wanted to be in the back to pummel him.

"Don't listen to him, Camille. He's a maniac asshole. You saw him."

"We follow the knife," Laurin repeated.

"We'll see where that leads us," de Bernonville directed them all. "Play it by ear. I've seen how cops work in this city—it's the same as everywhere else. They're slow. They'll take their time. At some moment, somebody will think to do something with the murder weapon. We'll be on hand to see that. Then we'll act."

"Act? What does it mean when you say 'act'? Kill somebody?"

"I'm sure it won't be necessary, Mr. Mayor. The appearance of force may be necessary, but—"

Houde spun around in his seat to address Laurin. "Do you hear what this guy is saying? Do you *understand* what he's talking about?"

"No further violence, he's saying."

"That's *not* what he's talking about."

"Mr. Mayor," Laurin pointed out to him, speaking ever in a flat, emotion-less voice, "my prints are on that knife. As are yours. If I am discovered, I will not be the only one."

That brought everyone in the car to a point of silence, and a choice hung in the balance.

Vimont understood his own stake in this now. "My prints are on it, too. And the cops have my prints on file."

Houde cleared his throat. He whispered, "Will you sell us out, Michel?"

"To stay out of prison?" Vimont answered. He let them deduce the answer for themselves.

"All right," Houde said. "We'll check it out. If there's an opportunity to seize the knife, then okay. But only if there is a clean, safe opportunity. There's no point for us to go to prison."

"If I go, you go," Laurin stated flatly.

"There's no need for that," Houde pleaded, but he had no hope of convincing anyone.

An ambulance raced past them.

"It'll be the same as when we were on foot. The cops are preoccupied with everything going on. Michel will drive us to our freedom. He's a calm man, I can tell. A man of few words. I like that. A man of action. I misspoke before, sir, when you could not pull out the knife. I tried myself. It was impossible."

Vimont listened to him, but did not speak. He did not turn his head around. His eyes moved between the rear-view mirror and the front windshield.

"So who goes? Into the park, I mean?" Laurin asked.

"Michel should go," Houde suggested.

The driver turned his head slightly. Nothing more.

"We need Michel to be behind the wheel of this car," de Bernonville said.

"Then you go," Houde told him.

"If we have to go after someone, with Michel driving, I will have to be in the car. You never know. We might have to act quickly."

"I can't go," Houde objected, fearing that the task might fall upon him. "I'll be recognized. I can't stand around in a crowd."

"I'll go," Laurin offered.

"Yes," de Bernonville agreed. "That's best."

They moved the car closer to Dominion Square and parked. Laurin got out and looked around, bundled himself up more tightly in his coat, then moved off into the park to investigate the commotion there, down by the Burns statue. Police cars had their lights on, and a crowd milled around.

When the signal came, it arrived in a fury, with Laurin walking back briskly, clearly agitated, at least for him, then catapulting himself into the limousine again. "It's in the coroner's van. In the glove box. The van is leaving on its own." He slapped the back of the front seat, behind Houde's head.

"Step on it!" de Bernonville shouted out. "Go! Now!"

"What are we doing?" Houde demanded as the car raced forward. He was pushed against the dash when Vimont braked, blocking the path of the departing van. De Bernonville was immediately out of the car, waving casually at the driver, as though he required urgent information. He went around to the passenger side and Claude Racine, the coroner, rolled down his window.

De Bernonville shot him. Point-blank. The other two guys in the van were screaming as he flung open the door and fought to find the glove box. He opened it. He warned the driver not to move. "I just want the knife. You don't have to die." Then the glove box fell open, and the knife was his again. As he moved away from the van, the coroner's body slumped onto the pavement.

The limo was already moving before de Bernonville got back in, and Laurin had to open the door for him and slide over quickly to the opposite side to give him room. The count grasped the door and had one foot in as the car took off. He had to fight to hang on, but he pulled himself inside, helped by Laurin, and the car vaulted forward. He was not complaining about the difficult entry when he yelled at Vimont to "Go! Go! GO!"

Vimont's foot hit the floor. The tires squealed. They heard glass shattering and the blast of a shotgun.

"Oh my God!" the old mayor cried out. "They're shooting. Get us out of here!"

The car careened into the chaos of the night.

†††

One more negotiation remained. Who would possess the knife when they split up?

De Bernonville volunteered. Houde pointed out to him that that meant the knife would be in Brazil by dawn.

"So you take it," the count suggested.

"So you can kill me in my sleep?" That idea didn't appeal to Houde either. Apparently the fugitive from Brazil was staying over in his apartment. "I'm sorry, but I'm kicking you out. I don't want a killer sleeping on my couch."

"Mr. Mayor—"

"No! Get a hotel room. I'm sure Michel can bring you where they won't ask for ID if you pay cash. They'll even give you a girl. I'll give you the fucking cash."

"I don't want to be where I'm not wanted. But the knife comes with me."

"I'll take the knife," offered Laurin.

"If you do, I want to sleep on your couch," de Bernonville countered.

"And I'll sleep in the spare room. You must have one," Houde said.

"I have a safe deposit box," Laurin stated. "I'll have it in there by two minutes after ten tomorrow morning. If someone wants to sleep in my apartment, and walk me to the bank, you're free to do so."

"I'll do that," de Bernonville consented.

"Not you," the doctor told him.

"Why not me?"

Laurin only looked across at him.

"If you don't trust me, I don't trust you."

"Dr. Laurin will take it to the bank," Michel Vimont announced.

"Oh, yeah?" de Bernonville mocked him. "Who are you, the pope now?"

They heard a click. Vimont raised his hand and aimed a pistol at the count's glistening forehead.

Vimont addressed them once again. "We can all go over to the doctor's house. Right, Doctor? We'll walk him down to the bank in the morning. That way we will know, if the knife gets stolen, who stole it. There can only be one person, and that one person will be the doctor."

They nodded.

"I get you," de Bernonville said. "Do you have enough beds, Doctor?"

Vimont answered instead. "Don't be stupid," he said, still aiming his gun. "Who's gonna sleep?"

Houde acknowledged that it sounded like a good plan. At least two men in this car carried weapons, which surprised him. He wondered if he should have thought of that and carried one, too. Roger had never suggested it, but he couldn't chastise him for that now.

"We're agreed," Laurin said. "Now, will you put the gun down, Michel?"

"The count's gotta give me his first."

That seemed less equitable to everyone, yet no one argued. De Bernonville knew he was up against a man with experience, and handed over his pistol. "Will you kill us all?" he asked. "When we get to the doctor's house?"

"That's the difference between me and you," Vimont told him.

Then he drove on, out of the alley in which they were hiding onto the street, hoping the cops were too busy to notice a limo with a black-eyed tail light.

CHAPTER 27

1970

THEY'D BECOME CAPTIVES OF THEIR OWN CONSPIRACY.

Interminable nights. Days passed as a bellyache. Barricaded within an apartment devoid of charm in bland North End Montreal, on nondescript Avenue des Récollets—working-class without the patina of age, modern, bereft of style—the James Cross kidnappers were fearful of anything that twitched beyond their booby-trapped doors. Their sole entertainment derived from listening to neighbourhood children play, and switching channels, hoping to hear news of themselves.

Soon, winter would bind the kids indoors.

And they weren't on the tube anymore. Outings were restricted to foraging at a corner *dépanneur* or running errands to pick up packets of cash scrounged by sympathizers. Supporters they'd relied upon for money had been rounded up in the random sweeps, so they developed a second tier of contacts. Risky. Their nerves were shot, their collective will sunk.

Walls inched closer. The ceiling crept down as they slept.

Fresh and stale sweat mingled in their airless rooms.

In her bed at night, the lone woman perpetually wept.

They had each craved the publicity their grand gambit created, and had come to depend upon their anonymous notoriety. Now the press had been muffled by the War Measures Act, and attempts to garner more attention—letters dictated for the hostage to write, criticisms of the government—ceded no intended result. On most days, nary a soul, it seemed, nor the soulless government, gave a hoot.

Their morale slumped deeper into depression as none of the three predictable consequences to their actions—capture, killing James Cross, or being slaughtered in a shootout—interested them.

The man Cross had come to depend upon—the others called him Jacques whenever they forgot themselves and mentioned a name, which had become more common of late—had been infuriated by Laporte's murder. That gave Cross a paltry hope. The kidnappers lost their course of action, their impetus. Now they prepared for capture. Would capture mean jail? A shootout to the death? Or a flight into exile?

Polls charted the growing support for the federal government and Pierre Trudeau. How could this be? Off shopping, the woman overheard a stranger remark that the FLQ ought to be machine-gunned against a wall. The cashier suggested burial alive. In line, the anonymous kidnapper smiled at the suggestion, as though she tacitly agreed. *I am buried alive already.* Nobody wanted a second murder, unless it was a member of the FLQ swinging at the end of a taut, gristly rope. Everyone wanted the crisis at an end, the soldiers off the streets, the FLQ vanquished from their lives. For the kidnappers, their dreams of revolution ended. Their beloved Front de Libération du Québec, that imposing title, had been reduced to another pack of absurd, irresponsible boys in the public's craven mind. They once yearned to emulate the experience of Algiers, at least as they saw the revolt there portrayed in a movie called *The Battle of Algiers,* yet experience had demonstrated that Quebec was not North Africa, that their revolution would never become the movie they once imagined.

From the lonely well of his room, Cross listened to his captors' whispers. They spoke in hushed tones, often bitterly now. Where once they professed conviction and resolve, now they bickered amongst themselves, trying to sort a way out. They were coming undone, unglued, which did not bode well for him. He presumed that, aside from their primary reluctance to kill him, he was kept alive because he constituted their ticket to freedom—their escape hatch. When the police came, which they now believed was inevitable, they'd trade his life for passage to Cuba. He was all they had left. No more dreams or ideals, no revolution. Just Jasper Cross, their prisoner, and Cuba, their hope.

In recent days, discussions concerned only escape. On a foray for supplies, one of their number returned with groceries and beer, but he also popped into a travel agent. He showed them a flyer. Initially, his comrades were furious about the detour. If they couldn't go out themselves, they didn't want him gallivanting around town like a tourist, or an ordinary citizen. And yet, Cross overheard them comment one by one on Cuba's white sand beaches and the pink open-air haciendas in the publicity shots. They were dreaming of another place, another life. Their hope in the future shifting.

Cross thought them mad. A government that would not negotiate when it did not know where they were would not negotiate once it had them surrounded. But he left them to their reveries. He was done trying to talk sense in this house.

The potential manner of his death disturbed him the most. He dreaded Laporte's experience—strangulation by wire. The indignity, the horror of losing his life in the vile grip of a lesser man's hands made him squirm against his restraints, and when he despaired, tears moistened the back of his blindfold.

He thought he'd silently cried himself dry, but he hadn't.

He would prefer, when the time came, to be shot. Once, he had been on the brink of saying so. "If you need to kill me, then please, shoot me." He rehearsed the plea in his head and nearly uttered the words aloud. Surely, he could appeal to their humanity to grant this one frail mercy. At the last moment, he successfully resisted the impulse. Saying those words gave his captors a convoluted permission to kill him. That satisfaction, that *approval*, that willingness to assuage their guilt by allowing them to bequeath his final request—he'd deny it to them. Even if it meant that, in the end, he endured the terrible agony of the wire.

The thought caused him to soak his sheets at night.

So be it. He'd die badly, if necessary. He'd not give them any hint that he condoned their actions against him. He would hate them—the woman who had made his ordeal so unbearable and the others equally, forever, whether his life was long or short. He might die, but he was not willing to surrender.

Always a struggle, though.

His worst moment had come after Laporte was butchered. The national television network, the CBC, reported that his own body had also been located. He was watching TV and the announcer, listening to a report through an earplug, told the world James Cross was dead. Then advised that the report was inaccurate. Then declared that, no, he was dead after all. Cross knew his wife would be listening to that broadcast, that her heart would wail as her mourning took hold.

Another terrible moment followed, when the letter dictated to him by his captors and written in response to the broadcast had been analyzed by reporters, also on television. He had deliberately misspelled a few words, tricking his French captors with his English, and the journalists had deduced—*in public, on television*—that he was trying to get a message out. The Cross message, they pronounced, had indicated, if nothing else, that the words were not his own, but those of his oppressors.

Who did those reporters think they were talking to? Did they not know that the FLQ had ears? That they fastened their eyes to every broadcast? *The FLQ is listening, you pricks. They're watching. They're sitting right beside me. Damn you!* The ignominy of that betrayal. His captors hauled him back to his room and denied him television privileges. For a few days, no one talked to him and they fed him less. The woman came into his room at night and woke him with a stiff shove to his chest. She berated him until her husband dragged her back to bed, then he returned to apologize. "It's the stress," he said. *Stress? Stress? Do you want to talk about stress? Have a chat with* my *wife.* Left alone, he felt so helplessly betrayed by those reporters that his body reeled from an internal, dull, wretched nausea.

A glimmering despair.

How despicable could this world be? Those damned reporters. Why did he have to suffer for their wanton stupidity? He fell into a more egregious tangent. *Are reporters working on behalf of the terrorists, tipping them off deliberately? Is the whole nation conspiring against me?* That worry provoked a new, untapped wellspring of anguish.

Lately, his captors were sensing that the end was near. He'd been bound up and either blinkered or blindfolded for almost sixty days. Perhaps they craved the finish, too. His imprisonment had become their own. He had noticed an incremental improvement in the household's food rations. Cross doubted that they had tapped a fresh supply of cash, money being a constant irritation among them. Instead, they were burning through their resources more quickly, spending more on beer, as if they no longer counted on a lengthy siege. As it happened, one was out shopping and two others were preparing breakfast when a fourth, Cross guessed, had peeked around a back curtain.

"*Flics,*" he whispered.

Cops.

Cross felt his bones congeal.

His comrades, apparently, ran from the kitchen to see for themselves, but saw no one. But where had the children gone? They always played in the street—now they were absent, their voices silent. The captors couldn't confirm seeing cops. But still, they were beginning to feel police around them. As if they could sniff them. Was this what paranoia felt like? *Flics,* gazing back at them through the bathroom mirror, listening devices embedded in their clocks and radios? Although they did not know that *flics* had taken up residence on the third floor of the building in which they lived, and across the street also, they could feel them everywhere, like stains on a wall, dust motes scurrying on the floor as they walked, as if the echoes of their own steps were being recorded and measured.

†††

This is how it happened.

Anik Clément took a seat in the rear booth of a restaurant on Jean-Talon Street, in the Greek neighbourhood of Park Extension. Within eight minutes, she was joined by Émile Cinq-Mars. They had little to say, having recently chatted at length. Cinq-Mars dared to place his hands over hers, to comfort his former girlfriend, and she did not pull hers away. He broke the intimacy only when Captain Touton entered and peeled off his hat and overcoat, which he hung on the hook next to their booth.

"Crappy weather, eh? Only December. Just the beginning. It's a sin to live in this climate," he groused, then sat down. "So? How's it going, Anik?"

She was reaching into her substantial handbag. "I have a couple of leads."

"Leads?" Touton snapped back. "I was expecting more than leads. I was expecting you to take us straight to the kidnappers. Patrolmen are standing by."

She looked up, both hands still in her handbag, and demonstrated that she would brook no guff from him tonight. "I could follow these leads myself, if you like, then take you by the hand to the kidnappers. Or, you could do your job and follow up the leads in a tenth the time it'll take me. It's up to you. Let me know by midnight. After that, I smash my glass slippers and go to sleep drunk."

He studied her. That stubborn look. "All right," he relented. "Show me your leads."

"You've neglected the women," she advised him. "Wherever there are men, there are women, even in a war. You're right to have Jacques Lanctôt's picture in the papers, but I take it you haven't located his wife and son?"

"We're looking."

"She's pregnant."

"I see." He nodded, taking that in, although he didn't see how it was of any immediate use.

"Do you? Check out the birthing hospitals to see where she's expected to deliver. Find the physician who's treating her. But first, look at this."

She placed a large black-and-white photograph down on the tabletop. Touton was staring at the snapshot of a young boy when the waitress came by. He ordered a coffee, and the other two indicated that they'd appreciate a refill.

"This is the son?" Touton asked.

"Boris, yep," Anik told him. "Now check this out."

The second photograph was of an older woman, somewhat rotund, wide in the hips, with an ample bosom and a shy moon face. Beside her, at her hip, stood the lad Boris.

"Who's this? Somebody's Ukrainian grandmother?"

"The babysitter. Look."

The next snap showed a man entering a second-storey home by the back entrance.

"You showed me this before. It's not the hideout?"

"This is where the babysitter lives. Boris is living with the babysitter. Among the women in my circle, she was known as a good sitter. So I put a photographer up a tree to guard her back door. Sometimes, Jacques goes to see her, we found out, but Suzanne, that's his wife, she goes more often."

"Which Jacques?"

"Lanctôt. Keep up, Armand."

"So we can wait there for Jacques?"

"That might not happen again," Anik cautioned him. "When he arrived this one time, in the picture, he had to talk his way in. I don't think it's a common visit, I'm saying. Put a tail on the babysitter. She takes the boy on excursions. Mostly to the local park. When she does, expect Suzanne to visit, at least once in a while. I guess she's just too busy right now to look after the boy full time."

"Busy? She's a kidnapper?"

"I'd say no. But a courier? Probably. Does she go to the hideout? Likely."

Leads never got much better.

"Next thing. Like I said, you've neglected the women. You have Jacques Lanctôt's face in the papers, but you don't have his sister's, Louise."

"His sister?" Touton hadn't heard of a sister.

"You see? I know the women. Louise is Jacques Lanctôt's sister and Jacques Cossette-Trudel's girlfriend. I noticed that her name didn't show up on the lists Émile gave me of people you've put in jail. Which makes no sense. I would have put her on the top ten of any list. She was radicalized years ago, she's committed. More so than people you have behind bars. So where's Louise? I think she's married, actually, but in any case, she uses Cossette-Trudel's last name. We call him C.T."

"Holy shit," Touton sputtered out. This changed a few things. It helped.

"It's about time I got a reaction out of you. Do you know the Taverne Boucheron, Captain?"

"Of course." On rare occasions, he went there himself to enjoy a few glasses of draft. Back in the good old days, he'd followed more than one perp into the establishment to see what company he chose to keep.

"Stake it out."

"Who and what am I looking for?"

"It's a rendezvous point. C.T.'s favourite spot. Always was. Apparently, that hasn't changed. Here." One more photograph. Of Cossette-Trudel emerging from the Boucheron Tavern.

"Who does he meet there?"

"Sympathizers. Doctors. Lawyers. Pipefitters. Men with cash—the ones you haven't rounded up yet. Couriers."

This was gold. Touton couldn't help but smile. He wanted to say that it felt like old times, meaning that part of this experience invoked those days when he had worked with her father and mother, but he thought he'd be better served keeping that opinion to himself.

"Thanks," he said.

He could tell that she was a bit proud of herself, but the moment was not about satisfaction. She turned away, unable to be fully content with her work.

After downing their coffees, they were each set to depart in different directions. This time, Anik did meet the captain's look. She held his gaze quite steadily. Then she turned, kissed Émile's cheeks, and tore off.

They watched her go.

She was almost running by the time she went through the door, and she got her handbag jammed up. She wasn't accustomed to carrying one, and had to free herself to get loose.

"Good work," Touton told his protégé.

Cinq-Mars merely shook his head. Nothing accomplished here felt remotely related to police work. "You'll keep her out of it?" he asked. "She doesn't want any of this coming back on her. I've made that promise, that it won't."

Touton didn't need to treat a young cop with such deference, but these were brutal times. He'd never lived through anything like it. They were engaged in the largest manhunt in human history, and today the two of them were on the brink of cracking it wide open. Yet neither man would ever receive credit. That was the price to be paid to broker this deal.

"We'll pass along Anik's tips to the Mounties."

"How come?"

"For her security. This way, none of the people who break the case will know where the good juice came from. They'll say it was from Montreal cops, and laugh—think we were too lazy to follow up on the leads ourselves, maybe too dumb to recognize their value. Our force will have to eat more shit. But Anik stays secure this way, and the job gets done, because a few of those Mounties do good work."

"They might not listen to you. They might think a tip from a Montreal cop can't be worth a plugged nickel."

"First off, it won't come from me. They'll take me too seriously. Later on, they might mention that it came from me, and we don't want that. So you tell them. You'll look like a dumb lunk for not knowing you had a good tip. You aren't worth mentioning because you're too junior. Then I'll follow up, to make sure the news gets checked out. Émile, we're going to get these guys. We'll put a stop to this."

Nodding, Cinq-Mars pulled on his woollen overcoat. For close to sixty days, the city had been in torment. "That's our job. It's good to finally get it done."

His captain clamped a hand over his near shoulder and gave it a good hard squeeze. Cinq-Mars could feel the man's legendary strength in that grip, not all of it lost to the passage of time. "A case like this could make your career, set you for life. You don't mind giving up the credit?"

He shrugged, then pointed to where Anik had gone. "Keep her safe. I mean it, Captain. That's all the credit I need right there."

†††

Yves had been away, and was overdue. He strolled down the block with his usual loping stride, oblivious to the world, and rang the bell of their street-level apartment. Inside, the men detached the dynamite booby trap on the door and admitted him.

"They didn't stop you?"

"Who?"

"The *flics*! They're all around us."

"You're imagining things."

They booby-trapped the door again. Later, the lights went out. After that, someone trespassing on their lawn tried to turn the water off to their building. Yves pointed his M1 at the intruder and told him to bugger off. The man scampered back to the other side of the street, fearing he might be shot in the ass.

So now it was official. They were under siege.

Then the phone rang. They were expecting the call. The woman answered and listened, then suddenly hung up.

"It's not only the *flics*." She spoke calmly, quietly. She'd been crying in her bed lately and getting angry at odd moments, but now she could not fake surprise or show emotion. "The army's here, too."

"What did he say?"

"'We have you surrounded.'"

They did not run to the windows to check. Instead, they seemed to observe a minute's quiet, although the time could not have lasted that long. To Cross, the interval seemed endless. He detected a change in the atmosphere, a charge. Suddenly, he was the most powerful person in the apartment, no longer the weakest. Before they spotted cops, someone had gone to fetch him water and had left the door open. Blindfolded, he saw nothing, but he listened through his pores for any indication of news. Had the woman really mentioned cops? The army? Was something going on? Was he dreaming? Then he heard the boots of the heaviest man pound across the kitchen floor, towards the window. The venetian blinds rattled slightly as they were parted. Then they shook again, as if suddenly pushed back. Cross tried to see every sound he was hearing and visualize the silences.

The man said, "Shit." In his inflection of the word, Cross registered sorrow.

The phone rang again, and they all jumped.

"Should we answer it?"

It buzzed a second time.

The woman answered again. "We have demands," she said.

She remained quiet.

"What the fuck's he saying?"

"Wait!" She listened a little more. Then she hung up the phone.

"What did he say?" the man asked, quietly this time.

"He said they don't want any more violence, nobody has to get hurt, we've all been through enough, it's time to give up peacefully. The usual cop bullshit rhetoric. He asked for our demands."

"Read the fucking manifesto!" one guy said, but his companions failed to goad him on. Manifestos read over the airwaves were hollow gestures now.

"What did you tell him?" one guy asked, and even Cross wanted to slap him awake.

"You were in the room, weren't you?"

The phone rang again.

"I'm answering this time."

"Why?"

"Why is it always you?"

The man who answered was the one who had gone to fetch Cross his water.

"Yeah?" he said, and listened. He put on a snide voice. "You don't need to know who you're talking to." A moment later he repeated, "You don't need to know that." He still sounded as though he wanted to pick a fight, but the next time he spoke, he was subdued. "Yeah, so? That's me. So?"

"Don't tell him that," the woman hissed at him.

The man suddenly shouted into the phone, "No, asshole! You listen to me. We want a plane to Cuba."

"Holy shit," another of their number said. This was feeling real to him.

"That's right. We got Cross in here. We're prepared to kill the fucker. A bullet between the eyes, maybe one in each eye. You want no more violence, get us a fucking plane." He waited for a response. "Yes, he's still fucking alive, do you want to talk to him?"

He walked straight to Cross, but the cord got stuck in the door. The woman yanked it free again.

"Tell them who you are," he demanded, and thrust the phone against the side of his captive's face.

"This is Jasper Cross," he said. He realized suddenly that these were the first words he'd spoken in his own language in two months. He wanted to bawl. "I'm all right."

The man stomped back to the kitchen. "Get us a plane or we'll have a shootout. Cross goes down first, then a few cops." Suddenly, he bellowed to one of his pals, "Get away from the fucking window! Do you want to get shot?"

"Give me the phone," the woman demanded. Apparently, her colleague acquiesced, because she spoke next. "Who the fuck am I talking to?" A moment later, she spit out, "You don't need to tell me about my fucking language, pig! I'll say whatever the fuck I want. No, *you* calm down." She took in the caller's response and shot back, "Go fuck yourself, all right? I'm not talking to you. I'm not talking to any fucking Mountie. . . . No! I'm not going to put the other guy back on. You talk to me, only it won't be you. You guys want to talk to me, put somebody on from the SQ or a city cop, then call me back. We're not talking to Mounties in this house."

She hung up.

Quietly, somebody said, "Fuck."

Another man said, "Somebody calls back, says he's SQ. How will you know? He could just be a Mountie saying he's SQ."

"There's TV cameras," a man said.

"Get away from the fucking window. I'm not going to fucking tell you again." Someone slammed a tabletop, then kicked a wall.

The woman was pacing, her clicky shoes tapping out a rhythm on the floor. "That's how we'll do it," she said. "Television. They'll have to show us who we're talking to."

"That'll work," someone said.

"No, it won't," another man said. "The power's off. Anyway, we still won't know who we're talking to. We'll be talking to some *guy*. That's all. Some guy in a suit. We won't know who he works for."

"That's true," the woman conceded.

"Does it matter who we talk to?"

"I'm not talking to any goddamned Mountie. I'm a Quebecer. It's humiliating! I'll only talk to one of our own."

"Mounties can be Quebecers, too."

Now she was furious. "Don't talk to me about those turncoat pricks. I'm not talking to a Mountie and that's that. I'm not talking to one of Duplessis's goons, either. That's not a legitimate government of the people. A city cop. That's it. That's all. That's the only *flic* who can negotiate for their side. You don't like it? Go fuck yourself!"

"Calm down."

"Don't tell me to fucking calm down." Cross could almost see that she was speaking through clenched teeth. "That Mountie shit said that to me."

"Okay, look," another man interceded. "She's right. Mounties, they take training in negotiations. We don't want to talk to somebody like that."

"Make it some cop we've seen before. We've seen some guys on TV. Pick one of them. That way we know who it is."

"What about Touton? We know what he looks like. It's probably bullshit, but he's got a reputation for integrity."

The phone rang again and the woman picked up. She listened. "We changed our minds. . . . No, you're wrong, I can do that. . . . Well, I'm sorry, but I didn't know you were dropping by tonight. Maybe we're not fully prepared." She waited a longer time before she spoke again, and when she did, her voice was low and threatening. "We've got James Cross in here, alive. We're willing to kill him. Now, listen to me . . . NO! You listen to me right now. We don't want SQ. All those old SQ guys were handpicked by Duplessis to be his thugs. We'll negotiate with a city cop. Armand Touton, that's our guy. Don't call us back until he's on the line. We want to see him on TV, so turn the fucking lights back on."

They were pleased with that episode. They felt they'd won a round.

"Now what?" somebody asked. Cross strained to listen. He was confused for a while, as were his kidnappers, but he gathered that big searchlights now shone on the exterior walls of the building.

"Don't worry about it," somebody suggested. "It's only for the TV cameras."

"Are you kidding me?" the woman shot back. "It's for the goddamned snipers."

††

They caught the commentary of their demise on television.

The five sat on the kitchen floor as army sharpshooters took aim at their apartment bathed in bright lights. In the distance, a perimeter of spectators formed, and they saw for themselves that no one demanded their freedom. The atmosphere verged on the festive. People were having fun, sharing jokes, waiting and watching, and probably a portion hoped to witness a bloodbath— some kind of action. They wanted to be nearby if the kidnappers fell in a rage of bullets and dynamite.

They wanted *Bonnie and Clyde*, the movie, but just the ending.

A hail of bullets.

This could look like war.

Behind the barricade, a TV reporter conducted people-on-the-street interviews. A few people spoke of their sadness that "the boys" had been caught. "What about me?" Louise had demanded of the TV set, then laughed, although a twinge of bitterness could be detected in her complaint. In his room, Jasper Cross, bitter also, thought to himself, *Yeah? So what about you? Nobody's sad that you've been caught,* and inwardly laughed at his private joke.

One wizened old guy said that the cops should blow up the house and be done with the nasty business. "What about James Cross?" the reporter asked, and in his darkened chamber, Cross thought, *Thank you, sir, for asking that question. At least there's one journalist left with half a conscience.* The old geezer teetered, perhaps in a drunken stupor, and waved his hand at waist height as if polishing the hood of a car. He was fighting for his words, then concluded, "Blow them up!" The reporter moved on, guessing that the old guy didn't really understand the question.

The phone kept ringing. They kept answering. The Mounties were right on what they said about that. They weren't going to shoot James Cross just because the cops made a phone call, now, were they? So the Mounties won that one. They could always take their phone off the hook, but the cops said that

Captain Armand Touton was on his way. If that's who they wanted to talk to, then he'd be the guy. But they had to be patient. Give him time to cross the city. He couldn't fly, now, could he?

They knew how long it took to cross the city. He should have arrived by now.

"While we're waiting," the woman said, "you should be getting a plane ready for us. We need lots of fuel. If you won't give us a plane, then pick out a coffin for your precious Mr. Cross. If you want, you can hear his preferences— what kind of wood and all that. I'll get him to write you a list." She hung up. Her voice sounded tired, her responses half-baked. Cross sensed her defeat. He presumed the Mounties could sense it, too. He didn't know if that helped his situation, or not.

Then the Mounties called to say they should select an intermediary as well. Someone to be a runner between them and Touton.

"How come?"

"Because we're cutting the phone line now."

"Don't—"

The line went dead.

Each of them took turns listening to the silence on the line.

No dial tone.

Like death.

"They're punishing us," one of the men said.

"For kidnapping Cross?"

"For cutting them out of the negotiations."

"I need to go to the bathroom," Cross called out.

"It's the excitement," somebody muttered.

"Keep your pants on," the woman called through to him. "I'll take you."

One more humiliation before they were done with him.

She told him the news. "They've cut the phone line. We need an interme- diary. A go-between, to talk to their go-between, whom we named for them. We got more go-betweens than we got hostages." His piss flowed out of him while she listed all their troubles.

"You only have one hostage," Cross reminded her. "Me."

"That's it. We got to take good care of you from now on."

†††

They threw a message out the window in a cardboard cylinder they took from a roll of paper towels. Mistaking it for a stick of dynamite, the nearest cops ran away. Inside the house, they had a good laugh over that. For an interval, a measure of their stress dissipated. The cops crept back and picked up the message, and seeing them so tentative and frightened was good for another laugh.

†††

Captain Armand Touton waited outside in his car and once more leaned on the horn. This time, it had an effect. Émile Cinq-Mars dashed out the door of his second-floor apartment. Then braked on the stairs, scooted back up, locked the door properly, and scampered all the way down the stairs again. He went around to the side and got in the front passenger seat, surprised that it was just him and the boss.

Touton slapped a flashing magnetic cherry on his rooftop, and they were off at high speed.

He didn't tell Cinq-Mars where they were going, and the young cop didn't ask. Along the way, the junior officer asked him, "Why do you want me there, anyway?"

"You've been watching the news?"

"Who hasn't been?"

"I've been asked to do the negotiating."

Cinq-Mars could not contain his surprise. "You? By the Mounties? Why?"

"Not Mounties," Touton snapped. "Would that make sense?"

Cinq-Mars was confused. "I didn't think so. Then who?"

"The terrorists. Who else?" He spoke as though he did not expect the young man to believe him.

He was still confused. "I didn't know you knew them."

The senior cop shrugged. "Neither did I. But they like my style." He smiled. "A lawyer, his name's Bernard Mergler, he's the go-between, but I negotiate for our side."

They carried on, fast, pell-mell, slowing for intersections, but barrelling through them the moment other cars caught his flashing light.

Cinq-Mars returned to his original question. "So why do you want me there?"

"Somebody has to bring me coffee." He honked at a bus and got it to move over. "Which reminds me."

"What?"

"Give me back my badge. The next time you want to come out on the job with me, wear a uniform."

Émile Cinq-Mars was a detective no more. But he was still a smart cop. He told Touton, "I'm not here to bring you coffee. I know what I'm here for."

Touton kept driving, but looked over at him a few times. Eventually, he bent his head down and back up again, as though to concede the point unspoken between them. "I may need you to talk to Anik."

"I know."

†††

The prime minister had chosen to watch the proceedings from his official residence at 24 Sussex Drive. Gérard Pelletier kept him company and interceded whenever the Justice Department called.

"We're going to close this out," Pelletier assured him, much relieved.

Television commentators were asking police officers how the discovery of the FLQ hideout had occurred. The cops talked, their lips were definitely moving, but they weren't explaining much.

"How *did* this happen?" Pelletier inquired.

Trudeau didn't take his eyes off the screen. "Remember the Cartier Dagger?"

Pelletier nodded.

"That's the price I paid."

The secretary of state took in the news, observing his old friend for any untoward reaction, or any reaction at all. "Should I ask?"

Trudeau shook his head. "You won't get an answer."

They both watched the tube awhile. Then Pelletier noted, "Expensive, no?"

The prime minister dug a hand down the middle of his back to give himself a serious rub, working out the stresses there. Then he shrugged. "Not if this works."

A while later, thinking politically, Pelletier posed another question. "If you can't tell me the reason you're letting them go, how will you explain it to the public?"

He delivered another of his famous shrugs. "The Brits put pressure on me to free their guy. In the end, I decided that his life was worth a lot more than the pleasure of incarcerating his kidnappers. If someone wants to know if I was negotiating with terrorists, I'll just say that the British made me do it."

"The Brits are tough. If they made you do it, then it had to be done."

"That's what I was thinking."

The old friends smiled. A few minutes later, evaluating everything, Pelletier assessed the situation with a positive nod. Fair enough. If it had been his decision, he'd probably do the same thing. Get the hostage back. Say good riddance to the rest. Nobody needed the kidnappers around being heroes in their prison cells, and Trudeau had already abolished the death penalty. Just get rid of them.

"This is a tough country to hold together," he opined.

Trudeau looked over at him briefly, then back at the TV. Pelletier had always been a master of understatement.

†††

Touton walked the long distance across the street. He remembered a day, years ago, when he flushed a syphilitic gunman from his home by tossing stones into one room after another until he showed himself. If the terrorists opened the door a crack for him, they first had to defuse the dynamite, then he could crash it down. He had the strength. His reflexes might be suspect, but if his legs performed to an old standard, he'd be on them so fast no shot would be fired. The kidnappers would be face down, their hands behind their necks, before they had a chance to blink. If they did blink, they'd be in handcuffs, wishing they'd never sipped mother's milk.

Still, he had Cross to worry about. Something to keep in mind.

Anik telephoned after Cinq-Mars had gotten in touch through a clandestine exchange. Touton ordered everybody out of the command truck to talk to her. "Mounties might be listening," he warned. "I can't be sure."

"Okay," she said, "I get you."

"I'm going over there, to talk to the kidnappers in person."

"I'll see you on TV," she told him, and laughed a little. "I'm watching now."

"I'll try to remember to fix my tie."

"Don't wear your hat," she advised him.

"My hat is my trademark."

"That's true. All right. Wear your hat."

He exhaled. "I need to know something."

"What?" Her voice was tentative, worried. She'd made a few tough decisions lately. She didn't need to make another.

"Somebody you once knew—I'm saying it this way because the Mounties are listening—he wanted the object to go into the right hands. What he considered to be the right hands, anyway."

"I believe that," she said.

"Not the fascists, or the commies or the unions, not the Church or the government—but into what he considered to be the proper hands. He might've been right, he might've been wrong, it's not for me to say. But he wasn't looking to make a quick buck, even if he had some deals cooking. I think it's fair to say that."

"I don't have any deals cooking," she said.

"Because that might've been his downfall."

"I'm looking to put the knife into the proper hands."

"That's what I'm asking, I guess. Because it's fair to say it's been in the wrong hands before. And for too long."

She needed a moment to think. "I'm not taking it from the man who has it to give it to the man I used to be sleeping with, if that's what you're worried about."

"It's a concern."

"Those two have to fight it out on their own. They're big boys. They have to get by without any props."

"All right. I guess what I'm asking is—"

She waited for him to say it. When he didn't, she provoked him. "What? You think I have my own FLQ cell now?"

"I want to know that you'll look after the knife. That it'll be your decision. Not somebody else's. Just yours. You, I can trust. But if you're being manipulated, or coerced, or influenced—"

"It'll be me," she said curtly.

"I don't mean to insult you."

"No? You're doing a pretty good job of it." He could hear her breathing become calmer. "It'll be me," she said. "On that part, you just have to trust me."

"I wanted to know. Before I go over there."

"I'll be watching," she said.

"Maybe I won't wear my hat."

"Yeah, it's the seventies already. Nobody wears hats anymore. You should change your style."

Touton smiled as he crossed the street, knowing that commentators on television would be wondering what amused him so much. Other cops standing around looked aggrieved. This one was smiling. He wasn't wearing his hat, so his face was easy to see on the cameras, and that must mean something. One analyst mentioned that he had never seen the captain without his hat. Probably, he suggested, it was a way to help put the kidnappers at ease.

They made the absence of his hat a turning point in the negotiations.

He entered the building. A man spoke to him from behind the door to the first-floor apartment. As if he was reading his mind, or recalling his reputation, the man warned, "We got a gun on Cross. Try anything, he's dead—like that." The young fellow snapped his fingers, and Touton decided to forgo any heroics. On his rickety legs, he'd need better odds than those he was facing now.

"Don't put ideas into my head. We just want to get through this negotiation. I understand it's hard. But you brought me in here because you figured I'd be a stand-up guy to talk to, right?"

"We want to stick it to the Mounties. Keep them out of the picture."

The comment made Touton chuckle. "You're doing a good job. They're peeved. Us Montreal guys, we appreciate it. We've had a few bad turns during this manhunt. We haven't come across so well. So it's nice to look like we can walk and talk at the same time."

The man inside also chuckled. Then he asked, "What did you want to tell me that you couldn't tell the lawyer, Mergler?"

"Bernie's a good guy. Trust him. Some secrets are secret though, you know what I mean?"

The man said he didn't have any idea what Touton meant.

"Getting you on a plane to Cuba has been authorized by the prime minister of Canada. He talked to Castro himself to make it all happen."

"That's nice if it's true. How do I trust you? How do I trust him?"

Touton realized the man was sitting on the floor, so he slumped down as well. There were three apartments in the building, two of which were above them. For more than a day, a cop had been residing on the top floor, with a make-believe wife, in a place borrowed from a school crossing guard.

"In the course of this investigation," Touton said, "we found something out about our Mr. Trudeau. About a lot of people, if it comes down to that. But we've got something on him, that if it comes out, he loses the next election."

"Oh yeah? What?" This was unexpected, a carrot tossed into the stew.

"I can't tell you that," Touton said. "The truth is, I don't know. But somebody who does know will talk if Trudeau doesn't keep his word to you guys, if he doesn't make the flight to Cuba happen. He's aware of the situation. He knows it'll all come out if he lets us down. Trust me. He doesn't want the embarrassment." The policeman adjusted his sitting position, becoming more comfortable, which was meant to indicate to the man inside that he was being more trusting himself. "Anyway, you should understand this: he wants you out of the country. He doesn't need any of you becoming martyrs—that'll only make his problems worse. He doesn't want you sitting in jail cells, either, becoming folk heroes. We don't want people writing songs about you. You want to know why you're going to Cuba? Because you're holding James Cross? Don't believe that. Hey, if you were just a gang of bank robbers who'd taken a hostage and it was just you and me, I'd have raided by now. I'd have smashed the door down and taken my chances. 'Fuck the dynamite,' that's what I would say. 'Just go get 'em.'"

"Try it," the man inside threatened.

"I won't," Touton thrust back, commando-style, hard and fast, as he was trained to do—only not with his fists this time, but with words. "Why won't I? Because nobody wants another killing, and because I have my orders. We all do. Nobody wants you dead, sir, and nobody wants you in prison and nobody wants you in the system. You think going to Cuba is your best answer? Guess what? It's everybody's best answer for you."

The man inside was quiet awhile, but Touton could tell that he was thinking. Something told him that more than one person had been listening. Probably the terrorists were exchanging hand signals, and Touton was vaguely tempted again, because he knew that they would have taken their fingers off their triggers. But that was an old self speaking to him, powered by adrenaline and instinct. Given the state of his knees, and his present position down on the floor, in any assault he'd need about thirty to forty seconds just to stand up. Some charge that would be.

Then the guy stipulated what he had been waiting to hear. "Send Mergler back and we'll work it out. Listen, I don't want a bunch of Mounties escorting us. That would be humiliating. City cops. Only."

"It'll be mostly city cops," Touton promised. "We'll escort you through the streets. A Mountie or two, and some SQ will ride along. Please, don't say that can't happen, because, to tell the truth, I've got enough headaches right now without going through that discussion with them."

"One more thing," the man inside said, without disputing what he was told. "How come there's all those plainclothes cops outside, walking around with red armbands?"

"Two reasons," Touton told him. "In case of a shootout, they want to be able to identify who's a terrorist and who's a cop. If I were you, I'd wear a red armband. You'll be safer."

"What's the other reason?"

"They want to scare you, because the truth is, nobody wants a shootout. So far, that's worked."

"I'm not scared," the man said, but who on this earth would believe him?

"I am," Touton told him.

The man inside locked the door again, and Armand Touton pushed himself up to his feet, groaning a little from the pain in his legs. Then he went outside and crossed the street.

TV commentators noted that he was limping on the way back. One suggested that the legendary captain of the Night Patrol might be showing his age, and he and his partner beside him chuckled into their microphones over their mean zinger.

Back in the command truck, Touton told the go-between, "Bernie. Good man. Go. Do your lawyer thing. End this."

†††

In Canada, only the queen of England on an official royal visit could command such a motorcade. Marc drove his relic of a Chrysler, the one in which Cross had been kidnapped, his foot heavy on the gas. A replacement car was driven along behind in case his broke down. Twenty-two motorcycles and eight cars raced through Montreal towards the island named after Champlain's child bride, Île Ste.-Hélène. Streets along the route were closed to traffic, with cops waving the entourage through the intersections. Thanks to live television coverage on every channel, the route was lined with the curious, as if for a parade. In this instance, rather than welcoming a monarch, they were watching kidnappers flee the country. Tens of thousands stared as they sped to the makeshift Cuban consulate at sixty miles an hour, while the rest of the country watched their history on television.

The process seemed very Canadian—polite, without drama or fanfare. In the former Canadian Pavilion from Expo 67, temporarily designated as Cuban soil, the kidnappers surrendered their weapons and Cross was taken into Cuban custody. He said goodbye to none of them, and shook only Cuban and British hands, no others. The terrorists waited, then were joined by Lanctôt's wife and child. She was close to giving birth, so a physician would accompany them on the flight in the event that a delivery became necessary.

They enjoyed, and had negotiated to assure, TV coverage. The cameras helped guarantee their safety and, they believed, helped advance their cause throughout the world. That satisfaction took a bad turn. They deposited suitcases in the trunk of Marc's rickety Chrysler, and now could not open it. "The damn lid's jammed." Rather than make a spectacle of themselves on international TV, trying to break into their own car and possibly failing, they abandoned most of their belongings. What they had taken in the back seat, however, across a pair of their laps, was the big old television they watched so intently over the previous sixty days, and they lugged that into the Cuban embassy, all set for passage. They would not be arriving in the Caribbean without a few trappings of home. They would bring what was most important, for sure. Their revolutionary gear. A few books. Their TV.

Once they were in the hands of the Cubans, they were off the airwaves. For posterity, and for broadcasts later that evening, film of their departure was made, but live coverage had been concluded. A military Sikorsky helicopter took them to the city's airport, where, as they waited on the tarmac, they horsed around a little. They boarded their aircraft, a Canadian Forces CC-106 Yukon, fitted out to transport dignitaries, in silence.

Inside, they briefly broke the tension.

"Hey! We're going in style."

"Like princes."

"Like presidents."

"Like kings and prime ministers."

"Like queens."

"Like revolutionary heroes."

Were they that? They didn't know.

Their plane—Military Flight 602—rose unobserved into the sky above the city of Montreal, and above the province of Quebec, and as the land fell away, they soared among the sparse clouds, pleased that they had killed no one, but also that they had saved themselves. The men and women wondered about the others, those who killed Laporte, guessing that they were observing their escape on television, for they did not know that their friends were hiding out in a tunnel dug beneath a barn thirty miles from the city. From there, they'd be flushed a few days after Christmas to face a rowdy trial and imprisonment. Those who had not killed continued to rise above the land and took succour in hopes they'd see those friends again, or any friends, and those with window seats noticed that, below them, the higher landforms had whitened with the advent of winter.

They cleared Quebec skies, heading south.

†††

Onboard, C.T. was thoughtful. His girlfriend slept fitfully in the cradle of his arms. Whenever she awoke, she looked around, then wept, then curled more closely into him again. She was already missing her homeland, already dismayed by exile.

He had learned some things, he knew. He had learned that he was no terrorist. Che, his hero, had talked about becoming a killing machine, but he wasn't one and wanted no part of becoming one. He told Cross one time that they planned to let him go after a few days of captivity, and his cell would have done so, except that Laporte was kidnapped, too, and that changed everything. Then Laporte was murdered, and that changed everything again. Che had never talked about what to do when you discover that you're not a killing machine, and didn't want to become one, either.

So, in the end, they weren't killers. Consequently, neither were they revolutionaries. They committed a revolutionary act and affected history. But they discovered other dimensions that embodied who they were, and they were not people who killed middle-aged British diplomats, no matter what their cause. C.T. had seen his colleagues change during the action. Jacques grew into their leader, directing that Cross not die. That made him their leader, because they were thinking the same way, yet Jacques had the courage to state it, to instruct the others accordingly. Initially, Marc was their leader. He was ten years older than anyone else, they had followed him, but now Marc followed the others and did as they decreed. Yves, who was passing himself off as Pierre Simard and held a passport in that name, was the only one among them from the upper classes. He embraced his new life, his new identity, but he was not a killing machine, either. None of them were made of that material. Had they been, the only man to die in the previous months would not have been a fellow Quebecer, while the English captive walked free. Under the pressure of the time, they found their true selves, and uncovered strength, and fortitude, and the substance and supremacy of their own humanity, their own care for life. They uncovered the courage to follow through on a newly determined objection to violence.

Which surprised them all. Astonished them all.

In committing a violent act, they discovered themselves to be peaceful. That irony was almost overpowering for C.T.

He was sad, too.

They had made history, in a way. They'd stirred the pot. He worried that they were now celebrities after a fashion, that books would be written, documentaries filmed, and he would probably be identified as the stutterer, the young one who tripped over his own words. People might laugh at how he was portrayed. He'd been through a lot, though, more than anyone knew, including those who went through it with him, even Louise. He helped keep her together, as she was wired pretty tightly. He supported Jacques against Marc and helped Yves from getting too depressed, from bolting, as Yves was inclined that way. He kept Marc feeling that he looked up to him, because Marc needed that, having thrown away so much to do this action, not least of all his wife and family. So C.T. knew he had contributed, and as the youngest among them he was not finishing this episode as the weakest, or the least valuable. In the end, he was stronger than when he began. Throughout the two months, he continued to read the same books that so influenced his life, so opened his mind to injustice in the world and to change. He again read Che, Mao, Pierre Vallières, sometimes out loud to Cross, but increasingly his analysis was different, the context altered. He began picking holes in the philosophy. Mao maintained that violence created a necessary repression by the government. Repression instigated an uprising among the people. And C.T., having hours to kill during which he merely watched over Cross and mused about things, thought, *The role of the revolutionary is to make the people suffer so that they will rise up. We did that. People are suffering under the War Measures Act, and we brought that on. But when you break it down, doesn't that mean that the role of the revolutionary is to be an enemy of the people? If the revolutionary is to be an enemy of the people . . . then I'm an enemy to my own people. When did I sign up for that?*

Life was more complex, he was discovering, than he previously believed.

Starting out with this, he had been young. He was still young. His heart, and a small voice, told him that that was his gravest sin. This conclusion made him sad, yet made him strong, as well. He and the other Jacques did not speak of these matters, but he could tell, he just knew, that the other Jacques also felt and experienced similar changes. Despite his unending love for the spotlight, to be on TV, the other Jacques had grown as he had grown. When Marc said to them, "*Nous vaincrons,*" they didn't repeat it back to him anymore. The words sounded hollow now. Even a little silly. They were not defeated—he still believed that they might conquer, but not in any way that Marc intended. He'd rather be useful somehow.

Cuba.

Exile.

Forever?

As they touched down on the tarmac in Havana and shuffled off the aircraft to commence their new, ungainly lives, far away, in Montreal, Jasper Cross was released from Cuban custody to resume his old life again, although to a posting perhaps more secure than Canada.

They began their new lives in Cuba. No sooner were they settled than they sold their TV. Their faces weren't on it anymore.

CHAPTER 28

1970–71

ON A QUIET SUNDAY EVENING, TWO WEEKS PRIOR TO CHRISTMAS, as Constable Émile Cinq-Mars arrived at the prime minister's residence at 24 Sussex Drive in Ottawa, snow alighted gently upon the grounds, pleasantly decorating trees and shrubbery. Lamplight sparkled on the large, moist flakes, and each vista conveyed a wintry enchantment worthy of the season. Dressed in spiffy, casual attire—a cream jacket, an ascot, dark blue shirt and blue serge trousers—Pierre Elliott Trudeau welcomed him warmly, as though they were old friends.

A fire crackled in the hearth.

"Promise me, Émile," he requested after they were settled before the blaze, "that the dagger will not fall—directly or indirectly—into the rapacious hands of René Lévesque." The whimsy in his tone suggested that he was trying to make light. "Or those of his ilk," he added.

"Actually," Cinq-Mars began. Then hesitated.

"Don't tell me."

"I don't think it will," the policeman, equally spiffy in his dress uniform, tendered. "Rumour has it that they're lovers, though."

"Lovers! Who?"

"The woman who'll be receiving the knife, and our Mr. Lévesque. Which is regrettable, on I can't tell you how many levels." Unable to restrain himself, Cinq-Mars sighed. "That said, she expects the two of you to duke it out as men. Neither of you will possess the advantage of the knife."

"If it is an advantage," Trudeau scoffed. He had offered his guest cognac, coffee and coffee cake, and the policeman, having driven two hundred kilometres up from Montreal, with plans to return that night, consented. The prime minister quipped, "I'm happy to proceed on my own. I'm tired of the dagger taking credit for my success, at least in some circles."

Cinq-Mars appreciated the man's humour about this transaction. Although it helped put him more at ease, he still had to give himself a swift boot in the rump—heel to arse. Here he was, a country boy from Saint-Jacques-le-Majeur-de-Wolfestown, Quebec, and a mere patrolman, kibitzing with the prime minister of Canada. *In his home.* As if he were a visiting dignitary himself.

"She's a stone thrower, our mystery girl. A tosser of rocks," the prime minister recalled. "That's helped me to rationalize this transaction."

At moments, Émile felt a trifle dumb in the prime minister's presence.

"She strikes me as someone opposed to the Order of Jacques Cartier, those windbag neo-fascists."

"For sure," Cinq-Mars happily piped up. "No doubts there."

"Then I'm content," Trudeau added pensively. "We shall see what designs fortune has upon our dagger."

"Actually, sir," Cinq-Mars contradicted him, "I doubt it. Time will tell, but what happens next will remain secret, I suspect. Beyond our purview."

Trudeau chose to soften the young man's defences. "You're an educated man, Émile? You don't talk like an average street cop."

"I have a degree in, ah, animal husbandry."

Trudeau seemed to be enjoying a private laugh. "So that's why."

Cinq-Mars was stumped. "Sir?"

"Your boss. Captain Touton. He asked me to inquire about your education."

"He likes to embarrass me, sir. It amuses him. I think he'll have to get used to educated cops. It's the future trend, in my opinion. But he can't get over my choice of subject. He equates the phrase with fornication. Sheep, in particular. *Husbandry,* you see. He's even more amused that I was once headed for the priesthood—which, come to think of it, he also may equate with fornication."

Trudeau honoured Émile's humour with a laugh, but also offered a small, dismissive gesture of his chin. "Why be embarrassed? You're an intelligent, small-town boy from the countryside, although not a farmer your-self. You went through the most logical progression there can be in Quebec. Priest, until that didn't hold, then veterinarian. Then you found your true vocation, a Montreal cop. That's different, but it tells me you're on your proper course."

"Thank you, sir. I believe I am."

Sagely, the prime minister administered a light rub to the bridge of his nose, as if to sharpen an astute thought. He was unaware that individuals often touched their noses in the presence of Émile Cinq-Mars, as though they felt a need to be thankful for their own modest beaks in the shadow of his mon-strosity. Trudeau's was eminent and decisive, yet well proportioned and no match for the policeman's. Cinq-Mars noticed this, as he usually examined other men's noses. He characterized the prime minister's as intelligent, and the nose of a physically active man.

"I'll be sad to have the knife gone from my hands, but I'm also glad that you have come to retrieve it."

"Why's that, Mr. Prime Minister?" In crossing his ankles, he realized that he had emulated the posture of his host, and quickly uncrossed them again.

"Mainly," Trudeau attested, "I welcome the chance to thank you for your work on the FLQ file. The country owes you—and your colleagues—a tremen-dous debt. In recent days, I've been advised that your contribution must never be publicly acknowledged. Yours or Armand's."

Cinq-Mars sipped his coffee. "You've been talking to my captain."

"Do you possess remarkable powers of deduction to surmise that instantly? A worthy attribute in a detective, I'd say."

The younger man blushed slightly. "Given that I stormed in here that day, raving, demanding to strike a deal for a valuable relic, I assumed that you'd call Captain Touton."

"We had you investigated. But I didn't talk to Armand back then. Only a few days ago, now that matters have calmed down."

Something about that statement struck the policeman as odd, and he jot-ted a mental note. "I don't mean to be falsely modest, sir. I hope to get better at figuring things out. I think I have a knack, but whenever I stumble across what

I believe is a clever deduction—or walk blindly into some lucky ray of comprehension—usually I feel like punching a wall that I didn't think of it sooner. I'm working on my abilities though. I haven't given up." He smiled more broadly then, somewhat embarrassed to have said so much.

"So you agree with him, then?"

The query was issued out of context, yet the young man had no need to pretend that he did not trace the connection. "I do, sir. We're linked to our informant. To associate either of us with solving the case will implicate her. It's imperative that we never be acknowledged or thanked."

"Except privately. Tonight. Here. With my words."

Cinq-Mars lowered his head. He could feel his face burning. "That's a fine exception, sir," he said quietly. "I was only doing my job. But I thank you."

Raising his right hand near his ear, the prime minister drew a few circles in the air, as if stirring a memory. "Last time we met, Émile, you were a detective." As the hand lowered, his forefinger began to shake at him. "Since then, you've helped break the most grievous case in our history." Cinq-Mars followed the hand down to the armrest. "For your troubles, it appears that you've been demoted. You're in uniform. Explain this to me."

Cinq-Mars smiled again. "Sir, I was temporarily upgraded to help with the case. Now that it's solved—it's back to the beat for me."

The prime minister did not appear mollified. "The mayor owes me a favour. After all, I invoked the War Measures Act at his behest."

"I'm willing to earn my rank as I go, sir," Cinq-Mars assured him.

"I'm convinced that you've already earned a promotion."

They finished their cakes and coffee with talk of the debacle in the Montreal Police Department and discussion of the climate on the streets and in the taverns. The prime minister poured another glass of cognac. Perhaps as a prelude to returning them to the business at hand, he displayed a few prized treasures. "I didn't buy these on the black market," he quipped. "I didn't steal them. In my youth, I was wandering through the ancient land of Ur—Iraq, today—and I picked up these tiles, right off the desert floor. I've had them assayed. The inscriptions are Sumerian. They date to the time of Abraham."

The young man dared not touch them, but examined them closely while standing and sipping his cognac, and permitted himself to feel the presence of that ancient time reflected in the artifacts. He acknowledged the allure of antiquated objects. To imagine a figure from Abraham's time—or the great patriarch himself—inscribing a tile, not knowing that one day it would be present in the home of a leader of a foreign country unknown, upon a continent as yet undiscovered to that people—his mind boggled.

The reflective moment was interrupted by a ring at the door, in coded sequence. "Security," the prime minister stated. He moved to the foyer and Cinq-Mars trailed behind. An officer admitted himself.

"Our silent alarms have been triggered, Prime Minister," the snow-covered man informed him, already dripping on the carpet as he removed his cap. "We believe by a dog, but we are investigating. Is everything in order here, sir?"

"We're fine, thank you. We've had no interruptions. Give Lassie my regards."

The excitement over, they returned to the hearth, where Trudeau tossed a log on the fire. "Last month it was a family of raccoons." He remained standing, and stated, with evident solemnity, "I can bring out the Cartier Dagger now, Émile. As you may recall, I had requested a final courtesy."

Cinq-Mars promptly put down his snifter. "Sir, I'm hoping that you will entertain a reasonable condition. The young lady in question will honour your request. She'll reveal what was said on Houde's deathbed. First, she must receive the dagger. She may be turning your condition from the last time back around, by asking for delivery in advance. At least, that's my assessment."

The prime minister put up his hands, as though to brush away his concern. "No problem. I hope you'll forgive my momentary indiscretion."

"Sir?" This time, the sly, older man did have him confused.

Trudeau directed him back into his chair and sat opposite him again. He knitted his hands together and leaned well forward as his voice went lower and became more directed. "I was curious, Émile, to know what the girl in the closet overheard as Houde lay at death's door. Who wouldn't be? He struck quite the figure, Houde did. He lived through astonishing times. In retrospect, I realize that I was requesting highly confidential information—an account, really, of a communication between a dying man and his priest. Initially, I was overcome by curiosity, but I've since reprimanded myself. I no longer seek to hear a word." He brushed his hands together, as if dusting them of crumbs. "I've been paid sufficiently. Overpaid, by the outcome of our difficulties." He resumed his upright posture. "So I want to thank you, Émile, and shall do so by bringing out the knife. No further restitution is required. Our deal is done. Our arrangements concluded."

"Thank you, sir. I have to tell you, although I realize that the stakes were high, you've been a good sport about this. You are losing a valuable posses-sion." He had to remind himself that he was talking—*so casually*—with the prime minister.

"Mmm." Trudeau touched a finger to his lips, and something in his man-ner suggested that he required a meditative moment to pull a thought together. Then he said, "It worked out well." The finger rhythmically tapped his lower lip, before he continued. "Émile, you know that I purchased the knife. A mer-cantile act. So it was never really mine to possess, not in any proper sense. The idea was to remove it from the control of potential fascists, that was one fear, or foreign collectors, that was another. My role, it seems, has been to act as its guardian through a transitional phase. The high road, certainly the legal path, would have been to restore the knife to its rightful owner, the Sun Life company, and to their designated hero, Clarence Campbell. But he was never accepted as the most worthy of recipients, and when you look at the history, really, at a moment in time, Sun Life itself stole the knife. Theirs had been a legal scam—the knife in exchange for an insurance policy—but its value could have insured a man's family for a thousand generations. So, is Sun Life the rightful owner? Legally, perhaps. Morally, it's questionable."

Cinq-Mars weighed in. "The legal is paramount in our society, as a rule."

"I'm a lawyer. I should know, and, I ought to know better than to disagree. We're Catholics, Émile. We both know that, at times, the moral and the legal, if not in opposition, arrive at a place of mutual agitation. I'm not trying to rationalize anything here. I admit that I'm in possession of stolen property. You, on the other hand, you're young, your hands are clean, but you will take the knife from me and, rather than return it to its legal owners, bequeath it to a young woman who mourns her father's death. You don't have a legal leg to stand on, do you?"

"I suppose not, Mr. Prime Minister."

"And yet, not only will you not lose sleep over this, but your conscience probably shines."

Cinq-Mars wound his hands together, and conceded a smile. "I'd say that as a moralist, sir, you make a compelling jurist."

Which made the prime minister chuckle. "Thank you. I'll take that as a compliment, even if it wasn't intended as such. But I still have a point to make, about why surrendering the knife is all right with me. Why it is that I'm comforted by this transaction."

"Comforted?" He wished that he could drop every last residue of self-consciousness and self-awareness and boundless amazement that he was here, in the prime minister's home on a snowy night in December, and just fall utterly into the conversation. He was perpetually outside the talk, seeing himself in it, which was an aspect he just had to endure. An affliction of youth. He knew, though, that he did not want this night to end.

"Sir Herbert Holt determined that the knife should be imparted from war hero to war hero, in perpetuity. Apart from the fact that that meant we'd have to keep going to war, forever, it was a grand design. One that I support. But wait, Émile, have we not recently emerged from a major battle? I had to invoke the War Measures Act, did I not? Did Roger Clément's daughter not commit herself to a heroic undertaking, one with a measure of self-sacrifice? Her effort helped our country resolve its crisis."

"That's true." He felt humbled by the direction the talk had taken, privileged to be the only one to hear this posit.

"She had to experience loss of life. I'm not referring to Pierre Laporte, though there's that. So the knife is being bequeathed to a true patriot. In this case, a heroine. And so, I was a temporary caretaker. With a measure of satisfaction, my stewardship ends, and a proper heroine now receives the relic."

Cinq-Mars nodded. "You've given this some thought."

Trudeau considered that, and shrugged. "The knife did my thinking for me," he said. "I don't mean to be enigmatic. Any *objet d'art* is worthy of our meditation. In dwelling on the knife, on its history, these matters came through, as did my resolve to not ask questions of the dead. I'll leave Houde's final words alone, then, and fetch the knife."

"Sir?" Before the prime minister stood, Cinq-Mars stalled his rise. He held up a hand, as though to physically restrain him. "I apologize, but I have also come with a request."

"Certainly." Trudeau sat back down. "As your mayor owes me, I owe you. What is it?"

"There's no debt, sir. I was doing my job. I don't mean to take up your time, but as you've observed, I'm in uniform tonight. To drive here, I borrowed a squad car from the department."

"I see."

"I told Captain Touton I'd be talking to you, but I also informed him I'd conduct official business. He doesn't know about the dagger changing hands tonight. Nor should he. Nor should anyone." He smiled, amused by his own subterfuge, and regarded his host closely. He noticed Trudeau's eyes dart to the right and down, then return to meet his. "If I may attend to other business then, sir, I'll not be negligent in my duties, or fraudulent in borrowing the car. Also, this other matter gives me a reason to be here, to explain my presence should I need to, without having to mention the old knife."

His host nodded and shared in the subterfuge with a smile. "By all means, Émile, proceed. I'm at your service. What's this about?"

"Thank you, sir. I don't know whether you've been informed, but you have been cited as another's man's alibi. If I may, I'd like to follow that up. I'm still on the case, you see, to solve the original theft of the dagger. More particularly, to solve the murders that occurred that night."

Crossing his legs, and clearly intrigued, Trudeau invited him to proceed.

"On the night of the Richard riot—needless to say, you remember it . . ."

"I was there. Only one man might suggest me as his alibi for that evening."

"Who might that be, sir?"

"Father François Legault. But you're not inquiring after him?"

Cinq-Mars dismissed the concern with a grimace and a shake of his head. "To unravel an old crime, where the trail's gone cold, it's necessary to start from scratch. That means talking to a lot of people and rechecking what they say."

"I see." He crooked his head a little, smacked his lips slightly, then declared, "I did meet up with Father François that night, if that's what you want to know."

"And how was that?"

Trudeau moved his hands apart in a gesture of openness, then brought them together again. "Like me, he was away from the riot, as I recall. I just arrived and assumed that the action would come towards me, to Phillips Square, so I waited for it to present itself. Father François was also in the square that night, apparently to recuperate. He'd had a bit too much excitement already."

"What sort of excitement?"

Animated whenever he spoke, Trudeau waved his hands and flipped through an impressive repertoire of facial expressions. He possessed a mercurial mind and a core moral foundation, but his principal asset as a politician had become his ability to communicate effectively, and to do so wonderfully on television. His wit, which he sprinkled with derisive remarks, snapped into a microphone while faultlessly avoiding the clichés that so riddled the speech of his rivals. He also utilized a plethora of gestures, his mouth, eyes, eyebrows, cheekbones, chin and the tilt of his head active in his cause. In the comfort of the official residence at 24 Sussex Drive, with views from the high escarpment down through the trees and over the Ottawa River partially lit by lamps, he gave Cinq-Mars a brief sampling of those tics, and said, "A weak heart. Which we know about, right? I remember having a terrible thought that evening. Perhaps I shouldn't admit it. But his jacket was undone, you see, and I thought, *It's because he's fat.* A skinny man, such as myself, would have buttoned up. After we sat around for a while, chatting, he buttoned up. Yet—not at first. We were together quite some time—I presume that you want to know all this?"

Excited, Cinq-Mars leaned in. "So the riot was in progress before you met?"

"I didn't go downtown until after things had heated up. Émile. You don't think *he* was involved in the theft of the knife and the murders, do you?"

"Did he initiate your interest in acquiring the knife?"

"I'd say yes, however—" The prime minister suddenly stopped.

"Curious," Cinq-Mars said.

The young man extracted a notepad from his inner jacket pocket to jot down a few lines. Looking up, he wore his grin somewhat sheepishly.

"Forgive me, sir, but were the two of you, or either of you, rioting?"

Trudeau broke from his spell and had a good laugh. "Father François may have wanted to, that's my opinion, but he was restricted by his health. He verbally harried a police officer, I remember that. Come to think of it, I may have pitched in. But no, we were not *rioting*. We were there as interested observers. I'm afraid I can't help you very much, except to verify that, if called upon, I can honestly present myself as the good friar's alibi—and he mine, come to think of it, should either of us require one."

"Has it ever occurred to you that you may?"

The prime minister eyed him curiously. "Your interest, Émile, is in discovering who committed the murders on that fateful night, is it not?"

"That's correct, sir."

Trudeau crossed an arm over his torso, offering his wrist to support the opposite elbow, and placed two fingers, meditatively, along his left cheek. Cinq-Mars presumed that the man had something to say, but the words did not appear to be forthcoming. Instead, the prime minister posed a question. "How did you know that Father François initiated my purchase of the knife?"

"I didn't, until you just told me."

"You appeared to have known that."

"I guessed, sir. But it was a reasoned guess."

"How?"

Cinq-Mars hesitated, sorting through the detritus that had delivered him to that conclusion. "My friend, the young woman, told me that you possessed the knife. I examined everyone who was potentially involved, of course, and the only one from that night with a connection to you was Father François. He named you as his alibi. He didn't know it, but in doing so, he tipped me off that he might be involved. Father François associated you with that night. When it came time to find a buyer, your name popped to mind—his mind. As well, of course, he's incriminated as being a part of Houde's deathbed confession. Though what was said on that specific matter is not known to me."

Browsing through the policeman's thinking, Trudeau lightly drew his right hand up and down his opposite forearm. "All right, then. But how did you come to consider Father François, of all people, 'potentially involved,' as you put it? I find this quite alarming, I must say."

Cinq-Mars rocked his head from side to side, as though sifting theories. "I search for connections. Another man murdered around that incident was Michel Vimont, a friend of Roger Clément, who was driving a limo for a mid-rank gangster at the time named Harry Montford. Tracing the tracks of Vimont's life, I discovered that he used to be the chauffeur for Monsignor Charbonneau."

"There's a blast from the past."

"The much-maligned, much-reviled, Monsignor Charbonneau."

"And much-revered," countered Trudeau.

"Yet he had many enemies. I decided to discover if he had any friends. The one name that shone through on that list—"

"Father François Legault. Makes sense. Those two, I mean."

"Father François was Houde's priest, he was Roger Clément's friend—he's maintained close contact with the family—he was Charbonneau's confrere—"

"And he also knew me."

"From your *Cité Libre* days. If the dagger had been heisted by the right, how could any of those right-wing clowns go to *you* to help them out by buying the dagger? The idea is ludicrous. So there had to be an intermediary. Another. Someone who both thought of you and could approach you. Among all the names I've dealt with, which one was leading me back to you?"

"Father François."

"Although I did not know it for a fact until you just told me."

"Émile, I hate to think what kind of detective you'll make after you develop the powers of deduction you seem so willing to disparage in yourself."

Cinq-Mars smiled briefly and realized in that instance that he had managed to forget himself and his frets for quite a few minutes. He was feeling good. This conversation had become an excellent dress rehearsal for what still lay ahead. He asked a few questions to draw out what Trudeau was willing to impart about how he acquired the knife, and the prime minister seemed to enjoy the retelling.

"The thug's name was Harry, or Larry, or—Barry!" Trudeau said at one point. "It's probably of no importance now, but he told me the name of his boss, too."

"He did?"

"De Bernonville."

"Whom you met in Asbestos, sir. Maybe that's why he was willing to sell to you. Not that he had scruples."

Trudeau rose to fetch the knife, took a few steps, then retraced them. "Émile," he asked, "do you know why I admitted you into my office that day? You arrived to see me without an appointment, carrying just the tip of the dagger."

Surprised by this turn, the cop put his notebook away. "No, sir. I presumed that presenting the knife's tip to you snagged your attention. Perhaps, are you saying—? Did it have to do with what we previously discussed?"

"Which was?" the prime minister quizzed him.

"You said that the commissioner thought I looked intelligent. That you were only talking to reporters in those days—"

The prime minister, while smiling, was now waving him quiet. "I was only having a bit of fun with you. But before that, before I asked the commissioner to check you out—why did I even go that far, rather than have you turfed out on your backside?"

"I don't know, sir," Cinq-Mars acknowledged.

"The knife kept you in the building."

"Sir?" Their eyes locked momentarily, until the prime minister broke that connection.

He returned to his chair, and stood behind it, resting his weight upon his forearms interwoven across the top of the chair's high back. "The previous night, I solicited the knife's help. Hearing that from me, you may want to reconsider your vote, if it happens that you voted for me. But it's true. I've done it before, even though I'm really not inclined towards magic. We all remember the debacle with Mackenzie King, all the spirit-talk he was engaged in—*brother.* I wouldn't want that on my record. If you tell the press, Émile, I'll deny it, of course."

"Sir, I wouldn't—" He didn't finish, realizing that the prime minister expected no response and was even having some fun with him.

"I asked the knife to help me. Call it a prayer, if you will. The next day, I heard that a police officer was trying to barge into my office. I was having you dismissed, when—out of the meditation from the previous evening, or out of some intuitive power that the knife itself possessed, I felt that I should admit you. A swift hunch."

Cinq-Mars nodded, not knowing how to respond further.

"I still did not act completely on that intuition. First, I asked for your evidence. Then, when the commissioner attested to your intelligence, and mentioned that you were representing Armand Touton—who once tried to recruit me, did you know?"

"Really?" A surprise, but he wouldn't put anything past his boss.

"I passed on that opportunity, but not without giving him a bit of a head's up. The episode gave me respect for him. After you had evoked his name, I felt strongly that I should see you. The tip of the knife clinched it. So I did."

Trudeau kept glancing down at him, then looking away, as though evaluating how his words were being received, as though to determine how much he might dare reveal to this young man.

"But the primary reason—" He stopped. This time, his gaze travelled through the window, to the falling snow. They both heard a dog bark three times. When he spoke again, his voice had gone sombre. Cinq-Mars could hear him, clear as a bell, but he guessed that if he moved five feet away the man would seem mute to him. "I felt the work of the knife in this . . . in your presence . . . but earlier than that, in the reports I was hearing of a half-mad Montreal police officer making a scene in the outer office. That was sufficiently bizarre to warrant my attention. So you see, Émile—and I trust that you appreciate the irony—only now that I am about to surrender the dagger to you have I come to believe in it. To trust it, in a way. In the past, I've had my suspicions that the rumours about the relic might have some faint validity. Those suspicions have grown. That's one more reason why I want you to do your level best to protect it."

The policeman did not feel he could mislead the prime minister in any way. "I will exert my influence, sir, on behalf of the knife's security. Once out of my hands, it will be beyond my control."

Trudeau nodded, conceding to that reality. "Do your best, Émile. That's all I ask. I've come to believe that that might be significant." He looked to the window again, as the barking had resumed, sounding closer now. "Lassie," he noted, smiling, "seems chagrined."

†††

On the drive home that night, Émile Cinq-Mars had a little over two hours on his own to stew over a dilemma. He wondered if he was capable of exercising a similar restraint to that shown by the prime minister of Canada. Anik Clément was willing to tell him what she had gleaned in the closet as Houde lay dying, expecting that he would then submit the information to Pierre Trudeau. Would he have the willpower to let her know that that information was no longer required? Or would he listen to her story anyway, for his own edification?

After all, was he not a policeman, an aspiring detective? Did he not traffic in secrets? Did he not still have a crime to solve?

Along the highway, he pulled over. He put on his flashing cherries so that passing trucks and cars would be less likely to ram him from behind.

Snow fell lightly, enough to thwart visibility.

He snapped on the interior overhead light and picked up the modest wooden box that housed the Cartier Dagger.

There, by the side of the road, he took it out.

If the prime minister believed in it, and had asked the knife to help him with a national crisis, then why should he not request help to solve his own critical case? What possible harm could that cause? Besides, was the knife not intricately involved in his investigation, given that it had been the murder weapon? Given that it already knew the answers he sought?

He held it in his grip awhile.

Then, carefully, he put the knife back in its cradle and turned off the interior light. He had to wait for a car to pass before pulling out onto the road. The driver slowed, then braked again, not atypical of a speeding motorist passing a police cruiser, but perhaps overdone. As the car passed him, Cinq-Mars spotted a collie in the rear seat turning to look at his vehicle. Cinq-Mars remained still—frozen. *Lassie!* The car carried on, and vanished over a low crest down the road. Slowly, he pulled away from the shoulder and drove on. He kept his speed down awhile. His blood ran cold. After a mile or so, he remembered to turn off his flashing overheads. Then he sped up, but never encountered that car again.

†††

Émile Cinq-Mars met with Anik when she was alone at her mother's house. He carried the treasure, within its wooden case, inside a shoebox.

"You look like a terrorist," she said, "toting a homemade bomb."

"I feel like a thief. Toting a bomb."

He opened the box on the kitchen table, but suddenly Anik did not want to look at it. Not yet. This was the foul weapon that had killed her father, which remained her governing interest. Her curiosity about the knife, its appearance, its effect on her, still resided across an emotional and turbulent divide.

"I'll check it out," she promised, "when I get my courage up. On my own."

Anik had recently rented an apartment, but her old bed remained available to her in her mother's house. She hid the knife under the box spring, then the two of them ventured outside for a walk in the winter air.

"Nobody followed you, right?"

"Already you're paranoid. Owning that knife won't be easy."

Anik smiled, while willing to take his point seriously. She told him, "I don't really own it. Nobody does. Or can. Don't worry, it won't be under the bed for long."

"I took precautions getting here. Every trick in the book. Nobody followed me."

For a while, they strolled along in silence.

"What about the other guys?" she asked. "Laporte's killers, Paul Rose and them? Any news?"

"Do you know where they are? Can you help?"

She appeared a bit cross, knitting her brow. "I don't know where they are, and I'm not going to help. I've meddled too much already. But you'll find them. I have a really strong impression that they have a lot of friends who aren't feeling quite so friendly anymore."

"That's been my impression also. They got away with hiding behind a false wall once. That won't happen again. They shouldn't have shown up the cops the way they did. Smearing their fingerprints around, that sort of thing. Now every cop takes it personally. Next time, we'll do better."

"I can imagine." She seemed far away from him, adrift.

"Next time, cops will blow up a building before they risk leaving someone inside undetected."

He didn't receive the smile he was hoping for, and they resumed their quiet time together.

Without speaking, the pair decided upon a mutual destination—a scruffy, nearby park. Each year, the grass came up, and each year, it was worn back down to dirt by children at their summer games and by adults wandering through for a small dose of tranquility. Now it was well groomed with about an inch of fresh, powdery snow. The benches had been cleared, most likely by teenagers needing a place to neck in winter, or somewhere to sit and smoke, and by aging, saggy bachelors who'd arrive each morning with small sacks of cornmeal for the cooing pigeons. As the pair sat down, a flock flew into the park, appraising the possibilities.

"I'm presuming that you understand the risk, Anik. No one can ever know that you possess the knife. That kind of information makes you a target."

"You know," she said. She smiled.

He shook his head. "I'll keep it to myself. But I don't want to know anything about the knife—what you do with it, its whereabouts, whatever. Not unless you donate it to a museum."

"I'm not giving it to a museum," she revealed. "It's stolen property. But why don't you want to know? Can't you trust yourself?"

The question was valid—a good one, really. He knew he'd take knowledge of the knife to his grave, and never betray her, so that wasn't the source of his anxiety. "I don't want you to trust a soul. Beginning with me. Tell me what you tell everyone else—absolutely nothing. If you were to tell me about the knife, I'd be afraid that you'd speak to someone else someday. A future boyfriend, a husband, a child. That won't be good, Anik. It'll never be good."

She sat still on the bench, observing a pigeon. She thought it looked like a juvenile delinquent. Maybe the bird had been studying the attitude of kids in the neighbourhood. "Trudeau knows I have it," she said.

A valid concern. "I haven't mentioned your name, but he knows it's going to Roger Clément's daughter. So, yeah, he knows you have it."

"So I'm at risk."

"That's what I'm saying." Cinq-Mars nodded. "Truth is, I want you to think that way. I believe Trudeau's accepted the loss. He feels it's been a good trade. He won't seek you out. He won't be inclined to blab about it, either, not as long as he's a politician. How can he bray that he had once owned a murder weapon? Then again, there's not much stopping him. Someday, he'll be out of office. That's why I want you to be wary of everyone."

If her friend was looking to scare her, or at least make her especially cautious, he was succeeding. "Armand knows I have it. That means you told him."

"He'll keep your secret." He placed his hand on her wrist. "But, Anik, you see, this is what I'm talking about. I didn't tell him."

"You must've. Émile—he knows. He called me while he was negotiating with the kidnappers. By then, he already knew I bargained for the knife."

Cinq-Mars did not dispute her argument—rather, he nodded to confirm it. "He had a few things to go on, that's true. But you see? I never told him. He just called you and made you admit to having the knife, or to say that you were expecting to get it soon, by pretending that he already knew. It's an old technique. I didn't tell him."

She crossed her ankles, just for the relief of getting one foot off the frozen ground, and squeezed herself more tightly against the chill. "It's a nice lecture, Émile. Armand said similar things. He was worried that other people would come after me. I didn't think he was only digging for knowledge. Look, I intend to keep quiet. I'm not telling anyone. Not even my mother."

"Good for you. That's how it has to be. Whatever measures that go beyond your death—"

"Oh, will you stop worrying. I'm not a child, Émile."

"Just don't trust people."

"I heard you the first time. Honestly. Who are you, anyway? Émile Cinq-Mars, country boy. Comes to the big city and now distrusts everyone. He's rational about all things. What's happened to you, country boy?"

He shrugged, and offered back a smile to her tease. "I've figured out a few things, I guess."

"Like what?"

"I have my secrets, too," he said, being cagey.

"I'm sure you do."

"Anyway, I still have a job in front of me."

"Trudeau's report?" she inquired.

"What you heard in the closet. Yes. The report to our prime minister." Cinq-Mars nodded, thinking, wondering. "I can set that up."

She shook her head no. He expected that she'd choose the method they had already agreed upon. "He might throw stones at me." The remark broke them up a little. "I'll tell you what I heard in the closet. Then you can tell him."

Cinq-Mars stared straight ahead then, at a few cars in their bright progress down the adjacent boulevard. He was waiting to hear himself say something of ready importance, waiting to hear himself stop her from speaking. From a distance, a dog's bark distracted him.

"Émile?" Anik inquired.

†††

As the priest admitted a friend into the church house from out of the snapping cold, Teilhard, the parish cat, poked its nose through the front door. Before its passage could be blocked, he scooted outside. The animal did not go far. This was a day for neither man nor domestic beast. The temperature had plummeted not long after Christmas, staying that way into mid-January. With its first full breath of icy air, the tabby appeared to freeze on the porch, then, stiffly, tried lifting all four paws off the mat at once, doing a dance. Bending down, laughing, the visiting policeman snatched the cat up to return it to the temperate climate of the rectory.

"You have a way with animals."

"Poor thing's in shock. He didn't imagine it could be so cold out."

"Now he'll be depressed. Teilhard is miffed to be cooped up inside with the likes of me. Émile, you wanted to be a vet. What would you prescribe for my disgruntled feline?"

Cinq-Mars set the animal down on the hall runner, petting it a little more and receiving appreciative purrs in return. "A youthful playmate might do," he suggested. "A female kitten."

"Ha! There's a thought. Are you sure you're not thinking of yourself?"

"Father. Please." He blushed, though.

The priest laughed, his big belly jiggling in his merriment. Cinq-Mars peeled his boots off by prying the heels down with his toes, then allowed Father François to give him a hand in removing his overcoat. "You'll have a cup of tea, to brace yourself from the cold?"

"Thank you, Father."

"Good!" He relayed the request to his housekeeper, and the two men made themselves comfortable in the living-room armchairs. "Now, to what do I owe the grand pleasure? I'm on to you. I know you're not checking up on me without a good—probably a devious—reason."

The younger man chuckled lightly. "Don't you visit parishioners, Father, to see how they're doing? Why be suspicious of me?"

"When I check on the welfare of my flock, I don't do so equipped with the power to put them in jail. Perhaps I can ship them off to a lower inferno— although that's arguable—but they still have the option of an audience with St. Peter—who's tough, we're told, but fair. The War Measures Act, on the other hand, or whatever it's called now—the Public Order Act—is a powerful instrument without recourse to the courts or the saints. You could click your fingers and have me locked up, Émile. Is that just?"

"I'm not sure, Father. But I'd like to try it sometime, just for fun."

The remark caught the priest by surprise, and he responded with another chuckle. Evidently, he was in a good mood, and smiled broadly as he watched the tabby leap onto the policeman's lap. Cinq-Mars helped the animal settle in, petting its greyish, black-streaked head.

"You've made a new pal."

"Indeed."

"Teilhard believes priests have private pipelines to God, to dial up the weather. I've tried to explain, my God lets the weather take care of itself. My God maintains the attitude of a parent, one who believes His children ought to be seen but seldom heard. God will heed my prayers," Father François continued in a whisper, "but only if He has nothing better to occupy His time, and never to effect a change of weather for a cat." Then he returned to his usual voice levels. "But Teilhard—try telling him that. He's not been persuaded. He blames the current cold snap on me."

The cat looked over at him as though to agree.

"The workings of God—for that matter, of men—confuse us all, not just cats," Cinq-Mars offered.

"Touché. That's a hint, though, isn't it? You're here on a serious errand." While he was doing his best to flaunt a relaxed manner and keep things light, Father François gave the impression of a man trying hard to be at ease, coming across instead as worried.

"As you can see, Father, I'm not in uniform."

"Plain clothes."

"Off-duty."

"Ah. I wished I realized. But it's not too late. There's still time to cancel the tea and break out the port."

"Or have our tea," Émile suggested, striking a compromise, "and a brief, serious discussion, then move on to the port."

"Fine with me. A warning, though. Our electric kettle's on the fritz. The water takes awhile to boil. But I'm eager, Émile. What's on your mind? Now that Laporte's killers are behind bars, you and your fellow officers must be feeling vindicated. What did my old friend call me—a bleeding-heart liberal? Well, Trudeau, not Teilhard, is the cat who's swallowed the canary now. Insufferable, don't you think? The luck of that man, although I'm also pleased with the final outcome."

The nod Cinq-Mars proffered, rocking his chin slightly, appeared noncommittal. He was playing his hand close to the vest. "My colleagues are relieved, sure. We pulled double shifts for months."

"You could probably use some time off yourself. Instead of interrogating me."

Cinq-Mars cocked his head. "A harsh word," he pointed out. He tried to not let his tone go grave. "I want to check a few facts, Father, as I've been doing for months, with respect to the Richard riot."

Father François shook his head. "You'd think that man would give it up, once and for all."

"Captain Touton? No, Father," Cinq-Mars corrected him. "I'm here on my own. I'm the one obsessed by those old events now."

"Then poor you. Too bad you can't take a pill for such an ailment. So tell me, how may I help alleviate your wretched curse?"

"Father," Cinq-Mars spoke quietly, his fingers lightly caressing the ears of Teilhard, "if you don't mind, I'd like our tea to arrive, then I'd appreciate closing the doors, to assure our privacy."

The priest clucked his tongue. "I have a wee problem with that scheme. My housekeeper. I tend to close the doors on her whenever I open the port. She'll be arching an eyebrow for a fortnight."

Cinq-Mars lifted the cat onto the floor, weary of the weight. "Then we'll have to break open the port, so your punishment won't be in vain."

"A shrewd mind." The priest nodded. "You're unorthodox. I admire that."

Ensconced, finally, to his liking, with even Teilhard dispatched from the room after the tea's arrival, Cinq-Mars asked the cleric if he had anything to say about the night of the Richard riot.

"Say?" the priest asked. "You once aspired to the priesthood, but that old desire does not elevate you to be my Father Confessor."

"She was in the closet, Father," Cinq-Mars told him.

"Excuse me?" He hesitated before asking his next question. "Who was?" And hesitated again. "What closet?"

Cinq-Mars nodded, as though to relay that his host had managed to figure out the question, even if he wasn't willing to admit to it. "Anik, Father. She was in the closet when you took Camillien Houde's last confession. As the English say, 'The jig is up.'"

The priest's natural jocularity dissipated, and he sought momentary refuge in his tea. Cinq-Mars noted that his first concern, when next he spoke, was for his office. "Émile, a privileged conversation. I have never repeated what was said back then, but more importantly, no one should. Not even Anik."

"She's no more bound by your oath than I am."

The padre's head jerked back as if from an impact. "Both of you are bound by the moral issue here. The mayor's confession was between himself and God—I was merely an intermediary."

"I understand that, Father. Nonetheless, information has been obtained."

The priest's second concern, Cinq-Mars observed, was for Anik. "That poor child. We talked about the death of her father, Houde and me. And it was, in a word, grotesque."

"I know," Cinq-Mars told him.

They gazed at one another steadily.

The priest revealed, then, a third concern—this one for himself. "What she must think of me."

The cop did not respond, but studied his hands.

Father François declared, "I think we're past due for the port."

"As you like," Cinq-Mars concurred.

The tea was set aside, the port poured, and Cinq-Mars was content with his first sips, warming bones that still felt a chill from his trek through the cold.

"That's better," the priest surmised. "Now, what is it you'd like to know that you have not already gleaned from Anik's wayward eavesdropping? Oh, that *child*."

Cinq-Mars carefully formed his question. "Her testimony gives me information, but not explanation. You were involved in the sale of the murder weapon, but why? How did that come about? Why would anyone ask you, of all people, to be an intermediary for that task?"

The large man shrugged and resorted briefly to his port. "The sellers found themselves in desperate straits. Their precious knife had become a liability. De Bernonville wanted only money. Houde desired his legacy enhanced, so that he might be seen as a great Quebec hero. How could that happen with two men dead? One, a friend of his. The other, a public servant. The knife not only had the power to incarcerate him again, it now had the power to pummel his legacy. Potentially, he might be remembered only as an accomplice to murder."

The telephone rang, but Father François indicated that the housekeeper would answer.

"And the other one?" Cinq-Mars dared to ask.

"What other one?"

He smiled. "Politics makes strange bedfellows, they say. That must be equally true of crime."

"More so, I expect," Father François admitted, and offered an affirmative guttural grunt.

A knock sounded against the door from the kitchen, and the housekeeper poked her head in. "Telephone, Father."

"I am not to be disturbed, Madame Caron."

"The port!" she called out, and almost stormed in. "At this time of day!"

"We are discussing a matter of the utmost gravity, Madame Caron. The *utmost*—" Father François paused on the word—"gravity." After she had vanished once again, he confided, "Our code for death. Please depart with sombre visage."

"Of course."

Impossible to fathom now, Cinq-Mars was thinking, but his life might have gone this way. Were it not for the upheavals in Church and state, slipping into a priest's cassock might have become his most natural and available endeavour. He, too, might have brokered his days negotiating the terms of his existence with housekeepers and cats. As the lives of priests went, Father François had not settled for the common routine, having chosen instead to be politically active and involved, perhaps, in criminal conspiracy. Yet he, too, had failed to evade the curse of the cassock, and slowly, steadily, succumbed to a lonely bachelorhood. Cinq-Mars felt relieved, and thanked God on the spot, that he might hope to avoid that destiny.

"Where were we?" Father François inquired.

Cinq-Mars did not want him to feel that their discussion was anything less than friendly. He lifted his wee crystal glass and declared, "I was sipping my port, Father. You'll forgive me, but that's where my concentration lies at the moment."

The priest winked at him and raised his own. Finishing, he poured himself another, and held the bottle across for Cinq-Mars to stretch out and receive.

"The other fellow," Father François embarked. "Camille Laurin, you mean? As Houde was keen on his legacy, so was Laurin dedicated to his political future. He no more wanted to be associated with a murder weapon than he wanted to contract leprosy. Of course he wanted to sell—everyone was desperate to sell. The problem was how. No one had experience pawning stolen artifacts. What they *did* know was that two men besides themselves had been involved in the heist—you don't mind if I use that word? A fun word. Heist."

"Go ahead. Now, when you say two other men, you're referring to . . . ?"

"Duplessis. Because he initiated the idea of stealing the knife. Roger was commissioned, shall we say, by him to swipe the knife. But nobody, not even Roger, wanted Duplessis to have it. I'm sure Carole Clément would have had his scalp had that occurred. When it came time to sell the knife, the premier might have presented himself as a potential buyer, except that he was notoriously poor, a pauper in his personal life. While he was a man of many marvels, no one figured that he could tap our tax money to purchase stolen property. Even if he could, it would have rotted Houde's socks, not to mention Laurin's, to see Duplessis acquire the knife. So he was out of the picture in the blink of an eye."

"So that left the second man," Cinq-Mars intimated.

"Me. Who represented the Catholic Church. Never mind that I didn't really, and that Monsignor Charbonneau, whom I did represent, was poorer than Duplessis, and poorer than me. Which is saying something. Like *le Chef*, we were willing to receive the knife from Roger for free, but we did not have the means to purchase it ourselves. But the sellers were not aware of our circumstances. They figured that, since I was a priest, I was probably representing the Church that dreadful night in Dominion Square as we stood below the heels of the Scottish poet. My resources, then, might conceivably be the resources of the Church. Perhaps, it's true that I guided them into thinking that way. Also, their culpability was already known to me, so I was a safe person to contact. So, they called. Would I like to buy the Cartier Dagger?"

Cinq-Mars encouraged him, tipping his glass. "That put you on the spot."

"It did. I had to grasp this matter quickly. If I did as they desired and brought it to the attention of the bishop, I'd risk allowing the conservative element within the Church to get their hands on it. It's alleged to have properties, you know. The liberal element—we're stronger now, but at the time we were an endangered species. So I concocted the scheme to get Trudeau interested in buying the knife. He had money, he was a risk taker, an adventurer—the illicit side of the bargain would not likely deter him."

"You gave it considerable thought," Cinq-Mars praised.

Father François ignored him, and in rhythm to his words, scratched his kneecap. "Unlike Houde and Laurin, he'd never been on the periphery of killing anybody. And I thought I could exploit his romantic weakness for the mythology of the knife, its cultural and historic properties, even for its purported magic. That was a hunch, but a good one. As well, he's Catholic—more religious than he lets on—which was important to me. So a door opened, at least in my mind. I could imagine that someday he might bequeath the knife back to the Church, should the Church become more interesting to us all, more progressive. That was the best I could do under the circumstances."

"Speaking," Cinq-Mars mused, "as you were a while back, of rotted socks—"

The parish priest waited, his head dipped low and tilting forward, his body slumped well back in his chair with his hands knitted together again, resting upon the hillock of his bounteous belly.

"—it must have rotted yours dealing with de Bernonville, to know that money Trudeau paid for the relic would support him."

Father François sighed, as though the burden remained with him. "Especially after that night in the park, him going off half-cocked like that, stabbing Roger—to see him benefit in any way, that was difficult to accept."

"Why did he do it, do you think, stab Roger? Go off half-cocked? Again, it's the explanations I'm hungry for." Cinq-Mars could not dwell upon the matter at the moment, but he noted to himself that he'd become quite an adroit liar. A good thing that he laboured as a cop, for he might have made a formidable miscreant. He had to hold his exuberance in check, pretend that he had already known what he had only just now discovered: *de Bernonville killed Roger. I've solved it.*

The priest tossed up his hands briefly, as though to appeal to the realm of chaos for an answer. "The man's a madman, a maniac. What did anybody expect? They thought he was a nice guy, a charmer, an entertaining fop? A dandy to invite up to the cottage for a barbecue and a swim? A bon vivant to deliver a bon mot over whiskey and cigars? What excuses did they make for the man? He liked to chat up the teenagers. About what? Methods of torture? I wanted to scream in Houde's ear, even while he lay dying, 'You idiot. He's a Nazi! He tortured his own countrymen. He killed men himself. He sentenced others to the firing squad. He sent decent men and women, French Jews and Catholics alike, to graves, to concentration camps, into forced labour. What do you expect from a fiend like that? Witty conversation? What, exactly, did you expect?'"

By the conclusion of his spiel, the heavy man was half-bounding out of his chair, the veins in his reddening temples more marked. He settled back then, and his guest had the impression that Father François had reminded himself to be calm, for he did not possess a constitution for intemperate outbursts.

"Sometimes, in this land, we delude ourselves. That's a great part of our heartbreak."

"In any land, I think," Cinq-Mars considered.

"We have a knack. A genius."

The policeman gave the priest time to collect himself. He had come to the rectory to undertake a subterfuge. So far, the matter was going well.

"You ask why he killed Roger. A good question. One that's unanswerable. Among ourselves, those who were there that night, we have tried to delve into his heart and mind. Why else did Houde ask that I become his priest as he lay dying, if not to discuss that night with me, alone, under the seal of secrecy? And me, the left winger. I've broken bread with Laurin, who puts on a good show now that he's in the Parti Québécois. Really, in his heart, he sits to the political right of Genghis Khan's hangman. What did we discuss? A priest who is meant to know the hearts of men, and Dr. Laurin, the psychiatrist, who is meant to know their minds? We discussed the heart and mind of Count Jacques Dugé de Bernonville."

The port gave him an excuse to pause, and this time they leaned across, at the priest's instigation, to clink glasses. Both men drank to their own good health.

"What did you surmise, the two of you?"

"Laurin had his cockamamie notions, his usual psychobabble. This is what I intuit, Émile, and I trust this thought: de Bernonville was more like me than I care to admit."

"I don't follow." The thread was unexpected, for he'd be hard pressed to discern two lives more divergent than the Nazi's and the rebel priest's.

For a few moments, it appeared as though Father François really didn't care to admit to the similarities between himself and the count.

Then he began. "In my youth, my politics took me further to the left than I care to acknowledge today. I believed in revolution, even that. I also believed that revolution was as inevitable as the next ice age. A matter of an interval, sluggish though it may be. But my politics then, Émile, are best summed up as *idealistic*. I was fiercely derisive of the status quo, conscious of every failing of whatever regime had assumed power—which was never difficult, not here in Quebec, under that megalomaniac's consumptive gaze. But one tyrant is not necessarily the equal of another."

"Duplessis, say, compared to a Hitler." Cinq-Mars felt the need to contribute.

The priest shrugged. "Same birthday, those two—a year apart, but oceans apart politically, despite the natural sympathy of one for the other. Duplessis was a quaint potentate, no worse. In the fifties, we were learning more about the tyranny of Stalin, and that dashed a few lefty illusions. When I reflect upon how the young people we recently dispatched to Cuba think, I know that there but for fortune, go I."

"Really?" He was not surprised that Father François would vouch for them.

"I might have been persuaded, in the right company, or the wrong company, to commit such acts. Trying to acquire the dagger—I assumed there'd be no violence. I could not imagine that two men would die. There I was, a naïve priest, involved in an illicit enterprise that came to a tragic end. Idealism walks on the wild side and gets crushed by the real world. Is that so different from the experience of those now in Cuba?"

"Speaking as a policeman, they committed the more heinous crimes. Your crime, and it is a failing, has been to be a closed-mouthed witness."

"I don't disagree with you. Yet there, but for fortune."

Cinq-Mars adjusted his weight in the chair and moved a hand down his jaw and neck in the midst of his contemplation. "But how," he asked, "does that make you at all like the count? Are you suggesting that he was once an idealistic young Nazi, deserving our sympathy?"

"He was never deserving of a sympathetic nod from a soul on this earth. God may find the capacity to love such people. Mortal men need not bother." He chuckled mildly, making his large belly quake. "All right. So the socialist in me is talking, not the priest, but life is jam-packed with contradictions."

"I'll forgive you, Father."

"Thank you, my son. And yet, I tell you, de Bernonville and I were more alike than I care to acknowledge. You see, the count *recognized*, as have I, belatedly, that those who aspired to one movement or another—my left, or the right of Houde and Laurin—were innocent in the ways of the world. This society's eminent names, Abbé Lionel Groulx and Henri Bourassa, and that slew of followers and potentates, many of whom should've known better, all enchanted by the rise of some great leader to reshape their existence, to reconstitute their paltry lives as men—infantile! Philosophically, socially, psychologically, politically—infantile! The count wanted to make that point. He'd grown weary of aimless discussion. What uprising could there be without action, without death, without carnage, without murder? And so, he *murdered* poor Roger, to deliver us from our innocence, to stain our lives and our souls for all time, to *demonstrate* the difference between our idle chatter and pathetic posturing and what it really meant to be a Nazi."

Cinq-Mars was finding knots amid the threads that were difficult to unravel. "Are you suggesting, Father, that we'd be better off if we all went around killing each other?" He was trying to lessen the other man's earnestness.

The priest didn't seem to mind the question, initially. "According to de Bernonville, yes." He wet his lips. "But the glory of our people, our greatest blessing, which is something that a man like him could never appreciate and would only seek to destroy, is that we've remained peaceful. Our penchant for rioting and outbursts aside—you know, for a Latin people, we've stayed within the bounds of decorum, don't you think? Especially when you consider that we derive from rowdy stock, Émile. We're not a nation of clockmakers. Of priests and nuns, perhaps, and of farmers, but our forefathers also explored every nook and cranny of this continent, long before the Americans knew it was there. Lewis and Clark go west, and who do they find? Indians and French-men. They ask, 'Where do we go?' And a French guide says, 'Follow the trail I marked.' So no, my son. Guard your tone in the future or you'll be served no more port—we should not go around killing each other. We've managed to do very little of that and must stay the course. For the sake of all humanity, I suggest it. At this point, if *we* can't be peaceful, who can? Now, you'll for-give me for preaching, but what has happened here, Émile, while hard won, has all been *forming*. We don't know our way. Partially because we lie to our-selves, and defeat ourselves, and do not accomplish enough on our own, and partially because it's all been so difficult and—I know, I know, the Church, despite its extraordinary history has also gotten in the way of our progress. And the English, well, I'm not one of those who blames them for everything, for that *is* infantile, but there's so many more of them on this continent and they've only been forming, too, finding their way. Canadians would probably be Americans if not for our influence. So I say, Émile, let's accomplish a whole lot more. Learn more and do more so we won't always act out of weakness. We have driven down a few dark roads, but we have miraculously avoided the great tyranny of war. We can build on that. Let's accomplish much, then, out of our potency, if a priest may use such a word, and out of our strength—the opposite of Laurin's vision—we can decide how things will be with us. Soon enough we'll know what to do with our rugged, cold, astounding homeland."

The priest had begun sermonizing, and respectfully, Émile assumed a med-itative posture to reflect upon his words. He was impressed by the sense of time and long struggle, the wrestling with processes, and ideas, and one's own con-science embedded in the man's acquired wisdom. *Experience*, he thought, might be the word he was searching for. The priest had perhaps not accomplished so much in his time upon the earth, but he had been involved in many projects, and had examined the world, at least as it had been presented to him in his vicinity. Cinq-Mars admired that in the man.

The young cop had taught himself—and his mentor, Touton, had under-scored the lessons—to lose neither the objectives nor the threads of a conversation. He felt obliged to pull the priest back to the raw core of this discussion.

"Father, you are both a material witness, and, arguably, an accomplice, in the death of Roger Clément. Would you not agree?"

Reluctantly, the priest did. "We heard that de Bernonville has expired, although no one knows for sure. So I doubt that your investigation will result in a trial. If it comes to that, then yes, Émile. As the English say, the jig is up."

They sat in the gloom of the afternoon awhile and continued to sip port. As he stood to depart, Cinq-Mars thanked his host, then suggested that he owed him a few words of apology.

"Why's that, Émile? We only speak truth today. What apology is required?"

"We've spoken truth, Father. But I've not been thoroughly forthcoming."

"How's that?"

His boots on, Cinq-Mars adjusted his coat over his shoulders and fixed the collar, which had gone inside out. From the pockets, he retrieved his hat and gloves.

"Forgive me, Father, but I must tell you that Anik Clément was in the closet, and heard everything that passed between you and the late mayor."

"As you said," Father François noted.

"I asked Anik to tell me nothing of that conversation. To keep it between herself, you, Mayor Houde and God. That's what she's done."

The rotund man stepped back and cast his glance away to consider this report. When he returned to gaze upon the aspiring detective, a smile bent the corners of his lips. "So you have tricked me, Émile."

"I have, Father."

"But I don't understand. How did you acquire a confidence, shall we say, in my guilt? You told me that I sold the knife."

"Trudeau let slip that part. He also told me that when he met you during the riot, you were physically exercised. Your coat was unbuttoned. To me, it sounded as though you might have been running. You've never been a jogger. What had occurred that night, I asked myself, to burn a fire under the seat of your pants?"

The priest blew out a gust of air and smiled again. "I should be enraged. Instead, our talk today has left me strangely unburdened. I will deny it, of course, in a court of law," he said, but he was enjoying the game now, "but you have proved yourself today, twice over, and require no forgiveness."

"Twice over, Father?" He pulled his wool cap onto his head and donned his gloves for the frigid burst of air soon to assail him.

"You've succeeded in your work as a detective, Émile. You've succeeded also in the work of a priest, in allowing me to unburden myself after all these years. Thank you. But next time, I'll be sharper. I shall not drink port with you so early in the day again."

The cat bolted past them once more, and again the policeman made the arrest, depositing Teilhard back from where he came. "I don't think he's too bright."

"Right you are. I would never allow a smart cat into my house. You've been the only exception, and look what's happened here."

Cinq-Mars went on his way, hunching his shoulders to fend against an Arctic howl.

CHAPTER 29

1971

TIME HAD PASSED, YET ÉMILE CINQ-MARS STILL NEEDED MORE TO bolster himself for his next planned encounter. He pored over files and notes, rehearsed set speeches, and did his best to anticipate any countervailing argument. He revisited witnesses to harangue them again with the same innocuous questions he asked previously, until he could detect them lapsing into the onset of comas. Gaston Fleury, the director of the Department of Research and Strategic Planning, threw him out of his office four times, although on the fifth attempt he examined the substantive details with him and gathered up the pertinent information. On the young cop's third visit to interview Captain Sloan, he caught a glimpse of the the retired cop skipping out through the back door of his rural home, jumping into his pickup and driving off. He was a widower now, but his housekeeper, in for the afternoon, reported that she didn't know what had gotten into him.

"He was complaining about a tummy upset. I guess he's gone to the doctor's."

Instead, Cinq-Mars found the truck parked outside the local watering hole.

An end to his period of preparation and procrastination had to be broached. He felt ready, and if that meant being prepared to kiss his career goodbye, so be it. What good was he as a cop, or as a man, if he was not willing to lay everything on the line? The time had come. But he still needed to think about things a little more, sift through further possibilities.

Then, one day, he woke up early and knew that the time had come.

Do or die.

That night, wearing casual attire, including a much-loved leather bomber jacket, he knocked on the open door to his boss's office and found him sitting with both feet up, his face a vaudevillian act of pained twitches.

The captain's shift had commenced ninety minutes earlier. Touton had dispatched his detectives, while Cinq-Mars had the night off.

"Let's get out of here," he advised his mentor.

"I'm working."

"You need a drink."

Touton reached for a lower drawer.

"I don't drink on the job," Cinq-Mars reminded him.

"You're not on the job."

"You are."

"Cut me some slack, twerp. Special dispensation." He pronounced the words as a cascade of syllables. Touton, it appeared, had already imbibed that evening.

"Captain," Cinq-Mars said.

"What, laddie?"

"Let's get out of here."

"Why?"

"These walls have elephant's ears."

He was all set to take him for whiskey or beer when the captain decided that he was famished, opting for pizza. The parlour was crowded, and they spent most of their time talking hockey. Did *les Canadiens* have enough to win the Cup? Few around town thought so, it wasn't their year, but Touton had not given up hope. "They'll pull it out, laddie."

"Will you quit with the 'laddie' stuff? Why are we speaking English anyway?" He had chosen a Hawaiian, which caused Touton to sneer.

"Will you tell me why we're here?" The captain had ordered extra pepperoni with extra cheese.

"Not in here, I won't," the young cop told him.

"What a gripe. I suppose you want to join my squad again. I see guys like you every day. You're a dime a dozen. Walking the beat's too hard on your toes? We all walked the beat, laddie."

"Some walked less than others," Cinq-Mars grumbled. "You got promoted pretty quickly."

"I was promoted through a department decimated by war and corruption. Get that straight. Times have changed."

"That's not what I want to talk about anyway."

"I walked out of Poland all the way to Germany in the dead of fucking winter."

"Sorry I brought it up. Actually, no—*you* brought it up."

"I had no boots."

"That was tough. A winter with no boots."

"Tough? Tough? What do you know about tough?"

Cinq-Mars sighed. Perhaps he hadn't chosen the best night for this.

"Out with it, laddie," Touton commanded, chomping down on a fresh slice. After he chewed and swallowed, he snarled, "I have things to do. Some of us work for our salary, you know."

"That's not all you work for."

The tone took the captain aback. He smiled, to have seen this burst of nettle from his young friend. He enjoyed getting under Cinq-Mars's skin. The country boy was always so calm, so aloof. "What's that supposed to mean?"

Cinq-Mars stared back at him. He could feel his heart beginning to thump. He wondered if he'd still have a job by the end of this talk. Either he'd stake his ground as an investigative policeman, or fall—*kerplunk*—upon his face.

"It means," he said, then hesitated. The lights were bright. "Let's take a walk."

"More with the walking," Touton complained as he hauled himself out of the booth. At least the young guy was paying for dinner. They were released to the mild evening and this particular March night was the first three weeks in which the temperature was forecast to ride above freezing through to dawn. Spring, finally, while not causing much of a disturbance, was at last making an entrance.

They strolled down Rue St. Jacques, past the great stone banks with vaulted ceilings and gold-leaf trim and the stolid office buildings from another era. Every time Cinq-Mars glanced through a window and noticed high ceilings and vast open spaces, he thought to himself, *a bugger to heat.*

"So, what's up?" Touton asked him, granting the benefit of the doubt by not being snide. He limped excessively these days, and while the exercise was not unwelcome, he kept to a measured pace.

"What do you think it costs to heat that bank in winter?"

"More than I got. Less than they got. Why are you wasting my time? I don't care what it costs to heat a goddamn bank, as long as they keep my money warm."

"I've solved it, you know," Cinq-Mars told him.

Touton looked at him. "The cost of heating banks?"

"Not that," he said.

Unaware of cases the young man might be working on—or if he had any, as he was only a patrolman—Touton drew one conclusion. He took his time answering, then said, "Roger's murder?"

"Yes, sir."

The older man walked on. Every few paces, he shook his head, as if to deflect a bad or a cumbersome thought. "All right," he said. "Before we break out the champagne, run it down for me."

Émile Cinq-Mars took a deep breath. Now he must perform, be meticulous and thorough, or his whole theory might unravel and leave him standing with a ball of delicate thread wrapped tightly around him in Gordian knots.

"Let me tell you who was in the park."

"Good to cross-reference."

"Why? Do you think you know?"

"I've got my guesses. Who was there?"

He started with an easy one. "Father François Legault."

"Do you have a screw loose? Okay, Fifth of March, explain to me why you think that. I'll explain to you why you're still a monkey in a tree. This should be good for a laugh."

"He's admitted it."

Touton stopped walking. Cinq-Mars went on for half a dozen strides before he stopped also, and looked back.

"Admitted what?"

"Being in the park."

"But he didn't kill Roger?"

"He's a material witness."

"He's admitted that? He saw what happened?"

"Right before his eyes."

"How far away was he?"

"Closer than me and you."

"He said that? He told you so?"

"Yes, sir."

Hobbled, as if stiffened further by the brief pause, Touton resumed walking. As they ambled along, Cinq-Mars told him who else had been in the park that night, who killed Roger Clément and why, or at least what various people thought might be the reasons why.

"Why do *you* think he did it?" Touton asked him.

"I like what Father François has to say on the matter. I'll add that the count was a frightened man. He was on the run. He was afraid of Roger, a man that strong. Roger's wife hated him—he remembered her from Asbestos, where she dressed him down in public once. But I'm never going to tell her that her tirade against the count might have cost her husband his life. Maybe the count remembered the incident too well, and was such a demented bastard that he wanted revenge. So he took it."

"Father François told you all that?"

"Reggie Chartrand. I went to see him to get his account of the fight."

"What fight?"

"Never mind that now. It's not the point."

"That's what I want to know. What *is* the point? Tell me what you fucking know, Cinq-Mars, or I'll beat the crap out of you."

Cinq-Mars took a breath. "Let me finish. It's simple, really. De Bernonville killed Roger to make the Cartier Dagger worthless to his partners. That's what I believe. After the killing, they needed to sell it for money. He was that mercenary. The others had discussed keeping it—Laurin for his politics, Houde for his good name, Duplessis for more power, the Church to revive itself. De Bernonville understood that he had to change their point of view in a hurry. He wanted cash."

Touton liked this young cop, and appreciated that, for all his recalcitrant, small-town, priestly heritage, his mind comprehended the darker side of men's souls.

"The point is," Cinq-Mars went on, without any prodding this time, "anyone who studied the Sun Life Building, who took the time to gaze at those pale cement blocks and columns, who bothered to take in the view of the place, knew categorically that a man cannot expect to crawl down the face of such a building at the end of a rope without being spotted, without creating a major stir."

Touton was expecting more, and when it appeared that Cinq-Mars had finished, asked, "How can a smart guy talk so dumb?"

Cinq-Mars crossed his arms, as though marshalling his defences before an onslaught. "Detective Sloan told me—sorry, it's Captain Sloan—"

"That's right. Respect a man's rank."

"Retired now, of course."

"Lazy, lucky bastard. At least he made it out alive."

Cinq-Mars fought harder to keep this on track. "He told me that on the night of the riot you gazed up for a long time at the Sun Life Building. He remembered it because nobody knew what to do with themselves, while you just stood there staring. In the end, the other cops stared up also. You had to have seen it, Captain." He was looking directly at Touton now, who didn't blink, staring back. "No man could crawl down the face of that building undetected—"

"I saw that it was possible. I remember thinking exactly that. It's possible."

"But unlikely. So unlikely that no crook would have *planned* it that way. No crook would ever have *counted* on sliding down unseen. Too risky, riot or no riot. Any cop would've rejected the possibility—"

"I'm not any cop. I saw that it was possible. It *is* possible."

"—or at least categorized the effort as highly unlikely and gone on to other choices. A cop like yourself, a great cop, would have known to check out other possibilities with due diligence."

"You and your use of big fucking words, Émile."

They were quiet awhile, standing still. Cinq-Mars kept his head down, and moved his feet around, kicking a chunk of ice that had probably fallen from a rooftop. He wondered if it had nearly killed anybody. Then he looked up and saw that his captain was gazing at him.

"So what are you saying?" Touton asked him.

"You failed to address the issue that it had been an inside job."

"You're saying I screwed up? I reject that point of view. I *know* how hard I worked this case."

The young cop remained adamant, in tone and stance. "The guy who came out and identified the body, the security guard from Sun Life, he knew it was Roger right off the bat—supposedly, from his days as a hockey player, more than fifteen years earlier. But Roger had changed. He was older, and he was a corpse. He didn't look like his old self. So how was he able to identify him so fast?"

Some signal passed between them, and both men began walking again. Traffic at this hour alternated between light and nonexistent. The older section of the city was losing its prestige as a business centre, with companies moving up the hill into new glass-and-steel skyscrapers downtown. Stone buildings were out of fashion. There'd been a lot of talk about finding a way to revive this part of the old town, but other than being an attraction for summer tourists, these blocks continued to sag. The two policemen left Champs de Mars behind them, the square abutted on one side by the massive Notre Dame Basilica. In its centre stood a statue of Maisonneuve, for here he fought Indians, killing an Iroquois chief while being wounded himself.

"I interviewed that guy. He knew Roger from a bar," Touton said.

Cinq-Mars asked, "You believed him?"

"Why not? Nothing made him credible as an insider. You're barking up the wrong tree."

"Woof woof."

"Hey, kid, maybe I can't walk, but I can still punch. I can take you on."

"I don't doubt it."

Touton nodded, as though satisfied.

They stopped at a red light. No traffic. Montreal culture demands that pedestrians walk when the path is clear, heedless of signals. Yet they stood on the curb in the near glow of the red, and, when the light turned green, walked on.

Cinq-Mars issued a sigh. "I don't doubt that you can knock me out. I also don't doubt that your guy was innocent. I know you were right, just as you knew you were right. The point is—"

"We're back to the point. In your world, a man can't climb down a building."

Cinq-Mars smiled briefly, then returned to his argument. "I'd have interviewed him and everybody else in the Sun Life Building to death."

"Even the innocent."

"Especially the innocent. In order to eliminate them. From all future investigations, for instance."

"So I reach obvious conclusions more quickly than you. It's called experience. Get over it."

Cinq-Mars looked petulant. "You had an advantage."

"What advantage?"

"You knew he wasn't involved, because you already knew the insider."

"Pardon me? What are you on about, laddie?"

"It's the only explanation. Any cop working that case would have thoroughly run down every employee and eliminated any question of an inside job. You didn't, Captain. Not because you were doing a poor job, but because you knew the insider."

"Sometimes you confuse me, Fifth of March. So tell me. Go ahead. Who's the insider?"

"You are," Cinq-Mars revealed.

Cinq-Mars didn't stop walking. He didn't look at Touton. This time, the captain didn't stop walking, either. He stayed alongside him, glancing over at his junior colleague, then looking ahead.

"Before I belly-laugh my way through the rest of my shift, fill me in on how you reached that conclusion."

Cinq-Mars nodded. "Thank you, sir."

"What are you thanking me for?"

The younger man bobbed his head, did a little feint. "You honour me by not denying anything."

"Give me time. I want to hear you out first. I'm hoping to be entertained. By the way, just so we're clear, are you suggesting that I killed Roger Clément?"

"Your alibi is airtight. Half the police department can vouch for your whereabouts."

"So tell me what you got on me."

"I'll begin with a question," Cinq-Mars told him.

"Am I a suspect now?" Touton finally laughed, and his amusement seemed sincere. "Forget the questions. Just tell me how I'm the insider."

"You didn't look for an insider with all due diligence. Why not? Because you knew it was you, not anyone else."

"So you said. That's nothing."

Cinq-Mars pressed on, calmly, aware that this was the moment he had prepared for and dreamed about for months now. "You had the keys, Captain Touton. You emptied the building beforehand. You made sure everyone was out and you took away the usual security for the building."

"It happened to be my job. Your Honour, may I point that out to the over-zealous district attorney here?"

"Then you did not discount an outside entry as being implausible. You went along with it. You helped everyone else involved to believe that that's how it took place."

At the next red light, they both glanced quickly in either direction and promptly stepped off the curb, crossing over. The way wasn't entirely clear, as a cab slowed slightly for their transit.

"At least now I'm understanding how you got yourself muddled up. Don't feel bad—it's your first complex case. What you're telling me is all good, but there's not a lawyer in the land who won't find it circumstantial, or a sober judge who'd disagree. But go on. I feel enlightened. There may be a sliver of hope for you yet, Cinq-Mars."

"Your relationship with Captain Fleury, boss. That's another thing."

"What? Oh, come on. What does he have to do with the price of peas?"

Cinq-Mars raised his eyebrows and tilted his head away momentarily as though to deflect the derision. "You value courage, sir. After his car was bombed, Captain Fleury backed off his investigation of limousines. He wasn't going to have anything to do with that, and returned to pushing a pencil. At the time, he was getting awfully close to Harry Montford. But he let that go. I can understand what happened to Fleury, how he got weak in the knees. He began to see that accounting wasn't such a bad life. But for a long time it was hard for me to understand how *you* could go along with it. Until it hit me, of course."

"Okay," Touton responded. "I'll bite."

"He wasn't your friend because you had great respect for him. He was your friend because you needed him. Specifically, you needed someone in his position."

"I didn't know he had a position."

"Neither did I, for a while. Until I asked myself what it might be." His expression indicated that the answer was obvious. "To make sure he didn't discover what he might have discovered, and to take care of your next move. That's why you kept him close to you. I'll talk about that later. Do you want a drink in here?"

They'd walked onto Rue de la Commune, where a bar had presented itself. Touton stooped slightly to peer into the place, saw that it was quiet and consented to drop in for a whiskey. The street had once been a small river, and somewhere nearby, it was rumoured, was the island's first European settlement. Maisonneuve, then, and Jeanne Mance, had lived just down the block. Cinq-Mars felt aware of that passage of time as he entered the bar, perhaps because their discussion turned on the Cartier Dagger, which used to be housed near this place in a fort called Perilous.

A pretty girl served them in a corner booth. Her smile seemed to lift the spirits of both men, and they clinked glasses before enjoying the first nip.

"Okay, kid. What else you got?"

"You must visit all the bars around here."

"This one's new to me."

"Back during the FLQ hunt, I put a tail on Father François. Guess where he led me? To a bar near here. Guess who he was talking to?"

Touton smiled. "I practically invented these techniques. I would never answer a question where you're pretending to already know the answer."

"You two have a working relationship," Cinq-Mars pointed out to him. Secretly, he was feeling pleased with himself. Even if his boss didn't like what he was saying, he had to be impressed.

"I have a working relationship with God. So? We're talking about your flimsy case against me."

Cinq-Mars shrugged, the gesture of a man on top of the situation. "You get into places, boss, that's my—" He decided to change his word. "—observation. You get in everywhere in this town, any club—it's your city—and especially, you can get into the Sun Life Building when you're the one holding the keys."

Touton took a longer slug than usual, and before bringing his glass down to the table, signalled the pretty waitress for a refill. "I figure you're paying."

"Dutch treat," Cinq-Mars corrected him.

"I don't know what that means," his boss told him. "I'm not Dutch."

"This is what it means. You put Detective Sloan in charge of the Sun Life Building and surrounding area. I know he had his good points as a cop, but being meticulous, or energetic, or hard-working, those attributes were never painted across his brow. So you split the work and gave the Sun Life, which required the most attention, to your weakest officer. Suspicious, no?"

"Coincidental, no? Circumstantial, no? I put my officers where I put my officers. Someday, you may have a command of your own. See if you make all your decisions based on who has the most energy. For crying out loud, laddie."

The bar was dark, narrow and long, with soothing piano jazz playing over the sound system that made conversation both easy and private. Eight others were in the room, and no one was having a particularly good time, sombreness being the dominant mood.

To their right, against the wall, a lonely candle flickered.

"All right, I'll concede that point. But it's all part of the grand design. You cleared the building. You didn't catch the man who was—may I point out, *your friend*—who was alone on the roof. I'm saying that only one person could have helped him stay hidden until the coast was clear, and then take a safe way out, and that person was Captain Armand Touton of the Night Patrol."

"Émile—"

"I know what you're going to say."

"It's circumstantial."

"I knew you were going to say that. I've got more."

"Let's hear it."

Only now did Cinq-Mars choose to slip off his bomber jacket, letting it fall back on the chair behind him.

"Your relationship with Carole Clément," he said.

"What about it?"

"You looked after her. Brought her into the department as a police informant—essentially replacing her husband. You've taken care of her as though she were your best friend's wife, which she is. You've watched out for her, as any man might do who felt guilty about her husband's death."

"I'm not impressed," Touton told him. "You're fishing without a hook."

Cinq-Mars ignored him. "Your relationship to Anik Clément. Forgive me, sir, but you have a daughter of your own you've all but ignored—"

"She was adopted," Touton reminded him.

"Meaning?"

"You said 'daughter of my own'—"

"She is your only daughter, Captain. You adopted her, but anyone looking on might think you adopted Anik."

"Move on, Cinq-Mars." For the first time that evening, the captain's tone expressed anger.

"The death of Michel Vimont. You let that one lie because it might have pointed back to Roger, and after that to you. I know you pursued that one on your own, but you kept it tight to your control, not wanting anything to leach out."

Touton seemed to be formulating a reaction, but Cinq-Mars decided to blow through his objections.

"Pensions," he said. He was developing a technique, and wanted to perfect it. Move information around, in and out, fast and slow, and come back to aspects seemingly at random, so that whomever he was interrogating could not anticipate what was coming next in order to properly formulate a defence. "That's what scared you about Detective Fleury."

"Me, scared of him? Are you doped up?"

"The pencil pusher might connect the dots. He was working with materials hazardous to your health. Numbers. Figures. Contracts. Arrangements.

Confidential deals. Pensions. The civilian you were lobbying the department to receive a full pension, Roger Clément, was the guy killed in a park. Lately, you've made the same case for Carole. You want her to collect her husband's pension, although you're calling it her own, for all the work she's done. A tough sell, but you have the people in place—the mayor, the police director, and Fleury, the administrator of pensions, or whatever the hell his trumped-up title is now, who will do your bidding. I've checked, by the way. So let's not pretend that none of what I'm saying is factual."

"But not incriminating. Carole deserves her pension just like Roger did."

Cinq-Mars took a swig of his Scotch. "Okay, but another piece of the puzzle."

"You've tied yourself up in knots over this." Touton didn't realize he had touched the junior cop's primary insecurity—that he was in knots, and that he could unravel, as could his case. "Let me ask you a question. If I was so all-fired hot to conceal the truth, as the insider on this heist, why did I choose you to keep the case going? I could've shut this case down years ago, put it to bed. Drop that question into your think tank, Cinq-Mars, then imagine it being asked in front of a jury. Your so-called case falls to ashes. The first stiff breeze, *poof*, it's blown away."

The smile Cinq-Mars exhibited in response was that of a man who had anticipated the question and, having agonized over it himself, had devised an answer. "Boss, I never said you don't want to solve the case. I'm not saying that now. Fact is, it's one of the reasons why you're so obsessed. You're not just a cop on the job here. You're also an interested party—the *wronged* party. Of course you want to solve the case. Your friend, your partner, got killed. One of your longtime colleagues, the coroner, also got killed. You don't do this out of a sense of duty. Your motivation has been for justice, and for revenge."

Touton shook his head and laughed a little. "I'm slowly becoming impressed again. Not with your evidence, which is bogus, but with your pig-headedness. Let me warn you about something, one old man to a young fellow. This is where conspiracy theories come from, before they evaporate into thin air. Cockamamie, trumped-up ideas. But don't let me discourage you. Go on."

"Let's talk about your relationship to the Cartier Dagger."

"What relationship?"

"You deserved it. You hit the beach at Dieppe. Your friends went down around you. They died horribly. Sometimes slowly. You remember their voices in your sleep and you remember the stench of the dead. You swam out to a destroyer, which you thought blew up in front of you. Men around you drowned because of that ruse. Wounded, you swam back to shore to face either death or capture. Clarence Campbell did important work and a good job, you may want to agree with me on that, but who was the war *hero*? The lawyer, who didn't arrive overseas until after the ceasefire, or the man who'd fought on hell's beach, then was captured, interned and force-marched through winter?"

"Without boots."

"Without boots."

Touton raised an eyebrow. "I never thought of it that way before. How can a man be designated as a war hero when the war was over before he got to do his job? Had I thought of that years ago, I might have become a bitter man."

Cinq-Mars shook off the lie. "Oh, you were bitter all right. I don't blame you. You wanted the knife because you deserved it. You had an incredible war record, and after the war you continued to serve as an officer of the law. You weren't a CEO or a president, so you didn't meet the letter of Sir Hubert Holt's charter, but you were well within its spirit. Especially so when you made captain. When Roger Clément came to you with a plan to acquire the knife, how could you resist him? That's why he thought to come to you, the squeaky-clean cop, but this one caper you could not resist. The knife was going to get stolen anyway—wouldn't Duplessis see to it? And wouldn't that be maddening? That fart, with the dagger. You knew who else wanted it, too—half the world, once people knew about it. Sooner or later, someone was going to snatch it up. Why not you? For the sake of those who died in battle right beside you, and died in the camp, and died on the march back to Germany. If for nothing else, you had to honour their lives and pay homage to their deaths. You owed that to them, not only to yourself."

Touton was clearly becoming agitated during his spiel, but chose not to interrupt. Once Cinq-Mars was finished, he said, "One problem, Émile."

"What's that?"

"I never knew the knife existed. Remember? Sorry. But that sound of shattering glass? It's your case crashing down."

"No, sir," Cinq-Mars claimed. "You just made it. Not for the first time."

At least, the young man noticed, his opinion was not being quickly discounted. Touton took a drink, then asked, "Why's that?"

"The French newspapers didn't take an interest in the subject—an old soldier, English, receiving an award from an English institution, Sun Life. They should have cared about the dagger, but it had been dormant for so long, its significance had eroded. For that reason, I think, you weren't aware that an English newspaper, the *Montreal Star,* reported that Clarence Campbell had been honoured for heroism in a time of war and been granted possession of a special artifact."

Touton shrugged. "You're right. I was not aware of it. That's what I'm trying to tell you. Knowledge of the knife had been lost to our countrymen. I knew nothing about it, either. The ironic thing is, we only really got interested again after it was stolen, after we found out about it."

Cinq-Mars pulled his bomber jacket out from behind him, and from the liner pocket extracted an envelope, which was not sealed. From it, he withdrew a copy of a newspaper clipping.

"The article, Captain, details an awards ceremony. It mentions that Clarence Campbell, at the luncheon where he was presented with the knife, was accorded an honour guard of Montreal police officers who were also veterans. Sir, you're mentioned by name. In the snapshot of Campbell—look for yourself. Who's that in the background, to the right—the handsome young man in dress blues?"

Accepting the article, Touton perused it. He paid attention to the photograph. "You're right," he said. "He is a handsome young man."

"Detective Sloan has told me—repeatedly, he's a clear witness—that you denied having heard of the knife on the night of the riot."

The older man nodded and pursed his lips.

"This is evidence," Touton agreed.

"Yes, sir."

"What happened here was personal. I'm a good cop."

"I know you are, sir."

"You've got some of it. Good going. But not all of it. I admit, this was personal. Men died on that beach. Within minutes. Their hearts blown out their backs. Their bellies lay across the sand. Eyes gone. Brain bits all over our faces. I probably swallowed brain bits in that crazy time. Like they were bugs."

"Yes, sir."

He pointed a finger at the tabletop and used a stabbing motion to make his points. "Not for myself, Cinq-Mars. For a commemoration. Somebody who'd been in battle should have it, as a soldier. For the boys who died, that's how I was thinking back then. The memories were still close to me. They're not so far away now."

"Yes, sir."

"And poor Roger. He wanted a pension. For his family. If we'd gone a little further, his family would have been looked after. But he died too soon. We didn't get that part done."

"So you looked after his family for him."

"He sacrificed his life. His big score. He didn't want a million dollars. He just wanted a police pension, to show that he led an honourable life, that he done something right, and to make sure that his wife and daughter were provided for and respected him."

"Yes, sir."

"You're not being snotty, are you?"

"No, sir. I'm not being snotty. In my opinion, you made a mistake."

"Yeah, and you're a self-righteous farm boy with a pitchfork up your butt. You could've been a priest. Should've been, maybe. Stayed out of my hair."

"Yes, sir."

"The best part of what you said is this: the knife would have been stolen anyway. It didn't need a riot—that only helped. But a break-in would have occurred. It was being talked about, even without de Bernonville. When he came along, he just bumped everything up."

"You know this how?"

"Roger. He was my snitch. I had to let him be part of stealing it, even though he told me to make it impossible to steal. Making it impossible made it necessary for Roger to be the one to do it. Otherwise, he'd have been cut out of the action. For my part, I had to let Roger be in on the theft whenever it went down. Otherwise, the dagger would have disappeared forever. I'm not saying that Roger or I would have taken it. Stolen property? Not me. But after it was stolen and then recovered, I bet it would have been treated with greater respect. And greater security. Delivered to a museum, maybe."

"When you found Roger dead—"

"Heartbreaking. I have no words. But at least, at that moment, we hadn't lost the knife. His death was not in vain." Touton looked away. "Until minutes later."

"I see," Cinq-Mars murmured. "I get it now."

Touton seemed to gather his strength under him. "Émile, being found out by you, that makes everything worthwhile. Know why?"

Cinq-Mars had no answer.

"Because now I know who killed Roger. Now I can go to his wife and tell her who did it. I can tell her who else was involved. And that's going to mean a lot to me. As a police officer, and as a man who was her husband's friend."

"I'll tell Father François that maybe he should leave town. Lay low for a while."

"That might be a good idea. She might knock his block off."

They were quiet awhile then. When their glasses were empty, they rose from the table.

"Know what?" Touton asked.

"What?" Cinq-Mars asked him back.

"I'm going to pay for this round."

"Oh yeah?" He smiled. "They say the dagger possesses magic. I guess I can believe that now."

Touton laughed, and the fullness of it, the lack of emotional detritus, surprised his companion, as did the drift of his next words. "I've enjoyed your big spiel, Émile, but now I have to tell you something."

"Sir?"

Standing, the older man flexed his legs, which had stiffened under the small table, and grimaced as he did so. "You're wrong."

"Excuse me?" The remark bothered him. He expected that, faced with his evidence, Touton would not try to duck this.

"I did not steal the knife with Roger, although I knew he was going to try. With one limitation, I did everything in my power to stop him. I put my cops in position to defeat him. That they failed is to his credit. Although it cost him his life."

For the first time that evening, Cinq-Mars felt out of his depth. "I'm not sure what you're saying. You told people he was working for you. We just didn't know it was as a crook."

"I told people he was working for me because I wanted to get him a pension. I failed in that."

"I see."

"You don't have a clue what I'm telling you."

"Okay. I don't."

Touton reached around into his pocket and produced his wallet. He dropped a few bills onto the table. Then he looked Émile in the eye. "We're taking this outside." The two walked out into the night air, and the captain of the Night Patrol put a hand on the younger man's shoulder. "This way," he said.

He led him over the tracks across the street, through a hole in the fence, towards a dock for steamships that plied the Great Lakes. The boats were lit up with activity. Ice was melting. Soon the season would begin in earnest. Crews were working to awaken vessels from their winter hibernation.

Both men placed their arms on a railing and looked over the water.

"Roger came to me. He said he had something to steal. I asked what. He said none of my business. But you know, we talked about it before, so I guessed. I asked him why it was none of my business, and he said he had powerful friends. So I asked, 'Why are you telling me?' He said because I had to back off and let him do his job. I said, 'Job? That's not a job.' He said, 'You know I have friends in high places.'"

Touton went quiet, and Cinq-Mars took out his cigarettes. He opened the pack and let his boss take one for himself, then the two lit up.

"What did you say to that?"

"I was quiet awhile."

They were quiet awhile.

Touton smoked. Then he said, "I knew this was no ordinary conversation. Roger had never come to me before to say he was going to commit a crime. But you should understand, together we were cleaning up the city. By this time, he was really an undercover cop, as far as I was concerned, which is why I wanted to get him a pension. We took out the gambling dens and raided secret whorehouses. Some of those used underage girls and boys. When bank robbing became organized, we disrupted that, and when the shakedown artists got too tough, too big, we shook them down. Roger contributed."

"So you owed him," Cinq-Mars concluded.

"Not only that," elaborated Touton, "I needed him to stay right where he was. To do that, he had to remain a thief. So I said to him, 'What do you want from me?'"

"What did he say?"

"Roger asked me to do everything I could to stop him."

"What? Why would he ask you that?"

"Think about it." Touton didn't give him much time to come up with any answers. "The theft was going to go down on my turf, under my nose. So he wanted me to cover my ass by doing everything in my power to stop him. Also, by making it tough for him, it wouldn't ever look as though we might be connected. This kept him safe—we thought—as well as me. I remember him telling me that I was going to take shit for what he did, so I'd better be able to show that I didn't actually screw it up. So I asked him, 'What if you fail?' And he said to me, 'There you go.'"

"There you go?"

"I didn't know what he meant either. But I caught on. If he failed, he wanted a damn good excuse, and the only excuse that would work was that I had pulled out all the stops, that it wasn't his fault. You see, he had some serious friends. If he screwed up, he had to demonstrate he wasn't to blame. Tit for tat."

Nodding, Cinq-Mars didn't feel like smoking his cigarette down, so he tossed it into the dark water. Touton had taught him, so he knew how to keep the tangents of a conversation together. "You said that you had one limitation to deal with."

"Two, really." The senior cop gazed at the smouldering tip of his cigarette between puffs. When he inhaled, he drew the smoke more deeply into himself than usual, and held it longer, watched as the smoke he exhaled drifted up into the sky, then gazed at the red tip again. "He said he was going to tell me what he was going to steal. But that I could not know it."

"Huh? What the heck did that mean?"

"I asked him the same question. He said I could defend the building it was in, but I could not defend the thing itself, because theoretically I should not have that knowledge. I had to find some other reason to defend the building, but the prize, that had to be left alone. So I said, 'Just tell me what building it's in.' And he said the Sun Life, which I had already guessed. I told Roger, 'I know what you're going after.' And he said, 'You can't be there.' He said I could oversee everything, but on the night in question, I could not be the cop on duty."

"In case something went wrong," Cinq-Mars noted.

"I agreed for that reason. I told him I'd make the building so impenetrable he'd have to quit before he started. He just smiled, said we'd see about that."

"Then how'd he do it?"

"An inside job."

"Do you know who?"

"In a way."

"Then what I am doing on this case if you're not sharing information?"

"It was your job to prove what I suspect."

"You mean I failed."

"We all have. It's part of being a cop."

"Who do you think was the insider?"

"Can't tell you."

"Why not?"

"Because I can't."

"I don't get this."

"You will."

Now Cinq-Mars wanted another cigarette. Touton declined.

They walked away from the water, and crossing the tracks they saw a man strolling beneath a rising moon with a collie on a leash. Cinq-Mars felt watched, followed, examined from the inside out. "Do you know him?" Cinq-Mars asked.

"Do you?"

"I feel like I should. My hair is standing up on the back of my neck."

"Easy, laddie. You've got a long way to go until retirement."

They squeezed back through the hole in the chain-link fence, then leaned back against it, as it was comfortable enough. Touton rocked against the wire, hands thrust deep in his pockets. His protégé put his shoulder against the chain and waited.

"Laurin was the key," the captain said.

"Why him?"

"Why was he there? Except for de Bernonville, everybody represented someone else. Vimont was there for Montford, who was involved in exchange for favours from Duplessis. Houde was also there for Duplessis, as well as for himself. He expected to be remembered as one of the wild men of that night. The priest was there for the Church and for Father Joe. But why Laurin? He was there for Roger's insider."

"Who was?"

"Can't tell you."

"And you know this, or suspect it, through what information?"

"Can't tell you that either. Think about it."

The young cop looked back towards the water. Then, suddenly, it hit him.

"Father François knows. That's why you wanted me to start questioning him, after I told you about Anik being in the closet."

The old cop shrugged. "Look, I knew about the closet. Carole found out about some of it from her daughter, but she instructed Anik to stay mute. She taught her that it was sacred, what a dying man said to his priest. She wouldn't let Anik tell her what she heard. We're all old Catholics here, and some traditions never die, even among the radicals. But yeah, I never thought the priest would divulge anything, so I never went after him. Then again, he never seemed like a real priest to me. More socialist than spiritual. But I was wrong. He wouldn't tell me, but he found a way to pitch in, as much as he could."

"Now I get it," Cinq-Mars said.

"Get what?"

"Why you brought me onto your team."

"Why? I ask myself that question every day."

"You met me with Anik."

"That was a night. You arresting her."

"You noticed that we liked each other." Cinq-Mars crushed his smoke under his shoe.

"If you got close to Anik, she might give you a name. Laurin represented the old fraternal sect—now extinct, one hopes—the Order of Jacques Cartier. He wasn't a criminal, he was a psychiatrist and a politician. Someone of power sent him there, the same powerful interests who put Roger inside the Sun Life."

"He worked inside the building, then, a CEO?"

"I checked them all. They're mostly English. But a man of great power can get almost anything he wants. Including a set of keys, and help from others."

"So it could be anyone."

"Or someone so well known that the mention of his name caused a child in a closet to weep."

Instinctively, they both began walking towards the street.

"You think so?" Cinq-Mars asked him.

"I think not. I did once. But you see, that's why Roger was working for me. Sort of. He wanted to participate in a share of that knife. I wanted to find a way to get it into the hands of a soldier."

"Not you?"

"Not me. That would be a criminal act I couldn't duck. There were other heroes. Plenty of them. Together, I thought we might be able to do something. I didn't count on so many other people thinking exactly the same way. I figured Roger could handle himself. And he could. But only to a point."

They listened to their steps on the pavement.

"I might've come close once," Touton revealed. "An old friend of mine, a restaurateur, Lu Lee, gave me a call one night. Someone had been whispering about the Cartier Dagger at his place. The guy had nasty things to say, too, about certain minorities. I got up there as fast as I could, but he was gone before I arrived. The bastard paid cash. No paper trail. When I talked to Lu Lee, he made the customer sound like somebody high up inside the Order. Just the things he said. I hoped the man would go eat there again, but he never did. Lu Lee is no longer with us."

Cinq-Mars cleared his throat before he made his admission. "I almost had the name. I could have had it."

"Why didn't you get it?"

"The priest in me. I chose to respect the last words of a dying man to his priest, so I let them go unspoken. Anik was going to tell me. But I stopped her."

"So we just missed twice. We're just Catholics. Maybe third time lucky."

They walked a bit, crossed after a car passed, and stepped onto the opposite sidewalk.

"You're still more priest than cop," Touton noted. He put a hand on the younger man's near shoulder again, as he did when they left the bar. "That's all right. We can use some of those."

"I'm sorry, sir."

"Don't be. You made a decision. As a young man, I was a soldier. I went to hell, but that's a part of me I won't trade. You're part priest. Never work against yourself, Émile." He removed his hand. "I'm going to walk back to the station alone. I could use a little time on my own right now."

They remained standing where they were.

Cinq-Mars didn't know why, but he didn't move and neither did his boss.

"Unless you were planning to bust me," Touton said.

"No, sir." He tried to smile, but failed somehow.

"If I was you, I'd bust my ass. I turned my face away to let that crime happen."

"I'm not you."

"You're too soft. You have to be hard in this life. Sometimes."

"Since we're on the subject, I'll be hard. I wrote a report."

He noticed the man's shoulders rotate back. "To whom?"

"Nobody. As long as you give up your interest in acquiring the knife. Don't ask me how I know, but I know. You've found out who has it now, but nobody can ever hear that information from you. Take it to your grave."

The young man was not so soft after all. In a terse tone, Touton said, "Apologize, laddie, because that's the first time you've insulted me tonight and I won't have it."

Cinq-Mars determined what was meant by those words, and what his answer ought to be. "Yes, sir," he said. "I'm sorry, sir."

"All right, then," Armand Touton said, and he turned away, facing the direction that would return him to his office. He reconsidered, and asked for a smoke for the walk back. "I've fixed it for Carole Clément to get a pension. Just so you know. If you do bust me ever, wait for that to go through first."

"Don't go insulting *me* now. You've done so well all night."

"So we're even."

"For my part, I just want you to understand the situation," Cinq-Mars said.

"I heard you the first time. Listen, laddie, you think we lost this one? We let the leader of the Order slip free? Don't be so sure. One thing I know, there's always some dark figure walking his dog down the railway tracks, some man who makes your hair stand on end. Like when we close down the whorehouse and the pimps rise up instead. If we kept the whorehouses, I bet my daughter never would've found her way into one, and never would have come in contact with a pimp, and so never would've run away back to him."

"I'm sorry about that," Cinq-Mars said.

"So am I. But this is the thing, Émile. There's always some dark figure. Doesn't matter who we bust or what we do. There's always a dark figure on a track."

"With a dog."

"Who makes your hair stand on end. The best we can do is keep him in the dark, don't let him stand out in the light of day. That's why I work the Night Patrol. To keep the day bright and sunny on these streets." Touton extended his hand. "Good night, Émile."

Cinq-Mars was surprised by the abrupt departure.

"Good night, boss."

The two men parted company, one going back to work, the other heading home, even though initially he had to walk in the opposite direction to get there. That stroll took him over and through the grounds where the city had begun, and in the quiet night he could sense that old wooden fort—stout still, its devout inhabitants dwelling under the dread of attack one moment, wrapped up in the ecstasy of their wild adventure the next. Fort Perilous had become a cosmopolitan enterprise. Recently, distant travellers had dropped by for a World's Fair. Since then, after that grand party, the people had made it through the throbbing fever of rebellion. Yet they were still standing. The first of their people had prevailed against every onslaught, and taken the measure of every challenge. Some things did not change.

Cinq-Mars was happy to take a long way home, content to walk the streets of his city at night, through the old *quartier* that was feeling like a ghost town, the aged buildings as quiet as tombs. Then up the hill to the vibrancy of downtown, the sidewalks animated with lovers and wanderers, the scent of spring in the air, the bars spilling customers from their doors, drawing others in. He thought he'd head for a bar himself, but his legs kept moving, and he ambled all the way home.

There he sat in his living room, on the sofa, then on the floor, where he thought about things. He pondered the future and dwelled upon the past. He had rationalized losing Anik when that sad moment had occurred, and had poured himself into work and the dark case of her father's murder. Which had meant pouring himself into the history of the Cartier Dagger and of his adopted city. In a way, solving it all had been meant to prove his love for Anik. To show her his love. Having done so, he found himself alone anyway. His heart had been broken once, but he administered the antidote—work, obsession, forging on. Now he could wholly feel the loss, and he grieved for a love that might have been, that in the overall scheme of things could never be revived.

Dawn would find him on the floor, slumped, doubled up, asleep. Rousing himself at first light, he stumbled through to his bed and peeled back the covers. He curled up in bed, clothes and all. He didn't possess the energy to undress, as though a great weariness had overtaken him and needed to be served through a long sleep. His eyes snapped open once. He wondered if he was wearing his uniform. Then, remembering that this was supposed to be his day off until nightfall came around again, he managed to work his trousers off, then his shirt. Then he resorted to a substantial rest.

CHAPTER 30

1971

E ACH HAD A SHOVEL. THE LIGHT OF A HALF-MOON GLOWED UPON the few remaining patches of snow and the shelf of tombstones. Black, grey and white marble emerged from a winter hibernation to breathe cool mountain air again. In its devotion to all seasons, the earth had sufficiently thawed to admit their trespass, yet the pair of women were vigilant not to disturb the ground in any grievous way, or to awaken ghosts who might prowl that realm.

Slurping noises accompanied their travail, as the mucky clay was lifted from the hole their diligence had created.

Anik Clément bent down and with a stick measured the depth.

"One more," her mother said.

"One or two," the daughter agreed.

Anik's terrier, Ranger, examining the cavity, seemed to approve.

Anik pulled him away.

Carole Clément wedged her shovel down their neat, square hole to pry free a section of mud. Scraping it up the side walls to the surface, she deposited the clump upon their small pile.

"There," she said.

Anik tested the depth again.

"That does it," she said.

She rose to her feet again.

Her eyes scanned the vast sky.

"It'll rain," she said, "right?"

"The forecast says so. I can feel a change in the air."

Upon the ridge where they stood, they could see across the city to the west and north. Moonlight illuminated the distant Laurentian hills, with a scud of clouds brightening and darkening as they sailed the higher winds directly above.

"Now's the time," Carole said quietly.

Beyond their small pile of muck, Anik's backpack lay waiting. She unzipped the inner pocket, having to shove Ranger's nose out of her way several times, and extracted the protective box for the Cartier Dagger. She placed it on the ground. Crouching over it, she opened the case and gently removed the relic. Still bent low to the ground, she kissed the handle lightly, then stood up.

She passed the knife to her mother, who kissed the handle also.

Anik held the handle to her lips again, then the blade to her cheek, then moved over the hole dug thirty-six inches deep into the soil above her father's grave.

"Do I say something first or after?" she asked her mom.

Carole Clément's lips were trembling, her eyes moistened in the light of the moon.

"Now," she managed to suggest. As if to confirm that choice, Ranger sat squarely on his haunches, waiting to hear what words might be spoken.

Anik had to catch her breath first. Her lips quavered. Her small frame began to shake. Carole stepped across to stand more closely beside her, slipping an arm around her waist. Sudden stray tears from both women slid from their cheeks to drip upon the wet earth.

"Daddy," the young woman said to the air, to the ground. "We got the knife back for you. You can look after it from now on. You deserve to have it with you."

Anik held the dagger, and Carole covered her daughter's hands with her own, then spoke the words she had spent days preparing. "We're burying the knife in the soil of this place we call Quebec, of this city, once known as Hochelaga, once known as Fort Perilous, once known as Ville-Marie, now called Montreal, to help make this a good ground, a sacred earth, for everyone who lives here, for everyone who arrives, in our time, and for all time. We entrust it to your care, Roger, my love." She paused to wipe away her tears. Then, more quietly, as though only between herself and her dead husband, she said, "You were my war hero, Roger. You are my love."

Anik squeezed her mom's fingers, to let her know she heard her words. "Daddy, in a time of war, you went to prison for love. That makes you my war hero, too."

Kneeling, Carole added, "You deserve the Cartier Dagger as much as anyone."

At the time of her father's funeral, Anik was too young to fully comprehend the loss. In her own way, then, this became her solemn commemoration of his life, and of her love for him.

"Hold Ranger," she said, and her mother did, hugging him in her arms. Bending low, Anik introduced the knife into the cavity, planting it upright there, in the soil of the mountain on the river city. She shoved the blade down to the hilt. Then she stood again, gazing upon it.

Composure, briefly surrendered, returned. Anik stepped over to the case, and from it retrieved the broken tip, which she showed to her mother. "I'm keeping this," she said. "As if it's my daddy's heart."

Her good friend, Émile, had asked her out again. She had to tell him that what was done was done. He understood, although they were both saddened. He gave Anik the tip of the knife then, without her asking, and without saying a further word.

She placed it now in her jacket pocket, which she zipped closed.

Mother and daughter hugged each other. They held on tight.

Then they attended to their noses, and eyes, and laughed a little.

Anik and Carole began to backfill the cavity, easing the earth around the knife until it was completely covered. Anik tamped the ground around where the knife stood, then backfilled the rest of the soil. Carefully, they returned the square patch of grass they'd removed to its original location, and did their best to eliminate any evidence of their trespass there.

"It'll rain by morning," Carole assured her daughter. "That'll wash away our footprints, and the bits of dirt."

"I'll come back once the sun's out again. Pay a proper visit. Bring a bouquet and some grass seed. Just to make sure everything's tidy."

"Good. It'll be all right, sweetie."

"It will. Daddy's watching, you know."

She knew.

The mother waited for her daughter to come away first. This was the young woman's time. Her moment, when a murmur nurtured in the heart flew above this sacred soil, across time and sky, forward and back, imbuing the earth and the history of the world with her regard, her terrible trepidation, her immense love. She remained still, and finally her mother tugged her arm, gently whispering her name. They gathered up the empty case, the backpack and their tools, and haltingly made their way down the mountainside in the ambient dark, led by an aging, still spry terrier. They did not take a route common to pedestrians, but chose a difficult path scouted on previous trips. They moved through the trees and over boulders.

They did not wish to be seen.

Two women with shovels and a dog. Departing a cemetery in the dark. On a mount called Royal. They drove down the mountainside into the thrum of their city on the frozen river, although the ice was breaking up now, and the water flowed freely once again.

THE END

ACKNOWLEDGEMENTS

Novels that draw a substantial portion of their narrative from history cull their information from many sources, while permitting fact and fiction to commingle. Stories recounted by Captain (retired) Jacques Cinq-Mars, the former captain of the Night Patrol with the Montreal Police Department, were crucial and inspiring to this writer. I hope that the accounts were put to good use here. I am greatly indebted also to a broad range of published material. Listed alphabetically by author and indicating publication dates for the editions at my disposal, I especially credit: *Duplessis,* by Conrad Black, published by McClelland & Stewart, 1977; *Montreal: The Days That Are No More,* by Edgar A. Collard, published by Doubleday Canada, 1976; *Storied Streets: Montreal in the Literary Imagination,* by Bryan Demchinsky and Elaine Kalman Naves, published by McFarlane, Walter & Ross, 2000; *The Revolution Script,* by Brian Moore, published by Holt, Rinehart and Winston, 1971; *Montreal: From Mission Colony to World City,* by Leslie Roberts, published by Macmillan of Canada, 1969; *Memoirs,* by Pierre Elliott Trudeau, published by McClelland & Stewart, 1993; *City Unique: Montreal Days and Nights in the 1940s and '50s,* by William Weintraub, published by McClelland & Stewart, 1996. Of assistance were websites operated by the government of Canada on early French-Canadian history. To editors and readers Shea Lowry, Anne McDermid, Lina Roessler, Andrew Hood, Lloyd Davis and Iris Tupholme, great thanks.

A NOTE ON THE TYPE

This book is set in Minion, the first version of which was designed for Adobe Systems in 1989 by Robert Slimbach. The name comes from the traditional naming system for type sizes, in which *minion* is between *nonpareil* and *brevier*. Inspired by the classical, old-style typefaces of the late Renaissance, Minion is also, in a typographical sense, quite economical to set, offering a few more characters per line than most other faces without appearing crowded or compressed—a useful attribute in a text as lengthy as *River City*.